These ruthless des
choice bet

THE SHEIKH'S DILEMMA

Three exciting Mills & Boon authors bring
you three red-hot desert heroes' romances!

We're proud to present

MILLS & BOON
SPOTLIGHT™

A chance to buy collections of bestselling novels by favourite authors every month – they're back by popular demand!

June 2010

The Ashtons:
Paige, Grant & Trace

Featuring

The Highest Bidder by Roxanne St Claire
Savour the Seduction by Laura Wright
Name Your Price by Barbara McCauley

The Sheikh's Dilemma

Featuring

A Bed of Sand by Laura Wright
Sheikh Surrender by Jacqueline Diamond
The Sheikh Who Loved Me
by Loreth Anne White

THE SHEIKH'S DILEMMA

LAURA WRIGHT

JACQUELINE DIAMOND

LORETH ANNE WHITE

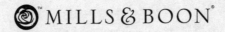 MILLS & BOON®

THE SHEIKH'S DILEMMA © Harlequin Books S.A. 2010

First published in Great Britain 2010
Harlequin Mills & Boon Limited,
Eton House, 18-24 Paradise Road, Richmond, Surrey TW9 1SR

The publisher acknowledges the copyright holders of the individual works, which have already been published in the UK in single, separate volumes, as follows:

A Bed of Sand © Laura Wright 2004
Sheikh Surrender © Jackie Hyman 2004
The Sheikh Who Loved Me © Loreth Beswetherick 2005

ISBN: 978 0 263 88039 7

64-0610

Printed and bound in Spain
by Litografia Rosés S.A., Barcelona

A BED OF SAND

BY
LAURA WRIGHT

Laura Wright has spent most of her life immersed in the world of acting, singing and competitive ballroom dancing. But when she started writing romance, she knew she'd found the true desire of her heart! Although born and raised in Minneapolis, Laura has also lived in New York City, Milwaukee and Columbus, Ohio. Currently she is happy to have set down her bags and made Los Angeles her home. And a blissful home it is – one that she shares with her theatrical production manager husband, Daniel, and three spoiled dogs. During those few hours of downtime from her beloved writing, Laura enjoys going to art galleries and movies, cooking for her hubby, walking in the woods, lazing around lakes, pottering in the kitchen and frolicking with her animals. Laura would love to hear from you. You can write to her at PO Box 5811, Sherman Oaks, CA 91413, USA or e-mail her at laurawright@laurawright.com.

Look for another novel from Laura Wright out this month, *Savour the Seduction*, part of THE ASHTONS: PAIGE, GRANT & TRACE.

To all my fellow romance readers
who love a tall, dark and sexy sheikh…

Prologue

There is a place in the northern desert of Joona where a man can race his stallion straight into the coming sunset. A place where amber veins run through pale sand like a thousand snakes beneath your feet, and white rocks rise straight up into a seamless blue sky. A place where the air is scented with heat and spicy wild brush, and the gods—the watchers of this land—stand erect in their sacred pools and welcome all those who risk so much in coming here.

This place is Emand.

An ancient land, rich with oil, beautiful valleys and vast cultures. But a land great with sorrow and bitter hearts.

This land bore three sons before claiming their fa-

ther. Though broken in spirit, the eldest son understood his position and remained in his homeland to rule. The younger son, destined to follow his great father, surrendered to the gods at just fifteen years of age. And the second son, Sheikh Sakir Ibn Yousef Al-Nayhal, left his home in search of his soul. But what he found instead were the strange deserts of Texas and the emptiness of a man who belonged nowhere and to no one.

One

"**W**hat a waste," Rita Thompson muttered, taking one last look at herself in the full-length mirror.

It was all there. Everything to be admired in a late-summer bride. Killer white dress—strapless, of course—white satin sandals to give her a little height, tulle veil to cover her anxious expression and a classy French manicure on both fingers and toes.

Fabulous.

And she hadn't forgotten those simple traditions of a bride-to-be either. She'd assigned her eyes as the sacred "something blue" and her sister's pearl earrings as the "something borrowed." But when it came to the "something new," she'd decided to pass.

Hey, she'd foot the bill for this entire ceremony and

the "I'm-really-sorry-about-deceiving-all-of you" re-ception afterward. She wasn't about to pay for anything else. Especially for herself.

She grimaced at her wedding-white reflection. "Maybe someday, kid. If you're lucky."

"If who's lucky?"

Rita turned, saw her dad in the doorway of the Par-adise Lake Lodge, looking very dapper in his dove-gray suit and matching boots. "Me. I'm lucky. Got a great family and I'm not too shy to say it."

"Rita, darlin'," he said, walking toward her, "you've never been too shy for anything."

A deep pang of guilt invaded Rita's heart as her fa-ther stood before her, his eyes so kind and loving. She'd never lied to him before. Sure, she'd omitted certain things as a rowdy teenager, but this situation was en-tirely different.

She'd directly deceived him.

A cold knot formed in her stomach. Hopefully he'd understand why she'd gone to all the trouble of faking her engagement and marriage, and forgive her.

"You look very handsome, Dad."

"Thank you. Thank you." Ben Thompson grinned and poked out his elbow in her direction. "Ready to be escorted down the aisle, beautiful lady?"

Though a little forced, she returned his smile and slipped her arm through his. "As I'll ever be."

Her father squeezed her to him, then a sudden seri-ousness crept into his tone. "You're sure about this, right?"

She swallowed hard. "Of course."

He shrugged, said, "Alrighty," then led her down the Lodge steps and out into the glorious sunshine and easy lake breeze.

"You know," he continued, obviously undeterred by her assurances of premarital happiness. "I tried to have a little talk with your intended, but he hadn't arrived as yet. Cutting it pretty close, isn't he?"

"He's a very busy man."

"Maybe so, but I don't like it." He led her toward the lakeside where fifty or so guests sat in white chairs facing a lacy canopy. "Not the best way to start off with a new family."

"Don't worry. He's wonderful, Dad—and he'll be here." Interesting, she mused. She sounded completely convincing. Just the way a woman ready to take the plunge with the man of her dreams would sound.

Well, the *dreams* part was actually pretty accurate. She'd had a serious crush on her boss, Sheikh Sakir Al-Nayhal, for close to three years now. He was intelligent, intense and over-the-top sexy.

Her type in a nutshell.

But alas, the man didn't even know she was alive—below the neck, at any rate.

Rita was the best at what she did, an assistant to die for, and Sakir treated her as such, with the utmost respect. But he never looked at her as anything more than a highly competent business associate. At least, he'd never shown any signs of interest. No requests to stay late for work—unless, of course, it really *was* for work.

No lengthy glances at her legs or a knowing smile when she'd worn something just a little bit revealing to work, hoping he'd notice.

Of course, that lack of interest—though thoroughly depressing for her as a woman—was exactly why she'd chosen him as her mock fiancé. Well, that and the fact that he rarely came to Paradise and was just this minute having a business lunch with Harvey Arnold in Boston—a lunch she'd set up two months ago.

"I still can't believe we haven't met him." Her father sighed as they reached the little staging area several yards from the altar. "It's not right."

"Save your breath, Dad." Ava, Rita's older sister, sidled up to them, looking like a goddess in her pale pink satin bridesmaid dress. "Rita knows what she's doing."

"Listen to my matron of honor, Dad."

"*Maid* of honor," Ava corrected her with a smile. "For three more weeks, anyway."

Rita glanced past her sister to a gorgeous Cheyenne man sitting near the altar. His grandmother, Muna, was on his right and his newly found daughter sat perched like a happy little bird on his lap. Rita smiled, felt a deep sense of peace. She'd really done it. This little bit of deceit had been worth everything. Ava was back with the man she loved, their daughter finally had a father and a loving family, and the marriage that should've, but never had, happened four years ago was now just weeks away.

Rita gave her father's arm a squeeze. "Let's get this party started."

"Just waiting on the groom, daughter."

Rita mentally rolled her eyes. "He'll be coming out with the preacher."

Or not.

Her father led her to within feet of the white carpet stretched out over the grass, the carpet that led straight to the altar. Several of the guests turned and saw her, then quickly dropped into a low hush. Beside her, the string quartet sat at attention, ready to play.

Rita took a deep breath, released it, and clenched her fists around her sweaty palms. All she wanted to do was get this over with, get jilted and get going, off to New Orleans for beignets and Hurricanes.

"There's Reverend Chapman," Ava whispered from beside her.

"Where?" their father asked.

"Right there, Dad. He's—" Ava stopped short.

"Holy hell," Ben said, his eyes narrowed.

Nerves punched in Rita's blood.

"He's alone," Ben whispered. "What the devil is going on—"

"Dad, please." Ava touched her sister's shoulder, squeezed.

Rita lifted her chin. She was ready to hear the cheerless whispers of her friends and family as they realized her fiancé wasn't coming. She was ready to blush and force a few tears.

She was ready to flee in shame.

Then suddenly her gaze caught on a decidedly male figure, proud as a prince and dressed in a white caftan striding across the grass toward the lonely Reverend Chapman.

Rita's heart jolted, and she felt as weak as one of the reeds blowing against the lake's surface.

This wasn't possible. Not possible.

But then again, there he was.

Her boss, her fictional fiancé and her bone-melting crush, Sakir Al-Nayhal had arrived.

Uninvited and totally unabashed.

With her heart fluttering somewhere between her chest and her white satin sandals, Rita watched him walk, stared as he came to stand at the altar, tall, broad and desperately gorgeous, his dark skin eating up the paleness of his caftan.

Then he turned and looked down the aisle, looked straight at Rita, his dark green eyes and firm, sensual mouth humorless.

Rita swallowed hard as her mind raced and the world spun.

Sakir arched an eyebrow, thrust out a hand toward her as if commanding her to come to him.

"Wow," Ava said beside her. "I hadn't expected him to be so…"

Panic welling in her throat, Rita cursed under her breath and muttered, "And I hadn't expected him—period."

Two

Sakir studied her closely, wondering if she would turn around and run from him and from this place.

But escape was not in this woman's nature, he believed. Rita Thompson was the only woman he knew who walked straight into conflict and faced it head-on. She relished the opportunity to fight for what she wanted and continually asked to be challenged. These were the primary reasons he had hired her to begin with, and why he had insisted she work with him on all projects.

But he was not looking for conflict from the beautiful woman before him—not today.

He was here on a matter of business.

He needed Rita Thompson to marry him, and although this wedding day had started as a charade, he would go to any lengths to make certain it ended in a legal union.

The quartet to Rita's right began a soft, simple rendition of *The Wedding March.* The light sound filled the air around them all, causing the crowd to hush and rise to its feet.

Rita continued to stare at him, confusion and panic flashing in her spectacular blue eyes. Then, just as he wondered if perhaps she might surprise him and turn and leave, she blew out a breath, picked up the skirt of her gown and walked toward him.

Sakir watched her hips sway with the movement, watched her breasts—full and pale under the bright sun—rise and fall.

Why must the woman look so beautiful?

Over the last few years, he had rarely allowed himself the pleasure of watching Rita Thompson. She was his employee. And very valuable to him, in that respect. He would do nothing to risk losing her.

But there *were* times, at night, in his bed when he thought of this woman in ways and in positions he knew he should not. There were times when he could not help but wonder how her mouth would taste, how her sweet curves would feel beneath him, how she would turn wild in his arms as he raked his hands up her back, up her neck until his fingers threaded deep into her long tawny hair.

Sakir felt need in his groin and a surge of possessiveness in his gut, but thrust both aside. This was how he always felt when he was near her—just as he always forced himself to respond with cool indifference.

Rita was his assistant, the one woman he trusted and relied upon above all others. No matter how strong his desire for her, he knew he must suppress it in order to keep her, for a woman rebuffed—as she would most surely be in time—would certainly leave his employ straightaway.

Sakir stood tall as she approached him with an uneasy expression. The music gracefully fell away and he reached for her hand. But, as he expected, Rita was not to be appeased. She raised a severe brow at him and kept her arms stiffly at her sides.

Her chin set, she turned to Reverend Chapman. "I need to speak to my...fiancé for a minute."

"Now?" the man asked, his mouth creased into a frown.

Rita nodded, said firmly, "Now." She then faced Sakir and through gritted teeth, whispered, "Can we talk, please?"

This was the woman he knew. Sakir suppressed a grin. Rita Thompson would not enter into anything without a discussion, and it pleased him to know that even in matters such as these she was a cool thinker.

He nodded. "Of course." And again, offered her his hand.

But she looked at his hand as if it were a venomous spider and didn't touch him. She turned to her father, sister and the crowd and said calmly, "If you will excuse us for a moment."

Clearly, the guests were stunned, and no doubt intrigued, by this strange turn of events, but Sakir saw that Rita was too preoccupied to notice. She was gone from his side in a flash, hurrying down to the water's edge. She was already pacing back and forth by the time Sakir joined her.

But when he did, she whirled on him and flipped her veil over her head. "What the hell do you think you're doing?"

His voice remained low, calm. "Should I not be asking you the very same question?"

She avoided this. "You're supposed to be in Boston."

"When I had heard I was to marry, I returned home at once."

Her gaze flickered to the grassy wetness beneath her feet, her teeth tugged at her lower lip.

He shrugged. "I thought it appropriate to attend my own wedding ceremony."

Again, she whizzed past the central question of the morning. "So, who squealed on me? Sasha? No, I'll bet it was Greg. He was always a butt-kisser."

"This does not matter, Rita."

"It does to me—"

"It is a policy of mine to know what my employees are doing. At all times. Especially when *I* am involved in what they are doing."

She narrowed her eyes, stepped closer to him. "Are you spying on me, Sakir?"

The sweet, honey scent of her stroked his senses and he felt the urge to take her in his arms and make love to her mouth. But he would not. "No, I am not spying on you. But it seems I would have good reason in doing so."

She looked away.

"What is this all about, Rita?"

Rita felt completely deflated and just wanted to lie down in the grass and cry. Her flawless plan had just exploded in her face. And the man before her, this gorgeous man with native dress and a knee-buckling gaze, was the one who had lit the stick of dynamite. And he wasn't about to back off. Sakir wasn't a man for playtime in serious matters. Sure, he'd given her some leeway here, but he was starting to bristle, his full mouth thinning in unmasked irritation.

She had little choice but to confess. "I needed to get my sister, Ava, and my niece back here to Paradise."

Sakir crossed his arms over his broad chest. "For what purpose?"

"For...well, romantic purposes."

"Romance?"

The word rolled over his tongue with smooth sensuality, and Rita's skin tightened in response. "To rekindle an old flame—Ava's first and only love. This...this wedding was the only way I could get her home, get her daughter to finally meet her father." She shrugged. "Well, it seemed like the only way."

"I see," he said.

She gestured at him flippantly. "Then you had to show up." *Looking all tall, dark, handsome and impassive.*

He gave a bark of laughter. "Your fiancé should come to his wedding, should he not?"

"Don't look so smug, Sakir, okay? There wasn't supposed to be any wedding or any fiancé. He was imaginary. I just had to pick a guy, any guy."

"But it was not any *guy* that you picked, was it Rita?"

He took a step toward her, close enough for her to feel the heat off his body. "No."

"Did you stop to consider what the people of this town would think of me when I did not come? When I left a woman at altar?"

Rita stilled, heard his query once again in her mind. Shame enveloped her. No, she hadn't thought of what the townspeople would think. She hadn't thought of anything or anyone but her sister and niece.

She glanced over at the waiting crowd, several groups of them huddled together talking, their expressions perplexed. "No, I didn't think of how the town would react."

"I thought not."

"I didn't think of them and I didn't think of you." She faced him, totally sincere. "I'm sorry."

He nodded. "I accept your apology."

She paused. "You do?"

"Yes."

"That was quick."

"I do not believe in making one suffer for her transgressions."

That was big of him, Rita thought. But after all she had done, his manner was a little suspect. She asked, "You're not going to fire me?"

"No."

A wave of unease moved through her. "But that can't be why you're here, why you stood up there in front of all those people—just to get an apology out of me."

"No, I confess it is not."

"Was it revenge, then?" she asked through nervous laughter.

"I have something to ask of you, Rita," he said slowly.

"Okay." Unease suddenly morphed to apprehension.

"I have a business proposition."

"Business?" She glanced over her shoulder at the waiting crowd. This was madness—standing here with her mock fiancé, discussing business. Lord, how could she have let things get so out of control? How would she explain herself to her friends and family? "Can this business venture of yours wait? I need to get back and try to explain this mess to my guests."

"No, it cannot wait," Sakir said tightly.

"All right, what is it?"

He inhaled sharply, raised his chin. "First, I must ask if you are interested in a partnership. A temporary partnership in marriage for a permanent partnership in my business."

Rita's mouth dropped open.

"I offer you partnership in Al-Nayhal Corporation," he continued, "for staying married to me for three weeks' time."

"You're nuts." She gave a choked little laugh. Her voice hoarse, she cleared her throat, then began again. "You've got to be kidding."

"Do I ever 'kid,' Rita?"

She just stared at him. "No."

"I must go to my homeland for three weeks, and I need you there with me as my wife. Your...little plan here has given me the idea. Marriage shows stability, reliability, and this—though it is of no interest to me—is important for the businessmen in my country."

Rita listened, half expecting him to say, "I have made a joke. Yes, there is a first time for everything," but he never did. He kept going, kept explaining...

"I have been asked to come, to consult on the oil fields in Emand. I want this task to be done perfectly and I will go to any lengths to make sure that happens."

She watched his handsome face darken, his green eyes burn with determination. "I don't get it. Why is it so important to you?"

The passion dropped away, and possessiveness took its place. "That is my own affair."

"But you're making it mine, Sakir."

"When we return from Emand, the marriage can be dissolved, no harm to anyone—and you will become my equal."

She arched a brow at him. "Excuse me?"

"You understand my meaning."

She didn't understand any of this. "This is crazy. Listen, if making a show of marriage is that important to you, I could go with you as your pretend wife. I certainly owe you that much after this fiasco. But it doesn't have to be legal."

"For the people of my country, it must be."

He was completely and utterly serious. "How would they ever know?"

His eyes were shuttered. "My brother will know."

"You have a brother?"

He didn't respond. "Do you accept this offer?"

Did she accept this offer? She mentally rolled her eyes. She'd have to be mad to accept such an offer. Marriage for three weeks to a man she didn't love for partnership in his company.

…and she didn't like the way that last part sounded.

But then again… Then again, there was a part of her that wanted so desperately to travel, to experience a different kind of life, perhaps to lie in Sakir's bed and have him see her as a real woman for once. That part of her was shrieking the word *yes* inside her muddled brain.

"There's no marriage license—" she began.

"I have procured one."

"What? How—" She sniffed, shook her head. "Forget it, I know how." Money and power could make any-thing happen.

"Make no mistake regarding my intentions, Rita." He studied her face. "This is strictly business. I swear to you. No touch—" his jaw tightened "—no intimacies—"

"Right." It was strictly business on his part. She released a weighty breath. Well, of course it was. He had a job to do and as usual he'd called on his faithful as-sistant to help. Plain and simple.

"So, you agree, then?" he asked.

Why the hell not, she thought. She wanted to make partner. She wanted to travel. She wanted to get out of Paradise, and this was just three weeks of work—as usual. "All right."

He nodded. "Good."

She didn't wait to shake hands on the deal. She turned away and started up the easy hill toward the guests and waiting preacher. But suddenly, she paused and glanced over her shoulder. "I must warn you, as my *husband* and all, when I'm out of the office and not your assistant, I can be a little hard to handle."

A hint of amusement gleamed in his green eyes. "I know this. But like you, I have never shied away from a challenge."

Three

He was no proponent of marriage.

To Sakir, the thought of being held, captured or owned made him see red. But the idea of losing the biggest contract of his career, a contract that stemmed from his home country no less, had him seeing nothing but the victory and retribution he'd desired for far too many years.

He nodded to the preacher and said, "I will," then without being instructed to, leaned in and gave his beautiful assistant a quick kiss on the mouth.

It had to be quick, he knew. The woman tempted him far too much to give in to slow and deep and wet. And after all, he had given her his word to remain impassive.

With a calm smile, he took Rita's hand and led her back up the aisle as the crowd cheered and threw rose petals. Sakir chuckled. Just ten minutes ago, these people had been wearing expressions of unease, perhaps even pity, for they had thought the bride ready to call off her wedding.

She had not.

She had indeed married him.

As they walked toward the Lodge, Sakir took Rita's hand. He found it cold and shaky. What she had done was just dawning on her. Now she had to face her friends and family, lie about why she had taken her fiancé down to the water's edge and pretend that she was deeply in love. It was no easy feat.

Within seconds of them stepping inside the colorfully decorated Lodge, Rita was whisked away by several women. From the back of the Lodge, Sakir watched as she was urged into throwing her bouquet, grinned as she toyed with the excited females, laughing uproariously, until she finally turned around and hurled the flowers over her shoulder and into the waiting crowd.

"Fine day, isn't it, son?"

Son. Sakir bristled, turned and saw Rita's father walking toward him. He would *not* tell the man that not even his own father called him something so familiar, for he suspected that Ben Thompson was just looking for some sense of familiarity with a proud groom he had never met before.

Sakir inclined his head. "After a somewhat stilted beginning, the day is looking very fine indeed."

Ben grinned knowingly, then stuck out his hand. "For a minute there I thought all was lost."

Sakir shook the man's hand. "As did I."

"Well, it's good to finally meet you. When you didn't show up to my prenuptial lunch this week, I wanted to tan your hide—even with you being royalty and all. Then today when I didn't see you standing beside the preacher—well, you can imagine what was going through my mind."

"Yes."

"But all's well that ends well, eh? What'd she say to you down by the water? She can be pretty stubborn when she wants to be. Did she ask you to give up your throne or—"

"Dad." A beautiful blonde came up beside them, the shape of her eyes and mouth so similar to that of his bride.

"What is it, daughter?" Ben asked.

"The minister is waiting to speak to you. You have to get ready to make the toast."

"Right. Right." Ben shrugged, shook Sakir's hand again. "Well, congratulations, son—that's all I'm saying. You're a lucky man."

Sakir nodded. "I believe so."

When they were alone, the woman turned to Sakir and smiled. "I'm Ava, Rita's sister."

"Ah, yes, it is good to meet you."

"You, too." She hesitated for a moment, something on her mind, no doubt. Then, she said, "Look, my sister and I are really close. We love each other very much."

"It is good to care for one's siblings." He knew he must acknowledge as much, but the words were bitter on his tongue.

"I think so." She lowered her voice, leaned in just a little. "I know what she did for me, and I know what she's doing for you."

Surprise sliced through Sakir's easy manner "She has told—"

"Don't worry," Ava said quickly. "She just told me. Everyone thinks you're a happily married couple who had a few things to work out before they got hitched."

"Well, the last part is true, certainly."

"I just want to thank you."

"For what?"

She shrugged, her eyes sparkled. "Being a gentleman about Rita's little ruse. You could've really embarrassed her if you wanted to."

"As you said, she is doing me a favor as well."

Again, Ava shrugged, and softly said, "I hope you both get what you want out of this."

"No more than I."

She bit her lip. "Just do me a favor, okay?"

"Of course. If I can."

"Take care of her. She's wonderful and funny and loyal. She is a treasure to me and I don't want to see her get—"

Sakir put his hand over hers. "She is all of these things, and I will care for her."

Ava smiled. "That's all I wanted to hear." She walked away and called over her shoulder, "Have a great honeymoon, brother."

Again, with the familiarity. Sakir sighed. "We are not going on—" he began, then stopped short, the people around him staring.

"We're not going on what?" Rita came up beside him, a piece of wedding cake in her hands.

Sakir didn't say anything, just let his gaze roam over her foolishly and covetously. If he were ever to truly marry, if he were to ever believe in such a state, he would wish for his bride to be like Rita. In looks and in manner and in intelligence. She was all the things her sister had said and more.

Yet, to him, Rita would always have to remain untouchable.

She grinned at him, accepted his lack of reply and held up the plate of cake. "Before we have our first dance, we both need to eat some of this."

"Why?" White cake with thick white icing was not his idea of a sweet celebration.

"It's good luck," she said, then proceeded to take a small bite.

"I do not believe in luck."

"Well, I do. And we need as much as we can get with what we're about to do—so eat up." And with that, she took a piece of the cake and thrust it into his mouth.

Four

With wide, eager eyes, Rita gazed out of the tiny window into the dark night. "Well, this is some ride you got here, Sakir."

Now casually dressed in black pants and a black cashmere sweater, Sakir glanced up from his goat cheese salad and rack of lamb and gave her a nod. "Thank you. I find it very comfortable."

A silly laugh erupted from Rita's throat. *Comfortable.* That didn't really seem the appropriate term for a million-dollar Learjet with tan leather seating, matching carpets, mahogany cabinetry, a marble bathroom and a luxurious bedroom suite.

No, insanely awesome was far more appropriate.

"And to think," Rita said with a mock sigh of melancholy, "I could've been flying around to meet clients in this instead of tooling all over town in my Chevy Suburban."

"Your work keeps you in the office on most occasions."

She smiled widely. "Well, not anymore."

Sakir inclined his head. "No, not anymore."

Contemplatively, Rita returned to her meal. Here she was married to Sakir, sipping champagne and eating this fancy dinner aboard a private plane, when just hours ago she'd been back at the Paradise Lake Lodge bidding fond farewells to her sister, father and all the guests.

Totally surreal.

Yet absolutely the most exciting adventure of her life.

She took a sip of champagne and grinned as the bubbles tickled her nose. For three weeks, she was Sakir's wife. This gorgeous man whom she had fantasized about for years—used as her ideal in a marriage that was never intended to come off—was her lawfully wedded husband. Her smile faded a touch as she looked down at the plain gold band on the fourth finger of her left hand and recalled the "fine print" of this marriage. *It was only a business arrangement, a way to gain clients.* If she knew what was best for her, she'd do well to remember that.

She turned to Sakir and proceeded to look him over. So dark, so dangerous and so delicious in his black pants, black sweater and black mood. Resisting the urge to fling herself at him was going to be near impossible.

Boy, was she in trouble.

She pushed all thoughts of intimacy into the back of her mind and forced on a light façade. "I can't believe I was bargained into this marriage."

Sakir sniffed. "And I cannot believe I had to resort to such foolishness for an oil contract."

"Why did you, then?"

He returned to his meal and said nothing.

"Is impressing the folks back home worth all this?" she asked.

He looked up. Annoyance hovered in his eyes. "I am not looking to impress."

"No? Then what?"

"This is the 'hard to handle' you were speaking of, yes?" he asked drily.

She grinned. "Pretty much."

His expression was inscrutable, but a glimmer of heat swam in the depths of his eyes. "I was hoping it would surface in a much more pleasurable way."

A shudder of awareness moved through Rita. Maybe it was the craziness of the day or the fact that he was traveling to his homeland, but never in all the time she'd known Sakir had he said anything remotely like that. Teasing and just a little bit sexual. She had no idea what to say.

But in seconds, the look was gone and so was the casual manner. Control ruled Sakir's gaze again. "It is late," he said. "We have a long flight. I think it is best for you to rest now."

"I'm fine."

He continued as though he hadn't heard her. "I will remain here. I have much work to finish. Please—" he gestured at the door behind her "—take the suite."

Heat rushed into her cheeks. His suite? His bed? "I don't think so."

"It is very comfortable."

"I'm sure it is." And terrific torture for a woman with a massive crush.

Sakir looked very stiff and formal sitting in his leather captain's chair. "We have an agreement, Rita, and I would not break this agreement, no matter how…fatigued I become."

Rita's shoulders drooped and she suddenly felt weary. Of course he wouldn't. No matter how into him *she* was, Sakir just wasn't attracted to her. And never would be. His teasing manner had meant nothing, and she would do well to remember that in the future.

"All right." She stood up and moved to the door.

"One moment, Rita."

She turned around. "Yes?"

"I wish to thank you."

"For what?"

"Making this trip with me. It has been many years since I have been back to Emand. It will be a strange homecoming."

Sakir clipped her a nod, then returned to his meal, seemingly unaffected. But Rita was sure she'd seen a trace of vulnerability flashing in those green eyes—a foreign emotion to the cool sheikh, she assumed—and couldn't help but be intrigued.

He stared at his work, seeing nothing but a jumble of lines and shapes that seemed to be forming the outline of a woman on a bed.

With a growl of frustration, Sakir tossed the papers

aside and reached for the little gold case on the table beside him. He rarely indulged in fine cigars, but the special blend of herbs that came from his country called to him now as he imagined Rita slipping out of her clothes and crawling into his bed.

He lit the thin cheroot, inhaled deeply and relaxed back in his chair, as outside the plane's thick window the black night flashed by.

He was going home.

After too many years incommunicado, he was not entirely sure what to expect. No doubt, his brother would scorn him, but that mattered little. Sakir wanted only to win this account and, in the process, prove to his eldest brother, the reigning crown prince of Emand, that he had been mistaken in thinking Sakir wouldn't amount to anything outside his country.

Sakir switched off the overhead lights, sat in the darkness and watched the smoke from his cigar drift upward toward the vent, making the shape of a woman's curves.

She slept in his bed, between his sheets.

His wife.

He shook his head, took another drag of his cigar. She was not his wife. She was his business associate.

No woman would claim him that way.

Since leaving Emand, Sakir had become cold and hard—in body and in spirit. He wanted only to be immersed in his work and to build an empire of his own. When his body ached, he took a lover, but he gave himself to no woman.

In his mind's eye, he saw Rita and felt her mouth beneath his as he kissed her once, quickly and without passion, at the altar. She had wanted more; he knew the taste of desire on a woman's lips—and, God help him, he had wanted to give it to her. But he would not. He had grown to depend on her and he was not about to allow his desire to overshadow his responsibilities.

His manservant entered quietly. "Do you need anything, Your Highness?"

The woman who lay sleeping in his bed.

"No."

When his servant left, Sakir took another drag of his cigar and reveled in the peace of the darkness.

Five

The Emand airport buzzed with activity. Tourists and locals bandied about looking for luggage and unoccupied taxis, while airport personnel shouted at them for not having the proper tickets and identification.

But for Rita Thompson, or rather Rita Al-Nayhal, things were far simpler. Meeting her and Sakir at their private gate were ten guards and four attendants, all ready to do as the sheikh and his wife bid them.

Within ten minutes of landing, she and Sakir were whisked out of the airport and deposited in separate limousines. Rita had little time to be shocked, not to mention annoyed, by the strange gesture, because in seconds the door to her limousine opened and Sakir stepped inside, wearing a white caftan with gold trim and a staid expression on his handsome face.

An enormous guard with wide brown eyes and olive skin stood in the doorway. "Your Highness, this isn't wise."

"I did not ask for any of this, Fandal," Sakir said, irritation threading his voice. "I did not come to Emand on ceremony."

"Yes, Your Highness, I understand this, but you see His Royal Highness—"

Sakir shot the large man a look so paralyzing he actually took a step back. "I see only that my brother has a hand in this. And I do not accept." Sakir reached out, grabbed the handle and shut the door.

"Drive on," he commanded the chauffeur.

Rita watched Sakir as they took off down the city streets. His face showed little emotion as he seized several documents from his briefcase and began to study them. In his offices in Texas, Sakir was a serious and intense businessman, granted; but in his country, he seemed rigid. He looked as though he needed to lighten up a little before he cracked in the desert heat.

"You know, I'm really flattered, Sakir," Rita said, her tone relaxed, almost playful.

"Why is that?"

"Well, you wanted to ride in *my* car and not one of your own."

He glanced up from his work, his gaze impassive. "It is tradition for royalty to ride separate from their family."

She grinned broadly. "I like a man who breaks with tradition."

A hint of a smile ruffled his sensuous mouth and his eyes softened—just a touch. "I ride here with you because I must make a statement to my family. I am no longer one of them."

"A member of the family or a royal?"

"Both."

"You might reject that notion, Sakir, but look at this." She gestured about. "Limo, private plane, bodyguards— I'm afraid you'll always be a prince."

A muscle twitched in his jaw. "I may have been born to this life, Rita, but I am not a part of it. Not anymore."

"Does that mean I won't be meeting your brother?" she asked as outside the desert landscape whizzed by.

"I imagine you will meet him."

He didn't sound pleased about the introduction and Rita couldn't help but wonder what in the world had happened between Sakir and his family that had driven him out of Emand and driven the people closest to him out of his heart.

"Do you have other family besides your brother?" she asked.

"I have a nephew."

She was surprised. "Your brother's married?"

"No. He fathered a child. The woman did not want the boy, she wanted financial freedom instead."

"How horrible."

Sakir didn't agree or disagree, just explained. "Zayad gave her riches in exchange for his child."

Rita couldn't imagine such a thing. "Your brother sounds like a good man."

Sakir's eyes darkened, as did his mood. "Perhaps we should talk of protocol now."

"Getting too personal, am I?" she said in jest, determined to keep the mood as light as possible.

"You are." Sakir gave her a dangerous smile, his gaze intense. "But I was prepared for personal."

Butterflies in the belly, she thought drily. Well, she hadn't felt that in years. "You were saying something about protocol?"

He nodded. "You are my wife, Rita. This does not mean the same here as it does in America."

"Is this about my clothes," she asked, smoothing down her blue silk dress. "Do I need to be wearing something more traditional?"

"No. You look—" he paused, his gaze moving over her, slowly, intently "—very beautiful. The color of your dress is magnificent with your eyes."

She felt her cheeks warm. "Thank you."

His gaze remained fixed. "No, this is about behavior."

She laughed with piqued amusement. "I'm not curtsying or kissing your feet or anything, Sakir, so you can just forget it."

"There will be no curtsying."

"Good to know."

He shot her a penetrating stare. "And I would never ask you to kiss my feet, Rita."

Heat coiled within her at his gaze. How did he do it? How did he make her weak and wanting with one look? It wasn't fair.

"What are you asking of me, then?" she asked.

"I would wish for you to treat me with respect, that is all."

"Of course. And you will do the same?"

He nodded.

Rita's gaze suddenly shifted out the window and to the view of a lifetime. Breath rushed out of her lungs. "Holy cow."

"What is wrong?"

"Wrong?" She pointed past him. "Look at that. I've never seen such an amazing hotel."

Surely Aladdin must've asked the genie in the lamp to conjure him up such a place, Rita thought, completely stunned. Situated high on a rugged desert landscape, with mountains behind it, sat an enormous fortress. Domes and balconies stretched high into the cloudless blue, the exterior brilliant in shades of gold and terra-cotta. "It's like something out of a fairy tale," Rita said with deep awe threading her voice.

Sakir didn't even glance over his shoulder. "That is not a hotel."

"What? It's got to be—"

"That is my family home, Rita."

She turned, stared at him. "You're kidding?"

"No."

"But it's so beautiful and…"

"And?"

She laughed. "Well, enormous for such few to live there."

He shrugged. "It is comfortable."

She laughed again, this time at his apathy. "Just like the plane, right?"

"Yes."

She shook her head. "I don't get it. You left all of this for Texas?"

His gaze remained shuttered. "I left what is inside."

Curiosity curled within her. His words were so daunting, so mysterious. More than anything in the world, she wanted to know what had happened here, happened to him and his family. But she seriously doubted that Sakir would ever share his past history with her. He was far too proud a man to let her see his scars, emotional or otherwise.

But she could, perhaps, scratch the surface.

"There's something I don't understand, Sakir," she said.

"What?"

"You don't want to be a part of this—of this royal life—yet we're staying in the palace?"

He sighed. "I would not wish it. There are many places for us to stay. But for our clients, I'm afraid the palace is the only option. They are traditional. They would not understand my staying at a hotel when my family is here. Their trust in me would be compromised."

"So you're willing to toss out your principles for this deal?"

Sudden anger lit his eyes. "Do not speak to me of principles. Was it not you who fabricated an entire ceremony for the sake of your sister?"

"That's different."

"How?"

"It was a sacrifice. For her happiness."

"You lied to many. Principles were tossed out, yes?"

"Yes, okay." She shifted in her seat, faced him dead on. "So who are you making happy in this deal besides yourself, Sakir?"

His nostrils flared. "You could not possibly understand."

"No, I think I understand pretty well," she countered. She knew in her gut that he was back for more than scoring a major business deal, though she was pretty sure he wouldn't acknowledge that fact.

"I see you wish to debate, Rita. And on most occasions I would be pleased to accommodate you." His cool stare drilled into her. "But not today."

"Fine." Rita said nothing else, just eased back against the seat and watched Sakir's family home grow closer. She wouldn't push him for more—not right now. He had demons to wrestle with, a history she didn't know anything about, and he had a right to his privacy.

For now.

They drove through three gates, each with several armed guards until finally they rolled up into a circular drive. A man waited at the top of the steps, handsome and almost familiar in his looks and manner. He wore a crisp white caftan and stood with his hands behind his back, very tall and proud as he watched the car approach.

Fandal, the olive-skinned uniformed servant who resembled an oak tree, opened the door, bowed low. "Your Highness."

"He was not to be here," Sakir hissed at the man as he stepped out of the car.

"He insisted, Your Highness."

Sakir said no more. He helped Rita out of the limousine and then walked up the steps.

"Hello, Zayad," Sakir said, his tone cool and his hand outstretched.

Zayad grasped his hand. "Hello, brother. It has been a long time."

Sakir nodded, then turned to Rita. "I would like to introduce you to—"

"Your wife. Yes, I know." Zayad grinned at Rita, then reached for her hand. "A pleasure."

"It's nice to meet you, Your Highness."

"Zayad, please." The handsome man with intense black eyes bent and kissed her hand. "After all, we are family now."

Rita smiled. "Thanks for having us, Zayad."

"You are most welcome." He turned and motioned for them to follow him up the beautiful marble steps and into the palace. "You are a lucky man, Sakir. If I could only find a woman as beautiful as your Rita, perhaps I would take a wife myself."

Sakir didn't reply, but his arm snaked around Rita's waist. "Are our rooms ready?"

"They are."

"Good."

The hall they entered was spectacular. It had gilded coffered ceilings with geometric moldings and landscape murals on the walls. Rita simply stared, her eyes widening as she took in the red marble floor that stretched out to meet a gold staircase.

Zayad gave them an easy smile. "I'm sure you would like to relax and perhaps take some refreshment."

"We would," Sakir said.

"Gana will take you to your apartments, then." Zayad inclined his head before turning to leave. "I will see you both at supper."

Sakir's voice boomed through the hall after his brother. "We will take our meal in our rooms as you must be busy."

With a chuckle, Zayad didn't turn, but called back, "Not tonight, Sakir. Not tonight."

Rita could feel the stiff annoyance of the man beside her and she reached for his hand. But Sakir moved away, clearly not able to accept her comfort.

A petite, dark-haired woman—very pretty and in her mid-twenties—bowed low and said nothing, but motioned for them to follow her.

They ascended the gold staircase and walked down a long hallway that sported several balconies, heavy with flowers and plants. The warm, jasmine-scented breeze wafted in through the open balcony doors, reminding Rita that she was in a foreign land—traveling and exploring for the first time in her life.

She smiled, said to Sakir, "Your brother's very charming."

"Yes," Sakir said drily. "Women tend to fall in love with him at first sight, so I would ask that you remember you are my wife for the next three weeks. After that, you may do as you wish."

She tossed Sakir a wry glance. "Is that anger or jealousy in your tone, Sakir? I can't tell."

"It is neither," he muttered, though a nerve jumped in his jaw.

Rita smiled as she followed Gana into the rooms she and Sakir would be staying in for their three weeks of marriage. But her smile quickly faded as the room came into view. It was far too grand for a simple girl from a small ranching town in Texas, that was for sure.

The large living area was both opulent and warm. Painted in pale green and gold, it had an almost Asian flair, with Chinese tapestries and furnishings inlaid with mother-of-pearl.

"This is extraordinary," Rita said, walking from the living area into a massive bedroom, which boasted a painted domed ceiling, royal-blue silk bed linens and a gold-encrusted canopy.

Rita stopped short. "Ah, Sakir?"

"Yes?"

She turned, saw him in the doorway of the bedroom, his green eyes burning with amusement.

"There's one bed," she said.

"I see that."

Her heart tripped. "I understand that we need to keep up pretenses—"

"We are married, Rita."

Was it her imagination, or did his gaze caress her? Was it her imagination, or was he implying that they sleep together for their own enjoyment and not because they were thrown together through a business deal?

"And it is a rather large bed." His mouth was so firm, so sensual.

Heat pooled in Rita's belly, then snaked lower.

He grinned. "Of course, I can sleep on the floor if that would make you more comfortable."

Why was she so nervous? She was attracted to Sakir and had fantasized about sleeping with him. Rita swallowed hard, opened her mouth to say something, anything; she could barely think.

But before she could get one word out, Gana appeared beside Sakir, her gaze lowered. "Your Highness?"

Rita looked expectantly at Sakir, who in turn grinned at her and said, "She is speaking to you, Rita."

"Oh," she said, suddenly a little flustered. She smiled at the young woman. "I'm sorry."

Gana looked up shyly. "Will you follow, Your Highness?"

"Of course." Rita walked past Sakir, then paused. "Will I see you later or—"

His eyes burned with intensity as he said, "You will see me soon."

Attempting to mentally cool her heated skin under such a gaze, Rita took a deep breath and followed Gana into a lavish changing room. There were gold accents and polished antique Chinese porcelain everywhere.

"I have drawn a bath for you, Your Highness," she said.

The ever-present "Your Highness" title was slowly bringing Rita back to, well, reality—if that were even possible here. Especially as the pretty young woman before her started to remove Rita's clothing—a very strange feeling, as no one had undressed her since her mother. And that had ended sometime around the second grade.

But Rita didn't fight with the woman. She was here in this exotic, fantasy world for only three weeks. No matter what oddities turned up, she was going to go with the flow and hopefully have an interesting, educational and fabulous time in the process.

After Gana helped her into a lovely silk robe, she led Rita into a large, pale blue marble bathroom with high ceilings, French doors leading out to a terrace and two dark blue marble tubs, each the size of a small swimming pool.

Rita sucked in a breath at the vision before her, her mouth suddenly dry as the desert outside the open windows.

Rose petals skimmed the surface of one bath, while her gorgeous sheikh husband skimmed the surface of the other.

Six

She wore the cream silk robe he'd chosen for her, Sakir noticed, a lethal combination of pride and savage desire rising up to claim him as he reclined in the bath.

Just two days ago, he had glimpsed through several books brought to him by his personal shopper. Books of fine women's clothing from all of the best houses in Paris and Milan. Granted, Rita owned many fine business suits, he knew, but she had little clothing that befitted a woman of her rank.

A princess of Emand.

Sakir let his gaze travel over her like a starving man. The pale silk clung to her hips like a lover's hands. Her waist, small and supple, begged to be encircled. And her full breasts swelled pink and enticing beneath the gaping fabric at her chest.

It was a good thing he sat in deep water, Sakir mused, as the lower half of his body was hard as the marble that surrounded him.

With a cool smile, Sakir motioned toward the pool. "The water is warm and scented with herbs."

She glanced down at the water, then back up. She raised a brow at him.

"Please join me, Rita."

Surprise remained steadfast in her eyes. "I think I'll wait for my bath until later."

"I have never known you to be shy," he said.

"Only in certain naked situations." She gave a smart little laugh. "I've been pretty busy lately—"

"Planning a wedding?"

"Right," she continued on quickly. "So I haven't been working out all that much. No crunches or leg lifts. And don't get me started on the chocolate addiction that's taken over my life."

Sakir slowly smiled. "I am quite certain that what dwells beneath your silk robe is a paradise that needs no apology."

Rita's mouth dropped open and two splashes of pink stained her cheeks.

Sakir was a little surprised at the bold compliment that had slipped so easily from his lips, but he did not retreat. He grinned at her, his brow lifted. "But I will keep my eyes averted, if that would make you more comfortable."

Rita snorted at this. "Not sure anything's going to

make me feel comfortable at this point. I'll take a rain check, Sakir."

Behind Rita, Gana entered quietly, her arms laden with fresh towels. She was too fine a servant to show her confusion at the scene before her, but Sakir detected something behind her dark eyes. Perhaps she was wondering why a wife would still be clothed and dry before her husband. Her husband the sheikh...

Sakir leaned back against the cool marble. It would not do to have Gana telling tales to his brother's man-servant about problems within Sakir's marriage. His mission here was too important.

"Wife," Sakir began, using a tone he'd heard last from his deceased father. "I command you to join me."

Rita's gaze shifted from apprehensive to savage blue fire in seconds. "Excuse me?"

Sakir glanced pointedly at Gana, back at Rita, then lifted his brow.

Rita's lips thinned, clearly understanding his meaning, but she refused to budge.

"I would ask that you obey me at once."

"Obey you?" she fairly growled.

"Rita..."

Eyes narrowed with annoyance, Rita muttered the word, "Fine."

In a great show of importance, Sakir put his hands behind his head, took a deep breath, smiled and waited for what would come next.

Rita, on the other hand, looked stiff as a poker as she reached for the edges of her silk robe. "I can't believe this," she muttered. She bit her lip; then, suddenly, she stopped and gave Sakir an acerbic smile. "Averting the eyes would be good now, Your Highness."

His grin widened and he dropped his gaze to the bathwater before him. "As you wish, my love."

The first sound he heard was her snort of derision. The second sound was the tantalizing whisper of silk hitting tile. And the third, the soft splash of nude, pink curves meeting warm, scented water.

Sakir felt tense, on edge with need.

No doubt he would be damned for all eternity, but he could not help himself—his gaze flickered upward.

Only a brief glimpse of her smooth belly and the soft curve of her breast were his.

And only for a moment.

But it was enough to cause him great torment in mind and body.

He released an impatient breath. Only a moment ago, he had plied Rita with silly compliments about what was beneath her robe. Never could he have imagined how just a taste of that vision would send him reeling with a desire he'd never known.

"Thank you, Gana," he heard Rita say. "You can go. We're good from here."

Sakir glanced up just in time to see the young servant's back as she walked out the bathroom door. And just in time to find Rita glaring at him.

"We're alone now, Your Highness," she said, her tone threaded with ire. "Any other commands you wish to give me?"

The question gave him pause, as he saw himself lying beneath her, commanding her to take whatever she wished from him, whatever would please her. A very impractical and foolish vision, he concluded. "I apologize for my brutish behavior, but I am afraid it was a necessity."

"I sure hope so, because that was completely humiliating."

"I do not see how."

"Oh, really?" She waved her arm at him and lowered her voice, "'I command you, wife.' Not something you hear everyday around Paradise—or want to hear for that matter."

He chuckled. He could not help himself. She was so spirited. And…correct. "You did bring this on yourself, you know."

"How's that? I just thought I was taking a bath after a long flight."

"You agreed to be the wife of a sheikh. This comes with certain…expectations."

"And you agreed to mutual respect," she countered.

Sakir paused, thought about this and then nodded. "True. You are right."

"Again," she said, her eyes brightening with a tinge of amusement.

"Do not push matters," Sakir said, his chin lifted. "But yes."

She smiled. "And you apologize?"

"Perhaps."

Rita felt the fight in her ease somewhat. Getting a man to admit he was wrong was a pretty tough task, but with Sakir such admissions were rare. She shrugged, her smile broadening. "You're forgiven."

"Very good."

With all the talk of propriety and apology, Rita had forgotten for a moment that she was naked, in very clear water and close to Sakir. Feeling a little too exposed, she reached for a cluster of fragrant herbs and steered them toward her chest.

"Oh, and Rita?"

She glanced up. "Yes, Sakir?"

"You have nothing to be ashamed of."

He sat there, staring at her—dangerous, sexy, his skin so dark and threaded with sinewy muscle.

She swallowed tightly. "What do you mean?"

His gaze dipped. "Your body is quite beautiful."

Her pulse skittered alarmingly. "You promised you'd look away."

He shrugged. "Normally, I am a man of my word, but—"

"Not today?"

His full mouth twitched with amusement. "I am afraid not. I am afraid the temptation was too great."

"I don't understand you, Your Highness."

"What is it you do not understand?"

"Back in Texas you were Mr. Straight-laced, Mr. Reserved, Mr. Concealed, Mr.—"

"I understand, Rita, please go on."

"Well, now look at you." She gestured at him.

"What is it you see?" he asked with a smooth, sensual grin.

Her stomach flipped over. Literally, flipped. "You've been home for an hour and you're so…you're…" The words—*relaxed, teasing, on fire*—died on her lips as Sakir calmly and coolly stood up and stepped out of the bath totally and utterly naked.

"I am what?" he asked.

Through the haze of desire that leapt from brain to breasts to belly, she came up with just two words to that query.

My fantasy.

Not an appropriate response, but oh, so true.

Sakir stood there, above her, before her, resplendent, and she allowed her gaze to travel the length of him. His calves were hard and finely muscled; his thighs were lean and toned; his buttocks were sculpted and curved in at the sides.

And then there was his pride. Long, pink and hard.

Heat snaked through her heavy, tight body, and her breathing fell labored. She'd never thought such things in her life. And in such a way. It was being here, in this land of spice and decadent sunsets, that had her conjuring such descriptions. It had to be.

"I will dress now," he said.

"Good idea," she muttered.

"I will send Gana to assist you. We have dinner in thirty minutes' time."

He didn't take a towel. Just walked back into the dressing area, his broad, tan back glistening with bathwater.

Rita inhaled deeply, her body wound tight as a drum.

She was in serious trouble.

With a meek little whimper, she plugged her nose and sank beneath the herb-scented water.

A half hour later, Rita stood in front of her bedroom mirror and smiled at what she saw. Exquisite blue and green silk encircled her torso and pooled at her feet. True, the dress covered her far more than what she was used to, but with the many beautiful items of clothing Gana had laid out for her, the traditional Emand dress had seemed perfect for a dinner at the palace.

"Thank you."

Rita spun around, her heart in her throat. Just a few feet away, knee-bucklingly handsome in a white and gold caftan stood Sakir.

"Thanks for what?" she asked.

"Wearing that dress." He walked to her, his gaze searching hers. "I picked it out myself, but I did not expect that you would want to wear it."

"Why not?"

"In Emand, it is a fairly modern costume, but for an American woman—"

"Well, for this American woman, it's beautiful."

Sakir took her hand, brought it to his lips and kissed her palm. "You are beautiful, Rita."

Her heart thundered in her chest. From the bathwater to the bedroom, little had changed—in her feelings, at any rate.

Lord, she thought, drinking him in. What in the world did she do now? Could she tell him he was beautiful, too? That she loved his kiss? Could she ask him to move a little closer? Whisper to him that she'd take that very same kiss on her mouth, her neck, her shoulder?

Rita exhaled. What a crazy notion. He'd surely reject her. And she couldn't handle that—not right now. Maybe when she got back to Paradise and they were going their separate ways…but not now.

No, she'd just wait and see—and maybe hope a little, too—that Sakir's transformation from perfectly balanced boss into sexy suitor would continue.

She gave him a pleasant smile. "Thank you for the compliment."

Sakir nodded, placed her hand on his forearm and led her out of the room.

Silence fell between them as they walked down the elaborate hallway. Rita wondered if he was having some of the same thoughts she'd been having. But, of course, she wasn't about to ask. So instead, she racked her brain for some significant, yet light, conversation. "So, when you were a little boy did you run up and down these hallways like a maniac?"

Sakir turned, gave her a wry glance. "What do you think?"

Rita laughed. "To be honest, I can't imagine you as anything but a serious child, Sakir."

"I do not remember a time when I was not." He led her down the staircase. "Except…"

His voice trailed off and Rita tugged on his arm. "Go on."

"It is an uninteresting anecdote, to be sure."

"I'll be the judge of that."

Sakir snorted.

Rita laughed. "Don't you dare leave me hanging like that. I'll…"

"You will what?" He stopped at the bottom of the stairs and found her gaze.

She shrugged, said mysteriously, "I don't know, but whatever it is, you don't want to risk it."

"Perhaps I do."

Heat moved between them, solid and dangerous.

Rita fought for her voice, which was lost in the haze of desire that shrouded them both. "I want the story, Sakir."

A grin ruffled his full mouth. "All right. I did have a rather fervent desire for figs as a child. I would do just about anything to have them."

Now, this was interesting. "Really? Like what?"

He leaned close, whispered in her ear. "There was a night or two in which I scaled the palace walls and escaped into the dark night—"

"Good evening."

The mood had been heated, sensual and intimate, but the steely timbre of the sultan's voice brought a cold wind lashing between her and Sakir. They moved apart as Zayad walked toward them.

"I trust you had time to relax and recover from your trip?" he asked with all politeness.

"Yes, thanks," Rita said.

Zayad turned to Sakir. "And you, brother? I hope you have found some rest."

Rita watched Zayad, confused. Deep interest threaded his tone, as though he really cared about his brother's well-being. She had been under the impression that Sakir and Zayad were at odds with each other, but Zayad's manner, just as it had been when they'd arrived, didn't hold an ounce of antagonism.

Unlike Sakir's cold indifference, she noted.

"I would expect your staff has informed you of our every move, Zayad," Sakir said.

Zayad shook his head. "Still the cynic, brother?"

"A realist, I think."

Zayad said nothing, merely nodded and then beckoned for them to follow. They left the hall and walked through several exquisitely furnished rooms. There were silk tapestries and gold moldings, jeweled frames with artwork that clearly belonged in a museum and priceless crystal chandeliers.

It was a sight to behold.

"Here we are."

Before Rita sat a massive dining room, done in red silks and velvet, with luscious gold accents. The splendor and sumptuousness of the room were to be expected after seeing the rest of the house, but Rita still felt in awe of her surroundings. A royal palace, to be sure. Very different than her comfy little two-storey back home.

She was seated next to Sakir and across from Zayad at a table that could easily sit fifty. Candles burned cheerfully, and while the meal was served and the wine flowed, the conversation began.

"How long will you be staying?" Zayad asked.

After taking a healthy swallow of wine, Sakir said, "Three weeks."

"Is that all?"

"I am afraid so."

"Your wife and I will hardly be acquainted in such a short time." Zayad turned to Rita and smiled.

"Pity," replied Sakir, his tone as dry as the desert outside.

Zayad continued to focus on Rita, perhaps knowing he wouldn't be getting much out of Sakir tonight. "You once worked for Sakir, is that right?"

"She still does," Sakir said before Rita could answer.

Zayad raised a brow. "Is that so?"

Rita nodded, her mouth full of tomato and cucumber salad.

"Ah, partnership in business and in marriage," Zayad said. "How fulfilling."

"Yes." Sakir glanced at Rita, his eyes a strange combination of heat and impatience. "It can be that."

With a quick nod to his personal servant, Zayad's plate was filled with a luscious-looking beef dish. "Americans marry for love, do they not?" he asked Rita.

"Most do," Rita said, also accepting the fragrant meat.

"We were never afforded such a luxury, were we, brother?"

"No."

Rita smiled at Sakir. "Living abroad has its perks, doesn't it?"

A flicker of a grin touched his lips. "Indeed."

Zayad watched them, watched their interaction. "But you must pine for the desert of Joona, Sakir, and the waterfalls up north."

Sakir's jaw went tight as a trap. "I am content."

"Well then, I am happy for this. But there are others to consider."

Sakir said nothing and took another swallow of wine.

"The people of Emand—your people—have missed you." Zayad leaned back in his chair. "They are throwing a celebration in honor of your return. You and Rita, of course."

"What?" Sakir fairly snapped.

Zayad nodded. "Tomorrow. Noon. In the marketplace. It is tradition."

"I do not think—"

Zayad did not let him finish. "There would be much disappointment were you and Rita not to attend."

Rita watched Sakir—watched his hand curl around his wineglass in a death grip, watched his nostrils flare. "I would not disappoint the people of Emand, as you well know."

"I do know." Zayad lifted his brow. "So you will be there?"

"We will be there," Sakir said through gritted teeth.

Zayad nodded. "Good. I must leave you now. My son is calling from school and I would speak with him." He bowed to Rita. "It has been a pleasure. Good night."

Rita forced a smile. "'Night."

Zayad faced Sakir. "Brother."

Sakir said nothing, though his gaze never left his brother as the man walked out of the room.

"Well," Rita began. "What do we do now?"

Sakir took a long time in answering. "There is always work to be done."

"Yes, there is always work."

Rita sighed, feeling a little melancholy—not to mention a little confused about what had happened between her and Sakir in the hall earlier and, just now, between him and his brother. But getting answers out of her "husband" seemed like an impossible task right now.

"Have you finished your meal?" he asked.

"Yes."

He nodded, stood. "Good. Because there is something I wish to show you."

"Contracts or stats?" she asked with a soft chuckle.

"Neither." He offered her his hand. "We have gardens here that are purported to be hypnotic in their fragrance and beauty. I wish to see if this is still so."

The warmth that had dwelled within her earlier, in the tub and standing with Sakir in front of her mirror, returned. Smiling, she stood up and took his hand. "Well, a little hypnotizing sounds good."

Yes, it did, Sakir thought as he led Rita down the hall, toward the back of the house, through a massive open-air atrium and out into the night.

Anything to ease the tension that had surged through him at dinner, in the presence of his brother.

At the entrance to the grounds, he stopped and watched Rita as she took in all fifty-seven acres of magnificence. Or what he'd always referred to as his childhood playground.

The thought made Sakir smile. He'd had a good childhood, for the most part.

"Wow," he heard Rita utter from beside him.

"What?"

She pointed to their right. Sunset was creeping silently into the rose gardens, with fingers of red and burnished orange hovering above the rare trees, shrubs, conifers and palms beyond.

Sakir released the breath he'd been holding since landing in Emand.

He was home.

Truly home.

Where the palace had always served as a watchful keeper, the gardens had been his sanctum.

"This is just amazing," Rita said.

"There is much to see," Sakir said, guiding her down the stone pathways to the medicinal gardens, rock wall and succulents.

"I feel as though I'm stepping into another time, as though this is sacred ground," she said with a lilt to her voice. "Does that sound crazy?"

"Not at all." Sakir led her over a bridge and toward one of the many glass atriums and lath houses that were used for indoor plants. "This garden was started thousands of years ago, so you are right about stepping into another time."

A perfectly kept stand of fruit trees followed, the tart scent of fresh lemons heavy in the air. Then orange and plum. It was like Eden. Yes, a true biblical setting, and Sakir wondered how many sins he was willing to commit to have the woman beside him.

"Let's stop for a moment," he suggested.

The sounds of the garden, the insects and the wind in the desert beyond filled the disquiet between them.

"Sakir," Rita said quietly.

"Yes?"

"Do you think your brother suspects that we're not…"

"Truly husband and wife?"

"Yes."

"I am not certain." At that, he turned to face her. His gut twisted violently. She was so beautiful, with her skin glowing in the light of the sunset and her eyes filled with a longing he knew all too well. "But I do think he believes we are lovers."

She looked surprised. "Why? We really don't show any signs of being lovers."

This brought a smile to Sakir's face. No doubt Zayad had seen Sakir's covetous manner and sensuous gaze whenever he looked at Rita.

"And what would those signs be, Rita?"

She smiled, her eyes dancing with amusement. "Looking at each other with desire in our eyes, bathing together, holding hands."

He grinned, his hands closing around hers as he moved closer to her.

She chuckled. "Now, if he'd have seen the kiss at our wedding, he'd have known we're not lovers."

"Yes, that was rather formal."

"Yeah, it was."

Without checking his actions, Sakir reached out and touched her cheek, his thumb brushing over her lower lip. "It was not the kiss I had intended."

She tipped her chin up. "Really?"

He shook his head slowly. "The kiss I had intended would not have been suitable for others to view." Sakir eased her into his arms. "Shall I show you?"

"Sakir…"

With his mouth inches from hers, he said, "You may tell me *no* at any time, Rita—tell me to release you."

She looked tormented and as on fire as he was. "There is no command this time?"

"Only from you."

"Then," she said, her breathing labored, "I want you to kiss me."

He smiled.

"We're breaking the rules…"

"Yes," he said before covering her mouth with his own.

Seven

Rita melted against him, her knees turning to water as every nerve in her body flooded with desire. In her mind, she'd imagined this—standing hip to hip with Sakir, her breasts crushed against his chest as he made love to her mouth with reckless abandon.

But nothing in her fantasy had prepared her for the decadence of reality.

Or with how highly skilled her fantasy lover truly was.

Sakir kissed her with severity, his passion desperate as his hands raked up her back, his fingers digging into her neck as he held her steady. Rita could do little but shiver and moan with the sweet force of his movement.

As the sunset turned to quiet twilight around them, Sakir turned Rita to liquid both inside and out, his tongue moving between her lips slowly, tasting her need. Then, when she'd had enough of his playful torture, when she'd whimpered and thrust her hips up against his erection, he feasted on her mouth once again.

He crushed her lips, then eased back into soft, wet kisses.

Rita moaned, her body begging for his—on top of her, beneath her, it didn't matter as long as they were naked and close.

Lord, it had been so long since a man had touched her this way, held her so tight that she felt his heart beating against her breasts. She'd almost forgotten what it felt like to be wanted.

Years ago, she'd given her body to a man she'd thought she was in love with. But her judgment had been skewed by hope and a young woman's romanticism. Her lover had used her for just one night and then dropped her flat. Something had closed around her heart that day. She'd allowed herself only fantasies since then.

Until now, that is.

Until Sakir.

As if hearing her thoughts, Sakir pulled her even closer, changing the angle of his kiss. His mouth felt so hot, so warm as he raked his hands down her back, down, down until he cupped her backside.

Rita whimpered. Her breasts tingled, and between her thighs a fire raged. She thrust her hips against him once more. She wanted to say, "Take me. Make love to me now before I melt right here." But she didn't want to move her mouth from his.

She hoped her body spoke for her.

But the only one to speak was Sakir. And his word was a muffled oath against her mouth.

"What?" she whispered, still deep in a passion-filled haze. "What's wrong?"

"We have company." Sakir straightened slowly, his eyes still on Rita, and still burning with danger and unquenched desire. "They will be upon us momentarily."

Breathlessly, Rita fought for her composure as she heard the sound of male laughter behind her.

"Maybe we should go inside?" Rita suggested, desperate to hold on to the heat of the moment. Yes, they could go upstairs—undress each other quickly, lie down in their bed, beneath those luscious silk sheets, and continue what they'd started here.

"Yes," Sakir said, his gaze shifting to the palace doors.

Rita reached for his hand, but he moved away. A chill moved through her.

"You are right," he said, a coolness to his tone as well. "Let us move inside. I fear I have neglected my work long enough."

It was as though a knife had been thrust into Rita's heart. Sakir had completely misinterpreted her suggestion. But if it was pointed or by accident, she didn't know. Though honestly, she didn't really want to know.

"I wasn't talking about work, Sakir." She tried once again to take his hand. "There's so much more to life than work, Sakir."

"Not for me," he said proudly, taking her hand and slipping it into his arm.

Rita felt herself nod. Her mind and body were floating somewhere between lust and shock; she fought for the light of reality. She knew she needed to see the truth here—that she'd just been rejected. Sure, she'd felt this kind of brush-off before, but with Sakir it felt so much worse.

A moment ago, he was making love to her mouth.

Sakir led her away from the lemon grove and toward the house. "I must apologize, Rita."

"What for?" she asked roughly, though she already knew the answer.

"I went too far, took things to a place they were never meant to go."

His words bit into her, but she remained poised. "I went there with you, Sakir."

"Yes, but there is a difference—"

She wouldn't let him finish. She stopped just outside the doorway and faced him, her chin lifted. "I enjoyed myself back there. I'm sorry you couldn't allow yourself to do the same."

A muscle under his eye twitched, his lips thinned. "You can find your way back to the suite? Or shall I escort—"

Rita shook her head. She wanted to be alone, feel her anger and frustration as she tried to figure out just what had really happened here. "No, I'll be fine. You get your work done."

She gave him zero chance for a comeback. Any more apologies, explanations or excuses and she'd get in a cab and head for the airport.

She walked into the house, away from her husband and the man she had an enormous crush on, and refused to look back. But as she took those steps, she realized that for the first time since she'd come to Emand, she wished she'd kept Sakir as a fantasy.

For the reality was becoming far too complicated.

The grounds, desert and city stretched out before him. Sakir leaned against the balcony attached to his tower offices at the palace—the offices that had once belonged to his father—and breathed in the spiced scent of Emand and the fading warmth of the surrounding deserts. For many years, he had put this world and all of its memories to rest. He had put aside the notion of family and, in return, had become a cool, sharp and impassive businessman.

But things were starting to shift.

Ever since he had stepped off the plane today onto the soil of his homeland, that impassive shield had begun to slip.

The lights of the city began to flicker on and the sight made him smile, though he couldn't stop the deep ache of homesickness that filled him.

He ran a hand through his hair and sighed. Feeling homesick—he would not have thought such an emotion possible, but it was clearly present within him.

As was another, perhaps more detrimental—sentiment. Affection.

Not just desire, but actual affection. And for a woman he had sworn to himself he would never touch. A woman that meant a great deal to him and his business.

Sakir closed his eyes and saw Rita beneath him, saw

her eyes flicker with desire one moment, then vulnerability the next, as he took her beaded nipple into his mouth, as he palmed her, as he slid deep within her body.

Sakir groaned, forced his lids to lift, forced his eyes to focus on the black sky littered with stars.

But it helped little.

Her kiss still lingered on his mouth. Her intensity and need. The way she'd exposed herself and her heart to him. The scent of her hair—it intoxicated him even now. And then there was the memory of her eyes as he had pulled her tightly to him...

He wanted more from her, and he would have taken more if his brother's servant hadn't come upon them in the garden.

His body tightened with the urge to run.

He could go to her now...

Just a few floors below, she lay asleep in his bed. Their bed. They were married after all. A legal union that bound them together...

Sakir's chest tightened painfully.

How would she react if he went to her? If he ripped back those silk sheets and lay atop her, his mouth ready to please her however she wished and the lower half of him hard as stone?

Sakir inhaled deeply, calling for calm within his skin, begging for the control he had spent too many years cultivating.

Rita Thompson was his assistant and soon to be his partner. But she would never be his wife. He would do well to remember that. He would also do well to remember that she held the key to his success here in Emand. If things went as planned, she would help him secure one of the largest and most important contracts of his career, while making his brother see what he could do without his family's aid.

This task was of utmost importance.

Sakir straightened. He would remain up here, in the tower, at his desk, at his work.

And Rita would remain in their bed, alone.

Sakir pushed away from the balcony and went inside. For the next three weeks, he would keep his distance, keep his lust in check and hope not to lose his mind in the process.

Eight

Nothing in the world felt better than a great big stretch beneath fine silk sheets in an extra-large bed in a delicious foreign country, Rita thought.

Well, nothing except having the man you'd just been dreaming about in bed with you.

Rita rolled onto her stomach, flipped a wave of tawny hair out of her eye and stared outside at the pink morning. Did the Emand sky always hold such a gorgeous pink hue in the morning? she wondered. And if so, would she be willing to consider transferring her work and her life over here to enjoy it on a daily basis?

Stop.

Rita buried her head in her down pillow and released a little scream. Some amazing kisses, some killer touch-

ing, and she was seeing pink skies and imagining a life
in Emand. Never mind Sakir's cold impassivity after
their encounter. No, she just wanted to remain in the red-
hot moment where that beautiful, impassioned man had
held her like no other, kissed her breathless and, honest
to God, made her bones tingle and shake.

What a fool she was.

A soft knock sounded at her door and for a second
Rita felt a flash of excitement in her belly when she
thought it might be Sakir. But then a young woman's
voice called, "Good morning, Your Highness," and Rita
frowned and flipped onto her back.

Gana stood in the doorway. She smiled shyly. "I am
sorry to startle, Your Highness."

"That's alright, Gana."

The young maid's smile brightened and she moved
into the room with the grace of a ballerina. "Your breakfast is waiting in the living area."

"Thank you." Rita's gaze flicked to the room behind
Gana as she asked casually, "Is Sakir— Is... Has my
husband been waiting long?"

Gana bit her lip. "His Highness arose very early. He
has already taken his meal—"

"Oh?" Why was she surprised? Sure he had to wake
up early—didn't want the servants to know he slept on
the couch and not in bed with his wife.

Gana continued, "But he has asked me to tell you that
he has gone away."

Rita sat bolt upright in bed, her heart in her throat.
"What?"

"Just for a few hours, Your Highness," Gana said quickly.

"Oh." With a little laugh of relief, Rita asked, "Do you know where he's gone?"

The young woman shook her head. "I am sorry, Your Highness."

Rita sighed and scooted to the edge of the bed. Obviously, Sakir wasn't all that anxious to see her. Unlike her, he obviously hadn't been that affected by their encounter last night. Or maybe, she mused, with just a little hope left in her heart, maybe he *had* been affected and taking off was his best defense against doing it again when he saw her this morning.

She didn't know whether to be frustrated or flattered.

Well, one thing she wasn't going to be after today was available—sexually, emotionally or otherwise. She'd left herself wide open for hurt last night and had gotten what was coming to her.

No more.

She was through with this fantasy thing. She would uphold her end of the "rules" she'd agreed to with Sakir and try to remember that they'd come here for one reason—business.

"Gana, would you do me a favor?" Rita asked, stepping out of bed and slipping on her robe.

Gana bowed low.

"Would you call me Rita?"

The girl looked horrified. "I could not, ma'am."

"Please. Just when we're alone?"

A smile crept into Gana's face.

"All this formality is getting a little crazy. I need one friend." Rita raised a hopeful brow. "Okay?"

"Okay," she said softly. "Rita."

Rita laughed. "Perfect. Now, let's you and I have a little breakfast together."

Again the young woman looked horrified. "Together?"

"Yep, together." Rita grabbed Gana's hand and led her into the other room. "And if I have to, I'll command it."

As the limousine whisked them into town that afternoon for the welcome feast in the marketplace, Sakir couldn't help but notice the curt set of Rita's mouth as she sat spine-straight on the seat opposite.

She was angry with him.

Even though he knew why she carried such a look of reproach in her blue eyes, the need to change that look to one of heat and pleasure—like the one she'd worn last night—almost corrupted Sakir's sensibilities.

But he knew such a move was unwise. He knew that to touch her again would only lead to both their ruins. He had acted the cool rogue last night to remind them both. They were married but they were not lovers.

Then again, he did care for her. And he was no callous prince. He sat back against the seat, his manner reserved, yet concerned.

"Are you all right, Rita?" he asked.

She stared out the window, into the bright light of day. "Perfect."

"You are cool, distant and professional—it is as though we are at the office."

"Well, we are, aren't we?"

"No, we are not."

She turned, looked at him. "Oh, c'mon. We came here for Emand Oil. That's work in my book."

Sakir glanced at the driver, who was trying to be discreet but could not seem to help looking back at them. Sakir pressed a button on the panel to his left. The privacy glass lifted and set in place. He turned back to Rita. "Yes, we are here to work, but under the guise of marriage."

"Am I not acting enough like a wife, Sakir?" she asked, her tone rich with frustration.

Frustration Sakir also felt, in mind and in body.

His wife…

When they had met in the hall earlier, walked to the car together and took their respective seats inside the limousine, Sakir had made every attempt to keep his gaze from moving over the woman across from him. But at this moment, he felt compelled by some scheming force of nature to take in every inch of her.

Minus the frown, she looked extraordinarily beautiful. She wore a bright blue dress, simple and tasteful, the silk fabric falling softly over her amazing curves. Her hair was pulled back in a pretty bun at her neck, and her skin glowed with health and the fire of a woman whose needs had yet to be met.

His wife.

At that moment, it was a monumental offense that she was not.

He eased out of her complicated question with a comment of his own. "You are angry with me, I know."

She chuckled. "You're quick."

The sarcasm in her voice caused the edges of Sakir's mouth to flicker with amusement. He liked her defiance. He was so accustomed to being catered to and flattered at every turn that he had always appreciated Rita's blunt and spirited attitude. Yes, he liked her fire. Now, if he could only stoke the fire within her in the way he wished.

"You are upset with me for not being at breakfast this morning?" he said. "It could not be helped. I was working and—"

"You are really arrogant, you know that, Sakir?"

"Yes, I do, but to what do you refer?"

She released an irritated sigh. "This isn't about breakfast. This is about last night—"

A rush of need moved through him as he recalled their kiss, her body, his arousal, last night. "Ah, I see."

"No, I don't think you do."

"The kiss, yes?"

"No, Your Highness—the promise."

Sakir paused. "I do not understand, Rita."

She leaned back against the seat, crossed one long, smooth leg over the other. "We agreed to rules. You set them up, Sakir. Don't you remember?"

Of course he remembered. Back in the States when he had honor and a clear head, and no beautiful wife in his bed, he had made those rules.

His jaw tight, Sakir muttered, "I remember."

Tossing her hands up, Rita said, "Then what the hell happened?"

Sakir just stared at her. For the first time in his life, he was without words. Well, not exactly. He had the words, but they were the wrong ones. These words would get him into trouble. How could he explain his actions? Was it wise to admit the truth? That he wanted her and could not control himself? That for the first time in his life he did not want to be in control around a woman—around her? That this is why he had taken her in his arms last night, kissed her like a starving man and forgotten the rules that he himself had set down as law?

She was watching him, her fiery blue eyes digging into his mind, his soul.

He inclined his head. "Again, I apologize for my behavior last night, and for breaking our agreement. It will not happen again."

She shook her head. "That's no explanation, Sakir."

Yes, he knew that. But he also knew that he could not tell her that, just as her mouth had called to him last night, it was actually driving him mad this very minute. He could not tell her that his body craved her almost to the point of pain, that he would bound across the limousine floor, strip her bare and make love to her right now in the light of day if she gave him any sign that she was interested.

Such erotic thoughts had his gut tight and his heart thudding hard and fast against the wall of his chest as the limousine slowed and then stopped.

"We will talk more of this later," he said, forcing back the raging need that was attempting to consume him whole. He gestured to the window. "We are here."

Nine

Rita had loved the Food Network ever since she'd gotten cable one year ago back in Paradise. Friday nights would bring her adventures from Rome, with the best of wine, cheese and pasta, or from Madrid, with seafood paella and Asturian cider, or closer to home, from Chicago, Italian beef sandwiches with all the trimmings.

But her travels only consisted of those through the "boob tube," as her mother had called it, so she'd never felt a part of the experience—never smelled the smells, tasted the wares.

Today, she had stepped into a real live Food Network episode.

Stretched out before her was a glorious marketplace. Under the warm sun and the shade of many vibrant-colored tents, men and women sold fresh vegetables and fruits, breads and succulent meats cooking on spits. They barked at each other, bargained for the best price and then exchanged money and a smile before going on their way.

And in the middle of it all, in the center of so much activity, heat and killer scents, was a decadent red and gold tent with the flag of Emand whipping animatedly at its roof.

"Let us walk," Sakir said from beside her. Then he took her hand and led her from the car into the marketplace.

As they approached, as the royal guards led them closer to the tent, the people stopped what they were doing and looked over at them. For several moments, neither prince nor people said or did anything. Both seemed to be waiting for something to happen. Rita wasn't at all sure what that was. She was about to ask Sakir when he suddenly raised his hand high in the air.

The crowd hushed.

Then Sakir called out to them. Rita didn't understand what he was saying, as it was in Arabic, but it seemed to please the people of Emand very much. When Sakir had finished speaking and his hand had returned to his side, the hands of his people rose to the heavens, followed by joyful shouts and hoots and whirls of sound.

"They welcome us," Sakir said and then turned to Rita. "They welcome you."

Rita glanced up at Sakir. His expression was stately and impassive, but his eyes shone brilliantly. He looked extraordinarily handsome and so princely in his white caftan with gold trim. She wanted to ask him what he was thinking and feeling at that moment as his people cheered him, but she didn't have the chance as he took her hand once again and led her away from the crowd and into the tent.

Once there, Rita's mouth literally dropped open.

She hadn't known what to expect from a welcome-to-the-family type meal from Sakir's people—but certainly not something as lavish and...well, as sensual as what was laid out before her.

Handmade carpets, that in any auction house would surely sell for an astronomical price, covered the floor, their medallion patterns set in bright blues, red and browns, accented with silk. There were pillows strewn everywhere in every color, silk with delicate hand embroidery. To her right stood a buffet-like table of solid gold, laden with trays of food and drink. And in the center of the tent were two sumptuous gold place settings laid out on the carpet floor, with more food and more pillows to lounge upon.

Rita shook her head, awe threading her tone. "They must care for you a great deal to do all of this."

"This has been done for the royal family for centuries," Sakir informed her. "It is a show of respect, that is all."

"Respect. Ah, yes." Rita sat down on the soft rug and eased herself back against one of the pillows. "Hard to believe that anyone could care about you this much, Sakir."

Sakir sat down beside her. "I am not looking for anyone to care for me."

"Are you sure?"

His dark brows lifted. "Where would you get such an idea?"

She shrugged. She wasn't sure herself. Maybe it was that faraway look in his eye when his people had cheered him, or maybe it was this whole mess with Zayad, or maybe it was the way he had looked at her in the limousine when he'd refused to answer her question about last night—with such desire, yet with such conflict. "I suppose I see you differently here. You're not as guarded in Emand as you are in Texas. Your feelings actually rise to the surface once in awhile—" she smiled "—for us common folk to see."

"It is good to see my country and my people." He picked up some flat bread and offered it to her. "As for you being common folk—" his gaze found hers, dark and intense "—make no mistake, you are anything but that, Rita."

A shiver of awareness moved through Rita at his words and at his gaze. "Thank you."

He nodded. "Have some of this." He placed a rich yogurt dish on a plate, followed by a few strips of meat, then handed it to her. "The meat is dried pastrami, aged well. It is delicious."

He was right, of course. Both dishes were wonderful, and Rita ate alongside him very happily. Fried eggplant, pumpkin salad, spicy cheese with tomatoes and onions and a tender lamb shish kebab. Everything was perfectly prepared and seasoned, and soon Rita felt quite satiated.

"I'm surprised we're all alone," Rita said as she relaxed back against her pillow with a cup of Turkish coffee. "That's a first."

"I asked for us to be alone, but if you wish for service it is a simple—"

"No, no." She smiled. "I like this."

He flashed her a devilish grin. "You like that *I* serve you, yes?"

"*Sakir, my humble servant*—yes, I could get used to that."

His eyes darkened as he leaned toward her and whispered, "What may I do for you, Your Highness?"

Rita fairly melted right there. This whole scene was too much. Delicious food, sensual atmosphere. Then there was the man before her, who looked too intense and too sexy, and who was acting as though he would do whatever she asked—no matter how wicked and unwise.

What may I do for you...

Did she dare say, "Kiss me, touch me…"

No. Not after what had happened last night.

When she didn't answer him, Sakir reached behind himself and took a piece of pastry from a nearby tray. "There is another custom that must be adhered to today, in this tent."

Rita's heart fell into her full stomach. "What's that?"

That wicked grin returned. He knew exactly what she had been thinking, imagining…hoping… "It is custom for the husband to feed his wife a piece of baklava at the end of the meal."

She could've slugged him for tormenting her so,

but she fought back with words instead. "Even a royal husband?"

"Especially a royal husband."

"But we aren't 'technically' married. And no one is watching us, so they really wouldn't know if we didn't follow the custom."

Sakir's gaze went dark and reckless. "Perhaps I would like to feed you."

Rita swallowed, her breath a little high in her throat. In the pit of her stomach, a fire raged and the blaze grew more and more out of control with every moment Sakir looked at her that way. How she would quench such an inferno, she did not know, nor did she know how to stop it from snaking lower and lower still down her body.

Sakir held the sweet pastry to her lips. "Would you allow me?"

What else could she do?

She nodded.

"Open your mouth for me," he commanded softly.

With her breath held and her eyelids drifting closed, she did as he asked, hoping to forget all that was behind her and all that remained to be seen and said between them.

She waited, and when he finally placed the delicate pastry in her mouth, time slowed, sweet played her senses and heat rushed her womb.

"Look at me, Rita."

Her lids fluttered open. Her heart thundered in her chest as she looked up into his handsome face. He gazed at her mouth and she silently begged him to kiss her, to run his tongue over her bottom lip and then slip deep into her mouth and make her moan with need.

"How does it taste?" he asked, finding her gaze once again.

"Wonderful. It's wonderful, but…"

"But?"

"I want…"

"More?"

God help her, she nodded again.

Pure desire raged in Sakir's eyes, and Rita felt utterly and gleefully responsible for it. She thought of seizing his face and pulling it toward her, but Sakir was already taking the lead.

He leaned forward, his mouth a whisper away from hers. But it wasn't as she'd hoped. He didn't kiss her. He stayed where he was, so close, not moving, hardly breathing.

Then he turned his head away and cursed darkly in Arabic.

Her body on fire, Rita forced herself to be calm—forced herself to realize the truth. Nothing had changed since last night. This fantasy moment in time that she'd just been imagining—the one with no future and no past—wouldn't give her the kind of pleasure she'd hoped for. Sakir would not allow himself to follow the desire that thundered in his eyes. No. He just sat there, totally in control of his body and his heart, while Rita fought to hold on to the desperate yearning racing through her blood.

"Maybe we should just toss custom right out the window," she began tightly, "and feed ourselves the baklava?"

Sakir nodded, his jaw tight, his lips thin. "Yes, that is one solution."

"You have another?"

Again he cursed and then reached up, touched her face and brushed his thumb over her lower lip. "There is nothing I hate more than leaving you unfulfilled, Rita—" he dropped his hand "—but as you said, we made an agreement. And I must honor it, yes?"

Rita forced herself to nod, feeling rejected, vulnerable and deeply discouraged. She would not fight him, beg him or cajole him into taking what she was so willing to give.

With a sharp exhalation, Rita reached past him, took a slice of the baklava and, this time, fed herself.

"Emand welcomed you and Rita with great enthusiasm today, yes?"

Sakir shut his book with a little too much force and turned to face his brother, who was walking into the palace library where Sakir had been holed up for the last hour with dubious apathy. "They were most gracious."

"They have long awaited your return, Sakir."

"Well, I am afraid they will continue to wait, as I have *not* returned."

Zayad sighed heavily and dropped down into the leather armchair opposite Sakir. "Will you always fight me, brother?"

"I do not know what you mean."

"Yes, you do."

Sakir leaned forward in his chair, his tone tight. "It takes passion to fight. I have none for you."

"No?" Zayad countered, his black eyes filled with indignation.

"No."

"I suppose your only passion is your work, then."

Sakir clipped his brother a nod. "As it will always be."

"That is a lonely business."

Sakir chuckled bitterly. "You lecture me on time spent at my work? What are you but a lonely man of business yourself?"

"I make time for a woman, Sakir."

"Of course. There are many at the sultan's disposal, I know."

Zayad's lips thinned. "I treat all women with respect, and with care." He lifted a brow. "Which is more than I can say for you."

"What the hell does that mean?" Sakir demanded.

"What of your wife?" Zayad leaned back in his chair once more, crossed his arms over his chest.

"What about her?"

"Is she a 'passion,' Sakir?"

Sakir narrowed his eyes. He did not like his brother's presence here, nor did he like this line of questioning. "Rita is none of your affair."

Zayad snorted. "Nor yours, I am told."

Sakir shot to his feet. "I will let you have your library, Your Royal Highness."

Zayad also stood and met his brother eye to eye. "What game do you play, Sakir? You come here with this woman, whom you obviously lust after, and admire as well, I think, but I hear from—"

"Zayad, you would do well to curb your tongue," Sakir warned.

Zayad released a bark of bitter laughter. "You command me?"

"I do." Through gritted teeth, Sakir added, "But I fear not your reprimand. What more can you do to me that has not already been done?"

For a moment, Zayad only stared at his brother, his breath coming tight and clipped. Then he said, "You act as though I banished you from Emand, that I took our parents from us—that I killed Hassan—"

"You did kill Hassan," Sakir uttered darkly.

Zayad turned bloodred. "Our brother's death was an accident."

"An accident he met with because you forced him into the army before he was ready."

"It was his wish!" Zayad bellowed.

"You were the elder brother!" Sakir shouted. "You were to know better."

"What's going on here?"

Both men whirled toward the doorway. Rita stood there, her brow creased. "I could hear you two all the way up the stairs."

Sakir looked away, feeling as though he would explode from the fury in his blood.

"I apologize if we disturbed you, Rita," Zayad said,

his tone princely once again. "We were having a disagreement about the past."

"There is no disagreement about the *truth*," Sakir said. Then he left his brother where he stood, stalked past Rita and left the room.

He heard Rita call after him, "Sakir? Wait, stop." But he kept going, his pace hectic. He was still caught up in that confrontation with his brother—a confrontation that had been a long time coming. Sakir had always thought that saying those words to Zayad would finally release him from the pain of loss.

But he felt only more burdened.

His hands balled into fists.

Rita came running after him. "Where are you going?"

"Out," he barked. "Where I can breathe."

He didn't look back, didn't care if his strides were those of a panther. But Rita kept up somehow. She followed him outside, through the gardens and down a flight of steps. The warmth of the day was starting to fade, but Sakir's blood ran too hot to notice.

When he finally reached the stables, he whipped open one of the stalls and led out one of his brother's large gray stallions.

"Sakir, talk to me."

"Go back to the palace, Rita," he barked, quickly bridling the stallion.

"No. You need a friend right now even though you're too damn stubborn to admit it."

In one swift move, Sakir hoisted himself onto the back of the horse. "You should not be around me right now."

"Why not?"

Damn her. Why could she not just do as he asked for once? "I am in a dangerous mood."

She sniffed. "I'm not afraid of you, Sakir."

"Perhaps you should be."

She ignored him. "Well, I'm going all the same—on your horse or one of my own. And I'm not that good a rider. I have no idea how to put on a saddle, so I'll have to go bareback like you. And I could fall and break a bone or get a concussion or—"

She never finished her sentence as Sakir growled with frustration, grabbed her under the arm, lifted her up and placed her behind him.

"Wrap your arms around me," he ordered.

This time, she did as he commanded. It was a good thing, because when he bellowed at the stallion in Arabic, the animal nearly flew out of the stables, racing toward the desert and the coming sunset.

Ten

The stallion's hooves pounded the sandy floor below as Rita and Sakir rode hard and fast with absolutely no communication. Rita could only guess at how long they'd been gone. A half hour seemed likely, as around them the sun set in a fiery dance of orange, pink and red. It was a jaw-dropping sight, and even though her backside felt bruised from the constant smack against the stallion's spiny back, Rita wouldn't have traded the view for anything in the world.

She'd seen many pictures of the desert of Joona, imagined its snakelike patterns in the sand and wondered if the air would be heavy with heat and spices. But as it was in the marketplace today, the reality was so far from the fantasy it wasn't even funny.

The desert stretched for miles and miles, tawny in color with just a hint of rust thanks to the setting sun beyond. The air, as it brushed her face, was scented, not with spice, as she had imagined, but with the rain that had fallen so light and fresh that morning.

It was like something out of a movie to be riding bareback, behind a handsome sheikh, his white caftan whipping in the wind.

But this was no movie.

There were real feelings here, real emotions at play, and all of it was incredibly complicated. In the marketplace today, Sakir had practically seduced her and then pulled away, angry and unfulfilled—again. Then later, he'd been in one heck of a knock-down, drag-out fight with his brother, whom he then pulled away from, angry and disgruntled.

Rita tightened her hold on his waist.

Would he ever let anyone in? Would he ever let her get close enough to see what pain was in his heart?

The questions in her mind evaporated as Sakir slowed his horse and brought him to a stop. The beast was breathing heavy and glistening with sweat. He snorted and pranced in a circle, then came to a stop once again.

"Where are we?" Rita asked, her throat dry from the sandy wind.

"Mid-desert."

"It's beautiful."

"Yes."

"And peaceful."

Sakir slid easily off the stallion's back. "Thankfully, it is that as well."

"It's so vast. You can't see a thing but sand for miles." She glanced down at him. "Are you sure you know how to get back?"

He offered her his hand. "I would never be lost in the desert."

No, she imagined he wouldn't. Where the heavy traffic of the Texas highways, even the moderate amble of the streets in and around Paradise, might pose a hazard to this man's sense of direction—as he always relied on his chauffeur to get around—he was definitely at home here in this wild vastness.

And for Rita, nothing could be sexier.

Sakir helped her down from the horse, then released her and dropped to the sand. He lay back, looked up at the peach sky.

Rita sat down beside him. "Listen, Sakir—"

"I do not wish to talk."

"I know, but—"

He sighed. "But you will continue anyway."

"I think it's a good idea."

"And force me to speak, yes?"

She didn't bother agreeing. "I heard what you and your brother were saying and—"

"Listening to another's conversation—"

"It's rude and dishonest, I know. I didn't mean to listen." She picked up a handful of warm sand and let it filter through her fingers. "I came to find you and didn't know how to interrupt gracefully."

He put a hand behind his head. "You would do best to forget what you heard."

"From the way you two were arguing I'd say that's easier said than done." Without thinking too much about what she was doing, she lay down beside him and looked up at the same sky. She felt close to him, close enough to ask, "You had another brother?"

Sakir said nothing.

She tread lightly. "You accused Zayad of causing his death?"

He inhaled deeply. "I did."

"Why?"

"Dammit, Rita."

"I know. I'm a pain in the butt. But I think you need to talk about this."

"You think?"

"Yes."

"You are my assistant, not my psychologist."

"Actually here in Emand, I'm your wife," she said with a lightness in her tone. "And I think that entitles me to nudge you a little."

Sakir groaned and cursed again. But to Rita's amazement and satisfaction, he also began talking.

"Hassan, my younger brother, he wanted to follow in our father's footsteps. He had the mind and the heart of a warrior. He wished to enter the army before he was of age. I opposed this, but Zayad allowed him to go." Sakir paused. He seemed to be waiting for someone else to say what came next. But no one did. "Hassan was killed in a foolish training exercise only a few short weeks later. It was a training assault on several abandoned buildings near the east end of town. There were explosions and rifle fire, and the attack caused a nearby building to burst into flames. Hassan perished in the blaze."

Rita turned on her side and faced him, touching his arm. "Oh, Sakir, I'm so sorry."

"I want no pity from you, just as I want no explanations from Zayad."

Rita held fast to his arm. She wasn't put off by his abrasive words. She knew they stemmed from pain. She also knew that it was best for him to get everything off his chest. "Did you leave Emand when Hassan died?"

He nodded brusquely.

"Why?"

"After that, I wanted nothing to do with my family, with Zayad."

Rita watched him, so proud and in such pain, and she wanted to comfort him. But how? This man was such an island unto himself, unapproachable at times. Could she cuddle up next to him? Kiss him? Tell him that she was here for him, if only he'd just accept her?

Slow and easy, she reached out and touched his face. She waited for him to flinch, to turn his head, reject her show of care. But he didn't.

He let her touch him.

Rita smiled. He was so warm, and she reveled in the feel of his strong jaw and the roughness of his day's growth of beard against her skin.

Sakir turned his head toward her, took her hand and kissed her palm. The simple gesture of acceptance and thanks was too much for Rita, and she released a soft sigh of pleasure. She silently prayed he wouldn't stop there, that his mouth would search for hers.

"I have made a promise to you," he whispered, his voice husky and tight.

"I know," she said breathlessly.

"This is the danger I spoke of when you insisted on coming with me."

"I'm not afraid of this happening." Her gaze searched his, the ache in her body loud enough to echo over the miles of the desert. "But you are afraid."

"Rita…"

"Why, Sakir?"

On a growl, Sakir rolled, was poised atop her in seconds. "It is the need I feel for you that I fear." His gaze roamed her face, his eyes forest-green and heavy-lidded. "There is such desperation running through my blood that I fear."

"What are you desperate for?" she asked him, her thighs brushing his as warmth surged into her.

"I have wanted you since the day we met. I want you now."

Rita couldn't believe what she was hearing. Her illusive fantasy was admitting that he wanted her.

Was it the magic of the desert that had spurred this on or pure truth?

Well, she didn't care what it was. She pressed her hips up, felt Sakir hard against her belly. "Take me, then."

He said nothing, but his thigh moved in between her legs.

"Take what you need, Sakir."

"And tomorrow?" he asked, his gaze steady, but passion-filled.

"I won't question tomorrow," she said in all honesty. "We'll leave whatever happens between us right here."

Sakir didn't move for a moment. Then he lowered his face to hers and brushed his lips over hers. "It is impossible."

She wasn't sure what he was referring to. Maybe it was everything. A day making love in the desert was impossible to forget, or trying to stop what was happening between them. She didn't know and didn't care. She said, "Impossible, probably. But inescapable, I think."

"Yes. I agree."

Sakir watched the flush of desire surge into Rita's cheeks. No woman made him feel as this one did, and he imagined no one ever would again. Life was unjust. In all things, he was master. Always controlled, always assured. But in Rita's company, he became a man—just a man—with a lust so reckless he believed he'd be close to death if it were not satisfied.

At this moment, he cared not for promises made and broken.

He wanted her mouth, her tongue, her skin.

His hands went first to her face, then moved to her neck and threaded into her hair. On a soft sigh, she closed her eyes, parted her lips and smiled.

Such perfection made him mad and he covered her mouth with his.

Instantly, her hands wrapped around his neck. Sakir sunk into her warmth and deepened his kiss. She tasted like honey and heat, and he wanted more, more, all she would give him. He changed the direction of his head, slipped his tongue between her lips and met hers with wet, warm passion.

On a groan, Rita thrust her hips up. Sakir answered her call, pressed his thigh up between her legs.

Rita sucked in a breath, her hands raking down, gripping his backside.

Sakir moaned. "You demand and give at the same time."

"To you, I would give anything," she uttered breathlessly.

Her words filled his soul, made him want to rip her clothes from her body and plunge deeply inside her.

But he took his time.

She kissed him with such passion as she gripped his buttocks. "Do you like this, Your Highness?"

"I like it very much, as you most assuredly can tell."

"I wasn't certain," she said coyly.

He took her hand and tunneled it between them, placed it on his shaft. "All you, my love."

He felt her go still beneath him at his words. He was such a damn fool. He had to learn to curb his wicked tongue around her. What had made him speak so?

He knew the answer—the heat, the moment, her long, sensuous body wrapped around him.

He nuzzled her mouth, felt he should explain, say something. "Rita—"

"No, don't." She lifted her chin and lapped at his lower lip with her tongue. "Please."

Sakir felt himself nod. All right. Yes. Forget. It was good for them both.

He sucked her tongue into his mouth, played with it, then kissed her intensely as the sand blew around them and as the sun dipped dangerously into the horizon. It would be twilight soon, but it mattered little to Sakir. He needed to feel Rita, taste her skin.

He eased to the side, took her face with him, his mouth working hers with needful passion. With true access to her now, he moved to the edge of her blouse, slipped his hand beneath and crawled up her hot skin. He felt her shiver and release a whimper into his mouth. The anticipation of cupping her breast and laving her nipple almost caused him to climax right then and there.

But he fought for control.

Up he moved, his fingers inching over her stomach until finally, finally he met with the silky fabric of her bra. With a quick snap, he released her heavenly flesh from its confinement and moved in.

His groin pulsed, seized with need as he cupped her breast. The heavy weight, the hard nipple stabbing into his palm. Madness took him and he ripped away from her mouth, whipped up her blouse and dipped his head.

Paradise was here.

His mouth closed around her nipple with perhaps

too much force. But she didn't cry out in pain. Instead, she took his head and pulled him closer.

Searing heat shot through Sakir and seed leaked from his arousal. With all thought gone, he found the button to her pants and tore, then tugged the flaps apart. He couldn't get to her fast enough—to her heat—to see if she too burned with their shared passion.

And when his fingers finally found her, finally moved through the soft tuft of hair between her legs, pleasure suffused his lungs.

It was as he'd hoped.

She was soaking wet.

Without a word or a sound, he slipped two fingers inside her. He smiled against her breast when he heard her gulp for air, but quickly continued his ministrations to her taut nipple, suckling, nipping.

Around them, the desert warmth started to ease, but between them a fire raged.

Sweat broke out on Sakir's forehead as he worked her body, his fingers plunging deep into her, further, higher, until his knuckles barred the way. Her hips pumped to his rhythm, as inside he felt her core begin to shudder. The walls around his fingers pulsated. Electricity ripped through her into him.

And she cried out into the desert air.

Sun faded, wind whirled around them as the moments passed, as hips slowed, as cries turned to whimpers, then to breathy sighs.

Sakir assumed that Rita would pull away when her body eased, when her body tired, but she did not. She turned to face him and frantically wriggled down his belly. Without a word, she undid his pants and released his erection.

He felt her warm breath and then her hand on him.

She wrapped the base of him in her fist, then began to move in slow, rhythmic strokes. Up, down. Her hand was so tight on him, he nearly passed out. But he kept his sanity.

For he needed it.

As only moments later, she took him into her mouth.

Sakir roared to the heavens in Arabic, asking for control. But no one answered him.

She played him, suckled him, her tongue dancing over the tip of his erection as her free hand cupped him.

An invisible fist slammed into his gut.

He would climax, lose his mind in mere seconds. Lose his control. Panic warred with desire beneath his skin.

He could not believe what he was allowing to happen. No woman had loved him this way in over ten years. It was the ultimate in power, in control. Could he allow the paltry grip he still held on control to be taken from him?

The answer was no.

"No further," he called out, his voice husky, weak, frustrated.

He knew she would be angry with him and totally perplexed, but he could not help that.

Rita released him, sat back, her gaze fixed on him. "Sakir…"

"I did a very selfish thing in marrying you, Rita," he said as he stood up, righted his clothing.

Rita said nothing, but he imagined she agreed with him.

He watched her snap and button her clothes, then scramble to her feet. She didn't look at him.

Sakir breathed in the scent of her. Felt his muscles, his arousal, still desperately hard, stretch and pulse. He gazed heavenward, took a breath. All for the sake of a contract—and the proof to his brother that he was worth something outside the gold gates of Emand—he had married this woman and turned her life upside down, possibly even damaged her heart in the process.

He was selfish.

He was ashamed.

Without further discussion, Sakir lifted Rita up, placed her on his horse and then swung up in front of her.

"I will ask you to hold on to me one last time," he said.

The words held a double meaning, but Sakir brushed them aside as Rita encircled his waist. This time, her grip on him was just enough to keep her safe and held little warmth.

Around him, the desert grew as dark as his soul. But it was a path Sakir knew well and was comfortable taking. He gave the stallion a kick and felt the wind in his face once again.

Women's lib had come to Emand in slow, though deliberate, strides, and Rita was happy to note that the movement hadn't skipped over the aged man sitting before her and Sakir in the grand offices of the Emand Oil Company.

Asad Qahhar, the head of Emand Oil, was definitely old

school in his dress and manner, but he had a warm, welcoming smile as he listened intently to their presentation.

Naturally, Sakir was doing most of the talking. Which might not have been the best idea, as he was slightly off in his pitch, a rarity for him. And although Rita still had a deep anger running through her veins regarding what she'd come to refer to as "his final rejection" last night in the desert, she couldn't help but feel a little sorry for him. She knew how badly he wanted this deal, and to what lengths he had gone—lengths they had both gone to—in order to get those papers signed.

Asad Qahhar placed the prospectus on the table in front of him, leaned back in his chair and addressed Rita. "I am delighted to see that you have traveled with your husband, Your Highness. It was certainly a pleasure to meet you."

"And you, Mr. Qahhar."

"Wife and business associate." Asad grinned widely at Sakir. "You are a lucky man, Your Highness."

"I think so," Sakir said tightly before returning to the business at hand. "You have seen my proposal, what say you, Qahhar?"

Rita tried to not show her frustration. He'd never acted this way. He was always smooth and easy with clients, no rushing to the finish line. Not today. Today, he was blowing this deal with his cold, quick manner. Didn't he realize this was why they'd come here, why they'd gotten married? His business. Emand Oil.

"It looks very good," Asad told him. "My only concern is that you are living in America now."

Sakir snorted arrogantly. "I fly all over the world for my work. I have never had a complaint regarding my performance."

Asad nodded his head sagely. "I am sure that is true, but you must understand my caution."

"Of course."

"I would like time to think, yes? We will meet again in, say, a week?"

"One week," Sakir repeated, his lips a little thin.

Rita mentally shook her head. The man wanted to think about things over the next week. This wasn't good.

Asad stood, shook Sakir's hand, then bowed to Rita. "Once again, it was a pleasure, Your Highness."

Rita gave him her most brilliant smile, not that she expected that to change the man's mind, but a warm gesture couldn't hurt after Sakir's coldness. "It was wonderful to meet you, too, Mr. Qahhar. Let's hope it's the first of many meetings."

The man returned her smile. "I must come to America soon. I like her people very much."

Rita didn't know what hit her at that moment, but she couldn't stop herself. After all she and Sakir had been through in the last several days, she wasn't about to let him lose this deal and let all her heartache be for not. "Mr. Qahhar, America is wonderful," she began, "but Emand is where true beauty lies. My husband and I plan on spending a good deal of time here."

Asad turned to Sakir, a look of fresh interest crossing his face. "Is that so? Why did you not say as much before?"

Sakir felt as though he'd been punched in the gut. What the hell had made Rita say such a thing? He whirled to face her, but she was avoiding his gaze. Qahhar on the other hand, was not.

"Well, this changes matters, Your Highness," he said. "I will see you both in a week."

Sakir inclined his head. And with a low bow, Qahhar left the room.

Sakir turned to Rita, his tone sharp. "What did you do?"

"We were losing him."

"We were not." Sakir snatched up his briefcase.

"I don't know what's going on with you, if it's about last night or this war with your brother, but you were totally off today and if I hadn't said what I said, this deal would be in the toilet."

Sakir didn't want to hear her explanations. True or false. He only wanted to bark. "'Spending much time in Emand.' I would not consider this, Rita, no matter how much I want the account." He raised a fierce brow at her. "I will have to restate this when Qahhar and I meet again."

"You mean when *we* meet with him again," she corrected.

"I am not certain. Not after what you have done."

She lifted her chin, looking so proud, so determined and so beautiful in her dove-gray suit and flawless complexion. "Oh, I'll be there, Sakir, you can bet your title on it."

Black rage threatened to drown him. He wanted to punch the wall, duel his brother, tell Qahhar to take his contracts and burn them—but most of all he wanted to haul this woman against him and make her body scream with pleasure. If he would allow himself, he would take her in Qahhar's office this very moment.

But he would not.

He had spent the majority of last night on the couch, reminding himself that with her, around her, in her, he was no longer in control.

"So, what's next on the business agenda?" she asked him, her tone flat, all business.

"I have work to finish back at the palace."

She nodded. "Do you need me?"

Fire fisted around Sakir's groin. Damn her. But looking into her impassive blue gaze, he saw that her query was not double-sided.

"I think not."

Again Rita nodded stiffly, slipped her purse under her arm. "Shall we go, then?"

Sakir walked with her out the door and into the halls of Emand Oil. Living life alone was what he had chosen long ago, and it had served him well. This life left no scars, no regrets.

It was safe.

The woman beside him threatened that strange sense of peace. She made him wonder what could be if he chose something different—a fact that made her even more dangerous than he had once thought.

Gana stood beside Rita as she packed some clothes, shoes and personal effects in her overnight case. "This is not wise, Your Highness."

"Relax, Gana," Rita said, her face set with determination, her body rigid with purpose. "I've hired two guides for this journey. A husband-and-wife team, no less. I'll be safe and sound and—" she gave a flash of brittle laughter "—maybe I'll get a little perspective in the process."

Clearly not able to appreciate the beauty of a "little perspective," when a woman was frustrated by her husband, Gana clasped her hands together and sighed. "The sheikh will not approve."

Rita grabbed her bag and headed for the door. "Right now, I couldn't give a damn what the sheikh thinks. I need some alone time."

Without further discussion, Rita left the room. But duty still called Gana, and she would not be so easily lost. She followed Rita down the hall and stairs, out the front door of the palace and into the bright morning sunshine.

"Your Highness," she called. "Rita?"

This made Rita stop and turn around. "What is it, Gana?"

"What is this alone time?" she asked, a little breathlessly from her dash to keep up.

Rita gave a wave to the older man and woman in the Jeep at the far end of the driveway, the couple that knew her as just a visitor, not as a princess, and then said to the sweet little maid, "It's what every woman who's been dumped by a man must take to regain her sanity." She gave her a rueful smile. "Bye, Gana."

"What shall I tell His Royal Highness?" Gana called after her.

With her hand on the door of the Jeep, Rita paused. Then, with a grin, she called back, "Tell him I'll see him in a few days."

The words felt good. As did the open-air Jeep. She was off, headed for the adventure of a lifetime. She'd been wasting time, energy and tears in this place. No more, she thought as they hit the beginnings of the desert.

Caramel-colored sand carpeted the Jeep's way and the hotel-like sounds of the palace gave way to peaceful nothingness, barring the wind and lazy hum of the motor.

All those lovely oases in the desert—the ones she'd read about on the plane ride over—would be part of her experience over the next several days.

And Sakir—well, he didn't need her around, did he? Not until the next meeting with Qahhar, at any rate. And even at that, he'd acted as though she could be miles away and it wouldn't matter.

Well, he was about to get his wish.

Rita sat back, closed her eyes and smiled. A little adventure, no, a lot of adventure, was just what she needed and deserved.

Rita woke with a start. She knew she must have dozed off for a while because the sun was overhead in the sky, and the peaceful sounds of wind and motor had been replaced by a loud whirring sound of a plane.

"We have to stop, Your Highness," her female guide said as her husband brought the Jeep to a sand-skipping halt.

"Why?" Rita asked, still a little lost in sleep.

"Sheikh Al-Nayhal comes."

"What?"

Her heart in her throat, Rita glanced out the window. She saw no other vehicles, no horse and no rider. Above her, the loud whir of the airplane intensified. She looked up. It wasn't an airplane in the sky. A white helicopter fairly floated above them—and it was descending.

Rita watched openmouthed as the enormous machine came to land directly in front of them. The inside of the Jeep felt like a wind tunnel as the blades of the copter still swung. Two seconds later, the door opened and Sakir jumped out.

He wore a dangerous frown as he approached. "Have you gone insane?" he shouted through her window, the noise of motor and wind almost deafening.

"No, I don't think so," Rita shouted back.

"You have run away from the palace, Rita. This is not done."

"Don't tell me what to do, Sakir."

His jaw went rigid.

"And by the way, you're the one who's always running away." She didn't stop, couldn't—even when he gritted his teeth. "Today, it's my turn."

"You will go no further."

"I am not your prisoner, Sakir."

He swung the car door wide. "You are my wife."

She snorted. "Do you really want to go there?"

In the front seat, her two guides were desperately trying to fade into their leather bucket seats.

"I need a break, Sakir," Rita began, her tone serious. "Part of this whole…adventure was seeing and exploring, and I plan on doing both."

He turned away, looking as though he was trying to gather patience or cursing or something equally mannish. "You will continue to fight me on this?" he asked.

"Hard to handle, remember." She cocked her chin. "I did warn you."

He shut the back door, then walked around to the driver's side and said something to her guides in Arabic. Rita's guides nodded and then quickly got out of the car.

"Hey," Rita began.

Without a word to Rita, Sakir shouted something to the helicopter pilot. The man also nodded and then beckoned the tour guides toward the chopper. Rita watched in frustrated anger as the husband and wife climbed into the white machine and closed the door. In seconds, the helicopter was off the ground and flying away.

Sakir walked back around to her door, opened it and said in all politeness, "Please sit in the front with me."

Rita blinked, didn't move. "What the hell did you just do?"

"I will answer you as soon as you change seats."

Rita practically growled as she did as he commanded—slamming doors, dropping into her seat, crossing her arms over her chest.

When Sakir was in the driver's seat, his hand clutching the gearshift, he said, "If you are determined to do this, I will be your tour guide."

"I've already had that kind of adventure," she said, her tone flat. "And you know what?"

He glanced over at her. "What?"

"It wasn't nearly as fulfilling as I'd hoped."

His eyes flashed green fire and he gunned the engine. "What you had, Rita Al-Nayhal, was a taste—just a taste." Then he shoved the gearshift into first and took off.

Eleven

Desert turned slowly into mountain, just as an hour's worth of stubborn silence inside the Jeep turned to frustration. Finally, Rita gave in and spoke. "I believe this is kidnapping."

Sakir glanced over at her, gave her a derisive smirk. "You make a joke, yes?"

"Hardly." She straightened her spine. "I was going along fine, minding my own business, having a nice little adventure, and then you show up—helicopter in tow—and sweep me away."

"Sweep you off your feet, you mean."

"No, that's not what I mean."

"Rita," he said with that patient tone she knew so well. It was the same tone he reserved for impatient clients. "It is a dangerous endeavor what you have tried to do."

"Why?"

"You must understand something. You are royalty now. My wife could be a target to many—"

She snorted. "Your wife."

"That is correct," he said firmly.

Her gaze moved over him. His long, hard body was decked out in a simple pair of tan pants and a white linen shirt. His handsome face was so stubborn; his eyes, gorgeous and intense.

Sigh.

His wife. If that were only true. If only he could stop acting like such an idiot and let that be true. But it wasn't and he wouldn't, so she was no wife—just a business partner. A business partner who was growing tired of all the games being played between them.

She shifted her gaze to the window and the view of the rugged mountains. "So, where are we going?"

"Lake Shami," he said, thrusting the car into second gear as they drove up a steep hillside. "Then we will travel just above it to the palm tree forest."

Rita snapped to attention, forgetting their troubles for a moment to concentrate on something far more intriguing. "Palm tree forest? That wasn't on the tourist maps. I've never heard of such a thing."

"No, you would not. The forest is a very special place, revered and cared for by my people…" He paused, his jaw tightening. Then he released a weighty sigh.

"What's wrong?" Rita asked.

"It is nothing."

Rita replayed the last thing he'd said, then smiled sadly. The "nothing" he didn't want to talk about was obvious to her. "You don't have to be embarrassed for calling them 'your people.'"

"I do not feel embarrassment," he said quickly.

He was so stubborn, so proud. "I'm just saying that for you to feel warmth and show you care for the people of Emand is normal."

"Look ahead, Rita."

Confusion hit her. "What?"

Sakir pointed. "Lake Shami is just over that rise—"

Rita shifted in her seat to face him. "Why is it so hard for men to communicate their feelings?"

"Why must women force these feelings from a man?" he countered.

She shook her head. "You're answering a question with a question."

"My point is thus," he said with deep sincerity. "Why can a woman not be patient?"

At that, Rita paused. She'd never heard him say such a thing. He'd barked, bitten, commanded, but never asked something with vulnerability attached. And she found that the anger in her heart melted a touch.

She took a deep breath. He made a valid point. Had she been pushing him? Not just about releasing his desire for her, but about his feelings regarding Emand, his life here, his relationship with Zayad and his grief over his younger brother?

Perhaps, she thought. Maybe it would be easier and

less stressful for everyone if she just let things happen or not happen, let Sakir make a move, or not, let Sakir confide in her…or not.

"Patience, huh?" She shrugged. "Okay."

Sakir glanced over at her, his brow lifted. "Okay?"

"Yes."

"As simple as that?"

She broke out into a broad smile. "Yes. Now, tell me more about these palm trees."

"See them for yourself." Sakir gestured out the front window.

There it was. Beyond the thick pane of glass. Utter magnificence. Rita could barely breathe as she stared at the sight in front of her. Hundreds of massive, waxy-leafed palm trees grew out of a glorious hillside like an earthy chessboard. And just beyond sat a beautiful and highly inviting lake in the shape of an eight.

"Look there," Sakir said, pointing to a rock wall above the right side of the lake where rain seemed to trickle down.

"Waterfalls?" she asked, excited.

"Yes. One of many."

Reverent silence took them both as they drove down the hillside, between the ancient palms to a vacant stretch of land where Sakir parked the car.

Rita got out of the Jeep first, stretching as hot, wet air enveloped her. She walked a few feet to a small clearing and then looked up. Palm tree leaves framed a patch of blue sky. "This is amazing."

"You know," Sakir said, coming to stand beside her, "you would not have seen it with the guides."

"I know."

"You thank me for coming to get you?"

She laughed. "Let's not get crazy here."

He laughed with her, his eyes crinkling. "Would you care to see the lake? Perhaps take a bit of lunch at the water's edge."

"Lunch?"

He held up a leather satchel.

"But how?"

He grinned wickedly. "I am a man of surprises."

Even in the supreme heat, a shiver of awareness moved through Rita. "Is that so?"

"Yes." He reached out and gently took her hand. "Are you ready?"

She smiled, nodded. "Lead on."

"Ah… So, I am a suitable tour guide, then?"

"Not bad." Her grin widened. "We'll have to see how the day goes."

"That sounds fair," Sakir said. He led her down a makeshift path of sand and rock and palm tree branches to the edge of the lake, and just adjacent to one of the lovely waterfalls. There, he delved into the satchel that she assumed was her tour guide's and came out with a blue and red carpet. He rolled the lovely rug out on a patch of sand, several feet from where the water lapped elegantly at the rocks.

"A carpet…" she began, playing along. "What else have you got in there?"

He raised a brow at her, then proceeded to take out several pieces of flatbread, some delicious-smelling meat and what looked like a cucumber salad.

"Dried lamb," he said, presenting her with his wares just a little bit dramatically. "Olive salad with cucumber and tomato, bread and some cold wine. A meal fit for a princess, I think."

Rita beamed. She couldn't help it. "It's perfect," she said. The whole thing, she mused. The meal, the view, the man—oh, and the possibilities.

No.

She couldn't go there. Wouldn't go there. Whatever happened, if it happened at all, it would come from Sakir and with absolutely no pressure *for* her.

Under the shade of a massive palm tree, they ate their lamb, bread and salad, drank their sweet, cold wine, then promptly relaxed back on the soft carpet and enjoyed the view.

"I love the water," she said, sipping her wine. "Comes from being a Pisces I guess."

"What is this Pisces?"

"It's an astrological sign for those born in March and the symbol is a fish."

He nodded. "Yes, I see now. I am August first. What does this make me?"

Rita started laughing.

"What?"

"You're a Leo, Sakir."

He raised his brow, clearly not understanding.

"The lion," she prompted.

An arrogant grin broke on his face. "Lion. I like that."

"I thought you might," she said drily.

"Lions love the desert as fish love the sea."

She nodded. "Although lakes are my favorite. They're so calm, so peaceful." She took another sip of wine. "Do you know if this one is spring-fed?"

"I think it is. And reported to be rather cool in temperature." He cocked his head, grinned. "But welcome on such a hot day, yes?"

His black hair was damp with sweat at the temples and nape. He looked sexy and full of sin, and, God help her, she was ready to ask him to kiss her.

How could one man make her so weak? She had her principles, she had a code of honor among women—the code that clearly stated, "I will not beg for sex." But around Sakir, when he looked at her with those dark eyes and come-hither mouth, she was lost.

"We could take a swim if you wish," he said.

A flush of excitement warmed her cheeks. "You're not restricted to waiting one hour?"

"What?"

"In America, there is sort of a waiting period after eating."

"Interesting." He grinned. "I suppose I like to live dangerously."

"Do you really?" she asked, unspoken questions threading her tone.

Sakir stood, seeming as tall and imposing as the palms around him. "I suppose I would not be a proper tour guide if I did not accompany you into the water."

Rita swallowed thickly, the heat in her belly pulsating, then dipping low. "I think it's only right."

Before Rita had time to think, Sakir was unbuttoning his shirt. With greedy eyes, she watched him as he so casually removed the pressed linen. Her hands itched to touch him, run her fingers down his chest, her nails over his washboard stomach. His bronzed chest was smooth and thick with muscle and she thought she'd never want to look at anything else ever again.

Until her gaze slipped a few inches.

Her breath caught in her throat, and the muscles in her womb contracted.

His pants lay a foot away, and he wore no underwear.

He was glorious. Long, lean and hard from head to foot.

"So, you're going skinny-dipping, huh?" she asked weakly, lust running rampant through her body.

"Did you have another suggestion?"

She shook her head. "No, you look amaz—" She shut her mouth, took a breath and began again. "What I mean to say is, I was going to wear my bra and panties. It's sort of bathing suit-like and—"

"What happened to living dangerously?" he asked.

"That was you."

A grin flickered at the corner of his mouth. "No, Rita. That is you as well. For as long as I've known you."

She didn't know how to respond to such a statement. If she looked back at her life since knowing Sakir, she wouldn't call herself bold or dangerous. Well, not in romance anyway. In business, perhaps. And then there was her fantasy life…

Okay, there she was bold. There she lived dangerously.

"You disappoint me," Sakir said, a thread of boyish discontent in his tone.

Rita rolled her eyes. "Well, I would hate to do that."

"You have a beautiful body, Rita. There should be no shame in revealing it."

Her cheeks burned and she tried not to stare at his burgeoning arousal. "There is definitely shame when you have big thighs and a bigger butt." She shrugged. "I keep meaning to join a gym, but—"

"Take off your clothes."

She looked up at him through her lashes. "Are you commanding me again?"

"Yes. Do as I say."

Rita inhaled deeply. She knew Sakir was only half-serious in his order, that he was being playful in such a sensual setting. And God help her, she wanted to play along with him. After all, she'd decided only an hour ago to leave the decisions and the come-ons to Sakir.

She'd decided this and yet she felt so odd, so vulnerable suddenly. He stood before her, totally at ease—barring nine and half inches of arousal.

If only she could be so calm.

Slowly, and very unsurely, she stood up and began to peel off her clothes from her hot, sticky skin one piece at a time.

She felt Sakir's gaze on her and wanted to run behind a palm, but she held her ground. Finally, she stood before him in her bra and panties.

Sakir shook his head, grinned with sinful intent. "You are not finished."

Rita's breasts tightened, tingled, begged for release, perhaps for this man's hands. She made a futile groaning noise, then said, "Fine."

First, she removed her bra and sighed as warm air moved over her jutting nipples. Then she slipped her fingers under the band of her panties and eased them down.

She stood before him nude, feeling his stare, feeling embarrassed and totally vulnerable.

Sakir walked to her, his hand slipping around her waist. "You make me weak with need, Rita. Feel how weak." He eased her close, and she felt him hard against her belly. "You are so beautiful, perfect, with a woman's curves."

Rita shut her eyes, her legs weak as water, her mind filled with chaotic thoughts and visions of making love to this man in the lake beyond, under the waterfall.

Sakir touched her chin, lifted her eyes to his. "Let us enjoy the water."

She smiled, wondering idiotically if he'd heard her thoughts as the heat rose and suffused them, and as Sakir led her into the cool water.

The sand yielded to her steps as they waded deeper and deeper, until the water was up to their shoulders.

"This feels too good," she said.

"I know," he said, wrapping his arms around her and pulling her close.

This time there was no discussion of what was right or wrong. His mouth collided with hers, his tongue dipping into her mouth, searching for her. Rita sucked in a breath, wrapped her arms about his neck and deepened her kiss.

"I am a weak man," Sakir uttered.

"And I am glad for it," she whispered.

His hands raked down her back, squeezing her buttocks, the pads of his fingers digging into her flesh. Rita trembled furiously, but thanks to the buoyancy of the water, she managed to wrap her legs around his waist.

His mouth slipped from hers and went to her ear. "I will bring you such pleasure, Rita."

"But will you ever take pleasure?" she asked, her voice hoarse.

He thrust two fingers inside her, silenced her. "Watching you *is* my pleasure."

Rita gasped for breath, the sensation of liquid fire hugging stiff fingers that bucked up against her womb so wonderful she thought she'd collapse or slip beneath the water and drown.

But she was meant to live, meant to ride his fingers, cry out as he used his thumb, rough and experienced on the bundle of nerves at her core.

His mouth moved to her neck, his teeth grazing her flesh as her heart pounded a rhythm of sex. Water splashed around them, and despite its coolness, sweat broke out on Rita's forehead. Climax was imminent. Her legs shook, her breath was coming in short, raspy waves.

Sakir pulled out his two fingers, then plunged three deeply inside her. Rita opened her mouth in a silent scream of pleasure. Her release was so close, as Sakir flicked her between his thumb and forefinger.

Suddenly she tensed, her body shaking, her mind blank, and let the rush of orgasm pound her senses.

Then all she felt was water and air. She sagged against Sakir, her breath coming in gasps. He rubbed her back and whispered soothing words in Arabic in her ear. She wished with all her heart that she could have this moment forever.

But then the fantasy turned to reality again, just as the fine weather turned to gray.

Sakir kissed her mouth, both with gentleness and with desire. "The clouds move in. Rain is coming."

"We haven't finished this."

"No, we have not."

Hope surged into her heart. "Really?"

"Back at the palace, in our bedroom, we will start this and we will finish it." He lifted her in his arms and started back to shore. "But we must go now."

"I don't want to," she said, turning into his chest, his warmth, knowing she sounded like a child, but not particularly caring.

When Sakir reached the sand, he set her down with supreme gentleness and said, "Nor I," then began to help her on with her clothing.

Midnight.

Sakir stared at the moon.

Midnight, and he still hadn't gone to the rooms he shared with his "wife."

When he and Rita had returned to the palace, the sky had been dark and she had just been waking from a nap in the Jeep. Sakir's immediate thought had been to take her upstairs and make love to her in their bed. He was ready, in mind and most assuredly in body. But something had kept him from that wondrous task.

Perhaps it was his spirit.

With a tone of regret, he'd told Rita that he had several phone calls to return and he would see her later. She gave him no fight, as no doubt she was growing used to his change in mood and in mind. A fact that shamed Sakir to his very bones. Though he gave himself to no one and gave pleasure whenever he was given pleasure, he had always remained a forthright and honorable man when it came to women.

The problem was Rita.

She was not just any woman.

She was fire and life, and he was growing too close to her. Wanting her too much. And, most troublesome of all, needing her too much.

Sakir walked further into the garden and let the scents of jasmine assault his muddled senses. He passed the sculpture of his grandfather, bronzed and ominous. He passed the walled rock garden and mint bushes. He passed the koi pond, knowing exactly where he was going and refusing to stop.

Finally he did.

The stone erupted from the ground before him.

Exotic plants Sakir himself had chosen surrounded his brother's grave. In the daytime, the plants attracted a variety of butterflies, for Hassan had loved butterflies as a child. At night, there was only a lush stillness to the spot.

Sakir stood there for a long time, meditating on all the years lost to his brother. Anger pulsed in his blood.

What a waste.

"Sakir?"

He didn't turn around. The voice acted like a balm to his anger. Rita. He felt her come up beside him, then watched from the corner of his eye as she knelt down and brushed her fingers over the words he'd had carved into the stone.

"What does this mean?" she asked.

His throat tight, Sakir uttered, "'Your brother misses you, little one.'"

Rita stood, then did the strangest thing. She took his hand and held it in her own. She felt warm and real and he wanted to pull her close and gather her up in his arms.

But he did not.

"How did you find me?" he asked.

"You like this garden."

"It is late."

"I know."

"You should be in bed."

She squeezed his hand. "So should you."

He sniffed. "Sleep has eluded me for ten years."

"Who said anything about sleep?"

Sakir turned. She stared up at him, her gaze soft and tender. On any other night, any other day, Sakir would have worried at such a look. But not tonight, not with her. He needed her warmth and care, and was ready to take it.

His gaze flickered down her body. She wore a pale

blue silk nightgown that molded to her curves and she carried the matching robe in her hand.

"I chose that gown for you," he said, desire cleaving to every muscle, every bone.

She smiled. "I know."

"You are breathtaking, Rita."

Her smile widened. "Let's go to bed, Sakir."

He nodded, then slipped his hands underneath her and lifted her into his arms. When she raised a brow at him, he said, "It is tradition."

"What is, exactly?" she asked as he walked through the garden.

Sakir said nothing until they were up the palace stairs and standing before their bedroom door. Once there, he leaned in and kissed her softly. "It is tradition for the prince to carry his princess over the threshold on their wedding night."

Rita laughed softly. "A little past that, aren't we?"

Sakir opened the door and headed for the bedroom. "We have never made love, Rita." With great care, he placed her down on the bed. "We had no wedding night." With slow, tender fingers he eased her nightgown up, up over her knees, up past her thighs. "I think this will be our wedding night, yes?"

Rita felt as though she were dreaming. Sakir talking of wedding nights as he removed her nightgown, her lace panties and his own white caftan. Sakir standing above her, totally nude, his body tight, his erection thick and ready.

Yes, this had to be a dream.

Sakir gazed down at her. "I wish to give you pleasure first, but I do not think I can—"

"Sakir I want you inside me," Rita said, her arms reaching for him. "You have no idea how much pleasure that will give me."

He released a weighty breath. "I want to tease you, taste you, feast between your—"

"I have been teased long enough."

A slow grin moved over Sakir's face. "Yes. We both have."

Rita watched as he quickly sheathed himself. Her breath held tight with anticipation, she waited. What would he feel like? Would she stretch enough to accommodate him? Would she please him? Would she make his climax as intense as he'd made hers?

Sakir moved above her. His gaze fixed on hers, he spread her thighs apart with gentle insistence. Then he lowered his hips.

Rita felt him, up against the entrance to her body. Just from the anticipation alone, she was very wet. Sakir moved up and down, teasing her as he watched her. But that's as far as he went. Never in her life had Rita been so excited, so curious.

His face so near hers, his breath so close, she asked, "What's wrong?"

He shook his head. "I do not know. This seems sacred somehow. I have never known such intensity of feeling."

Rita's heart thundered in her chest. She had known

nothing like this, either. But she did know how to name it. She was in love with her husband and no words, no reason, could keep her from it.

She wrapped her legs around his waist, urging him down, inside, deep into the wet heat of her body.

On an oath, Sakir slipped his hand underneath her hips, lifted her up and pushed into her.

"Yes," Rita uttered, tilting her hips up further as she reveled in every slow inch he gave her.

He was hers.

For now.

For this wonderfully delicious moment.

"Move with me," he said, as his slow strokes quickened.

"Yes." She slammed her hips to meet him, following him to that fast and frantic pace that knew no end but orgasm.

She just wanted to release, wanted to remove all thoughts of the past and how she and Sakir had gotten to this point. She just wanted now. Over and over again, if he'd oblige her.

Her muscles tightened around his shaft as Sakir drove into her. Sweat trickled down her back. Her breasts rose and fell. Time evaporated.

"When you climax," Sakir said through fraught breaths. "I want to hear you. Scream, cry, call out to the gods. Whatever is in you. But I must hear it. Do you understand?"

She nodded violently. Yes. She understood him. She would not hold back. Lord, anything he asked of her she would do. And his request was timely. The love in her heart was ready to explode; the volcano bubbling inside her was ready to flow, rip a hole in her heart, make her see stars.

And when Sakir lowered his head and took her nipple between his teeth as he drove into her hard and fast, she did just that.

Explode. Come.

Die. Live.

"Come with me now," she cried out, gripping his back with her fingers, her nails, she wasn't sure.

Sakir pounded into her. Over and over. His breathing rapid, his body wet with sweat.

Rita let her head fall back. Deep in her throat a cry erupted as torrents of fire, rain and electric shock rippled through her.

And Sakir went with her, uttering her name a thousand times as he spilled hot seed deep into her core.

Twelve

Sakir watched the pale pink light of sunrise play over Rita's nude body, just barely covered by the blue silk sheet from their bed. Up he roamed, his gaze moving from ankle to knee, to hip, to belly, to full breast and supple nipple.

Glorious.

He shuddered and rolled to his back.

What had he done? What had he allowed to happen in this bed? Had his lack of control and propriety disintegrated under the burning light of desire?

And did he care?

The answer to the final question was spirited away as Rita shifted beside him. The tangled silk sheet covered only her woman's curls, leaving the full view of her chest and belly to his roguish eyes. No, he did not care for control or propriety. He wanted to wake this sleeping beauty with a kiss on first one set of lips, then the other.

He felt himself grow hard at the thought. He turned to his side, faced her.

Again, she shifted. This time she rolled to him, snuggled into his chest. Her mouth moved over his skin, and her throaty whisper clawed at his groin. "You're up early?"

"You are very observant."

She laughed, her warm breath fanning against his chest. "You know what I mean."

"I sleep little."

"You told me." She nuzzled her nose against his nipple. "A lot on your mind?"

She would never know how much... "Yes."

Rita glanced up. "But I must be patient and not ask, right?"

Her wide blue eyes fairly drew him in, deep into pools of an understanding heart. He wanted to jump most sincerely. Get lost—or found.

He fairly sighed. Never had he expressed what lay weighty on his heart. Never had he wanted to. But the burden was growing heavier as of late. Rita had offered him her ears too many times to name; as he looked into her blue eyes, he saw empathy.

The words slipped from his lips far too easily. "With so much death and destruction in my family, I fear I am dead inside."

Yes, far too easily. His gut clenched with shame and he wished for the words back. But Rita was already set on her task. She wrapped her arms around his neck, her leg around his groin and pulled herself to him.

"I can assure you, you're very much alive."

Sakir's chest constricted with a tenderness he'd never had before today. He ran his hands down her back to her buttocks and pulled her closer.

Rita searched his gaze. "Tell me what you're thinking."

"I wonder if I am capable of loving. I wonder if I will ever allow myself to fly free." He wanted to look away as shame gripped him. Men of his rank did not say such things. In fact, they should not even feel such things. "I wonder if I will ever feel trust for anyone again."

"Sakir…"

He shook his head. "I do not say this for answers or for your pity, Rita."

"I know that."

"I tell you this because I care for you and want you to understand who I am and what I cannot give."

He saw her once steady gaze flicker, but she said firmly, "I've never asked for anything."

"No, but you deserve all."

A sad smile touched her beautiful mouth. "I don't want to talk about this anymore."

"You wished for me to tell you my feelings, yes?"

"Yeah, I did, but not now—not here, not today." She pressed her hips to him tentatively. "We have almost a week of fantasy left before reality sets in."

Sakir released a bitter chuckle. He understood only too well the need to suspend reality for as long as possible. Had he not attempted such a feat with this unsound romance several times before?

They had two weeks before they returned to the States, and to something resembling reality. Soon enough, he would have to face all those fears, those devices of protection, he had shared with Rita and decide once and for all if he could release his death grip on them.

"You wish for fantasy?" he asked, a slow grin cutting across his mouth.

Rita smiled and nodded enthusiastically.

"Done." Sakir rolled to his back, lifted Rita up over him and then slowly eased her down on his hard shaft.

She let out a joyful moan and white-hot pleasure ripped into Sakir. The wet glove of her body seemed to suckle his erection as she began to move, as she ground her hips against him.

Back and forth.

Deeper.

She grabbed his hands, thrust them to her breasts. She arched her back, let her head drop. And she rode him. Hard and intense.

Sakir couldn't take his eyes off of her as she slammed her hips against him, thrusting, going wild, her breasts quivering with the movement.

But the sight was too much for him to bear and he closed his eyes, let his mind run blank, let his body sink into the oblivion of pleasure.

Rita watched him as he ate his lunch, so perfect, so refined in his manner. She hid behind a potted plant and wondered if she should approach him as he sat before the grand marble table in the most exquisite of atriums. Granted, she wasn't a meek little mouse. But the guy was a sultan, for goodness sake. Pretty intimidating for a girl from a small ranching town in Texas.

Then again, she wasn't the intimidated type.

Rita took a deep breath, stepped out from her leafy cover and started toward him. But she only made it about five feet before she was grabbed from behind and hauled forward.

Panic jumped in her blood as she struggled against decidedly Neanderthal-like muscles. "Hey. Let me go! What's the big idea?"

Without explanation, she was dragged forward. Her heart was in her throat; she wondered what was about to happen to her. What kind of punishment she would receive for approaching the Sultan of Emand unannounced?

"Your Royal Highness." The very low, masculine voice came from just behind her left ear, from the Neanderthal. "This woman has been watching you."

Zayad Al-Nayhal turned casually and gave Rita an inquisitive smile. "Is this true, Rita?"

"Can this guy let me go, please?" Rita said tightly.

"Of course." Zayad motioned to the man behind her. "The princess wishes to be released."

"Princess…" The man sputtered, then quickly stepped back.

"And for the record, I wasn't watching you." Rita

sniffed proudly. "I was waiting for you to finish your lunch before I came to talk to you, that's all."

Zayad nodded at his servant. "You may go now, Laul."

Rita glanced back just in time to catch a glimpse of her captor. Big, brawny and totally bold, Laul bowed low, then turned and left the room.

"I apologize for my servant's brutish behavior." Zayad lowered his head a fraction. "But one cannot be too careful."

"When one is in power, is that it?"

Zayad smiled. "You understand." He motioned to the chair beside him. "Would you care to join me?"

She arched a brow. "Will I have to be strip-searched beforehand?"

His grin widened. "I will leave such a pleasure to my brother."

Heat shot into Rita's cheeks.

Zayad chuckled. "Please sit down. What can I do for you?"

Struggling to gain her composure, Rita took a deep breath and dropped into the chair beside him. "I want to talk about you and Sakir."

The smile fell away from the sultan's face. "As you have seen and no doubt heard, there is no love lost between brothers." His gaze clouded with pain, but remained steadfast on hers. "He believes me responsible for our brother's death and will not hear my opinion on the matter."

"I know. He told me."

"So if you do not come for answers, what do you come for?"

"The thing is, Your Highness, I believe that the circumstance surrounding Hassan's death isn't the real reason for Sakir's antagonism."

Zayad looked startled, though intrigued. "No?"

She shook her head. "I think he's scared."

Zayad snorted and puffed up his chest. "The men of my family do not feel fear, my sister."

Rita rolled her eyes. "Well, that's ridiculous."

Zayad's black eyes hardened, and for the first time since she'd met him, Rita felt very small and very insignificant. But she forced herself to remain calm and focused. She was here to make Zayad understand where his brother was coming from, because the spirit of the man she was in love with was at stake.

"You lose your mother, your father and your little brother," she began gently, "and you don't feel scared about losing the only other member of your family you've got left?"

This seemed to interest Zayad, though his supercilious attitude remained. "Explain further."

"Sakir has lost everyone he's trusted and loved. He takes off from the only home he's ever known and hasn't spoken to the one remaining member of his family in years. Why?" She waited for him to say something, but he didn't. "It can't be just because he's angry with you. He could be angry with you from here. He went halfway around the world, Zayad. Think about it."

Zayad looked thoroughly perplexed.

"If something happened to you," Rita explained.

"He wouldn't be around—he wouldn't be here—to feel it. If he despises you, if he convinces himself that you're responsible for Hassan's death, he won't feel the pain of losing another family member if that should happen."

Zayad shook his head. "How do you know this? Has he said—"

"He's never come out and admitted such a thing. He has too much pride."

Zayad nodded, his eyes deep with understanding.

Rita took a breath. "But I know him. I know what's going on inside him."

"And you love him."

It was a statement, not a question, but Rita felt herself nod.

Zayad was quiet for a moment, his fingers playing with the beads of water inching their way down the sides of his crystal tumbler. Then he turned back to her. "I must speak to him of this."

"No, you can't," Rita insisted, coming to her feet. "He would never forgive me for talking to you about this."

Zayad threw up his hands. "What would you have me do, then?"

"Just try and understand him. For now. Please." Her gaze implored him. "Know that he cares for you and this country more than you'll ever know. Know that in time, he'll make peace with you and with the past."

His jaw tight, Zayad said, "He must."

As Rita walked away from the formidable Sultan of Emand, she hoped to God she hadn't made the biggest mistake of her life. She hoped that her concern for Sakir's heart, and his future with his homeland, people and family hadn't driven her to create more problems, when all she'd wanted to do was make peace.

He had spent the day in meetings with members of Emand Oil's environmental group. But that hadn't stopped Sakir's mind from conjuring images of her, of last night, of this morning.

His chest went tight, as did the rest of him, as he took the palace steps two at a time. Anticipation filled him. More than anything, he wanted to be with Rita—alone, naked, fulfilled. But he would have to be content with seeing her face, perhaps kissing her sweet mouth, and postponing all sensual pleasures until later. His brother was expecting them for dinner tonight.

A frown threatened his good humor as he strode the hallway, but he forced his anger at Zayad away. He was going to her now. Yes, that had his smile returning full force.

He chuckled. Never in his life had he experienced such a pull. They were like moon to tide.

He chuckled once again at the foolish thought, his hand on the doorknob. He would do well to abandon all pangs of romance, concentrate on the real reason he was here in Emand.

Impossible.

When he opened the door, candlelight, driving music and the sensual scent of vanilla met him. The shot of anticipation from a moment ago intensified and all puny thoughts of work disappeared.

There were fifty or so candles in small glass jars lighting a pathway through the suite. Like Hansel and Gretel, a very curious Sakir walked the pathway, all the way through the living room, into the bedroom and out onto the large private terrace.

After that, Sakir noticed nothing. No candles, no scents or sounds. No desert or wind or falling stars.

Nothing but the half-naked woman before him.

Dressed in the native costume of an Emand Saka dancer, Rita smiled coyly at him. "Good evening, Your Highness."

He nodded. "Yes, I would say that it is."

With just that beautiful and highly seductive smile, she took his hand and forced him to sit down in a chair at the table.

The desert breeze blew around them, and he only noticed because it blew the blue gauzy skirt up her amazing thighs.

He licked his lips.

Then she began to dance.

A slow, swaying movement that only the ancient women of the Saka knew. How she was able to learn the dance, he knew not—nor did he care at that moment, for the music was enveloping the space, the sway of her hips was turning his brain to water and everything below his waist to rock-hard need.

Sakir was famished. Not for the wine or the olives and sweetmeats on the plate before him, but for the woman who danced with such abandon—her waist so small, her barely covered breasts rising and falling, her face so happy as she stared at him.

"Rita, please…" He stood, held out his hand. "I have had all I can take."

She grinned, danced to him, thrust out her right hip playfully. "You do not enjoy the dance, Your Highness?"

His gaze went lethal. "I enjoy it very much, Princess."

"But?"

He growled, warned her again. "Rita…"

"I have prepared a few hors d'oeuvres before dinner," she said, then asked coyly, "Are you not hungry?"

Sakir picked her up and slung her over his shoulder. "Famished."

Rita laughed.

At least until he had her on the bed, that filmy skirt up to her waist, her panties down to her ankles—and his tongue in a most heavenly spot.

Thirteen

Rita woke up beside her husband and smiled with happiness. Just lying there, with his nude, dark and heavily muscled body mashed deliciously up against her own, she felt like sighing.

Sakir made her feel so young and sexy and thankful to be alive. All those years of wishing that her gorgeous boss would notice her—or, if we're getting real about it, take her in his arms and make mad, passionate love to her—had not been in vain.

That wish had certainly come true.

For how long, she wasn't certain. But she was content with that. Had to be. She had gone into this love affair with her eyes wide open and she refused to act sad and worried about a future she couldn't control. She would enjoy right now, every moment.

"Good morning."

So intent on her thoughts, Rita hadn't noticed that Sakir was awake and staring at her.

His green eyes nearly drank her in. "What shall we do today?"

She bent down, nuzzled his neck. "We could always do more of this."

A husky moan eased from his throat. "I would be honored, Princess."

"But, then again…" She smiled.

Sakir paused, glanced up, his brow arched. "What are you thinking of?"

With the excitement of a little kid, Rita jumped on top of him, straddled him, grabbed his hands and squeezed. "I want to take you somewhere."

Falling easily into her play, Sakir grinned. "We can go anywhere in the world you wish."

"No, I mean here, in Emand. There's something I have to show you."

"How could this be? You do not know Emand—"

She leaned forward, her face just inches from his. "I'm full of surprises, Your Highness, you should know that by now."

He pulled her to him, kissed her on the mouth. "I do not like surprises."

She chuckled. "Why is that?"

"I wish to know the outcome at all times."

"You can't possibly know the outcome every time."

"I said it is my wish."

Her smile wide, she leaned down again, brushed her lips across his. "Sakir," she whispered, then gave him a thorough kiss—one hot, wet, teasing kiss that lasted a good thirty seconds. Her skin warmed and she thought herself very powerful as she felt him hard and jutting against her thigh. Finally, she sat up and asked, "You want to be in control, is that what it is?"

His eyes burned with the fire of a man who needed release. "Perhaps."

She took his hands and spread his arms back over his head. "Letting others take control now and then can be a very pleasant experience, you know?"

He lifted his head, opened his mouth and ran his tongue across her nipple. "You must convince me further."

Rita sucked in a breath at the intense pleasure of his touch. Her body tight with electricity, she gave him a decadent smile. "Well, our adventure can wait an hour or so."

Sakir grinned, tightened his grip on her. "You are a wise and wonderful woman, Rita Al-Nayhal."

His words swam over her, but she didn't analyze them. She was too busy melting as Sakir lifted his head, took her nipple into his mouth, suckled…

"You may be wise and wonderful, but you are also a reckless driver." The comment came from Sakir, who was now sitting in the passenger side of a black SUV, fully dressed and masked with that I-am-royalty-and-above-it-all attitude.

Rita felt the need to correct him. "I am a confident driver, you mean."

He fairly snorted. "No, I believe reckless is the correct description." He shook his head. "I should have never allowed you to—"

"Allowed me?" she began with mock severity.

"After this driving experience, yes—allowed." He threw his hands up. "When we made that turn back there the car was suspended on two wheels—"

"Oh, c'mon."

"Did you not almost hit that bush right afterward?"

"I tapped it a little bit."

"If I was tapped like that, I would be dead."

She turned and looked at him, then burst out laughing. He followed suit with a rather carefree chuckle.

Rita turned back to the desert road. Was it possible that the sober, always-in-control, rarely-found-life-amusing Sakir Al-Nayhal had changed? And in her care?

Was she too bold to think that she had something to do with this new light and loving side of him? And if she did have something to do with it, would she be responsible for bringing it out of him always—like back in Paradise, back home—

She mentally rolled her eyes. That was a ridiculous thought, not to mention an incredibly sneaky way of allowing herself to hope for a future, a way to stay near and dear to the man she was desperately in love with.

"Are we almost at our destination, Rita?"

She smiled at him. "Be patient."

"Impossible."

She laughed. "Just give it your best shot, all right?"

It was barely ten minutes later when Rita pulled over to the side of the road. Sure, it had been a long drive, but to her, the journey had definitely been worth it. Lord, just for the view alone.

The beautiful Bari Mountains stretched out before her. She took a deep breath and smiled. This land never ceased to amaze her. Mountains and deserts and the palm tree forest and waterfalls. Oh, how much she would love to bring her sister and father here.

She stopped herself from traveling farther with that thought. Emand belonged to Sakir and his family, which she was not part of—not really.

"Let's go," she called cheerfully, grabbing a pack out of the back of the SUV.

"Are we to hike?" Sakir asked, his gaze filled with interest as he took the pack from her.

She liked to see him this way, anticipation on his face. "Just a ways. Our spot is over there, in the flatlands."

Rita was happy to note that the walk wasn't all that rugged, but very pretty. Juniper woodlands encompassed the high flat plains, along with acacia trees and milkweed shrubs. Eagles soared overhead, playing chicken with the cliff faces just below.

Finally, they came to the spot Tureen, one of the sultan's men, had told her about—a rich, well preserved valley floor with a stream, several beautiful old acacia trees and one massive fig tree.

When Rita stopped, Sakir followed suit. "I have never been to this part of the Bari Mountains before."

Rita grinned. "I know."

He frowned, but humor burned behind his eyes. "I do not like this...this secrecy, going behind my back."

On a laugh, Rita grabbed his hand and pulled him toward the surprise she'd been planning since they'd returned from the palm tree forest. "Oh, just relax, Your Highness, and come with me. You'll like it plenty when you see where we're going."

In just under a minute, they stood before it.

Rita turned to watch Sakir's face as he took in the most enormous fig tree in Emand, or so Tureen had told her. His eyes widened and his mouth curved into a handsome smile. With great care, he reached up, cupped a giant piece of ripe, black fruit that hung from the tree's large puzzle-like leafs.

She squeezed his hand. "I thought a picnic under this tree. Bread, cheese, fruit, a little wine. And all we have to do is reach up for dessert."

Sakir said nothing, and she wondered for a moment if he was displeased or worse, unmoved by her sentiment. But after a moment, he turned to her, pulled her into his arms and whispered against her hair. "How did you know?"

"You told me." She pulled back slightly, looked into his eyes. "Don't you remember?"

He blinked, no doubt trying to recall a time when he'd allowed himself to be so open with another human being.

His hands threaded her hair. "Why would you do such a thing for me?"

She smiled a little sadly, stared up at the man of her dreams, knowing full well that she couldn't tell him how much she loved him. It was as though a hand fisted around her heart, but she managed a clear, "I don't know."

"You don't know?" he said, his gaze warm, safe.

She shrugged, not willing to believe she was ever safe enough with him to tell him the truth about her feelings. "I guess I thought you'd like to see it, that's all."

"I do." He smiled. "You are amazing, Rita."

"I hope that doesn't end with 'and any man would be lucky to have you.'" She gave him a playful grin.

He lowered his head, kissed her on the mouth. A soft, tender kiss—not heated as it was this morning. "This is true. Any man *would* be lucky to have you."

The ultrafeminine genes that dwelled within her sprung to life and she wanted to ask him if he would be that man. That lucky one. But she stopped herself, for she wasn't sure if she wanted the answer.

Not now, anyway.

And not here, in this perfect setting.

There would be enough time for truths, she knew. And although she hated to admit it, in her heart she was hoping that with all this time they were spending together, perhaps Sakir would knock down his wall of anger and resentment and embrace a future with her, fall as deeply in love with her as she was with him.

It was, of course, wishful thinking. But hopes could not be helped.

Sakir reached up again. This time, he picked that luscious, black fig from the tree and brought it down between them.

"Have you had a fig from Emand, Rita?"

"Never."

"The taste is unlike anything you have ever known. It is pure and it is pleasure."

Rita's breath caught in her throat. He could be speaking of them, of their time here—of her love for him.

She grinned.

Sakir did, too. "Open your mouth for me."

Resisting the fruit seemed foolish, but resisting Sakir seemed futile. She did as he asked and sighed as warm, sweet fruit met her tongue.

When Sakir and Rita returned to the palace later that day, happy, full and sexually content, there was a message waiting for them.

A message that tossed their relaxed and carefree mood right out of the palace's extravagant floor-to-ceiling windows.

It was from Asad Qahhar and asked for the prince to return his call at his earliest convenience. A deep sense of regret filled Sakir's blood as he left Rita in their suite and went up to his offices in the tower. He was not ready to hear the man's answer, nor was he ready for his time with Rita to end. But in his life, business always came first.

The call took just five minutes, but the outcome brought Sakir little happiness. He was slow in traveling back down to the suite, uncharacteristically awkward as he sat beside Rita on the bed. She was taking off her shoes, looking very content after a day filled with food, figs and lovemaking. He too had felt such contentment.

Until just a moment ago.

When reality had returned.

"Qahhar wishes to meet with us tomorrow afternoon," Sakir said at long last. "He has made his decision."

Rita looked up, her brows knit together. "So soon?"

"I'm afraid so."

She exhaled heavily, her shoes all but forgotten now. "I thought we'd have more time."

"As did I."

The air rushed from Sakir's lungs in a melancholy wheeze. What the devil was wrong with him? He did not understand the depths of his own feeling. This was what he had wanted, what he had come home for. He was poised, ready to take what Qahhar was about to offer him. Hell, he had heard as much in the man's voice. No secretary calling. The man himself, sounding very pleased.

And yet Sakir could muster no excitement.

The thrill of the chase had always been a pleasant one, but it was the capture that truly pleased him.

Not today.

A vise fisted his chest. He did not want to examine the reasons—*or reason.* He did not dare.

"Well," Rita began, a forced enthusiasm to her tone. "A positive and very profitable answer from Qahhar is why we came to Emand, right?"

"It is." No, he reminded himself, she could not read his thoughts. But it was as though she had.

She looked over at him, her eyes filled with questions. But she only asked one. And a general one, at that. "So after we get his decision, we could go back home?"

Sakir nodded. "Perhaps as early as tomorrow night."

Rita said nothing, just gave him a tight-lipped smile. Sakir wanted Rita to force his hand, remind him of their lovemaking, remind him of their time together, remind him that if he were an honorable man he would ask her to be with him—to make their "union" a true and honest state.

But he would not ask for this, just as he knew Rita would not. For very different reasons, of course—where he could never give love to another, Rita was far too proud to ask it of him.

"Do you want me to call him in the morning?" she asked, her back straight, her countenance one of a good and solid business assistant. "Confirm our meeting?"

Sakir put his hand on hers. "Thank you, but no, I will make the call."

With amazing warmth, Rita covered his hand with her remaining one and squeezed.

The action nearly tore Sakir apart.

Where, hours ago, this woman had been his—body, heart and soul—she now had once again become his assistant. He hated the fact, but knew he could have it no other way.

He released her, then stood up, bowed. "I will leave you to get ready for bed."

"Where are you going?" she asked.

"I think I will take a walk in the garden."

"Would you like some company?"

The muscles in his body tensed. He looked down, into her eyes and wanted to get lost there, wanted to say yes. Hell, if he had his preference, he would stay right here, in this bed. But such dreams were impractical. If he continued this impossible romance now, he would not be just a careless rogue, he would be a heartless one.

Rita deserved far more than that.

"I should like to go alone."

She nodded, but stopped him as he turned to walk away. "You know, Sakir," she said, her voice alive with passion. "What you're looking for isn't in that garden. And it's not in an eighty-hour workweek or a sprawling ranch in Texas."

He stopped, but didn't turn around.

"God, I hope you find it."

His jaw tight, he asked, "Find what?"

"Whatever it is that's going to make you happy and fulfilled." She paused, took a breath. "I'd truly love to see you that way."

Anger surged into Sakir, but at what—at whom—he was not sure. Madness had come over him the moment he had stepped onto his plane with this woman beside him.

Did she not understand?

He did not care for happiness and fulfillment. They were fleeting. No, he wanted only to find sanity again.

A muscle twitched beneath his right eye, but he ignored the uncontrolled movement, stuck out his chin proudly and walked out of the room.

Fourteen

The time was 1:00 p.m.

The place: the grand library in the sultan's palace.

Beautifully bound books swelled to the rafters; leather sofas and chairs were dotted about atop silk carpets to make the space a comfortable one; gold and marble tables held platters of cakes and cookies, while in the royal china were full servings of hot Turkish coffee.

It was glorious, and very overwhelming for the laymen, a class to which Rita and Emand Oil's Asad Qahhar definitely subscribed.

Rita had not been surprised at Sakir's quick change of venue. He liked the home court advantage, so to speak, when closing a deal. And there was nothing that rivaled the palace, save the White House.

Asad did not lean back in his chair as he had in his own offices in town. No, he remained straight-backed in his posture and deferential in his manner. "I am pleased, Your Highness. Al-Nayhal Corporation will do well for Emand Oil, I am certain of it."

Sakir, who had yet to sit down, nodded from his place behind the sofa. "We look forward to working with you."

"I feel the same," Asad said, then paused. "I cannot tell you how pleased I am that you will be in Emand several times a year. This makes me feel very comfortable in my choice."

Rita could feel Sakir stiffen all the way across the room. Although she didn't have to, she caught the quick glare he sent her way. She wasn't sure what he was going to do here or say to Qahhar. Perhaps he'd ignore the man's comment or amend Rita's previous and imprudent offer from their last meeting. Either way, it would surely quash the deal for them.

"I will be here two or three times per year," Sakir announced, then proceeded to pour himself another cup of coffee.

Rita nearly fell out of her leather armchair and choked on a pecan cookie. Had she heard him right? Had he just agreed to come home several times a year? She had no clue what had brought on such a change of heart, but she vowed to ask him about it later.

Asad nodded. "Two or three times, you say?"

"If this is not sufficient, I am sorry," Sakir said tightly. "But, alas, it is all I will commit to."

Asad shook his head. "No. This is very well, Your Highness. I am very pleased indeed."

"Good." He stuck out his hand. "We have a deal then."

Asad Qahhar stood and the two men shook on it. Rita just stared at them, her brain in some type of fog. She couldn't wait for the older man to leave so she could ask Sakir what had just happened here. And when he did, she pounced on Sakir.

"I don't understand."

"What don't you understand?" Sakir said, still standing, still looking as tight and professional as ever.

"You have agreed to come to Emand several times a year."

"I have."

She rolled her eyes. "Are you going to make me spell this out?"

Sakir sighed. "I did what I had to do to make the deal."

This made her pause. For a moment, just a moment there, she'd thought perhaps he'd really changed. She'd thought that maybe he'd forgiven his brother, wanted to come home again, wanted something different than deals and contracts and work, work, work. But that— again—had been just wishful thinking.

"You did what you had to do for the deal," she repeated. "Just as you did with us, right?"

"Yes," he said tightly. "That is right."

Rita stared at Sakir, her heart bleeding. No longer was he the sensual, carefree man she had known over the last several days. The man she loved and had made love to in her bed. No, the man that stood before her now

was the same man who had left her last night and who
had slept on the couch in their suite.

Her boss.

All business. All the time.

"I must see to some paperwork," he said, then
quickly downed the cup of coffee. "We will see each
other later, yes?"

"Of course." Her heart thoroughly ached, and she
wanted to curl up in her chair with a big, fluffy blanket
and cry for a few hours. But she didn't have that luxury. She had to be all about business as well if she was
to survive this. "Do you need any help with the work?"

"No. Thank you."

It was funny. Even in her anger and frustration, she
wanted to help him. Well, that was love, folks. What
an idiot she was for thinking she could get through this
unscathed.

She watched him walk out of the room, then fell
back against the chair and downed her coffee. She
wanted to take a few minutes, a little time to sit and feel
sorry for herself, but the library suddenly felt very con-
fining and she decided to get up and get out. Once in
the hall, she headed out to the gardens. It seemed the
place for thought and reflection—perhaps even regrets,
if she had a mind to list them.

The morning sun warmed her skin and the desert
breeze cooled her down as she walked along the rows
of roses. She was just bending down to smell a perfectly lovely yellow variety, when someone came up behind her.

"We must talk."

Rita whirled around, nearly stabbing her palm with a thorn in the process. "Zayad. You scared the life out of me."

"I apologize," he said, but didn't look the least bit sorry.

He stood before her, hands behind his back, his handsome face etched with tension as his white caftan whipped in the soft wind. "I know I have agreed to keep silent on the subject of my brother until he is ready, but I can do this no longer."

Rita's heart leapt into her throat. "Why?"

"I know the bargain you have made with Qahhar. This means your business is done here. You will leave Emand very shortly and I will never be able to confront my brother."

Rita's mind whirled with thought. Zayad was right, of course, but if he talked to Sakir now, about what she'd said, Sakir would be livid. He would admonish her for interfering, but he would probably never speak to her again for having his pride crushed before his brother.

She shook her head. "I'm sorry, Zayad, but—"

"I am sorry, too, my sister, but Sakir and I must speak."

"He's got to find his own way back home and to you," she said passionately.

He stood tall before her, his arms crossed over his broad chest. "Are you really asking me to forget all that you have said to me?"

"For now, yes."

"Well, I cannot. I will not." He turned away, his head

high, his manner defiant. Then he turned back. "I brought Sakir here to end this war, not to—"

"What?" The blood in Rita's ears began to pound. "What did you just say?"

Zayad shook his head, his lips thinning dangerously. "I want our family back together. I want my brother to know his place here. I want him back in Emand where he belongs. It is important to all—"

"Stop." Rita couldn't believe she was speaking so boldly, commanding a sultan in his own home, but she was beyond reason. "You *brought* Sakir here?"

Zayad sighed, said nothing for a moment and then, "Yes. I arranged for the meeting between Sakir and Qahhar."

"Oh my God."

"The interest in my brother for Emand Oil was my doing. So what?"

"So what?" she fairly choked out. "You speak of pride and honor. Sakir has these in spades."

"He would come no other way."

She threw her hands up. "He thought he got this all on his own, his talents…"

"It was on his own merit that he landed this account, Rita. Make no mistake. But Qahhar did come to me for counsel, and I gave him my advice. I told him who I believed was the best man for the job."

Above them, a cloud rolled in and covered the sun. The air cooled and the flowers seemed to wilt slightly. Rita swallowed, shook her head. "Sakir is going to be furious when he finds this out."

Zayad lifted his chin. "Just as he would if he knew you discussed his fears of loss regarding his family with me?"

Her belly clenched, she nodded. "Yes."

"Well, it is too late for the both of you, then."

Rita whirled around, her heart in her throat. No, no, no. It wasn't him. Not now.

But her silent plea went unanswered.

Eyes filled with hatred, Sakir stared at her. "From him I would expect such deceit—" he shook his head, his voice brutal "—but never from you, Rita."

Stunned, sickened by his withering gaze, Rita could only shake her head. But aloud, she could take nothing back. The situation before Sakir looked just as it was. Two people discussing him, covering up their previous conversations—conspiring to hold back things he had a right to know.

Rita felt raw, exposed and utterly defeated.

In her hope of helping him, she had deceived him.

"Brother," Zayad began slowly and with much patience.

"We are no longer brothers," Sakir uttered with thick revulsion.

Tears pricked Rita's eyes, but she swiped at them and took a step toward the man she loved. "Sakir, please listen to me—"

He stopped her cold. Full-blown reproach burned in his green eyes. Then, as he'd done earlier that day, he turned and walked away.

Fifteen

Rita Thompson had courage.

It had been a big trait of her mother's. The woman had been known to rise from the ashes in times of crisis, and do what needed to be done—say what needed to be said—regardless of the consequences. And no matter how badly she had wished to escape the discomfort of a confrontation, running away with things left unresolved just hadn't been an option for her.

This had been an invaluable, though difficult, lesson for Rita through the years. But things had always turned out better for it in the end.

She hoped today would be no different.

As she walked into the palace and took the stairs to her room, Rita heard her mother's voice in her head. She was urging her daughter to go to Sakir, apologize for how she'd handled things with Zayad and tell him what was in her heart.

Rita knew full well her regrets would not be taken with any sense of forgiveness, just as she knew her feelings of love would not be reciprocated. But when she arrived at the suite door, she didn't flinch. She turned the knob and went in.

She didn't see Sakir at first, and she wondered if he had gone to another part of the palace and had his things sent to him—or if he was already on his way to the airport. But then he walked out of the bedroom.

He had changed from caftan to jeans and a white shirt. He looked so handsome, so angry, so lost. She wanted to throw herself into his arms and cry her way to absolution, but she was no child. She would handle things as a grown woman, without entreaty and tears.

She swallowed the grapefruit-size lump in her throat and began. "I screwed up. Really screwed up. I'm sorry."

He lifted his chin. "It is forgotten."

Everything in his gaze, everything in his manner, screamed the opposite. "I doubt that."

"The bottom line is I have Emand Oil and you have your partnership. We will focus on this."

His words cut deep. She couldn't care less for the partnership. She wanted him to understand why she did what she did. And if God was handing out miracles, she wanted Sakir to give in to his feelings—feelings she knew in her soul were there, behind the thorny wall around his heart.

She wanted him to love her.

She walked over to him, stood a few feet away. "Sakir, we need to talk. I mean, really talk."

"I have much to do."

"It'll take a minute."

"I have papers to go over before we leave in the morning."

Leave in the morning...

The shock of that statement assailed her, dropped on her heart like a steel weight. Yes, they were getting on a plane tomorrow.

Back to real life.

Back to Paradise, Texas, and working and living under the pretense that this whole marriage—the nights of lovemaking and the days of friendship—had been a sham.

Rita took a deep breath. "Fine, but at least hear me out before you go."

He clipped her an impersonal nod. "Speak then, but understand, my heart is lost to you."

Pain seared into her soul at his words. But she knew she had to say what she'd come here to say. Sakir needed to hear it. He needed to hear the truth.

"The people of this country love you," she said. "Your brother loves you. And I love you."

His eyes blazed green fire; his nostrils flared.

Rita released a shaky breath. "I understand your fears about losing those you care about. The pain is unimaginable, I know—"

"You do not know anything," he replied in a voice taut with fury.

"I lost my mother when I was young, Sakir," she countered vehemently. "Believe me, I know."

This statement stopped him cold. For a moment, the ire on his face dropped away and genuine interest took its place. For once, perhaps he was thinking about her family and not his own painful history.

"I am sorry about your mother," he said at long last.

"Thank you."

"But it is different."

She agreed. "I know. When she died I was very angry, but I didn't blame anyone else for her death."

Rage filtered back into his gaze. His glanced at the door. "What more have you to say?"

What more besides, "I love you."

The midmorning sun inched its way into the room from the terrace windows, bathing both her and Sakir in its light.

"I went to your brother because I care about you," Rita explained.

Sakir scoffed at this.

"You can believe it or not. But it's the truth." She cocked her head, tried to get through to him with words and eyes filled with tenderness. "You needed the help, the push, whatever you want to call it—you needed it to get past this darkness you live in."

Through gritted teeth, Sakir uttered, "I needed no help. Especially regarding Zayad."

"Don't make the mistake of pushing him out of your life again," she said, her tone imploring him to listen. "He's all the family you have left."

Something close to vulnerability shone in Sakir's eyes at that declaration.

"If you do," Rita continued, "you'll regret it for as long as you live."

"I do not indulge in regret, Rita." He lifted a brow. "For anything or anyone."

Rita exhaled heavily. "You can toss out all these self-righteous one-liners and pretend none of this matters to you, but I know better."

"How is it you know?" he bated.

"I know because I see you, Sakir. I see you and your heart."

His green eyes narrowed and hardened. "Just because we fell into bed a handful of times does not mean you know who I am."

Rita felt as if she'd been stabbed. Her stomach threaded into knots and she could hardly catch her breath. No one had ever said something so cruel to her. Out of pain, fear, resentment—it didn't matter. Sakir had crossed a line today and no matter what happened, things between them would never be the same again.

Just as she would never be the same again.

He stared at her, still proud and unaffected. "Is there anything more you wish to say?"

"Only this." She mustered up every ounce of aplomb she possessed and looked him straight in the eye. "I quit."

And this time, with a bruised heart and a numb spirit, she was the one who turned and walked away.

* * *

What he needed was a smooth cigar and a very tall glass of whiskey.

Sakir sat in the worn leather chair his father had always used to think on important matters. He'd been cooped up in his father's study in the back section of the palace tower for close to three hours now—doing nothing, saying nothing, trying like hell to erase everything he'd heard and said today.

He was very good at that.

He had erased the past decade from his mind with ease. He had thought one day should be nothing to him.

He had been wrong.

As she had from the first moment they had met, the moment he had kissed her at their wedding altar, the moment he had first slid inside her body and the moment she had taken him in search of figs, Rita Thompson had insinuated herself into his mind and held steady.

He could not get her eyes out of his memory, just as he could not expunge the repulsive words he had uttered to her. Words that had meant to shock, to hurt, to drive away this woman who had come to mean far too much to him.

And he had succeeded.

With eyes filled with pain, she had told him that she would no longer be working in his employ.

Bitter laughter fell from Sakir's lips. He had lost her heart and her mind. And her love...

He growled, let his head fall into his hands.

This was a good thing, the right thing. He did not

want this woman's love. He did not want such a burden. Yet every time he played those four daunting words— *I love you, Sakir*—over in his head, his chest seized and his body ached for her.

He drove his hand through his hair. Dammit, he had been a fool for bringing her here, for making that agreement. Marriage, even one crafted on subterfuge, was a very risky undertaking. And he had taken the leap without a thought. All he had seen was Emand Oil, spurning his brother and getting close to a woman he had longed to touch and taste for years.

In truth, he deserved whatever wounds he got.

All thoughts died right then and there, as suddenly a sword whizzed past his head and dropped onto the table beside him, the steel blade smashing against the wood with a loud clatter.

"Let us resolve this."

Sakir whirled around, saw his brother standing over him and threw him a sneer.

Zayad's grin held no humor, either. In fact, he looked ready to do battle. "Unless all that time in America has left you soft."

Through clenched teeth, Sakir uttered, "You provoke me?"

Zayad inclined his head. "I do."

The anger that raged inside Sakir, the anger that had been eating at him for too many years to count, rushed to the surface in electric currents. His blood pounded in his veins, and his every muscle tensed.

Sakir and his brother had worked with swords for

many years, both excelling at the art. But today, at this moment, they were not playing a child's game. This was a battle, true and without fear.

"Not here." Sakir grabbed the sword and held it to his side. "Not in our father's room."

"Agreed."

Zayad walked out of the room. Sakir followed, his gaze like that of a hawk's. They both knew where they were going. The large terrace that spanned the entire third floor had always been used for formal occasions and state dinners.

Today, it would serve as the field of a final conflict.

The sun glared down on Sakir's back as he walked out onto the stone. But he cared little. His mind and his body were set like an animal's, ready to pounce, to strike. He never looked away from his brother as he positioned himself and waited—for it was the honor of the sultan to begin the match.

Zayad also positioned himself, then without a word he lifted his brow just slightly.

It was enough.

Sakir rushed him, his sword first held high above his head, and then slamming down. Metal crashed against metal.

Zayad's footwork was excellent and Sakir was forced back, back against the balcony wall. But he wasn't about to be defeated so easily. With a grin, he lunged at Zayad. Again, swords clashed as his brother was ready for him and struck back. Hard and heavy.

The sun beat down on them without mercy. Over

and over, back and forth, the two brothers battled. Sweat dripped from Sakir's brow into his eyes, but he allowed the sting to replenish his energy. And he used all the rage that dwelled inside of him.

He blocked and slashed and attacked, sparring with Zayad back almost to the railing.

Suddenly Zayad cried out. Sakir paused, his breathing labored. He watched his brother look down, turn over his hand and stare. Blood dripped from a gash in Zayad's palm.

Zayad looked up and gave Sakir a deadly glare. Again he cried out, but this time it was the cry of a warrior.

Zayad attacked like a man possessed. His sword fell to Sakir's leg, his waist, his chest.

Time seemed to hold still as they battled.

But not for long.

It was Sakir who howled next, who backed off. Blinding pain seized his arm. Blood seeped eagerly from the rip in his white shirt.

He looked at Zayad, his brow raised questioningly. Zayad knew that look, knew what it meant and nodded, sweat dripping from his forehead. Shedding blood was enough for them both; they quit and backed off.

"You have remained quick, brother," Zayad said through weighty breaths.

Sakir pressed the palm of his hand to his wound. "And you have remained slow."

Zayad chuckled and let his sword fall. "Shall we go again, then?"

Sakir shook his head and snorted. "I would like that, but alas I am too old."

Zayad walked to him and then fell to his backside onto the stone floor. "As am I."

Sakir also sat, exhausted. He no longer felt like the man of business, the man of indifference, the man of anger. Sitting here, on the floor with his brother, bleeding and trading gibes, he felt like a child, battled and bruised and ready for a nap.

The brothers sat in silence for a moment, then Zayad knifed a hand through his wet hair and sighed. "I miss Hassan."

Sakir looked away, the pain in his arm nothing to the pain he felt for the loss of his younger brother. "You could have kept him at home."

Zayad wiped the blood from his hand onto the stones beside him. "Sakir, do you not remember our brother?"

"Of course I remember him."

"Then you will recall that while on this earth he was a wild little monkey, a proud eagle—he could not be contained."

Sakir ripped off the sleeve of his shirt and handed it to Zayad for a makeshift bandage. If he thought back, if he allowed himself to think back on his little brother, he would see a boy just as Zayad had described. Hassan had been as stubborn as the rest of them.

Sakir glanced up, nodded. "He was a true son of Al-Nayhal, that is certain."

Grief moved through Zayad's gaze. "But for my son,

we are the last of this family. Can we not resolve our differences and be brothers once more?"

No biting comment found its way to Sakir's lips this time. He had fought a weary battle over the last ten years. Perhaps it was time to throw down his sword and face his fears, accept that his brother had no control over life and death, just as he, Sakir, did not.

"Perhaps we should resolve this," Sakir said with just a touch of humor. "For I fear I could not survive another clash of swords."

Zayad laughed again. It was a good sound. One Sakir had missed, though he would never admit it aloud. Once upon a time, when his mother and father had been alive, the family had sat together, taken a meal and laughed.

It had been a long time ago.

"You will forgive Rita, as well?"

Sakir shot out of the fog of memory and fairly choked. "What do you say?"

"Rita is owed an apology, my brother."

Sakir did not want to hear such a thing. He bit back. "This is none of your affair. And besides, she had no right—"

"She had the right of a wife who loves her husband."

Sakir snorted with derision. "Wife. She is not my—" He stopped short, stared at his brother. "But I gather you already knew that."

Zayad's brows knit together. "I thought I did. I thought your marriage was not based on love. But now I am not so sure."

"What does that mean?" Sakir asked, irritated.

"You may have married her out of necessity, brother, but much has changed, yes?"

Sakir opened his mouth to speak, to refute his brother's claim, then promptly shut it. Although he did not care to confess such foolishness on his part, he could not deny the change in his feelings, either.

He had married Rita to have respectability with his conservative clients, yes. But somewhere between the plane ride to Emand and the palm tree forest, things had turned and morphed into a genuine affection.

Zayad glanced down at his wounded hand. "Pride will keep you from this woman you love."

"Love," Sakir said with much flippancy. "What do I know of love?"

"Not much, that is true. But I am a man with eyes. I see how you look at one another." He grinned. "There is much feeling there."

"Bah."

Zayad placed his wounded hand on his brother's shoulder. "Sakir, will you do something for me?"

"What is it?"

"For one moment, think of your life without her."

It was as though he had been stuck by his brother's sword once again. But the words Zayad had uttered were far more painful than a mere nick on the arm.

His life without Rita.

But no, he would not be without her, he reminded himself. She would be at his side, his partner in the firm. All day they would be together. Then, of course, at night they would go their separate ways; she to her home and he to his—

Sakir stopped right there.

There would be no working together. He would not see her.

She had quit her job.

Under the hot sun, Sakir felt deathly cold. Even when Rita had told him that she quit, he did not think it possible. He did not think of her as gone, out of his life and his bed. Forever.

He lifted his head to the heavens and cursed into the wild desert air.

"It is as I thought." Zayad gave him a brotherly rap on the arm.

A sharp sting bit at Sakir and he let fly a groan.

Zayad chuckled. "Sorry, brother. But as you have already seen, no pain compares to the loss of a woman's favor."

"That may very well be." Sakir shook his head. "But it matters little now."

"Why?"

"I have said foolish, malicious things to her."

Zayad stood, offered his brother a hand. "She will forgive you."

The look in Rita's eyes this morning spoke differently. Yes, Sakir knew there was still love there. But she was clearly resigned to his snarls and her decision. Resignation was far worse than being angry.

Sakir grabbed his brother's hand. "She would refuse me now."

Zayad pulled Sakir to his feet. "I think not."

"You do not know her as I do."

Zayad shrugged. "You give in, then?"

One word sat on Sakir's tongue, refusing to stir. "Never."

Sixteen

She would miss this place.

Rita stared out the airport's soaring windows at the desert in the distance. The sun was slowly setting, tossing that exquisite pinky-peach glow her way, making her smile a little sadly. In a million years, she'd never have thought that she'd become as attached to this land as she had. Heck, she was supposed to be a Texan through and through. But Emand had snagged her heart.

Just as its sheikh had.

Her heart squeezed, but she forced the feeling away. She'd have to get used to this empty feeling. She'd have to remember that she had no Sakir, no job, no romance. She was going home with nothing, with only the hope of rebuilding her life. Thank goodness her sister Ava's wedding was just a few short weeks away. Getting lost in last-minute wedding details, helping the nervous bride with her makeup and dress would surely keep Rita's mind occupied. Then when Ava and Jared finally left for their honeymoon, Rita would get to work on finding a new job.

"Flight Fourteen to Paris, France, en route to Dallas, Texas, will be boarding at Gate Six."

Rita didn't even glance up when her flight was called. She'd booked a commercial flight back to the States, with a short layover in Paris. She hadn't told Sakir she was leaving, as she sure didn't want to ride back with him.

Her stomach clenched. Just the thought of hours on a plane with the man who had rejected her…it would be way too humiliating.

"All first-class passengers traveling on Flight Fourteen to Paris, France, en route to Dallas, Texas, should be boarding at this time."

Rita flipped through her magazine not even seeing the pictures. She didn't want to run in the direction of the gateway, not just yet. She had a little time, sure, but it wasn't that. The truth was she wanted to hold on to Emand and the memories she'd made here for as long as possible.

A fact that made her want to kick herself.

Oh, well. Soon enough she'd be on that plane, climbing into her snug little coach seat and flying home.

Back to Paradise.

Rita smiled a little sadly. Right now, her hometown

sounded like just that—heaven for a woman who felt like hell.

Unbidden, an image of she and Sakir making love, laughing underneath that massive fig tree, popped into her head.

Her throat ached with unshed tears. How could she have been so stupid? Thinking all the time that a future with this man never mattered, that all those wonderful days and nights and moments and memories would just fade into the scrapbook of her mind—forget the emotions that had come with them.

Well, Rita. That's what you get for marrying the boss.

Boss…

She shook her head, feeling unbelievably defeated. After today, Sakir would no longer be her boss. She'd quit, and no matter how hard it was going to be to find a new job, there was no way she was going back to Al-Nayhal Corporation. She couldn't see Sakir again and work with him every day, as her heart continued to pine and to break.

"At this time we would like to invite all coach passengers traveling on Flight Fourteen to Paris, France, en route to Dallas, Texas, to board."

On legs of water, Rita stood up, her carry-on feeling like it was filled with boulders as she walked slowly toward the terminal.

"Where has she gone?"

Sakir stood over Gana, who, up until a moment ago, had been stripping the sheets on the bed he had shared with Rita just a few nights ago. Zayad was beside him, not saying much, just giving his brother the support he had claimed he did not need.

The young woman bowed low. "I do not know, Your Highness."

"She said nothing?" he demanded, his arms crossed over his chest—a chest that had been constricting every time he thought about Rita leaving the palace, leaving him without a word.

"She embraced me, Your Highness. Thanked me for my service."

Sakir could barely contain his frustration, but he forced calm into his voice. "Think Gana, please. She packed her clothes—"

"The princess left most of her clothing, Your Highness," Gana said quickly.

A cold knot twisted in Sakir's belly. Of course she would not take his gifts. She was far too proud to take from him after what had happened, after what he had said to her. "Fine," he said tightly. "She packed the clothes she brought to Emand then, and…?"

The woman looked up to the ceiling, sniffed, clearly racking her brain for more of an answer than "I do not know." Finally, her weary gaze returned to his. "I am sorry, Your Highness."

Zayad, who had remained quiet up until now, stepped forward. "Did she want to travel to the mountains again? Perhaps tour the deserts?"

The young woman took a deep breath, shook her

head. "Not that I am aware of, Your Royal Highness." Her brow furrowed then. "Wait a moment."

"What is it?" Sakir demanded.

"There was one thing she said that sounded strange."

Zayad looked ready to shake the maid. "Well, out with it, Gana."

The young woman's eyes widened. "It was about the French."

"The French?" Sakir repeated. "What the devil does that mean?"

"She asked me if I thought the people in France call their string potatoes *French fries* as she would in America."

Zayad grinned at the amusing query, said to his brother, "She means to leave Emand."

Sakir nodded, his gut tight. Routes back to the States on commercial airlines went regularly through London and Paris. Odds were that she was at the airport this minute, or already on her way out of the country.

On his way up to the suite moments ago, he had thought that perhaps she had made her way to the airport. But he had not been certain and did not want to alert the airport security, and whoever else might be listening in, of a missing Emand princess.

Sakir walked to the open balcony and looked out. His heart pounded wildly in his chest; his mouth felt dry as the desert beyond. Never in his life had he been so afraid to lose something, someone. He had been a fool to hold on to the past with an iron fist. Now he was paying the price.

"Sakir?"

He turned. His brother raised a brow in unspoken query.
What to do?

Well, he would not let her leave, certainly. Not until he had said what was on his mind and on his heart. Odds were good she would refuse him, but if he did not see her one last time, apologize and profess his truths, he would lose not only the woman he loved, but his sanity as well.

"Shall I call for the car?" Zayad asked.

Sakir nodded, reached in his pocket and took out his cell phone. "But first, I will speak to my men at the airport."

"Rita Al-Nayhal?"

The man who had spoken her name so quietly and with such reverence stood before her, his head inclined slightly. He was joined at the hip with a far larger man, very bodyguard-esque in his searching eyes, meaty fists and tight-lipped mouth.

"It's Rita Thompson, actually," she corrected, her heart dipping just a bit as she said the words.

The man didn't acknowledge her amendment, just said very seriously, "Would you follow me, ma'am?"

"I'm about to get on a plane." She shook her head, confused. "Is there some problem?"

"No problem at all, ma'am." The man lowered his voice once more. "There are a few security measures for members of the Al-Nayhal family that we must adhere to."

Rita opened her mouth to reiterate that she was no longer a member of the family, but the man said far too quickly, "We have changed the gate for your flight, that is all, and wish to escort you there."

A shiver inched up Rita's spine and she turned. She saw many of her fellow passengers stopping where a woman collected boarding passes and stamped their tickets before they went through to the gate. "I don't think so. This is my plane right here. It's going to Paris, then to Texas."

"Your Highness, we do not wish to make a scene."

"Neither do I. And by the way, how do you know who I am?"

"We are security, ma'am," was all he offered. "It is important for you to come with us."

Panic shot through Rita's blood. "I'm not going anywhere with you people."

Just then, the bodyguard stepped forward. He said nothing, but he didn't have to. He was pretty imposing. The smallish man continued to speak, "You will come with us, ma'am." He lifted a brow. "*How* you come with us is entirely up to you."

Anxiety turned to anger inside of Rita. She knew who was behind this. Her "husband." No doubt, Sakir had called the airport and was having her sent back to the palace.

Why, she didn't know. He didn't want her anymore.

She eyed the bodyguard, knew she couldn't take him down or run from him, so she acquiesced. But she knew that when she got back to the palace, she was going to give that arrogant sheikh a piece of her mind.

The two men escorted her through the airport and

down several hallways. Soon the exit to the airport came into view, but the men didn't lead her in that direction.

"Where are we going?" she demanded, fear twisting in her blood.

"To your plane, ma'am."

"My plane—" she began, then paused.

There it was, sitting pretty outside the floor-to-ceiling windows.

Sakir's plane.

Of course.

A deep sadness filled her, and a lump formed in her throat. Sakir wasn't bringing her back to the palace for a chat. He was letting her leave. No fight. He just wanted to make sure she left in the same way she'd come—safe and sound and in style.

As if that mattered to her at all.

But no one was going to accuse Sakir Al-Nayhal of not being a gentleman.

Rita lifted her chin and proudly walked out into the sunshine, onto the tarmac and up the steps of the plane. A week ago, she'd come down these steps with a light heart and a wave of excitement.

What a heartbreaking turnaround.

When she entered the body of the plane, Rita felt thankful to leave the jerk security guys behind and to see the same flight attendant who had worked on her last flight over to Emand.

The man bowed to her and gave a warm, "Welcome aboard, Your Highness."

"I'm not a 'Your Highness' any more," she said drily.

The man only inclined his head.

"Can I take any seat?" she asked, just wanting to curl up in a ball and pray for sleep to hit her.

"The sheikh has requested your presence in the back of the plane, Your Highness."

She rolled her eyes. "Well, you can just tell the sheikh to go—"

She stopped short, her brows knitting together.

The sheikh requested…

Oh, God, no.

Her heart slamming against her ribs, she struggled to think of what to do next. She didn't want to see him and she sure as hell couldn't let him see her—not with love still shining in her eyes.

"Where is it that I should go, Rita?"

Rita stood stock-still, letting that voice seep into her heart and soul like honey and chocolate. If she wasn't as strong as she was, there would be nothing to stop her from running to him and throwing her arms around his neck.

But she was strong.

She turned around and faced him. As always, he looked too gorgeous for words, casually dressed in jeans and a black shirt. "What are you doing here?"

"We came here together. We will leave together."

"Honestly, there's no need to act all chivalrous," she said rigidly. "You should go home, back to the palace, to your people, where you belong—and let me go home to Paradise, where I belong."

His eyes were intense and passion-filled. "You do not belong in Paradise."

She sniffed. "More than I do here, that's for sure."

"I do not agree."

"Sakir," she said quickly, done with all this small talk. "What am I doing here? What do you want?"

"When did your mother die, Rita?"

Rita sucked in a breath, the question taking her completely by surprise. Tears filled her eyes and she choked out, "What?"

Sakir shook his head. "I am sorry that I never asked about her, about the pain you must have experienced in losing her." He shrugged sadly. "I was caught up in my own history—too caught up to see anything else."

Confusion spun in Rita's mind. "I don't understand. Why are you doing this? It's—"

"Important?"

"No. No, it's cruel." She took a step toward him, her voice breaking. "Don't pretend to care about me now. It's over, okay? I'm fine. There's no need to apologize, or have regrets." She threw her hands in the air. "No harm done."

His eyes filled with tenderness and with disbelief.

She sighed and sagged a little. "Well, maybe that's not entirely true, but I'll get over it." She paused and said words that were killing her to say. "I'll get over you."

"I do not wish for you to get over me."

"Why is that? So I'll stay at Al-Nayhal Corporation?"

"I will not pretend that you remaining in my company is not important to me, but it is nothing to having you beside me in other ways." His gaze went soft, tender. "In my arms, my bed, my heart."

Rita just stared, a flicker of hope winding its way though her. "Sakir…"

"Please come to me." He held a hand out to her.

She shook her head.

"Why?" he asked.

"I don't believe you. I don't believe any of this."

"And?"

"And…" Her throat was so tight. "I'm afraid."

"Of what, Rita?"

"Your words. They hurt too much."

He frowned. "I know. God, I know. I am beside myself with shame for what I have said to you. It was wrong and wholeheartedly untrue. My only excuse is one of fear. I knew I had fallen in love with you. I thought the only way I could regain my power was to hurt you." He shook his head, drew a jagged breath. "I was a coward, Rita."

Rita held her breath; on the verge of tears, she thought she'd bust out at any moment. She didn't know what to think, what to believe. She loved this man so much she ached with it. But she was so afraid; her heart couldn't take another rejection.

"Words can hurt, dearest," he said with supreme tenderness in his tone. "But they can also heal. I know this because my brother and I have talked and reconciled."

"You have?" she said, overcome with astonishment. "But I thought—"

"You thought I was a fool who would continue to hold my brother responsible for a life he had no control over in the first place just to protect myself against further pain."

"Yes."

"I am a new man, Rita." Sakir grinned, his eyes filled with warmth. "You have made me thus. Just as you have given Zayad and me a new beginning. Make no mistake, dearest. We both know that it was you who brought our family back together."

Tears spilled from Rita's eyes. She shook her head. "No."

"Yes, dearest." Again, he held his hand out to her. "I want to thank you. And if you will let me, I want to give you the family you have given me."

"Sakir…"

"Forgive me. Please."

Rita could hardly say the word. All the emotion, all the love in her heart had settled in her throat. But she couldn't help herself. She felt herself nod, felt herself running to him, wrapping her arms around his neck, sighing as she felt him so strong and safe and real.

He nuzzled her neck and whispered in her ear, "Thank you."

She clung to him.

"I love you, my dearest," he said.

"And I love you," Rita said breathlessly.

Sakir pulled back just an inch, dipped his head and covered her mouth with his. His kiss was tender at first, so loving and open. But it quickly grew heated and sensual, his mouth moving over hers as he murmured words of love she'd longed for, hoped for and wished to hear.

After a few moments, he eased his mouth from hers, though his gaze remained steadfast, true and so open at long last.

"Dearest?"

"Yes?" she said, loving this new and heartfelt endearment he was calling her.

Sakir lowered to one knee, grinned up at her. "I ask for your hand in marriage."

She gave a chirp of laughter. "Again?"

"This time, I will do things properly."

With a grin, he opened a small box. Rita looked down and snaked in a breath. An enormous pink diamond winked up at her.

"Will you have me?" he asked.

"Oh, Sakir, always and forever." She smiled at him, watched and held her breath as he slipped the ring on her finger.

Just a short time ago, she had been standing at an altar with a man who knew no love, no forgiveness and no true happiness. Because she wanted him and believed in him, she had been willing to go with him, see a different side of life, experience new and exciting adventures.

Sakir stood then, kissed her softly on the mouth and then hauled her to him.

Around them, the engines of the plane roared to life. The sound was a metaphor for them and for new beginnings.

Rita melted into Sakir's arms, knowing deep in her soul that she'd found all that she'd been looking for— her ideal husband, her loyal fiancé, her one true love and so many magnificent adventures to come.

* * * * *

SHEIKH SURRENDER

BY
JACQUELINE DIAMOND

A former Associated Press reporter, **Jacqueline Diamond** has written more than sixty novels and received a Career Achievement Award from *Romantic Times* magazine. Jackie lives in Southern California with her husband, two sons and two cats.You can write to her at PO Box 1315, Brea, CA 92822, USA, or e-mail her at jdiamondfriends@aol.com. Keep up to date online with her new releases at www.jacquelinediamond.com.

In memory of Jane Jordan Browne

Prologue

Sheikh Fario Adran, governor of the country of Alqedar's Yazir Province, halted his sports car in the small parking bay. He swayed rhythmically to the closing bars of a rap piece on his CD player before killing the engine.

Late-afternoon sunlight slanted across the windshield. Crisp mountain air, tangy with the scent of autumn leaves, filled his lungs. What a strange land, he thought, where a man could drive a couple of hours from Los Angeles and enter an entirely different climate.

And, in a few minutes, meet an entirely different sort of woman.

From the bucket seat beside him, Fario lifted the picture he'd printed out of his Internet sweetheart, Jenny Sanger. Her dark blond hair color looked natural, although you could never tell, and those moss-green eyes gazed at him alluringly. It was the delicacy of her bone structure and a hint of uncertainty in her face that particularly drew him.

She was a woman meant to be dominated by a man like him. Young, too, although with the Internet, he supposed he ought not to assume she was exactly as she appeared. Her skin couldn't be that perfect, could it?

He'd been skeptical at first when a friend at UCLA graduate school suggested trolling the Web for women. Fario had never had any trouble in that department while attending school in Switzerland and university in England. American women, however, were too assertive for his tastes, and a bit suspicious of Middle Easterners as well, although Alqedar was a U.S. ally.

Jenny seemed different: warm and enthusiastic. She wanted a strong man, she'd told him, someone to fulfill her sexual fantasies.

At first, she'd questioned Fario's claim of being a sheikh. He'd e-mailed her a shot of himself and suggested she compare it with his portrait on the Web site his older half brother and chief adviser, Zahad, had set up as part of his campaign to modernize the province of Yazir. That had done the trick.

Zahad was always doing things like that since their father had died two years ago, after a long and debilitating illness. In addition to establishing a Web site, he'd sought international funding and hired an economic consultant. Fario appreciated this, since he preferred to spend as little time as possible in their dusty, backward province.

He would not like to have Zahad as an enemy. There was something hard and dangerous about his half brother. But his loyalty, Fario believed, was beyond reproach.

From the seat, he lifted the red-and-white checked headdress he seldom wore in America, except when he made the rare diplomatic appearance, and fitted it over his head. Jenny would love this, although it went oddly with his tailored jacket and designer jeans.

She'd promised to be waiting for him. As for her wardrobe, she wasn't going to be wearing a stitch.

Collecting the bottle of French champagne he'd brought as a gift, Fario slid out of the sports car and took stock of his surroundings. The land here was rugged, and from where he stood, he could see peaks rising to the north. On one side, a ravine filled with tangled brush bordered Jenny's property. On the other, a downward slope led to a couple of small houses tucked behind a screen of trees. There was no sign of anyone around and not even a hum of traffic from the narrow road.

The one-story home had a quaint roughness typical of the mountain residences he'd passed on the way, and utterly different from the mud-brick houses back in Alqedar. Fario liked the privacy. If all went well, he planned to visit here often.

Zahad had drilled him with warnings about potential assassins and insisted he exercise caution everywhere he went. To Fario, this seemed unnecessary. It had been a dozen years since Zahad and his comrades had freed Alqedar from its dictator. No one was going to attack a sheikh in the placid ski community of Mountain Lake, California.

Fario's Italian leather shoes whispered along the walkway from the parking area to the front steps. Perfume drifted from a flowering bush that defied the early-December chill.

Fario pressed the doorbell and heard the chimes peal within. He saw no movement at the window, although he'd expected Jenny to be watching through the blinds. Nor could he hear footsteps inside.

Growing impatient, he pressed the bell again. It was true that he'd given Jenny only an approximate arrival time, but she'd been so eager to meet him that he'd assumed she would be waiting. He didn't see any other cars around, but hers must be parked in the garage set past the house at the end of the long driveway.

Suddenly he smiled. The door appeared to open outward; if she answered it in the nude, someone might see her. Even in such a remote setting, it paid to be discreet.

He tried the knob. It turned easily.

"Hello, Jenny," he called and opened the door.

A blast destroyed the peace of the afternoon. A crushing pain spread through Fario's chest as the gunshot sent him sprawling backward down the steps. The bottle hit the walkway and shattered, spraying him with glass and champagne.

As darkness closed in, he formed one last fierce wish. "Avenge me, Zahad," he whispered, and then he spoke no more.

Chapter One

Three days later.

There was a man in her toolshed.

As Jenny Sanger emerged from the garage, she saw the shed door standing open. An instant later, she glimpsed a masculine figure moving inside the rough-hewn structure less than twenty feet away.

Tools had been stolen from that shed to rig a murder weapon. Had the killer come back?

Behind her, the heavy garage door clunked shut, cutting off her retreat. No doubt it also alerted him to her presence, in case he hadn't already heard her drive up.

Inside her oversize purse, Jenny's hand searched for the clicker or for her cell phone. Her fingers scrabbled in vain through a sheaf of reports from the elementary school where she worked as principal.

Maybe it was the police, she thought frantically. But detectives had searched the property thoroughly and given the all clear. Besides, the only vehicle she'd seen nearby was an unfamiliar car parked a short distance down the road.

Under the papers, her fingers identified her lipstick, a tin of breath mints and a bottle of Tylenol. Why couldn't she find what she needed? The man would come out any second now.

At least her keys were still in her other hand. Jenny edged

toward the back of the house and winced when her pumps crunched on the fallen leaves.

The late-afternoon sun cast a shadow across the man as he stepped out of the shed. Even in silhouette, she could see that he was tall and solidly muscled. Although she stood five foot eight and had taken self-defense classes, Jenny knew she'd be no match for this guy.

Inside the purse, her hand closed over a tube of pepper spray. She jerked it out, heedless of the tissues and mints scattering onto the walkway, and took aim.

The man lunged. He was so fast that the tube vanished from her hand before she could press the button.

He stopped a few feet away, the spray canister engulfed by his large hand. They stared at each other in a frozen tableau.

The glare of sunlight revealed a sharp-featured man with white scars vivid against his tanned skin. He stood almost six feet tall, with dark, shaggy hair straggling across his forehead and his temples. In his black leather jacket, he put her in mind of a warrior.

He broke the silence first. "Miss Sanger, I presume?" It didn't surprise her that he had a deep voice, but she hadn't expected a British accent mixed with a trace of something exotic.

"It's Mrs. Sanger." Although divorced for three years, Jenny had retained her married name.

"My name is Zahad Adran," the man said. "My brother, Fario, was murdered here three days ago."

His introduction made her only marginally less alarmed. Fario Adran, she had learned, was a sheikh from the small country of Alqedar. There was no telling what notions of honor or revenge his brother harbored.

Jenny zeroed in on a little scar on the right side of Zahad's face. It was balanced by a jagged slash bisecting his left eyebrow, further evidence that a lot of people apparently disliked this man. Irreverently, she wondered what other scars he hid from view, until she realized what she was speculating about and banished those thoughts.

The best defense was a good offense. "I'm sorry about your brother," Jenny said. "But you have no business trespassing."

Zahad ducked his head. "I apologize for startling you. You startled me, also. I will return your property." He tossed her the tube.

Jenny's hand came up instinctively and snatched the small container from midair. She wondered if it would be a violation of etiquette to spray him with it. Not a good idea, she supposed, given the speed of his reflexes. Besides, its return implied that the sheikh had no immediate hostile intentions.

He picked up the items she'd dropped and handed them to her as well. "I came to bring my brother's body home, but the coroner has not released him. I took the liberty of examining your shed because I understand the tools were used to position the murder weapon."

A couple of deep breaths gave her courage. "Let me bring you up to speed on a few things," Jenny said. "Number one, this is not public property. It's my home. Number two, believe it or not, we have a police department in Mountain Lake. They already did all those high-tech things like check for fingerprints and collect DNA evidence."

"I am aware of that, Mrs. Sanger," he replied mildly. "Because of my connection to the deceased, they allowed me to read their report. I attempted to speak with the detective but he was out investigating a carjacking at the ski lodge. They have a small robbery-homicide detail, apparently."

"I still don't see why you're prowling around duplicating their work. I don't need any more footprints messing up my yard."

His mouth twisted in what might have passed for a smile in other circumstances. "I can see that no one bullies you."

"I spent too much of my life being bullied," Jenny said,

although she wasn't certain why she chose to reveal that to a stranger. "I refuse to let it happen anymore."

"Nor should you. Let me be honest. I want to find the killer for my brother's sake, but I am also acting out of self-interest. Because of the situation in my home country, there are those who suspect that I may have had a hand in his assassination."

"Assassination?" No one had referred to the murder that way before.

"Our father chose Fario to succeed him as sheikh and governor of our province, although I am the elder son by my father's first wife," he explained. "The position carries with it a certain amount of power and access to hereditary wealth."

She didn't need him to fill in the blanks. "So your brother's death makes you a rich sheikh. Or is there a third brother lurking around the oasis?"

Again, the man favored her with a ghost of a smile. "Just me, although I am certain my stepmother wishes she had another son."

"So you want to clear your name." It made sense, but Jenny wasn't about to take his problems to heart when she had more than enough of her own. "I apologize if I sound cold, but I really don't care what's going on between you and your stepmother. Someone's been cyber-stalking me, sending out photos from years ago when I used to model, and luring men here by promising them sex. As far as I'm concerned, that bullet probably had my name on it, not your brother's."

After a long pause, the sheikh said, "You believe someone was trying to kill *you?*"

"Someone hates me. The gun was in my house and it was almost time for me to come home from work. That makes it a logical assumption. Speaking of which, I just put in a long day and I haven't been able to get inside my house since Monday except to pack a suitcase. The police just gave me permission to reenter and I've got a lot of cleaning to do."

Today was Thursday, and her five-year-old daughter, Beth, would be returning on Sunday from a two-week visit with her father and stepmother in Missouri. By then, Jenny wanted everything as normal as possible.

"If someone is trying to kill you, how do you know there isn't another gun ready to fire when you walk in?" the man asked.

She'd been trying to reassure herself about that all day. "Because I had an alarm system installed and the locks rekeyed."

"According to the report, it is not certain the killer used a key," he said.

"That's true, but there was no forced entry." Several keys were probably floating around from the days when her great-aunt had owned the house. However, Jenny may simply have forgotten to lock the door.

"I would be pleased to enter the house ahead of you and ensure that it is safe," the sheikh offered. "I hope you do not interpret this as bullying. I assure you, Mrs. Sanger, if I wished to bully you, there would be no need to interpret it."

She didn't know whether to admire his gall or order him off her property again. She also wasn't sure she wanted to allow this man to look around inside, which was obviously what he sought. On the other hand, Jenny had been dreading the moment when she would have to step into the house.

Also, a part of her couldn't help hoping Zahad might find some piece of overlooked evidence. Much as she respected the local police, they were understaffed and possibly overmatched. Even after weeks of investigating, they still couldn't zero in on her cyber-stalker. What were the odds of their solving this murder quickly?

"I'll need to see some ID," she said.

From a pocket, he withdrew a gray-green passport stamped Republic of Alqedar. Inside, she found writing in both Arabic and English, along with a photo showing a younger Zahad.

In a flowing white robe and a checked headdress banded with dark cord, he projected an air of authority and, from the forward thrust of his jaw, impatience. "You don't like having your picture taken," she remarked.

"I loathe it."

The passport contained visa stamps from numerous countries, including more than one from the United States. "You've been to America before."

"I occasionally travel in the service of my country." He accepted the document back without further comment.

She could hardly refuse to let him help now that he'd cooperated with her request. "All right. But you can't stay."

"I only wish to take a look around."

"Do you really think you can find anything the police missed?" Jenny asked as she led him to the front. Although the back door was closer, it would make her uncomfortable to take him inside through her living quarters.

"I underwent special training in England. My goal was to become a security expert, not an investigator, but to be thorough I took several forensics courses."

When she reached the front, Jenny tried not to shudder at the bloodstains fading to brown on the concrete steps. "Watch out for glass. I doubt the police caught all the slivers."

"Ah, yes. The champagne bottle. Imported from France, no doubt, although the report did not specify the label."

"Your brother had expensive tastes?" She fitted her key into the new lock.

"Indeed." Zahad stepped forward quickly and covered her hand with his. His calluses brushed her skin, making her feel oddly protected. "Allow me."

"Okay." She retrieved her hand from beneath his. Jenny's gratitude at his apparent willingness to put himself in danger warred with a hard-won resistance to letting a man—any man—look after her.

"Stand aside, please," said the sheikh.

She moved away and braced herself as he opened the door. There was a pause, and then she heard the beeped warning that gave her one minute to disable the alarm.

As soon as Zahad cleared the doorway, Jenny input the code. She felt his eyes following her movements and reminded herself to change the code as soon as he left.

Indoors, a faint chemical scent lingered in the cool air. She hadn't been inside since Monday, when she'd arrived home to find police cars outside along with a fire truck and paramedic unit. She'd glimpsed a covered body on the sidewalk and smelled champagne and musky, unpleasant odors she hoped never to smell again.

Now Jenny took one look around her living room and wished she could twitch her nose and make the mess go away. Detective Finley had assured her the police were taking care not to damage things, but she'd be lucky if she could move back from the cabin she'd borrowed by the weekend.

All the furnishings had been pulled away from their usual resting places and the colored glassware in the china cabinet was disarrayed. Books sprawled across low shelves and some had tumbled onto the floor.

On the walls, painted china plates and framed reproductions of *Saturday Evening Post* covers hung askew. Dirt and black powder streaked the carpet and there were ashes around the fireplace. Some of the powder had drifted onto the skirted covers with which she'd updated the old sofa.

Seeing her home torn apart this way made Jenny feel personally violated. Until this point, she'd simply been terrified by the possibility that someone was trying to kill her. Now she felt angry, too.

"What on earth did they do in here?" She reached to right a vase that lay on its side atop the coffee table. "What's all that black stuff?"

"Fingerprint powder." Zahad's hand closed over her wrist before she could pick up the vase. "Do not touch anything."

"Why not? They're done here." She didn't think she could bear to leave this mess for one more second.

"*I* am not done," he said.

Jenny wanted to grab some rags and start righting this affront to her home. "The police have obviously gone over this house with a fine-tooth comb and maybe a sledgehammer for good measure."

"Yes, but they do not know my brother and I do."

"Your brother got shot on the porch."

"That's the way it looks, but looks can deceive."

Could the murder victim actually have come into the living room? Could other terrible things have happened in her home? If so, Jenny didn't want to know about them.

Zahad stared at a heavy chair upended directly ahead of them. "Would that be the one to which the gun was attached?"

"I guess so." Jenny didn't know how it had been done. She'd only heard that the killer had used wire from the toolshed to connect the trigger to the door.

Zahad indicated a couple of small holes in the wall. "That must be where he inserted the eye hooks."

"Maybe." She was reluctant to admit she hadn't known the killer had run the wire through eye hooks. The holes leered at her, yet another reminder of the violation that had occurred here.

"The gun belonged to you?" Despite his offhand tone, she knew this was no minor matter.

"I inherited it from my great-aunt, along with the house," Jenny said. "I fired it a few times at a target under Dolly's supervision. She's a retired policewoman who lives next door."

"She is the one who found my brother's body?"

"Right." That fact had been in the police report, of course.

"You kept the gun loaded?" Zahad asked.

"No. Unloaded and high up in a cabinet," Jenny replied. "The bullets were in a separate drawer." For good measure, she added, "This is an isolated place. My great-aunt once shot a rabid raccoon in the backyard."

"Surely you considered a gun good insurance against these unwanted suitors," the sheikh said. "Did you not even consider the possibility of rigging it as a form of self-defense in case one of them broke in?"

The suggestion that she'd set up the gun was ludicrous. "First of all, if I had, I'd have been more likely to shoot myself than anyone else because I'm about as mechanically gifted as a bunny rabbit. Second, if Dolly had checked the door to see if it was locked, she might have been the one who got killed. And third—wait a minute, I'm sure I've got a third point—"

"Perhaps you knew it was illegal to create such a deadly trap," Zahad offered.

"Well, I might have guessed that, if I'd thought of doing something like that, but I didn't," Jenny said. "Oh, I know. The guys showing up at my door weren't the real threat. Why would I want to kill someone who got suckered into coming here? It doesn't solve anything."

The sheikh lifted a hand to stop the flow of words. "You have persuaded me. Since I assume the police kept the gun as evidence, have you bought a replacement? It might not be a bad idea, if you are being targeted by a murderer."

One thing Jenny knew: She wasn't going to allow anyone to force her into taking steps that felt wrong. In retrospect, she should never have kept a gun, even unloaded, in a house with a child.

"No, and I don't plan to," she said. "I've never liked guns. My father was a military man, and he wanted my brother, Jeff, and me to learn how to shoot. I refused." She didn't add that it was one of the few times she'd defied her father.

Zahad studied the room. "What kind of music do you listen to?"

"Show tunes and pop," she replied puzzled. "Linda Eder, Audra MacDonald, Tony Bennett."

Releasing her, Zahad clasped his hands behind his back, crossed to her CD rack—which sat, displaced, on the floor by the coat closet—and made a cursory examination. "Very good."

"What were you looking for?"

"Rap CDs. If my brother visited often, he would have deposited some. I do not see any." He straightened.

"You mean, you thought I was having an affair with him?" Jenny retorted. "While I presumably stashed my five-year-old daughter in a closet?"

"Many women with children have affairs. Where is your daughter now?"

"She's out of state with my ex-husband." Jenny hadn't been happy about taking Beth out of kindergarten in the middle of the school year, but Grant had claimed those were the only weeks when both he and his wife, Shelley, could get vacation.

"It is fortunate that she was away when this happened."

"You're not kidding." Jenny was deeply grateful for this coincidence, and for the fact that she hadn't come home early that day.

She hated feeling glad that Fario had taken the bullet instead of her. She didn't want anyone to die. But, oh, she was glad that she hadn't been the one, for Beth's sake as much as for her own.

In her nightmares, the scenario played itself out repeatedly, with variations. Sometimes she arrived home in time to see Fario on the porch but too late to stop him. Other times she got here first, vaguely sensing danger but unable to prevent herself from reaching for the knob. Always, just as the door opened, she woke up on the verge of screaming and lay gasping for breath.

Zahad prowled through the front room. "The report indicated my brother carried several suggestive e-mails."

"That was the word the police used—'suggestive?'" She expected more direct language after reading a few brought by her previous unwanted visitors.

"I believe the term they used was 'explicit.'"

"That's more like it. I don't understand why someone wants to lure men here, but they didn't have any trouble doing it," she said. "It's amazing how gullible guys are."

"Your photograph obviously makes quite an impression." With one oblique glance, the sheikh let Jenny know that her features, from her high cheekbones down to her long legs, hadn't escaped his notice, either. To her dismay, she felt herself blush.

Although she considered herself on the thin side, with breasts barely large enough to fill an A cup, Jenny had been aware of her effect on men since her early teen years. It was the blond hair and green eyes, she supposed.

Usually, she wanted nothing more than to keep them at arm's length, but it was difficult to imagine any woman not reacting to this lean, restless man. Still, she didn't want anything from him except to be left alone.

"The kind of impression my appearance made on these men is something I could happily live without," she informed him.

"Tell me about them, these men."

When the first cyber-suitor had arrived six weeks earlier with a photo and expected to have sex with her, Jenny told him she must be the victim of a prank. Then she had to persuade a second visitor to leave. Worried, she'd called the police.

"They speculated that it might be a student's revenge for being disciplined," she explained. "They contacted an officer with a larger department who specializes in cyber-crimes."

He'd learned that someone was visiting various Internet chat rooms pretending to be Jenny and claiming to seek lovers. Whoever the cyber-stalker was, he'd covered his tracks by changing names and leaving false addresses. So far, four men had turned up at Jenny's home.

"At first, I figured someone just wanted to pester me," she said. "Then I began to worry that he wanted to harm me. Now I'm certain of it."

"It sounds like the behavior of an ex-husband." Keeping his hands at his sides, the sheikh shouldered through a swinging door into the kitchen.

There was more mess in there, Jenny discovered unhappily, although not as bad as in the living room.

"How do matters stand between you?"

"Grant and I were getting along fine until his wife discovered she can't have children," she admitted. "He started making noises a few months ago about wanting custody of Beth." Jenny had been stunned and furious. Every day since then, she'd expected to be served with papers.

So far, Grant hadn't taken any steps in this direction, although she had the impression he considered this two-week visit with Beth a trial run. Some women, she supposed, might have been tempted to coach their daughter on how to drive a stepmother crazy, but it would be cruel to treat Beth as a pawn.

"Sending these men here might give him leverage in court," Zahad said.

She'd considered that possibility. "Maybe. But I don't think he set it up. A couple of them confronted me when I was with Beth. Grant would never have endangered her that way."

"Does he have an alibi?"

"For Monday? I'm sure the police have checked. Besides, he lives in St. Louis."

"Perhaps so, but he may have some involvement." After removing a plastic bag from his pocket, he put it on, as if it were a mitt. The fact that he'd brought his own bag both impressed Jenny and made her uneasy.

If this man ever put his mind to committing a crime, he

would know how to avoid getting caught. She could see why some of his countrymen believed him capable of murder.

Yet she'd allowed him to come in here alone, even after he'd admitted he was under suspicion. That said something about Zahad's powers of persuasion. Jenny wasn't so sure what it said about her judgment.

He opened the refrigerator and inspected the contents. During Beth's absence, she hadn't done much cooking, and, of course, she hadn't been home in days. The sparse pickings included yogurt, pickles and a salad wilting under its plastic wrap.

"Is this necessary?" Jenny asked.

"It helps to substantiate your story," the sheikh replied.

"Because there's nothing in here your brother would eat?"

He closed the door. "The lack of wine and caviar speaks for itself."

Jenny recalled reading that many Middle Easterners avoided alcohol. "Is a sheikh allowed to drink?"

"My brother was raised in Germany, Switzerland and England." Zahad led the way into the guest room at the back of the house. "He chose which customs he wished to obey. He would have outgrown such notions in time." Beneath the critical tone, she detected a note of gruff fondness.

In the room, which doubled as a home office, the sheikh started toward her desk. She tried not to focus on the clutter of papers and computer disks the police had left in view. "That's enough searching, Mr. Adran," Jenny said. "I'm not going to allow you to poke through my personal things."

He glanced at her computer, no doubt itching to check for signs that she herself was behind the lascivious e-mails. However, the police had already searched it, which he must know from reading the report.

"Very well." He turned toward the door that led to the

hallway. "I understand the killer entered through the back. He must have come down this way."

"I suppose so."

On the office floor close to the hall sat a wastebasket containing a crumpled envelope. Zahad frowned. "They should have emptied this. Or, if that item was tossed there by the police, they contaminated the scene."

Jenny bent to take a closer look. "It's from a utility bill I got on Saturday."

"Allow me." The sheikh knelt beside her, so close that an edge of his leather jacket draped across Jenny's stocking-clad knee. Warmth fleeted through her.

Using the plastic bag, he moved the wastebasket to reveal a previously hidden scrap of paper on the dark beige carpet. "This is why the police should have emptied the waste-basket."

"It's just a piece of the envelope, isn't it?" she queried.

"I do not think so."

From a pocket, the sheikh took tweezers. By this time, Jenny wouldn't have been surprised if he'd produced a fin-gerprint kit and a test tube for DNA.

Using the tweezers, Zahad held the bit of paper up to the light from a window. "Do you recognize this pattern?"

"There's a pattern?" At an angle, she saw that he was right. There was a watermark in the paper, part of a logo.

Jenny recognized it, and almost wished she hadn't.

Chapter Two

"It's part of a crystal," Jenny said. "It looks like the logo of the First National Bank of Crystal Point. That's a town about five miles from here."

"Do you bank there?" Zahad kept a tight grip on the tweezers as he deposited the scrap into the bag.

"No." She hesitated. "I'm sure it doesn't mean anything."

"Who banks there?" he pressed.

"Lots of people. They offer free services that other banks charge for, including safe-deposit boxes." This wasn't a straight answer and they both knew it. Reluctantly, she finished, "One of my neighbors, Ray Rivas, started work there a couple of weeks ago."

Ray was no stalker and no killer, either. The affable man, who'd been glad to help Jenny with everything from plumbing problems to rototilling her garden, was married and had a four-year-old daughter. Most importantly, although he occasionally joked about her movie-star looks, she'd never felt any romantic interest or sexual pressure from him.

"A woman can tell if a man's trying to manipulate her," she explained to Zahad. "Believe me, I've got my radar permanently on alert."

"The fact remains that this bit of paper came into your house, possibly stuck to someone's pants cuff. And the po-

lice believe the killer walked down that hallway, although
he apparently covered his shoes."

"If Ray was smart enough not to leave muddy footprints
on the carpet, how likely is it he stupidly dropped something that indicates where he works?" she retorted. "Besides, he might have left it before Beth went on her trip.
His daughter, Cindy, is Beth's best friend."

Silently, she admitted that she didn't want to think someone she trusted could betray her this way. Was it possible
she could misjudge a friend to such an extent?

"Beth left nearly two weeks ago, correct?" Zahad's eyes
took on a hooded appearance that told her he was far from
convinced. "You must have emptied your wastebasket
since then."

"I might not have noticed a little scrap like that on the
carpet," Jenny said. "I'm afraid I don't vacuum as often
as I should."

This wasn't enough evidence to implicate Ray, to her
relief. She could see, however, that in the sheikh's esti-
mation her neighbor had just become a suspect.

"Where does this man live?" he asked.

"Next door." She gestured.

"I thought the woman who found Fario—what is her
name? Dolly?—lived there." He pronounced "Dolly" with
a hint of disdain, as if it were too frivolous a name for a
grown woman. "What is their relationship?"

"Her name is Dorothy Blankenship, although everybody
calls her Dolly. She's his mother-in-law." Jenny trailed Zahad along the hallway as he examined the carpet and moldings. "There are two houses on the property."

"They do not live together?"

"No, but Dolly owns both houses. She rents the front
one to her daughter."

Jenny sometimes envied the close family grouping. Her
own mother, who lived in Connecticut, had become absorbed in her husband and stepchildren after remarrying.

By contrast, Dolly was always there for friends and loved

ones. A dynamo at sixty-two, she tended to her ailing husband, Bill, and baby-sat for her daughter, Ellen. Since the cyber-stalking began, she'd also begun patrolling Jenny's property while she was at work.

Zahad peered into the master bedroom. Jenny saw the police had been here, too. Not only had they pulled aside her flowered coverlet, they'd also opened drawers and left black powder on the surfaces. She quailed at the thought of strangers pawing through her things.

Everything needed to be laundered. She wanted to scrub the whole house with Lysol and take a shower so hot it scalded.

"Do any of your neighbors have extensive knowledge of the Internet?" Mercifully, the sheikh's question pulled her away from her inner turmoil.

"Ellen designs Web sites at home. Everyone else uses it, too, I'm sure, except maybe Bill," she said. "He used to be a truck driver, but he's in poor health now and kind of forgetful. He might play video games."

"Who else lives close by?" He glanced into Beth's room but made no attempt to enter.

"The lot on the other side is undeveloped." As they returned to the living room, she filled him in on the people across the street. They included an elderly widow and a young married couple who'd moved in six months before. Directly across from her lived the police detective, Sergeant Parker Finley, along with his ten-year-old son, Ralph, and his housekeeper. His wife had died about five years earlier.

"Are you good friends with him?" the sheikh asked.

"Am I what?" She raised an eyebrow. It was the same expression with which she would greet a student's explanation that the cribbed test notes in his hand had fallen out of another student's pocket.

Zahad made a placating gesture with his hands. "I do not mean to insult you, Mrs. Sanger."

"It may come as a surprise, but I don't jump into bed with every male I meet," she snapped, and felt doubly annoyed when she recognized the note of hysteria in her voice. Jenny knew unflattering rumors about her had been circulating ever since the cyber-stalking began.

"That was not my implication. You may be completely blameless."

"Well, that's a relief." Her words dripped with sarcasm.

Frustration tightened his jaw. "I should have sent my cousin Amy to talk to you. You would love Amy. She is a rabid feminist who can never bear to lose an argument."

"Not with you, anyway," Jenny ventured.

He shrugged. "Yes, why me? I will never understand women and their prickliness. I am simply going about investigating this case in a rational manner. I had no intention of offending you."

"Oh, really?" She couldn't resist baiting him.

"It is not your fault if men react to your appearance. There. Have I apologized enough?"

"You haven't apologized at all." However, Jenny didn't feel angry anymore. She was beginning to find this man's clueless behavior around women almost appealing. He might be a male chauvinist, but at least he wasn't a smooth playboy. "You aren't exactly overloaded with social graces, are you?"

"I have had more important things on my mind." As Zahad spoke, his white scars stood out against his olive complexion. "I was forced to become a freedom fighter when I was young. Even after we liberated my country, assassination attempts were made against my cousin Sharif, an important leader for whom I served as chief of security. Now my brother is dead. I am sorry if I tread upon your delicate sensibilities, Mrs. Sanger, but it is in the pure interest of finding the truth."

The country of Alqedar, which had once been just a name on a map, began to seem more real to Jenny as the sheikh spoke, and so did the man himself. He had not merely led a colorful existence but a proud and distinguished one, which involved risking his life to protect his people.

It was hardly fair to expect him to behave like a politically correct Californian. Besides, she needed to find out who was stalking her, and he might be able to help.

"All right," she said, "let's make a pact. You treat me with respect and I'll do the same for you. That doesn't sound hard, does it?"

His bunched shoulders relaxed. "I can see that you must make a good school principal. Yes, that seems acceptable. May I continue?"

"Please do."

"If I may ask this without raising your hackles, I would like to know whether you have had any romantic entanglements with a man who might behave jealously. Any man."

"Okay, I'll answer that," Jenny said. "But I'm going to start cleaning up while we talk."

"Allow me to assist you," he offered. Despite some reservations, she agreed.

The sheikh not only helped move furniture, he volunteered to vacuum, although it took him a few minutes to get the hang of guiding the device over the carpet. When his longish hair flopped onto his forehead, he pushed it away impatiently.

As they worked, Jenny explained that she hadn't dated seriously since her divorce from Grant. Nor had she grown up in Mountain Lake, so there were no old boyfriends hanging around. With her father in the military, the family had moved frequently. They had lived in several countries, including Japan.

"I came here three years ago, after my divorce," she said. "Since I'd inherited a place to live, I applied for an opening as assistant principal at the local junior high." She'd been hired and remained there for two years before being promoted to elementary-school principal a year ago.

When the vacuuming was finished, Zahad borrowed her bottle of cleanser and a rag and tackled the fingerprint powder that had drifted to the dining table. "You have no inkling of anyone who wishes you ill?"

"Not aside from Grant and his wife," she admitted.

"Does your ex-husband have any friends in Mountain Lake?"

"He has no connections here that I know of." She paused in the middle of straightening her glassware to observe Zahad with mingled amusement and dismay. He was swirling the rag around the tabletop, smearing the powder rather than removing it. "I take it you don't do much cleaning at your palace. I suppose that's your wife's job."

"At the palace, the servants handle such matters. I have no wife. I have never taken the time to look for one." He frowned at his handiwork. "Why does this not look clean?"

Jenny started to laugh but changed her smile to a cough when she saw his mouth tighten. She *had* promised to treat him with respect. "Your technique could use some improvement."

"I believe I have assisted you sufficiently." With a grimace, he set down the cloth and went into the kitchen. She heard the water running as he washed his hands.

When he came out, Zahad said, "The detective is expected at his office by now. I believe he will want to see what I found."

"Do you plan to stay in town long?" she asked.

"A few more days, until Fario's body is released. I have taken a room at the Mountain Lake Inn."

Jenny felt a twinge of disappointment that he was leaving so soon. Despite his high-handed manner, there was something reassuring about the sheikh's confidence, not to mention his background in security.

No, she was being naive. This man was not her cyberstalker, but he might be the killer. He could have visited Fario in Los Angeles and seen an e-mail with her address and the date of the rendezvous. Zahad certainly knew enough to have set up the gun, and he had benefited from his brother's death.

She didn't really think he would have done something

so dishonorable. But she didn't intend to let down her guard with him.

"Well, have a safe trip back to Alqedar," she said.

The sheikh looked into Jenny's eyes as he extended his hand. When they touched, his strength enveloped her. At one time, she would have found it easy to yield to such a man.

And that kind of weak-mindedness, she told herself sharply, *is how you ended up being a thirty-two-year-old divorcée with a daughter to support and an arrogant ex-husband at your throat.*

She felt vulnerable, that was all. Shaky and scared and longing to turn back to childhood, when she had always had someone to protect her. But she couldn't and wouldn't turn to a man that way.

The sheikh held on to her hand a moment longer than necessary. "It is you who must be careful. You should hire a bodyguard."

"That's way beyond my budget." If Grant filed for custody, attorneys' fees would quickly deplete Jenny's modest savings.

"Then let us hope my brother was the intended target and you are in no further danger." Zahad released her hand. "Still, I am troubled about this cyber-stalker."

"Why do you care?" she asked.

"That is a question I cannot answer," he replied gravely, "except that I despise those who attack women and children. Also, you and I were brought together by a tragedy that will always haunt me and perhaps you as well. Such connections are not to be dismissed lightly."

Jenny had never given much credence to the idea of fate shaping someone's future. If there was a code of beliefs in California, it was that people made their own choices and determined their own futures. Yet the strength of Zahad's conviction made her less certain of that.

"I promise to watch my step," she said. "Good luck talking to Parker. I mean, to Sergeant Finley."

"Thank you. One more thing."

"Yes?"

"I suggest you lock your toolshed. If someone decides to do any further mischief, at least make him bring his own tools."

"Good idea," she said.

With a nod, he took himself away. The room seemed to shrink, as if adjusting itself to his absence.

Jenny waited until she heard the hum of an engine starting out on the street. Then she went to the alarm box and reset the code.

THE WOMAN WAS even more beautiful than she appeared in the photograph Zahad had seen at the police station. The passage of a few years since the picture was taken had given her an air of wisdom and maturity without diminishing the vulnerable look in her eyes.

She clearly had become cautious about sharing herself. The more he thought about her, the less able he was to consider her as the immoral temptress he had expected. Had he not read it in the police report, he still would have guessed that her ex-husband had been abusive.

Even if a woman infuriated him, Zahad would never strike her. That was the act of a coward.

Focusing his attention on the four-mile drive to town, he noted the way Pine Forest Road snaked between wooded rises and set-back, rustic homes. To those primarily concerned with aesthetics, Jenny's property would seem an ideal setting. To one concerned with safety, its isolation made it a poor bet.

Mountain Lake itself was a small town, distinct both from the dusty, ancient, spice-scented towns of Alqedar and from the medieval solidity of England, where Zahad had attended university. The buildings along its main street, Lake Avenue, blended frontier vitality and ersatz Swiss coziness with, at present, a garish overlay of Christmas lights and Santa Claus decorations.

He parked his rental car on the main street rather than tucking it out of sight at his nearby motel. It was harder for someone to tamper with a car in open view.

Across the street, the blandly modern building that housed the police department sat in a cluster of municipal structures beside an outdoor mall. Visible through a break between shops, Crystal Mountain Lake failed to live up to its name. In the dusky light, its surface appeared flat and leaden.

Nor was Zahad lulled by the apparent placidity of the town. Someone had committed a heinous crime here, and the list of suspects forming in his mind included the man he was about to meet.

In the glass-fronted lobby of the station, the desk sergeant called someone in the detective bureau and spoke in a low tone. The only other person there was a young man farther down the counter, filling out what appeared to be a theft report.

Thefts, traffic accidents and domestic disputes composed the majority of crimes in almost any jurisdiction. Zahad wondered how much experience Detective Finley had solving murders.

A middle-aged woman opened the door from a hallway. "Sheikh Adran?" She surveyed his leather jacket and slacks with a trace of disappointment. Apparently she'd been hoping for Lawrence of Arabia. "This way, please."

She led him past Traffic and Records to Detectives. An unoccupied desk in front bore a placard reading Mrs. Altoona. This, he presumed, was his escort.

The partitions that subdivided the large space failed to reach the ceiling and to dampen the clamor of ringing phones and beeping computers. Scuffed linoleum underfoot and acoustic tiles overhead, along with the uninspired ceiling fixtures, did nothing to soften the utilitarian planes.

Mrs. Altoona pointed the way to a corner office. "Sergeant Finley is expecting you."

"Thank you," he said, and took a moment to gird himself for the interview. Competent or incompetent, dedicated or corrupt, the detective he was about to meet would play a significant role in determining whether Fario received justice.

As Zahad entered, a man in a conservative business suit rose from behind his desk. Jenny's neighbor had regular features, a muscular build and the permanently tanned skin of an outdoorsman. From the touch of silver in the man's brown hair, the sheikh estimated him to be in his mid-forties.

"Sergeant Parker Finley," he said, thrusting out his hand.

The sheikh introduced himself and shook it firmly. At the detective's invitation, he took the only free seat, a straight wooden chair. A file cabinet loomed to his right, while a window behind the sergeant offered a view of a leafless tree and the municipal library.

"Sorry I wasn't available when you came in earlier." Finley resumed his seat behind the desk. "I understand you were allowed to read our preliminary report. It's not our custom to share the details of our investigations with the public, not even the families of victims. The desk sergeant shouldn't have shown it to you."

"I believe he consulted one of the captains before doing so." Zahad had no patience for bureaucratic stonewalling.

"I'm just letting you know that we won't be sharing our information from here on out," the man said.

"I, however, am willing to share whatever I come across," Zahad answered. "I think you will be interested in what I found at Mrs. Sanger's residence."

The sergeant's expression hardened. "You went poking around the house?"

"With Mrs. Sanger's permission, of course." He struggled to keep his tone even. He preferred not to get locked into a testosterone-fueled battle over territory, unless it was unavoidable.

"Please don't bother Jenny in the future."

"It is Mrs. Sanger's right to decide who enters her property."

The sergeant folded his arms. "You may be some kind of high official in your country, Mr. Adran, but you're in my jurisdiction now."

"Yes, and therefore I turn over to you the evidence that you overlooked." Zahad handed the plastic bag across the desk. "This lay underneath a wastebasket adjacent to the rear hall. It appears to bear the logo of the First Bank of Crystal Point. Mrs. Sanger will confirm that I discovered it in her presence."

The sergeant inspected the contents through the plastic. "Damn. I can't believe we missed this."

"Jenny—Mrs. Sanger—said she does not keep an account at this bank. A neighbor named Ray works there," Zahad added.

"A lot of people use that bank," Finley said. "Including me." He clamped his jaw shut as if he wished he hadn't volunteered the information.

"I'm sure a number of people could have accidentally contaminated the scene."

The detective's mouth worked angrily. But he replied with a terse, "We'll check it out." He retrieved an evidence envelope from his drawer and placed the Baggie inside.

"I will, of course, provide you with any other evidence I come across." Zahad waited for the explosion. He didn't have to wait long.

"Mr. Adran, you have my condolences about your brother," the detective retorted. "But if I find you interfering with my investigation, I won't hesitate to bring charges against you."

"As Fario's elder brother, it is my responsibility to uphold his honor."

"Not everyone in your country sees your relationship with your brother in such a benevolent light. I received a phone call this morning from a Mrs. Adran, whom I gather is your stepmother. She thinks you're behind his death."

That didn't surprise him. "Numa is distraught about losing her son."

"Apparently you should have inherited the—what do you call it?—sheikhdom from your father, but your half brother displaced you," the sergeant pressed on. "Now it's all yours."

"And you consider that to be a motive for killing him?"

"Wouldn't you?"

Zahad didn't bother to point out that what he had inherited was the lifetime burden of rescuing a province from the neglect incurred during his father's exile and subsequent long illness. Nor that, although he'd inherited substantial personal wealth, he intended to spend most of it on his compatriots. "Many people have motives."

"Did your brother have other enemies?" Finley asked.

"I was not his enemy. As to anyone else, there are people in my country who would prefer me as their sheikh in place of my brother. Others might wish to frame me and get rid of us both. But for any of them to have learned about Fario's infatuation with Mrs. Sanger and to take advantage of it in such a roundabout way stretches credibility."

The detective regarded him coolly. "Fortunately for you, even your stepmother admits you were in your country on Monday. That doesn't preclude the possibility of an accomplice."

"The same is true for Mrs. Sanger's ex-husband. I assume you have verified his whereabouts on the day of my brother's death," he said.

"We have."

"And where were you?" Zahad asked, in the slight hope that surprise would make the detective reveal something unintended.

Cold fury replaced the man's wariness. "This meeting is at an end." Finley got to his feet. "I don't want to see you around here again, Mr. Adran, and I don't want to hear about you bothering Jenny, either."

Zahad also stood. "When the coroner releases my

brother's body, I will leave town. Until then, I reserve the right to make my own inquiries. Particularly seeing that your department is not as thorough as it might be.''

Before the choleric redness could finish infusing the detective's face, the sheikh strode out of the office and past Mrs. Altoona's desk. Engrossed in reading a paperback with a knight and a large-bosomed maiden on the cover, she barely glanced at him.

He could almost hear his cousin Sharif chiding him for making an unnecessary enemy. *You shouldn't keep pointing out other people's incompetence. You make your life harder than it needs to be.*

It was true, Zahad reflected. When it came to diplomacy, he had a lot to learn.

But he didn't regret one word of what he'd said.

Chapter Three

By the time Jenny left her office on Friday, the secretary and the teachers had already departed. She checked the exits from the school's classroom wings and went out, locking the main door behind her.

In the field behind the school, a group of students was playing a pickup game of baseball despite fading light and a soft swirl of falling snow. Standing by her sport-utility vehicle in the adjacent parking lot, Jenny watched them for a few minutes. Although the forecast called for a storm and she wanted to put in another hour cleaning her house before heading off to the cabin, she enjoyed the chance to observe the students.

The boys, along with a couple of girls, appeared comfortable with themselves except for one undersize fifth-grader, a new transfer with the unfortunate name Elmer. When an opposing player struck out, he cheered so enthusiastically he tripped and fell, drawing catcalls from the rivals and smirks from his teammates.

"Some kids have a hard time fitting in, don't they?" Lew Blackwell, a fourth-grade teacher, said from a nearby space where he'd just unlocked his pickup truck. Reed-thin and balding on top, Lew was one of only two men on the teaching staff.

"He doesn't trust himself." Jenny's heart went out to the boy. "He's trying too hard."

"He'll learn," the teacher said.

"I suppose so." Jenny knew the boy had to find his own way of fitting in with his peers. Yet it went against the grain to leave him struggling.

"How's the cabin?" Lew asked.

"It's great. I really appreciate it." Lew, who lived in town, had loaned Jenny the cabin, which he'd bought as an investment and rented out to skiers and summer tourists. It had been a kind gesture, particularly considering that, as a longtime teacher who'd applied for the job of principal himself, he might have resented her winning the post.

Their relationship had been strained at first, after Jenny's promotion the previous year. It hadn't helped that Lew had asked her on a date while she was still assistant principal at the junior high. She'd declined, citing her recent divorce and the fact that she was in no emotional shape to start dating.

At forty-two, he seemed a bit old for her, and their personalities simply didn't click in romantic terms. Jenny felt glad she'd had an excuse not to go out with him. Nevertheless, he was a good teacher and had been courteous to her.

On the field, Elmer came to bat. He shivered as a cold wind hit him.

"Maybe we should go home," somebody said. "My butt's freezing."

"Let me strike him out first," called the pitcher.

"Don't count on it!" Elmer posed awkwardly with the bat.

"You couldn't hit a piece of cake." To demonstrate, the pitcher threw the ball right over the plate.

Elmer swung late and missed. The pitcher grinned. "See?"

The batter's team members grumbled among themselves. "He's going to blow it again," one of them complained.

Elmer's face crumpled. When the next pitch came in, he didn't even try to swing. Fortunately for him, it was high.

"If I were his coach, I'd tell him to let the ball hit him so he can walk," Lew said.

"Well, I wouldn't." Rummaging in the back of the SUV, Jenny found a pair of canvas slip-ons and exchanged them for her pumps. After tossing in her purse, she hurried to the field, heedless of the strange picture she must make in her tailored coat, suit skirt, stockings and incongruous shoes.

Elmer was grimly facing the batter as she trotted up. "Hold on!" she called.

"It's okay for us to play here, Mrs. Sanger," one of the boys said. "We do it all the time."

"I know." She smiled. "I'm an old baseball player from way back. Just thought I'd pass on a few tips." Her father had insisted his daughter spend her free time on the ball field, although she'd much rather have hung out at the mall with friends. Some of her most painful memories of her father involved their baseball games.

The children regarded her skeptically. It was too bad she hadn't had time to work with them during P.E., Jenny thought, because, willingly or not, she'd acquired a certain expertise.

"Elmer, pull the bat back like you're going to swing," she instructed.

Dubiously, the boy obeyed.

She could see him making the same mistake he'd made before. "You're locking your arm. That's going to slow you down and make your wrist roll." She sensed the others coming to attention as they realized she knew what she was talking about. "Keep your front elbow bent." She tugged on Elmer's arm until he achieved a more effective position. "That's it. Hands together, close to your body. No, not so far back. You'll lose the flexibility in your front arm." She stepped aside and nodded to the pitcher.

He threw another easy one over the plate. Elmer tensed as if about to swing, then got cold feet.

"Strike two!" shouted the umpire. One of the opposing players made a snorting noise.

"Here's another pointer," Jenny told Elmer. "Think yes! Every time, every pitch. Get ready to hit it. Don't second-guess yourself. It's yes, yes, yes. Track the ball with your eyes. Get ready to hit it right until the moment when you see that it's too far from the plate. Okay?"

"Okay!" He shifted as if getting a grip on himself.

The pitcher winked at the catcher. "He's going to throw it way off," one of Elmer's teammates said.

"Think yes!" Jenny hoped she wasn't going to screw this one up for the kid.

The pitcher sneered, wound up—and threw the ball straight over the plate. Teeth gritted, Elmer swung hard. With a *crack!* the ball went flying over the outfield. Two boys gave chase.

"Run, you idiot!" screamed a teammate. Recovering from his shock, Elmer raced around the bases and made it to third.

"Wow." His teammates shook their heads and grinned. "Way to go, Mrs. Sanger," one of them said.

"Way to go, Elmer," she corrected. "Okay, guys, don't play too long. If your fingers get numb, go home. I don't want to come back on Monday and have to dig your frozen bodies out of the snow."

A scattering of laughter followed her back to the parking lot. Her breath caught when she saw a man in a black leather jacket standing near Lew, his broad shoulders and masculine stance instantly recognizable. The sheikh's overgrown mane gave him a fierce air compared with the teacher's sparse thatch.

An unwanted shimmer of pleasure ran through Jenny. Zahad was the first man she'd met in Mountain Lake who made her think of tumbled bedsheets and late-night laughter. It was just her luck that a guy who probably thought women belonged in a harem made her knees wobbly and gave her the urge to check her lipstick.

"Hello, Mr. Adran," she said.

"You know this guy?" Lew asked.

She made introductions. "The sheikh's brother was the man killed at my house," she explained.

Lew blinked at the word *sheikh,* then caught up with the rest of the sentence. "I'm sorry for what happened. So you're only in town for a few days?"

"Correct," Zahad replied. Lew looked relieved.

"Is there something I can do for you?" Jenny asked the sheikh.

"I did not realize you would still be on the grounds. I wanted to familiarize myself with the town, and this place was on the list." To Lew, he explained, "As Fario's brother, I have a responsibility to make inquiries."

The teacher's eyes narrowed. "Jenny has enough to deal with. She doesn't need anyone hassling her."

"Your protectiveness is commendable," said Zahad. "Although unusual for a member of her staff. She is your boss, is she not?"

Tact really wasn't his strong point, Jenny thought. "Lew's also a friend. Now, if you don't mind, I want to do some more cleaning at home before the snow hits in earnest. So if you gentlemen will excuse me?"

They nodded stiffly. In her vehicle, when she glanced in the rearview mirror, she half expected to see them hissing and circling each other like tomcats. What was it about men that made them behave so possessively around a woman who was perfectly capable of taking care of herself?

Lew stood his ground. Zahad began strolling across the grounds, studying the one-story stucco building as if he might actually learn something from it. Most likely, he just wanted to provoke Lew.

With a sigh, Jenny headed home.

ZAHAD WASN'T CERTAIN what he'd expected to learn by visiting the elementary school. Despite what he'd said, he'd hoped to see Jenny, and in that he'd succeeded. The fact that she would sacrifice her dignity in order to coach her students in athletics impressed him. It showed real dedication.

He'd expected a very different sort of woman when he first saw her photograph. In person, too, Jenny gave an impression of soft femininity that went oddly with baseballs and canvas shoes, but she was also a serious professional. Her contrasts intrigued him.

Apparently they intrigued several other men, as well. The detective, for one. And now that teacher, the one glowering at Zahad as he pulled out of the lot—yet another potential jealous stalker.

This town was full of them. So was the Internet.

Last night, Zahad had e-mailed Viktor, a Russian programmer who worked under contract for the provincial government of Yazir, from his home base in central Russia. Viktor had promised to check chat rooms and see what he could come up with.

This morning, he'd forwarded some disturbing information. In the wee hours, California time, he'd found someone prowling the chat rooms pretending to be Jenny Sanger. The impostor had attached the same photo and urged the programmer to come visit her if he ever traveled to the United States.

Viktor hadn't succeeded in tracking down the sender's identity, but he had sent Zahad a copy of their conversation. The chat dialogue itself proved salacious but not very informative. A couple of misspellings might rule out a teacher as the perpetrator. On the other hand, one never knew.

At midmorning, Zahad had driven five miles to Crystal Point to look at the bank, which turned out to be a small, free-standing building with drive-up windows, ATM machines and a glass front. He'd ventured inside and spotted a desk whose placard bore the name Ray Rivas.

Jenny's neighbor was a stocky Hispanic man who'd been discussing loan terms with a young couple. When the man's gaze flicked upward, he'd fixed on Zahad with a glint of curiosity.

Withdrawing, Zahad had cursed under his breath. He should never have risked attracting attention.

So far today, he was batting zero, to use terminology those baseball players would understand. This made him wonder whether most American women were as knowledgeable about sports as Jenny. It seemed unlikely.

He found himself seeking an excuse to swing by her house. A poor idea, since she would no doubt insist that he work while they talked. Zahad could still smell the lemon scent of the furniture spray on his hands, despite repeated washings. Give him blood and guts over lemony freshness any day.

His cell phone rang. Since only key people had this number, he pulled into a petrol station—gas station, he corrected himself—and responded.

It was his cousin Amy Haroun. Although she had a knack for irritating Zahad, he'd hired her six months ago, with Fario's consent, as Yazir's director of economic development.

Together, she and Zahad had drawn up a master plan for revitalizing the economy of the province and bringing the infrastructure into the twenty-first century. Not only did she boast a business degree and an international background, she also understood the politics and the needs of their people. She worked hard, too, as evinced by the fact that she was telephoning in what was the middle of the night back home.

Amy went right to the point. ''Numa's asked President Dourad to appoint her nephew governor of Yazir until you're cleared of suspicion in Fario's death.''

Zahad uttered a few colorful phrases. Although the president couldn't take away the title of sheikh, he could reassign power. The tangle that would result from conflicting loyalties and arguments over who controlled what aspects of the provincial government would only harm its much-needed reforms.

''This must be stopped, but I cannot come back yet to

defend myself. Which nephew does Numa want appointed?"

"Hashim Bin Salem."

At twenty-four, Hashim was a playboy who'd been a close friend of Fario's. "Someone she can control," Zahad noted. "Or perhaps he has ambitions of his own."

"Could be."

It didn't surprise Zahad that his stepmother wanted to solidify her position as well as get revenge against him. He was sure she blamed him for Fario's death not only because she thought he'd arranged it, but because he'd encouraged Fario to attend graduate school in America. In addition, she must fear that once Zahad solidified his position, he would take revenge against her for persuading his father to disenfranchise him.

He had no such intention. To him, Numa was simply a nuisance that he wished to move aside.

"I require an advocate," he said. Since Amy worked for him, she was already compromised in the eyes of their countrymen. "Perhaps Sharif would be willing." Their cousin was a powerful sheikh who headed a larger province.

"He already called and offered to speak out on your behalf," she explained. "He wishes he could go to the capital in person, but Holly is expecting a baby any day."

Sharif had lost his first wife in childbirth while he was away fighting in the revolution. He would never leave his second wife at such a time.

However, President Dourad held Sharif in such high regard that his help would be valuable even at a distance. "I know he will do his utmost," Zahad replied. "Please ask him to point out that I am awaiting the release of my brother's body so I may escort it home. Surely there is no reason for hasty action during this time of mourning."

"I'll do what I can, but Numa's being a real pain in the butt," Amy said. "She has friends at court, so to speak." His stepmother was known for cultivating political friendships.

"I hope she is not treating you disrespectfully." The two women lived in the same palace complex.

"She doesn't dare. I've hinted that Harry's stockpiling bombs in his lab."

Amy's husband, Harry Haroun, a chemist, had moved to Yazir with her and their two children when she accepted the post from Zahad. In the laboratory furnished for him on the palace grounds, he was developing an improved fertilizer suited to the desert climate. Although bombs could be made from fertilizer, Harry had the heart of a kitten. But Numa didn't know that.

"Good thinking," he said.

"You know, I'm on your side in this one," Amy reminded him.

Although it pained Zahad to make a concession, he could see that he must. "I rely on you utterly."

"That must have hurt."

"More than you can imagine."

After he rang off, he sat in his car, seething at his stepmother. He hated it when people acted for petty personal gain, particularly when they got in his way. Why must he fight Numa and that callow nephew of hers simply for the right to improve his province's living conditions?

Perhaps it was a good thing that circumstances prevented him from flying back to Alqedar and giving the president a piece of his mind. Although he respected Abdul Dourad, he knew the country's leader must juggle competing interests. Zahad's take-no-prisoners approach to negotiating was unlikely to win him allies.

He wanted to get on with this investigation, and he wasn't making any progress sitting here watching people pump petrol into their tanks. Dropping by the elementary school and indulging himself in making conversation with Jenny hadn't helped his case, either.

Let the other men in town prostrate themselves at her canvas-covered feet. Zahad had better things to do.

JENNY GREW TENSE as she neared her house. In the aftermath of the murder she'd lost the sense of security she'd always associated with the place.

When she was a child, the house on Pine Forest Road had become a haven to return to as her parents moved around the globe. Whenever possible, she had visited her maternal great-aunt, Brigitte Ostergaard, a childless widow who'd operated a Swedish smorgasbord restaurant in town. After Brigitte died five years ago, Jenny had been deeply touched to learn she'd been named as heir.

For two years, as her marriage crumbled, she'd rented out the property. It had been wonderful to land a job in town after her divorce and to move here permanently.

Now she wondered if she would ever look at that front porch and walkway again without picturing the flash of emergency lights and the huddled shape she'd seen on Monday. If not for Beth, she might consider selling the place.

But what good would it do? The stalker would likely continue the harassment as long as she stayed in the area, and Jenny refused to be driven from her job. Besides, there was no guarantee she'd be safe anywhere else, either.

Resolutely, she pulled in to her driveway. Instead of proceeding to the garage, she halted in the parking bay. Given the rapid rate at which snow was accumulating, she'd only be staying a short while.

Her mind leaped ahead. She ought to change into jeans, and she also wanted to retrieve a pair of boots to take to the cabin. Absorbed in these thoughts, Jenny didn't see the man until he emerged directly in front of her.

"Jenny! It's me, Oliver." That broad, lascivious smile was all too familiar, although she'd never seen this bald, tattooed man before and didn't know anyone named Oliver. Her heart sank when she spotted the computer-printed photograph he held.

"Oh, for Pete's sake!" she snapped, silently rebuking herself for not paying more attention to her surroundings.

A quick glance told her the intruder had passed the parking bay and stashed his red sports car behind a tree near the garage. That's where he must have been lurking while he waited for her to come home.

She reached into her purse, but before she could find the cell phone or pepper spray, Oliver's beefy hand closed over her wrist. At close range, he smelled of alcohol. "No games, baby," he said, stuffing the photograph into his pocket and reaching for the front of her coat. "You promised me a good time and I want it."

The prospect of being pawed set off waves of fury and disgust. "Let go!" Jenny tried to twist away, but she couldn't get a firm foothold on the snowy concrete and the man was too strong. "Someone's played a trick on you. I never sent you that picture. I'm being cyber-stalked."

"Quit messing around," Oliver panted. "I didn't drive all the way from Nevada for nothing."

"Let go or I'll have you arrested!" Why couldn't he get it through his thick head that she hadn't invited him?

"I ain't letting you call no cops. I violated my parole to get here because *you* told me to," he growled.

Wonderful. Her cyber-stalker had found an ex-con to do his dirty work. "Just go away," she said.

"I don't think so." His lip curled.

Up close, she read Live Free or Die! on the tattoo snaking up his neck. As snow formed a curtain around them, Jenny realized how isolated they were. No matter how loud she screamed, none of her neighbors was likely to hear.

Who despised her enough to keep setting her up? And how was she going to get out of this?

Chapter Four

Almost subliminally, Jenny registered the buzz of a car approaching on Pine Forest Road. Even if the motorist could see them through the trees, however, there was no guarantee of help.

Oliver's head jerked toward the house. "Inside. Now!"

"No!" Although she was so frightened she could hardly breathe, Jenny tried to break away. "Leave me alone!"

"Shut up!" His grip like a vise, the man began hauling her up the walk. She felt as if her arm were being pulled from its socket.

Jenny tried to scream, but nothing came out. Although the sound of the engine grew louder as the car turned in to her driveway, it remained largely hidden from view.

Oliver halted. After an indecisive moment, he released her. "If you know what's good for you, you'll send them away."

Despite Jenny's desire to put as much distance as possible between herself and her attacker, her knees had turned to mush. She hated this paralyzing fear. What was wrong with her?

Then she caught sight of the car and its infuriated driver. Behind the wheel, Zahad had realized what was happening.

Barely taking time to brake, he came flying out and dodged across the snowy walkway as if expecting a bullet to whiz by. Jenny felt the shock of air as he slammed into

Oliver. The next thing she knew, the ex-con lay on the ground, facedown with his arms yanked back and Zahad straddling him.

"Are there any more of them?" the sheikh demanded as he patted the man down for weapons.

"I don't think so." The quaver in Jenny's voice embarrassed her.

Oliver struggled for breath. "Hey, man!" he rasped. "She sent for me!"

Zahad caught sight of the crumpled photo lying in the snow. "Count yourself lucky. The last man who showed up here caught a shotgun blast in the chest."

"Yeah?" the ex-con said. "Who the hell are you?"

"The victim's brother."

"Then you oughta hate this witch as much as I do."

Jenny's fists tightened with rage. The only problem was, she wasn't sure who or what made her angriest—this creep, her stalker or her own inability to act a few minutes earlier.

"Did he hurt you?" Ignoring Oliver's crude remark, the sheikh shook a wing of dark hair from his forehead.

She rubbed her wrist. "Just a bruise." Her shoulder was going to ache later, too, she thought.

"It ain't my fault," Oliver whined. "She made me mad."

"Do you want to press charges against this scum?"

"Who're you calling scum?" Oliver tried to twist around. Zahad drove one knee into his ribs and the man collapsed.

Furious as she was, Jenny had to face facts. Once the intruder showed the authorities the e-mails to prove he'd believed his advances were welcome, he would at the most simply be sent back to prison for a parole violation. He looked like the type to hold a grudge, and she didn't need any more people holding grudges against her, especially one who would likely soon be back on the street.

"Let him go," she said. "He's not the real enemy."

That wasn't entirely true, she thought, her teeth clenching. Any man who believed he had the right to subdue a woman by force was the enemy. Still, sending this creep to jail for a few months wasn't going to knock a sense of decency into him.

Zahad swung off the man. As Oliver staggered to his feet, the sheikh spoke in a low, menacing tone. "If I ever see you again, anywhere, anytime, you will be dead. I have killed more men than I can count. No dogs yet, but I am willing to start with you."

"Don't worry. I don't want nothing to do with you crazy people." The ex-con headed for his car. The engine turned over twice. Just as Jenny began to fear he might be stuck here for repairs, the guy took off so fast he nearly clipped Zahad's vehicle.

She took a wobbly step toward the house. Thinking the better of her bravado, she grabbed the porch railing for support. "Thank you," she whispered.

"You should let the police know what happened," the sheikh said. "He may hang around."

Jenny nodded. "I'll give him time to leave, then file a report in case he comes back."

She and Zahad regarded each other through the falling snow. He was breathing harder than usual, she noted, and then realized she was, too.

The world had just turned dark, and Zahad's watchful figure shone like a beacon. If he hadn't been here…

She refused to dwell on what-ifs. "Your timing was perfect. I'm grateful you came by."

"It is my intention to interview the neighbors." He glanced up and caught a snowflake right on his well-formed nose.

"Be careful you don't get stuck out here. There's a big storm forecast." On the point of fitting her key in the lock, Jenny felt a wave of aversion. After what had just happened, she couldn't face the sense of violation in her house. "Actually, I think I'll go straight to the cabin where I've been staying. I'll call the police after I get there."

"Are you well enough to drive?" Zahad asked.

Jenny could handle an automobile, but approaching the remote cabin alone in her current state of mind was another matter. "I'd appreciate it if you'd follow me."

"Of course." She felt glad he didn't fuss or insist on driving for her.

Zahad's car fell into place behind her vehicle along the curving two-lane highway, heading away from town. In the thickening storm, only two other cars went by. She kept checking her rearview mirror to reassure herself that he was still there.

Jenny reached the turnoff three miles down the road before it occurred to her that the sheikh didn't have four-wheel drive. She ought to send him away rather than let him risk driving an additional mile on a side road already dusted with snow.

But the prospect of arriving alone in the rapidly falling darkness stopped her. Although three or four other vacation cabins lay near the one where she was staying, she didn't know whether any of them were occupied at the moment.

There was no reason the cyber-stalker couldn't have found out her temporary address. He might direct someone here, too.

Shivers racked her, almost erasing the hard-won self-control. For once, Jenny didn't even try to give herself a pep talk. She just made the turn and let Zahad follow her to Lew's cabin.

Built of timber and glass, the A-frame structure was smaller than her house but more distinguished architecturally. Jenny halted in a double carport beneath the faint glow of a safety light.

On the approach, Zahad's wheels spun briefly in the snow before catching purchase. He pulled in beside her, shut off the engine and got out.

Yesterday, this lean, scarred man had been a complete stranger. But now, his presence was so welcome Jenny had to fight the urge to throw her arms around him.

"Do you mind waiting until I get inside?" Despite her determination, the words came out shaky.

"Does this place have an alarm?" he asked.

She shook her head.

"Then I will go in first." His gaze swept the wooded lot and the darkened houses nearby. "The owner should install one."

"I don't think Lew wants to go to the expense for a rental."

The sheikh finished inspecting their surroundings. "This cabin belongs to the teacher I met at your school?"

"Yes. He was kind enough to lend it to me for the week."

"How generous," the sheikh said dryly. "I presume he has a duplicate key?"

"I'm sure he does, but Lew isn't a threat." He'd only dropped by the cabin the first day to make sure she had everything she needed.

"How do you know this?" Zahad's shoes sank into the snow as they approached the porch. He wasn't exactly dressed for winter weather, Jenny noted.

"Instinct, I guess," she admitted.

"If your instincts about dangerous men are so trustworthy, why didn't they warn you about your husband?"

Jenny's temper flared. Although she'd mentioned Grant's abusive behavior in her statement to the police, it was nobody else's business. "My relationship with him doesn't concern you!"

"Except that he may be responsible for my brother's murder," Zahad said levelly.

He had a point, but he'd just pushed one of her buttons. "The fact that I made one mistake doesn't make me an idiot. Marriage is complicated, but I don't suppose you'd know about that, would you?" As soon as she heard the words slice through the air, Jenny regretted them. "I'm sorry. You just saved me from that creep. I didn't mean to be rude."

Although it seemed to pain him, Zahad said, "I am the one who should apologize. Tact is not my strong suit."

"Today, it doesn't seem to be mine, either." Much as the sheikh annoyed her at times, Jenny reflected, there were worse things than a man who blurted out what he was thinking.

"I will stick to the areas in which I have some expertise. Such as security." He removed the key from her hand. "Stand back, please."

She moved aside. When Zahad opened the door, Jenny braced herself. She wondered how long it would take before she stopped expecting the crack of a gun.

Inside, a trace of warmth greeted them. She turned up the thermostat and switched on the soft overhead illumination.

"Please remain here while I inspect the premises." The sheikh moved swiftly between the spare Scandinavian-style furnishings and climbed the stairs to the loft.

While she waited, Jenny put in the promised call to Parker, who as usual was working late. She felt sorry for his son, Ralph, although the housekeeper, Magda, appeared genuinely fond of the boy.

After Jenny described the incident, Finley promised to alert the patrol officers about Oliver. "What about Sheikh Adran?" he asked. "Has he left?"

"He's checking the cabin for me."

"You're there alone with him? I'll come and get you," Parker offered. "You can stay at my house tonight."

The detective hadn't asked whether she wanted his help, Jenny noticed, and the truth was, she didn't. The prospect of sleeping in his house made her feel smothered, not secure. "I'm fine here."

"How much do you know about Mr. Adran?" he demanded.

She recalled Zahad's statement that he'd killed a lot of people. "Not much." *Except that, no matter what he's done in the past, he protects me without trying to take over my life.*

"I don't consider him trustworthy. I certainly wouldn't want him spending time around you." Jenny pictured the detective's cool gray eyes narrowing as he spoke.

She'd found those same eyes assessing her from the day she moved into the neighborhood. Since then, Parker had occasionally dropped by to discuss matters ranging from his son's schoolwork to improving snow removal on their street. They'd attended a couple of community events together with their children, but Jenny had declined further invitations, and the detective appeared to have taken the hint.

He'd never entirely given up, though. Sometimes she got the impression he was just biding his time.

"Give me one good reason why I shouldn't trust him," she said.

"This guy was part of a rebel army that overthrew the government of his country about a dozen years ago," he replied. "We're talking violent revolutionaries here."

That must be when he'd killed people, Jenny reflected. "I thought Alqedar was a democracy."

"That I don't know," Parker admitted.

"Well, if he overthrew some other form of government to install a democracy, doesn't that make him a freedom fighter?"

"Maybe." The detective sounded gruff. "That isn't all."

"Let's cut to the chase," Jenny said. "Has he been charged with any crimes?"

"Not that I know of."

"End of story." She already knew Zahad had lived a rough life, one far outside her own experience. Since she had no intention of getting involved with him beyond her present predicament, none of that mattered. "Don't come and get me. What you ought to do, Parker, is go spend more time with your little boy before he grows up."

"I can take care of my own business," he snapped.

"I'm speaking as an education professional. It's good advice. Don't ignore it."

Coolly, he said, "I'll make a report about the intruder. Thanks for letting me know."

"You're welcome." If she'd thought it would do any good, Jenny would have added that it was going to be difficult to keep the police informed of developments if, every time she called, Parker became overbearing.

The sheikh descended the stairs, his dark clothing stark against the light decor. "Everything appears secure."

"That's all you have to say?" Jenny couldn't resist teasing.

"What more would you like?" He remained standing, making no move to take off the leather jacket he wore over a turtleneck sweater. As his unassuming virility filled the room, Jenny clenched her hands against the temptation to reach out and unbutton his coat.

"It's just that everyone else feels compelled to give me instructions, whether I want them or not," she said. "Parker Finley wants to carry me off to his house for safekeeping. A couple of my colleagues keep nagging me to stay at a motel."

"People can get killed in motels, too," Zahad replied.

"Well, that's comforting!"

"I am not here to comfort you. I am happy to help where I can, but you know my purpose."

To solve Fario's murder. Beyond that, he took no interest in anyone or anything in Mountain Lake. To Jenny, that was a mark in his favor.

In movies and on TV, beautiful women seemed to have all the advantages. There definitely were some, as Jenny knew from having helped pay for college by modeling. But after spending much of her life fending off unwanted attention, and now assailants, as well, she could see the disadvantages, too.

The funny thing was that she wouldn't have minded a

little more concern on Zahad's part. Just enough so that he would linger for another half hour or so until her nervous system returned to normal.

"We both want this case solved," she said impulsively. "Some mutual cooperation might be in order."

"You are offering to work with me?" He sounded dubious.

"You did find that piece of paper the police missed," she noted. "And it doesn't sound like Parker plans to take advantage of your abilities."

"I would be pleased to accept your input. The question is whether you have anything to contribute beyond your goodwill."

No one could accuse the sheikh of currying favor, Jenny thought with a touch of amusement. "You may have the security training, but I'm the one with an inside track," she retorted.

"Please explain."

"My neighbors are more likely to talk freely if I introduce you."

"And you will do that?"

Until now, she'd had no intention of it, but she doubted he'd get far without her. "Sure. Except maybe to Tish Garroway, the young woman who lives across the street. She doesn't like me."

"Why not?" Zahad asked.

"I honestly don't know." Tish, a waitress at the ski lodge, and her husband, Al, a ski instructor, had moved in six months ago. Although she'd made friends with Ellen, Tish was frosty to the point of rudeness toward Jenny.

"Introductions would be helpful," Zahad conceded. "Also, since this killer may be the same person who is stalking you, it would help me to gather more information about your life."

Jenny started to bristle, until she realized that guarding her privacy too jealously might cost her dearly. "All right.

We can compare notes over dinner.'' That would give her time to regain her equanimity—if he agreed.

Zahad's gaze had shifted to the upper windows in the A-frame. Unlike the curtained lower windows, they provided an unobstructed view of a rapidly descending wall of whiteness. Jenny could already hear the conventional demurral: If he stayed any longer tonight, he might get snowed in.

But she didn't feel ready to be left alone yet. The chafing of her wrist and an ache in her arm reminded her of how she'd been brutalized.

Zahad startled her by removing his jacket and hanging it on a rack. His turtleneck jersey clung to his broad chest. ''Very well. I presume you have food.''

''I'll rustle something up.'' She retreated into the small kitchen, separated from the front room only by a counter. ''How about omelettes?''

''What we eat does not matter.''

''Not at all?''

''Not as long as it does not violate my people's dietary customs,'' he added. ''Despite my brother's fondness for wine, I do not drink alcohol. I also do not eat pork.''

''I don't put wine in my omelettes. And the last time I looked, pigs didn't lay eggs,'' Jenny said.

A smile transformed Zahad, for the space of a heartbeat, into the handsomest man she'd ever seen. It vanished almost instantly. ''An omelette will be suitable.''

She preheated the oven for French bread and began fixing salads. Leaning against the counter, the sheikh watched without speaking. It was like having a puma in her kitchen, Jenny thought, but one that didn't appear likely to pounce, at least not at the moment.

''Tell me about the police report,'' she said. ''If they identified any suspects, they haven't told me.''

''There were no fingerprints other than yours on the gun or the chair. The killer was careful.''

''What about DNA evidence?''

"That has not come back from the laboratory. I believe it takes several weeks. However, if the killer had legitimately visited your house in the past, his or her residue would indicate nothing."

"Only if it comes from a stranger?" she asked. "Someone from your country, perhaps?"

"They would have to know who to test." Zahad drummed his fingers on the counter. "I doubt we will solve my brother's murder through physical evidence. Whoever set this up was clever and possibly knowledgeable about police procedure."

The implication chilled her. "You suspect Parker?"

"He must be considered, although many people know about police procedure from television. Your neighbor Mrs. Blankenship is also a former police officer," Zahad pointed out. "In any case, I doubt I am as suspicious of Sergeant Finley as he is of me."

"What makes you say that?"

"I met with him." The sheikh released a short breath that was almost a laugh. "He became insulted when I asked his whereabouts at the time of the murder."

Jenny popped a loaf of refrigerated bread dough into the oven. "No, I don't imagine Parker was pleased. But disliking you isn't the same as suspecting you." She set the salads and dressing on the counter.

"He pointed out, with reason, that I benefit most from Fario's death. Even my stepmother concedes that I was in Alqedar at the time, but the murder could have been carried out by a hit man."

Jenny shuddered. A hired killer in her house? "You think that's who did this?"

"I find it unlikely. The method was imprecise. It posed too high a risk of killing the wrong person."

"Don't remind me." She deliberately changed the subject. "Tell me, why did your father choose Fario over you? You seem like you'd have been a better leader."

"He did not choose my brother because of his superior

abilities,'' Zahad said with no apparent rancor. "Still, I grant that he was more sociable than I am. That is not difficult."

Jenny liked the fact that he was as uncompromising with himself as with the rest of the world. Still, he'd dodged the point. "You didn't answer my question."

"There were several reasons why my father elevated Fario. Of course, it pleased my stepmother, Numa."

While she waited for him to continue, Jenny cracked eggs into a bowl and stirred them. Perhaps if she refrained from asking questions, the sheikh wouldn't keep getting sidetracked.

His tone became reminiscent. "Seventeen years ago, when I was nineteen, a dictator named Maimun Gozen overthrew the legitimate government of Alqedar. We chose different paths, my father and I. I joined the forces training to fight Maimun. My father sought to appease him and to keep a low profile."

Vaguely, Jenny recalled reading about the troubles in the small Arabian country. But at the time she'd been a highschool student more concerned with grades and her overly strict father than with foreign affairs.

"My activities created serious difficulties for my father. He and Numa were forced into exile in Europe for nearly five years. Even after we overthrew Maimun, my father never forgave me. With Numa's encouragement, he blamed me for his continuing health problems and the economic troubles of our province."

"When did your father die?" she asked as she chopped onions and tomatoes, then sautéed them.

"Two years ago. I admit, I was as stiff-necked as he. After he rebuffed my first attempts, I never again asked for his forgiveness. Sadly, I was not called to his bedside and we never said goodbye."

"What kind of relationship did you have with your brother?" Jenny sprayed oil into an omelette pan.

"We got along well, considering that Numa and others

did their best to create ill will. Although with the title came the position of governor, Fario had no interest in improving the lot of our people. He asked me to serve as his lieutenant. Unfortunately, he wasted part of our family's personal fortune, which I believe should be invested in our province. He did allow me to make certain improvements and to hire a minister for economic development. We have been working to encourage foreign investment, but a tremendous amount remains to be done.''

Jenny finished cooking while he talked. She divided the omelette between two plates and retrieved the bread from the oven. ''Dinner's ready.''

Instead of remaining seated, the sheikh approached one of the front windows and pulled back the curtain. Jenny thought he was checking for intruders until he said, ''My car will not be able to negotiate this level of snow. I assume you sleep upstairs. I will take the couch.''

''Wait a minute.'' She hadn't planned on his staying all night. Since the loft opened directly over the downstairs, the cabin lacked privacy. Unless she decided to sleep in the bathroom, she wouldn't be able to close a door between them. ''That wasn't part of the arrangement.''

''It is now.'' Releasing the curtain, the sheikh returned to the counter. ''Believe me, it is with great reluctance that I expose myself to this awkwardness.''

''*You're* reluctant?'' She didn't know whether to be offended or amused. ''What exactly do you think will happen?''

Zahad downed a bite of his food before noticing that she wasn't seated. After swallowing, he said, ''Excuse my rough manners. Please join me.''

Jenny perched on a stool opposite him. ''Okay, I'm sitting. Now, what's your great reluctance?''

''The last thing I need is for anyone in Alqedar to learn that I have stayed at the home of the temptress who lured Fario to his destruction.''

Jenny stared at him in outrage. It embarrassed her to

realize that at some level she'd been attracted to this man, because he'd just thrown her vulnerability in her face. "I don't know how I'm going to control my irresistible urge to rip your clothes off, but I guess I'll manage."

The sheikh stopped with his fork halfway to his mouth, his startled expression almost comical. "That is not what I meant."

"And in case you've forgotten, I didn't lure anybody," she said. "Look, in the interest of protecting your precious reputation, you can take my four-wheel drive and get the heck out of here. You'd better hurry before the snow gets any thicker and you're really stuck. We wouldn't want the good people of Alqedar to question your maidenly virtue."

Zahad set down the fork. "We have not finished discussing the case."

"Yes, we have."

He leaned back and folded his arms. "I see I have given offense."

"You think?"

"I see also that I have been foolish. It is not my custom to allow the prejudices and suspicions of others to influence my behavior. If I leave you here with only my pathetic rental car for transportation, you will be at the mercy of anyone who comes along."

He might be right, but she felt so angry she didn't care. "That's not your problem."

"I think it is. As you pointed out earlier, I require your help to clear my name and win justice for my brother. As I suggested, you need a bodyguard, and you will never be able to find one better qualified than I."

"A bodyguard?" How had she gone from being a despised temptress to a damsel in distress? "Look, if you want to stay here tonight, fine. I'm sure both our reputations will recover. Beyond that, forget it."

"We will leave the matter for now." He tore off a hunk of bread. "By the way, you are a very good cook."

"Thanks, I guess." Obviously, neither her outrage nor

her sarcasm would have any effect on this man, Jenny reflected. Like it or not, she was stuck with him for the night.

She only wished that, deep inside, she didn't feel just a little bit glad.

Chapter Five

"Why don't you heave a hunk of that stuff at me, too?" Jenny said.

"I beg your pardon?" asked the sheikh.

She allowed her gaze to rest meaningfully on the serrated knife sitting untouched on the decorative cutting board she'd used to serve the bread. "Since we seem to be ripping it apart with our bare hands, please tear off a chunk for me as well."

Zahad glanced ruefully at the piece he was holding. "Sometimes I forget I am not camped out with the rebels. I will try to do better." He lifted the knife and sliced the French loaf neatly.

Jenny decided to press her luck. "While you're at it, you might consider getting a decent haircut."

Her guest studied her from beneath a lock that had, as usual, fallen across his forehead. With a subtle shake of the head, he dismissed the remark and handed her the cutting board. "As I said, we have not finished discussing the case. The list of suspects will be longer if the stalker and the murderer are not the same person."

"You think they might be different?"

"It is possible we are dealing with an opportunist."

"That would be kind of a relief," Jenny conceded as she buttered her bread more generously than usual. She felt in need of sustenance. "I mean, I'm sorry about your brother, but I've been terrified that whoever's stalking me may have progressed to trying to kill me. Can you think of anyone from Alqedar who could have taken advantage of the situation?''

Zahad's mouth twisted. ''Yes.''

''Who?''

''A young man named Hashim Bin Salem. He is Numa's nephew. She is proposing that the president of our country appoint him governor of our province in my stead. That would be a great step for Hashim.''

''Do you really think he could have managed it? How would he have found out about me?''

''He and Fario were friends. Fario might have told him of your intended meeting.'' The sheikh frowned at his salad as if uncertain what those shreds of vegetation were doing on the table. Or perhaps he was simply lost in thought. ''Removing my brother has presented him with a great opportunity.''

''Wouldn't he try to remove you as well?''

''I am not as easily led into a trap as my brother. Perhaps he wished only to frame me. Or I might be in danger. I am always on my guard. Still, we must not dismiss the possibility that you are the target.''

At his use of the present tense, Jenny set down her fork. Although she hadn't finished her omelette, she'd lost her appetite. Still, this discussion seemed unavoidable. ''Who's on your list?''

''The possessive Sergeant Finley. Your neighbor Ray, because he works at the bank. Also Dolly. She found my brother. And as a former policewoman, she should know how to cover her tracks.''

''Dolly has a key to my house,'' Jenny agreed. ''But there's no motive.''

She explained that Dolly, who'd bought the adjacent cabins as an investment and vacation getaway before her retirement, had become good friends with Jenny's great-aunt, Brigitte. Four years ago, Dolly had retired and moved in, bringing her husband and her daughter's family. She'd been delighted when Jenny arrived a year later. "She and I get along fine."

"In any case, we are blowing smoke," Zahad said. "The main suspect is obvious."

Although Jenny didn't like to think about it, he was right. "Grant."

"For motive, there is the custody issue. The police report states that he is a computer consultant, so he is capable of cyber-stalking. Also, he was a wife beater."

A wife beater. Jenny hated the way Grant had reduced them both to a cliché. She hated even more remembering the downward spiral of their marriage and the way she, conditioned to appeasing her domineering father, had tried to make peace until the night her husband crossed the line.

These memories had been haunting her all week, revived and intensified by Fario's murder. Today, she'd tried to shrug off the encounter with Oliver, but now a twinge in her arm brought that back full force as well.

Jenny started to shake. Embarrassed, she wrapped her arms around herself, fighting for steadiness.

All along, she'd believed that Grant couldn't be the cyber-stalker because he would never endanger his child. Well, even if he wasn't, that didn't mean he hadn't taken advantage of the situation.

Knowing their daughter would be safe at his home these past two weeks, he could have paid someone to eliminate Jenny. *A hired killer, in my house.*

"Are you ill?" Zahad leaned across the counter.

"No, I'm…" Her teeth chattered so hard she couldn't finish the sentence.

"It is a delayed reaction." The sheikh came around and helped her to her feet. "We must get you warm. You suffer from shock."

It had been a long time since anyone had taken care of Jenny, settled her on a couch, wrapped her in a blanket, talked to her soothingly. The sheikh even found a packet of hot-chocolate mix in the cabinet and made some for her. She didn't mind that it clumped together because he'd failed to stir it enough. At least it was warm and sweet.

After she finished drinking, he sat beside her and chafed her hands. The hard angles of his face softened as he worked. "Your family should be with you at such a time."

"My father died years ago," Jenny said. "My mom's remarried and lives in Connecticut. Her husband doesn't like her to travel."

"You should go and stay with your mother."

"I can't leave my job." Anyway, although she didn't like to talk about such personal matters, she didn't feel comfortable staying at her stepfather's. He was too possessive of her mother and seemed to resent her love for Jenny.

"There is no one else?"

"My brother's in the air force. He lives in Texas." He and his wife were wrapped up in their two children and their busy lives.

"This country is too large," Zahad remarked. "Families should stay close."

She refrained from pointing out that his family didn't appear to be very close. But at least he'd flown halfway around the world to claim his brother's body and try to solve his murder.

"I'd better turn in." She gathered the blanket around her. "This sofa folds out, and there are sheets in the linen closet."

"I require no such luxuries," he said.

"You have to stretch out or you'll get a cramp. I don't want my bodyguard getting a charley horse and falling on his face at the first sign of trouble." She managed a smile.

"Very well." He glanced with a touch of apprehension toward the kitchen. "Also, I will wash the dishes."

"Thank you." Gripping the arm of the sofa, Jenny got to her feet. At least, she intended to. Halfway up, her knees started shaking.

Zahad's powerful arms lifted her. Unsure how to respond, she lay pressed to his chest, the faintly exotic scent of his jersey intensifying her light-headedness. "You didn't put anything in the hot chocolate, did you?" she joked feebly.

"If I had, it would have been to make you stronger, not weaker." Carrying her easily, the sheikh mounted the steps to the loft. He scarcely seemed to register her weight, although at five foot eight Jenny was no trifle.

The upstairs room held a queen-size bed, a pine bureau and a desk. After lowering her onto the covers, the sheikh removed her shoes. "Can you finish undressing unaided?"

"Yes." She would sleep in her clothes if necessary.

"If you need anything, you have only to call. I will hear you." His dark eyes lingered on her.

"I'm glad you're here," Jenny said.

He nodded. "It is as it should be." When he stood up, the bed released him with a sigh.

After he went downstairs, Jenny listened to the clink of dishes being washed and, later, the creaks as the couch was transformed into a bed. Feeling more secure than she had in a long time, she fell asleep.

TEMPTRESS. He'd been wrong to use that word to Jenny's face, Zahad mused as he lay trying to ignore the lumps in the thin mattress. Yet that's exactly what she was. Not in the way he had once assumed, however.

He understood why men became fascinated with her. Superficial beauty was commonplace, but intelligence and wariness tempered by vulnerability were not. A man wanted to explore this woman and the sweetness beneath the peppery surface.

Not him, of course. Although possessed of normal drives, he had never been susceptible to feminine allure. As a soldier and fighter, he sublimated the needs of his body.

There had been women, of course. While a student in England, Zahad had dated a girl who considered his background romantic. She had not considered it romantic when he left to train at a military camp, however, and had soon found someone else.

His only other involvement had been with a French photographer who covered the revolution that restored democracy to Alqedar. She had seemed a kindred spirit, reveling in hardship and danger. But once peace broke out, she lost interest in Zahad and in Alqedar. The last time he'd seen her byline on a photograph, it had been from another wartorn country.

Until he became sheikh, Zahad had not considered marriage a desirable goal. Now that the title was thrust upon him, he supposed he would have to do so. He intended to choose a woman from his own background who cared about his people as he did. In the meantime, he took no interest in casual liaisons.

He smiled at the absurdity of contemplating a casual liaison. Jenny would slap his face if she even suspected him of harboring such intentions.

Amused in spite of himself, he finally found a comfortable position on the bed.

JENNY AWOKE IN BLUE-BLACK STILLNESS. Through the tall windows, she could see scattered stars against the deep sky. The storm must be clearing.

The hum of the refrigerator and the ticking of a clock reverberated from downstairs. These sounds were not yet familiar enough for her to ignore.

She'd been dreaming again. Certain images haunted her: a shadow moving in her yard, a hand clamping her wrist. When she moved her arm, her shoulder ached. Like some ugly burned thing, fear hissed and shriveled inside her.

Jenny craved reassurance. Was Zahad still here? Surely he was, yet she needed to be sure.

As she slid her feet into her slippers, she pulled on a robe. At the railing that overlooked the lower floor, she studied the angular shapes of the furnishings. It was impossible to see whether anyone lay on the pull-out couch.

He wouldn't have left. She should go back to bed.

It was impossible to sleep, though, in the aftermath of that dream. The tension in her lungs seemed to gain strength the more she tried to subdue it.

Perhaps she could fix a cup of tea without disturbing him. After a moment's internal debate, Jenny eased her way down the stairs. At the bottom, she decided to make a quick pass by the bed to satisfy her curiosity.

When she came close, she made out Zahad's solid shape sprawled across the mattress, a thin blanket bunched around him. Jenny listened with satisfaction to the regularity of his breathing.

Earlier, he'd said that she ought to be with family at such a time. Ironically, Jenny felt more at ease with this stranger than she ever had with relatives.

She'd grown up half-afraid of her rigid father. Despite an occasional show of tenderness, there'd been no predicting when his temper would flare and he'd lash out at her.

Only once had he physically hurt her: she'd messed up during a softball game and he'd become so incensed he'd deliberately thrown a ball, hard, into her arm. She'd wanted to take after him with the bat, but she hadn't been able to stir, just clutch her aching arm and stare at him in disbelief.

She hadn't fought back. Maybe that was why she still felt angry about it.

No matter what the provocation, Zahad would never vent his fury on a woman or a child. Jenny sank onto the edge of the bed and let his presence soothe her. If she sat here for a while, she might be able to sleep again.

Her eyelids drooped. Overcome by weariness, she lay down, just for a moment.

ZAHAD AWOKE with his arms around a woman. Sweet-smelling blond hair tumbled across his face and his body hardened with desire where it pressed into her back.

Although she was clothed, he wore nothing beneath the blanket. His instincts urged him to rearrange her garment and, with a few short strokes, unite them. Then he remembered where he was and who he held in his arms.

Instantly, he released her. She half turned and blinked in the morning light.

He sat up, adjusting the blanket to keep himself covered. "Why are you here?" he asked.

"I'm sorry." Jenny rubbed her eyes. "I had a bad dream. I just sat down here for a minute."

Zahad had no wish for her to guess his state of arousal. It was merely an instinctive response, after all. "It appears the storm is over." After pulling on the cloth robe that he'd left by the bed, he slid from beneath the covers and went to the window.

Outside, sunlight refracted off snowy branches and thick whiteness. Zahad wasted no time on sentiment. He had looked with some appreciation at the snowy landscapes in Europe as he passed by on a train, but he'd never had to drive through the stuff. On the positive side, the pristine surface gave no sign of any visitors.

Jenny joined him at the window. In her flowered robe, the woman was a rainbow of soft colors, Zahad reflected grumpily. He did not wish to have rainbows and gardens inflicted on him first thing in the morning.

"We should not delay," he said. "I may have only a few days, if that long, to conduct my investigation."

"And I have to get the house ready for Beth. Grant's bringing her home tomorrow," Jenny replied. "You use the bathroom and I'll make breakfast."

"Very good." Zahad marched across the room to retrieve his clothes.

IT WAS APPARENT TO JENNY the moment they stepped outside that the rental car would not be able to negotiate snow of this depth. She offered the sheikh a lift as well as an introduction to her neighbors.

"I'll be coming back here later to collect my things,"

she said. "It's warm enough, so the snow should start to melt and maybe you can get out then."

"You plan to stay at your own home tonight?"

"I think so."

As she unlocked her vehicle, Jenny hoped she would feel less spooked by the evening. She had to pull herself together before Beth arrived tomorrow, both for her daughter's sake and so she could stand up to any attempt by Grant to keep her. She was a little surprised her ex-husband hadn't called and demanded this already, since he must have learned about the murder from Parker.

Perhaps he realized she would never consent. And if he violated his visitation agreement by holding on to Beth longer than agreed, he'd hurt his potential custody case.

"I accept your offer," Zahad said, interrupting her train of thought. "It will help me make the most of my time." He took the passenger seat in the SUV.

He hadn't mentioned anything about her waking up in his bed this morning, Jenny reflected as she slid behind the wheel. She had a hazy memory of him holding her close, then pushing her away. She appreciated his self-control.

She tried not to think about the muscular body she'd glimpsed in nearly all its glory. A long white scar that zagged across one shoulder emphasized the sheikh's ferocity. His leanness, the absence of any wasted bulk, made even the athletes she saw on television seem soft in comparison.

Last night, she'd hotly denied any suggestion of being a temptress, and then crawled into his bed. Despite his rough manners, Zahad was more of a gentleman than most men would have been.

Her own response had been far from demure. The close contact and his tantalizing scent had filled her with longings she did *not* intend to act on.

As she backed out of the carport, Jenny noticed a stubble of beard darkening Zahad's jaw. He hadn't asked to borrow a razor and didn't seem to care that he lacked one. The man was obviously untroubled by vanity. She felt a bit alarmed by how much she was starting to like his raffish side.

Several inches of snow had fallen, with deeper drifts. No one had broken the surface on the side street, so it was slow going. Once she reached Pine Forest Road, where traffic had turned the snow to slush, she began to make better time.

Jenny rounded a corner near her home and slowed, her throat tightening at the sight of a group of neighbors standing across the street from her house. There were no emergency vehicles, but half a dozen people didn't stand around talking in the snow for no reason.

"Something's wrong," she said.

Although what she could see of her home through the trees looked undisturbed, frightening possibilities raced through her mind: Oliver had come back; another unwanted visitor had arrived; someone had broken into the house.

Jenny wished for one crazy moment that she could retrace their path to the cabin. She wished it were last night again and she lay curled against the sheikh, sheltered by his warmth.

Zahad studied the assemblage as Jenny halted in the entrance to her driveway. "Who is who?"

"I'll give you the short course." She pointed out widowed Louanne Welford, who lived on the far side of Parker Finley's house, and Tish and Al Garroway, the young couple in front of whose home the group stood. Dolly and Ellen, both stocky with short, reddish brown hair and freckles, were unmistakably mother and daughter.

Everyone turned to look at Jenny and Zahad, but only Dolly and Al Garroway waved. She saw no sign of Ray, who was probably working on his car as usual.

Jenny made her way across the street. "What's going on?"

"You know those carjackings near the ski lodge?" Dolly replied. "Someone jumped Tish last night. Got away with her Accord and her purse."

"Were you hurt?" Jenny was willing to set aside personal differences, even though she knew her neighbor had taken a dislike to her.

"I'm fine," Tish answered curtly. Of medium height, she had a bony build and blond hair with dark roots. Parker had said that, from a distance, she looked a little like Jenny.

Seeing everyone's attention fix on her companion, Jenny said, "I'd like you all to meet Sheikh Zahad Adran. It was his brother who was killed on Monday."

Ellen paled. "I'm so sorry." She'd taken the news hard, Dolly had told Jenny a few days ago. They'd all been shaken to realize that, had Dolly tried the door during one of her patrols, she rather than Fario would have caught a gunshot in the chest.

"I'm just glad my wife wasn't hurt last night." Al slipped an arm around Tish's waist. In his midtwenties, the ski instructor had dark hair, a narrow face and a scraggly goatee. "You guys don't think these carjackers are connected with the murder, do you?"

"How many carjackings have occurred?" Zahad asked.

"Five successful ones and three attempts," Dolly said. "They started about three months ago, targeting the ski area. People carry a lot of cash when they're on vacation."

"The police think it's some gang members from L.A.," added Louanne. Although wrapped in a coat, scarf and short, clunky boots, the widow shivered as a breeze stirred snow flurries. "We never used to have crime around here. I didn't even lock my doors until those men started pestering Jenny."

"Another one showed up yesterday, an ex-con," Jenny said. "Zahad chased him away."

"This is all about you, isn't it?" Tish snapped. "I'm the one who got shoved out of my car and lost my new Honda, and all you can talk about is how tough you have it."

"It's not a competition," Jenny snapped, and then wished she hadn't.

"She's got good reason to be upset," Al reproved.

"I didn't mean to imply otherwise."

"At least the cyber-stalking ought to stop now." Ellen's voice shook. "I mean, whoever's been putting this stuff on the Internet about Jenny, surely they'll quit when they find out about the murder."

"Unless the stalker is the killer and he isn't finished," her mother pointed out.

"Oh." Ellen blanched.

"I can tell you the stalker is still active on the Web. An associate of mine trolled the chat rooms yesterday and was solicited in Jenny's name."

"You're kidding!" Ellen hugged herself against the cold. "How could they…" She let out a short puff of breath. "I'm going to post the news of the murder everywhere. I'll make sure people quit falling for that maniac."

"Thank you," Jenny replied. "I'd be grateful."

"It is an excellent idea," Zahad agreed.

Tish eyed him coldly. "I'd like to know what the number-one suspect is doing hanging around here."

An uncomfortable silence fell over the group. "I don't believe a suspect has been identified," Dolly said after a beat.

"Parker was talking about him last night at the robbery scene," Tish went on. "I heard him grousing about this sheikh getting underfoot."

"This sheikh was in his own country on Monday and has witnesses to prove it." Jenny didn't know why she sprang to Zahad's defense, except that in a way Tish was impugning her, too. And despite her sympathy over the carjacking, she had tired of her neighbor's gratuitous nastiness.

"My brother deserves justice," Zahad added. "If the police are going to waste their time targeting me, it appears I am the one likely to solve this case."

"I can see why Parker doesn't like you," Tish said.

Al shook his head at his wife. "Why don't you cut people a little slack?"

"Because I don't feel like it," she said, and went into the house. Al spread his hands and followed his wife.

"What's with Tish?" Dolly asked.

"Oh, leave her alone. She got robbed and thrown out of her car. How would you feel?" Ellen stamped her feet. "My toes are going numb. Excuse me."

"I've got to go, too," Dolly said. To Zahad, she explained, "My husband, Bill, suffers from fibromyalgia. He's in a lot of pain, and he's absentminded, too. Last week he was going to the store and got on the wrong bus. If Ray hadn't found him wandering around Crystal Point, I don't know what would have happened. But if there's anything I can do to help, please tell me."

"Thank you," he replied.

That left only Louanne. "I'd be happy to help, too, but I'm afraid I don't know anything."

"It is possible you have observed more than you realize. May I accompany you to your house and ask a few questions?"

"I'd be honored." The widow beamed. "I never thought I'd have a sheikh visit me!"

"I will come by later," Zahad told Jenny.

"I'll be there, scrubbing away." Struggling to focus on the chores ahead instead of on the memory of yesterday's unwelcome visitor, Jenny crossed the street to her property. She couldn't keep relying on the sheikh to protect her.

She hoped he would learn something valuable in his questioning and that this whole mess would soon be over. Because she didn't want to go on feeling her breath catch in her throat and her hands grow moist every time she turned up her own driveway.

Chapter Six

If any uncluttered space had dared to present itself in Mrs. Welford's house, its owner would no doubt have hunted it down and stuffed it with bric-a-brac. Zahad had never seen so many figurines, doilies, souvenir plates and stuffed animals. Despite the scent of lemon cleanser, dust clung to the air particles.

The widow herself proved a font of neighborhood chit-chat, none of it very helpful. However, Zahad listened politely and filed everything away for future reference.

Over hot tea and crisp cookies, the widow described Cindy Rivas and Beth Sanger as two little dolls. She was glad Jenny had moved into the former home of her great-aunt, who'd been a good friend of Mrs. Welford's.

She also told him about Dolly Blankenship's marital history. "She and Bill were newlyweds when they moved here," the widow confided. "She was married twice before. Her first husband, Ellen's father, died of something—a heart attack, I think. They say her second husband won the Florida lottery after she divorced him. If you ask me, she should have waited!"

"Indeed." Zahad was more interested in learning about Dolly's son-in-law, who might have been the source of the scrap of paper he'd found. "I understand she retired. Why did her daughter's family move here?"

"Ray's a nice fellow but things never seem to work out for him."

His hostess offered him more cookies. He declined. A man who consumed too many sweets grew soft. "What do you mean?" Was Ellen's husband unstable?

"I heard he first wanted to be a pilot, but there was some problem with his eyesight. Nothing serious, but you know how picky the airlines are."

She seemed to require feedback, so the sheikh made an encouraging noise.

"After he moved here, Ray worked as a deliveryman but he hurt his back," she went on. "He started doing repairs, handyman stuff, but he didn't charge enough and he spent too much time chitchatting. I hope that job at the bank pans out for him."

"He must have spent a lot of time in people's houses." That meant Ray might have known where Jenny kept her gun. And a handyman would have had no trouble duplicating a key or rigging a booby trap.

Mrs. Welford nodded. "He's so friendly, you don't mind having him around."

"I must talk with him." With a smile that he hoped didn't betray his impatience, Zahad rose from the depths of his cushioned chair. "Perhaps he has observed something useful."

"He'd have been at work on Monday, when this terrible thing happened," she said, getting up at the same time. "Although I don't think he leaves until after nine. Maybe he passed someone suspicious on the road."

An elementary-school principal probably departed earlier, Zahad thought. Ray would have had time to do his dirty work after Jenny left. He'd had the means and the opportunity. Only the motive remained unclear.

After thanking his hostess, Zahad made his escape. Outside, he sucked in the cold, clear air.

From atop the small rise upon which Mrs. Welford's home was situated, he took in the lay of the land. Mountain peaks rose to the north, emphasizing the alpine quality of Jenny's neighborhood.

Straight across the street lay Ray and Ellen's modest house. There was a carport directly across the driveway and a garage on the far side of the house. The garage faced a rock retaining wall about three feet high.

Farther up the driveway stood a second home. Dolly's, obviously. An irregular line of snow-dusted greenery and rising terrain connected her property with Jenny's.

A man of peace might find it difficult to believe that Fario had been slain in such a picturesque setting. But having seen sunbaked villages smashed by tanks and colorful city markets dynamited, Zahad knew the swiftness and ruthlessness of death.

Once he had taken stock of his surroundings, he descended to the street. Several times he slipped in the snow and, although he avoided a fall, his shoes and pant cuffs became soaked. Zahad made a mental note to buy winter clothing.

He followed Dolly's driveway uphill. In the window of the first house, a little girl with light brown hair held her teddy bear to the glass. They both swiveled solemnly to watch Zahad go by.

He stopped outside the open garage, which was only wide enough for a single vehicle. It housed a classic car with shiny paint and a restored bumper. The occasional clanking noise from within drew his attention.

"Mr. Rivas?" Zahad called.

"You bet!"

The brown-haired man who ducked around the car had a typical American openness to his expression. Only slightly below Zahad's height, he had the kind of pudgy physique that bears testimony to too many pints, most likely consumed in front of televised rugby matches. Make that cans of beer and football, he reminded himself.

"Hey, you must be that sheikh fella my wife mentioned.'' Ray wiped his hand on a rag and stuck it out. ''Sorry about your brother. That's a real shame.''

His grip was firm and scented with motor oil. It occurred to Zahad that he might be shaking hands with Fario's killer. Before anger sharpened his tongue, however, he reminded himself that if Ray Rivas was innocent, he could be useful. He'd probably visited most of the neighbors' houses and ought to know who was fixated on Jenny.

''As you may have heard, I am making a few inquiries,'' Zahad said.

''Inquire away,'' the fellow replied cheerfully.

''Did you see anything suspicious on Monday morning?'' It was a relief to get right to the point. With Mrs. Welford, he'd tried to behave more sociably.

''Afraid not. I already told the police everything, not that there was much to tell. But I've got my theories.''

''Theories?'' Zahad asked.

''You know, about Jenny. I mean, she's such a babe,'' Ray told him. ''All the guys notice her but the one that might be motivated to go off the deep end is her ex-husband. I watch cop shows and the criminal is almost always somebody like that.''

''I see.'' To forestall any more unhelpful guesses, Zahad said, ''Do you know why the lady who was carjacked dislikes her?''

''You bet!'' He put one foot up on the bumper. ''Tish is just plain jealous. One time her husband said right in front of her that she looks a little like Jenny but Jenny's more glamorous. How's that for a poke in the eye?''

''Is her husband after Jenny?''

''I don't think so.'' Ray grinned. ''Hey, we all like to look at the scenery and Jenny's easy on the eyes. But that's as far as it goes.''

''What about Parker Finley? Does he like to inspect the scenery?''

''Sure, and he's single. But would he set Jenny up and harass her? And then fix a gun to kill whoever walked through the door? Man, I don't see it. Whoever did this has to be crazy."

"Have you met a teacher named Lew Blackwell?" Zahad might as well run through his list of suspects. "He loaned Jenny his cabin."

"Naw. My daughter doesn't start kindergarten till next year, so I'm not up on the teachers. I mean, none of it makes sense. Jenny gets along with everybody. Heck, we all get along."

Perhaps a bit too well. Dolly, for example, had a key to Jenny's house and, apparently, a finger in everybody's pie. Taking an oblique shot, Zahad said, "It can't be easy living next door to your mother-in-law."

"Aw, she's the salt of the earth," Ray replied. "You wouldn't believe how patient she is with Bill. He's getting senile and he's got some kind of muscle disease, too. He's so tightfisted he goes over their credit-card slips with a fine-tooth comb. She says he's always been that way. If you ask me, she should have stayed married to her second husband. He won the Florida lottery."

"So I heard." The topic seemed to fascinate the neighbors.

"You know what? You ought to stick around and protect Jenny. I hate to think about her and Beth being at that house by themselves."

"You wish me to remain here?" Ray had surprised him, after all. It began to seem less likely that he was the killer.

"Sure." The man scratched his scalp through his short, light brown hair. "The women around here might stop giving Jenny the evil eye and the men could quit tripping over their tongues. Maybe you'll even catch the guy who did it. You seem like the watchful type, if you know what I mean."

He couldn't resist mimicking the man's phrasing. "You bet."

They shook hands.

"I'm sorry I don't have one of my cards on me," Ray

added. "I saw you at the bank the other day. I'd be glad to assist you any way I can."

"Thank you." Embarrassed to have been caught spying and finding it hard to believe Ray was as guileless as he seemed, Zahad gave him a nod and headed for Jenny's house.

He could feel ice crystals forming in his socks. Time to take himself indoors.

JENNY WAS GLAD she'd turned up the heater when she saw how pale Zahad looked. If she'd needed further proof that he was chilled, it came when he accepted her offer of a pair of oversize sport socks.

"You can borrow my SUV and run into town if you'd like to change into some of your warmer stuff." She'd straightened the house but still wanted to wash the dishes and pots from the cabinets.

"I fear I have no warmer stuff," Zahad replied, his innate dignity unmarred even by the clunky socks. "Also, perhaps I should rent a more suitable vehicle."

"You can buy chains at the hardware store." When he didn't respond, Jenny explained, "You wrap them around the tires to get traction in the snow."

"Ingenious," he said.

From outside came the grumble of a car in the driveway. Zahad grimaced. "I suppose I should put on my shoes in case I have to perform kung fu."

"You know kung fu?"

"I learned a variation in military camp."

She glanced through the window. "Don't bother. It's Parker."

"He will not be pleased to see me." Zahad's mouth twisted.

"He'll love the socks." Jenny went to the door.

When she opened it, the detective was stamping his boots on the mat. "I wanted to make sure you're all right. After you told me that sheikh was hanging around, I got—'' He stopped, having spotted Zahad.

"As you can see, I am still hanging around." Her guest lounged on the couch with his sock-clad feet prominently displayed.

Parker grimaced. "What the hell is he doing here?"

Jenny raised an eyebrow disapprovingly. "Language, please."

"Sorry," the detective muttered. "No, I'm not sorry. I found out a few things about you, Mr. Adran."

"I have a lengthy résumé. Which part has aroused your interest?"

"The part where you were a suspect in a murder-kidnap in Orange County about three years ago."

Jenny's heart flipped into her throat. Zahad certainly hadn't mentioned that.

"Please note the use of the past tense," the sheikh told her. "I am no longer a suspect. The case was solved and my name cleared."

"I talked to a detective down there." The officer braced himself with his feet apart. "He says you may have pulled off a few things they never nailed you for, like breaking and entering."

To Jenny, Zahad said, "My cousin Sharif had a son by a surrogate mother in Orange County. She was murdered and I assisted him in recovering the boy and identifying the perpetrator."

"There was another woman involved," Parker warned. "The victim's sister."

"Her name is Holly and she is now Sharif's wife," Zahad replied. "In addition to Ben, they have a one-year-old daughter and another baby on the way." He didn't mention the breaking and entering, Jenny noticed. But in the course of rescuing a child and catching a killer, something like that seemed minor.

"Well?" she said to Parker. "It sounds as if he was more of a hero than a villain."

The man looked as if he'd bitten into something nasty. "It's a bad idea for people to take the law into their own hands. Innocent people get hurt that way."

"So do guilty ones," the sheikh countered. "You know, Sergeant, your suspicions of me lack logic."

"How so?"

"If I had arranged to kill my brother, why would I come here and risk arrest? You would have had a devil of a time extraditing me from Alqedar."

"Criminals return to the scene of the crime. And here you are."

Parker had a point, Jenny reflected reluctantly.

The sheikh didn't rise to the bait. "Speaking of criminals, do you see a connection to the carjackings?"

"Unlikely," Parker said. "They've all taken place near the ski lodge on the far side of town. We think it's an L.A. gang targeting women, taking their cars and purses, probably shipping the cars down to Mexico or selling them to a chop shop."

"If they're from L.A., why come here?" Jenny queried. It was a two-hour drive.

"Easy pickings. People are more trusting, plus we don't have the resources of an urban police force."

"How many robbery-homicide officers are there in Mountain Lake?" Zahad asked.

"Two," Parker replied. "And usually we're so under-utilized we help out with burglaries. Right now, we're a bit overworked, but that doesn't mean we need help."

"I commend you," the sheikh said. "But clearly you do not have time to guard Mrs. Sanger. That is why she has invited me to stay with her until my brother's body is released."

I did not! The protest never made it to Jenny's lips, probably because she dreaded remaining here alone. Besides, she didn't want to embarrass Zahad by contradicting him in front of Parker. Instead, she said simply, "Mr. Adran is a trained security officer."

"He's a trained killer," Parker retorted.

"A revolutionary," Zahad corrected. "One who must adapt to living in civilized society. I admit my manners have rough edges, but who better than a school principal to give me pointers?"

The situation did not call for humor, yet his cheekiness lifted Jenny's spirits. As if the sheikh would accept lessons in comportment from her!

The detective frowned. "I'll check with the medical examiner and see what's holding up your brother's release. Usually he finishes his work within forty-eight hours."

"He mentioned incomplete ancillary studies," the sheikh said.

"What kind of studies? Your brother died from a bullet wound." Jenny had assumed the cause of death was obvious.

"The M.E. has to make sure there isn't something else going on," Parker told her.

"This is a high-profile case," Zahad added. "No doubt the coroner wishes to avoid mistakes."

"By the way, your stepmother was pretty steamed when she called," the detective said. "I gather autopsies violate your customs. But our law requires them in a homicide."

Zahad inclined his head in agreement. He held his silence until Parker, realizing the conversation was over, excused himself and left. Jenny purposely hung back as he went out, to avoid giving him a chance to lecture her again about the sheikh.

One way or the other, she'd given her guest permission to stay. She turned to face him. "Well, what happens now?"

He arose fluidly. "I must go into town for supplies. Thank you for the loan of your vehicle. I will purchase chains."

Jenny hesitated only a moment before making a further decision. "I'd better give you a house key, too, and the alarm code."

"I know the alarm code."

So he *had* memorized it the other day. "I changed it."

A fleeting smile marked his approval. "Very wise. People rarely change their codes."

"How do you know?"

"I have sometimes found their carelessness useful."

Jenny could see why the police in Orange County hadn't caught him breaking and entering. Well, he wasn't going to have to break into her house. Whatever happened now, she would have no one to blame but herself.

IN TOWN, Zahad found that the main roads had been cleared and the stores were open. He was surprised by how many vehicles filled the streets and parking spaces, most of them bearing license frames with the names of other counties. Apparently skiers had arrived en masse to take advantage of the fresh powder.

He ate a late lunch at a café, after which he bought boots, a brown suede coat and groceries. At the hardware store, he purchased a set of chains to fit his rental car and a combination lock for Jenny's toolshed.

Before checking out of the motel, he hooked up his laptop and reviewed his e-mail. There was a message from Sharif, promising to do his best as an advocate, and another from Amy.

In a style sounding like her speech, she wrote:

I've been nosing around. Listen to this! Hashim flew to London about two weeks ago. Supposedly he was partying hearty, but nobody knows the details. It isn't even clear exactly when he got back. I'm looking into it. For all I know, he could have flown from London to California without anyone noticing. Will send more info when I have it.

Zahad wrote back with his list of suspects.

Please advise Numa, if she will listen to you without screaming, that I am doing my best to avenge Fario's death. She would do well to trust me.

He did not, of course, mention he planned to stay with the temptress herself. This would not play well in Alqedar. Thanks to cell phones and e-mail, no one needed to know his address.

He copied the message to Sharif and added a note of thanks. Then he typed up his recollection of that morning's interviews.

As he transferred his suitcase and computer to the SUV, it occurred to Zahad that it would be inconvenient if anyone attempted to carjack Jenny's vehicle at this point. He would be forced to defend it, possibly with lethal results. Sending another body to the M.E. might further delay the release of Fario's remains.

He took a moment to survey the busy sidewalk outside the motel for loiterers or thugs. There was no one of that description, only a steady flow of males and females who appeared almost interchangeable in colorful jackets, knitted caps and ski pants.

From the pharmacy next door emerged a figure oddly out of place among the physically fit masses. Thin and wiry with disheveled white hair peeking from beneath a hunting cap, the man moved with the aid of a cane. Although his coat hung unevenly, it was made of a fine herringbone tweed that matched his cap.

"Mr. Blankenship!" A young woman ran outside, waving a bag. She had thrown a coat over her white smock. "You forgot your medicine."

"Nonsense. I've got it right here." Grumbling, the man reached inside his coat and patted his shirt pocket. "Where the devil did it go?"

"Here it is." The clerk handed it to him. "Isn't there someone who can drive you home?"

"I may be old but I'm not senile." He snatched the bag from her hand. "I'm taking the bus."

"I heard you ended up in Crystal Point last week." The clerk hugged herself against the cold. "Why don't you come inside while I call your wife."

"They changed the durn bus route, that was the problem," the man said. "I'll be fine."

This must be Dolly's husband. Zahad had no interest in playing Good Samaritan to such a disagreeable figure, but he needed to interview each of the neighbors. Getting Mr. Blankenship alone in a car might be the only way to gain his cooperation.

He approached, keeping one eye on his loaded vehicle. "I am driving to Mrs. Sanger's house. I would be happy to give this gentleman a ride."

The clerk surveyed Zahad suspiciously. "Do you know Mrs. Sanger?"

He realized she suspected him of being one of the Internet creeps. "Yes. I am her houseguest. My name is Sheikh Zahad Adran."

"Oh, wow!" Her face lit up as if she were meeting a movie star. "I've heard about you! I mean, I'm sorry about your brother. Bill, this nice man is going to give you a ride home."

"He don't look so nice to me," the old man growled.

"I will ensure that he gets home safely," Zahad told the woman.

"Do you ever wear those robes and that head thing?" she asked.

"On occasion." Only when it was required by custom or suited his purposes, but he saw no reason to explain that.

"Wow!" Reluctantly, she moved back. "Go on, Bill. He'll take care of you."

"That's what I'm afraid of," Bill grumbled as she went in. On the sidewalk, a young couple with a baby approached. He made no attempt to move aside, forcing them to push their stroller around him.

Although the older man's hand shook as he clutched his cane, Zahad felt ambivalent about taking his arm. "Do you require assistance?"

"I don't require any durn thing. Are we going to get in the flipping car or are we going to stand here and freeze to death?"

Why had Dolly married such a snappish person? Zahad wondered. But perhaps he owed his ill temper to his pain.

When they reached the SUV, Bill struggled to ease himself inside but never asked for help. Ray had said his father-in-law used to be a truck driver. It must be difficult for him to accept his disability.

"You've been snooping around," Bill said as they pulled away from the curb.

"I have a duty to my brother," Zahad told him. He expected no sympathy and he received none.

"You sheikhs oughta stay in your own country."

"I will make sure to advise my fellow sheikhs of your opinion." He halted at a red light.

"I got no patience for small talk," Bill said. "Whatever you want to know, be quick about it. Once we get home, I'm heading for the bathroom, and I intend to be there a while."

"Very well. I would like your opinion of the neighbors."

"You want a rundown? Okay." The light changed and they started forward a little too hard, forcing the old man against his shoulder harness. "Hey! How'd you like it if somebody hit *you* across the chest with a board full of nails?"

"I am sorry." Zahad pointed to the bag. "Perhaps you should take one of those pills."

"They're laxatives."

"On second thought, never mind."

Bill cackled. "Naw, they're for pain. But I got to take them with water."

"Then I shall drive quickly. Please, fill me in on the neighbors."

Bill ran through the cast of characters, at least those he remembered. He didn't seem to know much about Tish and Al, who, Zahad recalled, had moved in recently.

According to Bill, Dolly was a decent wife although she snored and left hair in the sink. Ellen suffered from fits of jealousy, possibly because Ray had a wandering eye. "He's a hot-and-cold sort of fella," Bill added. "One minute he's your best friend and the next he won't give you the time of day."

Ray hadn't struck Zahad as volatile. He filed away the information.

"You don't need to know about the children, so I'll skip them," Bill said. "Jenny's a pretty woman. Ought to have a man in her life. Parker Finley, he'd like to be that man but he ain't her type."

"What is her type?" the sheikh asked.

"The kind that leaves her alone."

"How about Mrs. Welford?"

"Who?"

He dredged up her first name. "Louanne. The widow across the street."

"Don't have an opinion on her. Too boring. Now you tell me."

"Tell you what?"

"What they said about me."

The answer came promptly. "That you're tightfisted."

"I'm a retired fella with no pension and a lot of medical bills the government don't cover. You try living on social security. No, don't try it. You ain't entitled because you ain't American. What do they do with old people in your country?"

"Their children take care of them," Zahad said. Elders were respected and honored in Alqedar.

"What if they don't have children?"

He'd never thought about it. "I do not know."

"You're the sheikh. Ain't you got social programs?"

"I am a sheikh of recent vintage. I will look into it." He meant that.

Also, Bill's remark made him wonder about Numa. In her late forties, she didn't have much to look forward to with her only child dead. Of course, if her sole concern was her financial future, she'd have done better to placate the new sheikh than to antagonize him.

Nevertheless, Zahad knew his father would have wanted his widow to live in comfort. He reminded himself to set up a pension for Numa and assess the needs of elderly people who lacked families.

"Ain't you going to ask me anything interesting?" Bill asked.

"Such as?"

"Like whether I got a history as an ax murderer?"

"It is unlikely you would tell the truth on that score." Still, it couldn't hurt to sound him out. "Very well. How much do you know about the Internet?"

"I been on it a few times. My wife's got a computer. Seem to be a lot of dirty pictures on it." He didn't sound unhappy about that.

Zahad turned left into the driveway on Dolly's property. He passed the Rivas house and continued up a slope to the smaller cottage. With the snow melting rapidly, he had no trouble negotiating it.

The Blankenship house, constructed of dark wood with a deck visible in the back, lay in the deep gloom of overgrown pines. "You ought to get Ray to thin these out," he said.

"Didn't know you sheikhs was into that *Better Homes and Gardens* stuff. Wanna come inside and rearrange the furniture?"

"I will forgo the pleasure." Zahad got out and opened the passenger door. Although he didn't offer to help, he stood ready to catch the old man if he slipped.

The front door scraped and Dolly came out. "Bill! You should have told me you wanted to go into town. I'd have taken you."

"Just because I can't drive no more, that don't make me an invalid." The old man wiggled down from his seat, anchoring himself with the cane.

His wife shook her head. "He's going to be sore as heck tonight. I can't believe he walked all the way to the bus stop in the snow. Thanks for bringing him back, Zahad."

"Exercise is good for my heart." Bill regarded the sheikh. "I suppose you'll be expecting some kind of thank-you for the ride."

"It is of no importance."

"Don't encourage him," Dolly said. "His manners are atrocious."

"Who's this 'he' you're talking about?" asked her husband. "It can't be me. I'm standing right here."

"Sorry," said his wife.

To Zahad, Bill said, "Thank you. If my wife can be polite, so can I, I guess. Don't count on it happening again."

"I assure you, I won't." With a wave, Zahad got back into the SUV and traced the short distance to Jenny's house.

The afternoon sun hung low in the sky, casting harsh shadows across the snow. Against the looming darkness, the house glowed from within. And as he emerged from the vehicle, he caught a whiff of coffee. How easily a man could be lulled into a sense of comfort.

Zahad reminded himself that, beneath the snow, blood still soaked the earth. He had learned many things today, but none brought him measurably closer to solving his brother's murder. And, for him, time was running out.

Chapter Seven

In the late afternoon, Jenny and Zahad drove to Lew's cabin, collected her possessions and put chains on the car, although she doubted the sheikh would need them for long. Still, with another storm predicted in a few days, they might come in handy.

She made one last check of the premises and left a thank-you note. Then she locked up and dropped the key through a return slot, as Lew Blackwell had requested.

At home, they ate a quiet dinner of groceries Zahad had brought from town along with his possessions. Afterward, he excused himself to set up his laptop in her home office, which doubled as the guest room.

The dishes done, Jenny laid out scraps of fabric on a pad atop the dining-room table. She wanted to keep her hands busy and her mind occupied so she wouldn't dwell on the fact that an edgy and dangerously attractive man was sharing her home.

Flipping through a box of tiny dress patterns, she chose one for Beth's favorite doll. Even though Grant and Shelley usually showered her with expensive toys, her daughter would enjoy the gift. Like any five-year-old, Beth was susceptible to bribery, but only up to a point.

The last time she'd spent a week with them, they'd gone to Disneyland and the beach in Orange County, about a two-hour drive away. At first enthusiastic in her phone calls,

Beth had gradually wearied of the excitement. When she finally got home, she'd gone around the house touching the furniture and had stared at her favorite blue-and-white swirled glasses as if reassured to see them safely in their accustomed places. That was one of the reasons Jenny had been so eager to restore everything before tomorrow.

She and Beth both liked order and feminine frills. Simply laying the small pattern pieces along the bits of fabric, lining up the arrows with the grain and imagining how the seams would fit together gave Jenny an almost sensual pleasure. Her father had scorned fashion and disapproved of makeup beyond a bare minimum. She loved being able to indulge her child and the child in herself.

After a few minutes, she glanced through the kitchen to the office where the sheikh sat in profile at the desk. Wearing a loose-knit fisherman's sweater over jeans, he frowned as he typed on his laptop. Was he searching for the cyberstalker?

In spite of their tentative alliance, Zahad might take the opportunity while living here to go through her computer for signs that she'd been the one who'd e-mailed his brother. She didn't like the idea, but if he did, finding nothing should put an end to any lingering suspicions.

Jenny returned her attention to the dress. She loved the colors and patterns in the fabric scraps, leftovers from a craft project that one of the teachers had saved for her. Minnie, Beth's doll, would look pretty in flowered sleeves, a solid bodice and a striped skirt, all in shades of white, blue and burgundy.

Without looking up, she registered the sound of Zahad rising and approaching across the kitchen linoleum. He moved so lightly that she imagined he could easily slip past someone's guard.

Coming alongside, he regarded her handiwork. ''What are you making?''

''Doll clothes,'' she said.

''Your daughter is fortunate.'' He watched her hands ad-

justing the small pieces. Rather than feeling self-conscious,
Jenny enjoyed being the object of his attention.

"I suppose women in your country must be good at
crafts. Do they mostly stay home with the children?"

"Traditionally, yes," said Zahad. "However, these days
most families educate their daughters. We are a small country and cannot afford to waste human resources."

"There's a practical point of view." His nearness made
her conscious of the way her hair floated around her neck
and her sweater clung to her breasts. If he noticed, however,
he gave no indication. "What about your cousin Amy? I
presume she's educated."

"She is an economist. I have placed her in charge of
economic development for Yazir."

"Is she married? Does she have kids?" she asked.

"Both."

Jenny finished pinning the pieces in place. "Okay, you
get points for equal-opportunity employment."

He must have moved closer, she realized when his breath
tickled her neck. "I am a great believer in equality."

She made the mistake of looking up. She noted the bristle
of fresh beard along Zahad's jawline and the unruly fullness
of his thick black hair. His eyes were full of hunger, his
scars a vivid reminder of the battles he'd fought. His wild-
ness took her breath away.

Jenny edged around the corner of the table and picked
up a pair of scissors. Zahad made no attempt to follow.

"Did you have any luck on the computer?" she asked.

"I was trying to trace the movements of Numa's nephew
Hashim, the man who wants to be governor. Amy discovered he was out of the country these past few weeks."

"Do you consider him a suspect? I thought he and your
brother were friends."

"Young men may hang about together and share good
times. That does not mean they can be trusted when money
and power are at stake."

The sheikh remained on the far side of the table. Although she was the one who'd moved away, Jenny missed the frisson of excitement from being close to him.

"What's Hashim like? He didn't grow up the way you did, did he?" She was beginning to get a picture of two very different sets of people among his country's elite, those who had trained in desert camps and fought for freedom, and those who had lolled in the comfort of a European exile.

"Hashim is no warrior, nor is he, in my opinion, to be relied upon. He told everyone he was in England, partying, before Fario died, but tonight I heard from a friend of his in London who says Hashim disappeared for almost a week."

Her mouth went dry. "When, exactly?" Maybe Zahad really had found the murderer. It was almost too much to hope for.

It also would mean the killer was an opportunist, not the stalker. Hashim couldn't have been aware of Jenny's existence until he learned about her from Fario. Her troubles wouldn't be over even if he was caught.

"He was last seen in London twelve days ago," the sheikh said. "He returned to Alqedar last Sunday."

"The day before Fario died." Not guilty, then.

"Yes, if his friends are telling the truth, but that is far from certain." Despite Zahad's level tone, strong emotions strained beneath the surface. "Nor do we know where he went. We cannot rule out Los Angeles."

After cutting the last piece of the garment, Jenny began cleaning away the cloth fragments. "But he got home on Sunday."

"Still, if he was here, he might have made arrangements. Los Angeles is a big city and there are always people ready to sell their souls for money."

There it was again, the chilling scenario of a hired killer. Jenny kept trying to reject that scenario, she realized, because the idea of such a cold-blooded crime seemed all the more repellent. "How can you find out?"

"I will drive into L.A. tomorrow to seek my brother's acquaintances. Fario had been there almost four months and he made friends easily."

A wistful note in his voice caught her attention. "And you don't?" she guessed.

He gave her a crooked smile. "No, indeed. But the ones I make, I keep forever."

A longing enveloped Jenny to be taken into this man's inner circle. But what would it mean if he kept her forever? Obviously he didn't plan to stay in Mountain Lake.

Besides, she suspected that Zahad, if he ever loved, would want to possess a woman completely. And the only kind of man Jenny wanted was the kind who gave her space.

"Tomorrow's a good day for you to go into L.A.," she said. "It's best if Beth has me to herself for a while after Grant brings her back."

"When will that be?"

"The last time I talked to him, he planned to arrive around 3:00 p.m."

"I would like to know more about your ex-husband. Aside from Hashim, he appears to have the most to gain from this situation."

How could she sum up the man she'd been married to for four years? It seemed easiest to start with practical details. "You already know that he's a computer consultant. His wife, Shelley, is an attorney who handles contracts for him. She's twenty-eight."

"And she wants a child."

"That's right." Jenny felt the tension rising inside her. "They've been married maybe a year and a half. A few months ago, Grant told me she has a medical condition that precludes her having children and she wants Beth."

The half-dozen times Jenny had met Shelley, the young woman had seemed self-absorbed and brittle. She was certainly selfish. Just because Shelley couldn't have a child, that didn't give her the right to try to take someone else's.

"It would devastate my daughter to lose me," Jenny went on. "I told him children can't be handed around like possessions."

"What was his response?"

"He said she's as much his as mine and that he and Shelley can offer her a more secure two-parent home." Jenny's hands formed fists. She barely avoided pricking herself with the needle.

"Was this before the stalking started?"

She nodded. "About two months before."

"Has he taken legal action?"

"No. I expected Shelley to file the court papers by now, but maybe they need to hire a California attorney."

"Perhaps he hopes to harass you until you send your daughter away for her own safety."

"If that's his game, he doesn't know me very well," Jenny said. "I swore when I left him that I'd never let him push me around again, and I won't."

"I am surprised you ever tolerated his abuse."

She knew the sheikh well enough to detect the anger simmering just below his self-controlled surface. "Things didn't start out that way." Wanting him to understand that she hadn't been a doormat, Jenny sketched the circumstances of their marriage.

She'd been a teacher in Long Beach when she met Grant at a party. Twelve years older than she, he'd been a welcome contrast to the immature men Jenny usually fended off. Also, after losing her father the year before, she'd felt in need of stability. They'd married shortly after she turned twenty-five.

Given the difference in their ages, she'd fallen easily into letting Grant make the rules. Since he'd been reasonable and considerate at first, that hadn't been a problem. She'd felt they were building a future together.

After several years of teaching, Jenny had taken leave when Beth was born. During her extended leave, she'd completed work on a master's degree.

Slowly their relationship had changed. Looking back, Jenny supposed there were several reasons. Having a child meant not only that her attention was divided but that she assumed a more adult role. Also, after her husband's business suffered a setback, she needed to return to work. Gradually the balance of power between them shifted.

Grant started to drink and stay out late. At home, he became sarcastic and cold. When she was offered a job as assistant principal at a school in Long Beach, they'd needed the extra money but her added responsibilities and prestige had galled him. After that he'd criticized her almost constantly.

One night when he was drunk, he'd struck her. Jenny took Beth and left. Grant had begged her forgiveness and she'd given him a second chance. Things were fine for a few weeks, and then he began to drink again.

They'd had one last fight. There'd been a shocking moment when he'd shoved Jenny and tripped her. Lying helpless on the floor, she'd feared for her life. As soon as she could get away, she fled with their daughter, vowing never again to let a man control or intimidate her.

Although she'd had Grant arrested, she still felt angry that she hadn't been able to hit him back. No matter how much she told herself that it would only have made things worse, she hated feeling like a victim.

After Grant took an anger-management class, the charges against him were reduced to a misdemeanor. He hadn't contested Jenny's demand for custody as long as she agreed to regular visitation.

"If he does file for custody, I'll throw it all in his face," she said. "He's married a much younger woman, just as he did the first time. He's proven before that he can be violent. I won't let him take my child."

"Good for you." High color flushed Zahad's face. He looked ready to do battle for her, Jenny thought with pleasure. "A man who hurts someone under his protection is despicable."

"If you happen to meet him tomorrow, I'd prefer you didn't say that to his face."

"Why not?"

"We have a daughter together." It was a fact she'd reluctantly come to terms with. "I'm going to have to interact with him until she's grown. It's in her best interest for us to stay on good terms, unless he makes that impossible."

"I will exercise restraint," Zahad promised.

Actually, the prospect of facing Grant tomorrow was more daunting than Jenny wanted to admit. She almost wished Zahad wasn't going into L.A.

She wouldn't let her ex-husband pull any power plays. No matter how upset he got about the murder or the cyberstalking, he couldn't keep Beth until and unless he got a court order.

She wrenched her thoughts away from Grant. The sheikh was right in front of her, and they needed to deal with practicalities. "Would you like help making up the couch in the office?" Earlier, she'd set out sheets, blankets and a pillow.

"I will be fine. If I work late on the computer, I hope it will not disturb you."

"It won't." Tonight, Jenny resolved, she was not going to slip into his room, no matter how frightened she became. "I just hope you learn something useful in L.A."

"As do I."

After donning his coat, he went out to make one last patrol of the premises. When he returned, Jenny activated the alarm and gave him the new password.

It was her first night in the house since someone had been killed here. With the sheikh at hand, that fact no longer shook her to the core. She chose not to worry about what would happen after he left.

As REQUESTED, Amy turned up the name and address of one of Fario's Los Angeles friends. It was a tremendous advantage to have her as an inside source at the palace in

Yazir, Zahad reflected as he typed a thank-you for the information.

He no longer remembered why she used to rub him the wrong way. Because they were both bullheaded, he supposed.

After setting the information aside for later, he spent more than an hour incorporating the latest economic data from his province into its development plan. He forwarded a copy to Sharif to show to the president in support of Zahad's leadership.

Thank goodness for his cousins, Zahad thought. Jenny had been correct when she surmised that he didn't make friends easily. Nor did he walk smoothly along the corridors of power. He preferred an enemy he could fight in the open.

It was impossible to place himself in the shoes of a man like Grant, who had violated his wife's safety. The images that had leaped to mind as she'd talked had filled Zahad with fury.

He had never loved a woman the way his cousin Sharif loved his wife and most likely never would. That kind of all-consuming passion made no sense to him. Even so, when the time came to take a wife and father children, Zahad knew he would give his own life for theirs if necessary. If under some unforeseeable circumstance his mate turned against him, no matter if she attacked him herself, he would do no more than was required for self-defense. Even in the face of betrayal, a man must put honor first.

After logging off the computer, Zahad opened the bed and made it up with military precision. Yet he had never felt less like a soldier. The floral scent that wafted from the sheets carried him back to this morning, when he'd awakened next to Jenny.

His body had reacted instinctively and now did so again, tightening and aching as her scent filled his mind with pleasurable images. Jenny's delicacy stirred him, yet she was far from weak. Her beauty, all that glorious blondness and those eyes green as the depths of a hidden pool, were a bonus. What he valued most was her sharp mind and passion for life.

If she came from Alqedar, he would pursue her, but she did not. After Fario's body was released, she would remain in America to fight her own battles against her ex-husband and perhaps another hidden enemy. Zahad would go back to Yazir, where destiny had given him the sheikhdom denied him by his father.

Of course, it might be necessary to return to America if the local police proved unable to find Fario's killer and if Zahad himself could not do so in the time available. But he preferred not to come back. There was too much vital work to do at home.

From another part of the house, he heard a woman's low voice singing a melody he didn't recognize. When he caught the words *teddy bears* and *picnic,* he realized it must be a children's song. Rustling noises indicated Jenny was changing clothes, and then he heard water running in the bathroom.

It appeared she had become so unselfconscious about sharing quarters that she didn't hesitate to sing out loud. For however long he stayed here, he would prove worthy of that trust, Zahad vowed as he stripped off his outer clothing and laid it close at hand.

The silence of the wooded mountains amplified distant sounds. He fell into a warrior's slumber, awakening every few hours as he registered noises without becoming fully alert. Around 1:00 a.m., the eerie cry of an animal rang out, most likely a coyote. An hour later, he heard an ice-covered tree branch crack.

At four-thirty the rumble of a car brought him halfway to wakefulness. Zahad assumed the vehicle would pass by on the highway, but it grew louder, the engine reverberating through the predawn stillness. Close by, it stopped.

Someone had arrived. Someone definitely not expected.

The sheikh dressed and went into the kitchen to fetch one of the knives he'd seen in a rack. He would have preferred a gun, but Jenny's remained in the hands of the police.

As he moved quietly through the darkened house, he listened for any reassuring signs. Voices, for instance, carrying on a conversation. Or simply for the newcomer to walk to the front and ring the bell.

Neither of those things happened.

Instead, he heard shoes scrape on concrete as someone came around the rear of the house from the parking bay. If the new arrival was trying to be stealthy, he failed.

Zahad glided through the kitchen and eased into the doorway between his room and the rear hallway, avoiding the glow of a night-light low on the wall.

The killer had entered through the back, he remembered.

His brain leaped ahead, calculating what might happen. Should the intruder try the door, either he would find it locked and go away or he would turn a key in it.

The killer had a key. He might not know that Jenny had installed an alarm.

The rear door, like the front, set off a chirping tone that allowed the entrant sixty seconds to input the password into a security panel. Had Jenny consulted Zahad prior to installing her system, he would have instructed her to forget convenience and allow only one delayed entry point. Sixty seconds, plus whatever further delay occurred at the monitoring company and the police station, would give an intruder plenty of time to reach her bedroom before help arrived.

Both Jenny and Sergeant Finley had grossly underestimated the danger she was in. Although the detective lived across the street, he might not be able to arrive for as long as five minutes.

Assuming, of course, the detective himself wasn't prowling around the house.

Zahad adjusted the angle of the knife. If someone broke in, the sheikh could count on the element of surprise to buy him a few seconds against whatever weapon the intruder carried.

He tensed as a key rasped at the lock. So much for the possibility that this was a hapless Romeo summoned by the stalker. Whoever was out there had a key and didn't know the locks had been changed.

If Zahad did nothing, the intruder might leave them in peace. But he would lose the chance to find out his identity.

Sooner or later, he would return. Better to take a chance now and catch him in the act.

Moving quietly into the hall, Zahad tensed. He must act swiftly and give as little warning as possible.

The key scratched again. The intruder either hadn't grasped that it no longer fit or believed he could force it.

Zahad took a deep breath and flung himself forward. In a single fluid sequence, he flipped the dead bolt and yanked open the door.

And found himself staring into a gun barrel.

Chapter Eight

Zahad swung his arm hard and felt the gun fly from the man's hand. The intruder was slightly taller and heavier set but slow to respond. Certainly not fast enough to block a kick that landed square in his groin.

With a grunt, the man doubled over on the narrow porch. The sheikh wrenched him around, clamped his arm about the man's neck and pressed his knife to the pulsing throat.

Inside, warning chirps shrilled rhythmically. Everything had happened so fast that the alarm hadn't even begun alerting the security company.

"Zahad?" came Jenny's voice.

"I have him," he replied hoarsely. "Turn on the light."

A painful brilliance breached the hallway and lapped onto the porch. Blinking against it, Jenny came closer. She was pulling her bathrobe around her. "Who…"

The chirping grew into an ear-shattering screech. The man reacted. "What the—?" He broke off as Zahad clamped his arm tighter.

"Please turn off the alarm," he told Jenny. From this position, all Zahad could see of his prisoner was well-trimmed blond hair and a beefy build that, for all its bulk, lacked skill at fighting. With some relief, he realized that this was not Sergeant Finley.

Jenny input the code. The deafening noise stopped.

In the silence, she took a good look at the man he held. "Grant? Good Lord!"

"This is your ex-husband?" Zahad hauled the man into the house and forced him to his knees. "His gun is on the ground. Will you retrieve it, please?"

"Sure." Jenny grabbed a coat from a hook, slid her bare feet into a pair of canvas shoes and went out. A moment later she returned, gingerly holding a pistol. "I can't believe he came here armed."

"Also, he had a key. Obviously he was not expecting a new lock and an alarm. Or me."

Zahad had loosened his grip a little. On the floor, Grant said, "I knew about you. The gun's for protection."

"It seems to me that I'm the one who needed protection." Jenny handed the weapon to Zahad. He stepped back, pointed it at Grant and gestured at him to rise.

The blond man got up shakily. His face was flushed and he appeared to have difficulty swallowing. When he touched his neck, drops of blood speckled his hand. "Damn. He cut me!" As he leaned against the wall, his voice quivered with what Zahad could have sworn was indignation.

"You are fortunate to be alive. Count yourself lucky that your injury is so trifling."

"Where's Beth?" A dusting of freckles stood out against Jenny's pale skin.

"In the car. Don't worry. She's wrapped up," her ex-husband replied. "I know how to take care of my daughter."

"Yes, you're setting a great example of responsible parenthood," Jenny retorted. "Why did you try to break into my house, and where'd you get the key?"

"I have a right to check the premises," Grant blustered. "The detective called me yesterday with some more questions—" he coughed a few times before continuing "—and he said this assassin might be staying here."

"He called me an assassin?" Zahad couldn't believe Finley had been so irresponsible.

"Well, maybe he said revolutionary. Something like that. Anyway, I knew you were dangerous."

"I am not the one who tried to break in here with a gun," Zahad reminded him.

"It's not loaded." Another cough. "Anyway, you already did break in here and wiped out your brother. I wasn't leaving my daughter until I made sure you weren't around."

Zahad's civilized instincts held him in check only by a slim margin. "Jenny, please call the police before I do something I will regret." He examined the barrel of the gun, a small .32-caliber revolver. It was indeed unloaded.

Only a fool carried a gun without bullets. An armed opponent would not have hesitated to shoot him.

To Grant, Zahad said, "Do not make any sudden moves. I can kill you without this."

The man glanced at him warily. Reluctantly, he nodded.

"I'm going to call Parker and get Beth out of the car." When her ex opened his mouth, Jenny said, "Shut up, Grant. Zahad's a security expert and he's here to guard me. If he has to break your neck, I'll support any story he tells."

The beefy man fell silent. Zahad wondered if it was the first time in his life a woman had put him in his place.

He no longer felt quite so angry with Grant Sanger, however. What infuriated him more was that, if the man told the truth, Parker Finley had put them all in danger by warning Jenny's ex-husband of Zahad's presence.

A worthy opponent looked you in the eye. Only a weasel manipulated others into doing his dirty work.

TRYING TO SET ASIDE her fury, Jenny put her exhausted daughter to bed. She wanted Beth to feel secure in her own home, and apparently she did. Worn out from being dragged across the country on a red-eye flight, the little girl fell asleep almost instantly.

Although she could hear Parker in the front room trying to sort out what had happened, Jenny lingered to gaze at this child who owned her heart. The tangle of blond hair and the air of childish innocence filled her with wonder. Jenny wished she could take Beth away from all this darkness and cruelty.

But that wasn't right, she reminded herself. Her job was to raise her daughter in the imperfect world where someday she, too, would live as an adult.

With a sigh, Jenny pulled the covers up and went out to face the furor Grant had created.

He sat handcuffed in the living room, his face still flushed. Parker must have sent Zahad out of the room.

"Am I interrupting at a bad time?" Jenny asked.

"We're done for the moment." Parker clicked off his tape recorder and closed his notebook. She admired his thoroughness in using both. "I've got Mr. Adran's and Mr. Sanger's statements. I still need yours." As he ruffled one hand through his brown hair, she noticed dark circles under his eyes.

"Would coffee help?"

"Yes, thanks." He stifled a yawn. "I was up late with another carjacking. A tourist broke her arm trying to hang on to her purse." From his tone, it was obvious the robbers had escaped. "We're beefing up patrols. We're going to make it so hot around the ski slopes that those creeps will take their business back to L.A."

After reluctantly summoning Zahad to keep an eye on Grant, the sergeant accompanied Jenny into the kitchen. Over coffee, he took notes while she ran over the events of the past hour.

"Did Grant say where he got the key?" she asked when she'd finished.

"Apparently you loaned him one a few years ago in case he brought Beth back early from a visit. He made a copy."

"What an idiot. Under the circumstances, why on earth

would he tip his hand and risk us finding out that he's got it? It makes him an obvious suspect.''

"One thing that's never in short supply on this earth is stupidity,'' the detective replied.

"And the gun?'' It had occurred to Jenny that, thanks to security measures, her ex-husband couldn't have carried it on the plane. He couldn't have bought it after his arrival, either, because California law mandated a waiting period.

"He says he kept it in a storage unit near the airport. It's registered to him but he's not licensed to carry it concealed. He's lucky it was unloaded or he'd be in even more trouble.''

"A storage unit?'' Jenny hadn't heard about this before.

"He claims he makes business trips out here and doesn't like to schlepp his clothes and computer equipment on airplanes,'' Parker said. "Look, I'm sorry I mentioned Mr. Adran to him. I had no idea he'd decide to sneak in to see if the two of you were sleeping together.''

"Is that what he was doing?'' Jenny's temper flared. "And what was he going to do if he caught us?''

"He claims he just wanted to make sure the sheikh didn't shoot *him*.''

"Who I sleep with is none of his business or anyone else's.'' Jenny didn't bother to protest the false assumption. She had a right to do as she pleased. "You were out of line to tell him anything about my household situation.''

"I apologize. I don't know what I was thinking. But I do worry about you, Jenny.'' The darkness beneath Parker's eyes failed to soften their steeliness. "Sheikh Adran shouldn't be staying here. You've got an alarm for protection.''

"If Grant had been determined to shoot me, that wouldn't have stopped him. I feel safer with Zahad here, and it's my decision.''

The detective folded his hands on the table. "You should listen to me, Jenny.''

Frustration wiped away her tact. "Which part of 'it's my decision' don't you understand?"

"What I understand is that—"

He broke off as Zahad entered from the living room. Although they'd been talking quietly during the interview, they'd raised their voices during the last part and Jenny suspected he'd overheard.

Her hunch was confirmed by the glitter in the sheikh's eyes. "I am impressed with your efficiency, Officer," he said icily. "You have inspired a woman beater to attempt to break into his ex-wife's home. You have put a foreign dignitary at risk of being shot. You have also recovered a key and a gun from the prime suspect in a murder case. And on what do you focus your attention? On trying to control the sex life of the pretty woman who lives across the street from you."

Parker got to his feet faster than she would have believed possible. To Jenny's horror, she saw his hand poised above his holstered revolver. "Don't push me, Mr. Adran."

"Anyone would think you wanted Mr. Sanger to burst in here and get rid of me," Sahad said. "Why? Is it jealousy or do you have something to cover up?"

Couldn't he see the detective had no reserves of patience left? Jenny wondered. Glaring, she moved between them and made a time-out T with her fingers.

Zahad ducked his head in acknowledgment and Parker moved his hand away from his gun. She was pleased to see that the signal worked as well on testosterone-infused men as it did with schoolchildren.

"I'm sure Sergeant Finley will take appropriate steps to deal with Grant," she said. "Won't you, Parker?"

His gaze never left Zahad. "I'll arrange to have his home, office and storage unit searched. If he's your stalker, we'll find the evidence." He stretched his shoulders stiffly. "In the meantime, I'm taking him into custody for attempted breaking and entering and illegal possession of a gun. Satisfied, Jenny?"

"As long as you keep him in jail and away from me."
More and more, she believed Grant must be the one who'd
been targeting her on the Internet, although she wasn't convinced he'd killed Fario.

"That'll be up to the district attorney and the judge,"
Parker replied.

A bright spot occurred to her. "I don't think he's going
to make much headway trying to get custody of Beth after
this."

"Let's hope not," said the sergeant. "But right now,
who's watching the prisoner?"

Zahad, who stood close to the door, glanced into the
living room. "He appears unrepentant, but he is not attempting to escape."

"As I told Jenny, I'm sorry about this," Parker explained. "That doesn't change the fact that I think it's a big
mistake letting you stay here. You and Mr. Sanger both
have alibis for the day of the murder but that doesn't rule
out a conspiracy, for either of you."

"There is one important difference between him and
me," the sheikh said.

"I'm listening."

"He had a key to this house. I did not."

"From what I've been told, there isn't a lock in California that could keep you out if you really wanted to get
through it." The sergeant nodded to Jenny. "I'll stay in
touch."

"Thanks for coming," she said. "I know how hard
you're working."

A rare hint of warmth pierced Parker's stony expression.
"Nobody wants this case solved more than I do, Jenny,
believe me."

She walked into the front room with the two men. The
sight of her ex-husband sitting handcuffed threw Jenny back
to the night when he'd attacked her. Although she'd fled
before calling 911, she'd had to go to the police station in

Long Beach to make a statement, and she'd seen Grant in custody.

He wore the same air of offended dignity now as then. Some people never changed, she thought with a surge of anger.

"What about medical attention?" Grant demanded.

"Are you injured?" Parker asked.

"He damn near cut my throat open."

The detective glanced skeptically at the tiny wound. "We'll get someone to look at it. Come on, cowboy. I've had a long night."

"You're taking me in?" Apparently this was news to Grant. Despite the handcuffs, he drew himself up as if he were king of the world.

"That's what we usually do with men who try to break into their ex-wives' homes," the sergeant said. "Do I need to call for backup or are you going to cooperate?"

"I'll come along quietly, Officer." He spoke the line with a note of sarcasm.

After scooting awkwardly to his feet, Grant glowered at Jenny. When he opened his mouth to speak, she said, "If you're going to tell me this is all my fault, I'll slug you. And I don't care if Parker books me for assault."

Her ex-husband blinked. Slowly the aggression wilted from his stance. "I was going to ask you not to tell Beth I've been arrested. It'll upset her."

"I'll use my judgment." It occurred to her that Shelley wouldn't be happy with her husband, either, but that was between the two of them.

The detective called to let the station know he was bringing in a perpetrator and to arrange for someone to collect Grant's rental car. After he escorted his prisoner into the overcast morning, Jenny realized with a start that day had dawned.

She closed the door, swung around and ran straight into Zahad. He felt so solid that Jenny sagged against him, her energy depleted. If he hadn't caught her, she would have collapsed onto the carpet.

With her cheek resting on his shoulder, she felt the thrum of his heartbeat pumping strength into her. Jenny wound her arms around Zahad's neck and simply clung as the full shock of the past few hours rushed over her.

"I could kill him for doing this to you," the sheikh said.

"If you hadn't been here..." The gun hadn't been loaded and the key hadn't worked. But Grant was still larger and stronger than Jenny, and she'd have had to open the door to let Beth in.

"Do not waste time on what-ifs." Zahad steered her gently toward her bedroom. "Remember instead that perhaps the perpetrator has been caught and your troubles may be over."

"I hope it's that simple." Shock had temporarily evaporated all of Jenny's self-reliance. How strange, she reflected, that circumstances had brought a total stranger to protect her when she needed him. It felt right that he should be here, guarding her home, watching over her and Beth.

She knew her overstressed mind was playing tricks on her, but she didn't care. Zahad's company was a gift that she accepted gratefully.

"I appreciate that you defended me to the detective," he said as they entered her room.

"What did I say?" Exhausted, she could scarcely remember her conversation with Parker.

"That you felt safe with me." Zahad lowered her onto the bed.

Jenny thought about removing her robe and decided against it, not from modesty but because she was simply too tired.

"I value your trust."

"You've more than earned it." She struggled to keep her eyes open.

The sheikh pulled the sheet and the quilt over her. "You should sleep as late as you like."

"I'll get up when Beth does."

"I will make sure she is all right."

Jenny wanted to thank him again, but her muscles had gone slack and her tongue felt impossibly heavy. As if from afar, she felt his gentle fingers stroke her hair away from her temple.

Utterly at peace, she slept.

ZAHAD NAPPED FOR a couple of hours. At eleven o'clock, he arose, showered and donned slacks and a pullover. After checking his e-mail and confirming the address of Fario's friend Ronald Wang, he went into the kitchen.

Outside, the morning light filtered through cloud cover revealed a patchy vista of half-melted snow. Inside, it filled the house with soft radiance.

As he waited for the toaster oven to crisp the frozen waffles, he noted the welcoming effect of the red-and-white chairs against off-white linoleum and beige countertops. Jenny's spirit filled this house. Fario had come here to meet a fantasy woman, but the reality was far more complex and, in Zahad's viewpoint, far more desirable.

He had brewed coffee and was removing the waffles when a small voice asked, "Are those for me?"

Surprised that he hadn't heard the child approach, he made a brief examination of the pajama-clad pixie standing a few feet away. Beth was, Zahad saw with a twist of appreciation, a miniature version of Jenny, from the fine drift of blond hair to the assessing way she tilted her head. Only the eyes, blue instead of green, hinted at differences.

"I made them for myself, but I will give you half. Then I will make four more and share them also. Will that be acceptable?"

She nodded, but her forehead puckered. "Who are you?"

He took out another plate and a mug, decided that coffee might not be suitable and replaced it with a glass. "My name is Zahad. I am a friend of your mother's."

"I never saw you before." Beth climbed onto a chair and curled her bare feet beneath her.

Zahad poured milk into the glass. That was what Amy always served her children, who were a few years older than this poppet. "I am visiting."

"Did my daddy leave?"

"Yes." He saw no reason to elaborate.

Beth chewed on her lip as she watched him across the table. At last she transferred her attention to her waffles. "You forgot the syrup."

"A serious omission," Zahad agreed, and went to get it from the refrigerator. He put more waffles in the toaster, as promised. "I am not very familiar with children. Do you pour your own syrup or would you like me to?"

"Me." Beth took the bottle and glopped an outrageous amount on her waffles, pouring it all over the plate as well. "That's how you do it."

"I see," said Zahad, and poured the same outrageous amount on his own waffles and plate.

"You're funny," said the little girl, who had skewered her stack and was sawing raggedly with her knife.

"How so?" He handed her a paper napkin from a basket and took one for himself. On second thought, he gave them each an extra.

"The way you talk. I'm only five. You talk to me like I'm a grown-up."

"This is the way I talk to children," he explained. "Even to my cousin Sharif's son, Ben, who is three."

"I bet he likes you."

"I hope so. Many adults believe I am crunchy. Excuse me, I mean crusty."

Her smile reminded him of sunshine breaking through clouds.

"I want to be crunchy, too."

She scooped a huge dripping piece of waffle into her mouth. For a moment, Zahad feared it was too large and that she would choke, but she chewed mightily and downed the food with a gulp of milk.

It surprised him to discover he found this child interesting. He spent little time with youngsters and then usually in the company of their parents, so there was no need for him to interact. He had always had the impression that those below the age of adult reasoning were best left to their mothers.

As their conversation continued, what impressed him most about Beth was how seriously she took herself and everything in her world. Although she might look helpless, she had a strong sense of personal power and held to firm opinions.

She waxed scornful on the subject of her stepmother who, it seemed, believed that Beth ought to like the same clothes and toys she herself had once preferred. "Shelley's not a mom," the little girl concluded as she mopped the last syrup from her plate. "She thinks she is but she's not."

"You do not get along with your stepmother?" Zahad reflected that he had a similar problem, although on a larger scale. Such clashes were unfortunate but far from inevitable. After the war in Alqedar, he had seen many stepmothers become a blessing to motherless children.

"She's always mad at me," the little girl said. "Like when I painted my face with her lipstick."

"What did she do?"

"She called me a bad name." Beth's lower lip trembled until she got it under control. "I said I was sorry. But I wasn't."

"Sometimes I do things other people don't like, and I am not usually sorry, either."

At this remark, laughter erupted behind him. "Mommy!" cried Beth in delight, and nearly overturned her chair as she ran to Jenny.

Zahad watched with pleasure as the two blondes hugged each other. With a little assistance from Jenny, Beth climbed up her mother like a monkey until they were face-to-face. They played a quick kissing game back and forth on cheeks and noses. Then Jenny lowered her daughter to the floor.

"It's good to have you home," she said.

"Zod and I had breakfast," Beth explained.

"Zahad," her mother corrected.

"Zod likes his waffles the same way I do," her daughter continued.

Jenny eyed their plates. "Drenched?"

"Your daughter has expanded my range of culinary experiences." The sheikh cleared their dishes to the counter. "Now I must leave for the afternoon. It may be late when I return."

"Will you be here tomorrow morning?" Beth asked.

"That is my intention."

"Good," she said.

Hugging her daughter from behind, Jenny smiled at him. "I'm glad you two hit it off."

"We are very much alike, I think," Zahad said gravely.

He wasn't happy about leaving. Many things might go wrong for Jenny today, from Grant being released on bail to another Internet Romeo showing up. To his surprise, he found that he regretted leaving not only because of the danger but also because he was sure to miss a great deal of playing and perhaps some more doses of pint-size wisdom.

However, it could not be helped. He must talk to Fario's friend, whom he hoped to catch off guard. There were many things about his brother that Zahad did not know, including whether he had made enemies locally. And, of course, he must try to gather as much information as possible about Hashim's movements.

"Good luck with your mission." A shadow of anxiety fleeted across Jenny's face. For an instant, he thought she was going to ask him to stay, but she lifted her chin and remained silent.

"You will be careful." He knew better to say more in the child's presence.

"Of course."

He sketched the ladies a bow, the formal kind with one hand behind his back, and retrieved his coat before venturing out into the tingling air. Zahad briefly contemplated buying a gun on the black market but decided it would be too time-consuming and, in view of Detective Finley's suspicions of him, perhaps too risky.

As he got into his car, he hoped he would not regret that decision.

Chapter Nine

Jenny had known Zahad would take good care of her daughter while she slept. What she hadn't expected was to see him addressing Beth as an equal and behaving in a manner that could only be described as charming.

Grant rarely gave the little girl his full attention. He loved her, of course, but even when he played with her, he always seemed distracted.

The sheikh's behavior did not mean he was ready for fatherhood, she reminded herself. Nor did she want him to be. Beth had a father already, deficient though he might be.

She'd expected her daughter to stay happily at home today playing with toys she hadn't seen in two weeks, but the youngster had other ideas. Jenny had barely finished breakfast when Beth announced she wanted to play with Cindy.

"I don't know what her family's doing today." After all, it was Sunday. "I'll call them later."

"Call them now!" The little girl folded her arms and tapped one foot on the linoleum, a pose Jenny hadn't seen before.

"Is that the way Shelley stands?" she asked.

"I guess so." Beth relaxed her arms. "Please call them."

Since it was already afternoon, the Rivases had probably returned from church by now. "Okay, since you asked nicely."

The line was busy. "They're home but they're on the phone," she told her daughter.

"Let's go!" Beth pelted into the rear hallway and pulled down the coat Jenny had hung there last night.

"You haven't finished unpacking." She hated to barge in on her neighbors unannounced. "I'll call them again in a few minutes."

"I want to go now!" The little girl fumbled with her front snaps. Judging by her pout, she was on the verge of a tantrum.

Normally, Jenny didn't tolerate defiance. Today, however, she felt in no mood to fight, not after they'd been apart for so long. Also, Beth must be feeling off-kilter from yesterday's long trip.

The Rivases knew what little girls were like, and Cindy would be happy to see her friend. It wouldn't hurt to tell her neighbors what had happened last night, either.

"I'll tell you what," she said. "We'll walk over and knock on the door. If they're busy, we'll leave and you'll be a good sport about it. All right?"

Beth nodded. "Okay."

Jenny tucked her cell phone in her pocket. As they went out, she set the alarm and explained to her daughter how it worked. "There've been some strange men hanging around and we want to be careful," she added.

"I know." One of the would-be lovers had been waiting on the porch a few weeks ago when they got home from school. Fortunately, he'd backed off quickly when he learned the truth.

"Did your daddy say anything about what happened while you were gone?" She'd been debating with herself whether to mention the murder, but perhaps Grant had already done so.

"He said a man got hurt on the walkway and went to heaven," Beth told her.

"That's right." Silently, she thanked her ex-husband for

his uncharacteristic tact. "We're very sad about it. He was Zahad's brother."

Beth skipped ahead on the pathway that led downhill to the Rivases' house, but the rough terrain soon slowed her and she let her mother catch up. "I like Zod," she said as if the conversation had never been interrupted.

"Me, too," Jenny said.

After last night, no doubts lingered about her decision to let him stay with her. For all his concern, Parker hadn't been there when her ex-husband showed up.

But Zahad wasn't here now. Uneasily, Jenny glanced toward the street, checking for unfamiliar parked cars. She couldn't afford to let down her guard, not even on a quiet Sunday afternoon when the sun peeked through the clouds and Beth swung alongside her.

When they neared Ray and Ellen's house, Jenny heard the clink of china from inside. Although it was nearly two o'clock, they must be eating. She hesitated, but Beth raced ahead.

"Honey!"

Too late. Beth rang the doorbell and was hopping up and down with excitement. Reluctantly, Jenny joined her.

The door opened and Cindy's little face, surrounded by russet hair like her mother's and grandmother's, poked out. "It'th you!" she cried. "Bethy!" The two girls hugged. They were so cute that Jenny wished she had a camera with her.

"Cinders, you're not supposed to answer the door by yourself." Ray ambled into view. "Oh, hi, Jenny, good to see you." He gave her a lazy, welcoming smile. When she'd first met him, she'd thought he was flirting, but although he came over to help with repairs sometimes, he'd never so much as hinted at anything improper. She'd decided that he simply liked women.

"I didn't mean to interrupt," she said. "Your phone was busy and Beth got antsy."

"Sorry. I called my mom." He stood back to let her in. "Come join the neighbors."

Jenny felt a moment's trepidation as she caught sight of the group around the table that occupied one end of the front room. In addition to Dolly, Bill and Ellen, Al and Tish Garroway were drinking coffee and sampling muffins from a basket.

The look on Tish's face appeared far from welcoming. Ellen wore the same guarded expression she'd assumed around Jenny for the past few months.

"Tish brought over these delicious muffins," Dolly said. "Please join us." She, at least, seemed friendly.

"Just for a minute." Fleeing would only make the situation more awkward. Besides, she remembered, she had news for them. "I wanted to let you know that my ex-husband broke into my house last night, carrying a gun. Parker has him in custody."

A flurry of questions erupted. Over coffee and a muffin, Jenny answered them as concisely as possible. Ellen seemed very relieved to hear that the killer had apparently been apprehended.

"It's a good thing the sheikh was there," Ray replied.

Jenny remembered something Zahad had told her. "I'm glad you encouraged him to stay with me. Parker was giving him a lot of flak."

"You suggested he stay?" Ellen regarded her husband in surprise.

"It seemed like a good idea, with everything that's happened," Ray said.

"I don't like him snooping through the neighborhood." Al scratched beneath his scraggly beard. The ski instructor wouldn't be bad-looking without that ratty facial hair, Jenny mused, but perhaps Tish liked it. "Did you ever think that the sheikh might be hanging around to cover his tracks?"

"You sound like one of them gorillas that don't want no competition," Bill said. "One look at that sheikh fella and you started beating on your chest and howling."

Dolly's jaw dropped in dismay. "Oh, Bill!"

Although amused, Jenny couldn't let Al's remark pass. "Zahad's a security expert. In fact, he found a piece of evidence the police missed."

Heads turned. As everyone started talking at once, Jenny felt a pang of doubt. Maybe she shouldn't have revealed so much.

"I'd like to hear what it is," Al said.

"Maybe he planted it himself," Tish put in.

"Did it have anything to do with Grant?" Ellen asked.

Dolly waited attentively. While she focused on Jenny, Bill quietly slathered butter on a lemon muffin he'd sneaked past his wife, who tried to keep them both on a healthy diet.

Too late to back down now. "He moved a wastebasket that the killer must have walked by and found a scrap of paper." Remembering Tish's remark, Jenny added, "He'd just arrived at the house, so he couldn't have planted it."

"Was anything written on it?" Dolly asked.

"No, but there was a crystal watermark in the paper," she replied.

Al shrugged. Tish looked puzzled. Ellen bit her lip.

"Wow," Ray said. "That sounds like the documents at my bank."

"I know." Jenny wished she could read their reactions more clearly, but no one's response stood out as unusual. "Maybe part of a deposit slip."

"Were there fingerprints?" Dolly queried.

"Not as far as I know, but I'm sure Parker will check."

Ray smacked his forehead. "So that's why he was there!"

"Excuse me?" Al said.

"The sheikh. He dropped by the bank the other day," Ray explained. "I guess he wanted to check it out. Not that he could have learned anything just walking into the lobby."

Zahad hadn't mentioned stopping at the bank. Jenny

wondered what he'd hoped to find. Perhaps he'd simply wanted to look around.

"I can't see what good a scrap of paper is unless it has a fingerprint on it," Ellen commented. "Lots of us use that bank."

"We don't," Tish countered.

"It might have stuck to somebody's clothing and dropped off anytime," Jenny said. "Weeks ago, even."

"You never know." Belatedly, Dolly noticed her husband stuffing the muffin into his mouth, but she let it go. "If the police start to focus on a suspect, it might prompt them to look into his account."

"For what?" Al asked.

Ray brightened. He loved watching TV cop shows and had often recounted the plot twists to Jenny. "Suppose there was a hired killer and he put his blood money in an account. I mean, the police might notice that he'd made a large deposit. If it was a check, they could trace it to whoever hired him."

"The police can't look into an account without a subpoena, can they?" Al said.

"That's right," Dolly agreed. "They'd have to have reasonable suspicion."

"Yeah, but I'm not a cop," Ray said. "I could take a quick look at a few people's records, the ones that know Jenny. I wouldn't violate anybody's privacy or anything."

"How would you nose around people's bank accounts without violating their privacy?" Ellen asked.

He shrugged. "I don't know."

"In any case, I hope we're done with those awful men coming by," Ellen added. "I've posted warnings all over the Internet."

"Thanks. I appreciate it," Jenny said.

The phone in her pocket rang. After excusing herself, she moved to the far side of the room and answered, her spirits lifting at the possibility that it might be Zahad.

It was Parker, and she heard a tired edginess in his voice.

"I want to alert you that we're going to release Grant on bail."

"What?" Jenny nearly dropped the phone. "How can you do that?"

"He gave us permission to check his house, his office and his storage locker, so we didn't have to wait for warrants. He gave us his computer passwords."

"You mean for his home in Missouri?"

"Correct. St. Louis P.D. got right on it. So far, we haven't found one bit of evidence tying him to the murder or the cyber-stalking. We had to set bail and his wife's flying out to pay it. Actually, I think she left as soon as she heard he was in jail."

Jenny shivered. "I don't like the idea of him walking around free."

"It isn't up to me. I agree he might be dangerous. Speaking of dangerous people, is the sheikh with you?"

"No."

"Where is he?"

"In L.A." She refused to reveal anything else. In her opinion, Parker wasn't rational about Zahad.

"He'd better not be prying again."

"Oh, for heaven's sake!" Jenny's sympathy for the overworked detective evaporated. "I'm the one whose life is in danger, and I'm glad he's doing it."

"Jenny, you don't understand these matters. The more I look into this, the more suspicious that man becomes."

"Only to you," she snapped. "I'm coming down to the station to find out what's what. I'm not going to sit around my house waiting for Grant to show up."

"I wouldn't advise confronting him. However, I'll be glad to issue you a temporary restraining order. If he does approach you, we'll arrest him again and this time he won't get out so fast."

"I'll be there in fifteen minutes. Thanks for letting me know." After hanging up, she explained to the others what had happened and asked if she could leave Beth there.

"Of course." Ellen sounded friendlier than in a long time. "Cindy's missed her terribly. Don't worry about a thing. I'll even let them play with some of my makeup samples, if you don't mind." She sold cosmetics as a side business.

"Thanks," Jenny said. "I'll be at the police station." Her neighbors had her cell-phone number if they needed her.

Dolly, Ray and Al wished her luck. Bill slipped a blueberry muffin into his napkin and smiled at her like a Cheshire cat.

ZAHAD HAD VISITED his brother's apartment when he first arrived in the area. He'd flown into Los Angeles instead of directly to Mountain Lake so he could examine the premises, which the police had already searched, and ship home his brother's effects. The two-story white-stucco building where Ronald Wang lived lay about two blocks away, tucked into a side street near UCLA.

A two-hour drive—for which he had removed his tire chains—brought him to a different world. Here, palm trees replaced the pines of the mountain village, and instead of snow and a sharp wind, the city basked in filtered sunshine. Zahad parked on the street, fed a meter and headed for the building.

Casually clothed young people ambled past him, some carrying shopping bags. They had the open, comfortable look of Californians for whom a public street was merely an extension of their private space.

He reviewed what he'd learned about Ronald Wang from Amy and an Internet background check. At twenty-seven, he was slightly older than Fario and came from a middle-class family. A graduate of UCLA, he'd worked as a junior insurance executive for a couple of years before returning to get an MBA.

His family appeared to be of Chinese or Taiwanese descent, but the young man himself had been born here. The company with which Zahad contracted to run checks on employees had turned up a misdemeanor arrest years earlier for marijuana possession. Wang had avoided prison by undergoing counseling.

There'd been no mention of him in the initial police report. Amy had learned of his existence from one of Hashim's friends in London. Apparently Ronald had taken Fario and Hashim nightclubbing.

If Hashim had hired a hit man, it might have been this fellow or some connection of his. He was, after all, one of the few contacts Hashim could have made while he was here.

At the front of the building, Zahad found the name Wang and pressed the buzzer. Seconds ticked by and then a voice over the speaker said, "Wazzup?"

"I wish to speak with Ronald Wang."

"That's me. And the way you sound, this had better be—what's your name? Zad, Zan, Zach?—or I'm not letting you in."

"I am Zahad Adran." He hadn't realized that his slight accent and formal manner of address gave away so much, let alone that Fario had discussed him with his friend.

"Just for verification purposes..."

"Why do you require verification?"

"A—You sound foreign. B—Somebody killed Fario, who was my buddy, and the consensus on the Internet is that it had to be political, which means one of those wackos might come after me because I know something that I don't know I know. If you watch spy movies, you'll understand."

"I understand." Zahad wondered if Ronald Wang normally carried on such lengthy conversations over the intercom.

"I'm not finished. Let's see, oh, yeah, we're up to C. This isn't exactly in your favor but according to chatter on the Internet, the cops think you did it, only I don't. So, for verification purposes, tell me what Fario liked to drink."

"Champagne. His favorite nonalcoholic beverage was

goat's milk mixed with Mountain Dew.'' Zahad considered the concoction disgusting, but his brother had enjoyed it.

"Okay, I'm buzzing you in."

Inside, Zahad had no difficulty finding apartment 2C. An Asian-American man of medium height answered the door.

"Man, I gotta shake hands with you." He proceeded to do so. "Fario told me a lot about you."

"Did he?" The sheikh had assumed his brother rarely gave him a thought.

"He made you sound like James Bond." Ronald stepped back to let him inside.

The sunny front room was furnished with a white wicker couch and chairs. The other contents included an array of audiovisual equipment, a desk crammed with a computer and printer, and shelves loaded with video games and DVDs. Zahad noted a couple of textbooks, as well.

"Has anyone else come by to talk about Fario?" he asked.

"No."

"Where did you hear about his death?"

"It was all over campus," Wang said.

"The police haven't talked to you?"

A sideways shake of the head. Well, Zahad was certain the sergeant would consider this visit interfering with a police investigation, but if it weren't for him, the witness would never have been questioned at all.

"I'm really sorry about Fario," Wang said. "He was a great guy."

"Thank you." Zahad rather liked this young man. However, appearances could deceive. "Did he have enemies? Perhaps a rival for a woman?"

"The only woman he ever talked about was that one he met on the Internet. Can I get you a Coke or something?"

Zahad declined. He prowled the room, looking for anything out of place while asking Wang how Fario had come to "meet" Jenny.

"I used to date a woman I met in a chat room," the

young man explained. "I'm afraid I encouraged him. I knew it could be dangerous for women but I never heard of a guy getting hurt."

"You met his cousin Hashim?"

"Sure. A wild man." He grinned. "You Alqedarians or whatever you call yourselves sure know how to have a good time. Well, not you personally, I guess. Fario said you were kind of serious."

"When did Hashim leave?" Zahad asked.

"Saturday."

That would be two days before Fario's murder. "You are certain?"

"Fario drove him to the airport," Ronald said. "I went along for the ride 'cause he has such a cool car. I mean, had. What happened to it, anyway?"

"It is in police custody." Zahad would arrange for a buyer when the vehicle was released. "Is there anything else, however insignificant, that you could tell me?"

"Well, there is one thing." From a desk drawer, Wang removed a stack of papers. When he handed them over, Zahad saw that they were printed-out conversations from a chat room.

"I was mad about my friend getting killed, so I figured I'd get the goods on that woman," Ron explained. "I went online to see if I could find her. I wasn't going to try to meet her, just learn as much as I could."

"Jenny is not the murderer," Zahad said.

"If you say so. Anyway, look at those papers. Go on."

He flipped through the sheets. The ones on top contained chats between Jenny S and a writer called TheWiz. The ones on the bottom were between Jenny S and Arabprince. "Some are your conversations and some are my brother's," he guessed.

"Yeah. He made me copies because they were so sexy. Look at the way she wrote to me and the way she wrote to him."

One discrepancy struck Zahad immediately. "There are

more misspellings in the newer ones." They included "lushous" instead of "luscious" and "freind" instead of "friend."

"The writing's cruder, too," Ronald said. "Shorter sentences and more four-letter words. These were posted by two different women."

Despite his fluency in English, Zahad doubted he would have caught that distinction. Now that it had been pointed out, however, he could see that Wang was right.

"A copycat," he said. It might be someone playing a cruel prank. It might also mean that the original stalker had stopped and someone else had decided to continue the harassment.

"This could be useful," he told Wang. "May I keep these?"

"I'll make you copies." The young man ran them through the printer-copier. "What do you think it means?"

"I do not know."

"Do you have any suspects?"

"My stepmother has proposed Hashim as the next governor of our province," Zahad said. "He stands to gain a great deal by my brother's death."

"Hashim? The killer?"

"It is one possibility."

Ron shook his head. "He warned Fario not to go. He said this Jenny person probably had an incurable disease or was some kind of criminal."

This was a point in Hashim's favor. It didn't necessarily clear him in Zahad's eyes, however.

"For what it's worth, I don't believe you did it, either," Wang added.

"Why not?" Zahad asked.

The young man grinned. "Fario said you were hard-nosed. Man, he was right."

"Hard-nosed?"

"Tough. He was always bragging about you. How brave you were. How smart. Like you were some hero."

"Perhaps you misunderstood," Zahad replied. "My father was his hero."

"Not really." Wang fed more papers into the copier. "He said his dad always took the easy way out, like going into exile, and that you're the only one in the family with guts."

A sadness touched with regret came over Zahad. To receive this knowledge of his brother's admiration from beyond the grave was a rare gift, but also a reminder of what might have been had Fario lived.

"I wish I had known this while he was alive," he said.

"He came here because of you." The young man tapped the copies into a neat pile and handed them over. "He wanted to make something of himself so you'd respect him."

"Thank you for telling me these things."

"I'm glad to help any way I can. I sure hope you catch that woman."

"The person who lured my brother was not Jenny Sanger," Zahad said. "I suspect it was a man."

"No way!"

"Why do you say that?"

"Because he talked to her on the phone."

Stunned, Zahad took a moment to respond. "How did this happen?"

"She asked him to send her his phone number," Ron explained. "He told me she was curious to hear what a sheikh sounded like."

This was amazing news. "Did you hear her voice? Perhaps you would recognize it if you heard it again."

"Sorry, I didn't."

So the stalker had been a woman. Zahad had met four female neighbors, but of course there must be women teachers at Jenny's school who could have also done this.

"You must convey this information to the police," he urged. "Please call them on Monday, but do not mention that you talked to me."

"I don't know if I should," Ronald said. "I had this little marijuana conviction. He'll probably think I'm a suspect, too."

"He needs this information. Both about the second stalker and about the woman on the phone." On a spare pad, he jotted down Parker Finley's name. "It's the Mountain Lake Police Department."

"Yeah, okay," Wang said. "And I won't rat you out. You're doing exactly what Fario would have wanted."

"Thank you." They shook hands.

Zahad had just stepped into the hall when his cell phone rang. Retreating to the stairwell, he answered it.

"It's Jenny." He could tell something was wrong. "They're releasing Grant on bail. Apparently they searched his home and office and didn't find anything, so he's just facing charges from this morning."

"Where are you?"

"I'm at Ellen's, but I'm going to the station," she said.

"I will come as fast as I can."

After hanging up, he took the stairs at a rapid clip. On his way down, it occurred to him that Grant Sanger had a wife who wanted Jenny's child.

Could the voice on Fario's phone have been hers?

Chapter Ten

After calling Zahad, Jenny headed toward town. The day had warmed above freezing, although the weather forecast on the radio predicted lower temperatures tomorrow and a storm after that. She saw hardly any motorists on the way, but that wasn't unusual, since Pine Forest Road didn't connect to any major highways.

Her mind played over the conversation at the Rivases' house. She hoped Ray wouldn't do anything illegal at the bank. It seemed unlikely he could uncover clues simply by poking through people's account records, anyway. And if by any chance the killer really had deposited his hit money there, he might decide to come after Ray.

If Ray was in danger, so were Ellen and Cindy. Jenny shook her head at her own paranoid imaginings. Nobody was going to start killing people en masse in Mountain Lake. The worst thing likely to happen was that Ray might get fired from his job, which would be bad enough.

At least Ellen's hostility had eased. It wasn't hard to guess that she'd been jealous, although heaven knew why. Learning that Ray had encouraged Zahad to stay must have persuaded her he didn't have designs on anyone else.

At the thought of Zahad, Jenny began to smile. Wouldn't people be amazed if they had seen him joking with Beth across the breakfast table.

If only Grant had been so genuine and open. In retrospect, she could see how manipulative he was. Unfortunately, he exuded a superficial affability that she'd been afraid would work on his behalf in a custody case. Well, he'd just shown what kind of man he really was, and he had an arrest record to prove it.

Jenny rounded a curve and snapped back to the present. Ahead, a green sedan blocked her lane. While two guys peered beneath the hood, a third man in a windbreaker stood in the left lane, waving for help and blocking the road.

Normally, she would have stopped. Now uneasy questions nagged at her. Why hadn't the men pulled to the shoulder? Didn't at least one of them have his own mobile phone?

Carjackers.

She might be wrong. But why was that man standing on the left, endangering himself to force her to stop? A stalled vehicle only a few miles from town in clear weather hardly required such measures.

Jenny's stomach clenched. If she stopped, even with the doors locked, they could smash her windows and haul her out, grab her purse and take the SUV. She'd be at their mercy.

Jenny couldn't turn around on the two-lane road and she couldn't pass them to the right on the narrow shoulder. To the left lay a sharp drop into a creek bed.

She'd have to speed by in the left lane and hope no other car approached. And she must do it fast. As she drew closer, she made out a large wrench in the man's hand, plenty big enough to smash her window.

She was never, never going to let another man push her around.

Jenny hit the gas and steered left. A few dozen yards ahead, the man held his ground. He was daring her to hit him and smugly certain that she wouldn't.

He wore a smirk, just like Grant. Or like Oliver when he'd grabbed her arm.

Fury whited out Jenny's constraints. She didn't want to kill anybody. But if she veered off the road into the creek, she herself might be killed.

Her jaw tightened. She braced for the thump.

At the last minute, she made eye contact with the would-be robber. His sneer mutated into alarm.

As if in slow motion, she watched him dive toward his companions. Jenny flashed by inches away, her foot hovering between the brake and the gas. Her SUV slowed for a second until she realized she hadn't struck anyone, and then she floored it.

The men might have guns. They might come after her.

She flew along the road, watching for oncoming cars to warn but did not see any. She couldn't bring herself to pull over and she was going too fast to risk calling the police. She'd be at the station in a few minutes anyway.

Two miles passed with agonizing slowness despite her speed. There was no sign of anyone following, but on such a winding road they might not lag far behind. At last she turned on Lake Avenue and hit green lights all the way to the civic center.

Not until Jenny parked and slid out did she realize she was shaking. Holding on to the vehicle door, she forced herself to breathe evenly.

The realization that she'd won steadied her. She hadn't panicked. She hadn't let the criminals intimidate her.

She was no longer a little girl cowering from her father's anger. She wasn't Grant's wife, either, trying to placate him and save her marriage. She was a school principal and she'd stood up to carjackers.

Jenny marched across the pavement and through the front door of the station. The desk officer, a member of the PTA, recognized her at once. "Hello, Mrs. Sanger. Are you here to see Sergeant Finley?"

"Yes, but first I have to make a report," she said. "Three men tried to carjack me. At least, I think they did."

Her teeth started to chatter. Disgusted with herself, Jenny collapsed into a nearby chair. "I'm sorry."

"You all right?" He was dialing someone as he spoke.

"I could use a stiff shot of rum." She managed a tremulous smile. "Just kidding."

A minute later, a black-haired detective arrived. She'd met the officer, Hank Rygel, during the initial investigation into Fario's murder.

He was taking down the information when Parker joined them. Jenny described the men she'd seen and their car's color and possible make, but she didn't have a clue about the license plate.

After issuing an all points bulletin and assigning someone to warn Jenny's neighbors of the activity in their area, Parker escorted her to his office for further questioning. By the time he finished, Jenny felt as if her brain had been picked clean. Three interviews by Parker Finley in one week seemed more than any human being should have to endure.

The interviews weren't really the problem, she admitted silently. It was the fact that every criminal in California and maybe a few other states seemed to have her name tattooed on his brain.

Parker shook his head. "We thought we were driving the carjackers out of town. Instead, we just chased them into outlying areas where they'll be even harder to catch."

"Maybe they'll stop considering the locals easy prey now," she replied without much conviction.

"We should be so lucky."

"How's Grant?" she asked, getting back to the original reason for her visit.

"Beginning to see the error of his ways, I suspect. Mrs. Sanger—the second Mrs. Sanger—got here a few minutes ago. She stopped by the jail to pay him a visit. Hang on while I finish my notes, would you?"

"Sure." Sitting back, Jenny wished she didn't have to deal with her controlling ex-husband. Thank goodness Zahad was coming. It felt good to have someone backing her up.

She wanted him to stay a little longer. At least until they solved Fario's murder and she could shelve her imitation of Superwoman for next Halloween.

The phone rang. Parker answered, acknowledged the message and hung up. "Sanger's wife posted bail and they're releasing him. Are you sure you want to see them? You've been through one hell of a lot today."

It was tempting, but she wanted to see where Shelley stood on this custody business. In light of Grant's arrest his wife might have second thoughts about engaging in a lengthy court battle with Jenny.

"How could I miss this?" she said with a lightness she was far from feeling. "It's my own personal soap opera."

"In that case, I'm sorry I left my video camera at home," Parker joked, and escorted her back to the lobby.

The last time she saw Shelley, Grant's wife had worn an expensive business suit and perfectly coiffed hair. This afternoon, as she stood at the front counter, her eyeliner was smudged and the dark roots of her blond mane needed a touch-up.

She addressed Parker edgily. "My husband is willing to plead guilty to misdemeanor trespassing if you'll give him probation."

"The district attorney decides on the charge," Parker replied. "You should know that. And he'll have to enter his plea in court."

"I'm not a criminal attorney." With a clear effort of will Shelley forced herself to look at Jenny. "You could use your influence. I'm sure the D.A. would listen to you."

"What he did was serious, Shelley. He tried to break into my house with a gun," Jenny said.

"Unloaded."

"It was still a gun. He's fixated on me," Jenny added. "I want him out of my life and this custody business is going to make it worse."

Wearily, Shelley pushed a loose strand behind one ear. "You don't have to worry about that. I changed my mind. Your kid drives me crazy. I can't understand how you put up with her. As far as I'm concerned, the less we have to do with her, the better."

"She's just a normal five-year-old," Jenny said.

"If she's normal, I guess I don't have mothering instincts, after all." Shelley sounded surprisingly vulnerable. "My friends are all having babies and I thought I wanted a kid, too. Boy, was I wrong."

Jenny spared her a moment's sympathy. Beth certainly could get into mischief, but any competent parent would recognize that she'd been acting out because she missed her mother.

An inner door opened. "Oh, great," Shelley said. "Here comes Einstein now."

A rumpled Grant appeared in the company of a poker-faced guard. His gaze traveled uneasily between Shelley and Jenny. "What happens next?" he asked Parker.

"Your wife's posted bail but you need a criminal lawyer," the detective replied. "You'll be arraigned in court within a few days. As for the exact charges, that's up to the district attorney's office."

"We'll find an attorney," Shelley said.

"Because this is a domestic-violence situation, I'm going to give your ex-wife an emergency restraining order," Parker added. "It's good for five days, during which time she can get one that lasts up to three years. If you go anywhere near her or your daughter without a judge's permission, you'll be back in custody, Mr. Sanger, and this time you won't get out so fast."

The last scrap of pomposity wheezed out of Grant. "What I did was stupid. Believe me, I'm not planning to make it worse."

Jenny hoped she could believe him. Since their divorce, it was the first time he'd pulled anything like this. Assuming, of course, that he wasn't her stalker and Fario's murderer.

Through the glass, she saw Zahad striding toward the entrance. It was good to see him. Wonderful, really. She felt as if they'd been apart for much longer than a few hours.

Jenny ached to smooth back that shaggy hair and fasten a button he'd missed on his brown suede coat. And she wanted to tell him everything that had happened so he could help her sort it out and make it right.

The sheikh opened the door. Parker went rigid, like a dog scenting an enemy. Grant merely looked disgruntled.

"I asked him to come," she said. "He's acting as my bodyguard, remember?"

The detective nodded tightly.

Zahad caught sight of Jenny and his eyes lit up. She felt pulled toward him, and only held back by reminding herself where they were and who was watching.

As she greeted him, it saddened her to give him more bad news, but he needed to know about the attempted carjacking. Neither Grant nor Shelley had heard of it, either, and they all listened with varying degrees of dismay.

"I've put out an all points bulletin," Parker added when she finished.

"I hope they are caught quickly." Zahad looked grim.

"This was near your house?" Grant said. "I can't imagine how you can consider this place safe for Beth. Where is she now?"

"With a retired policewoman," Jenny snapped. "I might remind you, I'm not the one who left her alone in a car while I tried to break into someone's house."

Shelley held up one hand to forestall further arguing. "I don't think we're in any position to question Jenny's parenting decisions, Grant. Let's get going. I want to find a motel and take a shower."

Parker directed them to the Mountain Lake Inn down the street. After the couple departed, he said, "I'm going to get

Jenny a restraining order against Mr. Sanger. Then, Mr. Adran, I have to ask you to step into my office.''

"What for?" Jenny inquired.

"This is between the sheikh and myself." The sergeant's eyes never left Zahad's face.

"Of course, Sergeant. I am always ready to cooperate."

Jenny wished she'd never mentioned that Zahad had gone into Los Angeles. It was too late to do anything about that now, though.

THEY'D NO SOONER reached Finley's office than he turned on Zahad. "I told you to stay the hell out of my investigation. What were you doing in L.A?"

"Sight-seeing," Zahad said.

"The hell you were!"

He hated to lie, especially since Ronald Wang might slip tomorrow and admit having talked to him. That is, assuming Wang actually did call. On the other hand, if he told the truth, the detective would likely arrest him for interfering. "There is much to see. Have you visited the La Brea Tar Pits, Sergeant?"

"I know what you're up to," Finley retorted. "One of the neighbors called to complain about you pestering people. I want you to pack your bags and move to Crystal Point until the coroner releases your brother's body. Let me know where you're staying."

Which neighbor had called? Zahad hadn't interviewed the Garroways, but they seemed the most likely to object to his presence. On the other hand, perhaps Ray Rivas had more to hide than he let on.

"Mrs. Sanger has requested that I stay at her home. It appears she is in danger on several fronts and you are unable to guarantee her safety."

"And you are?"

"No one can guarantee safety. But I was there last night and you were not."

''Mr. Sanger would never have gotten into that house if you hadn't opened the door,'' the detective snarled.

His skin looked sallow this morning, a sign that lack of sleep and pressure were catching up with him. Zahad didn't spare him any sympathy. This man's bullheadedness was endangering Jenny.

''You have lost your objectivity,'' he told the sergeant. ''You dislike me for personal reasons and therefore you seek an excuse to get rid of me.''

''Oh, I'm biased, am I?'' Finley growled. ''I had an interesting telephone conversation this morning with a Mr. Hashim Bin Salem.''

This was unexpected. ''How did you come to contact him?''

''He said he was calling from Alqedar,'' the detective told him. ''Mr. Bin Salem informs me that your president may appoint him governor instead of you and he's afraid he's next on your hit list.''

''Hashim fears me?'' Zahad wouldn't mind giving the callow young man a fright, but he suspected an ulterior motive lay behind the phone call. ''What else did he say?''

''That's not public information,'' the sergeant replied.

''He called to stir your suspicion of me,'' Zahad speculated. ''Perhaps he told you that Fario also feared me.''

''He sure did.'' Weariness and resentment loosened the detective's tongue. ''He said your brother was going to appoint him chief adviser and kick you out of power entirely. According to Mr. Bin Salem, that's why you killed him.''

After talking to Ronald Wang, Zahad knew better than to believe his brother had intended any such thing. ''Hashim is playing you. He wants me out of his way. If he fears me, it is because my influence in our country interferes with his ambitions.''

This was disturbing news, all the same. Zahad had believed his young rival was simply falling in with Numa's plans. Perhaps that had been the case at first, but Hashim was now apparently determined to seize power even at the cost of lies and machinations. Zahad would indeed give him reason to be frightened once he returned to Alqedar. In the meantime, Hashim could pose more of a threat than anticipated.

"I can't force you to get the hell out of Dodge. But if I were you, I'd think seriously about leaving while I still could," Finley retorted.

Zahad refused to be intimidated. "I did not kill my brother. I am determined that one of us should find out who did. I do not care if it is you or I, Sergeant Finley. But I will not rest until it is done."

"Exactly where does Mrs. Sanger fit into this picture?" the detective asked.

That was a question to which the sheikh no longer had the answer. A few minutes ago, when he'd seen her safe inside the police station, relief had swept over him. He had not felt so happy since the time twelve years ago when he'd learned that Alqedar was free at last.

When she'd described the carjackers, he'd had to fight a near compulsion to race out and hunt them down. How could he leave her unprotected?

"I have pledged to protect Mrs. Sanger," he said in reply to the detective's question. "Her fate has become bound up with the crime against my brother. He would not wish me to abandon her."

"So once we catch this murderer, assuming it isn't you, you're history?"

"There are those in my country who consider me a part of history, and those who wish I would become history. I see you stand with the latter."

"You've got that right."

"Are we finished here?"

"Unless there's something you'd like to tell me about what you did in L.A." Finley waited with feigned patience.

"The Los Angeles County Museum of Art is also fascinating."

Wordlessly, the detective stepped aside and let him leave. He didn't bother to hide his disgust.

Zahad found Jenny alone in the lobby. One look at her pale face and he offered to drive her home. She declined, but at least she agreed that they should pick up dinner on the way.

Caravanning their vehicles, they bought hamburgers en route. Zahad was pleased to see that collecting her daughter and listening to the animated childish chatter helped restore some color to Jenny's cheeks.

After dinner, the three of them played a simple board game, which Beth won. Later, with Jenny's encouragement, Zahad sat on the edge of the little girl's bed and read her a story about small animals facing a moral dilemma. It was not only educational but also entertaining.

"I like the way you do the voices," Beth said as she snuggled under her quilt.

"I was not aware that I was doing voices. I simply spoke them as it seemed they should be spoken."

"You did a good job," Jenny added.

The sheikh was more pleased than he wanted to let on. He had never considered himself to have domestic skills other than basic cooking, a necessity in training camps.

Afterward, they drank decaf coffee at the kitchen table. Jenny explained that a search of Grant's home and office had come up clean. Zahad told her what he had learned from Ronald Wang.

They discussed the second cyber-stalker, debating who it might be without reaching any conclusions. The subject clearly distressed Jenny, as did the information about Fario's telephone conversation with a woman.

"It's easier to understand how a man could stoop to do something so cruel," she said. "I guess I expect more from women."

"I am sorry your experiences with men have made you so cynical." If he reached out to cup her shapely chin, her heart-shaped face would fit perfectly into his hand, Zahad thought. This did not seem to be an appropriate time for intimacies, however.

Jenny's shadowed green eyes met his. "Not all my experiences have been bad. I've had male friends, but never one like you. It's unfortunate..."

"What's unfortunate?" He very much wanted to hear what she'd meant to say.

"We both know how this has to end," she said. "Only the most bizarre circumstances brought us together in the first place. We're from different worlds and neither of us can change, even if we wanted to."

Zahad finger-combed an errant shock of hair from his forehead. He had never had such a personal conversation with a woman or, indeed, with anyone. "I suppose you're right," he replied at last, and regretted that it sounded inadequate.

Jenny went to bed a short time later. At the computer, Zahad found an e-mail waiting from Amy.

Holly, Sharif's wife, had gone into labor and was having difficulties. Her husband could not even think of leaving her to go to the capital.

She wrote:

Hashim must have found out that you're investigating him. He's doing his best to portray you as a threat to anyone who gets in your way. The latest word is that he and Numa want President Dourad to ban you from the country entirely.

Zahad's chest tightened. How could this happen? Surely the president was not so easily stampeded, but how could he be certain? He continued to read Amy's e-mail.

I doubt he'll take any immediate action. You're one of the men who paved the way for him to take office, after all, and he knows you're loyal. But this economic plan we're putting together may not be enough to show what a great leader you'll make. You need to plead your case in person.

He closed his eyes and remembered what Jenny had said. Unusual events had thrown them together, but it could not last. Soon they would be torn apart.

What must be, must be. After hitting Reply, he wrote:

Believe me, as soon as Fario's body is released, I will catch the next plane.

Despite his concern for Jenny, he hoped it would be soon. Otherwise Zahad might face the unthinkable: a future as a stateless person. For himself, he would find a way to survive. But for his people, it would be a disaster.

Chapter Eleven

In Jenny's dream, she drove along a street near the house in Long Beach where she'd lived during her marriage. There was a disabled car by the road and a man in the center, waving at her to stop. Grant.

She tried to steer around him, but he kept shifting in front of her. "I have to get by!" she shouted, but he refused to listen. The next thing she knew, she'd swerved off a cliff and was falling endlessly.

Someone caught her. The solid strength of his grip drew her up through layers of sleep until she lay in a man's arms, drinking in his exotic but now-familiar scent, feeling the scratch of his cheek against her temple as he sat cradling her.

"I am sorry to awaken you, but you called out," said a deep, gentle voice. Raising his head, Zahad gazed down at her. "Do not try to recall the dream. Let it fade away and you will sleep again."

"I'm not sure I want to." The sheikh had thrown on a robe, Jenny saw. Judging by the bare chest revealed in its gap, he wasn't wearing much underneath. She remembered waking up beside him at Lew's cabin and feeling drawn to the powerful, lithe splendor of the man.

"You must rest." His dark eyes reflected sparks of the moonlight flowing through the window.

"I'm too keyed up." With her head lying against his

shoulder, she became aware of the blood surging through her arteries. How much of her excitement was from the nightmare and how much a response to his nearness, she had no idea.

"A massage might help," he said.

"Don't tell me you learned how to do that in military camp!"

"In truth, I did." Zahad lowered her to the pillow. "Along with basic medical skills, we were instructed in techniques to ease muscle stiffness. A cramp can cause a man to miss his shot."

"I wouldn't want to miss my shot," she murmured.

"Turn over and cease disputing," he ordered.

Although she wasn't convinced it was the wisest course of action, Jenny obeyed. When he touched her, she felt a tingle, an almost electric spark.

As his hands roamed over her, she registered the coolness of his skin and the roughness of calluses. His palms were large enough to span her shoulder blades and surprisingly skilled as they probed the knots of tension along her spine.

A delicious ache spread through her. Warmth radiated to her lips, to the points of her breasts and between her legs. Jenny had never known such a sweet awakening, free from the need to defend herself against a man's demands. Beneath Zahad's healing touch, she relished her response.

It intensified as his thumbs found the taut small of her back and searched lower. Pleasure rippled through her, bringing with it a longing to touch this man and arouse him as he was doing for her.

She didn't fear growing close and then losing him. It was inevitable that he would leave. What she feared was never having a chance to know him.

Yet he had issued no invitation to anything beyond a back rub. For the first time, Jenny recognized how a man could act on his own sexual impulse without considering that the woman might not share it. It would be wrong to place Zahad in an awkward situation when he was only being kind.

She closed her eyes and concentrated on the lovely sensations and the longing to surrender. The heat of her blood burned away the helplessness and panic of her nightmare.

Utterly content, she drifted into a new and much more pleasant dream.

ZAHAD DREW the covers over Jenny, careful not to awaken her. He felt glad she'd found temporary peace and grateful that she had no inkling of the passion she aroused.

In his younger days, desire had existed as a simple physical response, a thing apart from the rest of his being. This longing for Jenny was the opposite. It touched his soul.

In her presence, all the disparate parts of him merged. He became a warrior who read bedtime stories to a little girl, a fierce avenger who wanted only to hold one woman close and keep her safe. He became a man he didn't know and, at the same time, his most fundamental self.

He was relieved that he'd restrained his instinct to kiss the nape of her neck. Too many men had tried to exploit Jenny. He would sooner suffer alone than have her think he resembled them.

Zahad sat for a while watching her sleep. When he left, he went to Beth's room and watched her, too. The child was a picture of innocence, her blond hair trailing across her closely held doll.

He thought of Sharif, half a world away, seeing his wife fight for her life and the life of their baby. Zahad had always valued children, but he had assumed it was because of what they might become. Now he felt how precious this little girl was and what a vast abyss would open up if she ever came to harm.

His cousin's pain and worry became his own. It was, he supposed, what people called empathy. Once, he would have believed that it weakened a man. Now he saw that it bridged the distances between him and the people he cared about.

He had Jenny to thank for this knowledge. Also for the restlessness that kept him awake for a long time afterward.

AS SHE GOT READY FOR WORK on Monday, Jenny drifted through her routine with a sense of disconnection. In a way, everything seemed normal. *Fix breakfast, make sure Beth dresses warmly, run through the day ahead.*

But nothing was normal, not really.

One week ago, Fario had died here. On Friday, an ex-con had grabbed her on the front steps. Yesterday, Grant had tried to break in, and three men had attempted to carjack her.

Thank heaven for Zahad. He made everything else tolerable. Sitting at the breakfast table in his robe, he looked thoroughly at home, untroubled by the dark stubble on his jawline and hair so rumpled she doubted a comb would make it halfway through.

"What are you going to do today?" she asked as she fixed a peanut butter sandwich for Beth and a tuna on rye for herself.

The sheikh buttered a couple of slices of toast and handed one to Beth. The two of them seemed to have entered into an unspoken routine of sharing their food.

"I believe I should keep my prying low-key. Detective Finley seems hypersensitive."

"You're sure this Mr. Wang won't make matters worse when he calls?"

"It remains to be seen." He obviously wasn't given to worrying about what-ifs.

"You'll try to find out who the woman is, won't you? The one who called your brother." She'd been trying not to think about the possibilities that came to mind. They were too close for comfort.

"If I can," Zahad said.

"Can we have something good for dinner?" Beth asked the sheikh.

"Would you enjoy a fresh roasted goat?" he inquired.

She made a face.

"Perhaps some stuffed sheep's stomach?"

"Ick!" She giggled. "You can do better than that!"

"Mr. Adran is our guest, not our cook," Jenny chided her.

"I will prepare the evening meal," Zahad replied calmly. "It will be a pleasure."

"No yucky stuff," the little girl said. "No vegetables. I hate them."

The sheikh and Jenny exchanged glances. "I will make it excellent," he promised. "But I do not guarantee the absence of vegetables."

Before she left, Jenny said she'd be home by five-thirty. "I have to pick up Beth at day care on my way home," she explained. Her daughter was one of about a dozen youngsters who rode a private bus to the nearby center after kindergarten let out at noon. "I can get fast food if you want."

He folded his arms. "I am not incompetent in the kitchen."

"No one would accuse you of being incompetent at anything." As she spoke, Jenny flashed back to last night and the expert massage. She turned away to hide a blush.

Zahad frowned. "I am not thinking clearly. Wait one moment while I throw on my clothes."

"Why?"

"I will drive you to town and pick you up later," he said.

Jenny glanced toward her daughter, who waited impatiently at the door. She appreciated his offer, but she couldn't accept it.

"Thanks, but no. You won't be around forever." She had to stand on her own two feet. "Besides, I might need my car at work."

Jenny expected him to argue, as most men would. Instead, Zahad simply regarded her for a moment before saying, "I admire your courage."

He respected her decision. The realization was both heady and disconcerting, because part of Jenny feared what might lie ahead today. She drew herself up. "Thank you."

"Call if you need me."

"I've got your number programmed into my cell phone." Jenny couldn't resist reaching up to cup his prickly cheek with her palm. When he blinked, startled, she quickly hustled her daughter out the door.

Please, she thought, just let us get through this one day without anything terrible happening. It would make such a nice change.

JENNY'S TOUCH LINGERED on Zahad's cheek as he showered. The tenderness in her eyes and her spontaneous gesture had surprised him. In only a few days, they had grown very close.

Yet she was correct: He could not protect her forever, Zahad told himself. It was a good thing Jenny possessed inner strength, because she would likely need it.

As a soldier, he had once doubted women's capacity to endure hardship. That was before he saw Sharif's first wife die in childbirth. Only then had he understood how ignorant men were of the courage required by women's lives.

Remembering the life-and-death struggle that Holly faced, he called Amy's number as soon as he finished shaving and dressing. "How is Sharif's family?" he asked when she answered.

"Holly had a C-section this morning and delivered a healthy girl," his cousin said. "They're naming her Jamila." The name meant "beautiful." "I'd have called you sooner, but I didn't want to wake you."

"How is Holly?"

"Still weak. Sharif wants to make sure there are no complications before he goes to Jeddar.'' That was the capital city, several hours' journey from his provincial capital.

"I understand.'' With Hashim seeking to send Zahad into exile, he could no longer wait. "I will call President Dourad myself and plead my case.''

"That's a good idea. I'm hoping he won't do anything before you return with Fario's body,'' Amy said. "But Numa's burning with a sense of injustice and she has plenty of friends in Jeddar. She honestly believes you killed Fario.''

"I will plead my case.''

After ringing off, Zahad put in the call. It was early evening in Alqedar, and he was only able to reach one of the president's aides.

"I'm glad you contacted me,'' the man said. "President Dourad has scheduled a session on Saturday morning to consider the governing of Yazir Province. He grows tired of the squabbling. I advise you to be present in person.''

"Thank you for your counsel.''

To reach Alqedar by Saturday morning, given the time difference and the possibility of flight delays, Zahad realized he must depart no later than Thursday morning. Ideally, he should go sooner. He hated to leave while matters remained so unsettled here, but Numa and Hashim were forcing his hand.

If Fario's body could not be ready, Zahad would of course have to return for it. Otherwise, he wished to come back anyway for Jenny's sake, but that would depend on the political situation.

He sent an e-mail notifying Amy and Sharif of the new development, then called the coroner's department. A deputy told him the medical examiner still had not released the body.

Although he felt tempted to point out that any competent physician could have harvested tissue samples by now, Zahad knew that insults were likely to backfire. He said a gruff thank-you instead and added that he needed to take the body back to his country for burial as soon as possible.

"Are you aware that the remains will have to be embalmed before any airline will accept them?" the deputy asked.

"No, I was not." Zahad massaged his forehead. Yet another bureaucratic obstacle!

"You should call a funeral home. They'll take care of it for you," the man said.

"I will do that."

In the Yellow Pages, Zahad located the Mountain Lake Funeral Parlor. The woman who answered assured him they would do their best to handle the embalming and assist with shipping arrangements on short notice.

He thanked her and provided information about Fario for later. Afterward, feeling too restless to remain in the house, he decided to talk to Dolly. She was, after all, the witness who had found Fario's body.

Outside, clouds layered a pale sky and the light breeze carried a nip. After setting the alarm, Zahad followed the path toward the Blankenship property. Near the Rivases' carport, he turned right and followed the driveway uphill.

The Blankenship cottage sat in a shaded patch, only a trace of weak sunlight filtering through the overgrowth. Standing on the porch, he heard the chatter of a game show inside. He realized the doorbell must have sounded like one of the chimes on the television, because it failed to catch anyone's attention.

Zahad rapped firmly. Dolly threw the door open as if she'd been expecting him and said, "Come on in."

Leaving him to close the door, she returned to the couch. With her short, reddish-brown hair and flowered blouse tucked into her blue jeans, she presented a sturdy, almost ageless figure. But he guessed she was in her sixties.

The home seemed even darker inside than out. The worn carpet and scuffed paint gave it a shabby air, but it smelled pleasantly of coffee. There was a great deal of overstuffed furniture, mostly oriented toward a large TV.

"Can you figure out what the phrase is?" Dolly indicated the screen, which showed a series of squares with some letters revealed. A clue appeared at the bottom.

"It would be difficult for me." Zahad lowered himself into an armchair. "I am not a native English speaker."

"You speak very well, if you ask me." She picked up a shapeless wad of knitting. In the show, a woman spun a wheel while people clapped encouragement. "She ought to buy a vowel, but people get overexcited and forget."

Zahad wished he could inspect the premises, since he wanted to know who else might be in the house, but it would seem indiscreet. "Does your husband not enjoy this show?"

"Oh, he went out. I practically had to hog-tie him to let me drive him to the senior center this morning," Dolly said. "He loves playing checkers but he always insists on taking the bus himself and he keeps getting lost. I can't tell him anything. You probably noticed how grumpy he is."

"Perhaps it comes from being in pain," Zahad said.

She didn't seem to hear him. "Oh, no!" It took a moment for him to register that the contestant had landed on the bankruptcy slot and lost all her money. "I hate when that happens!"

He had little sympathy for gambling. However, he had come to sound out Dolly, not promote his own opinions. "Perhaps you should apply to appear on the show."

"I wouldn't do well," she replied. "Besides, I don't need the money as much as other people, so it wouldn't be fair."

"A policeman's retirement must be more lucrative than I imagined," he said.

A commercial came on and she muted the sound. "I get a nice pension," she explained. "Plus I bought this property and a few rental units around town."

"You sound like a wise investor. You do not mind that

your second husband won the Florida lottery after you divorced him?''

The woman's laugh rang out. ''I don't begrudge Manley anything. We always got along as friends. Couldn't live together—the man's a slob and spends most of his time fishing—but he bought me this TV when he won because he knew I'd enjoy it. I call that darn decent.''

''Very decent,'' Zahad agreed.

She continued talking, more voluble now that the ice had been broken. As the contestants struggled to solve puzzles, he learned that she baby-sat her granddaughter after lunch each day and that she wished her son-in-law had more self-discipline.

Once the show ended, he steered Dolly to a more serious topic. Discovering Fario's body had been a shock, Zahad saw from the way her voice quavered when she described the scene. He learned nothing that hadn't been in the police report, however.

''Do you think you were in danger yourself?'' he asked.

''You bet. I can't stop thinking about it,'' she said. ''It's just good luck that Cindy was sick that day and kept asking for me, so I only made a quick check of the property. Usually I would have tried the front door.''

''Will you patrol after I leave?''

Dolly reflected briefly. ''Oh, what the heck. Sure I will. Jenny and Beth are my friends.''

Zahad hoped he could trust this woman with confidential information, because he needed her insight. ''Sergeant Finley says one of the neighbors complained about my inquiries. Do you have any idea who that might be?''

''I wouldn't put it past Bill, because he's such a crab. Or Tish Garroway. She's so possessive of her husband that I think she's a bad influence on my daughter. Something about Jenny makes them both insecure. It's nonsense. If a husband's going to cheat, he doesn't need to have a raving beauty next door.''

''What do you think of Parker Finley?''

"He's sweet on Jenny, but that's as far as it goes." Dolly stretched out her legs on the couch. She wore fuzzy blue slippers more suitable for a young girl than a grandmother.

"He would be displeased if he learned I had questioned you," Zahad remarked.

"Then let's not tell him. Parker's a good cop, but he's spread too thin right now. By the time he stumbles across the perp, Jenny could be dead."

"Thank you. If you think of anything later, please call."

"Absolutely," she replied.

Zahad let himself out. As he walked downhill, he reviewed his list of suspects.

If Fario was the intended victim, Hashim had the strongest motive. If the target was Jenny, he had to consider Tish's jealousy as well as Ellen's.

That left Ray and Grant, the most obvious choice. Zahad hoped the police would delve into financial records that might indicate whether he'd hired someone to get rid of his ex-wife.

The sticking point was the bizarre decision to attach a gun to a chair and tie it to the door. A hit man wouldn't take such an indirect route. Zahad had trouble imagining why anyone else would, either.

He was so lost in thought that only the scrape of a side door in the Rivases' garage alerted him to someone's approach. Sneakered footsteps crunched on a gravel path, then Al Garroway came into view.

Surprise and unease showed on his narrow face. No wonder. In his arms, he held a large battery-powered chain saw.

Zahad tensed. Although heavy and awkward to wield, this was a formidable weapon.

"Hey." The ski instructor made no threatening move. "I'm not stealing this, if that's what you think."

The sheikh assumed a casual stance. "Certainly not. I understand people often borrow each other's tools in this neighborhood."

"That's right." Al wedged the saw against his hip for

support. "I'm going over to Louanne's house to cut down some branches."

"You are kind to help an elderly neighbor." Zahad noted Garroway apparently didn't have to be at work at an hour when the neighborhood seemed virtually deserted. Last Monday, he could easily have helped himself to a different set of tools from Jenny's shed.

"I'm not all that kind," Al admitted. "See, being a ski instructor doesn't pay great and the hours are limited. Since Ray started at the bank, people have been saying they could use a handyman. He told me I could borrow his stuff, so I thought I'd try it."

It was a plausible explanation. Zahad tried a different tack. "I hope your wife has recovered from the carjacking."

"She's still pretty freaked out about it. We heard what happened to Jenny yesterday. It's a darn shame."

"Does your wife also work limited hours at the lodge?"

"Yeah, mostly on weekends. She's looking for a second job in town. We both liked the idea of living out in the country, but it's not what we bargained for."

"Your wife seems to dislike Mrs. Sanger." It was a bit off the subject, but Zahad didn't care.

"Oh, she dislikes any woman under forty who doesn't look like a prune. Except maybe Ellen," Al said. "Listen, I've got to get going. A big storm's due and Louanne doesn't want one of those large branches falling through her roof. One of them barely missed her on Friday."

"Please do not let me stop you." Zahad moved aside, a symbolic gesture since he wasn't blocking Al's path.

"Catch you later."

"Sure thing." The casual phrase felt unnatural to him, but it fit the local vernacular.

When Zahad reached higher ground, he turned and surveyed the street. Al was heading toward Mrs. Welford's house, as he'd said.

Inside, Zahad went online and checked a weather site, which did indeed predict a snowstorm for Mountain Lake.

He hoped it wouldn't delay his return to Alqedar. In any case, he needed to firm up his plans. Switching to another site, he checked international plane schedules for Thursday morning.

Chapter Twelve

Thanks to the local radio station, everyone at school had heard about Grant's arrest and the attempted carjacking. Just when the gossip about Fario's death had begun to die down, Jenny was inundated with more questions and expressions of concern.

She spent her lunch hour meeting with a lawyer and signing papers for a restraining order. She didn't put much faith in the power of a sheet of paper to protect her, but at least it assured that Grant would face dire consequences if he so much as showed up on her property.

During the drive home, she watched the road for carjackers. It would be a long time before Jenny made this trip without fear. *Please let us get back to normal,* she thought, and then realized that she hardly remembered what "normal" meant.

However, the changes in her life weren't entirely bad. If not for everything that had happened, she wouldn't have met Zahad. Thanks to him, she had learned how to relax around a man and enjoy her own instinctive sexual response without feeling threatened. Even if nothing more passed between them, he had affected her in a good way.

"Mommy, is Zod going to stay with us?" Beth's line of thinking apparently paralleled her mother's. They were both looking forward to seeing him in a couple of minutes, Jenny thought.

"He's only here for a few days." Her voice caught at the end.

"I want him to stay."

Jenny didn't know what to say. Thank goodness they were almost home.

Yet when she pulled in to the driveway, painful memories assailed her again. She trembled until she cleared some trees and saw the sheikh's car in the parking bay. *I'm turning into a basket case. I have to get over this.*

The trouble was, she couldn't get over it because it wasn't over.

When they entered the house, Jenny noticed the tantalizing smell of baking chicken. Then she heard Frank Sinatra singing "It Was a Very Good Year." The music must be coming from the boom box she kept in the kitchen.

"Hello!" she called as she and Beth hung up their coats.

"Welcome home, Mrs. and Miss Sanger." Zahad emerged from the kitchen, his red apron a cheerful contrast to his dark brown sweater and tan slacks. He carried salad tongs in one hand.

"You promised no yucky stuff!" Beth said.

The sheikh drew himself up to his full height. "I assure you, I have fixed no yucky stuff."

She pointed at the tongs.

"What I have created," he announced, "is Aladdin's Magic Salad." To Jenny, he explained, "My cousin Amy e-mailed me her children's favorite recipes."

"I hope I get a chance to meet Amy someday," she said. "I think I'd like her."

"What's that smell?" Beth asked, adding, "I like it."

"Camel patties," the sheikh replied.

"Camel patties?" Jenny regarded him dubiously.

"It is really oven-baked chicken nuggets, but 'camel patties' sounds more intriguing."

"Is it ready?" the little girl demanded.

"Give me five minutes."

"I'll go wash my hands!" Beth dashed down the hall.

Jenny wanted to tell Zahad how much she appreciated what he'd done but before she could form the words, she realized that she couldn't tell him what she really felt. It would mean revealing that he had given her violated home a new sense of solidity, and that he had brought joy into two lives she hadn't even been aware were lonely.

Even if such candor didn't embarrass him, it might give him the wrong idea. No matter how appealing he looked as he led her into the heart of the kitchen and no matter how much she longed to slip into his arms and tease him with kisses, Jenny knew she must not.

She understood both herself and their situation. During this magic time, while she and Zahad were united by a common goal, they had formed their own temporary universe. There was no use pretending it could last, even if they both wanted it to.

Jenny had found it impossible to establish a lasting relationship with any of the men she'd dated or with the one she'd married, even though they shared her culture and background. With Zahad, once the initial impetus ended, reason told her there'd soon be nothing left to build on.

She would hate it if this special relationship deteriorated into discomfort and misunderstandings. It seemed far better to have a radiant memory to cherish.

Zahad clicked off the boom box. "You are very quiet. Has it been a difficult day?"

"Better than yesterday," Jenny replied, "although that's not saying much. How about you?"

"Ronald Wang e-mailed me. He assures me he spoke to the detective but revealed nothing of my visit."

"Good." Jenny was glad Parker knew about the woman caller and the fact that there were apparently two cyberstalkers. She wished he was willing to work with Zahad, however.

"I hope it will help." The sheikh released a long breath, and the two of them stood in the kitchen simply looking at each other

Jenny didn't want to hear anything more about murderers or stalkers or carjackers. "I don't know how you feel, but I'm on investigation overload."

"We both need a respite," Zahad agreed. "During the revolution in Alqedar, sometimes the danger and loss threatened to overwhelm our morale. When that happened, we declared a camp evening. I suggest you and I do the same."

"What's a camp evening?"

"For a few hours, we became youths again." Picking up pot holders, the sheikh went to the oven. "We sang foolish songs, ran three-legged races and told jokes."

As he removed a tray of browned chicken nuggets, Jenny asked, "Is it fair to assume the jokes don't bear repeating in polite society?"

A trace of color appeared on his high-boned cheeks. "Assuredly not." He fetched grape juice from the refrigerator, poured it into three wineglasses and carried them to the front room. He'd already set the table—somewhat unconventionally, with the spoons on the plates and the napkins on the chairs. Perhaps he'd done so deliberately to make the occasion lighthearted.

Jenny picked up her napkin and sank into her seat. "Thanks for doing this."

"It is my pleasure."

When Beth bounded into the room, her eyes fixed on her wineglass. "Mommy won't let me have that. Will you, Mommy?"

"It's grape juice," Jenny said.

"All right!" Handling the glass very carefully, the little girl took a sip.

From the kitchen, Zahad fetched a large bowl containing salad greens strewn with some white flakes and brown bits. Jenny did want her daughter to eat vegetables, but what was this?

"Allow me to present Aladdin's Magic Salad," the sheikh announced.

Beth eyed the concoction suspiciously. After a long moment, she brightened. "It's got chocolate chips!"

"The white shreds are coconut." Zahad placed the bowl in front of her with a flourish. Next to it, he set a small pitcher of yellow dressing. "This is pineapple sauce."

Jenny tried to guess how chocolate chips, coconut and lettuce tasted with pineapple sauce. She decided to simply keep quiet and eat it.

Beth grabbed the tongs and plopped salad onto her plate, showering a fair measure onto the table in the process. She scooped it up and ate heartily. "Wow! Dessert in the salad!" she exclaimed when she came up for air.

"Why didn't I think of that?" Jenny had to admire the recipe's sheer inventiveness.

The sheikh brought in the nuggets on a serving plate and a casserole of scalloped potatoes sticky with cheese. "These are Camel McNuggets and Oasis Chips, according to Amy."

"I've absolutely got to meet this woman. Does she ever come to Southern California?" Jenny asked.

"It has happened. Perhaps someday she will return," Zahad said. To Beth, he added, "My cousin has a seven-year-old daughter. I believe you two would like each other."

"Does she have dolls?"

"Many of them from around the world."

"I'd like that!" The little girl stuffed a forkful of potatoes into her mouth.

Between mouthfuls, Beth told the grown-ups how her friends had welcomed her back after her two-week absence. The class had a new hamster, too, she explained with delight.

Once Beth ran out of steam, Jenny described the schoolwide winter decorating project she'd been coordinating. Older children were writing poems and stories to post throughout the building. Some artistic youngsters had been designing a mural to be assembled from many sheets of poster board, which the younger children would paint. The primary grades and kindergarten were supplementing this artwork with their own drawings and writings.

She also described seeing Elmer playing with a group of boys. "It looks like he's finally making friends," she said. "I think the baseball game broke the ice."

"The school is for you as my province is to me." Zahad studied her across the table. "It gives your life structure and meaning. Apart from your family, of course."

"Except that you are desperately needed, while I have a capable staff that was already in place when I arrived," Jenny replied. "I'm just putting on the finishing touches."

"Perhaps you would enjoy a greater challenge."

She'd had the same thought but it had always seemed so impossible. "At one time, this was everything I could have asked for. But it seems as if the more I do, the more I want to do."

"What is your goal, then?"

Jenny recalled the daydreams in which she'd indulged before the cyber-stalking and subsequent all-consuming events. "Someday I want to take on a bigger challenge, maybe work with underprivileged kids. When Beth's grown, I might move to an inner-city area and head up some kind of program there."

"Impressive," the sheikh said.

"It's just a pipe dream," Jenny conceded.

"What did you do today, Zod?" Beth asked.

"Many things. I talked with your neighbors Dolly and Al."

"Oh, really?" Jenny was glad to hear he'd been investigating despite Parker's disapproval. "Did you learn anything?"

"Perhaps." As he outlined his conversations, the sheikh avoided any direct reference to the murder, probably for Beth's benefit.

When he finished, Jenny saw from his hesitation that there was something more. "What is it?"

"I must return to my country Thursday morning. The

president will hold a meeting Saturday morning to consider who is to run my province. My enemies may have me banned from the country entirely if I do not present my point of view.''

''That would be terrible.'' Thursday morning. A hollow echo rang through her mind like the slamming of a steel door. Of course she'd known he was going to leave soon, but now that the day had been fixed, she realized she wasn't ready for him to go.

Amid the turbulence, the three of them had stolen a little time to be together. Now that the end loomed, she prized these family moments even more.

''Will you bring me a camel when you come back?'' Beth asked.

Trust her daughter to come up with the unexpected! Jenny would have laughed if not for a lump in her throat.

''He would be most uncomfortable on an airplane,'' the sheikh replied solemnly.

The little girl frowned. ''He could leave off his seat belt.''

That was too much. Shaking with silent laughter, Jenny gave Zahad a helpless look. She didn't want Beth to think she was being mocked.

He managed, heaven knew how, to maintain a straight face. ''An excellent suggestion, although I am afraid I cannot promise to return. Now, I believe it is time for dessert.''

''Yippee!'' Distracted by his last statement, Beth shot to her feet and cheerfully helped clear the dishes.

Dessert consisted of ice-cream bars coated with chocolate and ground nuts. ''Wow, you got the big ones!'' the little girl said.

''It is a special occasion,'' the sheikh told her. ''Also, I am very fond of ice-cream bars. The bigger the better.''

How strange, Jenny reflected as she enjoyed her treat, that in spite of everything that had gone wrong, she didn't recall ever being happier. She refused to allow herself to think about what life would be like without Zahad.

Some things couldn't and perhaps shouldn't be changed. The trick was to let the future take care of itself and concentrate on the moment.

After dinner, they joined Beth in watching a VeggieTales video. The sheikh found the smart-talking vegetables hilarious and announced that he would order one for Amy from the Internet.

"I'm glad your cousin will get something for her children," Jenny remarked. "She's been so helpful to me."

"To me also," Zahad said.

When they put Beth to bed, she insisted on sitting on the sheikh's knee to hear her bedtime story. At first he looked a trifle ill at ease while balancing the sprite, but the respectful warmth in the way he regarded her touched Jenny's heart.

"Tell me about your country," the little girl said.

"It is far, far away."

"Is it in Russia?"

"It is a separate country." Jenny wondered if the sheikh would grow impatient with the child's ignorance, but he simply gathered his thoughts and tried again. "Alqedar is on the Arabian peninsula. Unfortunately, we have no oil and we are not a seaport. The people used to be nomads— that means they traveled around and lived in tents. Now many of them farm and make crafts."

"That sounds like fun."

"Yes, we have a lot of fun," Zahad agreed. "The people wear colorful clothes at the marketplace. They make music and have big families, whom they love very much."

Jenny took a seat on the sturdy toy chest. It amazed her to see how gentle this rough man could be.

"Do you have any children?" she asked.

He shook his head.

"You should." Beth's forehead crinkled with thought. "Three. Two girls and a boy. Do you live in a palace?"

"Yes, although perhaps it is not as fancy as you might imagine," the sheikh admitted. "It is old and rambling and the plumbing has a bad temper. My stepmother lives there, too."

"What happened to your mother?" Beth asked.

"She died when I was seven. We did not have very good hospitals in our country, although we are building some now. My mother was a proud, brave woman, who taught me to put the good of my country before my own wishes."

"I do that," Beth said eagerly. "I recycle. And I conserve water." Honesty prodded her to add, "Sometimes."

"Good for you."

"Was your mother from a royal family also?" Jenny seized on this opportunity to learn more of Zahad's background.

"Yes. She came from the neighboring province of Bahrim, where she was sister to the sheikh, Sharif's father."

"What about your stepmother?" she asked.

"For his second wife, my father chose a woman from a prominent family in Yazir itself. Unfortunately for me, this makes Numa a local girl supported by many friends and relatives." Noticing Beth's large yawn, Zahad said, "It is time to say good-night, little one."

The girl hugged him. "You can stay with Mommy and me as long as you want to, Zod," she told him.

His dark eyes shone. "I wish it were that simple."

"Some things *are* simple. Like the fact that it's bedtime." Jenny said, lifting Beth into bed. She kissed her daughter and tucked her beneath the covers. The child curled up sleepily, pulling her doll close.

When Jenny and Zahad slipped out, she expected him to retreat to his room to work on the computer. It pleased her that he accompanied her to the living room instead.

"We are having a camp night," he explained as they sank onto the couch. "I am tired of thinking about evil people plotting evil deeds. The world is always full of them, but we need not let them control our minds."

"I couldn't agree more."

They had so little time together, Jenny reflected as a peaceful silence fell over the room. Only two more days. So little chance to explore each other.

The excitement she'd felt during the massage tantalized her. She wanted more of that, much more. She loved the person she became around him.

The truth struck Jenny with simple inevitability: She wanted to make love to Zahad. It would be the first time since her divorce that she'd slept with a man, but there was, she realized, no reason to hold back.

She didn't need to fear the slow, miserable breakdown of a relationship or the stifling attempts at domination she'd endured with Grant. Because the sheikh was leaving, they could enjoy a beautiful coupling that had at least a chance of remaining untarnished in their memories.

Shyly, Jenny stole a glance at the man beside her. He'd propped his feet on the coffee table, shoes and all, and leaned back his head. In profile, he had a nose strong enough to balance the pronounced cheekbones and firm lips. Her gaze trailed down the length of him and sparkles played through her as she pictured her legs tangling with his.

In his land, she wondered, how did he address himself to a woman? What conventions did they observe, or did they simply get swept away?

His head turned and he met her eyes. Jenny's breath caught as it occurred to her that he knew exactly what she was thinking.

"Many men seek you, but you elude them," he said in a resonant, contemplative tone. "Yet to me you have never seemed coy. Why have you not availed yourself of these lovers?"

"I haven't wanted any of them," she answered.

"How would a man know if you did?" the sheikh asked. "Forgive me if I am too much of a warrior but when it comes to women, I am not certain I can read the signs."

Anticipation spread deep inside Jenny. "I guess I'm not the temptress I'm cracked up to be or I wouldn't leave any doubt."

He gave her a rare smile. "Although I have much to learn with regard to reading signs, I am improving my skill at taking hints." His fingers drifted through her hair, parting the strands and lifting their fullness. Her eyelids lowered as she concentrated on the heat and smell of him and on the tug that progressed along her scalp toward the nape of her neck.

Zahad shifted closer. His breath stirred promises along Jenny's jaw and then his lips brushed hers. His mouth lingered for a long moment before letting go.

"I have no further doubts. Have you?"

"I'm the temptress here. I never had any doubts." With the edge of her thumb, she traced the small white scar on his jaw.

Easing onto her knees on the couch, Jenny leaned over and replaced her thumb with her tongue. A groan wrenched from deep within Zahad and he caught her by the hip. Emboldened, she traced his jaw up to his ear and took the lobe between her lips, relishing his shudder.

With a fluid motion, he swung her onto his lap. A little off balance, Jenny rested her cheek against his chest and listened to his heart thundering.

"I've been wondering about your scars," she murmured. "How many do you have?"

"I never counted."

"You have one on your back." She'd seen it at the cabin when he awoke beside her. "Were you attacked from behind?"

His cheek brushed her temple as he nodded. "By a treacherous coward. I dispatched him to a place where he can never betray anyone again."

This was the man who had dumped syrup all over his plate to please a five-year-old, Jenny reminded herself.

"There's a side of you that's so far beyond my experience I can't even imagine it."

"We are not so different. You are a woman of courage and resourcefulness. We have simply operated in different spheres."

She touched the white mark that bisected his left eyebrow. "That must have been a close call."

"Very close. Witnesses claim I was airborne for several seconds after my motorcycle hit a pothole. Alqedar is famous for its bad roads."

"You ride a motorcycle?"

"Sometimes it is the fastest way to get where I want to go." He slid her from his lap and stood, drawing her up with him. "I am accustomed to directness, Jenny." There was a question beneath the statement as he faced her.

He was offering her a chance to retreat. Even now, after she'd initiated the embrace, he didn't press her.

"Good. I like directness," she said.

Zahad gave a slight nod, accepting her decision. "Is your daughter asleep?"

"Let's find out."

They stopped by her bedroom. The little girl's regular breathing and complete relaxation told their own story.

When Zahad released her hand, Jenny glanced at him questioningly. He returned to the living room, from which she heard the beep of the alarm as he set it. On his way back, he switched off the lights.

Did he ever completely lose himself in passion? she wondered, and, with a flutter of excitement, realized she was about to find out.

Chapter Thirteen

When she drew the sheikh into her room, Jenny became aware of the lingering scent of sweet herbs from her drawers. In the intimacy of the boudoir, he loomed large and untamed.

"I wish to see you," Zahad announced. "All of you."

"You want me to strip for you?" She'd never done anything like that for Grant. He'd made her feel a bit self-conscious, and as a result she'd instinctively protected herself.

"You need not make a production of it." Zahad lounged across the flowered coverlet on her bed, forming a brown exclamation point in his sweater and slacks. He had removed his shoes, she noticed. "I want to enjoy the sight of you."

She nearly protested that she felt too shy, until she realized that wasn't true. Not with Zahad. She didn't fear he would find her too bony or too small-breasted or that he would compare her to some airbrushed, men's magazine standard. He always seemed to accept and appreciate the real Jenny.

She wanted to excite him. She wanted to make this tightly leashed man lose control. Jenny smiled. She was going to do it, too.

She replaced the overhead glare with the soft glow of a

table lamp. The golden circle shut out the rest of the world, creating a private realm.

She reached behind her and unzipped the blue dress. The cloth rustled as it slithered to the floor, unveiling a clingy, flesh-colored slip.

On the bed, Zahad swallowed. Jenny dipped her head to let her hair partially obscure her face, then tossed it back as a photographer had once taught her to do when she'd modeled. Then, she'd had to force herself to relax. Tonight, she felt safe enough to play at sexual fantasies with her sheikh.

Her sheikh. It amazed Jenny that this hardened desert warrior was here with her, fascinated by her, longing for her. In so many ways, he still seemed an enigma, and yet she was about to know him intimately.

Slowly, teasingly, she drew the slip up over her hips, her waist, her shoulders. When she tossed it aside, she enjoyed the sensation of his eyes feasting on her. As Jenny pushed her hair atop her head and then shook it free, the sheikh stirred restlessly.

She kicked off her pumps. The first one landed with a satisfying thump near the bed while the other fell onto the carpet nearby. Leaning forward seductively, Jenny eased down the waistband of her panty hose. As she lowered it, the tension in her midsection tightened into a knot of longing.

Zahad shifted to the bed's edge and reached out, his callused hand gentle as it traced Jenny's thigh. His fingers brushed so close to her yearning center that she gasped.

"Let me finish for you," he said, and swung his legs so that he sat straddling her where she stood.

Every brush of his fingers as he rolled down the silky stockings reverberated through Jenny. When he angled forward and kissed her bare navel, she had to catch hold of his shoulders to keep from losing control.

She wanted him more than she had ever dreamed of wanting a man. There was something deliciously liberating about the sensations he aroused, something that made her secure enough to surrender without a second thought.

When he left, Jenny would miss him terribly, but she would still be complete. She could give him everything without losing control.

The pleasure when he unhooked her bra and his hands closed over her breasts felt almost unbearably intense. Jenny shut her eyes but immediately opened them again so she could watch this scarred man radiate joyous desire.

Passion transformed the sheikh, softening his angular features. As his mouth and hands roamed over her, peeling away what little clothing remained, wonder animated his dark eyes.

From where she stood, Jenny bent to nuzzle the unruly length of his hair. She found the rim of his sweater and helped him take it off.

Beneath lay more scars than she had expected, some of them puckered and others crisscrossing savagely. The evidence of his courage stimulated her. Playing her breasts against his hair, Jenny caressed his back.

She could feel Zahad pulling free of his remaining clothes from where he sat on the bed. When they were both naked, he tipped back his head and traced his tongue across her breasts. She stood above his seated figure with nothing to hold them apart.

Their frenzy burned too fiercely to prolong as Zahad's knees separated Jenny's legs. He gripped her waist and lowered her atop him while their mouths claimed each other.

Catching her rounded bottom, he pulled her onto him. Jenny felt the incredible length of him penetrating her, the upward thrust searingly pure. A flame leaped between them, drawing her down, lifting her up again, intensifying until she ignited.

Zahad pulled her onto the bed. Cool fabric met the heat of Jenny's bare back as the sheikh lifted himself over her.

Although it had happened quickly, Jenny was glad to have spent her own desire so she could relish the climax of this amazing man. It thrilled her to see the wild yearning that overcame him.

He poised above, touching her in only one place, the one that joined a man and a woman in a thousand ways. Fiercely intent, he entered her again. His movements slow and deliberate, he drew himself in and out, eyes half-closed, breath rasping as he held himself in place with his powerful arms.

An ache grew inside Jenny. It was only a hint at first, but the incredible fullness of him and the sight of his strength poised above her rekindled the sparks. When he speeded his movements, the embers sizzled into fireworks.

The sheikh possessed an elemental maleness that let him please himself, vibrantly and without hesitation, while drawing Jenny into the brilliance with him. A blast of joy seized her when she felt Zahad's explosive shudders. They flew together, merging until they became a single glorious entity.

Then they were two again, their chests rising and falling rapidly, his arms encircling her on the bed. She felt the coolness of his damp skin against her cheek and inhaled his masculine essence. Inside her, a dozen unseen scars, as profound as the ones marring his body, were reabsorbed.

Zahad might depart on Thursday without a backward glance, but Jenny would regret nothing. He had healed injuries that, until tonight, she hadn't realized existed.

She hoped she had done as much for him.

WHEN HE ALLOWED HIMSELF to yield to temptation, Zahad had been reassured by the knowledge that, as a divorced woman, Jenny knew what she was doing. Also, she had no illusions about their situation, so their encounter would not leave her brokenhearted

He hadn't anticipated his own response. He was still trying to sort it out as he watched her snuggle into a pillow.

Zahad had spent decades building walls around his heart. In a flash, Jenny had torn them down. She had shown him a man who needed to connect with a woman at the most basic level, and who needed her in countless other ways as well.

He saw her eyes large and intense as they had appeared while the two of them talked earlier in the living room. He pictured Beth perched on his knee, assuring him that he was welcome here. He recalled the homey aromas of coffee and maple syrup.

Above all, his mind and body filled with impressions of the last half hour. Inside Jenny, he had felt whole for the first time in more than twenty years. They weren't simply two people who'd chanced to meet. This encounter had been fated, no matter what might come of it.

He rolled onto his stomach, fearing that his restlessness might disturb her but unable to keep still. This was insanity, to imagine bringing home as his bride the siren who some believed had lured Fario to his death. He himself might recognize her innocence, but how could he expect his people to accept her when they barely accepted him?

Zahad released a long breath. He would always cherish the memory of the past few days and especially of tonight. But he could not ask Jenny and her little girl to share the dangers that would confront him in his homeland or to face rejection by people who neither knew them nor wanted to know them.

With regret, Zahad acknowledged that he must begin putting up walls again. It would take a long time and involve more than a little pain, but eventually he would close off this weakness in himself.

Seeking rest, he struggled to clear his mind. At last sleep folded its wings over him.

He was deep within the darkness when a scraping noise reached him. He knew at once, even before fully waking, that it came from outside. Distinctly, he heard the clink of metal on metal.

Zahad bolted from the bed. Due to years of experience, he dressed without light in a matter of seconds.

"What's going on?" Jenny asked sleepily.

"Someone is breaking in to the toolshed," he told her.

"I'll call the police."

"Fine." He headed for the door.

"You can't go out there!" she protested.

It had never occurred to him to cower here. "Of course I will." Zahad put on his shoes. "If it is the murderer, here is my chance to catch him."

"You mean, here's your chance to get killed!"

He let the remark pass. "The flashlight by the back door—are the batteries current?" He should have checked them himself, he reflected.

"Yes." Jenny hesitated with the phone in one hand. "Take anything you need."

"I will." He had not intended to ask for permission.

Zahad grabbed a knife from the kitchen, threw on the coat he'd left in the rear hall and shut down the security system. He chose not to activate the exterior lights because they would give him away.

He took a key, as well. When he went outside, he locked the door behind him.

Cold air chilled his face and hands. Ignoring it, Zahad dodged to avoid becoming an easy target. No gunshot shattered the stillness, however, so he paused to listen for suspicious sounds beside the porch, where he was out of direct view. At the same time, he scanned the backyard for odd shapes and for signs of movement.

He heard only the breeze in the pines. He saw nothing but shadows.

In the faint moonlight, he approached the shed at a zig-zag. All the while, his senses sought evidence of the intruder. He spotted no one, but on a cloudy night like this a man could hide only yards away without being detected.

Once he reached the shed, he shone the flashlight on the lock. The shackle was gouged as if someone had tried to sever it with a bolt cutter. Zahad played the beam across the ground, hoping to find a footprint or an object dropped in haste.

Only frozen earth met his gaze.

If the interloper had driven here from elsewhere, he would most likely have parked nearby, yet Zahad had not heard an engine start. Since it was likely the man or woman remained in the vicinity, he decided to concentrate on the nearby area.

Overgrown trees and bushes filled the land behind and to one side of the property. Attempting to search such a large area alone struck Zahad as futile. Sometimes, however, the simplest course also proved the most effective one.

Moving to one corner of the shed, the sheikh stood silently letting the night carry its sounds and scents to him. When he heard someone stirring in the house, the trespasser might have dived for the nearest cover instead of fleeing. If so, how steely were his or her nerves?

Zahad waited. In the house, a light came on in Jenny's room. The thick curtains prevented him from seeing inside.

He jammed his hands into the open front of his coat for warmth. Although he preferred to stand at the ready, it would do no good if his fingers became so cold he fumbled the knife.

As his brain filtered out the murmur of the branches, he began to perceive sounds behind sounds. Nature had its own rhythm: in summer, a living hum of insects and birds; in winter, the subtle shifting and settling of stones and trees.

Attuned to any discrepancy, Zahad tried not to let himself be distracted by speculation. Yet his mind teemed with questions. If the intruder was the killer, why would he want to raid Jenny's shed a second time? Surely tools like hers could be purchased at the hardware store or taken from another neighbor's garage.

Perhaps the goal had been to lure Zahad outside. While he hunted the murderer, he might instead become the prey.

Inside the coat, his hand tightened on the haft. The sheikh braced himself in case he had to dodge an attack and throw the weapon. Even his deadly accuracy, however, might fail to bring down someone clad in heavy clothing.

He was allowing his mind to work against him. Harshly, he refocused his attention.

There's someone here.

He knew it without being able to pinpoint how he'd drawn that conclusion. Perhaps, subliminally, he'd heard a rasp of breath. Now, straining and keyed up, he could have sworn he detected a heartbeat reverberating through the frigid earth.

Was it his own heart? If only he had more experience at tracking in a wintry landscape. If only he understood how vibrations interacted with icy surfaces.

In the overgrowth behind the property, some thirty feet from Zahad, a twig snapped.

He swiveled to face that direction. If the intruder moved again, even slightly, he would have the location. Most people would bolt under such circumstances, thrashing through the brush and making a run for safety.

Any minute now. Any minute...

Down the road, Zahad heard a car approaching. *Let it pass quickly.*

Instead, tires crunched into the driveway. The police had had the good sense to leave off the siren, but whoever was hiding in the brush didn't wait around for the sheikh's reinforcements. Rustling and a sharp exhalation signaled his rush for deeper cover.

The sheikh raked the scene with the flashlight. He saw movement, too far away for an accurate throw of the knife. But he had the advantage for the moment. He pelted across the flat yard while his target struggled through rougher terrain.

"Police!" A voice rang out behind him. "Stop or I'll shoot!"

Every instinct urged him to keep going. A few dozen more steps and he could nail the person who might have killed Fario.

He could also die at the hands of an overzealous police officer.

Furious, Zahad stopped. "It is I, Sheikh Adran! Our target is escaping!"

"Come out where I can see you," the officer ordered.

Judging by the man's brittle tone, Zahad believed the policeman must be alone. He sounded young, also.

Barely restraining himself from showering the man with curses, Zahad strode into plain view. The officer crouched between the house and the garage, his gun positioned in a double grip.

The sheikh aimed the flashlight at his own face. When the officer failed to respond, Zahad experienced a moment of sheer alarm. If he had mistaken the voice, if this were Finley, he might seize the opportunity and shoot anyway. What better excuse for eliminating a rival?

"You can see it is I," Zahad called.

The patrolman lowered his gun. "Sorry about that." When he moved into the clear, Zahad saw that he was indeed younger than Finley and wore a uniform. "I'm Officer Franklin."

Zahad gave a short nod of acknowledgment. Then, with no further time to waste on ceremony, he gestured toward the terrain beyond the shed. "Whoever tried to break into the shed is out there. I heard him moving."

"We've got to catch him before he gets to the street," Franklin said.

"Or to one of the other houses," the sheikh added.

They spread out, keeping within view of each other as they searched. Either their target had found a well-hidden gully, however, or he or she was long gone.

They had given up by the time Finley trudged around the house, apparently having arrived on foot. When Jenny turned on the outdoor lights, they cast far deeper hollows on the detective's face than on Officer Franklin's.

It occurred to Zahad that perhaps this was their target and that the sergeant had conveniently covered himself by pretending to arrive from home. However, he saw no leaves or burrs clinging to the man's jacket and his pants were smooth and neatly creased.

"Did you find anything?" Jenny asked. Wrapped in a robe, she stood silhouetted in the back door.

"He got away," Zahad replied in disgust.

Finley regarded him wearily. "Tell me what happened."

Zahad and the patrolman ran through the details. When they had finished, the sergeant said, "So you never actually saw anyone?"

"That is true."

"I'll dust the lock for prints, but it's freezing out here. Dollars to doughnuts, if there was an intruder, he wore gloves," the detective said. "I'm not calling out a full-scale search team for what might be a raccoon. My men are stretched thin as it is."

"You have not yet apprehended the carjackers?" Zahad inquired.

"They've got to be staying around here, but we can't pinpoint where," Finley answered. "We're beginning to suspect they've got someone local helping them."

Zahad accepted the decision not to search further. At this point, even if they came across a trespasser, too much time had passed for them to be sure he was their man. If it was a neighbor, he could claim he'd come to learn what the fuss was about.

As it turned out, the only prints on the lock were a few partials too smeared to be readable, and they most likely belonged to Jenny or Zahad. At last the patrolman departed. Finley went inside to get Jenny's version of the evening's events.

"It seems suspicious, but we can't be sure it's linked to anything," he said when she'd finished. Zahad joined them in the living room. "Somebody clearly took a whack at that padlock, but it might have been a transient seeking shelter."

"We don't get many of those around here, but I suppose it's possible," Jenny told him. With hair rioting around her face and the bathrobe gaping at her throat, she looked vulnerable and, in Zahad's eyes, velvet with the aftermath of lovemaking. "Could it have been Grant?"

"He's staying at a motel in Crystal Point," Finley replied. "Obviously we can't take his wife's word for his whereabouts, but I'll check with the motel staff. I'll call now and have a cruiser swing by to make sure his car's where it belongs."

"I hope it's not him," she said. "For Beth's sake."

He shrugged. "He's being arraigned tomorrow, by the way."

"That was quick. Should I be in court?"

"If you are, you'll put him in violation of his restraining order," Finley said. "Also, there's no sense in provoking him. I'll let you know what happens."

"Thank you."

"Just doing my job. I'll talk to you soon." With a farewell nod, he went out.

The sheikh locked up. When he returned to the living room, he asked, "Are you okay?"

"A little nervous," Jenny said. "It's nothing. Parker's probably right about the intruder being a transient."

"Perhaps so." Zahad didn't believe that, but he didn't want to frighten her more than necessary. "I will make up my bed now. For Beth's sake, we should sleep separately."

"I'd rather have you with me."

"I assure you, there is nowhere I would rather be. But it is unwise."

She came and brushed a kiss across his mouth. Her lips felt warm and soft, and as he held her, Zahad longed to lose himself in her again. However, he must remain alert in case the intruder returned. "Good night, Jenny."

"I'm glad you're here, wherever you sleep," she said. "Thank you." After lingering for a moment, she vanished.

As he opened the couch and pulled out the mattress, Zahad wondered again why anyone would bother stealing tools from her shed. Had the killer left something behind that he was trying to reclaim, or had he recalled a particular item he needed?

Needed for what?

The answer, unfortunately, was that if the killer had been out there tonight, it probably meant he planned to strike again. Zahad only wished he knew when and against whom.

He sat up listening until his eyes refused to stay open any longer. If there were truths to be revealed tonight, he failed to find them.

Chapter Fourteen

Someone is going to die today.

Zahad awoke with this thought. Having dreamed of pursuing a shadowy figure through a darkened field, he retained an image of its hooded black robe and of the sword gripped in its hand.

"I shall follow your vehicle to school today. That way, there will be no difficulty if you need your car later," he told Jenny over breakfast. Unlike yesterday, he didn't intend to be dissuaded. "Please call me this afternoon when you are ready to leave and I will escort you home also."

She quirked one eyebrow but, noting Beth's rapt attention, didn't question him. "If you think it's advisable."

"I do."

He was about to suggest that he remain at the school and accompany her on her duties, but her warning glance told him she would refuse. Zahad decided not to press the issue. He needed to do many things today and it seemed unlikely the killer would be bold enough to attack in the middle of town. Whoever was doing this preferred isolation and subterfuge.

Zahad felt even more protective of Jenny this morning, perhaps because they had slept together. He wished they could acknowledge openly that they had become lovers, but, of course, they could not do so in front of the child. At least they had the prospect of two more nights together.

Zahad trailed Jenny's SUV into town beneath a leaden sky. According to the radio, a major storm was expected to move into the area on Thursday. His plane would depart just in time to miss it.

At the school, there were already a few cars in the lot despite the early hour. Zahad walked Jenny to the front. "Who opens the building?" he asked.

"The maintenance crew does, shortly before I get here," she said as they ascended the front steps.

"What do you do with Beth before school?" He wanted a complete picture of the situation.

"She stays with me until the kindergarten teacher arrives." Jenny pushed open the main door. "She sharpens pencils and gets supplies from the cabinet for me, don't you, sweetheart?"

"I'm Mommy's helper," Beth confirmed proudly.

Inside the front office, a balding man Zahad recognized as Lew Blackwell glanced up from filling out paperwork at the counter. "Good morning, Jenny, Beth." He didn't greet the sheikh.

"We had a disturbance at my house last night," she explained. "Nothing serious, but Mr. Adran was kind enough to escort me into town today."

"A disturbance?" Lew frowned. "Was it the carjackers or—"

"We do not know." Although Jenny was capable of answering for herself, Zahad refused to be dismissed by this teacher as if he had no importance.

"You weren't hurt, were you?" Again, Lew addressed Jenny.

"I'm fine." She held herself with confidence now that they had reached her territory. "I'd better get to work. I've got to pick the winners in the PTA art contest." The look she cast toward Zahad contained both her thanks and a strong hint that he should depart.

Surely she didn't expect him to leave her and Beth alone

with this man, he thought. Lew's possessive attitude made it difficult for Zahad to consider him a casual bystander.

"Perhaps I should remain until more people arrive," he said.

"Thank you, but that's not necessary."

Jenny's chin lifted. With her air of authority, she was nothing like the somewhat shaky lady he'd taken under his wing last Friday but a woman one hundred percent in charge.

"She's the boss," Lew said, evidently amused at seeing his rival dismissed.

As the sheikh hesitated, Beth broke the standoff by heading toward an interior hallway. "I have to go potty," she announced.

"I'll come with you." Jenny disappeared with her daughter.

Zahad glanced assessingly at the teacher. He knew it would be politic to make himself scarce before the two females returned, but he didn't share Jenny's apparent trust of this man.

"You seem to be spending a lot of time in Mountain Lake," Lew commented. "Don't you have a country to run?"

"Only a province," Zahad replied.

"Don't they miss you?"

"Perhaps less than I might wish."

Through the outer door came a heavyset woman, her cheeks pink from the cold. When she noticed Zahad, she said politely, "Is there something I can help you with?"

"This is Sheikh Adran," Lew explained. "Mrs. Buffington's the school secretary."

"So you're the one everybody's been talking about!" She surveyed Zahad with open curiosity. "What's it like being a sheikh?"

Her foolish question accomplished what neither Lew Blackwell nor Jenny had. It showed Zahad the wisdom of making a quick exit.

"It is most entertaining," he told her. "Good day to you both."

On a Tuesday morning, the town lay quiet and almost devoid of pedestrians. The small shops across Lake Avenue from the school had not yet opened. No one appeared to be coming or going from the police station down the way or from the lodge where Zahad had stayed until a few days ago.

In his pocket, the cell phone rang. He answered it en route to his car.

Before he could speak, a man said ominously, "There is going to be blood on the sand."

A chill ran through Zahad. His waking thought returned: *Someone is going to die today.* And he had dreamed of Death on the prowl.

Nonsense. He didn't believe in bad omens. "Hello?" he said.

"Sorry. I did not realize you had picked up." This time, he recognized the voice as Sharif's.

"What did you mean about blood?" he asked.

"I did not mean that literally. I was commenting to my aide," his cousin said. "Hashim's latest ploy is demanding that the justices in Yazir hold immediate hearings into the possibility that you killed your brother and are compromising the investigation in California."

In addition to presiding at trials, the justices formed a panel that served as the equivalent of a grand jury. Although they were appointed by the governor, once in office they operated independently.

"Hashim has become crazed with ambition." Perhaps so crazed that he had killed Fario in the first place? Zahad wondered. "Is Numa also seeking this madness?"

"She does not object. She is convinced that you assassinated her son and must be punished."

Zahad leaned against his car, the phone to his ear. "It would help if I could produce a testimonial from the local police detective. Unfortunately, he does not like me and objects to my inquiries." Remembering the difficulties Sharif's wife was suffering, he added, "How is Holly?"

"Much better. I will be able to go in person to represent you on Saturday in Jeddar," Sharif said. "However, I cannot be in two places at once, and it seems there is trouble also in Yazir."

"Have the justices agreed to hold the hearings?"

"Not yet but, according to Amy, they are nervous. They fear that if Hashim replaces you, he will find a way to exact revenge on anyone who stood against him."

"I am leaving here Thursday morning. Perhaps it must be sooner." He regretted losing one last night with Jenny, but there was too much at stake for him to delay. "How is Amy taking this?"

"She is furious at Hashim," Sharif replied. "She muttered something about taking matters into her own hands, which is why I fear there may be blood on the sand, figuratively speaking."

"I will call her. Thank you, Sharif."

"We shall prevail," his cousin said. "Hopefully, any blood that is spilled will belong to that worm, Hashim."

He expressed no such dire wishes about Numa. In her grief, she could not be held entirely responsible for her actions, Zahad reflected as he said farewell and dialed Amy's number.

A busy signal echoed in his ear. He waited a minute and tried again, with the same result. He would have to call Amy later.

Debating whether to change his airline reservation reminded him that it would be best if he could fulfill his original mission and return with his brother's body. He looked up the number of the coroner's office in his pocket organizer.

"I was about to call you," the deputy said when he came on the line. "Mr. Adran's body is ready to be released. What would you like us to do?"

"I have made arrangements with the Mountain Lake Funeral Parlor. I will telephone them at once."

"Sounds good to me."

The funeral home promised to embalm the body and ship it to Alqedar as quickly as possible. "I'm not sure how long it will take to obtain the necessary permits," the funeral director said. "We've never transferred anyone to your country before."

"I hope we can travel on the same flight. I have reservations from the local airport on Thursday morning. However, I must change that to Wednesday night."

"I should think so. They've moved up the forecast for that big storm. You'll barely make it out in time." The director offered to have his wife, a travel agent, coordinate their plans, and Zahad agreed.

"If you encounter any difficulties in paperwork, please inform me at once. I have connections in my homeland."

"Of course." The director cleared his throat. "The death of Sheikh Adran is a great loss. We will do our best to make sure he goes quickly—I mean, that the process goes quickly."

"Thank you." While clicking off, Zahad noticed that his fingers had gone stiff. The reference to death in connection with his own name and title—which of course had also been Fario's—was disconcerting.

He tried to dismiss his sense that this was yet another omen. Although many of his people believed in the significance of dreams, signs and portents, Zahad did not. The idea of destiny was another matter, but he didn't see it as something to fear.

If it was his destiny to die today, then so be it. Death held no terrors as long as he met it with honor and dignity. Yet it would be hard on Jenny and Beth, as well as on his cousins.

It would be tragic for his people also, or so he believed. Yet Zahad had reluctantly begun to wonder whether he was beating his head against a brick wall.

In the two years since his father's death, he had worked diligently on his tribe's behalf, keeping a low profile to avoid diminishing his brother. He had declined opportunities to take a position in the country's central government, instead devoting his efforts to building up his province's infrastructure.

Yet now that he was assailed on all sides, he saw no signs of loyalty to him among the common people. Although the cowardice of the justices infuriated him and he resented President Dourad's willingness to consider replacing him in such haste, the deepest cut came from the silence of his own countrymen.

Perhaps they didn't want to modernize. Perhaps they preferred to let themselves be led by his father's second wife and her opportunistic nephew. If they were so easily swayed by rumors, so quick to think the worst of Zahad, how could he count on their support in the years to come?

Troubled, the sheikh drove back to Jenny's house. He had only one more day to clear his name of Fario's murder and must make good use of it.

After parking, he went directly to the toolshed. Although last night's intruder hadn't managed to break in, something inside this building would likely hint at why he had returned.

He input the lock's combination and opened the creaking door. Through a large, low-set window with a warped frame, daylight played over a clutter of equipment and tools.

Nothing had changed from his last inspection five days before, except for the appearance of a few more spiderwebs. Traces of fingerprint powder remained from the initial police investigation.

What had the man been seeking?

The problem wasn't a lack of murder weapons but an abundance of them. Zahad dismissed the possibility of the killer planning to use an inefficient blunt-force weapon such as a shovel, given the lengths to which he'd gone to rig the gun device. Nor was he likely to select something as noisy and clumsy as the lawn mower or Rototiller.

There remained plenty of choices, however. A gasoline can held fuel for the mower and tiller. A row of shelves offered a selection of fertilizers, pesticides and weed killers. Long-handled implements hung from a rack along one wall.

Or had the man sought to erase a clue rather than to steal a weapon? The police had missed that scrap of paper in the house, so they might have overlooked something here as well, and he himself had given the toolshed only a cursory inspection on Thursday. A half hour's search, however, left Zahad with nothing more than dirty hands and a slight cough from the dust.

He emerged into a sharp breeze. After refastening the lock, he stopped at a startling sight.

In the western sky towered a black-edged cloud formation. The shape looked remarkably like a robed figure wielding a sword.

It held steady for only a few seconds. Then the wind shattered the weapon and dismembered the figure.

Zahad continued to stare at the jumbled clouds, disturbed. He had seen this shape last night in his dream. Phrases he had heard that day echoed in his mind. *Blood on the sand…the death of Sheikh Adran…we will make sure he goes quickly.*

Perhaps it was a warning after all. He had always known he might be the killer's next target, but it had made little difference in his investigation.

Now, however, he must consider that someone from Alqedar might wish to get rid of him. There was also the unnamed neighbor who had complained about him to Sergeant Finley. Perhaps his questions were hitting too close to home.

Sternly, he reminded himself of his training. The greatest enemy was one's own imagination. He must take all reasonable precautions and proceed with his probe. Above all, he must not allow emotion to rule his judgment.

Nevertheless, when Zahad unlocked the back door and eased it open, the warning chirp of the alarm gave him a start. Tautly, he entered the code.

Inside, he sat down to run background checks on the neighbors through his Internet service. That, he decided, was the logical next step, and he was determined to spend the rest of the day being very logical indeed.

ALTHOUGH CRISTMAS VACATION was two weeks away, the school took on a holiday air as students and teachers posted winter-theme artwork and poems in the hallways. Laughter and cheerful conversations created a music more pleasing to Jenny's ears than any choral concert.

Shortly after the children left for the day, Parker phoned from the municipal courthouse to tell her Grant had pleaded guilty at his arraignment on charges of attempted breaking and entering and carrying a weapon. He'd accepted a sentence of six months in county jail followed by three years' probation, which he could serve in St. Louis. While on probation, he would be allowed to return to Mountain Lake once a month for court-supervised visits with Beth.

"Judging by the way his wife was haranguing him afterward, she wants to keep him as far away from you and Beth as possible," Parker said. "It sounds like they may pass on those visits."

Jenny had mixed feelings. The less contact with her ex-husband, the better for her, but Beth needed a father. "That's up to them. I'm not going to stand between my daughter and Grant if he wants to maintain their relationship."

"Are you all right?" the detective inquired. "You've had a lot on your plate this past week."

"It hasn't all hit me yet," Jenny admitted. "I'm trying to take things one step at a time."

As if he'd just thought of it, Parker asked, "By the way, when is Mr. Adran leaving? I heard they released his brother's body."

"They did?" Jenny tried to tell herself that it made no difference, because Zahad had already scheduled his departure. But subconsciously, she realized, she'd been hoping he might delay. "He made reservations for Thursday morning."

"If you like, you and Beth can stay at my house until we get this thing cleared up. I'll lend you my room. I don't mind sleeping on the couch."

Jenny felt she should refuse. But was that sensible? She still hadn't spent a night alone at her house since the murder and she didn't look forward to it. And, after all, Parker had a live-in housekeeper, so there'd be another adult on the premises. "I'll think about it. Thank you. It's a very kind offer."

"Sure thing," he said, and rang off.

Jenny tried to concentrate on some paperwork, but her thoughts kept returning to what had happened between her and Zahad last night. It gave her a thrill to remember the pressure of his mouth and the glide of his skin over hers.

If only they had days or weeks to explore all the magical things that could develop between them. Not years or even months; she wasn't that unrealistic. Well, at least they had another two nights.

A knock at the open office door roused her from these musings. She glanced up and saw Lew Blackwell. "Come on in."

When he crossed toward her, she noticed a new energy to his stride. His smile seemed broader than usual, too, although she also caught a hint of regret in his expression.

He handed Jenny an envelope and took a seat facing her. "I'll save you the trouble of opening it. It's my resignation."

She blinked, taken aback. "You're leaving us? Lew, if it's anything I did…"

"No, no." He seemed completely at ease. "As a matter of fact, I want to thank you."

"For what?" She'd declined his romantic interest and

trumped him for the job as school principal. He'd responded with unexpected generosity in loaning her his cabin. She was the one who ought to be thanking him.

"For lighting a fire under me," the teacher said. "I'd completed the coursework for my Ph.D. but never finished my dissertation. I figured I didn't really need it, until you knocked me for a loop. Getting beaten by you was the best thing that ever happened to me."

She leaned back in her chair. "You're actually glad you lost the job?"

"Ironic, isn't it? If you hadn't come to Mountain Lake, I'd probably be right where you are now. And I'd still be there next year and the year after that and so on until what's left of my hair falls out and I'm ready for retirement."

Jenny chuckled. "What a grim picture!"

"Absolutely right. Instead, I finished the dissertation."

After receiving his doctorate, he explained, he'd applied for an opening as assistant superintendent of a school district near San Diego. He'd just learned he got the job, and would start after the late-January winter break. "It'll be good for me to move to an urban area, meet new people and face new challenges. I got lazy here."

"Congratulations." She was genuinely pleased for him but also sorry to see him go. And, in a way she couldn't put her finger on, a bit envious, as well.

After he left, Jenny sat trying to figure out why his departure left her so unsettled. Although she was going to miss Lew, this had more to do with her own feelings about her career, she decided.

Until the last few days, she'd never realized how much she wanted a broader scope for her efforts. Much as she enjoyed her job here, she longed for a chance to help a larger number of students with greater needs. As a single mother, however, she knew it would be many years before she was in a position to work on a doctorate.

Seeing Zahad's concern for his people had opened her

eyes. Now Lew, too, had whetted her appetite for a greater challenge.

It was, she feared, going to be a long time coming.

DURING DINNER, Zahad listened for sounds from the yard. He found it hard to concentrate on Beth's and Jenny's account of their day at school and to make casual conversation suitable for a child's company. He mentioned running background checks but, catching a warning look from Jenny, postponed giving her the details.

Halfway through the meal, it occurred to him he'd forgotten to call Amy again. Since it was now the middle of the night in Alqedar, that would have to wait.

After dinner, the doorbell rang. Motioning to his two companions to stay in the kitchen, he answered it himself.

It was Dolly, Ellen and Cindy, going for a walk. They'd come to invite Beth to accompany them, they explained when she and Jenny appeared.

"Ellen has some cosmetics to drop off at Tish's house," the older woman said. For Zahad's benefit, she added, "She sells them on the side. Anyway, it's nice brisk weather and we all decided to take a walk. Then we'll go back to Ellen's and have some hot chocolate."

"Please, please, can I go?" Beth begged.

Jenny looked to Zahad. "Do you think it's a good idea?"

"I believe it will be fine." He couldn't keep the child locked up and, in fact, since the killer was most likely targeting either him or Jenny, Beth might be safer away from the house.

"All right," Jenny told the women. "Give me a call when you return to the house, okay? I want to pick her up before it gets too late."

"We will," Ellen promised.

Bundled up and hopping with excitement, the little girl went off with them. Jenny made decaf coffee, and she and Zahad settled in the living room to catch up on the day's more serious events.

He took pleasure in the graceful way her hands curved around the coffee cup as she described Grant's plea bargain and told him of Lew's imminent departure for greener pastures. It seemed that Parker had also informed her about Fario's release.

"The funeral director believes his body can be shipped tomorrow night. With the storm forecast, I have changed my reservation."

"You're leaving on Wednesday?"

"A little after 9:00 p.m."

"I'm sorry." Green depths glinted in her eyes and she stared into her cup.

Zahad felt his own eyes sting. "I am, also."

He felt that there should be something more to say or do, an acknowledgment of what had passed between them and of the bond that had grown. There must be conventions to help a man and woman deal with such moments, facing a separation that might be permanent. Should he promise to write—but if so, what good would it do? Should he invite her to visit, when he knew she never would?

It was beyond him to put a good face on the need to say goodbye. He did not have the temperament or the social graces to smooth over this painful end to something precious. Having spent most of his adult life preparing for war and dealing with its aftermath, he had never learned how to deal with the subtler sorrows of peacetime.

And so, when he saw Jenny's lips tremble, he didn't offer comfort. Indeed, he had none to give her.

Outside, the wind picked up. Tree branches lashed the air. From the direction of the Rivases' house, Zahad heard someone gunning an engine. As a precaution, he went to the window, but he could see nothing in the deepening darkness.

"That must be Ray. He's always working on that car." Jenny came to stand beside him.

"I assume it is a hobby, since they have two operational vehicles." Zahad fingered the silken lightness of her hair.

Jenny caught her breath but made no move to return the caress. "It's a classic. He swears it will be worth a lot of money when he gets done."

Zahad could not resist touching her again. He laid his arm lightly around her waist, hoping she would not mind.

To his satisfaction, she swayed toward him. A slight shift and she was in his arms, her face upturned, her lips parting. Savoring the moment, he lowered his mouth to hers.

She kissed him fully, her tongue exploring his teeth and her arms winding about his neck. At once he was ready for her, but, unwilling to hurry their tenderness, he ran his hands along her hips as he nuzzled her cheek and neck.

A loud crunch resounding from outside startled them both. Instinctively, he released her and turned. Still he could make out nothing through the glass.

"I hope he didn't hit the retaining wall again," Jenny said.

"You mean Ray?"

She nodded. "One time the brakes failed while he was backing out and he hit that low wall. He spent a fortune for a new bumper on eBay."

"A fortune?" Zahad said. "I wonder if he truly cares whether he turns a profit or whether he simply enjoys the process. It seems to me there are more worthwhile ways to use one's spare time. In fact, we have hit upon one ourselves, have we not?"

"I..." Jenny wavered indecisively. Zahad hoped she would ease back into his arms, but instead she retreated. "We'll have to go get Beth soon."

"Yes, of course." He swallowed his disappointment. "Tell me what you learned today. You said you ran background checks."

"There was nothing definitive. My service filled in a few interesting details, that is all."

From a police standpoint, the neighbors were a relatively clean bunch, Zahad explained. Bill had a drunk-driving conviction from six years ago, and the police in Big Bear had arrested, but later released, both Tish and Al eight months earlier for engaging in mutual combat during a squabble at a restaurant. In addition, their credit reports were a mess, although they'd paid off quite a few bills recently.

"I'm sorry to hear they fight so much," Jenny said. "That doesn't bode well for their marriage."

"They do not strike me as a happy couple," Zahad agreed. "It might help if they had a large family nearby, as we do in Alqedar. The older men would counsel the husband, and the women would heap advice upon the wife. They might make peace simply to avoid being inundated with tender concern."

She smiled, but her smile faded quickly. Outside, a branch hit the side of the house as the wind stirred again.

Jenny checked her watch. "I hope Beth's on her way back. She needed to let off steam but…"

From the direction of the Rivases' house, a woman's scream tore through the air. The heart-stopping cry came again, filled with anguish.

"Beth!" Jenny cried. "Oh, please don't let anything have happened to her."

The two of them ran for their coats. Why had he been so fixated on himself? Zahad wondered in disgust. Why had he let the little girl go outside when all day portents had signaled that someone was going to die?

He barely remembered to switch on the alarm and lock the door as they exited. Jenny was already racing ahead of him along the path, desperately calling her daughter's name.

Chapter Fifteen

The night was pitch-dark, with only faint illumination from overhead, and the flashlight in Jenny's hand revealed little as she raced up the path. The cold air burned her lungs and she stumbled twice before slowing.

Zahad's long strides devoured the ground, and he caught up with her quickly. Although she didn't spare the time to acknowledge him, she was grateful for his presence.

As they hurried along side by side, she struggled against panic. Surely Beth wasn't injured. No one would want to hurt her. Something else must have happened.

Whatever it was, it must have been terrible. That scream had made the hair on Jenny's arms stand on end.

They rounded the carport and got their first clear view of the driveway. In the glare of exterior lights, she saw Ray's old car sitting outside the garage. There was no one in sight.

"Ray?" she called. "Is anyone here?" Maybe he'd gone in search of the woman who'd screamed.

The sheikh extended one arm to halt her close to the carport. "Do not put yourself in danger by rushing in," he said in a low voice.

"I have to find out..."

"It may be a trap."

A trap. In Jenny's mind this phrase triggered a terrifying image of the gun as it must have looked rigged in her living room. In her anxiety over Beth, she never would have thought of that. Had the killer lured them here by screaming? If not for Zahad, she'd have rushed forward heedlessly.

But where was Beth? And Ray and everyone else?

Motioning to her to stay put, Zahad eased toward the classic car, which looked odd to Jenny sitting right out in the open. It didn't appear damaged, however, at least not the part that she could see. So apparently Ray hadn't backed it into the retaining wall.

In advancing, the sheikh wove from side to side as if expecting to be shot at. Jenny scanned the area. It was eerie how threatening a familiar setting could seem, she thought, and shivered.

From the direction of the street, she heard girlish voices heading her way. Ellen entered the diffused brightness first, blinking as she called out, "Mom? Where are you?"

"Grandma!" Cindy seconded.

"Mrs. Blankenship!" Beth trailed her friend into the light.

Relief washed through Jenny. Her little girl was safe! For that instant, she didn't care what danger might lurk. She flew across the driveway and gathered Beth close.

The child giggled and hugged her back. "Hi, Mommy."

Cutting short his advance, the sheikh turned to them and positioned himself in front of the women. To Ellen, he said, "We heard a scream. We must make certain it is not a trap."

"We heard it, too. It sounded like Mom," she replied worriedly.

"Why isn't she with you?" Jenny asked.

"She decided to go home to check on Bill. He wasn't feeling well. The girls and I were just leaving Tish's when we heard her." Ellen stared past them. "Why's the car sitting there?"

"Get back!" Zahad grabbed Beth and hauled her to the side of the house, behind cover. "There's someone in the garage."

"Of course there is," Ellen said, following slowly. "It's Ray. Why are you acting like this?"

"We're taking precautions," Jenny answered. "Welcome to my world. This is how it's been for the past week."

"It's Mom." Ellen pointed to the woman coming out of the garage. She moved stiffly as if in shock.

"Don't go in there," she told Ellen.

"Is Ray all right?" her daughter demanded.

There was no answer.

"Mom! Tell me Ray's okay."

Dolly shook her head. Tear tracks stained her ruddy cheeks.

"What happened?" Ellen started to cry, too. "Come on, Mom."

Her mother released a long breath. "I was crossing the street when I heard a crash. The car must have shifted into gear while he was working on it. It…" She swallowed hard. "It pinned him. I backed it out, but I was too late."

That must have been the source of the crash, Jenny thought in dismay. The car had struck the inside of the garage. Ray must have been crushed.

"Call the paramedics," Ellen said shakily.

"I already did," Dolly replied. "I'm sure the police will come, too. Jenny, would you please take the children inside?"

"Of course." She shepherded the youngsters in from the cold. Her relief at finding her daughter safe had been replaced by wrenching sympathy for Ellen.

Despite the turmoil in their marriage, Jenny knew Ellen and Ray had loved each other. She couldn't imagine building a life with a man and losing him so abruptly.

In the distance, sirens wailed. Jenny was becoming sick of that sound.

"Let's have hot chocolate," she told the girls. "I'll put marshmallows in it if I can find some."

They needed a distraction. Cindy would need much more than that in the days ahead, but it was all Jenny had to offer right now.

ZAHAD WAS RELIEVED that Jenny didn't have to see Ray's shattered body where the car had smashed him against the back of the garage, and Dolly resolutely kept her daughter away from the scene, as well. There was no hope of saving him. The paramedics called ahead to the coroner to meet them at the hospital.

Despite the possibility that it had been an accident, Sergeant Finley brought in his crime-scene technicians and secured the area. Although no one had heard a car start on the street or seen anyone else nearby, he sent patrolmen to comb the neighborhood.

Finley ordered Jenny and the girls out of the house so it could be searched. He seemed inclined to take everyone to the police station for questioning, but Ellen was sobbing uncontrollably and Cindy was becoming more upset by the minute. After talking to another detective, a fellow named Rygel, he relented and allowed the witnesses to be questioned in the police cars and at Dolly's house.

As the night wore on, each of them submitted to a separate interview. Since she had found the body, Dolly underwent two interviews, before and after the others. By the time she emerged from Finley's car the second time, she was fuming.

"I don't understand why you keep asking me all that stuff about Ellen," she told the detective as they stood in her driveway. Zahad, who'd come outside to check out the source of some mechanical noise, was staring downhill toward the Rivases' house, where a tow truck had hoisted the classic car onto a flatbed. "She was at Tish's house when this happened. She'd never have hurt Ray, anyway."

"Dolly, you know she was jealous," Finley said. "It can't be any secret to you that she suspected Ray of having an affair."

"She has an alibi for tonight and you know it!"

"I grant you that, but his death isn't the only case I'm working on. Hank and I were on our way here to serve a search warrant when we heard your call."

"What?" Dolly shook her head as if she must have misheard. "A search warrant for what?"

"You know I can't discuss my investigation. I've already said more than I should."

"Parker Finley, she's my daughter!"

"Which is why you shouldn't hear this," he told her. "By the way, she needs to find somewhere else to sleep tonight. She might be able to get back in the house tomorrow, but the garage will still be off limits."

"They can spend the night at my place," Dolly said. "May I at least pack some of Cindy's clothes and her favorite doll?"

"I'm afraid I can't let anyone in the house yet."

She regarded him with distinct displeasure, Zahad saw when he glanced their way. "Well, all right. But whatever you're looking for, remember that Ellen just lost her husband. Cut her some slack."

"I have to follow procedure," Finley replied doggedly. "I'll give you a list of whatever we take. We'll need her computer."

"She uses that to earn a living!"

"I have to do what I have to do." He obviously didn't like being in this position. "Speaking of which, you'll have to excuse me. I've got a search to conduct."

"Go ahead," Dolly said. "The sooner you start, the sooner you'll finish."

Zahad registered the fact that the search warrant involved the computer. That might mean they believed Ellen to be the cyber-stalker. They must have had some fairly credible evidence to persuade a judge.

Mentally, he connected the dots. Yesterday, Ronald Wang had informed the detective about Fario's phone conversation with a woman. Finley must have searched the phone records of any woman known to dislike Jenny. Tish and Ellen both fit that description.

A call from this house to Fario's number would provide enough evidence to justify a warrant. Still, even if Ellen was the stalker, that didn't make her his brother's killer. And she obviously hadn't killed Ray.

Zahad wished he could figure out how everything fit together. He had the sense that either he was missing some key point or they might be dealing with more than one murderer.

The door opened and Jenny came down the steps from Dolly's house, her coat only half-buttoned. "I need to talk to Parker."

"He's down there." Zahad indicated the Rivases' house.

"I just thought of something I forgot to mention in my interview." She looked so cold with the wind whipping her hair that Zahad wanted to draw her against him to warm her up. Such a public gesture would be inappropriate, however.

"Who's watching the girls?" Dolly asked. "Don't tell me it's Ellen. She's in no shape to take care of anyone."

"They're sleeping and Bill's keeping an eye on things," Jenny replied. "He's trying to help in his curmudgeonly way. He does seem weak, though."

"Well, he's no Hercules, but he could roust everyone if an earthquake hit," Dolly said. "What did you remember?"

"It's cold out here," she said. "I want to go explain it to Parker."

The three of them trooped down the hill. The sergeant didn't look pleased to see them until Jenny explained the reason she'd come.

"On Sunday at Ellen's house, I mentioned the slip of paper Zahad found, the one with the logo from the Crystal Point bank," she said. "Ray suggested he snoop through people's accounts and see if anything funny was going on. I think he regarded it as kind of a game."

"That's right," Dolly said. "He was speculating about a hired killer, that he might have deposited his payoff in one lump sum."

Zahad hadn't heard this before, and judging by the way Finley's eyes narrowed, it was news to him, also. "Who else was there?" the detective asked.

"Ellen, Dolly, Bill, me and the Garroways," Jenny said.

Dolly wrapped her arms around herself. "What a stupid thing. He'd never have really done it. Please don't tell me he got killed over that!"

Finley made notes on a pad. "You're sure no one else was present?"

"Just the two girls," Jenny answered.

He tucked the notebook in his pocket. "Thanks. This could be useful."

"Do you require our presence any further?" Zahad asked.

He gave a sideways shake of the head. "I'd suggest you people get some rest."

Zahad didn't argue. He went with Jenny to collect Beth, who nestled against his shoulder on the walk home. When he lowered her into bed, she immediately fell asleep.

"Thank you," Jenny said as they went into the hall.

"It was no trouble."

"I didn't mean for carrying her." She tipped her forehead against his chest. "For being here. For being you. For keeping me sane."

When Zahad enfolded her against his heart, a warmth stole through him. He allowed himself to luxuriate in an unfamiliar sense of peace and wholeness.

"A part of myself exists only with you," he murmured. "The happy part."

Jenny gazed up at him. "I feel like we're living in a magic bubble with evil all around. What will I do when you leave?" She stepped back and with her hands made a little gesture of frustration. "Don't mind me. It's late."

"I am accustomed to death. You are not." But that

wasn't the point, he thought as he took her hand. The point was that he belonged here.

The impossible had happened. He'd fallen in love, and Jenny loved him back. Yet she was right: They *were* living in a bubble, and it was bound to break. He could even name the day and time: tomorrow, Wednesday, at 9:12 p.m., when his flight took off from Crystal Point Airport.

Zahad didn't like to think about what lay ahead for him in Alqedar or the cloudy future he would face if he were removed as head of Yazir Province. Yet if that happened, he would eventually find some other battle to fight, some other cause to live or die for. But he would never again find someone to love this deeply.

Jenny gave him a rueful smile. "It's hard to believe I've got to be at work in just a few hours. I'd better get some sleep."

"Indeed," he said.

Slowly she removed her hand from his. There was no need for additional words.

Once she had retreated, the sheikh sat in his room reviewing everything that had happened, beginning with Fario's murder. He kept trying to put the pieces together, hoping everything would fit into a pattern.

Something nagged at the back of his mind but he couldn't pinpoint it. Was it something from tonight or from his background checks on the neighbors? Or was it something Ron Wang had said?

The answer eluded him. Perhaps his thoughts tomorrow would become clearer. Zahad hoped so, because tomorrow was all he had left.

ON WEDNESDAY MORNING, he followed Jenny and Beth to school. Zahad had just pulled out of the parking lot when the point he'd been seeking popped into his head.

According to their credit reports, Al and Tish Garroway had paid off a number of bills during the past three months.

Yet Al had complained that neither of them was earning as much in Mountain Lake as they'd expected.

Where had the money come from?

At the next light, Zahad made a U-turn and headed back toward the police station, debating with himself the whole way. Three months ago seemed rather early for anyone to have received a payoff to commit murder. The cyber-stalking hadn't even started until six weeks later.

However, the timing corresponded with the onset of the carjackings. Until the patrols grew heavier, the perpetrators had targeted the ski area where the Garroways worked. They'd certainly been aware that tourists with bulging wallets frequented the area. On the other hand, Tish herself had fallen victim.

At the station, Zahad learned that Finley was out, so he spoke with Detective Rygel. The black-haired man, whom he judged to be in his early thirties, listened intently. "Why did you run a credit check on Al and Tish Garroway?" the detective inquired after taking notes.

"In my country, being a sheikh involves functioning somewhat like a CEO," Zahad said. "I subscribe to an Internet service to run background checks on prospective employees."

"The Garroways want to work for you?"

"I ran checks on all the neighbors. Someone killed my brother. If there are clues in their backgrounds, I wished to find them."

"Parker told me you'd been poking around." The detective regarded him with reluctant approval. "I have to admit, I didn't much like the idea, but this information is worth looking into."

They parted on amicable terms. Although he hadn't shed any light on Fario's death, Zahad mused as he drove home, if he had helped the police to crack the carjacking ring, at least they would have more time to devote to the murders.

But that didn't mean they would solve them in time to protect Jenny.

Uneasily, he recalled the nocturnal break-in attempt at her shed. Whatever the killer had been seeking, it didn't appear to have figured into Ray's death. Had he simply changed his plans and seized the opportunity to use Ray's car as a murder weapon or was he planning an additional crime?

The original target of the slaying might have been Jenny. If so, the killer wasn't likely to stop until he got her.

Zahad couldn't bear to think of her and Beth alone in the house. He might have asked Dolly to stay with them, but she had her hands full with a grieving daughter and grand-daughter.

As he drove along Pine Forest Road, he found himself considering something he once would have dismissed out of hand. He could delay his return and simply let matters fall where they might in Alqedar. If Amy and Sharif were able to stave off the attacks on him, fine. If not, perhaps it was time he set his sights elsewhere.

Zahad didn't delude himself into assuming he and Jenny could build a future together. It might be possible, but even if he were to remain in the United States, it might not. They both had independent natures and vastly different back-grounds.

But he wanted very much to keep her safe. As for the people of Yazir, he'd risked his life to free them and had struggled for the past two years to serve them, and what was their response? Indifference, at best.

At the house, after a quick security check, Zahad entered through the rear door. Warm air redolent of coffee and baby powder triggered delicious memories of Jenny and Beth. Their scents and smiles and voices overlaid the emptiness of the house and filled the void inside him.

He would stay and protect them, no matter what it cost.

Opening his cell phone, he dialed Amy's number. He had intended to call her today in any event, and she had a right to know of his change of heart. He hoped she would not take it hard.

She answered on the first ring. The instant she heard his voice, she said excitedly, "You should see this! You're not going to believe it."

"What?"

"I'm looking out my office window." Located on the upper floor of the palace, it had a view that extended past a freestanding perimeter wall and all the way to the market square. "Half the province is marching in the streets. You'd need a bulldozer to get into the town center."

"What do they want?" Zahad asked in alarm. If Numa and Hashim had brought civil war to Yazir, they would set back his public-works plans and devastate the economy.

"Didn't Sharif tell you?"

"Evidently not."

"I organized a little protest," Amy explained.

"A little protest?"

"Well, maybe not so little."

"You did this?" he asked, unsure how to react. "Amy, what's going on?"

"I figured the people have a right to decide what happens to their province."

There had never been a widespread protest in Yazir before. Zahad hoped she hadn't started something that would careen out of control. "Perhaps Hashim stirred them up."

"No way," she told him. "I run the Web site. And then there's Radio Yazir. They gave me fifteen minutes this morning for my spiel." One of Zahad's first actions had been to restore a long-neglected radio station and staff it with energetic young residents. It broadcast local programming for two hours daily.

"Tell me what you said." He sank into the desk chair, trying to absorb this turn of events.

"I reminded them of everything you've done and told them about your plans for the future. I made it clear that Hashim doesn't care about them, he just wants power. I said that if they don't make their opinions known, they can expect more of the same neglect they've endured in the past.''

"You did not speak ill of my father or brother, I hope." Much as he appreciated her support, Zahad wouldn't be party to blackening their names.

"I didn't mention them or Numa, either," Amy said. "People can draw their own conclusions. The citizens aren't stupid. They understand what's going on. Well, at least they do now."

"Now that you've leveled with them." He should have done so himself, Zahad thought. He'd assumed they would follow the lead of the foremost families, as they always had, but he'd been wrong. His cousin, who wasn't even a native of Yazir, had trusted them more than he had.

"Well, you should see them now," Amy crowed. "The market's pulsing with people waving signs and chanting. Hashim went out a while ago to try to talk to them, and they shook their fists in his face and chased him back to the palace."

"What do the signs say?" Zahad was starting to grin.

"I don't want to give you a swelled head." She clicked her tongue. "Oh, all right. One of them says, Zahad! Rightful Leader. Then there's, Zahad, Yes! Hashim, Never! And We Will Fight to Keep Our Sheikh. I didn't write that slogan."

"You wrote the others?" He chuckled at her audacity.

"Well, sure. Oh, wait, there's a new one. Our Hearts Belong to Zahad. I swear, that one isn't mine."

"Are you certain you are not exaggerating for my sake? Did you pay any of them?"

"Certainly not! And Radio Yazir just estimated the crowd at ten thousand. It's broadcasting overtime. I can't see them all from here. Apparently they're spilling in from the countryside."

"Ten thousand?"

"You bet!"

It was unheard of. The province's entire population did

not surpass thirty thousand. Even allowing for wishful thinking on the part of the broadcasters, this was an impressive showing.

Over the years, without realizing it, Zahad had developed an outsider's mentality. Accustomed to struggling in the background with little recognition, he'd never expected to be popular. His spirits soared.

"You have done a wonderful thing," he said.

"You're the star of the show. Everyone wants to see you," Amy said. "When are you getting back?"

"By Friday," he replied. It would take that long, factoring in the international flight and the time difference. "Amy, I can never thank you enough."

"I just lit the fuse. You're the one who built the bomb. Wait. I didn't put that very well."

"I got the point. Thank you."

"You're going to knock 'em dead," his cousin told him. "I'll bet Hashim's packing his suitcase now."

"Let us hope so." As they said farewell, he was already eager to return.

Hashim would never be able to govern the province now. Neither, Zahad suspected, would anyone chosen by Numa.

Never had he imagined his soul could feel so torn, joyful and anxiety-filled at the same time. Yet his path was clear. He must not put personal happiness before his duty to his countrymen. Other warriors, including his cousin Sharif, had lost people they loved while engaged in battle. Zahad hoped it would not come to that for Jenny, but beyond any question, he must return to Alqedar.

He had a suitcase to pack.

Chapter Sixteen

Jenny usually ate in the school cafeteria. However, as Wednesday was her last chance to be alone with Zahad, she took off for a longer-than-normal lunch break after calling to inform him that she was on her way home.

When she came through the door, he gathered her close. They scarcely needed to speak. What she craved was the feel of his hair beneath her fingers, his mouth covering hers, and more…

They left a trail of clothes en route to her room. By the time they reached the bed, they were naked. They barely stopped to use the protection Zahad produced.

He made love to her with all the fierceness of a desert warrior and the tenderness of a man who adored her. But Jenny didn't wish to think about emotions. There was a comfort in the reality of his body entering hers and the intense physical connection they forged.

She knew her future was not meant to include him. So she wanted as much as she could get in the present. And the present had condensed into a few stolen minutes of pleasure so keen it verged on pain.

As she writhed against Zahad, Jenny tried to imprint in her consciousness every detail of him. She relished the way his muscles shifted and his hands caressed her hips. She absorbed his scent and the deep groans issuing from his throat.

She let his fire roar through her. And when the flames began to die, she rolled on top in a sheen of sweat and aroused him all over again.

Zahad reached up and kissed her, completing the circuit. Exquisite sensations arced through Jenny at his thrusting. They rode each other in a white sizzle of electric longing until it blazed to an end. Breathing fast and in counterpoint, they sank into a damp tangle of sheets.

This man, a stranger less than a week ago, now seemed as familiar as her own image in the mirror, Jenny mused as she gazed at him. His scars, his broad shoulders, his angular face filled her days and played through her dreams until she felt she must have known him for years.

She wished they could stretch time. But already the clock on the headboard insistently returned her to reality.

"I have to go back to work." She sat up, fighting the languor of her body.

"I know." He traced the swollen tip of her nipple. "I wish I could stay here longer."

She wasn't about to dwell on impossible hopes. "We both knew we'd have to say goodbye. I hope you can win your battles at home, Zahad."

"Perhaps I already have." He told her about the protests spreading through Yazir.

"I'm pleased for you," Jenny said. "And I'm glad for your people. It must be marvelous to know they appreciate you."

"More than I realized."

She washed up and dressed. As she was leaving, Jenny paused in the bedroom doorway. Zahad lay uncovered except for a sheet thrown over his midsection. When he saw her, his smile lit up the room.

"I'll see you at dinner." It seemed inadequate after what had passed between them, but Jenny couldn't linger.

"I will buy some ice cream for Beth," he offered.

"She'll like that."

Her skin tingled in the cold air as she hurried to her SUV.

She felt alive and full of hope, although she wasn't sure what she hoped for.

It sobered her to remember that last night Ellen had lost her husband. Jenny wished she could find a way to prepare for what life had in store, but she knew better than to ask for the impossible. Who could have predicted the shape events had taken these past ten days, for any of them?

Only the killer.

Yet, as she drove back to town, she discovered that she didn't feel nearly as afraid as she once had. The discovery that she could love a man more profoundly than she'd ever imagined possible and yet find the strength to face the future without him had somehow armored her.

Since childhood, Jenny had battled the instinct to quail before a man's anger. After her marriage ended, she'd withdrawn from men as a defense against their attempts to dominate her.

What she'd also been fighting, she saw now, was her need for intimacy and her fear of rejection. The freedom to give love and receive Zahad's love without strings had liberated her.

Jenny realized her physical safety might be at risk in the days ahead. Yet her old wounds had healed, and she'd heard that scars were stronger than the bare skin they replaced.

She drove back to school and, despite her lack of sleep the night before, finished the day with her head held high.

ALTHOUGH ZAHAD HAD FACED death many times during the war of liberation, at least he had been driven by a single, unified purpose. Preparing to leave that night, he felt torn in two directions. In some ways, leaving was the hardest thing he had ever done.

Together, he and Jenny prepared oven-fried fish for dinner, served with sesame noodles and French bread. Beth helped make a salad. Gleefully, she tossed in handfuls of chocolate chips and coconut.

There was a homespun magic in the way the three of

them moved comfortably around each other in the kitchen. At one point, Jenny gave Beth a little hug, and a few minutes later the child repaid the favor to Zahad. He swung her up and, after a mischievous exchange of looks, he and Jenny kissed the little girl on opposite cheeks at the same time. Beth giggled and wiggled until they did it again.

They were becoming a family. How ironic that he had found these two special people in the wrong place and at the wrong time.

During dessert, Dolly stopped by. The stress of the past twenty-four hours had given her eyes a puffed look and her determinedly upbeat tone revealed a frayed edge. Nevertheless, she seemed under control.

After Jenny invited her inside, Dolly closed the door quickly behind her, shutting out a swirl of snowflakes. "Man, it's getting thick out there and the wind's nasty. I hear we're in for a real blizzard."

"It is moving in more quickly than expected." Troubled, Zahad checked his watch. Almost six-thirty. "I must leave by seven. Perhaps I should go now."

"You're flying out of Crystal Point? The roads won't fill up in the next half hour, but I wouldn't wait any longer than that." Dolly didn't seem surprised to hear that he was leaving. Word traveled quickly around here, Zahad mused.

"How's Ellen?" Gesturing to her neighbor to sit down, Jenny offered her one of the ice-cream bars.

Dolly declined with a polite shake of the head. "She's taking it hard. She blames herself in a way, although I don't know why. Mostly I think she regrets all the energy she wasted being jealous of Ray without cause."

Beth, who'd been squirming in her seat, lost patience with the adult chatter. "May I go play?"

"Sure, honey. Go ahead."

Although he hated to see Beth go, Zahad felt relieved as well. They could talk more freely now.

"Anyway, I came to tell you some news." Dolly rested

her elbows on the dining table. "The police arrested Al Garroway this afternoon."

"For what?" Jenny asked. Zahad hadn't had a chance to tell her about his meeting with Detective Rygel, he realized. "You're not saying he killed Ray!"

"We don't know yet," Dolly replied. "He was arrested in conjunction with the carjackings. It seems the perpetrators were paying him a percentage of the take."

"What was his involvement?" Zahad asked.

"Apparently he tipped off some men he knew from his old job about the easy pickings up here," Dolly explained. "I guess he figured it was a way to make some money. The idiot even rented them a cabin in his own name."

"But they robbed Tish!" Jenny said.

"Yes, the idiots. Her own husband was responsible for the men who attacked her, and she's furious." Dolly arched her neck to release tension. "She stormed over to my house a little while ago asking if I know a good divorce lawyer. Unfortunately, I don't."

"What happened to the carjackers?" Zahad asked.

"According to the radio, the police have surrounded their cabin up near the ski lodge. Parker hasn't had time to check whether there's any connection between Al and Ray's death."

If Al had put his stolen money in the Crystal Point bank, he might have been afraid Ray would figure it out. But he'd had no obvious motive to kill either Jenny or Fario. "We must assume the killer is still free," Zahad said.

"Agreed." Dolly stretched her shoulders. "Which, in a way, brings me to my other reason for coming here."

"Yes?" Jenny said.

"Ellen got permission to move back into her house tonight. I don't think it's a good idea, but she wants to start cleaning and she'd like Cindy to sleep in her own bed."

"I can understand," Jenny replied. "I felt the same way."

"Bill's being a good sport about my sleeping over with

them,'' Dolly explained. "He even suggested I invite you two to join us. Beth would keep Cindy distracted and you and I could keep Ellen's spirits up.''

Zahad nearly seconded the suggestion. What better way to safeguard Jenny and Beth than for them to stay with the other women?

Before he could say so, Jenny spoke. "It's a good idea but frankly, I'm exhausted, and we're all under stress. Having us around might make matters worse instead of better. Besides, with all the snow we're supposed to get, I'd feel more comfortable in my own home.''

"You're sure?" Dolly asked.

Jenny nodded firmly.

Their guest stood up. "Well, then, I'd better go back. Oh, we'll probably schedule Ray's funeral for Saturday, but that depends on the coroner. I'll let you know.'' She thrust out her hand to Zahad. "Have a safe trip.''

"Thank you.''

After she left, Jenny said, "I hope I didn't sound unsympathetic. It's just that I don't have enough emotional reserves right now to provide much support.''

"A wise choice.'' Zahad felt glad he hadn't encouraged her to comply. "Now, I, too, must depart.''

"I know.'' Jenny swallowed hard.

He retrieved his suitcase and put on the coat he'd bought in town. On the way back, he stopped to look into Beth's room. In a bright disk of lamplight, she sat on the floor talking to her doll and doing a simple jigsaw puzzle.

"Not that piece, Minnie,'' the little girl said solemnly, as if the doll were helping with the puzzle. "That one won't fit.''

"Your doll is not as smart as you,'' Zahad said.

Beth looked up. Her blond hair formed a golden halo. "Of course not. I'm her teacher.''

"Is that what you're going to be when you grow up?''

"Yes,'' she replied. "Or I might decide to be a principal like Mommy.''

"I must go." Zahad's chest squeezed. "I have enjoyed my visit very much."

Girl and doll came hurtling across the room. When Beth flung her arms around his waist, Minnie smacked him in the rear end.

The sheikh lifted them both for a proper hug. Reluctantly, he set them down again.

"I'll see you next time," Beth said.

Perhaps Beth was thinking that he would visit regularly, as her father had done. How could he explain to this tiny tyke that forces on the other side of the world might not allow him to come back?

"Goodbye," he said simply.

"Bye, Zod."

Jenny put on a coat and walked him to the car. Snow flurried around them, obscuring their view of the road, and gusts of wind tossed her hair. "Dolly was right—it's getting bad. I'm glad you put the chains on."

Zahad strove for lightness. "I will make a great racket going down the highway."

"I doubt there'll be many people around to hear you."

With all the padding on them, they embraced like two teddy bears. In a sense, they had said their farewells at midday, he thought. He much preferred the way they had done it then.

"Drive carefully." She didn't cry or urge him to return. He almost wished she would.

Jenny Sanger, the fragile-looking beauty in the photograph, had turned out to be as strong as Zahad himself. Perhaps, at this moment, stronger.

He cupped her chin in his hand. "I will e-mail to let you know when I arrive."

He was about to kiss her, when she said, "I just have one request."

"Whatever it is, I will be honored to do it."

Jenny stuffed her hands in her pockets. "When you face

those people who're trying to get rid of you, kick some good old Yazirian butt for me, will you?''

"I beg your pardon?" The earthy phrasing surprised him, coming from such a sweet-faced creature.

"I know you're not American, but that's the way we think," she said, stepping back. "Give 'em hell. Only don't tell Beth I used that word."

"I promise." Zahad admired her spirit.

"In a way, I envy you," Jenny told him. "You get to slay dragons. It'll be years before I have a chance to do that. In my work, I mean. But I'll get there."

"Of that I have no doubt."

And so he drove off, with the storm blowing and Jenny watching after him. Once she disappeared behind the trees, Zahad turned his attention to negotiating the road amid rapidly diminishing visibility.

He wondered if he would ever see her again.

JENNY DELIBERATELY hadn't kissed him goodbye. If she had, she'd have started to cry.

There was no point. Their paths had converged for less than a week, and now they were both continuing on their rightful courses. It was nothing to weep over, not like the deaths of Ray or Zahad's brother.

That was what she tried to tell herself. Yet the house echoed with Zahad's absence and rattled from gusts of wind hitting the windows.

Uneasily, Jenny checked to make sure the doors were locked. Then, quietly, so as not to call attention to her presence, she looked in on her daughter.

Holding Minnie on her lap, Beth sat on her bed in the midst of an array of stuffed animals. "We're all going to sing a song," she told them. "That way you won't be sad."

Tears filled Jenny's eyes. She felt proud of her little girl's courage and heartbroken at the same time that Beth had to endure so much.

When the tiny voice started singing a tune from *Sesame*

Street, Jenny tiptoed away. Much as she wanted to give comfort, she respected her daughter's attempt to take control of her own feelings.

In the living room, Jenny turned on the radio to listen for a weather report. The local station was playing music, but there'd be an update soon. To keep busy, she took out her sewing kit, chose a pattern for a doll's jacket and began sorting through fabric scraps.

The music trailed to an end. "In case you haven't noticed, it's snowing out there, folks, and we're clocking gusts up to forty-five miles per hour," the announcer said. "The weather bureau recommends you stay off the streets if at all possible."

After predicting more snow overnight and gradual clearing the next day, he segued into a commercial for snowblowers from the local hardware store. The news followed.

"We've had a report of shots fired at a cabin on Duck Hollow Road," the announcer said. "Police have cornered three suspects in that rash of carjackings. One local resident is already in custody but officers haven't released his name. Now back to the music."

As the radio played "Let It Snow," Jenny pictured her dark-haired neighbor with his thin face and unkempt beard. Al hadn't become a friend, but she'd never felt threatened by him, either. Of course, since he was responsible for bringing the carjackers who'd tried to halt her car, she'd been mistaken about that.

What would make an otherwise law-abiding citizen prey on his fellow humans? Greed, she thought. And selfishness and an incredible insensitivity to how upsetting it was to be the victim of a crime. She wondered how Al had felt when his own wife was attacked.

Her mind veered back to the sheikh. He would give his life rather than expose innocent people to danger, Jenny thought.

She forced herself to concentrate on aligning the pattern pieces along the fabric. She admired Zahad. More than that, she cherished him, but she couldn't ignore the vast differences separating them. Better that he'd left now, before Beth grew accustomed to him and Jenny started relying on him for things she could do herself.

After she finished cutting out the pattern, she put everything away and went to check on Beth again. The little girl lay beneath the covers, fast asleep amid her furry friends.

Jenny rearranged the stuffed animals to make sure none were in a position to block Beth's breathing. Then she turned the lights out.

In the front, she set the alarm for the night and peered out the window toward the street. Snow fell so thickly she couldn't see past the first few trees along the driveway. A dusting had accumulated on the ground.

The wind, which had quieted briefly, was picking up again. It battered the tree branches, raising an eerie, unsettling moan.

After drawing the curtains, Jenny tuned the TV to an old movie. Caught up in the mystery plot, she lost track of time until a loud thud caught her attention. Jenny muted the volume and listened.

For a moment, she heard only the groaning of the trees. Then another *wham!* echoed from behind the house. She could have sworn the noise had a metallic ring to it.

Dread rooted Jenny to the couch. Maybe the wind had blown something into the garage, she told herself.

Or maybe someone was trying to break into the toolshed again.

She was so angry she wanted to end this nightmare once and for all, even if it meant storming out there and confronting the intruder. For the first time, she wished she had her gun back.

No, she didn't mean that. She would never expose herself to danger that way or leave Beth in the house unprotected.

She went to the kitchen and picked up the phone. There was no dial tone. Puzzled, she tapped the cradle in vain until the truth hit her.

Someone had cut the line.

Jenny's chest tightened with fear. She forced herself to think clearly. The phones went dead and the power blacked out around here with annoying regularity, especially during bad weather. The wind might have knocked down the aboveground wire leading to the house.

Thank heavens for her cell phone.

Her hand trembled so hard she had to make two stabs before she pressed the On button. To Jenny's relief, she got a dial tone. She rapid-dialed the police.

"911 emergency." The dispatcher sounded a bit strained.

Jenny identified herself. "I think someone's trying to break into my toolshed. I heard a thud."

"Is anyone in immediate danger?" the woman asked.

"Not exactly." Her tight throat made it hard for Jenny to speak clearly. "It could be whoever killed the sheikh at my house. He took tools from my shed."

"Yes, Mrs. Sanger, I'm aware of that. I'm sorry but unless there's an immediate threat, I can't send anyone right now. I'd have to pull them off an emergency."

"I know about the carjackers," Jenny conceded. "But..."

"We just had a three-car pileup south of town with people trapped in their vehicles," the dispatcher said. "Everyone we can spare is at the scene. Is someone trying to get into your house?"

"No. At least, not yet."

"I promise to send an officer as soon as I have someone free. I'm really sorry... My other line just lit up."

"Thank you," Jenny said. "Send someone as quickly as you can." She clicked off and put the phone in her pocket.

Maybe she should have mentioned that her regular line had gone dead, she thought. On the other hand, that didn't prove anything, either.

She had to find out what was happening in the backyard. The dispatcher was right. Unless someone was actually trying to harm her, the other incidents took priority.

Despite knees that felt like gelatin, Jenny made her way down the hall and activated the exterior lights. As she went into her office, Zahad's lingering scent gave her strength.

Through the glass, she saw loose branches and unidentifiable bits of debris flying across the yard, but nothing that looked human size. Unfortunately, the shed door faced away from the house, so she couldn't tell whether the lock remained in place.

She was taking the phone from her pocket to call Dolly for advice, when it rang, startling her. Her hand jerked, and it was a moment before she managed to open it. "Hello?"

"Jenny?" The thin, quavery voice had a breathless quality. "It's me, Bill. I just woke up. I think Dolly slipped me a sleeping pill."

"Are you all right?" She remembered that he'd been left alone while his wife spent the night with Ellen.

"I heard them talking a while ago," the old man said dazedly. "Something about a fire. Jenny, you gotta get outta there. Take your little girl and go. Far away as you can."

"I don't understand." She could hardly hear through the pounding of her pulse.

"They're gonna kill you. Tonight, Jenny. They're both crazy, that's what, especially Dolly. Crazy with jealousy and I guess some kinda delusions. Been poisoning me all along. Now I know what her other two husbands musta died of."

"I have to call the police." Her thoughts were too jumbled to make much sense of what he had revealed, except to recognize with horror that she'd been about to turn to the very person who wanted to kill her.

"I'll do it." Bill wheezed a couple of times. "You get outta that house before they set it on fire. Better hurry. I don't want you to end up like Ray and that sheikh fella."

"Thank you," she said. "Are you all right?"

"She thinks I'm sleepin'. Don't worry about me. Just go." He hung up.

Fire! An image of a roaring inferno filled Jenny's mind.

The house of one of her students had caught fire last winter from a wood-burning stove and gone up in flames. Thanks to their smoke detector, the family had escaped, but they'd lost everything. And that fire hadn't been deliberately set to trap them.

Now Jenny knew what the intruder had wanted in the toolshed. Gasoline.

She ran to get her daughter.

Chapter Seventeen

Jenny had to get Beth away from here. Even the police couldn't save them if Dolly turned the house into an inferno.

She could hardly believe it. She'd been grateful for her neighbor's offer to watch the house and had trusted her without question.

It made sense now. She'd given Dolly a key. Her neighbor had seemed genuinely upset about finding Fario's body, but that was probably because she'd expected it to be Jenny's. Dolly had admittedly backed out Ray's car, a perfect cover for any DNA evidence inside it, although Jenny still didn't understand why she'd wanted to kill her son-in-law.

And Ellen. In retrospect, she had to be the cyber-stalker. She'd been wildly jealous of any attention Ray paid to Jenny and hostile to Jenny herself, and she knew the Internet inside and out. But she'd seemed so distraught about her husband's death.

None of that mattered now. Jenny had to focus on bundling a sleepy little girl into a coat and wrapping herself warmly. After grabbing her purse and Beth's favorite doll, Jenny peered out the front window to make sure the coast was clear.

Impossible to see anything through the thick, swirling snow. She had to take her chances.

When she thrust open the door, the alarm began to chirp. With her hands full, she couldn't shut it off. Besides, Jenny realized, the alert would add emphasis to Bill's call to the dispatcher.

Icy wind and snow scoured their faces. "Mommy, it's cold!" Beth protested.

"I told you, honey, we have to go." Jenny hadn't explained why.

"But where?"

"To a motel. I'm sorry, sweetie, but we can't wait."

Jenny was glad she'd parked by the front walk instead of in the garage. Because the structure was set far back, she hadn't wanted to face digging out an extra length of driveway. She'd been meaning to put in a carport as her neighbors had done.

Her neighbors. She shuddered. They weren't going to be her neighbors after this.

Struggling to move through the blustery darkness, she felt as if she weighed a thousand pounds. And at any moment, she expected to see Dolly loom into view, her face distorted by madness.

With agonizing slowness, Jenny unlocked the car and strapped Beth into her booster seat in back. "Minnie's scared." The little girl clutched her doll.

"She'll be fine," Jenny said.

The house alarm let loose with a screech. Beth clapped her hands over her ears.

"It'll stop in a minute," Jenny told her.

She clambered into the driver's seat. As she inserted the key into the ignition, another thought struck her.

Cars can burn, too.

Had Dolly rigged a bomb? Maybe the metallic noise she'd heard had come from the front, not the rear of the house. The way sound bounced off the hilly terrain, directions could be deceiving.

Jenny halted with her hand on the key. It was too risky

to try to drive. Maybe she should take her daughter and flee across the street to Parker's house.

With him at work, there'd be no one home but the house-keeper and his little boy. Would she be putting more innocent people at risk? Jenny didn't know. She simply couldn't think of what else to do.

The alarm was still screaming so loudly she could hardly hear herself shout to Beth, "We can't take the car!"

"Why not?"

Oh, heavens, she didn't want to terrify the little girl. Struggling to hide her fear, Jenny said, "There's something wrong with it. Let's go over to Ralph's house."

"I want to go to Cindy's!"

Jenny was searching for a plausible excuse, when a fierce gust jolted them. The SUV rocked and Beth uttered a shriek.

Nearby, trees swayed wildly. One large pine twisted as if alive, swayed to one side and, picking up speed, crashed across the driveway. The boom shook the car windows so hard Jenny feared they might shatter.

Mercifully, the house alarm shut off. Silence fell, or at least it seemed like silence, although after a moment Jenny realized the wind was still stirring.

She commanded herself to breathe. A quick look around indicated that the SUV wasn't damaged and neither was the house.

Scant comfort. Even if she'd dared to drive, she couldn't do it now with the fallen tree blocking their escape route.

"Mommy, I want to go inside!" Beth said.

Jenny found the strength to speak calmly. "We're going to have to walk. We're just going across the street."

She got Beth out of the car. The storm appeared to be worsening, although a few minutes ago that hadn't seemed possible.

"It's not far," she said. "Let's go fast!"

"We don't have to walk," Beth replied. "Somebody's coming."

Jenny heard it now, too: the mutter of an engine heading up her driveway. She couldn't see the vehicle through the tree branches and snow.

She had to take cover. They couldn't stand here waiting to be confronted. "We have to hide."

"But it's cold!"

Why did her usually cooperative daughter pick this time to get stubborn? "We'll just duck around the side of the house. Come on, sweetheart." She bent to pick up the child. "It'll be all right."

Jenny heard the other car come to a stop. Whoever was driving could easily walk around the fallen pine. If it was Dolly, she'd surely be armed.

Half pulling and half carrying Beth, Jenny struggled through the snow. Beyond the tree, a car door shut. Why had gravity suddenly doubled its grip and the wind turned against her?

"Jenny!" A wonderfully familiar baritone voice roared above the wind and the thundering of her heart. "Are you there?"

"It's Zod!" Beth wriggled with joy. "Mommy, it's Zod!"

Tears misted Jenny's eyes and threatened to freeze on her lashes. He'd come back. Her sheikh had returned to protect her.

She didn't want to need him or anyone. But right now, she did, desperately.

"We're here." Her voice caught, and she had to repeat the words louder.

"Are you hurt?" He was moving toward them.

"No," she called. "But we've got to get out of here."

He made his way around the tree, his strong, solid shape a refuge in the midst of chaos. Jenny and Beth headed toward him.

"I tried to call you from the airport." Reaching them, Zahad wrapped them in his arms. Jenny pressed close, her heart lifting. "The line kept ringing with no answer," he said. "When your cell phone was busy, I began to fear something might be wrong."

"The regular phone's dead. I was calling the police because I heard someone outside," Jenny explained. "But they're tied up with emergencies." She remembered suddenly how urgently he needed to make his flight. "How could you come back? You might not get home before Saturday."

"I will take my chances." Zahad's dark eyes shone with worry. "Why are you outside?"

"We must leave. I'll tell you on the way."

"Let's go, then." He didn't question her, she noted gratefully.

En route to his car, she outlined what Bill had said. She tried to soften the words for Beth's sake, but she had to share this information with Zahad.

"It is fortunate that I returned." He fitted the booster seat, which he'd taken from her SUV, into the back of his car. "I am only sorry I did not become suspicious of the right person sooner. She fooled me, also."

When they were all inside, the sheikh eased the car toward the street. Although they weren't yet out of danger, Jenny's anxiety lessened. As it did, the events of the past half hour began to replay through her mind.

The metallic thud outside. Her futile attempt to summon the police. The warning call that had saved her life. That reminded her of a point she hadn't mentioned.

"Dolly may be poisoning Bill," Jenny said. "He believes she might have poisoned her first two husbands as well."

"I was told she had divorced the second one. No one mentioned that he had died." Zahad stared through the windshield into the snow falling so thickly he had difficulty making out where to turn onto the road.

"Don't cut too sharply," Jenny advised. "There's a drainage ditch."

"I am aware of that, but thank you," he replied, and

pulled cautiously onto the street. "She told me her second husband bought her a television set when he won the lottery. It seems they were on good terms."

"That's strange." The discrepancy troubled Jenny. Perhaps it simply underlined Bill's increasingly confused mental state.

"What is that?" Zahad indicated a flare of reds and yellows coming into view off to their right. Blurred by the storm, it billowed upward with a surreal, hellish quality.

"It looks like a fire," Jenny said, puzzled.

"It is a fire." Zahad's nostrils flared as if smelling smoke. "It is a house burning."

"It's Ellen's house!" What on earth was going on? Had the women accidentally lit the gasoline in the wrong place?

"It burns very intensely." Zahad halted in the entrance to Dolly's driveway. "This is no accident. There is a ring of fire around the house."

"It looks pretty," Beth remarked innocently.

"Oh, honey!" Anyone inside would be trapped, Jenny realized. "Cindy! She might be in there."

She and Zahad exchanged looks. It took him less than a second to respond. "I will get her out." He left the key in the ignition. "Lock the doors after me. Call the fire department."

"Yes," she said. "Be careful." She didn't know what had happened except that they couldn't save themselves at the expense of a little girl.

He brushed a kiss across Jenny's mouth, his lips cool but his breath warm with promise. She wanted more but there was no time. He had to go.

There might be a world of differences between them, but she and her sheikh had one thing in common. Neither of them would risk leaving a child in a blazing building even to save themselves.

"If I do not come back quickly, drive away," he advised. Before she could respond, he opened the door and vanished into the white fury of the storm.

Jenny tried to imagine what had happened at Ellen's house. Had Dolly gone so insane that she'd tried to kill her own daughter and granddaughter? Had the women entered into some kind of suicide pact?

None of it made sense. The only thing she could deal with right now was the fact that Zahad was risking his life. Taking out her cell phone, she dialed 911, and this time she wouldn't take no for an answer.

THE SHEIKH FOUGHT his way up the driveway through the driving snow. The flames hadn't yet engulfed the house, he saw as he neared it. They were following the lines of some accelerant—gasoline, by the smell of it—poured around the foundation. The fire must have started only moments earlier or it would have spread.

He heard no screech of a smoke alarm from within. Perhaps it had been deactivated, or maybe they didn't have one. Whoever was inside might be sleeping, oblivious to the peril.

He saw no sign of a rampaging Dolly. But she would hardly stand here waiting for him, would she?

In a planter box, he spotted a loose brick. Seizing it, Zahad circled into the unfenced backyard. To rouse the occupants, he needed to target one of the bedroom windows.

Fire licked up the wooden siding, hindered slightly by the patches of stonework that decorated the exterior. In only a matter of minutes, however, it would reach the eaves and explode through the house.

Anyone who'd set a blaze like this wouldn't leave without seeing it to its conclusion. Again, Zahad looked around, but still saw no sign of the madwoman.

At the far end of the house, two windows flanked a smaller, rippled one that denoted a bathroom. Guessing that the corner room belonged to Ellen, he braced himself and heaved the brick.

It crashed into the glass. Through the gale, he heard the

pane break, but no one responded. Were the people inside unconscious or had they left?

Zahad considered it unlikely that this was a setup. Dolly wouldn't expect Jenny to rush into a burning building and she hadn't known of his return.

He had to brave the flames. Zahad crouched, meaning to roll in the snow to armor himself against the heat. As he did, a loud crack reverberated in his ears and a hot streak seared his right shoulder.

Startled, he lost his balance and jolted to his knees. When he put his hand down for support, pain wrenched through him.

He'd been shot. He knew that searing sensation all too well.

Out of the blizzard, a thin form materialized. Riveted by the gun pointed at him, Zahad took a moment to realize that the person behind it wasn't Dolly.

A hunting cap and a shock of white hair topped a narrow face contorted by fury. "If it wasn't for you, it'd be over by now!" Bill didn't look fragile now. He looked maniacal. "You're too damn nosey. You can thank yourself for getting Ray killed!"

"I don't understand," the sheikh said. "Why did you kill him? What about my brother?" He gauged the distance between them and the possibility of dodging the next bullet. The odds weren't close to zero.

"Your damn brother came sniffing around looking for sex. He shoulda minded his own business." Despite his rambling, the man kept one finger firmly on the trigger. "You think I married that witch so I could end up with nothing? More than two million dollars, that's what I got and I ain't giving it up. Goodbye, Mr. Sheikh."

A sudden movement registered on the edge of Zahad's consciousness and he began to turn. So did Bill just as a hard white ball smacked into his temple. His hand flew up and the gun roared into the air. A few yards away, Jenny ducked for cover.

Zahad launched himself onto the old man, his hand closing around the bony wrist. Bill held on, apparently powered by a combination of adrenaline and rage. Twisting harder than the sheikh would have thought possible, he brought up his legs and kicked out.

Battered full in the midsection, Zahad loosened his grip. In that instant, the gun swung back toward him. He barely had time to thrust at Bill's wrist with the heel of one hand before a blast slammed into him.

He landed on his back on the frozen earth, the breath knocked out of him and his ears throbbing. He knew he had to get up. He had to stop this viperish old man from killing anyone else. But his muscles refused to respond.

At last the ringing in his head diminished enough for him to hear sirens in the driveway. Help had arrived. He hoped it wasn't too late to save Jenny, because he had failed her.

"TWO MILLION DOLLARS," Dolly said hours later as they sat in the lobby of the police station. "I can't believe he sacrificed two lives out of pure greed. Heck, I'd have given him the money just to save Ray. Or Fario, either."

It was nearly daylight. Mrs. Welford had taken Cindy and Beth to her home, but no one else had slept. At least the storm had passed more quickly than expected, allowing the police to conduct their searches.

"You didn't even know your ex-husband was dead, let alone that he'd left you his lottery winnings. You couldn't have done anything." Jenny stretched her cramped legs. Except for giving her statement, she'd spent most of the night waiting, first in the hospital while Zahad's wound was treated, then here at Parker's request in case he needed more information. They'd nearly emptied the coffeepot provided for them and had consumed half a box of doughnuts.

Surreptitiously, she studied the sheikh, who'd refused to stay in the hospital for observation. Across the room, he sat talking on his cell phone, his sweater bulging over the bandage on his shoulder.

Mercifully, the bullet wound was superficial. He didn't appear to have suffered a head injury when the gun's recoil knocked him flat. Even so, he'd retreated into his own world.

He'd scarcely reacted on learning that Bill had died in the gun blast or that the brick he'd thrown had awakened Dolly, Ellen and Cindy just in time. Although he seemed relieved by the outcome, she sensed that in his mind he was already halfway back to Alqedar.

"I feel like an idiot," Dolly said. "I married a man who only wanted my money. I got suspicious a couple of years ago when he kept wanting me to put the property and my savings in both our names. When I announced that I was leaving everything to Ellen, we had a big fight. I told him I wanted a divorce."

"What changed your mind?"

"He got sick. I figured he was just playing on my sympathy until the doctor diagnosed fibromyalgia. I guess I'm a soft touch, because I hated to kick him out."

Judging by Bill's conduct last night, he must have been exaggerating the symptoms, Jenny thought. If she hadn't distracted him with that snowball, he'd have killed Zahad.

"About a year ago, he started acting nicer," Dolly continued. "I figured it was a sign I'd made the right choice. I had no idea Manley had died and Bill had intercepted the lawyer's letter."

A police search of Dolly's house in the past few hours had turned up papers forged with her name, claiming the inheritance. There was also a bankbook with a very large balance in the First National Bank of Crystal Point.

Apparently Bill had then set out to get rid of Dolly in a way that wouldn't cast suspicion on him. He'd played on Ellen's jealousy to turn her into a cyber-stalker and tried to take advantage of the situation to make it appear that Dolly had died as an innocent bystander.

Fario had simply wandered onto the scene at the wrong time. If he hadn't showed up, Dolly would have taken that bullet. Bill must have assumed the police would blame Jenny for rigging the gun as a form of protection.

Now Ellen was in jail facing stalking charges. After evidence turned up on her computer, she'd admitted that Bill claimed to have seen Ray and Jenny embracing. He'd talked her into the cyber-stalking, making it sound like justifiable revenge. She'd agreed—until Fario got killed.

Ray had died because Bill feared he'd come across the large amount of money in his account, although he'd already invested some of his ill-gotten funds in stocks and bonds. Jenny doubted they'd ever learn who had dropped that slip of paper with the bank logo in her house. However it had landed there, it had set off a lethal chain of events.

Based on what the police had found in Dolly's computer, Bill had continued the cyber-stalking for a few days, still hoping to set up some kind of smoke screen. When that didn't pan out, he'd made another attempt to kill his wife and frame Jenny. He'd spooked her into fleeing to make her look guilty, or at least, that was what she surmised, and a gasoline can stolen from her shed had been discovered at the scene.

Despite all that she'd been through, Jenny hoped Ellen would get off with probation. Losing her husband and her home seemed like more than enough punishment, and Cindy needed her mother.

Zahad flipped his phone shut and looked up. "My flight was canceled because of the weather. I can catch the same plane that will carry Fario's remains this morning if Sergeant Finley allows me to go."

"I suggested he write a letter of commendation for use in your homeland," Dolly said. "If it weren't for you, my family and I would have died."

"Thank you," the sheikh replied. "I am glad you escaped safely."

When Finley joined them a few minutes later, it turned out he had followed Dolly's advice. Producing an envelope, he told Zahad, "It's addressed To Whom It May Concern and says you aren't a suspect in your brother's death and have cooperated in my investigation. I hope that helps you.''

"Thank you. I would shake your hand if it were not too painful.''

"Understood.'' The sergeant looked a trifle sheepish but Jenny had to admire his good sportsmanship.

"I know there are many loose ends, but I must leave now,'' the sheikh told him. "If it is acceptable to you, I will catch a flight this morning.''

As Parker weighed his request, Jenny noticed pronounced pouches under his eyes. "Ordinarily, I'd ask you to stick around,'' he said at last. "However, I know you've got your brother's body to bury. And I understand there are some serious issues at stake in your homeland.''

"Very serious,'' Zahad agreed. "You have my phone number and e-mail address. I will be happy to answer any further questions.''

"Good luck to you,'' Parker told him. "As for everybody else, you can all go home. We're done for tonight. I mean, this morning.''

"I'd like to see my daughter,'' Dolly said.

"Her lawyer just showed up. You can talk to her when he leaves,'' Parker replied.

She nodded. "I'll be here.''

Zahad couldn't drive in his condition, Jenny realized. "I'll take you to the airport,'' she offered. "I can turn your rental in and catch a cab home.''

"Thank you.'' To Parker, the sheikh said, "Please have the bomb squad check out Jenny's SUV, just in case.''

"We already did. It's clean,'' the sergeant explained. "We removed the tree, too, so we could access the tool-shed.''

The men regarded each other with grudging appreciation. "Perhaps we are more alike than either of us wished to believe,'' Zahad said.

"I'll grant you that." With a rueful smile, the detective held the door. "Have a safe trip."

Outside, dawn light was breaking over a storybook scene of snow-laden buildings and cars. The mounds of white added an authentic note to the Christmas decorations.

Jenny appreciated the chance to spend a little more time with the sheikh. But despite his affability at the police station, he made no move to touch her as they walked to his car.

His thoughts must be flying ahead to what awaited him in Alqedar. Jenny wished they could hold on a little while longer to the magic they'd created amid tragedy this past week. Unfortunately, the bright light of day was dissolving the dream along with the nightmare.

HE HAD NEARLY FAILED Jenny. Lying powerless on the snow after the gun went off, Zahad had realized that nothing in his life mattered as much as keeping her safe.

He had never felt so helpless. Because once he admitted to himself that he loved her, he also had to face the fact that he desperately feared losing her to fate.

While fighting a revolution, the sheikh had never worried about danger. If he lost a battle, he could always regroup and fight again another day. If he died in a just cause, he would go to heaven.

Love was different. It made him vulnerable. A man could not always be there to protect the woman and child without whom his existence had no meaning.

Riding in the car as Jenny negotiated the freshly cleared road around the lake, Zahad collected his thoughts. For hours, he had been stunned by the shock of his wound, by the sudden turn of events at the Rivases' house and by being rendered defenseless, before he discovered the deflected shot had killed Bill.

His cousin Sharif had loved this deeply and his first wife had died. Years later, Sharif had been fortunate enough to love again, but Zahad knew that he would not. He did not form attachments as easily as his cousin. Jenny was his first love and she would be the last.

How much did he have the right to ask of her? Was she not better off staying here, now that her enemies had been routed, rather than coming to a land where his own rivals still flourished?

Beside him, she broke the silence. "I never thought I'd be so grateful that my father made me play softball. You probably didn't notice what good aim I had when I smacked Bill with my snowball."

"I did notice. It is too bad the students at your school could not witness your prowess."

"There's no need for sarcasm."

"I was not joking."

"Then you're forgiven."

She grew quiet again. Morning light danced through her golden hair.

In a few minutes, they would reach the airport and say goodbye. The bond between them, however, would not break. It seemed so strong to Zahad that he imagined it tethering the airplane and bringing it crashing down on takeoff.

Of course that would not really happen. He must take matters into his own hands.

"Come with me," he said.

Jenny blinked. "I'm sorry?"

"I do not mean this instant," he clarified. "I know you have obligations and you must make arrangements to bring your daughter. I am asking that you come to Alqedar and be my wife."

In the pause that followed, he recalled that a man was supposed to stage a production of asking a woman to marry him. He supposed he should have provided gifts and flowery promises, perhaps to the accompaniment of music.

Such affectations lay beyond Zahad's grasp. Simplicity and directness were all he knew.

"I can't," Jenny said with a sigh. "Zahad, I'm sorry.

You mean more to me than any man I've ever known. But I have my own dreams and plans. I can't give them up for anyone, not even you."

"I understand," he replied.

There, it was done. He had taken the risk he must take, and she had given the answer she must give.

Was this truly the end? The end for now, in any case.

They drove for a while longer without speaking. Jenny pulled to the curb in front of the small terminal. When their eyes met, he saw sadness but no uncertainty.

"I will keep you informed of what happens in my country," he said.

"I'll let you know what the police turn up." She swallowed. "Zahad, thank you for everything."

How should he respond? Pat answers evaded him even under the best of circumstances.

What he wanted to say was that someday he would return, that he would find a way to change her mind and that he would shower her with treasure if that was what it took. But to say such things would be an insult. He respected her decision.

"No thanks are due," the sheikh replied. "We have both accomplished our aims. It has been a successful alliance."

Jenny smiled tremulously. "Only you would say something like that at a time like this."

"There is one thing I can promise you if we meet again," he said.

"Yes?"

"I will have an interesting new scar to show you." Zahad nodded toward his shoulder and winced as it throbbed. He made no objection when Jenny came around to open his door. He might be proud but he was no fool.

Outside, they stood awkwardly facing each other. Jenny seemed too beautiful and too delicate to belong to a ruffian like him, but even so, he luxuriated in the sight of her.

"I don't want to hurt your arm, so I guess I can't hug you." Jenny reached to ruffle the ragged edges of his hair.

"You might want to get that cut. After all, you're a very important person."

"I will attend to it," Zahad said, and promptly put it out of his mind.

After a last regretful look, Jenny turned away. He started to reach for her and nearly cried out with pain. Perhaps he should have accepted the doctor's medication after all, he reflected.

In any case, he had lost the chance to touch her.

However, it wasn't his arm that hurt most as Zahad approached the security checkpoint a few minutes later. An ache formed deep in his chest, or perhaps his stomach. It grew more agonizing with every step he took away from Jenny.

By the time he reached the aircraft, it had grown into a fiery corona around a hard black lump. As he thought of what he was leaving behind, Zahad realized this must be what people meant when they spoke of a broken heart. Already, it began to seem familiar, like something he would have to live with for a very long time.

Chapter Eighteen

On a Friday in mid-January, Jenny gave a farewell party for Lew Blackwell during lunchtime. It was just cake and punch in the teachers' lounge, but she knew he treasured the heartfelt good wishes of his co-workers.

"I'm a little envious," Jenny admitted when the other teachers had returned to their classrooms.

"You're ambitious," Lew noted. "There are people who'll hold that against you, but you'll leave them in the dust."

"I guess so." She began cleaning up the paper plates. "We'll miss you around here."

"Don't stay in Mountain Lake too long. You might lose your fire, and that would be a shame."

His words rang in her mind for the rest of the afternoon. What she felt wasn't so much a longing for more money or prestige as a desire to help a large number of students who really needed assistance. Perhaps she could find a way to combine this with raising her daughter, but Jenny had been too busy during the past month even to think about her career path.

Since Zahad left, the days had sped by, although the nights seemed almost unbearably long. Even though they'd known each other for only a short time, she found it hard to believe he was gone. She kept imagining she heard his voice in the other room, or that at any moment she would roll over and see a smile light his scarred face.

Life went on, however. After Jenny spoke on Ellen's behalf at a hearing, she'd been granted probation. Dolly had put her property up for sale so the two of them and Cindy could move to a new community away from bitter memories.

At least they would never want for money. A paper trail had turned up a little more than two million dollars that belonged to Dolly.

The police had definitively linked Bill to both murders. They'd also learned that his description fit that of a man who, years earlier, had romanced then fleeced single women in towns that Bill had once passed through as a truck driver.

Pieces of the puzzle kept falling into place. Jenny remembered the time when Bill got on the wrong bus and landed in Crystal Point. In retrospect, she realized he'd gone there to conduct his banking and pretended to be lost when Ray spotted him.

Bill had been an instinctive liar and a devious plotter. Not all of his schemes worked, but he'd nearly gotten away with them.

As for Al Garroway and the carjackers, all faced trials and potential long sentences. Tish had filed for divorce.

That Friday afternoon, the teachers cleared out quickly at day's end. The following week was midwinter break and many of them planned trips.

Jenny left a little after five to collect Beth. They stopped for pizza at an Italian diner.

"Are you sure you don't want a party?" she asked her daughter while they ate. Today was the little girl's sixth birthday. They could still schedule a get-together for Saturday or Sunday.

Beth shook her head. "It won't be any fun without Cindy."

"I know. I'm sorry." Ellen had already moved away

with her mother and daughter. Although Beth had other friends at school, they weren't the same.

Grant couldn't be here, either. He'd even declined Jenny's offer to visit him at Christmas, saying he didn't want his daughter to see him in jail. The two of them had flown to Connecticut instead to celebrate with Jenny's mother.

"Can Zod come?" Beth asked over a slice of pizza. "I want him to have some of my cake."

Beth was always delighted when the sheikh asked about her in his e-mails. She'd also received one directly from Amy's seven-year-old daughter, Farhanna, and had gleefully dictated a response to Jenny.

"He's very far away," Jenny explained. "But I'm sure he's thinking about you."

"Maybe he can come next week. For school break." It wasn't a question, so Jenny didn't answer.

After dinner and an animated movie, it was nearly eight o'clock when they arrived home. Jenny felt the usual quiver of apprehension as she turned into the driveway. She wondered if her dark memories would ever fade.

"We can have some cake now and open presents," she said as they entered through the back.

"Okay." Beth didn't sound enthusiastic. Most likely she was just tired.

Jenny disarmed the security device and, for an instant, indulged in a fantasy that Zahad was waiting in the other room. He still knew the code, after all. Maybe she and Beth wouldn't have to celebrate alone, ever again.

Of course she found no sign of him when they went in. She'd been as blindly optimistic as her daughter.

The sheikh had asked her to marry him and she'd turned him down. She felt certain she had made the best decision, but sometimes it didn't feel right.

The phone rang. Beth flew by. "I'll get it!"

Who was the child expecting? "Honey, maybe I should—"

"Sanger residence," Beth said into the mouthpiece. "Hi, Zod! I knew you'd call!" The little girl beamed.

Zahad had phoned once before, several weeks earlier, to say that he'd been formally appointed governor of the province. Hashim, humiliated by the people's rejection, had left the country. After learning from news accounts how diligently her stepson had worked to solve her son's murder, Numa had apologized for her accusations. She'd accepted his offer of a pension and gone to live with her sister's family.

"Mommy!" Beth called. "Zod's sending me a doll! Farhanna picked it."

"That's sweet." Jenny was amazed that the sheikh had thought of sending a gift or even remembered her daughter's birthday.

"He wants to talk to you." Beth held out the receiver.

Jenny's hand tingled as she took it. He was right there, on the other end of the line, waiting to talk to her. "Beth's thrilled," she said. "It was kind of you to call."

Grinning, her daughter trotted out of the room. A moment later, Jenny heard her announcing to her doll, "You're going to have a sister!"

"I have often wanted to phone." Zahad's voice vibrated through her deliciously. "However, I know you are busy with your many plans."

Not so busy that she hadn't missed him every waking minute, she thought. "How are you? How are things going?"

"Matters are progressing. A Belgian company intends to build a carpet factory here. Also, a large charitable group will finance a new school, which we need."

"It sounds exciting." Jenny reminded herself to check Yazir's Web site to learn more about those developments.

"What about Mountain Lake?" he asked. "Are you still happy there?"

She didn't know how to answer. "There've been...many adjustments," she said at last.

''My offer has not changed.''

Her eyelids stung. In a way, Jenny had wanted to hear that, but she still couldn't accept. As she'd said, she had to plan her own future. ''Zahad...''

He must have heard the regret in her tone. ''I apologize. I should not have mentioned it.''

''It's all right. I'm really glad you called. Beth's been asking about you.''

''Farhanna wishes to meet her,'' he replied. ''Perhaps someday Beth can visit here. It would be educational.''

What was it like, this palace of Zahad's? Jenny tried to picture the scenes and the people he'd spoken of, Amy and Sharif and their families, and realized she would love to see them, too. ''Maybe when she's older.''

''Of course.''

Their goodbyes were muted. She hung up feeling as if the conversation was unfinished.

At the entrance to her daughter's room, Jenny saw that Beth had arrayed her stuffed animals and Minnie on the floor and was serving them with her miniature tea set. The little girl was holding her own birthday party.

The tears Jenny had held back earlier slid down her cheeks. She wanted more than this for Beth and for herself, as well. But she didn't know where to find it.

She retreated to her office and switched on the computer. In seconds, she made her way to Yazir's site.

She found the news about the carpet factory at the top of the page. Jenny skipped it to read about the new school. It was part of a major overhaul of the educational system, the article stated and provided a link to a job notice for minister of education.

She clicked on the link.

The ad referred to ''long hours, tremendous challenges and a modest salary. Knowledge of Arabic not required.'' Qualifications included a master's degree and experience as an education administrator.

Jenny stared at the screen for a long time.

ON MONDAY, a delegation of German businessmen pelted Zahad with questions during a luncheon at the city's newest restaurant, which was, ironically, French. They seemed impressed both by his blunt answers and by the full sheikh regalia that he had donned for the occasion. This included a long white robe and a red-and-white checked headdress, held in place with a black band.

Zahad hoped no one noticed that he was wearing jeans and a T-shirt underneath. Preoccupied with going over the plans for a new sewer system, he'd hurriedly thrown on his formal wear right before the meeting.

Back at his office, Zahad drummed his fingers on his broad desk. Where was Amy? He'd expected her to hasten into his office to discuss the results of the luncheon, which she had also attended, but she'd disappeared immediately afterward.

Swiveling, he surveyed the busy market scene beyond the palace wall. Even through the glass, he imagined he could smell the spices, perfumes and coffee. Jewelry glimmered in the sunlight and brightly colored clothing hung from kiosks.

A dusty four-wheel-drive vehicle wended its way between two camels burdened with market goods. While two ladies in European dress examined tooled-leather purses, a woman in a long cloak and black head scarf strolled past, talking intently on her cell phone. His land combined the old and the new, the high-tech and the traditional, and Zahad loved it.

After a tap at the door, his secretary entered. The young man had come to him the previous year at Sharif's recommendation. "There is a candidate here for the post of education minister."

"I was not aware I had an appointment," he replied.

"Mrs. Haroun set it up." His secretary knew better than to interfere in the sometimes tempestuous but mutually respectful relationship between the sheikh and his director of economic development.

"Very well. Show him in," Zahad said.

"It is a female."

A woman wished to move to this remote province and assume the job of education minister? He hadn't anticipated this. Indeed, the recruiters he'd contacted before posting the job had informed him it was unlikely he would find any qualified candidate willing to relocate to such a backward community.

"Show *her* in."

"Yes, sir."

On his computer, Zahad reviewed the job notice. When the door opened, he spoke without looking up. "Please sit down."

"That robe is fantastic," said the dearest voice in all the world. "Is that how you usually dress around here?"

He jumped to his feet so fast he banged his thigh on the desk's kneehole. "Jenny!"

Her green eyes looked luminous, as if lit from within. Distractedly, Zahad noticed that she'd tucked her blond hair into a businesslike twist and wore a powder-blue suit.

"I'm here about the job."

"Excuse me?" He stopped in midstride.

"I understand you need a minister of education." Jenny stated the fact calmly, as if it were the most natural thing in the world for her to appear in his palace. "I happened to have a week off so I decided to bring Beth on a little trip."

A little trip halfway around the world? "Where is she now?"

"Playing with Farhanna."

Although he wanted to sweep her into his arms and kiss her senseless, he stayed where he was. "You talked to Amy about the job?"

"I got her number from the Web site and called her Friday night. She thought you might be willing to interview me." Jenny gave him a *Mona Lisa* smile. "The job sounds like what I'm looking for and I'm sure we could get along, although I have to say, if you're going to dress like that, I might get sidetracked.''

He glanced down at his white robe. "Ah, this was to impress the Germans." Feeling a bit overdressed, he removed the headdress and set it aside.

"I'm sure they were very impressed," she said.

"Did you really come about the job?" He finger-combed his shaggy hair, no doubt the worse for wear. "Because if you did, you are hired."

"Just like that?"

"I have observed your empathy for children and I know of your experience in the field," Zahad replied. "When can you start?"

"I...soon. How's your shoulder?"

He flexed it. "Almost well."

"You promised me an interesting scar."

The air between them vibrated with unspoken longings. Jenny hadn't come simply to apply for a job or she would not make a personal reference to his body, the sheikh reflected.

This must be one of those occasions when a man was supposed to read between the lines. He felt grateful that this insight had occurred to him. Before he met Jenny, it would not have.

"I cannot show you my scar just now. However, I have something else for you."

From the desk drawer, he removed a carved wooden box and handed it over. Her face alive with curiosity, Jenny opened it.

He heard a sharp intake of breath as she stared down at the filigree-gold necklace and earrings. "I saw those in the marketplace," Zahad continued. "I meant to bring them to you one day soon."

When she raised her eyes, he saw love shining there. At least, he hoped it was, because he knew love was radiating from his own face and he didn't want to look foolish.

"They're exquisite. Zahad..."

His heart nearly stopped beating. He prayed she would not refuse him again. "Yes?"

"After we get married, you're really going to have to get a haircut," Jenny said.

If she had meant to add anything, she never got the chance. Catching her in his arms, the sheikh pulled her into an embrace that lasted for a very long time.

He was glad she had dreams and plans. He was even happier that from now on, he was going to be part of them. "I love you, Jenny," he said.

"It's wonderful to be home," she answered, and kissed him again.

THE SHEIKH WHO LOVED ME

BY
LORETH ANNE WHITE

As a child in Africa, when asked what she wanted to be when she grew up, **Loreth Anne White** said a spy…or a psychologist, or maybe marine biologist, archaeologist or lawyer. Instead she fell in love, travelled the world and had a baby. When she looked up again she was back in Africa, writing and editing news and features for a large chain of community newspapers. But those childhood dreams never died. It took another decade, another baby and a move across continents before the lightbulb finally went on. She didn't *have* to grow up. She could be them all – the spy, the psychologist and all the rest – through her characters. She sat down to pen her first novel…and fell in love.

She currently lives with her husband, two daughters and their cats in a ski resort in the rugged Coast Mountains of British Columbia, where there is no shortage of inspiration for larger-than-life characters and adventure.

This one is for Leslie Wainger and the eHarlequin
community, where the seeds for the Sheikh were sown.
And of course to Susan Litman for once again
making it all happen.

Prologue

Monstrous clouds of hot desert sand mushroomed in the fierce wind, blotting out a sun that boiled blood-orange over an angry black sea. Panic squeezed Kamilah's heart. She scrambled up the dune as fast her little six-year-old legs would carry her. She shouldn't be out in this storm. Her father would be furious.

But it didn't matter now. Nothing mattered. She had to get help or the mermaid might die. After all this time, all this waiting, she had finally come.

But she was broken.

Tears stung Kamilah's face. Her lungs burned. The wind clawed at the very roots of her hair. The ocean behind her boomed as she ran, heaving foaming water onto the outlying coral reefs, pounding it into the bay, making the ordinarily placid waters swell and surge with turbid life.

Daddy please help. Before the sea takes it away again.

The words screamed inside her brain, drowning out the gusts of wind. Words that wanted to be spoken out loud for the first time in a very, very long time.

Lightning cracked the sky. Kamilah flattened instantly to the ground, scrunched her eyes tight and waited for the crash of thunder. It resounded through her little body making her limbs tremble and her heart drum so fast she thought it might burst right through her chest.

But she had to move. She had to get Daddy. She scrambled up the sand bank, lurched over an exposed root, skidded back down. She grasped desperately for purchase as pain seared her hands, her knees. The sand stung her eyes.

But she could not give up. She would *not* let the sea take it back. Because Mummy had sent this mermaid. She just knew it!

David Rashid pushed a yellow pin into the large map that covered the entire back wall of his office. The pin denoted the last of the Rashid International oilfields to be reclaimed from the rebels. It too was now in full production, drawing rich black gold up to the arid Saharan surface, oil that had for centuries been buried deep under the northern reaches of Azar. Oil his father had known was there.

The smaller red pins clustered into the map up near the Libyan and Egyptian borders flagged the final desert strongholds of the now-straggling rebel army. The two big blue pins to the southeast of Azar represented the biggest prize of all, the Rashid uranium mines. And it was no ordinary uranium that Rashid International was drawing out of the earth. It had a unique molecular structure that made it invaluable in cutting edge nuclear technology. David's mines were among only a handful in the world in a position to deliver this particular uranium. It had put Azar squarely back in the game.

David stepped back, folded his arms, and smiled. It was a coup he could be proud of. One his father had dreamed of. One that would rebuild his nation by bridging the old world with the new, that would fuel the economy and give pride and spirit back to a forgotten people, the Bedu of Azar, the warrior nomads of a country wedged between Chad and Sudan with Egypt and Libya to the north.

David's only wish was that his father had lived to see this. And to see how he'd managed to heal the bitter rift between himself and his half brother, Tariq.

He rubbed the stubble on his jaw as he studied the clusters of red pins on the map, vaguely aware of wind tearing at battened-down shutters, swirling and shrieking in the old castle's protected courtyards. The only question that still ate at his mind was, who was backing the rebels? But before he could chew on it, his office door flung open with a resounding crash.

David jolted, spun around. The storm winds blew fine desert sand up out of the courtyard and into his office. His daughter tumbled in with it. Her hair was a wild, dark tangle about her bloodless face, her chocolate-brown eyes wide with terror.

"Kamilah!" He lunged for the door, slammed it, shutting out the storm. He dropped to his knees and took her slight shoulders in his hands. She was trembling violently.

"Kamilah? What is it?"

Her eyes were impossibly huge, and they stared straight at him. *Into* him. David could barely breathe. She was trying to tell him something with those beautiful expressive eyes, eyes that hadn't gazed directly into his for almost two years.

Every muscle in his body tensed. The sound of the storm faded into far recesses of his mind. He was afraid to move, to breathe even, fearful any slight gesture might sever the tenuous connection between him and his child. It was like a thread, fine as gossamer. He didn't know whether to grab hold and yank it in to him, or to tread softly around for fear of breaking it. God, he never knew what to do with his beautiful baby girl. He swallowed, tentatively moved a tangled strand of hair from her pale cheek.

She didn't back away. It fed his courage, his hope. He breathed a little deeper. He took her tiny hands in his own, looked deep into her eyes and dropped his voice to a gentle, reassuring whisper. "What is it, Kamilah? Can you tell me?"

She drew in a shuddering breath. Her lips parted. David's heart stopped. He waited. Not a muscle moved in his body.

The struggle to form words showed painfully in Kamilah's dusky features. Then she suddenly closed her lips, compressing them into a tight line. David's heart dropped like lead. His pent-up breath came out in a whoosh. He closed his eyes and his chin sunk to his chest. He shouldn't have even dared to hope. Hope only bred despair.

"The...mermaid," she whispered.

His eyes flared open. *She spoke!* His heart stumbled and kicked into a light stutter.

"She...she needs help," Kamilah said hesitatingly, shrinking back from the sound of her own words. But to David it was pure music, her little voice sweet like rain on the sands of a drought-ridden desert. A ball of emotion expanded painfully in his throat. Kamilah hadn't uttered a single word in twenty-one long months. Not since the accident. Not since she'd watched in horror as the ocean had swallowed her injured, drowning mother. Not since she'd witnessed her own father fail to save his beloved wife from the choking grip of the sea.

David had begun to believe his baby daughter might never speak again. And now that she had, he was absolutely terrified he'd do the wrong thing, say the wrong words, make her stop again.

He couldn't even begin to find his own voice. All he could do was take her soft cheeks into his hands, stare into the depths of her dark eyes and let the emotion spill hot and wet over his face.

"Daddy?"

His heart clenched. Oh God, how could a word be so painfully sweet?

She tugged at his shirt, her eyes widening in dark intensity. "She…she's dying, Daddy."

Confusion clashed with the euphoria in his brain. He'd been so focused on the sound of her voice, on the fact she'd spoken, that he hadn't heard the meaning in her words. He blinked, registered. With cognizance came a hot thread of panic. Was his sensitive little girl losing her tenuous hold on reality? Was she reliving the accident? Imagining things?

"*Who* is dying, Kamilah?"

"The…the mermaid."

"Mermaid?"

She nodded.

He hesitated. Hell, it didn't matter. Did it? Whatever it took to keep her talking, he'd play along, even with an imaginary mermaid. They could deal with the rest later. "Where is this mermaid?"

"Half-Moon Bay."

"*You* were at Half-Moon Bay? In *this* storm?"

Something shuttered in her eyes. She turned her face abruptly away from him.

"No!" *Don't turn from me. Not now.* "It's all right, Kamilah. Look at me. Tell me, baby, what's wrong with the mermaid?"

Those huge dark eyes lifted slowly to once again meet his. "She's hurt. You have to help before the sea takes her away again."

"Yes," he said, desperately trying to second-guess his child. "Yes, of course I'll help. I'll go find her."

Hope lit Kamilah's eyes making them once again dance with life. It made David's heart soar. It made every molecule in his body sing. "But listen, Kamilah, you must stay here, in the palace, with Fayha', okay? The storm is much too dangerous for you."

Her little fists clutched at his shirt. David tried to move but Kamilah's grip tightened, balling the fabric. He realized then that she wasn't convinced he'd actually go. She wasn't sure if she could trust him. *Like she hadn't been able to trust him to save her mother.*

A maelstrom of emotion crashed through David. He sucked in a deep breath, hooked his finger under her chin, lifted her face gently. "Listen to me, Kamilah, I *promise* to look for your mermaid. If she's hurt, I *promise* I'll help her. I won't let you down, baby." *Not this time.* He'd do anything to keep that sweet little voice talking. Whatever it was out there in that storm that had cracked her open, he'd find it. And he'd make damn sure it stayed on his island.

"Come here. Give me a hug." He swooped her up into his arms, felt her warm little body close to his. He felt her tiny hands creep up behind his neck and hug him tightly back. Warmth flooded him. Hot tears spilled down his face. For the first time in nearly two years he had found a connection. He was sure his heart would burst with the sheer joy of it.

With new fire in his blood, David set his daughter down. He had a storm to brave, a mermaid to find. And he had a little girl to get reacquainted with.

The wind was ten times more powerful on the battered beach of Half-Moon Bay. Froth whipped off the surface of the sea in fat globs, and bullets of hot rain beat against his face.

David squinted into maelstrom. What had disturbed Kamilah? What had she seen?

Then he saw it. A pale form among the debris. The symmetry of the shape was unmistakably human. And female. *Kamilah's mermaid!*

He kicked his stallion into a gallop along the packed wet sand. The form remained motionless as he neared. David dismounted, crouched down beside her.

She lay among scattered debris, limp as the pieces of broken jellyfish that had washed up with her. David pressed his fingers against the cold skin of her neck, searching for a pulse. She was alive. Barely. He quickly assessed the scene.

She was naked from the waist up. Her wet hair was almost hip length, and it tangled like amber seaweed about her upper body. She had the most perfect breasts he'd ever seen. Small with dusky coral-tipped nipples scrunched tight. Torn green fabric swathed her legs.

He glanced up at the perilous, churning ocean, the waves thundering over the outlying razor-sharp reefs. It was an absolute miracle she hadn't been sliced to ribbons.

He carefully moved the strands of hair from her face, looking for injury, and his breath caught. She was utterly exquisite. Her slanted eyes were closed, fringed with long amber lashes. Her honey-brown skin glistened with rain. But below the cosmetic appearance of a healthy tan, she was deathly pale. He could see why. A gaping gash split the skin on her temple. It had been washed bloodless by the sea.

He rolled her gently over toward him. There were more cuts, angry ones, down the left side of her torso. And a jagged wound on her left forearm, also bloodless from time in salt water. As he assessed her injuries, a rogue part of his brain noted she wore no wedding band, no engagement ring. A primal male awareness quickened the pace of his heart.

Thunder exploded above him and he winced. Lightning forked over the horizon. The wind shifted suddenly, thrashing in frenzied circles as if delirious at the prospect of even heavier weather. A solid wall of blackness begin to swell out over the water. It rose like a monstrous gray-toothed maw, filling the sky, sucking in everything in its path. And it began rushing in a towering, screaming wall toward the island. It was the brunt of the electrical sandstorm and it would hit any second. He had to risk moving her. Thank God Dr. Watson was still on the island. The foul weather had stopped him from flying out to Khartoum this morning.

David yanked the curved dagger from his waistband, slashed the fabric binding her legs. He ripped off his shirt, carefully slid his hands under the woman, winding the wet fabric around her. He then lifted her limp and unconscious form up onto his horse's back, praying she didn't have a back injury because this movement sure as hell would seal her fate if she did. But he had no choice. She would most certainly die out here if he tried to go for help first.

He mounted, gathered her in close to his naked chest and kicked his stallion forward. The horse bolted, stumbling wildly up the dune, eager for the shelter of home. David bent low over the woman, shielding her from the worst of the violent weather. His concentration was on speed, yet a part of him was acutely aware of the stinging sand and slashing rain on his bare back—and how the painful sensation contrasted with the soft feminine swell of the woman's breasts, of her smooth wet skin against his naked chest.

And even as he raced for his palace, deep down in his heart, David Rashid he knew he was in trouble.

Chapter 1

Where was she? Her eyes flared open. Dim light sliced through to the back of her brain where it exploded in a burst of sharp pain. She scrunched her eyes shut tight again.

She could hear an unearthly sound, like wounded banshees or a screaming wind. She couldn't make sense of it. She thought she could hear surf crashing far away. Like the drums of gods or rolling thunder. Or maybe it was just the dull thudding of her heart, the sound too loud inside her skull.

She tried to move her head, but it hurt. *Everything* hurt. Her whole body pounded with rhythmic pain as if her veins and vessels were too small and too fragile for the angry blood that was being thrust through them.

She tentatively tried to open her eyes again. Through her lashes she could make out shapes, shadows. Quivering. Firelight? Candles? An exotic scent stirred in warm currents of air. She couldn't seem to find focus. It was all a blur, so very foreign.

A wedge of panic rammed into her heart.

Then she sensed a presence. Someone standing over her. Her heart stalled. With a bite of fresh urgency, she forced her eyes open wider, trying to pull the dark shadow that loomed over her into some kind of recognizable form.

It was a man, staring down at her. A severely beautiful man with dark skin, sharp, angled features, raven-black hair and piercing blue eyes. Eyes that bored right into her soul.

Danger!

Her chest constricted. Her heart hammered up into her throat. She knew that face from somewhere. It set every alarm bell clanging. She tried to swallow, to calm herself, to breathe. She concentrated on the man's face, mentally cataloguing his features, desperately trying to find a match in her brain, to understand why he was supposed to represent a threat.

He was big, tall, with a wide chest and powerful forearms covered with dark hair. His wrists were broad, and his fingers, she noted in a distant part of her brain, were long and exquisitely shaped. His skin was an exotic mocha brown, a sharp contrast to the startling indigo of the eyes that bored into her, through her.

His brow was prominent over his eyes giving him a predatory look. In fact, everything about him was predacious, save for his mouth. His lips were full and elegantly sculpted, rescuing his features from the severity of harsh angles and planes, giving him a smouldering male sensuality, an air of refined yet dangerous aristocracy.

Her eyes moved slowly down the length of his body. He wore a loose-fitting and very white *galabiya* that offset the dusky tone of his skin. It was cinched at the waist by a brocade belt and into that belt was thrust an ornate *jambiya*. Her brain cramped. The world spun around her. A *galabiya?* It was the robe worn by most Saharan desert tribes. And the *jambiya?* Only Arabs carried the traditional curved dagger like that. But those intense blue eyes were *not* those of an Arab. *Who was he?* Where on earth was she? Confusion and fear tightened twin fists around her heart.

He was profoundly attractive, powerful, but he was also an enemy. Not on her team. She had to be careful, guarded. Her life depended on it. She knew this somehow. But how did she know all this? Why? A wild terror scrambled through her brain. What *did* she know?

Her eyes flicked nervously around the room. It was lit by lamplight, a kerosene lamp. That's what the smell was. That's what made shadows flicker on the whitewashed walls. A wooden fan turned slowly up on an exceptionally high ceiling. The room was furnished with artistic, antique-looking pieces of dark burnished wood. She noted the ornate arch over the heavy wooden door at the end of the room. The whole effect was high-end North African…or perhaps Moorish. Her heart stuttered into a crazy panicked beat. She didn't recognize a thing. She had absolutely no idea where she was. She tried to sit up.

He restrained her instantly, placing a hand firmly against her shoulder. "It's okay, relax, take it one step at a time," he said.

She stilled at the deep gravel tone of his voice. He had a British accent, yet it was underlaid with the low and sensual gutturalness of Arabic. His hand was warm on the bare skin of her shoulder, and his palm rough. She realized then that she was covered by only a white cotton sheet. Under it she was utterly naked. Alarm mounted, swamping any attempt at rational thought.

"Don't touch me." She warned, her voice coming out in a raw croak.

He withdrew his hand instantly. "As you wish. But take it easy. You've been unconscious."

"Where…where am I?"

"You're in my home on Shendi Island."

"Where's that?"

"The Red Sea, off the coast of Sudan. Shendi is a private island. I own it. My name is David Rashid."

"The Red Sea?" Her words came out in a panicked and painful rasp. Why was she anywhere near the Red Sea? The wind was making a terrible howling sound outside. She could hear it banging, tearing against shutters. It muddled her mind. She couldn't think.

Concern shifted into his eyes as he stared down at her. And that distressed her. If he was worried, she too had reason to be.

She held his gaze, fighting her fear, determined to show some strength. "Why am I here?" she demanded.

"You took a bad knock on the head. We found you unconscious on the beach. You're very lucky you didn't drown."

Drown? Knock on the head? She reached up, tentatively felt her brow where it throbbed dully. Her fingers detected a neat line of stitches along her temple just below her hairline. Alarmed, she fingered the length of what must have been a nasty gash.

"You have more cuts," he offered. "Down your left side, and along your arm."

Her eyes shot down to her forearm. More rows of tiny black stitches. Swelling. Blue-black bruising beginning to show. "What happened to me?"

"You washed up on the beach in the storm. We need to know if you were on a boat, if there were others with you. We have a search party out but have found nothing so far."

Confusion shrouded her brain. She tried to marshal her thoughts but couldn't. Her head hurt terribly. "I…I don't know…"

"That's okay." He lifted his hand to touch her shoulder again, thought better of it. "Give it time. It's probably the concussion. Let's start with your name."

She opened her mouth to say it, but she couldn't. It wouldn't come. Terror ran hot through her veins. Frantically she searched her brain, but she couldn't locate it. She couldn't remember her own name. She couldn't seem to recall anything. How she got onto the island. Where she'd been. Or why. The storm. Others on a boat.

Absolutely nothing.

His eyes sharpened again, cutting into her with laser intent as he waited for her to speak. Her mouth went dry. She clutched the sheet tight around her chest as if it would somehow shield her from the sheer horror at her predicament. The wind rose to an awful howl. Shutters crashed somewhere.

He was still watching, still waiting. But something else was shifting into his features. Pity. He felt sorry for her. And that made her feel infinitely worse. It also made her angry. She hated pity.

"If you tell me your name," he said, "once we get our communication system up and running again, we can let someone know that you're all right."

She remained silent. She had absolutely no idea who might be looking for her.

"I'm sure there are people worried about you."

She drew in a shaky breath, said nothing.

A crease deepened across the smooth skin of his brow. He studied her face, his blue eyes analyzing, stripping her down to her mental core, making her feel more naked than she already was under the crisp sheets.

"You don't know your name, do you?"

"Of course I do."

He arched a brow, waited.

"I...my name is...it's..." It still wouldn't come. She couldn't find it. She felt it was inside her head somewhere, lurking in a file folder in her brain. She just couldn't find the tab that identified the folder so that so she could grasp it, pull it out.

He touched her arm again.

She jerked back reflexively.

But this time his hand remained on her arm. "It's all right," he said, his voice suddenly incredibly gentle. His hand was warm. The roughness of his palm against her skin spoke of a man who spent a great deal of time outdoors. For some reason this grounded her. This time she found some small comfort in his touch. This time she didn't pull away.

"Just relax, I'll get Dr. Watson."

"Doctor?"

"He tended to you most of the night." He smiled into her eyes. "I took the graveyard shift so he could get some rest. I'll send for him."

Panic swamped reason. "No." She jerked away, fresh energy and determination surging through her system. She struggled into a sitting position. She clutched the sheet around her torso and swung her legs over the side of the bed. "I don't need a doctor. I'm fine."

She *would* be fine. As soon as she got moving. As soon as she got blood flowing back into her brain. Then it would all come back. Her name, everything. She was sure of it. "Where are my clothes?" she demanded.

He angled his head, tilted his dark brow, a hint of amusement lighting his intelligent eyes. "You haven't got any."

"What?"

A smile ghosted his lips. "You washed up on the shore as naked as the day you were born...apart from some torn green fabric wrapped around your legs."

She stared at him, mortified. "Who brought me up from the beach?"

"I did."

"How?"

"On my horse."

Oh, Lord. She closed her eyes, tried to find a center in the gray swirling blankness of her brain. She had to get moving. It was the only way. She was sure of it. Once she moved she'd be fine. She forced herself off the bed and onto her feet, clutching the sheet tightly around her body. Her legs felt like lead, her feet were as heavy and about as cooperative as dead stumps.

She took a step, and the world spun wildly. She wobbled, grabbed the edge of the bed, steadied herself.

He grasped her elbow. "You shouldn't move so quickly."

She jerked away from him. "I said don't touch me." She took a determined step toward the thick-looking bedroom door. Then another. But her body wouldn't behave. Her steps turned into a wild, flailing stumble, and the whole room spun. She swayed as a dizzying kaleidoscope of black and bright closed around her. She felt her legs collapse under her. Everything moved in slow motion as she sank to the floor, the sheet pooling embarrassingly at her feet as she went down.

He moved quickly, catching her head an instant before it thudded onto the cool tiles. She was vaguely aware of his callused hands against her bare torso, the brush of his forearm over her naked breast as he lifted her from the ground.

Then everything went black.

David yanked on a thick, tasseled bell cord. His housekeeper appeared almost immediately.

"Fayha', get Dr. Watson, please. Tell him his patient surfaced briefly. I think she's sleeping now."

Fayha' dipped her head in silent acquiescence, closed the door gently behind her. David turned to the mysterious woman lying in his bed, all the while listening for the approach of Watson's heavy footsteps in the stone corridor.

She looked like a wax sculpture in the golden glow of the kerosene lamp, a surreal angel. She was in her late twenties, he guessed, possessing an unconventional and exotic beauty, with high defined cheekbones, elegant arched brows and almond-shaped eyes fringed with thick amber lashes. She was tall, her muscles long and lean. But above all, it was those eyes that had undone him. They were closed now. And that made him feel a little safer.

But when they'd flared open he'd been stunned by the hugeness of them, the deep emerald green. And when she'd found focus and stared up into his own eyes, he'd been rocked by the depth he'd seen in them.

A man could drown in eyes like that. Eyes the color of the ocean.

Then a thought slammed him up the side of the head so hard and sudden he sucked in his breath. Aisha had drowned in an ocean that color. While he was diving, taking personal pleasure in the beauty and depths of a coral reef. He'd left her and Kamilah alone, up in the boat.

David swallowed against the hard knot of pain, of love and loss and irrational guilt. That was almost two years ago. The memories should be a little easier now. But they weren't. A part of him didn't even want them to be. A part of him relished the sharpness of the pain they brought him, as if hanging on to the hurt would preserve his love for his dead wife, as if it might absolve his guilt in some way.

He didn't deserve easy memories as long as Kamilah still suffered. And he didn't deserve to dive in waters like that, ever again. Which is why he hadn't. Not once since Aisha's death.

The woman in his bed moaned softly, jerking David's attention back to the present. He felt himself bracing for the incredible green of her huge eyes.

But she didn't wake. Her breathing settled back into a soft and regular rhythm, her chest rising and falling under the Egyptian cotton sheet he'd placed over her. Her hair was dry now, full of wave and curl. It fanned out about her face over the white pillows, the fiery color of a Saharan sunrise.

Her neck was sleek, elegant in the way it curved down to her collarbone. His eyes followed the lines of her body down to where the sheet rose gently over the swell of her pointed breasts. He thought of the soft and heavy weight of those breasts, naked against the palm of his hand, against his bare chest. He thought of the dusky coral nipples. David's mouth went dry. Unbidden heat spilled low into the pit of his stomach.

He wiped the back of his hand hard across his mouth in shock. This was sick, to be aroused by an injured and barely conscious woman. A woman who couldn't be more vulnerable if she tried. But by God she was desirable, in an unattainable and otherworldly kind of way.

Kamilah was right. If he'd had to conjure up the image of a mermaid in his dreams, this would be it.

A smiled tugged at his lips. Maybe he had more in common with his daughter than he dared admit. His smile deepened as he allowed his thoughts to go. Because in his dream the mermaid too would be naked with perfect coral-tipped breasts, waist-length amber hair, bewitching green eyes and an emerald-green tail.

He mentally shook his head. This was ludicrous. His thoughts and emotions were bouncing all over the place. This woman was real. A normal human being. And what might have passed for a tail was a swath of tangled green fabric. Still, he couldn't shed the deepening sense of unreality.

He reached out, tentatively touched her cheek, almost to prove to himself she was not a figment of his imagination.

She murmured again.

He jerked his hand back. His breath snared in his throat. His heart rapped a light and steady beat against his ribs. The lamplight quivered, teased by invisible fingers of warm wind that had found their way through cracks in the shutters.

He felt edgy. Finding this woman on his beach had totally unstrung him.

She groaned suddenly, wrenching her head from side to side, wincing from the obvious pain and discomfort the movement caused her. Instinctively he reached out and smoothed her hair back from her forehead. "Shh, it's okay," he soothed. "You'll be all right. You're safe here. There's nothing to hurt you here."

She stilled, as if listening for his voice.

"You're safe," he whispered again.

Her eyelids stopped flickering. The tension in her features eased. He'd managed to quell her angst, and that satisfied something primal within him. He began to move his hand away but was arrested by the silkiness of her hair against his skin. It was impossibly soft.

He lifted a long strand, let the curl twist around his fingers. And inside he felt a sudden, aching, vast and indefinable emptiness. His eyes flicked down to her left hand. There was definitely no sign of a ring, no tan line, nothing to indicate a ring that may have been lost to the storm. A hot thrill of promise speared through his chest and into his belly.

He jerked back, startled by the sheer power of his own physical reaction. He sucked in a deep breath, dragged both hands forcefully through his hair and told himself in no uncertain terms that he was only looking for clues to her identity.

But even so, he couldn't deny the spark of interest that had flared deep within. Even as he tried to quash it, he could feel the small, hot, ulcerous burn of it. He had a sinking sense it wasn't going to heal anytime soon.

The thought made his mouth dry, his head hurt. It was as if the freak storm had invaded his very brain, whipped up his normally razor-sharp and logical mind, clogging it with the rain-soaked sand.

The door banged open behind him. David just about jumped out of his skin. He swiveled around. Dr. James Watson stood there, medical bag in hand, his gray hair still slightly disheveled from sleep.

"I didn't hear you coming," he growled, furious at having been caught unawares. David Rashid was *never* caught off guard.

The doctor's wise gray eyes studied him silently, knowingly, irritatingly. "Sorry, David. Didn't mean to scare you." Watson jerked his chin toward the door. "Wind just grabbed it from my hand. Fayha' must have a door open somewhere. There's a bloody gale blowing down the corridors."

Watson closed the heavy door carefully behind him and ambled into the room with his customary air of casual authority. "So she woke up, did she?" he asked as he set his big black medical bag down on the nightstand and opened it. "How was she?"

David gave himself a mental shake, banishing unbidden images of mermaids and wedding bands to the farthest reaches of his mind. "She seemed fine. Apart from the fact she has absolutely no idea who she is, what happened to her, or how she got here," he told Watson. "Doesn't even know her name. She got up, tried to walk and went out like a light."

The doctor nodded, feeling for her pulse. He timed it, his face furrowed in thought as he focused on his watch.

David paced the room. Through the slats in the louvered shutters he could see the sky beginning to brighten. He glanced at the clock on the bedside table in surprise. It was almost 5:30 a.m. He hadn't slept a wink since he'd tucked Kamilah into bed.

Watson rested the woman's wrist back on the covers and joined David near the window. He kept his voice low. "Her breathing and heart rate are back in regular range. So far everything is looking normal."

"What about the amnesia?"

"It's not uncommon to experience some memory loss after a blow to the head. It may last seconds, days, months. It could even last years."

"Could it be permanent?"

"Possibly. She might never remember the accident that brought her here."

David studied the doctor's face. "But there's something else worrying you."

Watson pursed his lips. He glanced at the woman then back at David.

"What is it Watson?" he pressed.

"The retrograde amnesia, that's consistent with head trauma, with organic damage." The doctor chewed on the inside of his cheek, a furrow deepening along his forehead. "But the loss of sense of self…" He shook his head. "We really should get her to a hospital for a CAT scan. Maybe fly her into Nairobi, or north to Cairo. In the meantime, she'll need to stay under constant observation. And—"

But before the doctor could complete his sentence, their patient groaned. They both spun around.

Her lashes flickered against her cheeks.

David tensed, once again anticipating those incredible eyes.

Outside the wind was suddenly silent. The storm had finally died. Only surf boomed over distant coral reefs. Yellow dawn sun seeped through the louvered shutters, throwing patterns on the tiled floor as the sun peeked over the distant horizon.

Then her eyes flared open. She stared straight at David and blinked like a confused and trapped animal. Something snagged so sharply in his chest it clean stole his breath.

She looked so lost. So vulnerable.

She was straining to pull her whole world back into focus.

Lancaster's hulking frame filled the doorway of the Khartoum hotel room.

O'Reilly glanced up from his laptop. He stilled instantly at the somber expression on the big man's face. "Bad news?"

"Still no sign of her." Lancaster dragged his powerful hand over his brush cut and stepped into the room, momentarily blotting the early-morning sunlight from the window.

"And Gibbs?"

"Got picked up by a Sudanese fishing vessel last night. He's pretty bashed up. Damn lucky to be alive. He says he saw her go under, says there's no way she could have come out of that alive."

O'Reilly swore bitterly under his breath. "What the hell do we do now?"

"We find her. Dead or alive. We need to be damn sure either way."

O'Reilly turned to the window and stared out at the African city skyline. "If we go looking for her, if we send search parties out with guns blazing, Rashid's gonna find out."

"Then we do it another way, and we do it real quiet. And we kill any information before it gets out, starting with the embassy."

O'Reilly nodded. "If he finds her first…" He paused. "Rashid is a dangerous man," he said very quietly.

Lancaster studied him in silence. "Yes. But if crossed, *she* is one dangerous woman." His eyes narrowed. "And right now she is a loose thread we can't afford."

Chapter 2

"This is Dr. James Watson." David introduced the large gray-haired man to whom he'd been talking in hushed, guarded tones.

Why the secrecy? What were they hiding from her? Unfocused panic skittered through her system.

The doctor came over to her bedside. His smile was warm. "How're you feeling, Sleeping Beauty?"

From anyone else, the trite comment would have annoyed her, but she didn't mind it from this man. He seemed genuine enough, and he had the comforting look of experience in the deep lines of his weather-beaten face. "I...I've been better," she said, her voice still coming out raspy. Her tongue felt too big for her mouth, and her lips were dry and cracked. The skin on her face felt tight.

"I want you to follow this light with your eyes," Dr. Watson said, moving a pencil-thin flashlight across her field of vision. She followed the movement.

"Looking good." He clicked off the light, stepped back slightly and studied her face. "I hear you're experiencing some amnesia."

She tried again to recall what had happened, how she'd ended up on the beach of a Red Sea island in a terrible storm, but she couldn't. With a horrible, sinking realization she realized she still didn't have a clue who in the world she was.

"The most important thing is not to panic," he said.

Yeah, right. She swallowed, wincing at the raw pain in her throat. David moved instantly to the dresser, poured water from a jug into a glass, brought it to her.

She raised herself slightly on one elbow, accepted the glass from him and swallowed greedily. But before she could drain the glass, he grabbed it from her. "Whoa, take it slow."

She felt as if he'd snatched a life source from her. Her eyes flashed to his. "I'm thirsty," she challenged.

His eyes held hers, the ink of his pupils blackening his irises as he watched her face. "Too much, too fast," he said slowly, too slowly, his voice low like heavy mist in a dry and rocky canyon, "and you'll only feel worse. Trust me, I know thirst. I know the ways of the desert."

Trust him? Instinctively she knew she shouldn't. But she couldn't break his gaze. She couldn't tear her attention away from the smouldering male interest in his eyes. Her heart began to beat faster. Her breathing became more shallow. And with utter shock, she realized her body was warming under the intense heat of his gaze. She was reacting physically to the thirst in this powerful man's eyes.

He stepped slowly back from the bed, his eyes still holding her prisoner, even in retreat.

"I'd like to ask you some questions if that's all right?" The doctor's voice snapped her back. With sheer relief she turned her attention fully to Dr. Watson.

"Do you know who this is?" He gestured to David as he spoke.

She hesitated, unwilling to look at David, afraid to snare his gaze again, mortified at how he made her feel inside. Lord, she sure wished she *did* know who he was, why she was feeling these things about him. "Of course I know who he is. He's David Rashid. We…we met earlier. He…he said he brought me up from the beach." *Naked.*

"Very good. You're able to form new memories since your accident. That means no anterograde amnesia. Now let's see what you know about the past." He paused, thinking. "Okay, tell me, do you know who John Lennon was?"

"Of course."

"Churchill?"

She let out an exasperated breath. "Yes. I know who Churchill was. And Hitler. I know my history. I know about World War II. I know when the Berlin Wall came down. I know when Mandela was released. I know…" *that David Rashid is smuggling weapons-grade uranium.*

She froze. Her heart cramped tight and then hammered hard against her chest. Oh God, where had that come from? Heat flushed into her cheeks.

"Your parents?"

The doctor was talking to her, but her mind was suddenly blank.

"Do you know who your mother is? Your father?" he pressed.

She squeezed her eyes shut, trying to remember something about her childhood…*anything* about her childhood. But there was nothing. Just a black hole. She sucked in a shaky breath. "No," she said softly, opening her eyes, still trying not to look at David. "I don't know who my parents are."

"Can you recall where you went to school? To university? Your job?"

She shook her head.

The doctor was chewing on his cheek, his brow furrowed in thought. She could feel the heat of David's concentrated gaze on her. It confounded her thinking further. Unsettled her. She needed clothes. A hairbrush. Maybe then she'd feel less vulnerable.

"Do you remember where you grew up?" This time the question came from David.

She sucked in a breath and turned slowly to look into his face. She felt a flush rise in her cheeks again the instant his eyes caught hers. She fought the warming sensation, forced herself to scrutinize his features, to find a match in her brain. Why did she think he had anything to do with nuclear weapons? What did uranium have to do with anything at all? Where in heavens had that thought come from? She tried to dig it out of her memory. But it was gone, a wisp of smoke in the breeze. Had she fabricated the notion? Maybe it had been born of a confusing nightmare she'd had as she'd slept in his bed. She didn't trust anything about her mind right now. Or her body. And that scared the hell out of her. She didn't want to show just how frightened she was.

"This is ridiculous," she said. "If I can remember the Beatles, if I can recall historical events, why don't I know how I came about that information? Why don't I know where I went to school? Why don't I know who the hell I am? It just doesn't make sense." She felt tears burn behind her eyelids, which only frustrated her more.

"Give it time," Dr. Watson said. "I'll run a few more tests later. Meanwhile," he said, clipping his black bag shut, "try to relax. No use worrying about what you don't know, now, is there?"

Oh, yes, there was. She angrily sniffed back the thick emotion rising in her chest.

"You're British," David offered, his voice a little softer.

"Is that a question?" she snapped.

The hint of a smile tugged at his finely sculpted mouth. It only served to irk her further. Her belligerence, given her absolute vulnerability at the moment, obviously amused the man.

"It's a suggestion," he offered. "Your accent is English. You sound like you're from the U.K. Maybe you came on a diving holiday? Not many tourists come to the Sudanese region otherwise. Unless of course you live in the area. Or you're working here, with an aid organization, maybe?"

"*Those* are questions." And they made her deeply uneasy.

"Does any of it seem even remotely familiar?" he asked, a twinkle in the indigo of his eyes.

She closed her eyes, shutting him out. "No."

"Well...do you dive?"

Her eyes snapped open. "I don't know!"

"You *do* know where the Red Sea is?"

"Of course I know where the Red Sea is. I'm not brain dead. I just can't remember who I am." Frustration clipped her words.

David opened his mouth to speak. But Watson's hand restrained him.

"It's perfectly normal to feel frustrated," said the doctor, eyeing first David, then her. "Things will probably start coming back as you begin to feel better. For starters, you could probably do with something to eat."

God bless the doctor.

"Of course," said David. "Forgive me. I'll get Fayha', my housekeeper, to bring you some breakfast. Anything in particular you like?"

"I...I..." She racked her brain. "Dammit, I don't know!" She struggled into a sitting position, clutching on to her sheet. Something shifted suddenly in David's eyes. He was watching how her hands clutched the sheet over her breasts. "Don't worry," he said, his voice deeper, the Arabic accent suddenly stronger. "We'll find out who you are. We'll put word out as soon as we have communication up and running again. We'll contact the embassies in the region and the Sudanese Ministry of Interior. You can't get into this part of the world without a visa, and you have to register with authorities once you arrive. If you came to Shendi from Sudan, there'll be a record. We'll also put word out in Saudi Arabia and Egypt in case you were on a dive trip that originated from one of those countries. Someone will know who you are."

"Great," she muttered. "I sure as hell hope so."

"And once you've eaten," said Dr. Watson, "I'll come back and run a few more simple tests. In the meantime," his eyes shifted to David, "I need to pack for Khartoum. I have to leave this afternoon if we're going to get those medical supplies to the Ba'ar mine before the end of the week."

David nodded and Watson made for the door.

She panicked. The doctor was going to leave her alone with *him*.

"Are you a neurologist?" She called after Watson in an un-focused attempt to keep him in the room.

The doctor paused, turned calmly back to face her. He indulged her with his warm and generous smile. "No, I'm an internist. But I do have some basic neurological and psychiatric training. I'm in David's employ," he explained.

"Employ?"

"Watson works for Rashid International, my company," said David. "He sees to my employees in remote areas, and you're damn lucky he was still around when you washed up."

Rashid International. Something pinged faintly in the back of her brain. There was something familiar about the name… as if she had a role to play with the organization. But that wasn't possible…because then surely David and Watson would know who she was, wouldn't they?

A noise outside in the passage interrupted her thoughts. David heard it, too. He stilled, listened. And a grin spread slowly across his face. "Kamilah?" he called out. "Is that you lurking out there?"

The silky, dark head of a child peered around the heavy door. Huge chocolate-brown eyes stared straight at her. They were the eyes of a beautiful and nervous deer, she thought as she studied the girl. She had velvet coffee-brown skin, and her hair, the same blue-black as David's, hung thick below her slight shoulders.

"Ah, as I suspected." David held his hand out to the child. "Come on in, sweetheart." He turned to face her. "This is my daughter, Kamilah. She discovered you on the beach. I believe she saved your life."

She looked from David to Kamilah and back. Saved her life? This child?

Kamilah stepped cautiously into the room.

A band of tension strapped tight across David's chest as he watched his daughter edge toward the woman in his bed. Kamilah had not uttered another word since he'd brought her "mermaid" up from the beach, in spite of his best efforts to reengage her verbally.

At first his heart had sunk. But her eyes had looked deep into his, giving him a rare window into her little soul. And in her eyes he'd read gratitude. That look alone had shifted the ground beneath his feet. And her small hand had held his so very tight when he'd brought her to see the "mermaid" in his bed once Watson had stitched her up.

And when he'd kissed Kamilah's soft dark head good-night, she'd smiled, hugged him as if her little life depended on the contact. It had all been a precious slice of pure sunshine in a world that had been way too gray for way too long.

But still, he couldn't shake his feeling of unease as he watched Kamilah venture up to the woman's bedside. He watched his daughter's eyes widen in awe at the sight of the golden woman in his bed.

"Hello, Kamilah." The woman's voice was suddenly soft. Melodious.

"I guess I owe you a very big thank-you," she said. "How on earth did you manage to find me in the storm?"

She waited, expecting Kamilah to answer.

The room went dead quiet. Expectancy hung thick in the air. David felt the muscles in his neck go stiff. Would she speak again?

His daughter edged even closer to the bed. It had been a long, long time since David had seen such confidence in his baby. For the past two years, she'd all but coiled up in front of strangers. He tried to swallow against the odd mix of sensations in his throat. Would she speak in front of one now?

"I...I was waiting for you," Kamilah said so softly David thought he might have imagined the sound.

"Waiting for me?"

Kamilah's dark head nodded. "For a long time."

Emotion exploded instantly into David's chest. She'd spoken to a stranger! Just like that. When for the past two years she hadn't been able to utter a word to *him*. A curious cocktail of relief and resentment began to churn in his stomach.

"You were *waiting* for me?" the woman asked again, confusion knitting her brow. Her eyes flicked up, met David's. He could see the unspoken question in them. But he couldn't move. He couldn't say a thing. She scrutinized him, then she turned her green eyes on Watson. He said nothing, either. Neither of them were willing to break the spell.

The woman turned her attention back to Kamilah, obviously aware that something was playing out on a much deeper level. "Well, I'm very grateful that you found me," she softly.

And with those few words, she notched up a resenting respect from David. In spite of her injury, in spite of her memory loss, she had enough presence of mind not to call Kamilah on her statement. She'd simply gone with the flow.

David watched as Kamilah's eyes slid in wonder down from the woman's face to where her legs raised the Egyptian-cotton sheet. Then his daughter tensed visibly.

"What is it, Kamilah?" the woman asked.

Kamilah's eyes shot up to the woman's face, then back to the unmistakable shape of legs under the sheet. And David knew. He knew *exactly* what was worrying Kamilah. The woman didn't have a tail.

He had to do something, say something. He cleared his throat. "Kamilah…feels, uh, she believes that you should have a tail."

Everyone stared at him. He cleared his throat again. "You're…you're supposed to be a mermaid. With a tail."

The woman's almond-shaped eyes widened. Her jaw dropped. David's stomach balled into a knot. He had no idea what the woman might say, what words it would take to crush his child. He was petrified Kamilah would once again derail when she discovered the woman was not a real mermaid.

"A tail?"

David nodded. "Yes."

She studied his eyes, trying to read him, trying to guess his game, then she turned slowly to face Kamilah. "Should I have a tail, Kamilah? Please don't tell me I should have a tail. Have I totally lost it?"

Watson chuckled heartily, cracking the tension. "Well if you had a tail it's gone now, so yes, I'd say you lost it." The doctor continued to chortle merrily at his own joke.

David didn't find it at all amusing. He knew what this meant to Kamilah.

The woman sensed it, too. "But *you* seem to think I should have a tail, Kamilah?"

The little girl nodded, her face deadly serious.

"Hmm." Then the woman smiled. A warm smile. Like sunshine. It reached right into her emerald eyes making them sparkle with the morning light. And it made a dimple deepen in her one cheek. David stared, struck once again by her unbalanced beauty, by how white her teeth were against her soft tan. She'd been exquisite in repose, but the animation in her smile brought her beauty to full life. And it was dazzling. But it wasn't only her physical appearance that intrigued him. She possessed a latent confidence, and right now she was in control of this bizarre situation in spite of her loss of identity, in spite of the fact she was stark naked under that thin sheet, a fact he couldn't seem to erase from his mind.

Bemused, he watched as she placed her hand gently over Kamilah's. "You know, sometimes it happens when mermaids come on land," she said softly. "Sometimes they lose their tails in exchange for something else…like legs." She tipped her head conspiratorially closer to his daughter's, and lowered her smoky voice to a whisper.

"And, Kamilah," she said. "You do have to remember that sometimes things are not quite what meet the eye. You've always got to keep an open mind, because one can never be sure when it comes to the magic of fairy tales." She smiled again. "But I think you know that, don't you? I think you know all about fairy tales."

No one spoke. Tiny dust motes danced, glistened in the shafts of yellow sunshine sneaking through the wooden slats that covered the window.

"What's your name?" Kamilah's little whisper sliced the silence. David released a whoosh of air he hadn't realized was trapped in his lungs. His heart tripped back into a steady rhythm. His child was coping. She was going to be okay.

The woman studied his daughter carefully, looking deep into her eyes, as if seeing something there that he, a mere mortal, a mere father, didn't have the power to see.

"Kamilah," she said. "I don't have a name. Not right now, anyway. I can't remember it. I got a bad knock on the head, and I can't seem to remember where I came from."

Kamilah nodded solemnly, as if she understood completely, as if mermaids not only lost tails but that it was quite common for them to lose their minds when they got washed up out of the sea. Then his child turned suddenly and stared expectantly up at him.

David swallowed, taken aback by the spark of urgency in his child's eyes. He wasn't sure what she wanted. "What is it, Kamilah?" he asked.

His child waited, eyes eager.

"Kamilah?"

She said nothing.

Why wouldn't she speak to *him*? Why did *he* have to try and second-guess everything? What did she want from him?

Watson nudged him. "She wants you to come up with a name, Rashid."

"What?" His eyes flashed to the doctor.

"Give her a name," urged Watson. "She wants you to give the mermaid a name."

Kamilah nodded, her liquid eyes intent.

David felt suddenly cornered. He scrambled through his brain, trying to find some moniker for the mysterious woman. He couldn't.

Kamilah waited. Everyone waited.

Why was this suddenly his responsibility? He swallowed, cleared his throat. "Sahar," he said finally.

Everyone in the room looked at him. "Sahar," he said again, as if the repetition would somehow make it more real. Still the silence hung heavy and awkward. It was as if he now needed to explain his choice.

But he couldn't do it. Wouldn't. It was suddenly too personal, his choice too intimate. Because Sahar meant awakening. Dawn. A new beginning. And he'd chosen it because of what she'd brought to his daughter. This woman had made his precious little desert flower come alive again, long after she'd all but withered on the vine.

And she had hair like a Saharan sunrise.

The woman's eyes studied him from across the room. Something strange and unreadable shifted in her features. "Thank you," she said softly. "That's a beautiful name."

David shrugged. He felt awkward. This whole damn situation had knocked him off balance.

But he was rewarded with a brilliant smile from Kamilah as she nodded in happy agreement. David's heart torqued in his chest at the rare sight of warmth and animation in his little girl's face. He'd done something to make his baby happy. He'd taken another tiny step on the complex road he traveled with his daughter. And despite his portfolio of international achievements, nothing made him feel more proud, more worthy.

The woman, Sahar, turned to Kamilah. "Now, sweetheart, do you know where a mermaid could possibly find something to wear...and maybe a hairbrush?"

Kamilah hesitated. Then she spun on her heels and charged from the room, brushing David's legs as she ran past him into the hallway.

It was in that very instant that David knew *exactly* where his daughter was going.

"No!" he yelled, spinning around. "Wait! Kamilah!"

Watson grabbed his arm, held him back. "Let her go, David. She needs to do this. She needs to move on. You both do."

David clenched his jaw. His heart pounded in his chest. His hands felt clammy. He could feel the woman's eyes appraising him. And he suddenly felt exposed. Humiliated by his own irrational outburst.

He jerked free of Watson's hold, stormed from the room. Furious, he marched down the passage, his riding boots clacking loudly on the stone floors.

"Fayha'!" he barked. The sound of his voice bounced off the thick stone walls, resounded under the arches of his palace. "Fayha'! Where are you?"

His housekeeper came scuttling from the direction of the kitchen. "Sir?"

"Help Kamilah," he ordered. "I'm going for a ride."

"Where is she?"

"In—" he hesitated "—in the room. The room with her mother's things."

Fayha''s eyes widened.

"Just do it." He swiveled on his heels and headed for the stables. But inside he knew. *He* should be the one helping Kamilah. *He* should be with her in that room, going through Aisha's things. Working through the past, putting it away properly. But he couldn't. He just couldn't make himself go in there. He hadn't so much as opened the door since he and Kamilah had returned to Shendi Palace. He'd had his staff move all of Aisha's possessions in there after the funeral.

At the time, he hadn't been able to throw or give anything away. He loved his wife too much for that. At the time, he'd felt that getting rid of her things would be like trying to excise her memory.

And now...well, now it was two years later. What good

would it do either of them to dig into old memories now, to touch Aisha's clothes, to feel the silk of them, to smell her lingering fragrance on them?

His eyes burned.

Holding on to memories was one thing. Physically digging up the past quite another. He'd said his goodbyes. He'd come to terms with the fact she was gone. He had no need to go digging into the past, and neither should his daughter. They had to look forward. Not back.

This was all Sahar's fault.

David clenched his fists, gritted his jaw, strode angrily through the courtyard toward the stables. There was dust and sand everywhere, piled in miniature dunes and stuffed into every conceivable crevice. The whole bloody world had been turned on its head by the freak storm.

And by what it had blown in.

He shoved the stable door open, felt the soft and familiar give of pungent hay. It helped ease his mind. He made directly for Barakah's stall.

But even as he led his stallion out, deep down, David knew what was really irking him. It was the fact his little girl had responded to a total stranger. She had spoken words that had flowed so naturally from her mouth you'd think she'd never been mute. She had quite simply come alive. Because of a stranger washed up with the wind and rain.

After all he had tried to do for Kamilah, after all this time, a mysterious woman had simply blown into their lives and made it happen in the blink of an eye. It should have been *he* who'd broken through his daughter's shell. He *needed* that victory, dammit. He *needed* to know his daughter had forgiven him. Totally.

The woman had deprived him of that.

Resentment began to snake through him. But braided with

the bitterness he felt toward Sahar was a thread of gratitude for her having cracked open Kamilah's shell. And there was a third thread in that complicated braid. One he preferred not to think about. Because it forced him to face the fact that she had not only awakened his daughter, she had stirred something frightening and powerful in *him*. She'd made something come alive and burn, slow and deep inside his soul.

Trouble was, he didn't want to feel this way. He didn't want to feel this insidious burning in his gut, this low, raw longing for a woman with no memory. A woman who was surely going to leave Shendi, abandon Kamilah as soon as she figured out who she was.

David gritted his teeth.

It was best she left, sooner rather than later. Before Kamilah got too attached, he wanted her gone from his island.

David led Barakah into the storm-washed morning. In the distance the rising sun glimmered off the ocean surface, making it shine like hand-beaten copper. The color filled his mind. And as he mounted his stallion he could think only of how the color resembled Sahar's long sun-kissed curls, the way the gold and copper shades contrasted with the startling green of her haunting eyes. And the way her skin had felt against his.

He swore softly in Arabic. He needed her gone all right. He couldn't begin to feel these things for a woman who had another life, perhaps even another man. He *wouldn't* allow Kamilah to be hurt.

With a spurt of anger, he kicked Barakah into action. He needed a tough workout. He needed to clear his head. And by the time he returned, he expected his technician to have restored communication on the island.

Then he would set to work, find out who the devil this woman was and where she had come from.

Then he'd send her right back where she belonged.

Chapter 3

Sahar listened as David Rashid's angry footsteps faded to a distant echo. Confusion shrouded her brain. She lifted her hand to her forehead. Why in heavens did she know the meaning of the name he had just given her? Did she know Arabic? Or just the meanings behind Arabic names? And why did she feel honored, touched, by the name David had given her? Was it because of the raw look she'd glimpsed in his eyes as he'd spoken it? Or was she trying to read meaning where there was none?

Watson misread her confusion. "Your head hurting?"

"Uh…no. I…I'm just trying to remember."

He smiled. "No need to try and rush the process. The body is a wonderful thing in the way it can heal—and protect itself—but you must give it time."

Time. She didn't have time. Why did she feel she was running out of time?

"I'll come back once you've got some clothes on and had something to eat. We can do some more tests then, okay?"

She nodded, watched the doctor make for the door. "Dr. Watson," she called out. He halted, turned around.

"About Kamilah...the mermaid thing?"

He hesitated. "The child hasn't spoken a word in two years," he said. "Not since the death of her mother."

"What happened?"

"Aisha Rashid drowned in a boating accident not far off the coast of this island." He smiled sadly. "David took a huge gamble coming back here. Returning to Shendi was a final bid to bring life back to his child. He's done everything within his power to try to get Kamilah to speak again. Nothing worked until now—until you arrived."

"Me?"

He nodded. "That's right. Kamilah Rashid had not spoken in nearly two years—until she found you on the beach."

"And she...she really thinks I'm a *mermaid?*"

"The fact that she thinks you're a fantasy creature is key," he said. "You've helped bridge the gap between her silent, private world and the real one."

"So...so why is her father so angry?" The range of unguarded emotion she'd seen cross David Rashid's face in the space of a few beats of a heart compelled her to ask.

A broad grin creased the doctor's sun-browned face. "Ah, a couple of things have got his goat, I suspect. Rashid likes to be in control. *He* wanted to be the one to make his daughter well again. Now he's faced with a mermaid who's done the trick for him." Dr. Watson chuckled. "You've wounded the man's pride, but don't worry. He'll be fine once he's licked his wounds. He always is. I'll be back later."

Sahar watched as the doctor closed the heavy door behind him. She was desperately grateful to have some time alone.

She needed to think. She swung her feet carefully over the side of the bed and stood slowly, not wanting to repeat the fainting episode. The tiles were cool under her bare feet. She steadied herself against the bed, waiting for a momentary dizziness to pass. Then she wound the sheet neatly around her body and moved over to the long oval mirror nestled into a tall dark-wood closet at the far end of the room.

She hesitated, almost afraid to look. Then she sucked in air and stepped squarely in front of the mirror. She stared at the person reflected in the glass.

The eyes that stared back were her own. Logic told her that. She stepped closer, touched the reflection with her fingertips. There was something vaguely familiar about her image. It was as if she was looking at someone she'd crossed paths with once or twice before. But she couldn't place where or when.

She studied the face. It was a face she was comfortable owning. It felt like her. But how? How did she know what it felt like to be her?

Was she a tourist? Somehow she didn't feel like one.

Could she dive? She thought she probably could.

Slowly she unwound the sheet and studied the rest of her body. She had no jewelry. No necklace, rings, bracelets or earrings. No clues. Nothing at all to give her away.

That didn't feel right. Something was missing. The sensation niggled away at the back of her brain. And with a start, she realized she was fingering her left hand, exactly where she'd wear a wedding ring...if she had one. She frowned. Why did she feel as if it was missing?

She ran her hand gently over the cuts and bruising down the left side of her torso.

Had she been on a boat when the storm hit? Were there others who hadn't survived? Damn, damn, damn. For the life of her she couldn't recall a single thing about how she got to this island of David Rashid's. She scooped up the sheet in frustration, wound it tightly around her body and stomped over to the shutters. She flipped the catch and threw them open wide as if to cast clarity on her situation. But the harsh flare of yellow sunlight exploded against her eyes. She scrunched her face tight in painful reflex.

As the stab of pain slowly subsided, she became cognizant of the sun's rays. With her eyes still closed, she lifted her face to meet the light. The warmth on her skin offered a basic animal comfort. She breathed in deeply, feeling tension slowly begin to dissipate as she allowed the warmth to soak through her.

It dawned on her then—she was like a primal creature. No clothes. No identity. No past. Only the present. Only the sensation of warmth on her face to give her a feeling of being alive, a feeling of belonging in the world. This sensation was the closest she could come to a sense of home, of who she was. Because beyond that, she'd been reduced to nothing.

She didn't know if she had a family or if she had kids, though she guessed not—the idea seemed too foreign. Perhaps she had a lover, someone who right now was worried sick about her. Did she have a job? A house? An apartment? Did she have a cat or a dog?

Is this what it felt like to start from scratch? To have a blank slate and a chance to do things over? Because it sure as hell didn't feel like fun. It felt formidable. And claustrophobic, as if she was hemmed in by an invisible fortress.

Panic started to grip again. She pressed the palm of her hand against her stomach, trying to force calm on herself. The doctor had said she might feel like this. He'd said she would also likely experience anger, denial. That was normal, he'd said. But what in hell was normal about this? What in hell was normal about a stranger giving you a new name? A name that means dawn, new beginnings.

The distant sound of hooves thudding on packed sand registered in her brain, yanking her mind back into the room. Her eyes flicked open. She shielded them against the harsh glare of the sun with her hands and searched for the source of the sound.

The sight that greeted her clean stole her breath. Through the arched window, the sea gleamed a brilliant turquoise in the distance. Waves rolled relentlessly toward the shore and broke in long ribbons onto a beach of pure white sand, spraying spumes of white spindrift into the wind.

The beach turned gradually into shades of cream, amber, orange and ochre as the land curved in sweeping, undulating hills toward her. Then the sand gave way to rich vegetation closer to the castle walls.

She blinked. *Castle?*

She leaned out of the window. Yes, she was in some kind of Moorish-style castle. Walls, several stories high, ran off in either direction from her window. Arches were cut into them at regular intervals. At the end of the one wall, the building veered off into another wing and at the end of that she could make out a square tower with turrets along the top. In other parts, the roof was angled over the walls and covered with thick irregularly shaped tiles baked reddish-ochre by the sun.

The sound of the galloping hooves that had alerted her grew louder, echoing off the palace walls. She leaned even further out the window, searching for the rider. Then she saw him.

He came around the far wing of the castle and headed at breakneck pace across the sandy ridge on a huge and powerful white stallion. Her stomach muscles tightened automatically at the sight. David and the horse formed a dark and powerful silhouette against the glare of the sea. He rode with a fierce and reckless abandon. Bareback. Like a wild desert warrior born with the beast between his legs.

He and the creature on which he was mounted looked as untamed and dangerous as the Sahara itself.

How did she know that? Had she been to the Sahara? Her hands tensed on the thick stone windowsill.

As he reached the edge of the ridge, his horse reared up, hooves pawing the air. Her breath caught in her throat. But he moved naturally with the stallion, steadying him effortlessly. Then he reined in the horse and headed down the ridge. She could see the sheen of exertion glisten on the animal's white flanks and the blue-black glint of the sun on David's hair. Even from this distance she could see the powerful strength in the man's coffee-skinned forearms.

He kicked his horse into a gallop and she could feel the rapid, rhythmic pounding of the hooves echo right through her chest as he disappeared down the far edge of the ridge and headed into the hills that sloped toward the sea.

She tried to lean even farther out the window in an effort to catch one last glimpse. But he was gone. And she felt a small and inexplicable slip in her gut.

She stepped back into the cool of the room, suddenly aware of her quickened pace of breathing, the heightened rate of her pulse. Who *was* this man? She forced her brain to think. He said he headed up a company, Rashid International. A sinister sensation crept up the back of her neck. Maybe she had a role to play, something to do with him and with his company. Something subversive. She could sense it in the murky shadows of her mind. Fear began to edge in.

She tried to swallow, to fight down the fright demons. She couldn't allow fear to take over. She had no one in the world to turn to right now. She had to get a grip on herself. She had only herself.

The door banged open behind her.

Instantly she spun around.

But it was only Kamilah, a shy grin on her little face, her arms piled high with silky garments.

With shock, Sahar realized her hands were raised in front of her, her legs tensed for a kick, her whole body, every muscle, was primed to attack this child. Shaken by her instinctive aggression, she pressed her hands firmly down to her sides and forced a smile. "Kamilah, you startled me."

Kamilah entered the room and began to lay her armload of garments out on the bed. Sahar forced herself to relax. She moved over to the bed and fingered the sheer, exotic textures. "These are beautiful, Kamilah, where did you get them?"

Kamilah looked down at her feet. "They're my mother's," she said softly.

Sahar froze. "Oh, Kamilah, I couldn't possibly wear your mother's clothes."

Kamilah's big brown eyes lifted slowly up. Sahar could read the hurt in them. She crouched down to the child's height. "Kamilah," she said. "It's not because I don't like them. I think they're the most beautiful dresses I've ever seen. But I'm not sure your father would be happy if he saw me wearing these clothes. And I really wouldn't want to upset anybody."

Kamilah's bottom lip trembled slightly. Sahar was at a loss. The poor child seemed to desperately need this. She sighed. "Okay, how about I just try one dress on, then?"

Kamilah's face lit up. She immediately reached for a silky green dress and held the garment out to her.

Sahar took it from the child. "You think it'll fit me?"

Kamilah nodded.

Sahar held the fabric against her face and turned toward the mirror. Kamilah had made a fine choice. The jade-green silk picked up the dark flecks in her eyes. She moved closer to the mirror. But as she did, a bright-white light stabbed through her head. She gasped. Her hand shot to the neat line of stitches under her hairline. It was as if she'd seen something. As if dark glass had cracked and let in a painful bright shard of memory. A memory that had something to do with the color of this jade-green silk. Something more than just the color. But as sharp and fast as it had come, it was gone.

Sahar's heart pounded. She carefully set the dress back onto the bed. She couldn't possibly put it on. She had to find a way out of this without upsetting Kamilah.

But before she could speak, the unmistakable sound of galloping hooves once again thudded into her brain. *The Arabian horseman—David Rashid.*

She spun around and peered out the window inexplicably hungry for another glimpse of the man on his stallion.

She saw him coming back up along the ridge at a hell-bent pace, spurts of red dust shooting up behind the stallion's hooves, the horse's mane and tail flying free with the wind of speed. Her breath caught once again at the primitive image of the powerful man astride his white horse.

"That's my daddy," said the small voice at her side.

Sahar released her breath in a whoosh. "Wow, he sure can ride. What a beautiful horse."

"He's got lots of horses. That's Barakah, his stallion. He's just broken him in." Pride for her father had burst out in a spurt of words that left the little girl looking shell-shocked at the sound of her own voice.

Sahar chose not to comment, to go with the flow as if nothing was unusual. "You're kidding? He's totally in control. That stallion must be a devil to ride, but your dad makes it look like he was born on the horse."

Kamilah shrugged.

"So, *was* he born on a horse?"

A smiled struggled across Kamilah's lips. "Kind of."

Sahar crouched down again. "How so?"

"My...my daddy, he used to ride with *his* daddy, Sheik Omar bin Zafir Rashid, when he was very little, in the desert. That's where he learned how."

"Sheik? Your grandfather's a sheik?"

The little girl nodded.

"And does he live here, too?"

She shook her head. "He's dead now. Like my mummy. He was the leader of a nomad tribe in the desert. Now daddy is the sheik."

Curiosity quickened through Sahar. Somehow, instinctively she'd known David Rashid was connected with the Sahara. And the fact he was titled slotted into her brain like a missing puzzle piece. "So is *that* where your father is from? The Sahara desert?"

Kamilah nodded.

"But he's also got a bit of an English accent."

She nodded again.

"So he's from two places? From England *and* the desert?" She felt a twinge of guilt at pressing the child like this for information on her father, but she couldn't help herself.

The child smiled shyly. "Yes, and he's been teaching me to ride. Horses and camels, too."

"Your daddy must be very, very proud of you."

Kamilah shook her head solemnly. "He's upset with me."

"Oh, sweetheart, why on earth would he be upset with you?"

"Be-becau-because I...I can't talk." She stumbled over her words, suddenly self-conscious again.

"Oh, honey," she bent down, took Kamilah's hands in her own, "you *are* talking. Beautifully. Listen to yourself."

Tears pooled along the rims of the child's big eyes. "I...I can talk to you...but...I...I can't talk...to my daddy. Or...or anyone."

"Because I'm a mermaid? Is that why you feel you can talk to me?"

"Yes," she said in a tiny voice. "Because I knew my mommy would send you from the sea."

A swell of emotion choked Sahar's throat. "And that's why you were waiting for me? You knew your mother would send you something from the sea, because that's where she went?"

Tears spilled from Kamilah's eyes and ran in a sheen over her smooth brown cheeks. Sahar took the child's shoulders in her hands and looked into her eyes. "Kamilah, have you been able to speak to *anyone* since your mother died?"

She shook her head.

"No one at all?"

A sob shuddered through her body. "I…I…I had to…I had to tell my daddy you were on…on the beach. I *had* to speak or the sea would take you away."

"And you haven't been able to speak to him again, not since you found me?"

She shook her head. Another sob racked through her little body, and fresh tears streamed down her face.

"Oh, honey, come here." She drew the little girl into her arms and hugged her tight. She nestled her nose into Kamilah's hair. She could smell the apple scent of the child's shampoo. She could smell sunshine in her clothes.

And in Sahar's heart an unbidden sense of responsibility swelled. She hugged tighter. She wanted to tell Kamilah she wasn't really a mermaid. But she didn't know what she was. She had a fictional name. No past. No future. She wasn't a real person. Not in this child's eyes. Not in her own eyes. She was a one-dimensional fabrication with no sense of self. A half person. A fairy tale.

And the notion made her feel suddenly so very alone and desperately lost. As lost as Kamilah probably felt.

As much as Kamilah seemed to need her, Sahar also needed this child. She needed this connection, this hug, this human touch. It somehow grounded her in the frightening mental blankness of her world.

The child probably needed her own mother for all the same reasons. To feel grounded. Whole. Loved.

She *had* to help this little girl, whatever it took. Right now this child was the one thing that linked her to some sense of purpose.

She felt Kamilah's little hands stroking her hair. A hiccup of emotion tore through Sahar's chest. Even in her own state of distress the child was offering comfort. She was a deep little thing. Intelligent and full of silent, lonely agony. Kamilah's subconscious had cooked up a mermaid story to help explain the inexplicable—why the people you loved most had to die. The fantasy somehow helped justify the tragedy to the child. And perversely Kamilah now thought Sahar was one of the mermaids sent up from the sea by her mother to help her. A gift from the ocean in exchange for all the ocean had taken away.

And with that realization, Sahar vowed to herself that no matter what it took, she would do what she could to help Kamilah. She would *be* that gift from the ocean.

And hopefully, by the time she got her memory back, by the time she figured out who she was and where she belonged, Kamilah would be beyond the need for fantasy and mermaids and she'd be ready for her to leave Shendi Island.

"Kamilah, look at me, honey."

Kamilah's tear-streaked face gazed up at hers. "Listen to me, Kamilah. I'll make you a promise. I will help you find your lost voice if you will promise to help *me* find my lost memory."

The little girl's lips began to tremble.

"Is that a deal, sweetheart?"

Kamilah nodded, swiping at her tears with her little hand, smudging them across her face. Then she flung herself back into Sahar's arms and clung tight. "Please," she whispered, her little breath warm against Sahar's neck, "please don't ever…ever go away…like…like my mummy. Please don't ever go back to the sea."

"You think she's *faking* it?" David's hand tightened around his glass. He had to get a grip on the irrational anger, the strange swirl of unidentifiable emotions that tightened around him when he thought of Sahar.

"No, I'm not saying that."

David slammed his glass onto the table. "Then what are you saying, Watson?"

The doctor eyed him silently. "Why don't you sit down, David."

"I'm comfortable standing." He waited for Watson to continue.

"Okay, all I'm saying is that her amnesia appears to be psychological in origin."

"Meaning what, exactly?"

The doctor sipped his mint tea, ice chinking against the glass. "Meaning I think she needs a shrink. Her vitals are fine. I ran several basic memory tests and apart from the loss of personal identity and personal history, I can detect absolutely no other retrograde or anterograde dysfunction—no signs of organic damage."

"So it's all in her head, then?"

Watson smiled. "I forgive you the pun, Rashid."

David was not amused. He waited in irritable silence for the doctor to continue.

"She appears to have a dissociative disorder, most likely stemming from the trauma. It's probably some kind of coping mechanism. She really needs a specialist for me to be one hundred per cent sure, David. I don't want to jump to conclusions."

"You think she's mentally cutting herself off from her accident?"

"It's possible."

"Or faking it."

The doctor sighed. He set his glass down, pushed it to the middle of the table, leaving droplets of condensation in its wake. "It's always difficult to tell."

David dragged his hands through his hair. This mind business was so damned awkward. He'd been through all this with Kamilah. It had taken him months to come to terms with the fact the accident had shut his daughter off. A part of him always believed Kamilah held some control, that if she really wanted to, she would speak. That she had the choice.

He'd dealt with anger. Denial. He'd even come to a kind of acceptance. Yet a mad part of himself couldn't let the thought go that perhaps Kamilah was punishing him for not having managed to save Aisha.

Specialist after London specialist had not been able to help either of them. That's where Watson had come in. He'd helped David come to terms with the fact Kamilah did not hold control over her speech. That she was trapped in a psychological prison.

And now this woman. More mind games. He liked things up-front. Direct. Straightforward. He blew out a breath of pent-up air, reached for his tea, swigged. "Okay. So what you're saying is medical attention is not urgent."

"Not life-threatening urgent, but a good idea."

"Fine." He set his glass down. "My tech says the sat-phone system should be up again by tomorrow morning. In the meantime, when you get into Khartoum this evening, you get Sahar's details to the British Embassy and to the Ministry of the Interior. Hopefully they'll get bulletins out via Interpol, newspapers, whatever, and she'll be identified within the next few days. Her relatives can then come and get her and take her to a specialist in her hometown…wherever that is."

Watson drained the last of his tea, plunked the glass down and stood. "Good enough. I'll stop by and see the ambassador this evening. In the meantime, little things like a familiar scent or sound could help jog her memory. Once she grabs on to a particular thread, the whole lot could come cascading back in one go."

"Yeah, let's hope that happens sooner rather than later."

"It could be traumatic if it happens all at once, David. She'll need someone to help her through it."

"Yeah." David checked his watch. "The chopper should be ready. I'll see you out."

The doctor hesitated.

"What now?" David asked, words more clipped than he'd intended.

"Why the anger, David? The woman's helpless. It's not her fault."

"Ah, don't you go pulling the shrink stuff on *me* now, Watson."

"You're worried about the mermaid thing, about Kamilah."

David sighed deeply. He studied Watson's lined face. The man was his friend. He meant well. He had no right to take his frustration out on the doc. "Yes," he said. "I'm concerned about her grasp on reality, on her unnatural attachment to this woman." *And his own alarming physical attraction to her.*

"Kamilah has started to speak, David. You've both reached a major milestone. Things can only go forward from here."

"Kamilah thinks the woman's some kind of fictional creature. *That's* the only reason she spoke."

Watson chuckled heartily. "Mermaid, schmermaid, whatever Kamilah thinks, it broke through her mental barriers. Use it, David. Use the tools that have been placed in your hands."

David gave a derisive snort. "The *tool* I have been handed, Watson, is an unexplained woman coughed up by the sea in a freak storm. Why can't my life be simple?"

Watson grinned broadly. "Because you're not a simple man, Rashid."

David smiled in spite of himself. "Seriously, Watson," he said. "The woman will be gone in a few days. Where will *that* leave us?"

The doctor tilted a bushy white brow. "Us?"

"I mean Kamilah, where will that leave Kamilah?" His verbal slip shocked him. And it must have shown in face. Because the doctor angled his head and scrutinized him knowingly. "She's a beautiful woman, David."

"What the hell has that got to do with it?" he snapped, his voice harsher than he'd intended.

The doctor raised his hand in mock defeat. "Okay, okay. But any red-blooded male can't help notice she's one hell of a woman."

"And probably attached," he said in spite of himself.

Watson's weather-beaten face cracked into a grin. "Ah, so you *did* notice, Rashid. There is hope for you yet."

"She'll be history as soon as her memory returns. The sooner she goes, the better. I don't want Kamilah any more attached to the woman than she already is."

And *he* sure as hell didn't want to feel any more attracted to her than he already was.

The doctor nodded, the twinkle still in his eyes. "Word about our beautiful amnesiac should start circulating by this evening. People like her don't go unnoticed, David. Especially in a place like Sudan. We'll know soon enough."

David watched the doctor waddle off with his characteristic uneven gait. Damn him. That all-knowing gleam had never left Watson's perceptive eyes. Not once. He'd noted David's blatant attraction to Sahar, and that just made David angrier. He'd thought he'd at least demonstrated outward control of his libido. That his male interest was so obvious irked the hell out him. It meant Sahar had likely seen it, too. And that gave her a power he didn't want her to have.

Because David Rashid *always* made sure the balance of power was in his hands.

Chapter 4

David took his brandy out onto the tiled terrace that overlooked the lagoon and the ocean beyond. The sky was devoid of cloud, the air sultry and the black heavens peppered with stars.

Dinner with Kamilah had been really special. Just the two of them. She hadn't spoken to him again, but she'd engaged him with her eyes. Watson was right. It was progress. And he was going to hold on to that.

He allowed himself to relax. Cradling his drink, he watched the pale light of the moon shoot silver ribbons across the oily black sea with the rise and curl of each wave. In the calm of the lagoon below, his yacht swayed gently with the rhythm of the incoming tide. He could hear the distant chink of the halyard against the mast.

Having the occasional drink was one of the few Western luxuries he allowed himself. Being born of an English mother and Arabic father, being raised half his life in the desert, the other half in the hallowed halls of British aristocracy, he'd found himself torn between two cultures—a man with one foot in an ancient world and one in the new. His detractors saw this dichotomy as a weakness. But David had made it his strength, in business and in life.

He took a sip of his brandy, the fire of it burning down his throat. He felt its warmth diffuse through his system. He exhaled softly, stretched out his legs.

"It's so peaceful."

He jolted, almost choking on his drink.

"It's hard to believe there was a violent storm only hours ago."

He turned to look at her. She stood in the arched doorway. The lamplight from the dining room behind her set a halo of soft fire to the amber-gold of her hair. It was tied back loosely with a piece of ribbon, but fine tendrils escaped and wafted ever so slightly about her face in the warm, salty breeze. Her eyes were darkly luminous in this light. An oversize white muslin shirt hung to her thighs. On her legs she wore soft white muslin pants. She had oversize leather thongs on her feet. *Watson's clothes?*

He swallowed against the tightening in his throat. He'd expected—no, dreaded—seeing her in Aisha's clothes. And here she was in Watson's garb. And in spite of the getup, she remained ridiculously sensual and feminine, in the way of a woman confident and secure with her sexuality. That in itself was insanely arousing to David. He couldn't seem to find his voice. All he could do was stare at the shape of her body under the sheer African fabric, silhouetted against the lamplight. It made him recall her perfect breasts, the tight coral tips.

His pulse rate kicked up, and his breathing became light and shallow. This woman had a confounding effect on his body. He cleared his throat. But his voice still came out low and gruff. "Those clothes?"

She smiled. "The doctor's. May I join you?"

"Why are you wearing Watson's stuff? What happened to the clothes Kamilah brought you?"

She stepped out onto the patio and into his personal space. "It didn't feel right," she said. "I didn't want to upset anyone. I told Watson how I felt, and he gave me free access to his closet." She looked down at the garments and grimaced playfully. "I'm afraid this is the best I could come up with. Couture à la doc."

He couldn't help but smile. She'd floored him. Her sensitivity and tact, especially given her circumstances, made him feel like a brutish clod. He'd been so self-indulgent he hadn't begun to think about what she might be going through.

"You look great," he said. And he meant it.

"Thanks." She came up to his side. He felt his nostrils flare in reflex as she neared, drinking in the fresh, clean scent of her.

"You didn't join us for dinner." The banality of his statement belied how he'd felt about it. A part of him had hungered to see her again. Another was relieved when she hadn't shown. And then, when she still didn't appear, he'd felt slighted, even irritated.

"I ate in the servants quarters," she said simply.

"Why?"

She smiled at him, that dimple deepening in her one cheek. He couldn't take his eyes off the way her lips curved. He noted that one side of her smile was a little higher than the other. It gave her a mischievous look, as if she held some hidden secret, as if she was toying with him.

"I didn't want to interrupt your private time with Kamilah." She hesitated. "Dr. Watson told me about her...about her problem."

He stared at her in stunned silence, a grudging respect rising in him.

She came even closer to his chair. He felt the hairs on his arms rise, warmth stir in his groin. His body was powerless in her presence. Entranced, he watched the way the pale moonlight played across her exotic features.

"How was dinner…I mean with Kamilah. How was she?"

He was taken aback by her question, the intimacy of it. This was Rashid business. "Special," he said.

She waited, eyes watching him.

"She didn't talk to me, if that's what you want to know."

Her brow raised at the brusqueness of his tone.

He felt a pang of guilt, a need to elaborate. "She…she was there in a way she never was before." He grinned in spite of himself. "She even laughed at my silly camel jokes."

Sahar smiled. But it wasn't the same smile he'd seen before. There was a haunted look deep within her eyes, a look that betrayed her outward control. It was the look of someone adrift. Lost. Even a little afraid.

She was doing her best to appear relaxed, confident. She was looking beyond herself, beyond her own tragedy, caring about him and Kamilah. But he'd glimpsed the truth inside. She was hurting. Guilt knotted in his chest.

"I'm glad I found you," she said. "I've been looking for you all over the place. This palace is like a maze." Her voice curled like silk ribbon through him, tightening around his insides.

"You were looking for me?" She needed him. That pleased the primal male within.

"I wanted to ask you if…if you've had any contact from the mainland yet…about me?"

The question jolted him to his senses. He coughed, recalling his manners, stood up, pulled out a chair for her. "No, I'm afraid not. Communication is still down. Take a seat. Would you like a brandy?"

"No, thanks, I'm fine. I need to work on keeping my mind

clear if I want to remember anything." She sat with fluid grace but he could hear the disappointment in her tone at his answer.

"When I hadn't heard from you, I guessed there was no information. I kept telling myself you'd come and tell me the minute you learned something." Her eyes flashed up to his. "Right?"

Oh, God, she'd been waiting all day, anticipating word. And all he'd been thinking about was how to get rid of her, how to stop her impacting his personal life. And here she was being considerate of him, being tactful by not wearing Aisha's clothes, by not interrupting his dinner time with Kamilah. She'd even waited until the last possible moment in the day before coming to find him, although she'd been dying for some news, some clue to her identity.

The knotted ball of guilt in his chest tightened. "Of course I'd tell you right away," he said. "Hopefully we'll know something tomorrow. My tech reckons he'll have the satellite communication system up and running again by morning."

"It was downed in the storm?"

"Yeah, the sand out here gets into everything. We use a fixed satellite system which means the phones inside the palace can be operated just like landline sets. Only trouble is the radio antenna unit and junction box need to be mounted outdoors with a clear view of the sky. That means it's vulnerable to sandstorms."

She tensed suddenly. Her eyes widened, then the line of her mouth flattened. She turned abruptly away from him, shutting him out.

A frown cut into his brow. What had he said? He studied her profile. She was hugging her arms tight to her stomach, staring out over the inky ocean. What had caused this rapid shift in mood?

Perhaps she was wondering what befell her out there in the dark void, what had happened to the people she may have been with. Something snagged in his chest. What *had* she been through in that storm? Something so traumatic that it had shut off a part of her brain, made her dissociate from herself? Was what she experienced anything like the mad, awful terror that had gripped him as he'd watched Aisha, bleeding, being sucked down by the waves? Had she, too, known that huge hammer-heads swam like shadows between the reefs underneath?

If Watson was right, her memory loss was only a tempo-rary buffer against pain she might yet have to face in the next few days. Did she even have any idea that her amnesia was psychological? Would it help to tell her? Or would it only cause more distress?

She put her hand to her temple, pressed down on the stitches.

"You okay?" he asked.

She shook her head. "No. I mean yes. I'm fine. I...I just got a feeling."

"You remembered something?" He leaned forward.

"I...I don't know. Maybe." She forced a smile and ab-ruptly changed the topic. "You're a very lucky man to own such a slice of paradise, David. This place is truly beautiful."

"Yes," he said, his eyes holding hers. "Very beautiful."

She faltered at his loaded words but held his gaze. The jasmine-scented air grew warm and thick between them. She swallowed and then turned away, but not before David had glimpsed the flare of female interest in her eyes.

"Do storms like that happen often out here?" she asked, her voice smoky, thicker. Her obvious physical reaction to him did wild things to his body. Heat simmered in his belly. His throat went dry. He told himself this was ridiculous. To even begin to think of her in this way was a fool's game. She was vulnerable. She wasn't able to make rational decisions in her state. And she probably had a lover waiting for her somewhere.

He cleared his throat. "No," he said. "Storms like that are rare. And when they do come, it's usually without the rain." He angled his head, caught her eyes. "And without mermaids."

She laughed. The sound caught him by surprise. Husky. Rich. It socked him right in the gut. But even though she laughed, David noted she was rubbing her arm nervously. Inside she was still loaded with angst. He wondered if it would help if he tried to prompt her memory. And a part of him couldn't help thinking about the possibility she could be faking this. "What do you know about the Red Sea?" he asked.

"Nothing really...I think."

"Seems strange how you washed up out of a sea you know nothing about."

She stopped rubbing her arm. "You make it sound like you don't believe me."

He took a long, slow sip of his brandy, studying her face carefully. She didn't shy away from his scrutiny for an instant.

"No, I believe you," he said finally. "What would you stand to gain by faking something like this, anyway?"

"That's a rhetorical question, right?" Her words were markedly clipped. "I can't believe you'd even begin to think I was malingering."

"Right," he said, noting her use of the word *malingering*. Watson had used the same word in a medical context. That didn't necessarily mean a thing. But still, it alerted him, put him on guard. David was not a man who trusted easily. He'd never have gotten where he was now if trust had come easy. He'd learned as a child out in the desert that you always had to watch your back. And he'd gradually learned that the more powerful a man became, the more people tried to tear him down.

No. For David Rashid trust was a very rare commodity. For him trust was hard-won.

But his suspicion had offended her. She glared at him, fire snapping in her eyes. Even though he'd upset her, he was pleased to see her energy back. He could deal with anger. He couldn't deal with the haunting loneliness he'd glimpsed a few seconds ago.

"Believe me," she said in a low, cool tone. "I have no desire to be stuck out here on some lump of land in the Red Sea with a man who doesn't believe I can't remember who I am." She pushed herself up from the chair. "If you think for an instant that I'm enjoying any part of this, you're dead wrong. It sucks. And I can't wait to get off this bloody island."

He grabbed her wrist as she turned to go. "I'm sorry," he said, looking up into her eyes. "That really was uncalled for. It's just such a strange thing to have happened. And I can't even begin to imagine how it feels to have no sense of self. I do apologize."

She glared at the hand that restrained her. But he wasn't going to let go until he got through to her. "Will you forgive me?" He smiled slowly, deliberately, aware he was turning on the famous Rashid charm.

He felt her relax under his fingers. Male satisfaction spurted through him. His charm had effect on her. She was not immune to him. He released her arm. "Please sit."

She acquiesced, but a sharp wariness lingered in her eyes. He felt compelled to chase it away. "I should be doing more than apologizing," he said. "I should be thanking you for allowing my daughter to speak again."

Her eyes softened. "Dr. Watson told me she hasn't spoken in nearly two years, not since the death of her mother." She hesitated as if unsure of her ground. "I'm sorry for your loss, David," she said. "I'm sorry for what you and Kamilah must have gone through."

The muscles of his neck constricted. He shouldn't have opened this door. He didn't know what had possessed him to do it. He looked away. "It's in the past," he said.

She had enough presence of mind not to press him. They sat in uneasy silence, watching the pull of the moon on the ocean, keenly aware of each other's presence.

"David," she said suddenly.

His eyes shot to hers.

"I…I want you to know that I'll do whatever I can to help Kamilah."

"Why?" The word came out too terse.

"Because I feel somehow responsible. I…" She wavered. The light of the moon caught the glisten in her huge green eyes, giving her away. She swallowed. "I don't know how to explain it but I feel like I have a connection, that I can somehow relate to her…to what she's been through."

David wanted to reach out, to touch her pain, to share his own. Instead he slammed down the doors. "You'll probably be gone by tomorrow night," he said brusquely.

Hurt flashed through her eyes. She turned her face away from him. "Yes," she said softly. "I hope I *will* be gone by then." She got up and left.

And he let her go.

He cursed silently in Arabic and swigged back the last of his drink, relishing the angry burn down his throat.

It took all Sahar's control not to run. She walked calmly over the terrace and back into the palace. But once inside, she pressed her back hard up against the cool stone wall and scrunched her eyes tight, willing hot tears of frustration away. She was shaky, an absolute mess of conflicting emotions. She knew *exactly* how David Rashid's satellite communication system worked. The realization had hit full-blow between her eyes the instant he'd begun to explain it to her. And she'd gone stone-cold. Some remote part of her brain had recognized that how his communications system functioned was somehow vitally important to her. *But why?*

She shivered. The more snippets of recollection she got, the more ominous her whole situation seemed. She felt there was something really big she was just not grasping. But the more she tried to grab hold of those elusive feelings, the further it all seemed to retreat into the murky shadows of her mind. It made her feel vulnerable, as if an unidentified enemy prowled in the peripheral darkness of her brain, closing in. And Sahar knew that whoever she was, she *hated* feeling vulnerable.

And on top of it all, she was attracted to the man in the most basic way. He stirred things inside her she didn't want to begin to think about right now. Not when she didn't know if he was supposed to be an enemy. But even though David Rashid set off every warning bell in her system, an instinctive female part of her wanted to ease his pain, help him connect with his daughter. And she'd tried to do just that. She'd reached out to help. And she'd been burned by rejection.

Despite Sahar's best efforts to quash the rising tide of emotions, a sob escaped her. It shuddered up through her body, and the pent-up frustration spilled hot down her cheeks.

David was furious with himself. He shouldn't have let her go like that. He jerked off his chair, stormed across the terrace, swung into the dining hall. And froze.

She was pressed up against the wall, head back, eyes closed, a shimmering trail of tears down her cheeks.

His throat closed. He'd done this to her.

"Sahar," he said, his voice thick.

Her eyes flared open. She gasped, tried to turn away. He lunged forward and grabbed her arm. She stilled. He reached up, cupped her jaw, turned her slowly to face him. But she wouldn't look him in the eyes.

"I…I didn't want you to see me like this," she whispered.

"Oh, God, Sahar, I'm so sorry. I didn't mean—"

She pulled loose. "Don't. It's nothing. It's me. I'm just tired. I need sleep. I…I guess I get emotional when I'm tired." She forced a weak smile. "See, I'm learning something about myself."

"Sahar," he said firmly.

Those huge green eyes looked into his. Bewitching, mesmerizing eyes, filled with a shimmering ocean of emotion. He felt himself pulled inexorably toward her, he felt his lips move closer to hers. So close he could feel the warmth of her breath against his mouth. It took all his strength to hold back. To not press his lips down on hers. "Sahar." His voice came out rough and deep. "I meant it when I said thank you…for helping Kamilah."

She stared silently up at him, her lips parted. The look of hurt and frustration in her eyes tore at his heart. He moved a stray gold tendril of hair from her face, hooked it behind her ear. "In the desert," he said softly, "rain is a gift directly from the gods. There is nothing more spiritual than rain in the desert. Because it not only brings life, it *is* life."

He cleared his throat. The look in her eyes had forced him down this track. And he could no longer turn back. "You blew in with the rain, Sahar. And like the rain you brought the life back to my child. You awakened her. And me. That's the reason behind my choice of name. *Sahar.* It means dawn, to awaken. A time of new beginnings. Of growth. Life. I want you to know that. I want you to know why I chose it."

Time stretched as she stared up into his eyes, a range of unreadable emotions crossing her face.

"It's a beautiful name, David," she said finally, her voice

thick and husky. "Thank you." She looked away. "I wish it really was mine. I mean, to keep…forever."

And David suddenly felt sick. Because nothing about this woman in front of him could be forever. It was simply a matter of days before she was history. He'd do well to remember that fact. But right now trying to send her away seemed about as logical as trying to stuff the rain back into the clouds, as trying to roll the morning sun back into the night.

"I…I really should go to bed," she said. "Good night, David. And thank you for your hospitality, for your help." She turned to go.

He watched the sensuous sway of her hips as she walked the length of the dining hall, her spine held stiff, her chin held high, her luxurious reddish-gold hair rippling across the small of her back. He swallowed against the thickness in his throat. He hadn't been any damn help at all. He'd been suspicious, resentful and ridiculously turned on by this woman.

He'd been focused only on himself and Kamilah and how this woman was rocking their boat. Not on her anguish, her loss. And he could kick himself for the way things had gone tonight.

"Night, Sahar," he whispered as she slipped through the doorway into the corridor.

But there was no one to hear him.

O'Reilly peered through the dim blue haze of smoke. He spotted Lancaster at the far end of the bar. He made his way through the crowd, edged in next to him. "You'll never guess who dropped in on the ambassador's little soiree this evening."

"Who?"

O'Reilly glanced over his shoulder, leaned forward and dropped his voice so that it was drowned by the bar racket. "Rashid's very own Dr. James Watson."

Lancaster's body stiffened. "And?"

"They have her. On Shendi Island."

"Jesus, you've got to be joking—she survived the storm?"

"You betcha. And get this, she claims to have amnesia. According to the doctor, she has no idea who she is. Apart from that, she's fine."

Lancaster threw his head back and roared with laughter. He stopped almost immediately. "What did the doctor want from the ambassador?"

"Rashid sent him. Our sheik is trying to find out who she is. He wants the ambassador to get the word out."

"Kill it."

O'Reilly grinned. "Already done. Rashid will never be the wiser." O'Reilly motioned to the bartender to bring him a whiskey. He took a swig, then paused. "What if…I mean, what if she really can't remember? What if she's *not* faking?"

Lancaster studied his drink. "Then we're safe. In the meantime, we wait to see if she makes contact. If she doesn't, we pose as loving relatives, go in, neutralize her. If she does make contact—" Lancaster grinned devilishly "—then, partner, we're back in business."

Chapter 5

Soft yellow light seeped through the louvered shutters, throwing stripes of shadow onto the whitewashed walls. She blinked in confusion, then her heart sank like a stone. It was dawn. She was still on Shendi. She still had no memory of her identity.

The thought paralyzed her for a moment. She lay staring at the bars of shadow on the wall. They only served to drive her situation home. She was trapped. Imprisoned inside her own damn head, on a remote island with a man who scorched her insides every time he turned his laser-blue eyes her way. A man who might be dangerous—if only she could remember why.

A man who had named her Sahar.

Frustration burned her eyes. How in hell did one deal with this? Then she thought of Kamilah.

Kamilah understood something of the prison she was in.

Maybe that's why she felt she could identify with the child. If the little girl could cope, so could she. She closed her eyes, willed away the panic.

Everyone had their own pain, she told herself. It was all relative. Besides, today she might learn who she was. Today word might come from the embassy in Khartoum. Things could start looking up. She *had* to stay positive.

She shoved the covers back, sat up. She needed a run to clear her head. Maybe once she got blood pumping through her cells that darn gray matter would start functioning properly again.

She pulled Dr. Watson's clothes over the simple white underwear Fayha' had given her, then slid her feet into Watson's oversize thongs and slipped out of the heavy oak door into the long, cool hallway. She paused. Fayha' had shown her how to navigate two of the palace wings yesterday, but it was still a confusing labyrinth to her. Like her mind.

She turned to her left and wound her way through stone passageways and mosaic courtyards thick with the scent of jasmine and the hum of bees, searching for the archway that would lead her down to the strip of sugar-white beach she'd seen from the window yesterday.

The phone on his desk beeped. David's head jerked up from his papers. The sat system was operational. It beeped again. He stared at the phone. Watson perhaps? At six in the morning? Maybe he had an ID on Sahar.

It beeped a third time. David's muscles tensed inexplicably across his chest. And he realized a part of him wasn't quite ready to find out who she was. He picked up the receiver. "Rashid."

"David, it's Larry Markham. I've been trying to get hold of you for two days."

Relief slid through him at the sound of his lawyer's chipper voice. "Markham. We had a storm take our system down. We've been incommunicado until now. Everything okay at the London office?"

"All's fine. I just wanted to let you know I'm going to fax through those papers you wanted prepared. As soon as you okay them, we can have Tariq sign them. It'll put him in control of the second uranium mine and the last northern Azar oilfield."

"Thanks. Have you made the extra adjustments to the trust?"

"Done. In the event of your death, Tariq will retain management of those mines, but he'll remain under the control of the board you appointed. Your plans for Azar will stay in place no matter who takes the helm of Rashid International."

"Good. Send the papers. And, thanks, Markham." He hung up and his fax machine started to hum. David stretched, cricking his back into place. He stared at his phone again. He should call Watson. He should find out what happened at the embassy. He checked his watch. No, too early. And right now he needed his ride.

But as David strode toward the stable compound, he knew he was only postponing the inevitable.

And he really didn't want to think about why.

Sahar slipped the thongs off her feet and stepped onto the sand. It was already warmed by the morning sun. She curled her toes into the fine grains, savoring the sensation. She shaded her eyes and scanned the bright strip of beach. Nothing but sand for miles. Waves crunched rhythmically against the shore, ridges of swells feeding them from behind. She felt her spirits begin to lift.

She began to run. And her spirits soared as the salt breeze

played with her hair and blood pumped through her system. She picked up her pace, ran faster. Harder. The muscles warmed in her body. Her breath rasped at her throat. And she felt free. Truly free.

She ran even faster. And it felt as natural as breathing. She began to almost feel herself.

The notion brought her to a screeching halt. *Herself?*

But as fleetingly as it was there, it was gone. Nothing but the dull thud of blood in her head.

It was as if her body, her cells, had a physical memory. Her body remembered motion, how to run. And she'd listened to it intuitively. Her body had craved this feeling of release from the minute she'd woken up. But in her mind, she hadn't registered she was a runner. Or why. She'd simply moved instinctively. But the physical action itself had jolted her brain, given her a glimpse. Maybe she could do it again. Maybe there was another physical motion that could knock something free in her brain.

What else did her body know that she didn't?

David halted Barakah up on the ridge and patted his muscled neck. They were both damp from the exertion of the ride. He drew in a deep breath, surveyed the ocean below. He loved this spot. Here he felt above everything, as if nothing could touch him.

Then he saw her.

His heart bucked, kicked into a light, steady rhythm. She was running on the strip of sand below the ridge. He leaned forward on his horse, mesmerized by her fast, fluid, natural motion. Her waist-length hair fanned out behind her, whipped by the sea breeze as she ran. It caught the morning sun, glinting with gold and copper light. The skin on her arms glistened with a sheen of moisture.

He whistled softly under his breath. For a mermaid she sure knew how to move on her legs.

Then she stopped suddenly and bent over, bracing her hands on her knees, catching her breath. Intrigued, David watched as she stood up again and raised her face to the sun. She stood like that for a while. Motionless, hands at her side.

It made him wonder what she was thinking.

Then she began to move. He watched as she placed her palms together between her breasts, as if in prayer. She then moved her hands up along her body until she held them high above her head, palms still pressed together. She stepped forward with one leg and leaned into a lunge, her hands still held in perfect symmetry above her head.

She was doing some sort of yoga, as if in salutation to the morning sun. She turned her body sideways, bent at the waist. Then she faltered. Her movements became a little more tentative as if she were slowly recalling a sequence.

She crouched suddenly. Then lurched into a leaping spin as her leg kicked out to full length at her side.

The muscles in David's stomach tensed at the sudden and aggressive, yet exquisitely fluid movement.

Entranced, he watched as she continued her sequence, each kick and thrust of her arms flowing with fluid grace into the next. She looked like a golden warrior, balletic in her fighting sequence. Where in hell did she learn that? he wondered.

Then she stopped, looked around as if confused. She moved up to the high-tide line, searching for something among the scattered storm debris. She picked up a piece of flotsam, discarded it, hunted for another. Then she found what she was looking for. A long, slim and flat piece of wood, about as wide as her arm.

Holding it with two hands, wielding it like a sword, she began to swing it in front of her. Rhythmic. Fast. Sparring with

an imaginary foe. Faster. Harder. But even as her speed
mounted, each thrust of her weapon remained clean, smooth.

She was in control every inch of the way, perspiration
gleaming on her skin.

A smiled tugged at the corner of his mouth. She was a phe-
nomenal athlete. It didn't surprise him, given the state of her
body. Just the thought of her naked warmed him inside.

"Come, Barakah." He nudged his horse toward the steep
path that led down to the beach. "Let's go and see what's gotten our mermaid so worked up this morning."

The beach was empty when he rounded the ridge and came
through the grove of palms at the bottom. Puzzled, David
scanned the area. She'd been here only seconds ago. Then he
saw the neat pile of clothes on the sand. Doc Watson's clothes.
David's eyes shot immediately out to the waves breaking
along the shoreline.

She was there, playing in the waves. He watched as she
moved into a swell with long, smooth strokes. It crested into
a wave. She turned at precisely the right moment and rode the
wave in as it broke, her hair streaming around her in the water.
She ducked under the foaming surf, popped out behind the
froth and headed for another swell.

She was playing in the ocean like a young seal, showing
none of the fear someone who'd recently survived a boat
wreck might. David shook his head. The woman was an absolute enigma.

He watched as she rode another wave in. A smile quirked
along his lips and he felt his heart lift at the sight of her playful spirit. It made a part of him want to play too. He shook his
head mentally. He couldn't recall having felt this way in years.

She caught yet another wave, and he marveled at the way
she was toying with the power of the swells, the force of nature, becoming one with it. It excited him. He could relate to

t. He nudged his horse forward, watched hungrily from the shadows, the feeling mounting within him that this woman was some kind of wild and kindred soul.

She kicked out of her final wave and swam to shore. He watched her emerge from the turquoise water. Droplets caught the sun and slithered down her flat, tanned belly. She raised her arms and slicked her hair back, the movement highlighting the firm swell of her breasts.

Barakah moved under him, making him conscious of the heat in his loins as he watched her stride up the beach, her chest rising and falling from the exertion of her exercise, the sleek muscles of her thighs shifting under smooth wet skin.

As she came closer he could see the darker shade of her tight nipples under the wet, white underwear she was wearing. It hid nothing. His eyes slid down her body, drawn by the darker delta between her thighs.

His pulse quickened. His mouth went dry. His stallion stirred again, restless under him.

David swallowed and shifted on his horse, conscious of the beast between his thighs, of his own searing heat as his body responded involuntarily to the sight of the woman nearing him.

But he stayed in the shadows, just feet away from her.

She went straight for her piece of wood. With her back to him, she stooped, picked it up, swung it around…to face him. Barakah spooked, reared up violently. David grabbed the reins.

Sahar cried out in shock, dropped her piece of wood.

His stallion reared again at the sound of her cry. David felt himself slip. He clenched his thighs. "Whoa. Steady, boy, steady." He struggled to calm his massive horse. Then he coaxed Barakah gently out onto the beach and into the sunlight.

Sahar glared at him, hands on her hips, her eyes wide, breathing hard. "What the hell!" she demanded.

He grinned, couldn't help himself. He jerked his chin in

the direction of her weapon. "You planning on killing someone with that stick?"

"You were *spying* on me?" she accused, furious spots of
color flushing her cheeks.

"Last I recalled," he said lazily, holding a tight rein on Barakah, "it was my island and I was free to go where I willed."

Her jaw clenched and she held her ground, feet firmly
planted in the sand. David had expected her to lunge immediately for the protection of her small pile of clothes. She
didn't. Neither did she back away as his massive stallion approached. Instead she pulled her shoulders back, thrust her
chin forward. Even in that simple, yet very revealing, wet underwear she was as proud and regal as a lioness.

"What were you doing with that stick?" he asked. "Some
kind of martial art?"

She faltered. "I…I'm not sure. I was trying to remember…until *you* interrupted me."

He couldn't stop his eyes from sliding slowly, brazenly,
down her awesome body.

She didn't flinch under his scrutiny. Instead she caught his
eyes, held them, defying him to look away from her face. He
forced himself to hold her gaze. But her challenge excited
him, it shot a jolt of heat to his groin. His stallion pawed at
the ground, the movement making him exquisitely conscious
of his hot, pulsing desire. And for a moment he couldn't
speak, couldn't breathe even. He was pinned down by the dare
in her eyes, by the dark hum in his body. The world around
him seemed to slow to a standstill. The sound of waves breaking along the shore receded to a dull white noise in his head.

His horse snorted again, jerking him back to his senses. He
sucked in air sharply, trying to pull his scattered thoughts together. Seeing her standing like that in her underwear had sent
his brain and blood south.

"It was perhaps a mermaid fighting sequence?" he offered, provoking her further.

She pulled a face. "Yeah. Probably."

Right. It was more likely some fitness routine picked up in a swanky London gym. Despite her lack of any worldly possessions, Sahar carried herself with obvious breeding and grace. He suspected her life, once she figured out what it was, was well-heeled. She'd probably acquired her perfect biscuit tan aboard upper-class yachts and on the shores of exotic beach resorts. Yet there was something else about her that was innately earthy.

And something that told him he wouldn't want to confront her in a sword fight.

Although he was practically born with a *jambiya* in his hand and could wield a scimitar with the best Arabian horseman, he suspected she just might match him in that department. That only deepened his curiosity. Who *was* this woman? He was quite simply drawn to her, like a proverbial moth to a flame.

He leaned forward, slowly massaged Barakah's neck. "Want a ride home?"

"Home?" Her eyes widened like a child's. "You got news from Khartoum?"

Guilt bit at him again. "Sorry. It was a figure of speech."

Her features fell. She nodded silently, studying the form of his horse.

"I'm sure word will come soon," he offered, hoping at the same time it wouldn't. He wanted just a few more hours with this compelling woman. Because right at this instant he liked the way she made him feel. She'd made the blood flow hot in his loins in a way he'd forgotten was possible. And it made him feel powerful. Alive. It made the colors of the world seem brighter. It made him feel like a king.

She lifted her huge green eyes to his. "He's stunning," she said. "I heard you'd just broken him in."

"Yes."

"All primal power," she said, moving closer. From his vantage point David looked down into the valley of her breasts. She laid her palm flat on his stallion's flanks and rubbed him as if testing his muscle, his strength.

To David's astonishment, Barakah held steady under her touch, obviously reading her surety. The woman was confident around horses. And too bloody confident in her underwear. This was going to be his undoing. He couldn't take his eyes from the depression between her breasts, the way droplets of sea water clung to the fine blond hair there, drying into soft clusters of salt. He moistened his lips. He could imagine slowly licking that salt from between her naked breasts as he watched those exquisite nipples tighten. He could almost taste the salt. His vision began to narrow at the hot and delirious thought of it.

"Yes," she said, her voice shattering his illicit thoughts through his brain in a kaleidoscope of sharp shards.

He blinked, momentarily confused. He cleared his throat. "Yes, what?" His voice came out thick and rough.

"Yes, I'd like a ride home," she said, her eyes studying him intently.

"You're not afraid?"

"Of what? You?"

He shifted. She had to have seen the raw stamp of arousal on his features. And now she was toying with him. Or was she?

"My stallion," he said. "You're not afraid of Barakah?"

"No," she said simply.

"You're experienced, then."

Her eyes flashed to his and she raised a brow.

"I mean, with horses."

She gave a slow, sly smile. Damn she *was* toying with him. "I guess I know a thing or two." She stroked the stallion's neck. Then she angled her head, catching his eyes with a mischievous twinkle in her own. "He looks like one hell of a challenge, though."

David swallowed. She wasn't only toying with him. She was flirting. She was turned on. He could see it in the hardening of the nipples under that darned thin fabric. It spiked his blood clean off the Richter scale. "You afraid of *anything?*" he asked, his voice coming out an octave lower.

She held his gaze. "I guess I'll have to find out."

"Barakah's no easy ride," he warned. "And there's no saddle."

"You make that sound like a dare, Rashid."

He smiled slowly. "Maybe it is, Sahar."

"I don't believe I turn down a challenge."

"A woman after my own heart." He held out his hand, palm up. "Come on, then."

"Wait." She spun around, her hair fanning out behind her. It was almost dry already and the salt had plumped the curls, making her mane wild and full. With her back to him, she bent over to retrieve the pile of clothes. Her movement was so fluid he didn't have a chance to turn away. Even if he had wanted to.

He was held transfixed by her smooth back, the neat ridge of her spine, the way her panties skimmed her firm rump. He became insanely aware of the way her buttocks separated into two tight globes; of the neat gap at the apex of her thighs.

Blazing heavens. He blew out a hot breath, turned quickly to stare over the ocean as she slipped back into Watson's clothes. He couldn't do this. He couldn't have this woman, for all the reasons he'd mentally checked off last night. They were still just as valid. She had another life that could come back and bite them all, that could hurt Kamilah. And him. And her. In spite of her rebellious streak, she was vulnerable, even if she wasn't admitting it to herself. She wasn't in a position to make decisions like this. And it was up to him not to abuse that. He clenched his teeth.

"I'm ready."

He was not. He turned to face her. She was holding her hand out to him. He reached down, grabbed her arm and swung her up fast and hard. Too hard.

He bit back a curse. He hadn't meant that. His vigor had been born of sexual frustration. But she moved fluidly with his brusque momentum, straddling her legs over the flanks of his horse and slotting comfortably in behind him. She slid her arms around his waist. "Ready."

And he knew he was sunk. He swallowed hard at the sensation of her legs splayed open against him. He nudged Barakah forward and instantly he felt the tense and flex of her inner thigh muscles around him as she moved with the rolling motion of the horse. This was going to kill him.

He sucked in a gulp of air and urged his powerful stallion slowly back up the ridge, allowing both the horse and the woman to get used to each other.

Barakah topped the ridge and immediately strained against David's control in a desire to charge across the hills for home as they did each morning. He held the beast in, allowing only an incremental increase in speed. Sahar moved with surprisingly fluid ease behind him. He kicked up the pace—she handled it. He gave the stallion even more rein, freeing him to gallop.

Her arms tightened around his waist, the wind pulled at his hair and she laughed behind him. It kicked his spirits sky-high. He let loose, holding nothing back. And they sped with reckless abandon over the hills. Sahar moved as if she was one with his body. He moved as if he was one with his horse. And for an instant they *were* one. A most intimate union. Man, woman and beast. David felt a wild spiritual freedom. His heart sang. The horse's hooves thudded on packed dirt, his mane flying free.

Sahar knew in her deepest being she had never experienced anything like this with a man. She knew it not with her mind but the very molecules and cells of her body.

She'd never dreamed, when she'd seen the dark Arabian horseman silhouetted against the sea, that she'd be straddled behind him like this. One with him and his stallion. It was sublime. She felt the wind pull at her hair, draw tears from her eyes. And she clung with her thighs to the hard and powerful man between her legs, the sensation deliriously wild and intimate.

They raced along the ridge and over the hills, the sea gleaming aquamarine in the distance, the castle looming ahead. Sahar knew she'd have to wake up eventually. But right now she was existing merely in the moment. She was living a dream. A fairy tale. And a part of her did not want to wake from it.

Breathless, exhilarated, blood pumping, they came to a halt in front of the stables. David slid down from the horse, held his arms up to her.

She stilled.

He stared up at her. Silent for a moment. There was a blaze in his eyes she had not yet seen. An unspoken connection. His hair was tousled by wind and he was covered in fine desert dust. So was she. She swung herself off the stallion and into the steely strength of David Rashid's arms.

For a second he held her there, aloft, his eyes smouldering. They were at a crossroads. Her world stood still. She became conscious of nothing beyond the hot breathing of the horse, the rhythm of blood in her veins, the heavy-lidded intent in David's eyes. And a scorching ribbon of desire unfurled slow and deep inside her.

He brought her slowly down to him, drawing her closer into his chest, toward his exquisitely sculpted lips. He let her feet touch the ground. And his hand ran roughly up the back of her neck. He forced his fingers up into her tangled mass of hair. He tilted her face sharply up to his and he pressed his lips down hard onto hers.

Sahar's vision swam. Her knees buckled. Her lips opened under his aggressive firmness and his tongue slipped hot into her mouth. She felt herself go faint. He deepened his kiss as he slid a hand down the hollow of her back to the base of her spine. He pulled her pelvis sharply up against his thigh. Sahar gasped, her mouth opening wider. She could taste the salt of his skin, feel the roughness of the dark stubble on his jaw, the hard heat of his chest against hers.

Her body thrummed. Ached. With exhilaration, with need. Nothing existed beyond this moment. And in his arms she felt the way she had felt in the ocean. Natural. Wild. A primal being. She kissed him back, hungrily, trying to feed an unidentified need deep within.

Then he jerked back, releasing her instantly.

Stunned, Sahar blinked into the sudden sharpness of the sun. Why had he dropped her like that?

Then she saw. A little figure, in the far distance, barely distinguishable, was skipping along the path that led down to the stables.

"Kamilah!" His voice was hoarse. There was raw shock in it, as if he'd been caught off guard doing something illicit. As if the fact he was doing it at all rocked him to the very foundation of his being.

Sahar swallowed, still stunned. "She…she couldn't see us, David. She's too far away," she said, out of concern.

He turned on her, his face like hard granite, a blackness in his eyes. All trace of the man she was with a second ago was gone. The look on his face ripped the ground right out from under her, and her heart sank like a cold stone. "David?"

He glared at her. "This is *exactly* what was not supposed to happen!" He whirled on his heels, grabbed Barakah's reins, stormed off toward the stables.

Sahar reeled. She felt as though she was flailing in air. She watched his powerful form disappear into the stable buildings.

She sucked in a shaky breath and pushed her mess of hair back from her face. Reality began to seep back into her brain. He was right. She'd been a fool. They had both been crazy. Overpowered by the moment they had slipped across a line. But neither of them had any idea what other life might await her. *Who* might be waiting for her.

But whatever life she'd had, she knew for certain she'd never had a man like David Rashid. A deep loneliness seeped into her, but she shook it off. There could be no tomorrows for her. Not until she figured out who she was. It could be no other way.

She turned her attention to watch the dark little figure coming down the path.

Kamilah came to a halt in front of Sahar. Puzzled, the child looked from Sahar to the stables, to where her father had disappeared. A sadness slid into her eyes.

Sahar bent down. "Were you looking for your daddy?"

She nodded, still staring at the empty stable door.

"What did you need him for, sweetheart?"

Kamilah hung her head. "I guess he has to work again," she said softly. "He always has to work. He never has time to play with me."

She stroked Kamilah's cheek. "I think your daddy's got a lot on his mind. He's a busy man."

"I guess so," she said quietly. "But he used to play before mummy died. He wasn't so busy then."

And with those few words, Sahar got a whole picture. While Kamilah had cut herself off from her father and the rest of the world through the loss of her voice, David had cut himself off in his own way. He'd turned to work. He'd lost the ability to connect with his child.

The idea made her heart squeeze tight inside her chest. It was all so tragic. A father and a child who loved and desperately needed each other, but who couldn't find the way to each other. They stood on either side of chasm not even knowing they needed a bridge. And Sahar felt something surge through her. A need to help build that bridge.

She hooked her finger under the child's chin. "I tell you what, since your daddy is so busy, how about you play with me?"

A smile crept cautiously along Kamilah's mouth.

"Deal?"

Kamilah nodded, slipping her little hand into Sahar's, her warm fingers clutching tight. And Sahar's heart blipped at the sensation. Because in that instant she just knew she didn't have a child of her own somewhere. She just knew.

A part of her was beginning to feel like there really wasn't anything special waiting for her anywhere in the world.

At least she knew how to play. It was all she really could do right now, exist in the moment, for the moment.

And wait to see if her memory returned.

She tugged Kamilah's arm. "Come on, then. How about a game of tag?" And the two of them raced around the side of the palace.

Chapter 6

David stared blankly at the papers his lawyer had faxed him, unable to focus. He clicked a button on his computer, and the screen crackled softly to life, but he couldn't concentrate on that, either.

He'd showered, changed, but his insides still churned. It was as if he was in shock. He couldn't erase Sahar from his mind; the way he'd connected so intimately with her on his horse. He couldn't pinpoint exactly when it had happened. There was no clear line demarcating black and white. But at some point he'd slipped over the invisible boundary and been swept so completely into the moment that he'd forgotten the past…and the future. It had only been the moment—on that horse with her wrapped around him—the primeval sensation of just being. Man and woman. Fully alive, vividly and vitally so, in a world that was warm and free.

He blew out a shuddering breath.

He'd never felt anything like it in his life. He clenched his fist around a pencil. It snapped sharply. Startled, he looked down at the broken thing in his hand. The connection between them had snapped just like that, the second he'd seen Kamilah in the distance.

And as much as he wanted Sahar, the very last thing he wanted to do was hurt his child. Because when the time came for Sahar to leave, it would kill them both.

He had to stop this. It was too much of a gamble. She could leave anyday. Any minute. It could happen the instant the phone on his desk rang.

David rubbed his brow fiercely, then reached for the phone—and stopped himself. Surely Watson would ring if he had news. *Damn.* He couldn't even pick up the bloody phone to see if they had an ID on her yet. He *wanted* her to be Sahar. Not someone else.

He slammed the pencil shards onto his desk, turned to his computer, forced his mind to function and began to review the latest production report from the Azar uranium mine.

Things were looking good. Britain and France were snapping up all the yellowcake he could produce. He started to scan the numbers. But they blurred, her image once again shimmering in his mind.

He smashed his hand onto the desk. He couldn't take this. She lingered in his senses like opium. He needed to wipe his mind clean, but it was impossible.

He sat back in his leather chair, closed his eyes. And once again he could feel her long, sun-browned legs around him, the wind in his hair, the movement of Barakah under them.

She was so different from Aisha.

Aisha had been soft and dark, sweet and gentle, raised with a strong religious influence. She'd been bright, sensitive, creative. A wonderful advisor and a friend. Yet she'd deferred everything to him with a soft feminine subservience that had boosted his male ego. She'd stood by his side with a quiet luminescent beauty at social functions in London society. She'd carried herself with grace, walking the strange cultural lines of Azarian tradition. She'd been a perfect asset. A gentle lover. A wonderful mother. He never thought he could want anything more.

Until Sahar. This was a shock to his system. She challenged him in a way Aisha never had. She matched him. Her femininity was as strong as it was sensual. Her grace was that of a lioness. Fluid. Powerful. Proud.

And dangerous.

Because she'd snared something within him, made him lose focus. David Rashid *never* lost focus. Doing so meant making mistakes.

He gritted his teeth, jerked up in his chair, grabbed the phone and punched in Watson's number. The doctor answered on the second ring.

"Watson, any news?"

"Rashid, I was just about to call you."

David's stomach tightened. "You have word?"

"Not a bloody thing. It's too weird. The British ambassador here even volunteered to check in with the other embassies in the region for us, but so far, nothing. She's a complete mystery."

A quirky mix of relief and anticipation rippled through him. "The ambassador found nothing whatsoever?" he asked, just to be sure.

"Nope. It's the darnedest thing. No one has ever heard of this woman. No one has reported her missing. There's been zip from the dive operators, the embassies, the Ministry of Interior, the airlines. Nothing from the Interpol databases. It's like she never officially set foot in Sudanese territory."

"You mean she's *un*officially in the country?"

"Well, that's the question, isn't it?"

"Maybe she came down from Egypt on one of their dive tours."

"That's just it, David. The ambassador says his staff has checked everything, even the embassies up there. It's like she doesn't exist."

A dark thrill quirked through him. He couldn't begin to define it. Didn't want to.

"Women like her don't go unnoticed, Rashid." The doctor chuckled. "Maybe there *is* something to Kamilah's mermaid theory."

"Yeah. Right." She was an enigma all right.

"Or…" The doctor hesitated. "Maybe there's something *else* going on here."

David detected the subtle shift in Watson's tone. "What do you mean?"

"I don't know. Maybe I'm just being paranoid, but a part of me gets a sense someone over here in Khartoum might be hiding something."

"Such as?"

"Such as who she is."

"Why on earth would you think that?"

"You know me, Rashid, I'm the born conspiracy theorist. It's nothing I can put my finger on. Just a feeling."

David frowned. Watson might be a conspiracy theorist at heart but his instincts were solid as rock. Still, David couldn't begin to imagine why someone would try to hide Sahar's identity. "I think the African sun is getting to you, Doc," he joked. "Let's wait a couple of days to see what comes up, now that the word is out about her. When are you heading into Azar?"

"I've got the supplies I need. I'll be up at the new mine in about two days to set up the clinic. And, Rashid—"

"Yeah?"

The doctor paused. "Watch your back."

David laughed dryly. "Why? The mermaid's going to stick a knife in it?"

Watson was silent.

The image of Sahar fighting with her stick on the beach filtered into David's mind, but he shook it off. "Seriously, Watson, even if someone is hiding something, what can the woman do?" *Apart from unhinge me physically and mentally.*

"I'm just saying be careful, that's all."

David hung up and stared at the computer screen. He couldn't afford to think about Sahar now. Not in any way. He had work to do. He brutally shoved his thoughts aside and turned his attention to his work.

He leaned forward, his interest finally back where it belonged. But laughter drifted through his open windows, shattered his thoughts.

He cursed softly, lifted his head.

The melodious sound floated up to him on the warm breeze. A woman laughing with a child. The muscles around his heart tightened reflexively.

He got up, moved to the window, rested his hand on the cool sill. Sahar and Kamilah were chasing each other on the grass below the patio. A smile snared the corners of his mouth. They were playing tag, he realized. Intrigued, he leaned farther out the window and once again watched Sahar move. There was nothing self-conscious about the way she was charging about after his little girl. She was utterly free, unfettered of any inhibitions. His smile broadened. It was probably because she didn't know anyone was watching. And once again he was a voyeur. He wanted to keep it that way. He leaned back into the shadow lest she see him. He didn't want them to stop. Not yet.

Kamilah shrieked with utter childish delight, and he felt a heavy burden lift from his heart. His eyes moistened. This is what *he* should have been doing with Kamilah these past two years. Playing. He should have been tumbling on the lawn with his daughter, allowing her to be a child instead of bouncing her from specialist to specialist in an effort to solve her problems. Maybe the answer had been in his own hands all along.

Sahar tagged Kamilah and the two of them rolled like puppies in the grass. The sound of his daughter's infectious chuckle gripped him by the throat. It burbled from deep in her stomach, erupting like a bubbling brook.

It was a sound he hadn't heard in almost two years. Laughter hadn't rung through the halls of the Rashid household in all that time, and his heart lifted in sheer empathetic joy at the sound of it.

He forgot his need for hiding. He leaned forward, pushed the window open wider, hungry for more. He chuckled softly to himself. Sahar was still in the doctor's muslin clothes, still covered in dust from their ride. She was running barefoot, Watson's oversize thongs discarded on the grass. Her hair was a glorious wild tangle, her eyes alive with laughter, her cheeks flushed with exhilaration.

She was like something from another world. Her dusty attire reminded him of a desert traveler, at ease with few possessions, content in the arms of nature's awesome power. It was something he related to. Wholeheartedly.

It was that very sense of purity, of man alone against nature, that had kept driving him back into the harsh ways of the desert for most of his life. It was the clarity he found out there, the brutal honesty, the essence of life that drew him into the oceans of sand and endless horizons.

Out in the Sahara man was stripped to the bare-bone

basics. Hunger and thirst was a constant. And the focus was on the present. It was harsh. But it was true.

And as he watched her, he began to understand how she'd managed to suck him into the moment earlier in the morning. It was because it was a state he'd so often aspired to. It was the very thing that kept drawing him back to the wild open spaces of his beloved Sahara. And now he'd glimpsed it in her.

He wondered, though—would she be this free once her past came to reclaim her? Would she lose that unabashed magic when she found her place in the pecking order of the civilized world again, when she discarded Doc Watson's old garb and once again donned the lush silks and tailored linens he had no doubt she was accustomed to wearing?

He chewed on his cheek, wondering what she'd look like in silks and gold. Would the clothes and adornment change how he viewed her? Maybe if she dressed in the couture to which she was accustomed she might actually remember more about her past, about herself.

Again Kamilah chuckled. Sahar laughed heartily in response, the sound of it rich, enticing.

He could feel it inside him.

His smile deepened. And on impulse, he swiveled, reached over his desk, picked up the phone and punched in a number he hadn't called in a very, very long time. It was the number of a high-end boutique in Cairo. And as he waited for the sales clerk to pick up, he felt just a little playful. The sensation caught him off guard—and it felt good.

Sahar and Kamilah took refuge from the midday heat in the shadows of one of the palace courtyards. They sat on an intricately carved marble bench, sipping the iced mint tea Fayha' had brought them. While they sipped they listened to the soft tinkle of water spouting from the mouths of ornate stone lions that reared up around the fountain in the center of the enclosed garden. The air was heavy with sensual warmth and the heady scent of flowers.

The palatial surroundings seemed surreal to Sahar. She felt like Alice, slipping through the looking glass of her old world into the alternate reality of a Middle-Eastern fantasy. She was sure that any minute she'd wake with only a massive bump on the head to show for it all. She wiggled her toes in the jasmine-scented air, not sure if she actually wanted to wake up. Because this dream came complete with a dark and dangerously seductive Arabian prince. The memory of their morning ride began to stir her blood once again. She couldn't believe how she'd let herself go.

She laughed at herself. What a twit. Of course she'd slipped into the moment, because that's all she could do. She only had the present. No past. And therefore no future to contemplate—at least not until she had an identity. She'd be crazy to let herself go like that again. Besides, she still had the lurking sensation of danger when she looked into his face. But that only intensified his mystique. And despite the fact he set warning bells clanging in her brain, she knew if David Rashid so much as looked at her with those smoldering eyes again…she laughed nervously.

"What are you laughing at?" Kamilah asked.

Sahar glanced down at the little girl sitting companionably at her side. An old leather-bound book rested on her lap.

"I'm laughing because I'm a silly fool in a crazy dream," she said. "And if I don't laugh about it, I'll cry." Sahar nodded toward the book in Kamilah's lap. "What book is that you're reading?"

Kamilah lifted it, pushed it reverently into Sahar's hands. Sahar read the title and smiled softly. She fingered the embossed lettering. It was an old copy of Hans Christian Andersen's *Little Mermaid.*

Kamilah's liquid brown eyes watched her intently, waiting for reaction. "It's my favorite," she prompted.

"It is?" She was amazed at how Kamilah had opened up after their game of tag. It had broken down yet another barrier, and the child was almost talking with ease.

"It was my mother's. She used to read it to me a lot. Do you know the story?"

Sahar thought about it. "Yes, I do, actually. If I remember correctly, it's about a little mermaid princess, the daughter of the sea king. She was the youngest of five sisters and the prettiest of them all."

"Six," Kamilah corrected. "There are six sisters."

"Oh. Okay. Well, the youngest of the six mermaids, then. And she was not only the most beautiful, she also had the loveliest voice on earth. She fell in love with a human prince and she desperately wanted a chance to be on land with him. But," said Sahar, "before she could get legs and go on land she had to sacrifice her voice to a wicked old sorceress. And then, because she didn't have her voice, she had to try and make the prince love her without using words."

"So you *do* remember that." There was a strange mixture of curiosity and accusation in the little girl's statement.

"Kamilah, I know it's strange. I find it very difficult to understand myself. But I do remember a lot of things, just not who I am, or how I came to learn the things that I do know. I haven't the slightest idea when I read Andersen's *Little Mermaid.* I just know that once upon a time I did. Maybe *my* mother read it to me."

The dark eyes studied her with brooding intensity.

"Why is that story your favorite, Kamilah?"

The little girl fiddled with her fingers in her lap. "'Cause my mummy liked it and she used to read it to me."

Sadness clogged Sahar's throat. She stroked Kamilah's silky hair. "I guess you are like the Little Mermaid, too, huh? Because you also lost your voice." Sahar smiled tenderly.

"I guess." Kamilah sat silent a while. Then her eyes flashed up to Sahar's. "Do you think the ending in the book is happy?"

David made his way along the corridor. He needed to find Fayha' and inform her that Tariq would be dining with them tonight. He stepped out to cross the courtyard when he heard Kamilah's and Sahar's voices. Instinctively he froze in the shadow of a mosaic column.

They were just feet from him, sitting on a marble bench facing the fountain. Kamilah's little face was turned up to Sahar's. Sahar's wild hair cascaded down her back, the sun bouncing off glinting gold highlights among the auburn. They looked like a painting, a Madonna and child. He was held transfixed.

Then he heard his daughter's clear little voice over the sound of the tinkling fountain. She was asking Sahar if she thought the ending of a book was a happy one.

"Hmm, that's an interesting question," he heard Sahar say. "I guess it depends on how you look at it. What do *you* think?"

Kamilah pulled her legs up onto the bench, wrapped her arms around her knees. "The Little Mermaid didn't get to marry the prince."

"No, she didn't."

"Because the prince got confused," said Kamilah. "He mistook the Little Mermaid for someone else, and he fell in love with that person instead. I don't think that part is happy."

David leaned closer, greedy for the sound of his daughter's little voice, the sound of the words she'd had locked up inside all this time. For almost two years he hadn't had a window into his daughter's soul. And now here she was, opening up to Sahar. And he was getting a glimpse. But at the same time, a perverse jealousy twined itself around his heart. He wanted it to be *him* on that bench with Kamilah. It *should* be him.

"But even though the mermaid lost the prince, she did get her own reward," offered Sahar. "She sacrificed herself for her love, and for that she got a chance to have an immortal soul, which mermaids don't ordinarily have."

"I know," said Kamilah, her voice suddenly incredibly sad. "But I think she should have gotten the prince."

David's fists balled. An ache swelled in his chest. He wanted to step out into the bright sun, claim his place alongside his child. But he couldn't move. He was afraid he'd break the magic, stop the talking. He watched Sahar take his daughter's hand. "Kamilah," she said gently, "when the Little Mermaid threw herself into the sea, she started an incredible journey on her way to getting an immortal soul. She became like a piece of sea foam and she could float around the world bringing happiness to good children."

Kamilah's head drooped a little. "I know," she said resignedly. "When the Little Mermaid visited the good children, she was invisible. They never knew she was there, watching over them." Her eyes flashed suddenly up to Sahar's. "But *I* knew that if the child was very, very, good, she would get to see the mermaid one day. That's why I went down to the beach every day to wait. I thought maybe my mummy would send one to me. To be my friend…and to be daddy's friend."

The words grabbed David by the throat. He couldn't breathe. Is *this* why his daughter had insisted on going to the beach every day since they'd arrived back on Shendi? He hadn't had a clue. How could he not have known this? How could he not have been there in a more profound way for his child?

"So you waited at beach where you found me?" asked Sahar. David could hear the tenderness in her voice.

"Yes," said Kamilah. "I waited at Half-Moon Bay because it looks just like the beach in the book where the Little Mermaid used to watch the prince."

David watched in dumbstruck awe as Sahar tilted Kamilah's chin and looked down into the child's eyes. "Kamilah, you *do* understand that I am not really a mermaid, don't you?"

He stilled, waited for his daughter's response, petrified.

Kamilah silently studied Sahar, head to toe. Then she pursed her lips. "What *are* you then? You haven't got any clothes and you haven't got a house and you haven't got a memory. You *gotta* be a mermaid. I *want* you to be a mermaid." Her voice quavered. "'Cause if you're not…you will go away. I don't want you to go away."

Every muscle in his body strapped tight. *This was enough!* He had to stop this. Here in front of his eyes was the perfect example of why he couldn't let this continue. Because it was going to kill his daughter when Sahar left. They would all be back at square one. He *had* to step in, tell Sahar to back off.

She could stay on his island but she was to stay *away* from his daughter.

Sahar put her arm around his daughter's slight shoulders and hugged her close. "Oh, honey, right now I also wish I could be your mermaid. But you know what, whatever I am, *whoever* I am, something in the stars allowed you and me to meet. Something made me wash up on that shore while you were waiting. And for whatever reason that happened, we can give this story of ours its *own* happy ending, okay?"

Kamilah looked up at her.

"Is that a deal, Kamilah?"

David tensed.

"Yes," his daughter said. "I like happy endings."

"We all do, Kamilah. We all do."

David was furious. Sahar had no right making promises she couldn't keep. Happy endings were for fairy tales. This was reality. Reality had no promises of ever after or happiness. His nails dug into his palms, and he took a step forward. Then he went rigid as he heard her next words.

"Would it help you to talk about what happened to your mother in that accident, Kamilah?"

David's stomach churned violently. What in hell did she think she was doing?

Kamilah looked up at Sahar. "Do you want to hear it?"

"Sometimes it's good to talk about difficult things," she told his child. "Because then you can share the unhappiness with someone else and it can make things easier to bear. And sometimes it helps to get it off your chest because if you hold it inside too long, it can really hurt and make you feel sick in many different ways."

His little girl nodded with a wisdom beyond her years. When she spoke her voice was crystal clear and it ripped out his soul. "We were in daddy's boat, at the reef. We had gone diving—"

No!

He could not listen. Would not.

He did not want to hear the accusation come from Kamilah's own lips. For two years he'd lived with it in her eyes. He could not hear the words. Not now. Not ever. *Damn this interfering woman to hell!* He spun on his heels and stormed off in search of Fayha'. He'd get Sahar later, give her a piece of his mind. She'd gone way too far.

Sahar felt the muscles in her chest tense. She wasn't sure if she was doing the right thing, but she sensed deep in her gut that this was what the child needed. To talk. To put into words what she'd bottled up inside for two years.

"Mummy stayed up on the boat with me while daddy went under the water," Kamilah said. "And when daddy was deep under looking at the fish, there was a bang and a funny smell and then the boat caught fire. My mummy rushed for the extinguisher, but the end of the boat exploded. The explosion hurt mummy and the boat tipped up on the one end and we started to go under really fast. We both fell into the water and mummy was bleeding." She shuddered. "A lot."

Sahar's jaw clenched. She could almost see it. She could *feel* it. As if she'd been there.

"I was far away from mummy," said Kamilah. "She was way off to the other side of the burning boat and the waves were coming in between us. Daddy came up when he heard the explosion. He came up in the middle of us. I could see mummy going under the waves but she yelled for him to save me—" Kamilah choked "—to save me first." Tears streamed down her face.

A shiver chased down Sahar's spine. The blood drained from her head. She hugged the child tight. She could literally feel the water sucking at her, see the little girl going under behind the huge swells, taste the burning salt in her own throat, the claws of terror. Her body went cold. It was as if *she* was there. As if *she* was remembering. Something from long, long ago. But she couldn't pull it from the void.

"Daddy got me and he swam and put me on the beach. He went back for mummy." Another shudder racked her little body. "He was too late. She'd gone under already. He really tried. He tried so hard. I could see him. He went under and under and under and he was coughing and he was crying and screaming at the sky, and I was so scared and sore from the cuts and the bleeding and the fire." Another sob choked her little body. "Daddy tried so hard…but…the…the mermaids took her."

Sahar felt tears streaming down her own cheeks. She held Kamilah very tight. She stroked Kamilah's hair. "It's okay, baby, it's okay. It's good to talk about it. It's good to get it out. Because then you can deal with it. Your mummy did such a wonderfully brave thing. You must be very proud of your mummy and your daddy. Very proud."

Kamilah sniffed and rubbed her nose. "I am proud of them."

And as she spoke, Sahar's heart cracked. This family had been through an awful tragedy and it had barely begun to heal. She kissed Kamilah softly on the top of her head. And once again she vowed not to let this child down. Or her father. She would do what it took to help the two of them. Because somehow, buried deep in her memory, she sensed she knew just how this kind of tragedy could tear a family apart. And how, without help, the wound might never mend. And it would continue to destroy.

But she had to promise herself another thing. She had to resist the powerful physical attraction of David Rashid. Because until she knew who she was, who might be waiting for her, she could not possibly begin to think of a relationship at that level.

Chapter 7

David worked until the sun was in its zenith and the air thick and shimmering with heat. He knew Kamilah would be resting at this hour, along with most of his staff. It was the right time to confront Sahar.

He was clear about what he intended to tell her. Quit with the mermaid fantasy stuff and stay away from his daughter. She could be gone within days. He expected her to keep to herself until then. If she was going to be on his island, she'd best know her boundaries. And his.

David searched his palace, but he couldn't find her anywhere. His frustration mounted along with the heat. Anyone in their right mind was under shadow, grasping for respite from the oppressive noon heat of early summer.

Even the birds had gone quiet.

But Sahar was not resting in her room. She wasn't in any

of the courtyards. She wasn't in the massive pool, cooling off under the fountains that splashed into it.

The last place David looked was the kitchen. There he found Farouk, the only member of his staff not taking a siesta. Farouk didn't have a problem with the heat. He was busy cleaning the kitchen countertops.

"Have you seen Sahar?" David asked him.

The man's toffee-colored skin gleamed with perspiration. He wore the traditional head cloth of the Azar nomads. Farouk wiped his brow with the loose edge of the cloth. "You mean the woman from the sea?"

Irritation spiked. "Yes, where is she?"

Farouk tipped his head toward the wide, arched doorway that led outside. "She's in the kitchen garden."

"In *this* heat?"

"She asked if she could help." Farouk shrugged. "I told her it would be better when the shadows grow long. The sun is very hot today. But she said she needed to do something useful. She said she was tired of just sitting around, so I gave her a job."

A hesitancy sneaked in under David's resolve as he made his way to the door.

"*Sahar.* It's a good name," Farouk called after him. "Shendi has come alive since she arrived."

David didn't answer. He stepped out into the herb and vegetable garden that lay off the kitchen and a wave of heat slammed into him, knocking the breath right out of his lungs.

The garden was enclosed by tall stone walls and crisscrossed with paved pathways. It was a marvel in this climate and made possible only because of the sweet water pumped from the deep wells on Shendi. Creeping thyme filled the cracks between the paving stones. Vegetables burgeoned from beds and were identified by seed packets propped up on sticks.

Little stone benches rested against the walls under trees heavy with ripe fruit.

She was at the far end of the garden, bent over, jabbing a trowel into the moist earth, her back to him. An oversize straw hat, battered and crumpled, shaded her head. Watson's hat. She'd tried to tame her wild curls into a thick braid that hung down the center of her back, but soft spirals of fine hair floated free in the rising heat currents. The sun caught the amber and gold fire in the strands.

David walked quietly up to where she was hunched over, angrily thrusting her trowel into the ground, forcing it to yield up monstrous carrots. As she uprooted them, she tossed them with a clunk into a large blue enamel bowl at her side.

She'd changed out of the dusty muslin clothes but another oversize shirt covered her lean frame, also one of Watson's. Pale-blue cotton. It all but covered the khaki shorts she wore. Watson's shorts, bunched in at the waist and wide and baggy over her smooth thighs.

She was doggedly refusing to wear anything of Aisha's. She was more than going out of her way to respect his feelings.

Guilt niggled at him and his resolve wavered further. Suddenly nothing seemed simple. What was it that he was going to demand of her? Keep out of his business? His life? Stay away from his child? It suddenly seemed unreasonably harsh. He swallowed. The midday heat was making his mouth dry, his head thick. It didn't usually affect him this way. Heat was a familiar thing in his life. But there was nothing about this situation that was familiar.

David stood silent, watching her, trying to find his focus, listening to the hum of bees and clicking of tiny grasshoppers among the vegetation. Her garden tool scrunched against soil as she stabbed at the earth. Her movements were snappy in spite of the temperature. Her body language screamed frustration. He watched as she tossed another bright-orange carrot into the bowl with a clunk. The livid color was in stark contrast to the verdant green of the leafy tops that hung over the side of the deep-blue bowl.

David stared at the colors, the contrasts. Everything seemed unusually bright, his senses extraordinarily heightened.

He wiped his brow. It must be the sun, he thought.

He glanced at the sky. The sun was at its zenith and there was not a wisp of cloud in sight, not a hint of breeze in the air.

He turned his attention back to Sahar. Her hands were covered in soil. She was fully engaged in her task in the same way she'd been engrossed in her game of tag with Kamilah. He found this deeply alluring.

She unearthed another carrot, tossed it in with the others. The bowl was almost full now. Still David didn't speak, couldn't. He was fascinated. There was something so earthy, so organic about the vignette in front of him. Something basic and honest and life-affirming about the way she was digging in this time-old garden that had fed generations before them.

He cleared his throat.

She gasped, spun around, stared up at him, lips parted in surprise. "David, you startled me!" She rose slowly to her feet, trowel in one hand, carrots in the other.

There was dirt on her knees. The brown smudges drew his eyes down the length of her lean, tanned legs.

"Do you always sneak up on people like that?"

He dragged his eyes up from her legs, along the length of her body, to her face. Her features were dappled by the shade of her straw hat, her wide eyes an impossibly luminous and bewitching green in this light.

"I've been looking for you," he said, stepping closer. He could smell the musk of freshly turned earth. And he could smell her. The heat was lifting her fragrance into the air. Citrus. Warm. And female. His nostrils flared reflexively.

She angled her head to get a better line of sight from under the battered brim of her hat. Up close he could see a fine sweep of almost imperceptible gold freckles across her nose, her cheeks flushed from the kiss of the sun.

"And now you've found me." She smiled, hesitantly. "What did you want me for?"

Oh, he wanted her all right. Right now. Right here. He moistened his lips, trying to find focus. But he couldn't quite get his mind back on track. Her skin was slick with the soft sheen of perspiration. Mesmerized, he watched as a small bead of sweat shimmered down from the hollow of her throat toward the valley between her breasts. His eyes followed the droplet as it slithered down into her shirt. He felt a sudden dizziness. It was the sun, he told himself. The heat.

His eyes slid slowly back up to her face. She was watching him warily from under the brim of her hat, like a wild cat in the shadows. Time seemed to hang still, warped by the waves of heat. The buzz of the bees grew louder in his ears. His focus shrunk to another tiny jewel of perspiration that traveled like a tear from the side of her eye. David watched the glistening drop slide slowly down the subtle swell of her cheek to dangle precipitously on her jawbone. She sensed it, swiped it away, leaving a smudge of dirt along the side of her chin.

He reached out reflexively and wiped the dirt from her jaw. Her breath caught sharply in her throat.

His hand stilled. "You've got dirt on your face," he explained, his voice thick.

Her mouth tightened. "Thanks." She turned away from him, dropped back to her knees, tossed the carrots she was holding into the bowl, jabbed angrily again at the earth.

She was cutting him off. That's what he wanted, wasn't it? So why did it sting?

"Why were you looking for me?" she asked as she dug.

"I need to talk to you about Kamilah."

She glanced up at him.

"Why don't you come inside? We can talk there, get a drink."

"We can talk here," she said bluntly.

He blinked. He hadn't expected resistance. People seldom resisted his will. David crouched down beside her and reached for a carrot, as if asserting his ownership, his control over everything including the vegetables in this garden. He dusted it off against his pants, crunched his teeth into it, watching her as he chewed.

Something shifted again in her features. She turned abruptly away from him and concentrated on unearthing another root. "What about Kamilah?" she asked as she turfed the carrot into the bowl.

"I want you to stop with the mermaid nonsense."

She went dead still. Then she turned slowly to face him, her eyes narrowing. "What *nonsense,* exactly, David?"

Again he moistened his lips. The heat of the sun beat relentlessly through the fabric of the shirt on his back. A trickle of sweat ran down under his arm to his waist. "It's hot as hell out here," he said. "You'll get sunstroke. Come, let's go inside."

She didn't budge. "*What* nonsense?" she insisted.

He blew out a hot breath of frustration. Well, if she wanted this on her terms, her choice of turf, she'd get it.

"Kamilah has been through a lot, Sahar. I don't want to go into all the details because it's *not* your affair. This is Rashid family business, and I expect you to keep out of it. I want you to stop filling her head with fairy-tale garbage. Life isn't like that. There are no happy endings. I don't want you filling her head with unrealistic expectations."

Her jaw dropped. She stared at him. "You were listening to us?"

"It's my island. My palace."

She glared at him in silence.

He shifted uncomfortably. Another trickle of sweat traced around his underarm, slid slowly down the length of his waist.

Still she said nothing.

Irritation simmered under his skin. "Do you understand me, Sahar? You're welcome to remain on Shendi until your memory returns, but you are *not* to interfere in my life."

She jerked to her feet. "*Your* life?"

Her reaction startled him. He looked up. *Mistake.* Her legs were astride, feet planted angrily into the ground. He was uncomfortably conscious of a gap between the hem of the wide, oversize shorts and those smooth, long thighs. Fixated, he stared at the opening. Something hot and slick slipped low in his belly. He felt his blood rush from his head.

He quickly stood up, seeking the advantage of height, forcing his brain back on track. But it only made him dizzy.

"This is not just *your* life, David. I don't know if you've noticed but you've got a little girl who desperately needs to share what she's been through. She *needs* to talk. Have you even considered the fact that *you* may the one who's been blocking her efforts to reach out?"

She was lecturing him? How dare she? "Sahar—" His voice came out in low warning. But she refused to back off. She was on a roll and she was going to have her say.

"You're all cramped up with your own damn anger, David. You're so busy wallowing in your own guilt that you can't see what your child needs. I saw how you shut her out this morning. She came down to the stables to be with you. She was reaching out, David. And you snubbed her."

"*Damn you, woman,*" he snarled, grabbing her wrist. He

wrenched her toward him. It silenced her instantly. His fingers tightened like a cuff, digging into her skin as his eyes bored angry into hers. "How *dare* you? I love Kamilah more than anything in this damn world. She's all I have left. I've hired the best specialists, the most expensive tutors. I'd move heaven and earth for her—"

"David," she interrupted, her voice suddenly soft, caring, so gently feminine that it knocked him completely off stride. "Kamilah doesn't need heaven and earth. She doesn't need specialists. She just needs *you*. She needs her daddy. She needs to play. She needs to be a child."

His throat constricted around his words. Because he knew she was right. Her presence on Shendi had shown him that.

"She just needs you to hold her, David. Is that really so hard?"

His fingers tightened around her wrist. But she didn't flinch. She just stood there probing his soul with those haunting eyes, getting right inside his bloody head. She was scrambling his radar. He was primed for a fight, and she'd come at him sideways, knocking his knees out from under him with her soft voice and liquid eyes.

And words of truth.

He wanted to lash out at her, hurt her for doing this to him. He wanted to pull her to his chest, kiss that incredible mouth, plunge himself between her legs. But he didn't dare move. Because he wasn't sure what in hell he *would* do. So he held dead still. Too close to her mouth, to her beautiful breasts. So close that the scent of her filled his nostrils, his mind, drugged his senses.

"Why the anger, David?" she asked softly.

That's what Watson had asked him. He sucked in a shuddering breath.

She reached up, placed her palm against his cheek. The simple gesture cracked him. It took all his control to hold back the bank of emotion that exploded painfully behind his eyes. God, this woman was splitting him right open. She'd ripped back his barriers and exposed him. And now her simple touch was blowing salt into his wounds. He clenched his jaw and held on desperately to the volatility heaving inside him.

She moved her body closer to him. "Let me help you, David," she whispered.

"Why?" his voice came out hoarse.

"Because I can see your pain." She hesitated. "Because I've ridden with you on a horse and I know that inside is a man aching to be free again. Free like you felt on that stallion... with me."

She was unreal. She could see right into him. How could she possibly know the depth of what he'd felt on that horse? Where in hell had this woman come from?

Shocked, he pulled away.

As much as he wanted to take her into his arms, to believe in her, to make this journey with her, he couldn't.

He took another step back, sucked in air. He couldn't do this. She was going to leave. Anyday. Any second. Watson may have information on her right this instant. There might be a message waiting in his office that would take her away before nightfall.

"Sahar, just keep out of it. I don't need your help."

Hurt flashed through her eyes. She bit her bottom lip. He could see why. It was beginning to tremble. She was trying to stop it.

His heart twisted. She had her own pain. "Sahar—"

She looked abruptly away. But not fast enough to hide a fat tear that slid down her cheek trailing fine dust after it.

Great! Now she'd switched tables on him! What was a guy to do? "Sahar?" He stepped forward.

She wouldn't look at him. She held up her hand, shook her head as if warning him to back off.

He'd done it again. He'd pushed her too far. There was something so innately resilient about her that it kept surprising him when he hit her sensitive spot. She seemed too outwardly strong to hurt. But inside she was lost. And instead of offering comfort, he was doing his damnedest to chase her away. He was lashing out at her because of the way she clouded his mind. Because of what she did to his body. And if he was truthful, it scared the hell out of him. He was used to being in control at all times. He was *not* used to *this*.

"Sahar—" he took her elbow firmly "—come sit in the shade."

She acquiesced, allowed him to lead her to the stone bench under the fruit-laden tree. She seemed suddenly spent. The energy that had quivered around her was gone, and that threw him. He felt like a cad for having done this to her. She was probably exhausted, drained. She'd been through a terrible accident. And on top of that, she'd been physically going at it all morning, running, swimming, riding, playing tag with Kamilah and now jabbing a trowel into the earth under the fierce heat of the North African summer sun.

She slumped onto the bench in the shade. He sat down beside her. They both remained silent. As if afraid to take the next step in the bizarre game they seemed to have been thrust into.

"That came out all wrong," he said finally. "I'm sorry."

She swiped at a tear, leaving a smudge of dirt across her face. "It's okay, I...I totally understand."

How could she possibly understand?

She took Watson's battered old hat off, exposing the bruised look in her eyes. She swiped her damp brow with the tail of her shirt. It only streaked the dirt from one place to another.

"I should be the one apologizing, David. I can see I'm making you unhappy. It's not my intention to hurt you or Kamilah. I only wanted to help. I *needed* to help. I can't explain it." She smudged another tear across her cheek. "I'll go. I'll leave Shendi. I'm an uninvited guest and you've been good to me, and I thank you for that. But I'll leave in the morning. Dr. Watson left me his mobile number. I'll call him and ask him to help me find a place…somewhere…maybe Khartoum…while I try and figure out who I am."

Oh, boy. He felt like camel dung now. She hadn't asked to be washed up onto his beach unconscious. She hadn't asked to be placed in this predicament. Hell knew what she'd been through in that storm, what she may yet have to face when the nature of her accident began to reveal itself.

And Kamilah? She'd be devastated if she found Sahar gone in the morning. Damn, this was a double bind. This was precisely what he'd been trying to avoid in the first place. Hurting Kamilah. Allowing himself to *feel* something for this stranger.

Because suddenly she wasn't a stranger anymore.

She was Sahar. She was digging up carrots in his vegetable garden, riding with him on his stallion, telling him how to be a father, stirring feelings in him that were fit for sin.

When exactly had this started to happen? He blew out a breath.

This woman didn't play fair.

She didn't play by the rules.

He placed his hand on her knee. "Sahar, I want you to stay."

Her eyes slanted up to meet his. More tears pooled in her lower lids. Her hand fidgeted at her side.

"I want you to be my guest. Consider this an official invitation." He did his best to smile warmly, but inside he was a mess of conflicting, uncertain emotion.

"David—"

"No." He placed two fingers against her lips. "Enough. I apologize. I've been an abominable host. I want you to stay on Shendi. But I also want you to remember one thing. When you leave, Kamilah will be devastated. I just want you to consider that, when you interact with her. I guess that's all I was really trying to say."

She took his hand from her lips, held it in her own. "I know she will be sad. She told me. But I was hoping we'd have managed to work through the mermaid thing by the time I left, that she'd be ready for me to leave. But maybe you're right, David. I shouldn't have interfered. In her life or yours. But I couldn't *not* help. Maybe it is best if I do go now."

His stomach swooped out from under him and his pulse quickened. "No, Sahar. I can't let you go." It was too late. As much as he wanted her to leave, it was beyond him to actually let her go. He just couldn't. And even if he could, what kind of man would that make him? Sahar had amnesia. She was helpless. She had absolutely nowhere to go and not a possession to her name. "Give me a chance to be a better host, Sahar." He attempted a laugh. It came out a little hollow, a little desperate. "I haven't even shown you around my home." He cupped her jaw, tilted her face to his. "What do you say, Sahar? Will you stay? Be my guest? For as long as you need?"

Sahar hesitated, snared by the intensity in David's eyes. But more than anything it was the deep sincerity, the honesty and integrity in his voice that held her. This was a man struggling to do what was right. And she could only respect him for that.

Besides, she had nowhere to go. The thought of being nameless and alone in a place like Khartoum terrified her.

"Yes," she said softly. "I'll stay. Thank you, David."

David exhaled, ran his hands through his hair. "Good. That's settled then. *Now* can I give you a tour of my home?"

A shaky smile tugged at her mouth. "Yes." She said, swiping at the last of her tears, trying to pull herself together. "I'd be delighted."

He stood, thrust his shoulders back in mock gallantry, grinned like a pirate and held his hand out to her, palm up, steady as a rock. "Come, then."

She reached out, placed her hand in his. He closed his fingers around hers. And inside she felt as if she'd found a bridge, steady and dependable, one that would somehow get her to the other side.

Wherever that was.

Chapter 8

"My father bought this place when I was a child," David explained as he took Sahar's arm and led her into the enormous main hall.

She stared up in awe at the stained glass dome high in the centre of the curved ceiling. The midday African sun streamed though it, picking up hues of oranges, ochres and greens, imbuing the vast room with a cathedral-like quality. Except the architecture couldn't be further from the cathedrals she knew. "It looks Moorish in design," she said.

"You're right. Moroccan inspired," he explained, pushing open thick double doors at the far end of the room. "Shendi Palace was built by an eccentric French general in the early 1800s. He'd served for years in Algiers, Morocco and Mauritania before the jinns got him."

"Jinns?"

David grinned, a sharp twinkle lighting his eyes. "The evil

spirits of the desert." He tapped his finger against his temple. "The heat, the thirst, endlessness of the Sahara, it can drive a man crazy. The locals say that's when the jinns come and get you."

"So the general went a little loopy?"

"That's the story. He took early retirement and moved out here onto Shendi. He bought the island because of the unusual springs of fresh water. He dug the wells that feed these gardens, and in designing the palace, he copied the Moorish architecture from the areas he'd come to love, combining it with whatever other North African influence inspired him."

"It's absolutely stunning...eclectic," she said, studying the mosaic work in one of the recessed alcoves.

"Eclectic is the word. In some ways Shendi Palace is symbolic of North Africa itself. So much of this part of the world is a fascinating and often uneasy blend of past cultures, Arabian, African, colonial, each one trying to erase traces of the previous one, going all the way back to the Kingdom of Sheba and beyond."

The sudden deepening of his voice, the guttural catch in the honeyed gravel tones, forced her to look up.

He was staring at her. His face had changed. A sharp and fervent energy had shifted into the granite of his dark features. His eyes flashed dangerously.

Sahar swallowed. A tingle of foreboding trickled down her spine at the mood in his eyes. North Africa and the Sahara was something David Rashid obviously cared passionately about. The palace, the Africa he described, they were like the man himself, she thought. He too exuded a timelessness, as if the spirit of ancient warrior tribes, the wild and exotic spice of desert leaders, still shaped his thoughts. Yet his barely leashed and feral energy was veneered with the fine cultural sensibilities of British aristocracy.

David Rashid was a mystery in more ways than one. It

made her curious about his personal history…and more than curious about why she was feeling this shiver of portent down the back of her neck.

She cleared her throat, trying hard not to shy away from the hooded intensity of his indigo eyes. "Kamilah said your father was a sheik."

"Kamilah *said* that?"

"Yes."

His jaw hardened. He turned away from her, grabbed a brass ring and flung open a heavy wooden door to another room. He strode ahead of her into the vast chamber.

She caught up with him. "Does that make *you* a sheik then?"

He stopped, swung around to face her, the lines bracketing his mouth hard. "I am Sheik David bin Omar bin Zafir Rashid. I am the oldest son of my father. According the customs of my father's people, I now bear his title."

He paused, his eyes boring into hers. "But it means nothing." He swept his arm out in an expansive movement, dismissing the subject. "This is the hall where the French general used to host his famous balls."

Sahar was more interested in studying the face and architecture of David Rashid than the room. "Why do you say it means nothing?" she pressed.

His eyes probed hers, as if he were weighing her up, deciding her worthy of the information. "It would take time to explain. Come." He took her arm, urged her through enormous double doors to another enclosed courtyard, this one with a long, black marble pool sunk into the center. The pool was flanked by columns and surrounded by arched walkways fragrant with exotic blooms. Elaborately carved fountains splashed water into the pool causing ripples along the shimmering black surface. The pool looked darkly cool under the white-hot sky. Sahar could not see below the surface. She

looked from the pool up into David's eyes. The reflection of
the water rippled like wet ink through them. She couldn't see
below the dark surface of this man either. But she wanted to.
She *needed* to.

"I have plenty of time," she said, forcing a soft laugh.
"More time than I know what to do with right now."

He stilled. "You really are interested?"

She looked up into his smouldering eyes. She was interested all right. She was drawn to him by every cell in her body.
"Yes," she said. "I am."

He pursed his exquisite lips in thought, his eyes never leaving hers. "All right." He took her hand, drew her to a bench
in the shade of the arches facing the pool. He seated himself
beside her, eyes focused on the dark water.

"My father, Sheik Omar bin Zafir Rashid, was descended
from a tribe of desert warriors that migrated from Arabia and
down through Egypt into the Sahara hundreds of years ago,"
he explained. "The Bedu of Azar. A fiercely proud people.
They lived as nomads and hunters, and their lives were ruled
by the stars and the seasons. They killed oryx for meat and
they traveled from oasis to oasis with their camels and goats.
They lived by an ancient code of ethics and were both revered
and feared."

He stopped talking, his eyes distant, staring into the waters of the swimming pool as if he could see through them to
a distant desert oasis. "They were a noble people, Sahar. But
they are no more. I am the lineal leader of a tribe that no longer
exists."

"What happened?"

He shrugged. "The world changed. My people and their
ways didn't. The desert is dying, and with it an ancient way
of life. After years of relentless drought, traditional watering
holes have dried up. The oryx are gone. Famine has taken its

toll. Camels and goats died. And the Bedu were forced to abandon their way of life, the very existence that made them proud and free. In desperation they were forced toward towns and settlements, and they began to eke out an existence living in shacks on the outskirts of civilization."

David turned to look at her, his eyes glittering. "A once-noble people have lost their culture, the bonds that held their tribes together. They are now scattered, directionless and impoverished, subsisting mainly on supplies of American grain and other foreign aid."

The ferocity in his voice caught her by the throat.

"That is why I say the title means nothing." His jaw steeled, flint sharpened his gaze. "But I will give pride back to my people, Sahar. I will make them whole again. It was my father's dream. And it is now mine."

Sahar stared at him. So this is what drove the man. His raw passion for his people, for the desert, moved her profoundly. "How would you do that?" she asked. "How would give pride back to the Bedu?"

He smiled in a way she had not seen him smile. A smile so powerful it reached right to her heart, took hold of it and squeezed so that she could barely breathe.

"I told you, it is a long story."

"I want to hear it, David." She needed to. It gave her unique insight into the man, to what fired his soul. He possessed a depth, an integrity she had only guessed at.

He took her hand, and his thumb absently stroked the inside of her palm as he stared into the black water. Her insides went shivery, but she could not bring herself to pull her hand away. This man held an enigmatic power over her, something that defied her control. Did he even realize what he was doing to her?

"I spent half my life in the Sahara," he said, speaking into the distance, to a place way beyond the pool, a place that lived in his mind. "My father wanted me to see it, to experience the old ways firsthand. He wanted me to taste the ancient lifestyle of a desert warrior before it disappeared from the face of this earth forever." His fingers laced through hers, tightened. Her heart beat faster.

"My father realized when he was still young that the old ways were going. And he knew the only way to save his people would be to bring the ancient ways of the desert in line with the new world, to give the nomads economic control over their destiny." He paused. "My father made it his goal to be accepted at Oxford. He'd heard the Bedu legends about the black gold, the oil, that lay beneath the sands of northern Azar. And he wanted to learn how to find it. He came back a geologist, armed with both science and knowledge of the ancient ways of the desert." David drew in a deep breath. "He found that black gold, Sahar. After many years, he found it."

For a while they sat silent, her hand still held in his. Sahar looked up into his face. "And?" she prompted softly.

He turned to look down at her, his gaze meshing intimately with hers. "He brought something else back from England," he said. "A British wife...and a son."

"You? And your mother?"

"Some saw it as a sign of my father's betrayal."

"Because she was British?"

"Yes." A bitterness clipped his word. "A foreigner."

"What happened...to your mother?"

"She didn't take easily to the ways of the desert. She was the daughter of British privilege, and to her the desert was simply an adventure that grew tiresome. To my father it was life. My mother began to pine for her home, and my father loved her too much to trap her in a place she couldn't live. He in turn could not leave his beloved desert for a full-time life in England. Their relationship was doomed from the start."

"How awfully tragic."

He drew breath sharply in through his nose. "In the end my mother got ill. She decided to return to her homeland, her people. But she wouldn't leave me behind. I was four. I had been born for the ways of the desert but she took me to England."

Sahar looked up into his eyes. Below the surface of those dark-blue irises, somewhere deep inside this man, lurked a boy, a boy who had been torn between two parents. Two countries. Two cultures. A boy who had shaped this potent man of the present.

He squeezed her hand, gave her a wry smile. "Ever since, I've been divided. For six months of each year I lived in the desert. For the other half of the year I studied in England."

"What happened to your father after your mother left?" she asked.

"He eventually remarried…took an Azarian bride. He had another son eight years after my birth, my half brother, Tariq. Some felt Tariq should have inherited my father's title because he was the *pure* one." David dismissed it with a shrug. "Either way, like I said, it is a title that means nothing."

"Do you get on with your brother?"

His eyes flashed to hers and pierced her with a sudden laser sharpness, with suspicion. He withdrew his hand. "Why are you interested in this? It's Rashid business."

She stumbled mentally at the turnabout. This man had low flashpoints. "Because…" She felt warmth infuse her cheeks. "Because…I…care. About you. About Kamilah."

A muscle pulsed along his jawline. But he said nothing. He waited, watching her face, his eyes unreadable.

"I have nothing else to care about, David. I'm…I'm all alone. Until I find out where I belong."

His eyes softened slightly. He lifted his hand and briefly caressed the side of her cheek. "My brother and I did not get on until about two years ago."

"Why?"

"Tariq felt I was not one of them. Not pure." An anger glittered briefly in his eyes, then was gone.

"He thought he should have been sheik?"

"He thought I should have been dead."

"What?"

David snorted. "Tariq grew up resenting everything about me, Sahar, including my father's affection. You see, my half brother didn't agree with our vision for bringing Azar into the global economy. And because of his radical views, he was cut from my father's will. But that was then. Tariq is older now. Wiser. He is beginning to see beyond his narrow idealist window. He has finally come to accept my views. We share the same goal now, to build the wealth of our people, to marry the ancient ways with the new, using the resources of Rashid International, the company started by our father, the company designed to feed our father's dream."

"What finally turned Tariq around?" she asked.

"A promise." David absently fingered the hilt of the dagger at his waist. "I vowed on my father's deathbed to do everything within my power to heal the rift between myself and Tariq. And I vowed to continue his work to heal his people, the Bedu of Azar. He died with those dreams on his lips."

Sahar noted he said "his" people. Not "my" people. Even in his own mind, he wasn't wholly one of them. David's dichotomy was cleft deep into his soul. And she had a sense that healing Azar, bridging the divide between the ancient ways and the new, would in a sense make this man whole himself. It would make him feel worthy of his title. It would heal the scars of the four-year-old buried deep within the man.

"How did you manage to sway Tariq, David? I mean, a fundamentalist ideology is not something one gives up easily."

His eyes shot to hers. "You're right. But blood can be stronger than ideology. And I never gave up." His exquisite fingers moved absently over the ornate handle of his *jambiya* as he spoke.

He caught her looking. "My father's," he explained, curling his fingers tight around the hilt. "A gift from his deathbed. The symbol of my promise. I wear it always."

She swallowed at the sudden dark and possessive edge in his voice, the way he held his weapon as if he were about to yank it from its sheath. His eyes glittered sharply. She'd hit another of his flashpoints. It made her jittery. Anxiety began to swamp her again for some reason she couldn't identify. She had no doubt that the raw passion housed within the powerful man that was Sheik David bin Omar bin Zafir Rashid gave him the capacity to kill.

What would he do to her if he found *her* to be disloyal? What would *she* do if he turned out to be her enemy? She swallowed, tried to keep her voice light. "So…is…is Azar prospering now?"

"Not quite." He stood up, his one hand still resting on the hilt of his *jambiya*. "There is still much work to do. Come." He held out his other hand. She took it. He led her under the arches and escorted her back into the palace.

"Africa is complicated," he explained. "And in the tradition of Africa nothing goes smoothly." The mellifluous smoothness was back in his voice, the sharp twinkle back in his eyes. "Once all the oilfields were in full production, after my father died, I discovered a source of very unique uranium, something far more coveted than the oil."

David Rashid is smuggling weapons-grade uranium.

The thought speared into her brain. Sahar's chest cramped

tight. She tried to breathe. But this time she couldn't shake the thought. It began to diffuse through her brain like an explosion of ink in water, tainting, suffocating everything.

"And…and what is so special about this uranium?" She heard the catch in her voice.

So did he. He paused, arched his dark brow slightly. "It has a unique molecular structure which makes it very easy to enrich beyond power-station grade."

To nuclear-weapons grade.

Every muscle in her body froze. She stopped in her tracks. He halted beside her. "What is it, Sahar?"

"Ah…nothing. It's nothing." She forced her muscles to move, forced herself to walk. "Go on."

A frown creased his brow. He held her back. "Are you sure you're feeling all right?"

She nodded quickly. "Yes, of course. What happened then?"

"The uranium discovery sparked a coup attempt in Azar," David explained, his eyes searching hers, his frown deepening. "A dissident Azarian faction attempted to overthrow the government. The rebels gained control of the north and my oil fields, stopping a flow of cash into the country. Then they started moving south in an effort to seize Tabara, the capital."

Her mouth went dry. "Wh…what happened then?"

"I fought back," he said, watching her intently. "I hired a private army. I came to an agreement with the Azarian president that I would fund a private military presence on the condition that we would first fight to reclaim and protect my oil fields."

I know this. I know all of this. Every bit of it. She placed her hand to her temple. Maybe she'd read about it in a newspaper, seen it on the news.

The line of stitches under her hairline began to throb with each beat of her heart.

David misread her reaction. "Mercenaries are not all bad, Sahar. There are teams out there who do good. This is one of them. They have pushed the rebels back up toward the Libyan border. In addition, the mercenaries are stiffening and training Azar's own army. They will be able to stand on their own in a way never seen before. I am making my country strong."

She was at a loss for words. All she could do was nod.

"Come," he said, taking her arm. "I'll show you." He led her into another wing and along yet another arched corridor.

Her head pounded wildly. She was dizzy. She could feel the prickle of perspiration along her upper lip. "I…I'm just wondering why you are here, then, on Shendi, if your heart…your business is in Azar?"

"It's a safe home for Kamilah," he said. "England was not good for her, and Azar is still technically at war with the rebels. And while Azar is my dream, Kamilah is still my priority. Shendi is close enough for me to fly into Azar when needed." David opened another door and allowed Sahar to enter ahead of him. "This is my study," he said.

She stepped into a room that was masculine in decor with lots of dark wood and leather and an unmistakable North African stamp in design. The ceiling fan moved slowly up above, stirring soft currents in the warm air.

Sahar caught sight of the huge ochre-toned map on the far wall. A bolt of recognition stalled her heart. She knew instantly *exactly* who David Rashid was. A thousand little loose shards suddenly slammed together into a cohesive picture as sharp as glass. Pain pierced her head. She gasped at the sensation of it.

She knew the map depicted Azar, a country nestled like an inverted wedge of pizza between Chad to the west, Sudan to the east with Libya and Egypt to the north.

She even knew what the different-colored pins stuck into the map denoted. The big blue pins marked the two Rashid uranium mines. The yellow pins were his oil fields. And the clusters of red pins in the north marked the positions of rebel armies that had been pushed back by Rashid money, cash paid to a controversial new mercenary group grabbing international headlines, the Force du Sable, headed by none other than the legendary Jacques Sauvage and the formidable Hunter McBride and Rafiq Zayed.

The room spiraled in on her. Her heart pounded painfully against her chest wall. She groped wildly for the back of a chair.

David's arms shot out to steady her. "Sahar! Are you all right?"

"I…I…I'm fine. Just…a…a bit dizzy."

"It's the heat," he said angrily. "I shouldn't have allowed you to work in the garden. I'll send for Watson."

"No!" She shook her head. "No. No, I'm fine…really."

But she wasn't. She was a mess. Because in the instant she'd seen the map, she'd known that Sheik David bin Omar bin Zafir Rashid was one of the world's wealthiest and most influential industrialists, an enigmatic man with considerable interests in oil, uranium and diamond mines not only in Azar but around the world. She also knew he was a shadowy and mysterious figure who did his best to stay out of the press. But he was a figure who nevertheless fueled the hunger of tabloid journalists who'd touted him as one of the Europe's most eligible men since the death of his wife.

She didn't know *how* she knew all this. But she did. Her mind had somehow taken the bits of information he'd just given her and filled in all the gaps at once, hitting her brain like a bolt of electricity, instantly overloading her circuits. And she reeled with the shock of it.

She tried to force the river of jumbled facts roiling in her brain into some kind of sensible order. But she couldn't.

Somehow she also knew he was smuggling uranium into Libya as well as selling it on the black market to Korea. Uranium for nuclear weapons. Weapons that would be aimed at the U.S. and Britain. He was a bad guy. Her enemy.

She pressed her hand to her head, tried to stop the spinning. How did *she* fit into all this? Who was *she*? Why did she know these things? Had she read it *all* in newspapers, tabloids? Seen it on TV?

She couldn't have read the black-market stuff in papers, could she? Because if it was common knowledge surely he'd be behind bars? A wanted man? She pushed her hands harder against her temples.

But no matter how hard she pressed she couldn't stop the sickening spinning. And as the facts churned through her brain, they swamped in a suffocating flood. She tried to draw in a breath, couldn't. The room lurched wildly. She felt herself sway.

"Sahar, tell me what's going on? You're pale as a ghost." He tried to take her hand.

She waved him off. "I was just remembering..." She clamped her mouth shut. Instinctively. She'd been going to tell him she remembered who he was. But something inside made her stop. Dead. Something told her it was a matter of life and death.

Oh God, why? Would this man kill her if he knew what she knew?

Her stomach heaved. She was going to throw up. She clutched at her belly, bent over. "I...I think I need to lie down for a second." And as she spoke, her knees sagged under her.

David was there in a flash. He caught her, scooped her up, carried her to the door, kicked it open with his foot.

"I'm taking you to your room, and then I'm getting Watson." His words were clipped, efficient. His boots clacked loudly on the hard stone floors.

"Please no, David. I...I just need a rest. You...you were right, it's the sun, I shouldn't have been out. I'll be fine. Really."

And something cold sank in her stomach as he carried her to her room. Because she knew she had to hide her knowledge from him. She instinctively knew she couldn't tell him what she knew about him. Because her life...the lives of others depended on it. She just didn't understand why.

David kicked open the door to her bedroom and laid her gently on the bed. The ceiling spun madly. The fan was spinning, too. Or was it? Maybe it was just her head. She closed her eyes, but still everything swirled in a mad maelstrom of grays and blacks.

David moistened a piece of cloth using the jug on the nightstand and pressed it gently to her forehead. His touch was impossibly tender. She began to breathe easier. She felt the oxygen finally going back to her brain.

"Rest," he said. "I'm going to call Watson and ask his advice."

"I'm okay. Just a bit of sunstroke. I'm sure I'll be one hundred percent after a rest."

"Here." He raised her head slightly, put a glass of water to her lips. "You must keep hydrated."

She sipped greedily, looking up into his eyes as she did, reading deep concern there.

"I don't care what you say, Sahar, I'm going to speak to Watson. You might be having complications from the head injury."

Oh, she was having complications all right. He didn't know the half of it. But she couldn't try to think anymore. Fatigue pressed down on her. She lay back, closed her eyes.

David covered her with a cool cotton sheet and stroked her hand as she fell into a deep sleep.

* * *

David closed the door quietly behind him. Sahar had spooked the hell out of him by fainting like that. But she was probably right. It was most likely sunstroke. Still, he'd sound Watson out on her symptoms.

He leaned against the closed door, rested his head back against the wood. And as he relaxed, he began to smile. She was one hell of a character. Stubborn, strong, principled. Intelligent. Sexy as sin. Fun.

Fun? That hadn't featured in his life for two years. Yes, she'd put the word back into his existence. And for the first time in his life he had opened up fully to another human being, about his childhood, his family, his dreams. And it didn't leave him feeling the slightest bit vulnerable. It made him feel good. He'd shared, and it only made him feel stronger. He was able to share with Sahar because he connected with something deep inside her. Whoever she was, surely that would never change?

And she *cared* about him.

For the first time David Rashid dared feel hope. He dared to dream that once Sahar's true identity was discovered, things might not have to come to a grueling halt. That maybe, just maybe, she had a past that wouldn't necessarily tear her away from Shendi. At least not right away. Because he cared for her. A lot. In ways that went way deeper than the heat of raw desire.

That little seed of hope began to grow deep in his belly as he fed it with his imagination. His smile widened, and inside he felt light, exhilarated. Because in some way he felt as if he'd found a friend. And by God it felt good.

In the distance he heard the rhythmic chop of helicopter blades and sobered instantly. He was a fool to think this might last. To even begin to dream it was to set himself up for failure. And he didn't tolerate failure.

He checked his watch, listening to the sound of the chopper grow louder. That would be Tariq. Good. He needed to put his mind to work. The two of them had a ton of business to get through. They only had two days before Tariq left for the mines in northern Azar.

And continuing to build solid relations with Tariq was just as important as rebuilding a nation. David brusquely shoved other thoughts from his mind and went to greet his half brother.

Chapter 9

A soft knocking at the bedroom door roused Sahar from the sleep of the dead. She blinked into the shadows, confused. It was darker, a little cooler. She squinted at the clock. Goodness, it was early evening. She must have slept the afternoon away. And with that realization came the sinking recollection of what had happened earlier in David's office.

The knocking sounded a little louder. She tensed. She wasn't ready to confront David yet. She needed to think. "Who is it?" Her voice came out rough.

Fayha' poked her head around the door. "It's me, Sahar. Are you decent?"

Relief swooped through her. "Oh, Fayha', come on in."

The housekeeper pushed the door open wide, motioned to another young woman who wheeled in a trolley piled high with boxes each tied with a sleek burgundy ribbon and each embossed with the same little gold logo.

"What's this?" Sahar asked.

Fayha' beamed. "Clothes. Mr. Rashid had them flown in from Cairo. They just arrived on his helicopter with Mr. Tariq."

Sahar frowned. "David had *clothes* flown in? For me?"

"A whole wardrobe."

"From Cairo?"

"Mr. Rashid has his pilots fly in supplies weekly from both Cairo and Mombasa…as well as other places if need be. It's how he likes to run things on Shendi."

Fayha' ran her eyes over Sahar and smiled gently. "Besides, it's about time you got out of those old clothes of the doctor's. They need a wash." She gestured to the trolley. "Shall we leave it here in the corner?"

"Um…yeah. Thanks." Her head was still groggy from sleep, her brain still thick with unrelated facts and dark shards of memory.

Fayha' closed the door with a soft click.

Sahar swung her feet over the bed and padded over to the pile of boxes. The labels read Boutique L'Avalle, El Qâhira. She'd heard of L'Avalle, a distinguished and prohibitively priced world-class designer label. She'd also heard that El Qâhira, or Cairo, was the fashion capital of the Arabic world.

Intrigued, she removed the top box, set it on the bed, slid the ribbon off and lifted the lid. She peeled back the pale-green tissue paper and her breath caught. It was the most beautiful green fabric she'd ever laid eyes on. She fingered the texture. It was liquid silk. As she let it slip through her hands it caught different aspects of the light, which made the color shift and shimmer from jade to emerald to turquoise. She'd never seen anything like it.

Sahar held it up to her face, swung around to face the mirror. The entrancing fabric caught the light in her eyes.

But when she moved, the color shifted to a predominant jade green. Once again she stilled, and she had that strange gnawing feeling, like there was something vitally significant about this particular hue of green.

She shook it off, set the gown aside and quickly opened the other boxes. David had thought of everything. There was delicate lacy underwear, sports and workout gear, bathing suits, robes, eveningwear, cool sundresses, shorts, tees, tank tops…all in her size. The man just didn't cease to amaze her.

And she couldn't help smiling.

She felt like a kid at Christmas. She had no idea what she usually wore but she liked what she saw in the boxes. It was a mix of elegant femininity, sleek athletic lines and something a little playful, even a tad daring.

Is that what world-famous industrialist David Rashid thought of her? Or had the boutique owner second-guessed his taste? It didn't matter. Just the idea that he'd thought to do it was intriguing, endearing…intimate. And more than a little titillating. The whole thing sent a crazy spurt of warmth through her.

Then she saw the envelope that had slipped to the floor. She scooped it up, opened it, took out a card the same color as the ribbons on the boxes and embossed with the same gold logo. She read the bold handwriting.

"Join us at nine for a late dinner in the grand dining hall. P.S. Do *not* wear anything of Watson's."

Sahar giggled, her blood zinged. She felt slightly heady, as if she were a schoolgirl invited on her first date with the dark prince.

She almost immediately pulled herself together. This was ridiculous. This girlish reaction wasn't part of her usual repertoire of behaviors…was it?

She sat back on the bed, pushed her knotted hair back from

her forehead. David Rashid was confusing the hell out of her. And it didn't help that her head was a mess to begin with. She stared at the boxes and their beautiful bounty.

So he was famous. And wealthy. And mysterious. Perhaps even dangerous. It didn't necessarily mean he was evil, did it? She'd probably read about him. And if there was anything more sinister, well it was probably simply tabloid gossip and speculation worth zip. She felt in her heart, *her gut,* that he was a good man. A man of integrity and brutal honesty. That was the David Rashid she'd come to know in the short time she'd been on Shendi Island.

And the reason she'd felt so odd in his office, well, that *had* to have been because of the sun and overexertion so soon after her accident, she told herself. And because the heat had scrambled her senses she'd found herself filling in the blanks with dark nonsense.

But deep, deep down, no matter how much she tried to rationalize it all, there remained a sharp biting sensation that wouldn't go away, warning her to be cautious, telling her that being open could be dangerous. That lives were at stake.

And because of that, she knew she wasn't going to tell David about those dark thoughts. At least, not until she knew more.

And what did that make her? A liar? Dishonest?

Ah, what the hell. She jerked off the bed, made for the ensuite bathroom. Whatever it meant, it didn't mean she couldn't take a bath, put on an evening gown and enjoy his company over dinner. She'd just be careful. She'd go with the flow. Because what else could she do? She was stuck in the prison of her mind, and until she had all the facts, she wasn't capable of rational judgment or action. She felt it was now simply a matter of time until her memory returned fully, until she solved this mystery. She was sure of it.

She turned on the taps, and the water gushed from the fish-shaped mouths of brass faucets. Sahar tipped a capful of bath bubbles into the stream of water and watched it froth.

She stepped into the tub, sank down into the fragrant, foaming water, closed her eyes and let the warmth soak deep into her skin. She felt her muscles begin to relax and allowed her mind to go blank. Steam slowly curled up and filled the room, and Sahar felt herself begin to drift into a warm, dream-like haze. She imagined herself dancing in the beautiful green gown David had bought for her. She was in his strong arms, swirling, twirling under the stained-glass dome. Sahar smiled softly to herself. She could almost feel the motion, see the colors of the fabric of her exquisite gown shifting under the light from emerald to turquoise, to…

Jade!

It hit her like a bucket of ice. She gasped. Her eyes flared open and she jerked upright in the tub, her heart thumping hard. That was it! *That* was why she'd felt there was something so significant about that particular color, that shade of green. *That* was why it had felt so familiar, so right when she'd held the fabric against her skin. Jade…no, Jayde. Her name was Jayde!

Her heart almost tripped over itself in her excitement. She leaped up from the tub, spilling water onto the floor. She grabbed a towel, almost slipping on the tiles. She had to tell David. She had remembered her name! It was Jayde Ashton. Yes, that was it, her last name was Ashton. *She had her name.* And that alone would jog the rest of her memory free in minutes, hours. She was sure of it.

She rushed to her bedroom door and pushed it open. And froze. A bleak coldness descended over her. She couldn't tell David. Not yet. Because Jayde Ashton had something deep and dark to hide from Sheik David bin Omar bin Zafir Rashid. She was now certain of it.

But what, dammit?

She sank onto the bed, towel wrapped around her. She had her name, but she still couldn't make her mind go beyond that. She still couldn't grasp who Jayde Ashton really was and why she knew—and *felt*— these things about David. And she still couldn't explain the sense of ominous portent that grew stronger and more sinister with each snippet of memory recalled.

Jayde Ashton walked into the grand dining hall at five after nine, a thrilling cocktail of excitement and anxiety zinging through her blood. The new gown skimmed her high strappy heels, giving her stride a bold and feminine confidence. She knew she looked damn good. She'd washed her hair and piled it into an updo with tendrils escaping and curling along the nape of her neck. She'd also clamped an exotic copper band around her upper arm and added a choker with a single large amber stone that rested against the hollow of her throat. She simply felt like a goddess.

David sat at the head of a long table of dark wood set with ornate crockery and crystal glasses that shimmered in light cast by two massive antique silver candelabras. He was deeply engrossed in conversation with a man who had his back to her. The man was of remarkably similar stature to David and had the same blue-black hair, only longer. Music, a soft lilting African-Arabic mix underlaid with the gentle rhythm of drums, played in the background.

David's head jerked up as he sensed her presence. The man seated at his side glanced up.

Jayde's blood went ice-cold.

She recognized the stranger's face instantly.

He was Tariq Rashid. David's half brother. He had the same basic bone structure as David yet his face was wider, his skin slightly darker. His nose was a little broader, slightly crooked, as if it had been broken once. And where David's wild and dangerous look was somehow refined with an elegance, this man's was not. He looked rougher, coarser.

Nausea swooped through her stomach, but she fought it off with a forced smile.

Roll with the punches, Jayde. The pieces are coming together. Breathe. Think. Think. How do you know this man?

Although she recognized Tariq, she could read no obvious reciprocal recognition in his coal-black eyes as they studied her with brazen male appreciation. Jayde swallowed her anxiety and approached the table.

Then it hit her. *Lancaster!*

She almost stumbled on her high heels.

Gerry Lancaster, her handler, had shown her a photograph of Tariq Rashid. He'd also shown her black-and-white photos of David Rashid. He'd shown them to her...and agent Michael Gibbs. With David O'Reilly. In the briefing room. On a screen.

She and Gibbs had been sent to spy on David Rashid!

Her breathing faltered. She swayed on her feet. Oh, God, he was a spy. An agent for the British government. She had a handler. It was all coming back. That whole wretched ball of tangled yarn was unraveling in her brain, swamping it, strangling logic. She pressed her hand to her temple. She had to sort it all out. Quick. Before she made a horrific mistake. Dammit, why had she been sent to spy on him?

Because British and U.S. intel had recently discovered Rashid uranium was going into a covert Libyan nuclear weapons program. And some of it was also being sold to Korea in exchange for technological expertise.

Her heart stalled. Time warped into slow motion. Jayde Ashton now knew *exactly* who she was, where she had come from and why she was on Shendi Island in the middle of the Red Sea.

It was true. David *was* her enemy. Her jaw began to trem-

ble at the sheer power and emotion of it all. But she couldn't
cry. Not here. Not now. Not ever. Because Agent Jayde Ashton, MI-6, *never* cried.

He stood, came toward her, hand held out.

She clamped her jaw shut, pulled her shoulders back.

The light of the candles glittered in his eyes. His smile was
a wolfish slash of white against the darkness of his skin. He
took her arm firmly in his hand. There was a proprietary quality in his behavior toward her tonight. His eyes prowled down
the length of her body, a predator sizing its prey. She could
feel the electrical tingle his heated gaze left in its wake. She
held her breath, repressed a shiver.

"You look ravishing." His words growled through her resolve.

"Thank you," she said, trying to swallow fresh, hot panic.

He held her at arm's length, tilted his head to one side,
raised a dark brow. "Jade…" he said.

Blood drained instantly from her head. She gaped at him.
Oh God. Oh God, Lord Almighty. He knew her name!

"…it's a beautiful color on you. It suits you even better than
I thought it would."

Her heart jackhammered. Her mouth went dry.

He reached up, touched his fingers to the stone at her neck.
"And amber…" He smiled darkly, a twinkle rippling like ink
through his eyes.

Her breath congealed in her throat. Oh God! Amber! Was
he toying with her? He couldn't possibly know she'd had a
twin sister named Amber. What else did he know? That she
was a spy?

"…the colors in the stone complement your hair," he said.

Relief swept through her. *He didn't know.* Unless he was
teasing, testing her with loaded words…just to gauge her reaction. She had to change the subject, act normal, buy time

ink. "Is...is Kamilah not here?" she asked, anxiety skitter-
g through her belly.

"She's in bed." David spontaneously kissed her on the
heek. "She asked me to kiss you goodnight."

"She *asked* you?"

"Yes, of course." His eyes glistened with mischievous hap-
iness. "I took your advice. We played before dinner. I hugged
er a lot. And it's working. She is talking. *To me.*"

Emotion choked her throat. How could this man be bad?
How could he possibly be evil. She couldn't believe it.
Wouldn't. But...

He sneaked his arm around her waist. "Come. Meet my
rother." He led her to the table. "This is Tariq. He's here for two
ays on business. Tariq, this is Sahar." A wickedness danced in
is eyes. "Kamilah's *mermaid,* the one I was telling you about."

Tariq stood, inclined his head slightly in greeting before
eating himself again. He didn't deign to smile at David's mer-
aid reference. He remained aloof, distant. Sahar immedi-
tely sensed deep mistrust. The intensity of it only served to
eepen her apprehension.

David pulled out a high-backed chair. He motioned for her
o sit. She just stared blankly at him, trying to digest every-
ing that had just slithered into her consciousness. Had Gibbs
urvived the storm? What had happened to *him?*

"Sahar?" Concern shifted into his eyes. "Are you sure
ou're all right? You still look a little pale."

She mentally shook herself. "Yes...yes of course. I'm
ne." She smiled brightly, falsely, and sat in the chair he was
ffering her.

He bent to push in her seat and as he did, he whispered
arkly into her ear. "I see I judged your size just right." His
oice chased a quiver down her bare neck, raised the fine hairs
long her nape.

She swallowed. "Really, David, you…you shouldn't have And all the way from Cairo?"

He shrugged. "I fly things in daily. It's nothing. My dress maker would have taken weeks to make you a full wardrobe." He brought his mouth even closer to her ear. She could fee the warmth of his lips against her lobe. "Besides," he whis pered. "Watson's clothes were beginning to look a little tired, don't you think?"

She shivered at the heat of his words against the nape o her neck. She turned her head and looked up, deep into hi eyes, searching. For a sign. Any sign that would tell her if he knew who she really was. A sign that would prove to her tha he really was dealing in weapons of mass destruction. But i his expression she could see nothing but a dark and viscera hunger…and something else, something that went beyon concern, something that spoke of friendship, happiness. I was a look of…of love. Her heart twisted sharply inside.

"I…I can't thank you enough, David. And you chose s well, I—"

"Shh." He pressed two fingers to her lips, silencing her "Besides, I had an excellent muse. Now don't say anothe thing. Consider the clothes a gift in exchange for the lif you've brought back to Shendi, to me."

The dinner was lavish and the wine excellent. But Jayd could barely touch it. Her stomach was a ball of knots. It too all her effort to pretend nothing was wrong.

And that in itself was eating her. Because although th forced smiles and hollow platitudes drained her energy, as th evening wore on the deceit began to fit, to feel natural. An that horrified her. Was this who she really was? Was this wha it felt like to be Jayde Ashton? A hollow, fake persona?

And all through the dinner, Jayde had felt Tariq watchin

her from under his thick black lashes. There was something hidden in his hooded eyes. But whenever she'd sensed those eyes on her, she'd looked up and he'd looked abruptly away. It made her uneasy. And when he did hold her gaze, there was a dark male appetite in his eyes that bordered on threatening and disrespectful.

Although his words said otherwise, Tariq made her feel like she was an intruder in David's castle. And he kept mentioning Aisha as if somehow warning Jayde to step back from his brother's overt attentiveness.

After dinner Farouk brought out coffee, and again Jayde felt the heat of Tariq's gaze. Her eyes flashed up. She was sick of this. She stared at him in challenge.

This time he didn't avert his eyes. He held her gaze and he addressed her. "Your amnesia," he said, "I find it strange."

She kept her eyes locked onto Tariq's. "Why?"

"I placed a call," he said bluntly as he lifted the small espresso cup to his lips. "I have a colleague who is a neurological specialist in Egypt." He sipped, waiting for her reaction, as if trying to catch her out.

Her stomach turned over itself but she refused to show any outward sign of discomfort. "And?"

"According to him, your symptoms are psychological. Or they are…faked."

She reeled, her eyes flashed to David.

David said nothing. He was studying her. She suddenly felt betrayed, hurt…in spite of the fact she was the betrayer in this equation. "You *knew* this?" she demanded of him.

David nodded, placed his hand gently over hers. "Yes. Watson suspected as much."

"And you didn't *tell* me?"

"We weren't sure, Sahar. We decided to try and locate your relatives and take it from there. Since there was no immediate medical emergency, we thought it best you seek psychiatric treatment close to home…once we found out where that was."

She clenched her jaw, pulled her hand out from under his. She reached up, felt the line of stitches under her hairline. She'd thought her memory loss was from the gash to her head. Could it be… No! It couldn't. Her throat closed in on itself. Could it possibly have happened to her…again? After all these years?

"Sahar." David reached for her hand. "Come on, it changes nothing."

"It changes *everything*," she snapped, pulling away. And it frightened the hell out of her to think her memories, her very sense of self, the core of who she was, had been locked away by *her*. And that she alone had held the key to her prison.

Why had she done this to herself again? A mad kind of terror gripped her heart. And why had Tariq even bothered to check up on her? He had to suspect something.

Tariq's eyes continued to bore into hers.

She felt heat rising in her cheeks. She turned on him. "But you, *you* don't think it's psychological, do you? You think I'm faking. Is *that* why you checked up on me?"

Tariq simply shrugged. "Your situation is strange. No one has reported you missing. There is no record of a boating accident. You came out of the sea—" he snapped his fingers in the air "—just like that. And quite frankly, I find that suspicious. So I placed a call—"

"Tariq!" David warned.

Tariq's eyes flashed to David. "I have your interests at heart, David." He turned back to Jayde, leaned forward, his black eyes unwavering, his voice lowering in threat. "Many a gold digger has tried to insinuate herself into his life since Aisha's death."

Jayde jerked up from the chair. "Damn you!" For whatever

reason fate had thrown her up out of the sea unconscious and onto the beach of Shendi Island, this was not it. She did not have to stand for this.

David bolted up, restrained her. "Sahar, relax—"

She pulled out from his grasp. "No, I will not. How could you keep this from me? Is that what you think, too, that…that I'm after your *money?*"

Tariq smiled slyly. Jayde realized she was trembling.

David's eyes pierced hers. The muscle at his jaw pulsed. "I'll tell you one thing about myself, Sahar." His voice was low, fierce. "I don't lie. Ever. And I do *not* tolerate liars. I'd be lying if I said it hadn't entered my head, but—"

She didn't want to hear the rest. She spun around and stormed from the room, not out of the door that led back toward the bedroom wing, but out onto the patio. She needed air, open sky, freedom. The palace was suddenly claustrophobic, a structural maze of a prison that resembled her mental state. And she needed out. She needed right out of this convoluted mess she'd found herself in.

He came after her. "Sahar!"

She ignored him, made her way to edge of the stone terrace, slipped off her shoes and ran down the grass path toward the lagoon beach.

"Sahar!" She heard David call behind her.

She ran faster.

He started after her. But Tariq came swiftly up behind him, grabbed his arm. "Let her go, David. I need to talk to you."

David seethed, whirled around to face his brother. "How *dare* you!"

"How dare I check up on her?"

"You had no right."

"I have every right. We both have a huge amount at stake at the moment. And that woman—" he pointed to where Sahar had disappeared into the dark "—could be more than a gold digger, David, have you considered that?"

"What, exactly, are you trying to say?"

"I don't trust her. She could be working for someone."

He felt his jaw drop. "What in hell do you mean? You think Sahar is some kind of spy?"

"Even if she's not, look how easily she got onto your island, into your home." He jabbed his finger at David. "She got right into *you,* brother. You need to be more careful. And you need better security."

Rage boiled up through David's blood. It took every ounce of control to keep his voice level. "I have adequate security. And if you think Sahar is some kind of spy, you've lost your mind. What in hell's gotten into you Tariq?"

"You're a powerful man with enormous influence, David. And that means you have enemies. There are people, corporations, superpowers, who want to tear you down, take control of the oil fields, the uranium, rob you of your influence in this part of the world. You know it and I know it. And that woman could be faking, working for any one of them. Everything you…everything *we* have worked for could be at stake."

David heard the depth of sincerity in his brother's words. And he felt himself hesitate. That in itself infuriated him. Because he knew as sure as his heart pumped blood through his veins that Sahar was genuine.

He may have doubted her at first, simply because of the weirdness of her situation, because he was a man for whom trust did not come easy. But not now. He didn't doubt her now. Not after he'd seen her with Kamilah. Not after he'd spent time with her, not after he'd gotten a glimpse into her soul. He would *not* let Tariq's paranoia get to him.

"Sahar was injured, Tariq, washed up in a storm. I was there. I saw her. I saw the gash in her head, the cuts and bruises on her body. She was unconscious. No one fakes stuff like that."

Tariq shrugged. "You said it yourself, it had entered your head."

"Of course it entered my head. But that was before—"

"Before what?" His eyes dipped briefly down David's body. "Before you started thinking with…your third leg?"

David cursed viciously in Arabic. He stepped aggressively close to Tariq and lowered his voice to a snarl. "I may not know who Sahar really is but I have seen the person inside. And that person is *true*. I know it here." He struck his fist to his heart. "And from this point on you will stay out of my personal affairs."

Tariq smiled slowly, teeth glinting in the pale moonlight. "You've already slept with her, haven't you? Is she really that good, brother?"

David's anger spiked clean off the Richter scale. His fists balled, the muscles across his neck snapped tight. His hands shook against the force of control it took not to hit his brother square in the face, breaking his nose, just as he had done once when they were boys.

"No," he said through a clenched jaw. "I have not slept with her…*yet*."

He pivoted and stormed off down the stairs to the grass path and into the dark after Sahar, intending to do just that.

David knew it was an irrational fire that seared through him. But burn it did. Tariq's challenge had only solidified whatever he had been feeling for Sahar. Now it was clear as crystal in his head. He wanted her. More than anything in this world right now, he wanted to make her his, to stake his claim, to prove he had every belief that she was genuine and that she had his and Kamilah's interests at heart.

"Watch your back, David," he heard Tariq call after him into the night.

David's heart blipped at the reminder. It was the same thing Watson had said.

"Her name isn't even *Sahar,* it's simply a name you conjured from your head! You have no idea who she is." Tariq's voice taunted him in the dark.

And David realized in that instant how much he wanted her to be just that. His Sahar. The Sahar that belonged to him and to Kamilah and to Shendi Island. Not to another world lost to her memory.

And as it hit him, part of him realized he was a fool, a man made powerless by a bewitching woman with no name, a man wanting desperately to believe in a fairy tale cooked up by his daughter.

He cursed again.

And then he saw her.

She stood on the far edge of the stone pier that stretched out into the lagoon, a siren staring out over the dark water, the moonlight catching the shimmer in her dress.

He halted, caught his breath, stared at her statuesque silhouette.

He had a sense that if he went to her, if he walked out onto that pier, he would be crossing a final line. And if he took so much as one step over that invisible threshold tonight, there could be no turning back. Because this thing simmering between them was too powerful.

He thrust his hands into his pockets and studied the feminine form on the end of the pier, watched the way her hair lifted in the slight salt breeze. She looked so alone out there.

As he watched her, he became acutely aware of the soft susurration of tiny waves that licked and sucked at the white sands of the lagoon shore and he could her the rhythmic *chink, chink, chink* of the halyard against the mast of his yacht anchored off the pier, the soft slap of the incoming tide against its hull.

And he realized he could no more turn back the ocean's tide, the natural pull of the moon on the waters, than he could deny the natural force this woman exerted over his body and his mind.

He sucked the night air deep into his lungs. He had no choice. He had to go to her. He could no more deny his need than a sailor of old could refuse the ancient call of the mythical siren.

He took the first step over that invisible line and made his way down the pier.

Tariq watched David disappear down the path into the dark. He took a sleek silver box from his pocket, opened it, extracted a long cigarillo. He lit it, the flame flaring hot and orange into the dark. He blew out a stream of smoke and swore under his breath. He was troubled—gravely so.

David might have nothing to hide, but *he* did. David could afford to trust. But *he* couldn't. The woman was a professional. He'd stake his life on it. He knew her type. And she knew just how to get to his brother. She'd made him blind. She only had to look at them with those big green eyes and he went soft—not the David he knew. He'd never seen his brother like this, not even with Aisha.

This was different, and it worried him. Innocent or not, a woman like that could change things. Either way, to Tariq she was an enemy. An obstacle. And either way, she had to go. He had two options. Get rid of the woman. Or find proof that she'd been sent to betray David. He had to move fast.

And if she was some kind of spy, how had it been set up? That part puzzled him. Had she been dropped on the beach in the storm? David had said there was boating debris found with her. Had that been planted? Or had there really been an accident? Could there be more debris out there, possibly some clue that might tie her to a foreign government?

Tariq stubbed his cigarillo out in the flower pot. He'd call his men tonight, get them to scour the remote outer islands at first light, see if they could find anything he could use.

David walked slowly, deliberately along the pier toward Sahar, each step swelling the thrilling sense of anticipation that surged through his blood.

As he got closer to her he could see the soft night breeze toying with the loose tendrils of her fiery hair and ruffling the hem of her silk gown about her ankles. His loins tightened instantly in response.

He swallowed. He was already pumped from his argument with Tariq. Anger had heightened every sense in his body, heated his blood to feverish pitch. He moistened his lips, tasted the salt in the air.

And then he took that final step. "Sahar."

Chapter 10

His hand touched her shoulder, and a crack of heat jolted clear through her spine. She clutched her arms tightly against her stomach, against the sensation.

She didn't want him to see her face, to see that he possessed the power to melt her from the inside out, to see that he'd once again managed to push her up to the brink of emotional collapse.

But she wasn't crying, not this time. She was close. But she would not cry. Crying wasn't part of Jayde Ashton's makeup. Tears were a sign of weakness. She was not weak. Just stupid. A naive idiot for allowing herself to fall for David Rashid. For allowing her brain to do this to itself again after all these years.

Doctors had always said it could happen again. That she could slip more easily into a fugue-like state of dissociation a second time around. But in all those years, she had never believed it would happen. She thought she'd made herself too strong for it.

Now she knew different. She had an incurable fissure in her foundation. She had no control over it. And that terrified her.

But what horrified her even more than having slipped into that state again was the way her amnesia had lowered her defenses against emotion, how it had torn down the protective walls she'd been building around herself since she was eight years old.

How could that simple blank gap in her mind have allowed David Rashid in like that, allowed her to *feel* so deeply when feeling was a just not part of who Jayde Ashton had become?

And why in heaven was she actually feeling rejected and betrayed by David—her target, the man she was being paid to betray?

What was that about? Where in hell had that come from? He didn't owe her a damn thing. He had every right to be all-out suspicious of her story. Hell, it was barely making sense to her. One minute she'd been setting up a surveillance system, posing as Gibbs's wife on a diving expedition off the coast of Shendi Island. Then the storm…then next thing she knew she was lying in David Rashid's bed with not a scrap of clothing and not a clue how she got there.

Even though she'd been sent to spy on David Rashid, her amnesia was genuine. And the desire, the care that had grown out of it was genuine. Frightening as all hell, but genuine. She'd never meant to get into his and Kamilah's life like this. She would never consciously have done it. And she didn't know what the hell to do about it now. Jayde Ashton just didn't have a clue about this feeling. Period.

"Sahar?" The thick rasp of passion in his voice kicked her heart into a light stutter. His hand pressed down on her shoulder. "Sahar, I'm sorry, for my behavior, for Tariq—"

More than anything in this world she wanted to turn around, to bury herself in his arms. She wanted to *be* Sahar.

Right now, right at this very instant, it was all she wanted from life—to be Sahar. With no past to worry about. No handlers waiting in Khartoum for her to hand over the man she had come to care for. No worrying about whether or not David Rahid was helping a corrupt government secretly build nuclear weapons of mass destruction…

"Sahar, talk to me."

She drew in a shuddering breath. She still wouldn't look at him. She continued to stare out over the black water as she spoke. "You have nothing to apologize for, David." She tried to hide the tremor in her voice. "You have every right to doubt me. Don't you think *I* didn't wonder why no one came looking for me? And now you tell me there is no physical evidence of my amnesia, that my subconscious cooked it up all by itself. You're right. Tariq is right. It all sounds bizarre. How could I expect you to even begin to understand?"

"Look at me, Sahar." He grasped her shoulders, turned her body to face him.

She looked slowly, warily, up into his eyes. They were dark with a mad and feral kind of hunger. A thick visceral energy emanated from him in slow, heavy waves. He reminded her of a wild jaguar, one that crouched in the night shadow of a jungle, watching his prey, restraining every muscle, controlling every sinew in his body as he waited for precisely the right time to leap, make his kill.

It excited a reciprocal primal appetite deep within her and it wiped her mind clean of rational thought.

"I want you to know something, Sahar." His voice had lowered in tone and it curled through her body like dark-blue mist through a morning ravine.

"No matter what happens, I will be there for you. Do you understand that?" He traced his fingers slowly along her collarbone, awakening sleeping nerves, leaving them raw and tin-

gling in the salt air. Her breath caught in her throat at the sen
sation. He cupped his hand firmly around the back of her neck
drew her closer to him. "When your memory comes back, yot
won't be alone. Watson said it could be tough, that it coulc
all come back at once. But I'll be there for you. I want you tc
know that."

She choked back a lump of tears. "Why, David? Why
would you want to be there for me? You don't have a clue who
I am…who I might be."

He moved the rough pad of his thumb firmly along her jaw
bone, tilting her face up to his. She felt the latent power, th
absolute control in his hand. He could snap her neck in an in
stant if he wanted to.

What would he do when he found out who she really was.

"I don't need to know your name to know *you,* Sahar." He
scored her bottom lip with his thumb. She shuddered unde
his touch.

"I don't need a government identity document to reach ir
and touch the person inside." Her body responded to the dark
meaning wrapped in his words by sending a surge of molter
warmth down to her belly. With it came an instinctive desire
to open up to him, fully, to allow him to touch her inside, tc
feel the full, hot, maleness of him deep within in her core.

His mouth moved closer to hers. So close. She felt her knee:
go weak, felt her whole body go boneless at the anticipatior
of his lips taking hers. But he didn't. He just whispered hotly
against them. "I want you, Sahar. I want you so badly I ache."

Her vision narrowed. She opened her mouth to speak
couldn't. His lips almost touched hers. She could almost taste
him, his warmth, his maleness, his heat…his tongue.

He pulled back. "No. I can't do this, Sahar." His voice
came out thick as molasses. "I can't do this to you."

Yes, you can! Every molecule in her body screamed. She

needed him. It was as if he embodied the power of life itself. She needed to tap into that force, that hot energy, with a desperation that defied all logic.

She leaned into him, pressing the curves of her body against the hard length of his. And her world shrank to just this instant. Just this sensation of his solid strength, his maleness hard up against the silk of her dress. Absolutely nothing else mattered now. Nothing could. She pressed her pelvis against the thick muscle of his thigh, lifted a leg, driven by an aching and potent primal force, a mad hunger to feel him against her.

He caught her knee with one hand, held it against his hip and moaned as she moved against him, the sound guttural, animal. His other hand cupped her buttocks, yanked her hard up against himself. She gasped at the heat that seared through her.

"Sahar." His *R*s rolled in his throat, his Arabic accent swallowing the refined British as his smooth veneer fell away to reveal the rough warrior underneath. "You could regret this. There…there may be someone else your life…."

"No," she whispered, reaching up, brushing her lips along the exquisitely firm and sculpted line of his. "There…there is no one."

He stilled suddenly, grasped her jaw in a vicelike grip and pulled back. He held her face steady, forcing her to look up at him as his eyes bored down into hers, dangerously dark. "Are you *sure?*"

"I'm sure." She was dead sure. She'd never been consumed by this kind of fire before. She'd never felt this kind of emotional longing for a man. Jayde Ashton had never allowed herself to feel deeply for anyone…not since she was eight years old.

"How would you know?"

"I…I just know. I can feel it in my heart." She whispered. There *could* be no one else.

It was an answer that satisfied him. A slash of white teeth glinted in the moonlight as he smiled. A devilish glitter lit his eyes. And her adrenaline spiked at the wicked intent she saw there.

Then he kissed her. Hard. Fast. His tongue probing, stroking, his teeth scoring. She felt his hand move down her thigh. She felt him bunching up her silk gown.

Then she felt his fingers. Rough. Warm. Callused. She felt those beautifully tapered fingers searching, tearing her panties aside.

She lifted her knee higher, widening access. And his finger plunged roughly into her slickness.

A low moan escaped her throat. Her knees gave in and she sank down, melting onto the length of his finger, his hand.

He deepened his kiss, moving his tongue, his finger, inserting another, twisting them inside her. He moved his hand deeper and she felt his palm rub against the sensitive nub between her legs. She could hardly breathe. She moved against the palm of his hand, desperate, hungry, wild. Blind to anything but the instant.

"My yacht," he whispered thickly into her hair.

"It's…it's in the middle of the lagoon," she countered, her voice breathy, her heart hammering as though it would split free from her chest.

"We'll take the Zodiac." He scooped her up, carried her effortlessly in his arms to the small rigid-hull inflatable tethered to the pier. David reached the craft, set her down, leaped onto the boat and held his hand out to her over the water, beckoning her like the desert prince he was.

She reached for his grasp, but as she did a soft lagoon swell surged suddenly with the incoming tide, rolling the boat sharply away from her as she stepped forward.

It happened so fast. David felt her hand slipping from his grasp. He heard her sharp intake of breath. Then the splash. He sucked in his breath. "Sahar!"

There was silence. Darkness. He could see nothing but flecks of gold moonlight glinting on black ripples of water and white foam where she went under.

Oh God, Sahar.

And in that instant David Rashid knew he never, ever wanted to lose this woman. He would do what it took to make her his, no matter who she was. No matter who waited for her. He was going to keep her. On his island. For himself and Kamilah.

"Sahar!" he barked, frantically stripping off his dinner shirt, kicking off his shoes, ready to dive in. Then he heard her laugh.

Dizzying relief ripped through him. He spun around. *Where was she?*

And she laughed again, the sound of a clear brook running through his senses, floating over the swells.

A crazy bubble of happiness erupted low in his stomach and pushed up to his throat. But anxiety kept it locked down. *Where the hell was she?*

Then he heard her again. He spun to his left. And there she was. On the other side of the inflatable, sculling out into the black bay.

The moonlight glinted off the waves, off the slickness of her wet hair and off voluminous silk billows as her gown lifted and flowed around her with the swells. His initial alarm was replaced with a sense of bemused wonder.

She looked like a mermaid! *His* mermaid. She must have dived under the Zodiac and swum up to the other side—just to scare him.

"Sahar!" He said half in anger, half in relief, bewilderment muddling his brain.

She giggled at his shock. It shot a spurt of fuel into the strange cocktail of hot energy and warring emotions within him. She was challenging him. Toying with him. Playing. The way he'd seen her play in the waves. The way he'd seen her play with his child.

That odd, painful ball of happiness and delight spiced with shock exploded through the tension in his throat, erupting into mad laughter. Laughter that boiled from the base of his belly, reverberated up through his torso and out through his chest in glorious release. He threw back his head and just laughed into the night sky like he hadn't since he was a kid. And by Allah it felt fine.

She was laughing, too, sculling farther out into the shallow lagoon, toward the depths where his yacht was moored.

He stilled suddenly, heat stirring his loins once more as he watched her, floating, tantalizing, beckoning. Billows of wet silk fanning out about her.

She was luring him, a man of hot sun and dry sand, into her element. Water. Into depths he'd been trying for years to avoid. He'd known the instant he'd first looked into her emerald eyes that he would succumb and drown in their depths.

"You coming?" she called darkly out over the swells.

And he couldn't resist her siren call. Like an adventurer of old, he left the security of his craft and plunged into the sea, powerless to defy the song of her seduction.

But as he swam toward her, she kept moving just out of his reach, her rippling laughter taunting him, pulling him along like threads of moonlight.

She lured him over a sandbank. The water was now chest high. His feet found the sea bed, and he began to wade aggressively toward her. But still she kept infuriatingly just beyond reach, floating in her sea of silk, toying with him, tempting him until he thought he would burst with his desire for her.

In sheer desperation he lunged at her. But she ducked under, leaving only a ring of empty ripples and glittering phosphorescence in her wake.

He looked to his left, to his right. Nothing. Then he gasped as she grabbed hold of his legs underwater and pulled herself up along the length of his body to the surface. Surprise swirled with a titillating pleasure as she surfaced against him. The thick wet silk of her gown enveloped him as the ocean surged and fell, the folds of it tangling erotically about his legs.

Her hair was slick as a seal's, and water ran creamy over skin made luminescent by moonlight. Her eyes were dark and mysterious. Magic eyes. *Mermaid's eyes.* The eyes of a mythical creature with no name, no place, no memory. He stared into those eyes as the water lifted them slightly. Up, then down. A basic rhythm of the earth. The ocean responding to the moon. Gravity. Essential. Natural. Undeniable.

The water was cool against his skin, but heat boiled inside him. He kept a firm hold of her with one hand lest she bolt again. With the other he traced his fingers up the elegant column of her throat, the throat he'd admired when she lay unconscious in his bed. She responded by hooking one long and naked leg around his clothed one. She placed her palm flat against his bare wet chest, splayed her fingers, moved it slowly along his skin, down his belly. Lower. He swelled hard and hot against the wet fabric of his pants.

He slid his hand along her shoulder, slipped the thin strap of her gown down, exposing her breast. It was milky white, glistening with the sea under the lunar light. He caught his breath, touched her nipple with his fingertips. It reacted instantly, tightening to a hard nub.

He bent his head, sought out the hard tip of her aroused nipple with his lips. He flicked his tongue around it and then sucked, drawing it tighter, to a slick and salty point. He'd ached to do this since he'd watched her on the beach, since he'd watched the rise and fall of her breasts under the white Egyptian-cotton sheet as she'd lain unconscious in his bed, since he'd felt the soft weight of those breasts against his bare chest as he'd hunkered over her on his horse, riding ahead of the storm.

But the pleasure was more than he could even have begun to imagine. It drove his hungering ache to a feverish pitch. He scored her nipple with his teeth, bit.

She moaned, arching her back, pressing herself against him, offering all of herself to him. Her reaction drew a shaft of liquid fire that seared clean through to his groin. A low and hungry growl emanated from deep in his throat. He moved his mouth slowly up the column of her neck, tasting the salt, licking her skin, making her writhe under him with need.

Then he grasped the back of her neck firmly, lifting her face to his, and he forced his mouth down onto hers. He felt her open instantly under the pressure of his lips. Her warmth was salty. Elemental. Soft and deeply feminine.

With a groan he sank his tongue down into her. She responded, her tongue slipping, entwining around his. It cracked his world open into a dizzying rainbow of light. Colors spun riotously inside his head. Music seemed to swell though his core. He was feeding on her brightness, filling a void he hadn't even known existed within him.

He pulled back, stunned, breathless. "Are you for real?" he whispered. "Or are you really something conjured up from the sea?" In his wild sensual delirium, he almost believed she might be.

She murmured in his ear sending hot and cold shivers over his skin. "I can be whatever you want me to be, David."

"Be mine," he growled, lips against hers. *Be my Sahar.*

Jayde didn't want to begin to think about what was happening, what she was doing. What he was doing to her. Her walls had been breached and right now she was utterly defenceless against the raw power that was streaming through them. She was quite simply imprisoned in the present, by her desire, by her desperate passion for this powerful man.

All she could do was lift her face to his. Right now she would be his Sahar. Because deep, deep down, the forgotten part of herself had actually become Sahar. A woman with feeling, emotion, and aching love in her heart. A woman who had been locked away, many years ago, by an eight-year-old child who had been burned by life. Until now.

And now she was desperate. Now she wanted everything she had missed. She looked up into his face. Desire etched his features into dangerous feral planes, his eyes flashed. A quiver ran through her stomach. "Take me, David," she whispered. "Take me."

He crushed his mouth down hard onto hers. She met his urgency, her tongue seeking his, her hands tearing at the buckle of his pants under the surface. She felt him swell free in her hands, his need blatant, hot and hard against the cool velvet of the water. There was no stopping now. It was fast. Furious. Desperate. He shoved the wet, floating silk up high about her waist, grasped at her lace panties, ripped them off her. She wrapped both her legs around him using the swells of the ocean for buoyancy. He pushed his mouth hard onto hers, invaded with his tongue, roughly. Demanding. She was overwhelmed with her own aching need. She arched her back, opened her legs wider around him, aching for him from the very center of her being.

He gripped her buttocks and thrust his full length into her as he pulled her down onto himself. He was hot, hard against her softness. She could feel her own heat pooling between her thighs, around him. He groaned and he thrust deeper. The movement drew cool water into her molten fire. She gasped.

The contrast in temperatures inside her heightened every sensation, awakened every nerve. Her body screamed in delirious and silent delight.

She could hardly breathe. Each movement, each stroke sent her higher, made waves of watery resistance surge between them, their coupling creating a turbulence that fanned out in concentric phosphorescent ripples over the black waters of the lagoon.

Jayde felt as if she would burst. A desperate need to scream into the night air rose in her throat as he drove her higher and higher. She could feel the thick length of him inside her grow hotter. She could feel it quiver and she knew he was near.

That knowledge itself pushed her over the tip. Her vision blurred and she was blinded as scarlet waves slammed into her head and colored her mind. She swallowed her cry as the blinding sensation took hold of her. Her body rippled around him in wave after wave of hard contractions. And then he came, bucking, releasing into her with a final violent shudder.

They held each other, spent, bobbing gently in the water, silently in the swells, breaths coming light and fast.

He brushed his lips over her forehead. "Mmm…that was sublime," he murmured against her skin. "A fantasy."

Jayde began to feel the chill of the water against her skin as her body cooled. Cognizance crept back with the cold. With it came the sharp bite of reality. He was right. It was a fantasy. Only, he didn't know the half of it. And she felt suddenly sick. She was deceiving him. She couldn't do this.

But before she could begin to pull away, David reached up and ran his rough palm over her breast. "Shall we try to make it to the yacht this time?" His voice was dark with fresh promise.

Jayde was shocked by the bolt of new heat that shot to her belly. A pang of guilt touched her heart, but her desire pushed it away. "Yes," she whispered in his ear.

Tomorrow could wait.

Tonight she was stealing time. Tonight she was stealing lost years.

They made love through the night. And as dawn glowed peach on the horizon, Jayde wished in her heart she never had to leave Shendi Island. Or David. They were made for each other.

No, she corrected herself. *Sahar* and David were made for each other.

Jayde Ashton had been trained to be something very, very different. Only, it didn't seem to fit anymore. A part of her had actually become someone else, a woman with emotion and lightness and love in her soul.

She'd been rent in two. And she knew she could never become whole again. Not in the way she truly wanted. Not with David Rashid. Because when he found out who she was, he would never forgive her. He'd said it himself at dinner. There was nothing he abhorred more in life than a liar. And she believed he'd truly meant it.

Surely a man who abhorred lies could not be covertly shipping uranium to Libya and Korea? On the surface, Libya was dismantling its nuclear weapons program, but at the same time the Libyan leader was secretly backing the Falal, a radical extremist group charged with taking the country's weapons program underground—and using Rashid uranium to do it. Jayde was one of the few people in the world who knew about it.

She lay on her back on the large double bed in the cabin of David's luxurious yacht, staring up at the ceiling, listening to the slap of water against the hull, the chink of metal against the mast, the comforting sounds of David making coffee in the galley. And she drank in the heavenly scents of a domestic morning.

No. She could *not* believe he was involved. And she could

not continue lying to him. She would not. She had to find a way to get hold of Lancaster.

She closed her eyes. God, she wished she didn't have to do this.

"Morning, gorgeous."

Her eyes flared open. He stood, dark and totally naked, a Zeus, holding two mugs of steaming coffee, a sinful grin across his ruggedly handsome face.

She smiled in spite of herself, allowing her gaze to roam brazenly, appreciatively over his exquisite body, taking in the broad, dark-skinned chest, the whorl of dark hair that ran down the center of his washboard stomach and flared out to cover his godlike maleness.

"Uh-uh." He shook his head. "You look at me like that and you're gonna have trouble."

She laughed. "I can see trouble stirring already."

He pulled a face, set the coffee mugs down and grabbed a *kikoi*. He wound the brightly colored strip of African cotton around his waist, hiding his swelling interest.

Jayde made a mock moue. "What a shame."

He wiggled a brow. "We could fix that."

Heat spurted to her groin. He sat down on the bed, leaned over her. She pulled his kikoi free...

But the sound of an engine coming at full throttle over the bay made them both pull back.

Someone was speeding toward the yacht.

David jerked to his feet, grabbed his *kikoi*, wrapped it around his waist. But before he'd even made it up on deck, Jayde felt the bump of a small craft pulling up alongside the yacht. Then she heard Tariq's voice barking over the sputter of the motor. "I must talk to you, David. Now."

"What is it?" Undisguised irritation laced David's voice as he clambered up to the deck.

"Not here. In private. There is something you must see. It cannot wait."

Jayde heard David coming back down to the cabin.

"What does Tariq want?" she asked, nerves skittering through her chest. *Had Tariq found something out about her?*

He took her face in both his hands, kissed her full on the mouth. "Business. Wait for me. There's food in the galley. Help yourself."

"David—" she called after him in desperation.

He blew her a kiss. "I'll be right back."

Jayde's heart sank like a stone. She listened to the roar of the engine as Tariq took David away from her. A heavy sense of doom descended on her as the splutter of the engine faded into the distant sound of waves.

She just knew David would not be back.

Not in the way she wanted him back.

It was over.

David stared at the item Tariq had placed on his desk as if it were a poisonous snake from the pit of hell. "Where did you find *that?*"

"On one of the small outer islands. We did a search early this morning, found some boat wreckage, clothing, life jackets, diving gear—" Tariq jutted his chin in the direction of the package "—and that."

"Why did you search?" he snapped.

"I'm trying to help you, David. No one has claimed the woman. I was looking for some clues to her identity."

David picked up the waterproof document pouch and yanked open the ziplock closure. He tipped it upside down. The contents spilled out over his desk. Two diving passes. Airline tickets from London. Two British passports. A boat rental agreement…

And a gold wedding band.

His heart drummed in his chest. His throat went dry. He reached out, picked up the passports, flipped one open. The photo was Sahar.

Except it wasn't Sahar.

It was *Melanie Wilson*. He flipped the other document open. It belonged to Simon Wilson.

A lump swelled hard in his throat. He reached for the diving passes. Simon and Melanie Wilson. He grabbed the rental contract. It was made out to Mr. and Mrs. Wilson.

His heart shriveled in on itself. He struggled to breathe. Slowly he reached for the wedding band. It was cold in his hand. Smooth. A woman's size. He turned it over in his fingers, read the engraving.

"Simon and Melanie forever."

David sank bonelessly into his office chair, the gold ring clutched tightly in his fist.

Mrs. Melanie Wilson. He felt as if every bit of life had been sucked from his marrow. She was *married.* And, inside, a part of him died.

Tariq was watching him silently. David looked up at him, forced himself to ask. "Was there any sign of…of her husband?"

"No."

"Any sign of *anyone* else?"

"Nothing."

David closed his eyes, rested his head against the back of his chair. He tried to steady his breathing. He hated himself with a passion for even beginning to think what he was thinking— that if her husband had drowned there was still a chance for him.

His eyes flared open. He slammed the ring onto his desk, glared at Tariq. "Why has *Mr.* Wilson not come looking for his wife, then?" he demanded. "What man doesn't look for his wife!"

"David—"

"No." He held his palm up. "Don't talk to me. Just phone that damn diving operation and find out why no one is looking for *Mrs.* Wilson. Find out why no one is looking for that boat! Find out what in hell has happened to *Mr.* Wilson! And find out why the goddamn British Embassy doesn't know these British subjects are missing!"

He jerked to his feet. Nothing added up. But he had to go to Sahar. He had to tell her they had an ID on her.

No, he corrected himself, not Sahar. She wasn't Sahar. Not anymore. That fantasy was over. She was Mrs. Melanie Wilson.

And as David made his way back down to the bay, he caught sight of his yacht gleaming white on the water. He stopped and stared at it. She was on that yacht. Waiting for him.

His whole body began to vibrate against the tension in his muscles. Because now he couldn't have her. She belonged to another man. And that meant he had to keep his hands off her. Just the idea of not touching her again made him feel like a bomb ready to blow its casing. He knew it would take every ounce of control to hold himself in check. Both emotionally and physically.

He didn't know if he could do it.

Chapter 11

She had to think fast. There was a chance Tariq had simply wanted David for some other urgent business. And if Tariq had nothing on her, she had two choices. Continue to deceive David. Or come clean and tell him who she was.

She could do neither. Deceiving him now was out of the question. She was just not capable of consciously hurting him and Kamilah in that way.

And telling him? That would jeopardize an international sting operation. And it could endanger lives. It was not feasible.

There was one other option. She could abort the mission.

That's what she would do. She had to find a way to reach Lancaster, tell him she'd been compromised, that she needed to be brought in. ASAP.

Jayde glanced at the antique clock on the cabin wall. David still wasn't back. He'd been gone for over an hour.

It was nothing, she told herself. He was a busy man. He and

Tariq had business. And she could get herself back to shore with the inflatable if she really wanted, or she could swim.

But in spite of her reasoning, she had a sinking sensation something had gone horribly wrong.

She anxiously fingered her ring finger. Then it hit her. *It was missing.* The engraved wedding band she'd been handed as part of her cover with all the other "pocket litter" was gone.

She'd taken the ring off on the boat because wearing jewelry on her hands irritated her. She'd slipped it into the document pouch with the other papers she and Gibbs had been given.

Some people routinely took their rings off to wash their hands and do other things. So technically, it wasn't a mistake, she told herself. She'd been behaving as a normal married woman might have. But in this case, it had turned out to be a critical error. On a deeply personal level. Because maybe if she'd kept the ring on, maybe if she'd been able to read the inscription on the wedding band, she just might have remembered sooner who she was…and why she was anywhere near Shendi Island. Maybe she'd never have found herself this far down the road with David Rashid.

Jayde sat on the bed and sank her fingers into her mass of hair. How could this have happened to her? Why had she lost time again so many years later?

She closed her eyes.

It was the storm. The boating accident. It had to be. It must have shocked her right back to that terrible ordeal off the coast of Cornwall when she was only six…Kamilah's age. That's why she'd felt such a visceral connection to the child.

Jayde got up, made her way toward the bathroom. She leaned over the basin and stared into the mirror. She touched the clear amber stone that hung at the hollow of her throat.

Amber. The name of her twin sister. She covered the stone with her hand and closed her eyes. For a second last night she'd thought David had been on to her. But he'd only been talking about the stone. Not about the sister she'd watched drown with her father in that awful boating accident when she was six.

Jayde and Amber. Her parents had given the twins the names of precious stones. She and Amber had been inseparable. She choked down the balloon of pain in her throat, stumbled back to the stateroom and sank down onto the bed. Her body began to shake. Her breathing became labored. She began to relive the horrific memories her mind had tried once again to blot out.

They'd been on holiday, visiting her grandfather in Cornwall. She and Amber had gone out on a boat with her dad. A terrible storm had risen out of nowhere blacking out the sun and sky. They'd tried to outrun it, but it was impossible. Monstrous waves had swamped the boat. They'd ended up in the viciously churning and frigid sea. Her father had saved her first, shoving her into the heaving lifeboat as he choked and coughed out the salt water in his lungs

Hold tight baby, I'll be right back. Her father's words echoed in her skull. She clutched her arms tight about her waist and swayed.

He never came back.

He went after Amber. But he was tired, too tired to fight the raging sea. He was injured, bleeding. The waves were too big. The water too cold.

She never saw her father or sister again.

For two days she'd lain curled up in the bobbing lifeboat, adrift in the sea, shrouded in thick gray mist. When they'd finally rescued her she was unconscious. The newspapers had said it was a miracle she'd survived at all.

Her mother hadn't been on the boat that day—she'd gone to see a movie with an old school friend. The guilt at not havng been there to help had eaten at her like a cancer. And it had eventually killed her like a cancer, when she swallowed a bottle of pills and bottle of whiskey to hide from the pain. She never came back.

Jayde was eight years old when that had happened. She'd found her mother when she'd woken up in the morning. Her mother's skin had been ice-cold, a photograph clutched in her stiff fingers, the one where they were all together and smiling under the Christmas tree.

Jayde had called for help on the phone. Then she had waited by her mother's body until the police arrived. But it was no use. No one had been able to wake her mother up.

And when the police took Jayde away, she lost herself for the first time. She went into a dissociative fugue, as the doctors had called it. She simply forgot her name and how she fitted into the pain of her world. And it had taken her a full two years to come out it. Two lost years. Two years of hiding from the agony of her own memories.

Doctors had told her later in her life that the chances of re-experiencing a similar amnesiac state were much higher after it had happened once before.

Jayde scrubbed her hands brutally over her face trying to make it all go away again. That's what must have happened. When the storm hit off Shendi Island, when the boat she and Agent Gibbs were on started to go under, she must have regressed, started to relive those terrible memories as she was once again sucked under the waves. And her old coping mechanism had snapped in. She'd simply shut it all out again.

And now it was back. Every lurid detail. Just like that.

She scrunched her eyes tight. They burned, but tears wouldn't come. Because she was Jayde Ashton, agent for the British secret service. And everyone in the business knew Jayde Ashton never cried. They knew nothing touched her.

Ever. Because she would never let anything get close enough, and that had made her one of the best in the business.

But now? Now she'd been compromised. Now she would have to tell MI-6 about the mental weakness she'd kept hidden from them. She had never dreamed it could one day damage her or her colleagues. She had to assume that Lancaster and O'Reilly knew she was here, on Shendi. Did they know she had amnesia? Or did they think she might be role-playing? Whatever they thought, they were probably waiting for her to make contact. She had to find a way to reach them. But before she could figure out how to do it, she heard the roar of an engine cutting across the lagoon.

David was coming back!

Her heart twisted into an excruciating knot. Panic skittered through her blood. She took a deep, shuddering breath, tried to quell the shaking in her limbs.

She felt the Zodiac knock up against the yacht, heard him thud onto the deck. She held her breath.

David loomed into the doorway, strangling the light in the cabin. Under his coffee-brown skin his face was ashen. A muscle pulsed at his jaw. His neck was corded with tension, his mouth a flat, hard line.

And in his piercing blue eyes Jayde saw a look she'd seen only once before in her life—in the eyes of soldiers faced with an impossible mission, one they knew they would not return from. It was a look of emotional distance combined with fierce determination. A look of the haunted and damned. And seeing that look in him terrified her in a way she didn't think possible.

What had happened? What had Tariq shown him? Had he found out she was a traitor?

A hatchet of fear hacked into her heart. "David?" her voice came out hoarse.

He said nothing. He took something out of his pocket and eld it out to her. She stared at it. She knew exactly what it as. A passport. A British passport.

Then he took something else out of his pocket. The wedding band. Her eyes flashed up to his in horror.

"You're married," he said, his voice hollow, his mouth wisting in an effort to hide his pain. "Your name is *Mrs. Melanie Wilson*. You belong to another man."

He didn't know she was MI-6! Of course he didn't. He'd ound only her cover information. Relief plunged through er. Then it flipped straight over and reared up into a horrile black realization. David was devastated not by the fact she as a spy, but by the fact she was *married*. And the agony that choed through the hollowness of his voice ripped the very oul from her body.

David, the potent desert warrior, was destroyed by the fact he belonged to another man, another world. That she wasn't his.

She choked on the emotion that boiled up into her throat. *t's not true! I'm not married! I don't belong to anyone!* She vanted to scream the words, wipe away his pain. Her pain. She vanted him. Like she'd never before wanted a man in her life.

But she couldn't. She couldn't have him. She couldn't tell im the wedding ring in his hand was a lie. A lie devised to nare him.

More than anything she wanted to tell him the truth. But he truth could cost lives. And the truth was worse. Because hen he'd know she was a liar. And in his own words, he was man who abhorred liars. What would he do when he discovered the extent of her lie, her deception?

Her face dropped into her hands. And agent Jayde Ashton ried. Her whole body shook. For the first time in her life since he was eight years old, Jayde Ashton *felt*. And it was overvhelming her.

* * *

David wanted desperately to go to her, to hold her tight in his arms. He ached with the need. But he couldn't move. His limbs were numb, his brain thick. It was all he could do to clear his throat and say, "Tariq is making some more calls now that we have your details."

Her big green eyes lifted slowly to meet his. And in them he saw an echo of his own devastating pain. He watched as she fingered the amber stone around her neck.

They stared at each other in silence. There were no words that could possibly ease the tension or the hurt. There were simply no platitudes that could fill the void of space and time that yawned between them.

A few minutes ago they'd been so close. Now it seemed as though an ocean separated them. He'd known a moment like this would come. But he'd underestimated the raw power of it. He was an absolute fool for having entertained the notion that things might somehow work out. He deserved this pain. But *she* didn't. She was innocent in this. He should have protected her, not taken advantage of her. This was his fault.

She broke the silence, swiping the tears from her face. "David, I'm so sorry. I…I don't know what to say." She stood up, took a hesitant step toward him, reached out her hand as if to touch him.

He tensed, moved away from her. A small part of him took satisfaction in the fact she didn't seem happy with the discovery of her identity. And that meant she cared for him deeply enough to be sorry to lose him…and Kamilah. But if he allowed her to touch him now, he knew he'd be powerless to stop himself from grabbing her into his arms, holding on to her forever. "I'll take you back to shore," he said, his voice rough, thick. "Hopefully we'll get more details soon."

"Yes. Thank you."

He hesitated. "Now that you know...now that you know our name, does it help you remember anything else?"

Uncertainty flickered through her eyes. Then she nodded. "Yes. I...I think it's coming back, bit by bit. I...I believe I was n a diving holiday."

He felt his fists clench, but he had to say it. "With your husband, Simon?"

She looked away from him. "Yes," she said softly.

His stomach bottomed out so fast he felt ill. "I see," he said. "I hope he's all right."

She nodded, but she was shaking like a leaf.

"Do you remember if there was anyone else on the boat?"

"N-no, there wasn't. It was just us, the two of us."

He nodded. "Come, I'll take you back to my office. We'll ee if Tariq is making any headway. Do you remember now where you and your husband launched your trip from? The oat rental papers say Port Sudan. Is that right?" His voice trained against the effort to sound normal. All he wanted was o smash his fists into the wall.

"Yes. We launched from Port Sudan," she said, refusing to ook him in the eye.

He frowned. "Why do you think no one reported the boat— or you—missing?

"I...I have no idea."

"Did you register with the embassy in Khartoum when you rrived in Sudan?"

She shook her head. "I know it's recommended but we lidn't bother. We wanted to get out on the water as soon as ossible."

"And you remember *all* this now?" A strange cold shadow f doubt crossed his heart. This didn't seem right.

She was still shaking, clutching her arms into her waist as f she was going to throw up. "I...I guess I blocked everything out…because of the accident. Do you…do you mind if I make the calls myself? I need to do it…to find out if my…my husband is missing."

"Of course." And with that, David knew it really was final. She was looking for her husband.

There could be nothing more between them.

David showed her into his office. There was no sign of Tariq, and that relieved Jayde immensely. She couldn't face the man's accusing eyes right now. And she needed to do this in private. She needed to contact Lancaster and tell him to bring her in. She looked up into David's eyes. "Do you…do you mind if I do this alone?"

He hesitated. "You sure you don't need me?"

"Yes," she said.

Hurt rippled through his features. "Of course," he said and left the room.

Jayde swallowed her remorse, picked up the receiver on David's desk…and paused. Calling her handler from this phone was a risk. But she had to take it. It was the only way to make contact. She quickly punched in his number.

"Yes?" Lancaster's voice was gruff on the other end.

"It's Jayde," she said.

She heard a sharp intake of breath. "Are you all right?"

"I'm fine. Is…is Gibbs okay?"

"The lucky bugger is in excellent health. He was picked up by a fishing vessel. Good ploy with the amnesia, Ashton. We've been waiting for you to check in."

"It…it wasn't a ploy," she said. "It was for real."

Silence stretched over the distance. "But you're fine now, right? You remember everything now?"

"Yes. But I've been compromised. I need to be brought in, ASAP."

"They know who you are?"

"No. It's…I'm not able to…the amnesia compromised me."

"Ashton." Her handler's tone was gruff. "We *need* you here right now. You're right inside his home. We couldn't ave orchestrated this better if we had tried. You have to hold teady."

She scrunched her eyes up in frustration. *What did the an want? Did she have to beg?* "Lancaster, I can't stress this nough, I've been irrevocably compromised. Besides, I be- eve Rashid is innocent." *And I trust him. And he's made me el things I never thought possible. And I've made love to im. I…I love him.* She choked on a ball of tears that lurched nto her throat.

Again silence stretched. "You have any proof of his inno- ence?"

"No."

"And Rashid has no idea who you are?"

"No."

Silence again. "We have new intel, Ashton. It came in late ast night. Hear me out, *then* make your decision. If you still eed out, we'll mobilize ASAP."

"I'm listening."

"You just may be right. There is a chance David Rashid ould be innocent."

Her heart blipped, kicked into a light staccato beat. She *new* it! In her gut she just knew it.

"The CIA operative undercover in Libya has made a break- hrough. He saw Tariq Rashid leaving the Falal base in Libya ear the Azar border two days ago. He's one of them."

"Tariq is *Falal?*" she whispered.

"Yes. And according to the operative, Tariq is the one or- anizing Rashid uranium and oil shipments for the Falal. His rother may not even know about the deals, since it is Tariq

Rashid who is now in control of those mines. We have als
just learned that the Falal is funding the dissidents in Aza
The Falal is using the Azar rebels to disguise a renewed at
tempt to seize the Rashid oil fields and uranium mines. Onc
they have those under their full control, they'll be in a posi
tion to mount a coup and take the whole country."

"But the Falal is really just an underground arm of the Lib
yan government…" Her brain reeled as it hit her. "Lancaste
that means Libya is trying to annex Azar using the Falal. I
means David and the Force du Sable are not just fightin
against rebels, they're fighting a whole damn country."

"That would be the assumption from the recent intel, yes."

"But Tariq…it just doesn't make sense. Why would Tari
belong to a group fighting his own brother, a group fightin
to take over the Rashid mines, his own mines, his ow
country?" Then with a sinking realization she knew. Once .
fundamentalist, always a fundamentalist. Tariq had neve
forgiven his half brother. David Rashid had been deceive
by his own flesh and blood. He was being destroyed from th
inside out. And Tariq was running the show.

"There's still the chance that David Rashid could be be
hind this, Ashton. He could be orchestrating this."

"No, I don't believe it."

"One way or another the Rashids are central to whateve
is going down in Libya and Azar. And whatever it is, it'
going to end up compromising global stability. If David Ra
shid is innocent, we need proof."

"I'll get you proof." And by God she would. She'd stak
her life on the fact that Tariq was deceiving his brother. Th
bastard. "I'm staying on Shendi."

"Ah, there's the Ashton we know."

Fire burned bitter in Jayde's gut as she replaced the re
ceiver. She knew just how the revelation of Tariq's betraya

would cut David to the core. He would feel that he had failed to keep his promise to his father. This was the stuff that went to the very heart of what motivated the man. But...she couldn't tell him without blowing her cover.

Jayde's heart sank like a stone. Keeping her cover, staying on Shendi, meant she would now knowingly be deceiving the man she had come to love.

She couldn't do it.

But she had to. In order to prove his innocence, to protect him from a traitor, an enemy within the walls of his own home. His own brother. She stared at the phone. What had she just done?

She felt as if her very soul had been ripped in two by divided loyalties. She pushed her hair back from her brow with a shaky hand. God, David was going to hate her when he found out what she'd done. In trying to help him she was killing any hopes of a future with him. Who was she kidding? There *was* no hope for a future. David would never believe her amnesia was real once he learned who she was. He'd think she'd deceived him and Kamilah from the start. So what difference would it make to see the mission through now? None. Apart from the fact she might save him from the evil of his half brother.

Jayde sucked in a breath, filling her lungs until they felt they would burst. But as she did, she sensed a presence. Someone was watching her from behind. A cold dread seeped through her. Very, very slowly she turned around.

He stood rigid in the doorway, blue eyes crackling with sparks of fury, the muscles of his neck corded and tight.

"David!" she gasped. "How long have you been standing here?"

"Who were you talking to?" His voice was flat, dangerous.

Jayde's eyes shot to the phone, then back to him.

How much had he heard?

"I said, who were you talking to?" he demanded.

"I…I called the embassy."

"Bull!" He stepped into the room, slammed the door shut behind him, locked it, pocketed the key. "Who the hell *are* you?"

She forced panic away. She told herself she was trained for this sort of thing. But she couldn't kid herself. Nothing in this world had prepared her for the situation in which she found herself now.

He grabbed her wrist, tightening his fingers around her like a metal cuff. He yanked her toward him. His eyes lanced hers, stabbing clean through to her soul. "Who was on that phone?" he growled. "What's this about my brother? What about the Falal?"

She stared up into his ferocious eyes. Beyond the crackling anger, she could still read deep pain. A pain she had put there. And she couldn't lie to him. Just couldn't. She knew in her gut that he was innocent. And if his brother was working against him, he deserved to know it.

Jayde drew in a shuddering breath. Telling him would be one hell of a gamble. One that could cost lives if her gut was wrong. And it would most certainly cost her her job, right or wrong. But at this instant she didn't care about her career. Before she'd met David, her job had been her life, her colleagues had been her family, and a sense of duty to her country had been her sole driving force.

But this man had sneaked in when her guard was down, and he'd changed her in some profound way. He'd put the missing part of her soul back into her heart. And life was no longer simple.

Deceit or truth? The choice hung over her head like a sword of Damocles. Her mouth went bone dry. She tried to swallow.

His fingers tightened painfully around her wrist. He was waiting for her response...for the thread to break and the word to fall.

Tariq waited until he was absolutely certain she'd hung up. Then he clicked the receiver carefully back into place. His hand trembled. Perspiration pricked along his top lip. He swiped it away. He'd been exposed. This was far worse than he could have contemplated. He had to think fast. He had to move fast.

David's fingers squeezed her wrist, and rage circled his heart like the winds of a terrible storm. He'd been betrayed by a woman he desperately wanted to believe in. A woman who'd made him dream once again of a future.

He was an idiot. He should have listened to Tariq. Instead he'd fallen into a trap as old as time. He had little doubt after hearing her on the phone that she was some kind of spy.

The question now was simply, who was she spying for?

She stared up at him with her huge innocent green eyes. But this time he knew they were a lie. "Who was on that phone?" he snarled.

"David, I...I'm...I'm not the person in that passport. ...I'm not married."

A crazy wave of relief swooped through David's stomach so fast he almost threw up. *She wasn't married.* But the sensation bottomed out instantly. He tightened his grip, yanked her closer. And as he did, his nostrils flared in reflex at the scent of her. In spite of himself, his loins stirred involuntarily. Her body was so close to his he could feel her quick nervous breaths against his lips. His blood began to heat.

A dangerous cocktail of adrenaline, rage and furious desire began to spurt through his veins. A dark and primal voice whispered through him that she was fair game now. She didn't belong to another man. And she sure as hell wasn't the vulnerable amnesiac. He need feel no guilt, no shame in taking her now. Right here, on his desk. Hard and fast. His breathing quickened. His blood boiled with rage and lust. His eyes bored into hers.

But instead of challenge, instead of the latent confidence he was used to seeing in those bewitching eyes, a look of uncertainty…and of fear stared back up at him.

It totally threw him.

"Who the hell *are* you then?" he demanded, his voice hard and strange to his own ears.

She sucked in a shaky breath. "David, you have to understand, the *only* reason I'm going to tell you this is because I believe in you. You *have* to understand that."

The desperation in her tone, the insecurity in her eyes set him on edge. "What are you talking about?"

"What I'm going to tell you cannot go beyond these walls. Can you promise me that? Can I trust you, David?"

He could feel her pulse racing wildly under the pressure of his fingers.

"Trust?" He snorted. "Who are you to talk of trust?"

"My name is Jayde Ashton. I'm an agent for the British government."

Anger and an unexpected jolt of sharp pain pierced his chest. He grabbed her jaw with his free hand, jerked her face up to his. She winced in pain.

"What in hell do you want from me, *Jayde Ashton?* Did you get what you came for? Was I a nice, easy lay? Will it please the British government?"

"Don't do this David—"

"Don't do what? Pretend I didn't fall for a professional? Pretend I wasn't taken by your lying sinful eyes?" He shoved her brutally away from himself. "You're a spy!" He spat the words out in disgust. He raised a finger, aimed it at her face. "Tell me what you came for, then get the hell off my island!"

Shock, hurt, ghosted her features then was gone. She steeled her jaw, took a deep breath. "I'm going to give it to you straight, David. I owe you that much."

"You sure as hell do."

"If you are guilty, you will kill me for this." She straightened her spine, squared her shoulders. "*That* is the measure of my trust in you, David. I am prepared to tell you the truth. I am prepared to tell you what I am doing here because… because I just believe—" her voice caught "—I believe in you. With my heart. And if I'm wrong, I don't care. I don't care if I die." Her eyes glistened with hot emotion. "Because…I have nothing I want to go back for. Not anymore."

A spasm of shock quirked through him. *Him, kill her? Was she crazy?* His anger shifted. Confusion swirled through him. Then he clenched his teeth. This was probably just another game, another ploy.

"If I am guilty of what?" he demanded.

"I work for MI-6, the British secret service—"

"I know what MI-6 is," he snapped.

She swallowed. "My partner and I were sent to set up a perimeter surveillance system of your island—"

"Why?" he interrupted. "Why me?"

"You're a person of interest to the British Government."

"And *that's* why?"

"No." She cleared her throat. "Two months ago the U.S. National Security Agency picked up intelligence that led to the U.S. interception of a yellowcake uranium shipment from Libya to Korea. It was a rare kind of uranium, David. The kind that made headlines two years ago, the kind being used in cutting-edge nuclear technology."

His chest tightened. He knew exactly what kind of uranium she was talking about. It came from only a few mines in the world. He owned two of them.

"It came from *your* mines, David. It was being shipped to Korea by the Falal in return for sophisticated centrifuges and other nuclear-weapons hardware and technology. What the U.S. discovered is only a small portion of what is coming from your mines. The rest is going straight to the Falal and the Falal is enriching your uranium and using the Korean hardware to manufacture nuclear weapons for Libya. Falal, David, is a covert arm of the Libyan Government."

David's heart kicked against his rib cage. He said nothing. He felt sick. This couldn't be true.

"The U.S. also learned that illegal oil shipments from Rashid mines were making their way onto the black market and that the funds generated from them were going to finance the Falal. Because it's your company and because you are a British citizen, U.S. intelligence alerted MI-6. The agencies are cooperating. On the surface Libya had abandoned its nuclear-weapons program. But now we have proof the Falal has simply taken it underground. It still exists, and your mines are fueling it."

David felt the blood drain from his head. "It cannot be true."

"It *is* true."

"It can't be. I'd know about it. Or…or Tariq would. It couldn't be done without at least one of us being aware."

"Yes," she said, watching him intently.

He reeled at the implication. "You're trying to tell me my own brother knows about this!"

"Yes."

"No!" He slammed his fist onto the desk. "It's a lie!"

"David, Tariq was seen at the Falal base in southern Libya two days ago." She hesitated. "The U.S. has an undercover operative at that base. He has evidence that Tariq belongs to the Falal. He also has proof that the Falal is funding the rebels in Azar...the rebels you have been fighting."

His vision narrowed and his world spun. "You're telling me that my brother is a traitor not only to his family, but a traitor to his whole country. And that I'm not fighting a small group of Azarian dissidents but I am fighting Libya itself?" He paced the room angrily, raked his hands through his hair, halted, glared at her. "Why should I believe you? You are a liar!"

"Because I care about what happens to you and Kamilah."

"Bull!"

"David, you *have* to trust me."

He felt himself beginning to shake with bottled rage. "You faked an accident to get into my home, you faked amnesia, you insinuated yourself into my daughter's life to get to me. You...you *slept* with me. You are the worst kind of liar...and now you accuse my brother and you want *my* trust?"

She took a step toward him, her eyes burning with desperate urgency. "The accident, David, the amnesia, that was all real."

He stormed over to the door, unlocked it, swung it open. "Get out! Get out of my life! Get off my island!"

Jayde had pushed him too far. But she stood her ground. She had to see this through. She had to ensure the information she'd divulged stayed with him and him alone. "I can help you, David."

His eyes literally sparked with rage. Fury came off him in hot waves. He seemed to swell in size with the power of his anger. He was an awesome and frightening sight, and there was no doubt in her mind David Rashid was a man who could be driven to kill with his bare hands.

"Leave!" He pointed to the door, his voice quavering with rage.

Jayde made her way slowly toward the door, her mind racing for a way out. But as she reached the archway, a terrible scream echoed through the palace corridors. Then another. And another. Coming toward them. Both she and David froze at the awful sound.

They could hear footsteps. Someone running, stumbling. Gasping for breath.

Fayha' lurched around the corner and collapsed against the wall. She was pale as a ghost, her eyes as big as black saucers. Her scarf had been yanked back, leaving her hair uncovered. Her dress was torn and stained with dirt. She opened her mouth. But the only sound that came out was a coarse rasp. Her knees buckled under her and she began to slip down the wall.

David lunged forward, caught her. "Fayha', what is it?"

"Allah forgive me...forgive me."

The first thing David did was pull the scarf back up over his housekeeper's hair. The gesture moved Jayde deeply. David knew how important it was to a Muslim woman to keep her hair covered. The gesture also showed a respect for his housekeeper, respect he no longer had for her and would never have again.

He spoke gently. "Take it easy, Fayha'. Tell me what's wrong."

"Sh...she...she's gone."

"*Who*, Fayha'? *Who* has gone?"

"Kamilah."

David's body went rock still. "What?"

"He...he took her."

"Who?" he barked.

"Mr. Tariq...he...he took her in the helicopter."

David didn't move. Time stretched thick. Then his head turned, very slowly, and his eyes lifted to meet Jayde's. In them Jayde could see the harsh truth of his brother's betrayal beginning to sink in. His whole face began to change as she watched. She saw darkness bleed into the sharp blue of his eyes. His brows lowered, his mouth flattened, his features sharpened. The muscle in his jaw pumped wildly. And she was held prisoner by the intensity of the transformation.

Fayha' thrust a crumpled wad of paper at David. "He…he gave me a note."

David jerked his attention back to Fayha', grabbed the paper, stood up, read it.

And his face went white.

Chapter 12

David read the note a second time. The words had no less impact. It was written in Arabic, in Tariq's unmistakable scrawl. His daughter had been kidnapped.

By his own brother.

He couldn't get his brain around the fact. It didn't make sense. He read the note a third time.

"If you want to get Kamilah back alive you will do everything I say. Expect my call by midnight. Follow orders to the last detail."

This was not possible! How could his brother do this to Kamilah? Even if what Jayde Ashton had said about Tariq was true, surely he would not harm Kamilah, his own niece, Aisha's child? Tariq knew just how vulnerable Kamilah was, how she'd suffered since the death of her mother. This would utterly destroy her. How could he use her like this? Why? What could he possibly want?

David tried to swallow the orb of anguish ballooning in his throat. His fists balled, his jaw clenched, his vision blurred. He hadn't been there for her. He'd been distracted by a woman.

Once again he had failed his daughter.

Rage began to boil deep inside him, surging violently up through his body, his blood. He could feel himself begin to vibrate against the sheer steaming power of it. And he knew he was veering dangerously close to the outer limits of his control.

But he couldn't afford to lose it. He brutally clubbed his emotions back into submission. He sucked in a deep breath, willed the fire of his fury to flatten out into a deadly cold and laser-sharp focus. He had to think fast. Clearly. He needed to be both restrained and ruthless. And he had to move with lightning swiftness.

First he had to contact his insurance company in London. He had kidnap and ransom cover with Sudderby's. They would immediately dispatch Gio Moriati, a trained negotiator, the world's best. And he had to summon Jacques Sauvage to his island immediately. Sauvage would put together a tactical team and the tracing equipment needed to track Tariq's call. If he moved fast enough, they could all be in place and ready for that call by midnight. If the negotiating failed, Sauvage's team would be ready to go in and retrieve his daughter. And David would go with them.

He sucked in another slow, deep breath, filling his chest to capacity, filling his body with control. He exhaled slowly. He ignored the MI-6 agent watching him. He took Fayha''s arm, led her to a chair in his office and sat her down. "Tell me exactly what happened, step by step."

Fayha' was still shaking violently. "Mr. Ta-Tariq was on the phone in the great room. I...I came in to see what dusting needed to be done and I...I saw him there."

"Did you hear him talk on the phone?"

Fayha' shook her head. "No. He was just listening. The he put the receiver down and…and then…he saw me. His eye were strange. He asked where Kamilah was. I…I told him sh was in the kitchen helping with the dinner." Fayha' began t choke on her own sobs. "She likes to do that, you know… she's such a good child. I…I told him where to find her. I…"

David took her hand. "Fayha', it's not your fault. I need yo to think clearly now, we all need to. What happened next?"

She sniffed, smudged the tears from her face. "I followe him. I wasn't sure why he wanted to see Kamilah." Anothe sob shuddered through her body. "He…he took her to the hel icopter. I…I couldn't stop him in time. I tried. He…he wa too strong. He threw me to the ground. I…I didn't have tim to get help."

"Thank you, Fayha'. You did what you could. Go clean up," he said. "I'll have Dr. Watson brought in. He'll give you some thing to help calm you down when he arrives."

David turned to the woman at his side, the stranger h thought he'd known so intimately. Her eyes were wide and he skin was white with shock at the news of Kamilah's kidnapping

But *her* feelings didn't touch him. They would never touc him again. He never wanted to see her again. But right at thi instant he needed her on his side. He needed every ally h could possibly think of. Working with the woman who be trayed him might help save his baby. He wasn't going to mis a single possible play. He'd do anything in this world to brin his Kamilah home safe.

He glared at her. "Tariq must have heard you on the phone."

She swallowed. "I know. I have to call in. If Tariq heard m it means the American agent in Libya has been compromised." Her voice was small. "He will be killed if they find him."

He stared at her beautiful face, at the raw pain and regre

in her eyes. And his heart sent a ripple through him. He quashed it instantly. This woman had done more than betray him. Because of her actions, the most precious jewel in his life had been taken from him. He could never forgive her that. He had to hold on to anger, channel the energy of his emotion into hate, revulsion. It was the only way he would be able to keep functioning.

"I want all the information your people have gathered on Tariq," he told her, his voice cold. "And I want whatever intelligence you have on the Libyan Falal, their southern base, the black market exchanges, details of the Falal connection with the Azar rebels. You will deliver this to the Force du Sable tactical team in the great dining hall as soon as you have assembled it. We need the information by midnight. Use my phone."

She said nothing. She'd lost her fight. She was no longer challenging him. It was as if a part of her had died. It made something sink inside David. Again he shoved it brutally away. He watched her move woodenly over to his desk and pick up the phone.

Guilt weighed heavily on Jayde's shoulders. In allowing herself to open emotionally to David, in falling for him, she had allowed him to become her one weakness, the chink in her armor. And in trying to help David, in being honest with him, in being true to herself in the only way she possibly could, she'd ended up putting his daughter in jeopardy, and now possibly a colleague.

She'd done what she had for all the right reasons. She could not have behaved otherwise. And everything had gone wrong. There was no reward for being true. There was no justice in this world. This was life. Not a fairy tale. And life was cruel.

She swallowed against the dryness in her throat. She loved

that child. She understood her. And now she knew why. It was because she had been there. She knew what it was like to lose someone you loved to the sea, what it could do to your soul, how it could kill a part of who you were, and how it could destroy a family. She'd promised Kamilah a happy ending. A fairy-tale ending…

Jayde gritted her teeth suddenly. *By God she was going to do it!* She was going to do whatever it took to deliver that happy ending to little Kamilah, or she would die trying. She grabbed the phone and punched in Lancaster's number for the second time that day.

She knew that when she'd finished telling Lancaster what she'd done, she would be without a job.

She'd lost everything. First her memory, then her heart, then the man who'd stolen her heart. Now she'd lost his child and it would cost her career.

But she was not going down without a fight. She would not let Kamilah and her father down again. This was her fault. And she was prepared to do whatever it took to make it right.

By the time Jayde made her way to the dining hall it was eleven o'clock and dark, with a waning crescent moon low in the sky. She'd gathered her wits and was now sharply focused on the task that lay ahead.

Lancaster had seen the need to keep her on the job—for now. He made no bones about the fact he would deal with her later. He and O'Reilly had delivered the bag of gear and information she'd requested from them earlier in the afternoon. They'd flown it in by chopper and they were now on standby in Khartoum in case she needed additional manpower. Lancaster had also told her the American undercover agent was safe in Azar. He'd left Libya with a group of dissidents under the guise of picking up another uranium shipment. His cover was still tight. But most of all, he was still alive.

But it did little to ease Jayde's conscience. She would rest only when Kamilah was safe and back in the arms of her father.

She strode down the palace corridor dressed in light cargo pants, an olive-green T-shirt and army boots. Her hair was tied in a neat braid that hung down the center of her back. She'd pulled herself together and she meant business. She knew this was her last mission with MI-6, the organization that had been family to her for most of her adult life. And she was going to make it count.

She pushed open the double doors, entered the dining hall and did a double take. The grand hall had been turned into a war room in the space of hours. There were maps tacked onto the wall and spread over the table. Electronic equipment, computer monitors and wires covered another table. The telephone was connected to a microphone, to speakers, and linked into the computer equipment. Lights blazed brightly over the whole affair.

It was a far cry from the candlelit atmosphere she'd shared only hours ago with Tariq and David at this very table. She had to hand it to David, when he went into warrior mode, he sure as hell moved fast.

David was in deep conversation with three men gathered around the far end of the long table. One of them was the most powerful-looking black man she'd ever laid eyes on: bald head, gleaming ebony skin and bone structure worthy of an ancient gladiator. The other two were Caucasian, and equally potent in build. Both were deeply tanned. One had dark hair, another was sandy blond.

They looked up in unison as she approached. Each wore an expression of business. David's mouth flattened at the sight of her. He didn't bother to introduce her.

She nodded at the men, dumped her pack on the table. "I'm agent Jayde Ashton," she said. "MI-6."

The dark-haired man at the head of the table stood to a towering height. His icy silver eyes appraised her with cool and calculated concentration.

Jayde knew his face instantly. It was unmistakable. All hard angles with a scar that sliced from the corner of his left eye to the base of his sharp jaw. It was a ruthless and rugged face, one that had graced many a paramilitary magazine. It was the face of a man who had piqued the attention of the world's governments with the way he'd single-handedly challenged the international community's perception of mercenaries and armies for hire. He was the legendary Jacques Sauvage, the formidable head of the notorious Force du Sable. The founder of the first private military operation to lobby for United Nations sanction. The man giving soldiers of fortune respectability.

In spite of herself she felt a prickle of awe run over her skin.

"Jacques Sauvage," he said, holding out a large, roughened hand. She held out her own. His grip was as powerful as he looked.

"And this is December." He motioned to the large black man at his side. December tipped his head and lowered his eyes in sullen greeting.

"And this is Gio Moriati, K&R point man for Sudderby's of London."

Jayde nodded to each. She knew K&R stood for kidnap and ransom and that Moriati would thus be handling the negotiations with Tariq. But she suspected he would have little success. Tariq was not after money. He was after his brother's soul. And a country.

She sensed David's eyes on her. She turned to look at him and she felt color rise to her cheeks under his intense scruiny. She held his gaze, but his features remained implacable, his eyes cold and hard. Like the men he'd assembled around him, David Rashid was in combat mode. These were the men he'd chosen to guide him into battle. These were the men he was relying on to help save his daughter from his own brother. They made a formidable team. And she was going to show them she was every bit as good as each one of them.

Jayde pulled out a chair and joined the men. She had less than an hour to table everything she had on Tariq, Falal, the Azar dissidents and the black market trades.

She methodically laid out her case, her eyes continually trying to read David's as she did. But he'd make one hell of a poker player. Nothing she said about his brother seemed to touch him. She felt as if she'd never known him, never even glimpsed the man she knew lived under that shell.

By the time the clock ticked down the final minutes to midnight, they had a preliminary battle plan drawn up. They assumed Tariq would hold Kamilah at a Falal base just over the Libyan border. It was an old French fortress in the Sahara desert with a sheer ridge of rock to the north. They would trace Tariq's call with state-of-the-art satellite technology. They needed to keep him talking for only thirty seconds to confirm his location.

They would hear out his demands, and Gio would try to get proof of life and keep negotiating as if in good faith. They would stretch the negotiations out as long as they could in order to buy time for Sauvage and a small team of crack paratroopers to mount an offensive from the north.

"He will not expect us to hit from within Libya's borders," said Sauvage. "They will be looking for us to the south, to Azar. We'll launch from here, in the Egyptian desert near the Libyan border." He jabbed his finger at the map. "We'll fly in at night, low, under Libyan radar. We will drop off here, behind this ridge just north of the fortress." He moved his finger over the map. "We will approach the fortress from this direction using the ridge as cover."

Jayde tried to place his accent as she listened to Sauvage speak. It was a rich and eclectic blend of French and South African with the hint of American drawl. She could not pinpoint his origin. No one could. He'd come out of the French Foreign Legion, a man with no past.

"Once we have our package," he said, "we will radio for pickup at this point just south of the fortress. We will make it over the Azar border and fly in to Al Abèche, this small settlement here." He poked his finger at a spot in the desert.

Jayde studied the map. Al Abèche was nothing but a name in the middle of miles and miles of Sahara sand.

Sauvage glanced up at David. "You will wait for us at Al Abèche."

"I'm going in with you."

"No," said Sauvage with the ease of one practiced at command. "I understand your need, David, but you must let me do my job. Kamilah will need you when we get to Al Abèche. But she will need me and my men to get her to that point. While you are in Al Abèche, you will remain in constant contact with Gio, who will stay here on Shendi. Tariq must at all times believe you are still here. *Ça va?*"

Jayde watched David's Adam's apple move as he tried to swallow. His eyes, however, remained emotionless. When he spoke, his voice was flat. "Understood," he said. And Jayde knew just how torn this man must be in spite of his stolid exterior. It made her heart ache.

"Bien," said Sauvage. "At the moment this is a bit of a mug's game until we know exactly what Tariq's demands are and where he is. We will adjust as needed."

David glanced at his watch. Jayde checked hers. One

minute to go until midnight. The air seemed suddenly thick. Time stretched, and silence hung ominously over them as they all waited for the phone to ring.

The door behind her swung open. Jayde almost leaped out of her skin at the sudden interruption. But it was only Farouk with tea. She let out a shaky breath as he set the tray on the far end of the table. She hadn't realized just how tense he was.

The phone rang.

For a nanosecond everyone froze. Then December moved instantly over to the tracing equipment, seated himself in front of a computer screen. He held up three fingers.

David nodded, waited until the third ring, picked the phone up. It clicked over to the speakers.

"Rashid," he said, the strength and power in his voice belying the angst that most certainly had to be chewing him up from the inside out.

"I have Kamilah."

David's body tensed visibly. His knuckles whitened as his hand tightened into fists. Jayde's heart squeezed. She held her breath. Sauvage watched. December tapped quietly at the computer keys.

"Do what I say if you want to see her alive." Tariq's rough voice echoed dissonantly through the speakers, bounced off the mosaic walls and drifted up to the glass dome above them. Jayde could see the sliver of the sickle moon shining down through the reds and oranges of the stained glass high above their heads.

Sauvage made a fast rolling motion with his finger, indicating to David that he must keep talking. David nodded. "Let me speak to her, Tariq."

"No. You will do as I say. Until then, you will have no contact."

The muscle in David's jaw jumped wildly. Jayde could see the veins in his forearms, his neck, popping out. He was visibly straining against violent impulse. But they all knew the plan was to stay steady, to stay in control, to calmly sound Tariq out, to hear his demands without antagonizing him and driving him to make an irrational move. This would set the stage for Gio to take over negotiations. David had to make it clear to Tariq that he would have to deal with Gio and Gio alone.

"What do you want, Tariq? Why are you doing this?"

He laughed, the sound harsh. "You know what I want. My views have never changed. We want what is ours. The oil fields, the mines, Azar, the desert."

"We?"

"Those of *pure* blood."

David flinched. Fire began to crackle in his eyes.

Sauvage rolled his finger.

David nodded. He cleared his throat. "You mean the Falal?"

"The people to whom the desert belongs. The people you and my father sold out to the Imperialist West."

David's fists clenched. Sauvage made another motion with his hand, telling him to go slow, take it easy, stay calm.

Jayde knew it had to be killing David.

"I have sold out to no one." His voice leashed his fury. But barely. "You speak the propaganda of Falal, Tariq. You are a fool. A puppet. Nothing but a means for Libya to take control of Azar's wealth, a wealth that belongs to *my* people."

Tariq cursed in coarse and guttural Arabic.

Sauvage held up his hand, motioning to David not to inflame Tariq further.

David sucked air deep into his lungs. Jayde could see him straining for control.

"Why take Kamilah? She is innocent. She is harmless. She annot withstand this. It will destroy her. You know that."

He laughed. "It will destroy *you*."

And in that instant Jayde knew Tariq had no intention of ver returning Kamilah alive. They had to move in. And they ad to make every second count. She caught Sauvage's eyes, hen Gio's. And she could see they, too, had reached the same onclusion.

"You would not harm Kamilah! I cannot believe it. Not fter what she went through with the death of her mother."

Tariq snorted, the sound ugly and harsh. It bounced around he cavernous hall mocking them from all angles. "*I* took Aisha's life. You and Kamilah were meant to die with her."

Jayde gasped. The blood drained instantly from David's ace. He grabbed the back of a chair, steadied himself. All eyes vere on him. The tension in the room was suddenly as thick is pea soup. But David didn't speak. He didn't blow his con-rol. He simply waited for Tariq to continue. Jayde's heart bled or him. She got up, moved around the table and touched his irm. He pulled back.

"It was meant to look like an accident. And in the event of he death of your entire family, I was ready to mount a legal hallenge to take control of Rashid International, to take back vhat my father denied me. Except you didn't die. And you estructured your company, changed your will to put in place a trust to ensure your plans in Azar would go ahead in the vent of your death. Killing you was no longer an option, brother. So I found a new way."

David's grip on the chair tightened as the sheer scope of iis brother's betrayal set in. Tariq had never stopped hating iim. Not for an instant. He had killed Aisha. He had caused Kamilah untold pain. And he was prepared to do it again.

When David spoke, his voice was rough like gravel roll-

ing through a metal pipe. "What must I do to get my daugh
ter back?"

"You have exactly one week to withdraw *all* Force d
Sable troops from Azar. If one soldier is left in the country
Kamilah will be executed."

Everyone looked up, exchanged glances. Withdrawing
Force du Sable troops at this point would amount to a coup
The rebels would move in, and Azar would fall into the hand
of the Falal. It would in effect be annexed by Libya, and the
international community would be powerless to stop it. Ev
eryone at the table knew that. And everyone knew that the rip
ple effects of the takeover would shift the balance of powe
not only in the Middle East but the world.

December shot his fist into the air in victory. He'd pin
pointed Tariq's location. Sauvage jabbed a pin into the map
marking the spot. They were right. He was at the old fortress

"I want the country, David. Or I will take the life of you
daughter. Your choice."

"There is no choice. I will have my daughter back!"

"Then show me you negotiate in good faith. I want the
troops in Li'shal gone by nightfall tomorrow. The next day
you will remove troops from Benghusi."

Fury glittered in David's eyes. "Give your demands to Gio
Moriati," he snapped. "He is my negotiator. From here on, hi
voice is mine. And may God save your soul, brother. Because
I plan to send you to hell!"

David stormed from the room.

Jayde found David down at the cove, where he'd ordered
a bonfire lit to keep vigil for Kamilah. It was the same beach
Jayde had washed up on. It was where Kamilah herself had
kept a vigil for her mother, waiting for a mermaid to come
from the sea.

David stood in his daughter's place now, staring out over he black swells, straining to reach out to his child in every lesperate way he could.

Jayde could almost feel the man's mind calling out over he waters. Calling over the ocean, across the desert sands, to where his Kamilah waited for him. And Jayde knew that the most difficult thing for David to face right now had to be the waiting. He was a man of action. And this must be killing him.

He didn't hear her approach. The roar and spit of the bonfire drowned even the sound of small waves on the shore. And his mind was focused outward, on his daughter.

"David?"

He jolted, spun around. His eyes shot to hers, then he urned abruptly away from her to face the sea.

But in that brief instant, highlighted by the orange light of he flames, she'd seen the rawness in his eyes. It grabbed her y the throat, tore at her insides.

"I'm going with you to Al Abèche," she said.

He didn't move a muscle, didn't look at her. "No."

"I have to."

"I don't want you there."

"I can help you."

"No."

"David, look at me, listen to me, I can help Kamilah when hey bring her out. I know as well as you do how fragile she s. And you know as well as I do how she opened up to me, ow she needed *me* to be able to talk. Who knows how she vill have regressed, what this trauma will have done to her. She will need me there, David." Jayde hesitated. "She will eed *both* of us there. *Together.* It will make her strong to see s as a unit. After that I swear I will get out of your life. You'll ever have to look at me again."

His eyes flashed to hers, held. Jayde swallowed. The intensity she saw in his features put her on edge. But she coul also see she'd found a chink in his armor.

"Why would she need to see us together?" His voice wa cracked. He was a caged and wounded tiger that could strik a lethal blow in an instant. She had to tread carefully.

"It's part of her fantasy to see us together," Jayde sai softly. "I know how her mind works."

"How in hell would *you* know how her mind works?" h snapped.

"Because I've been there, David. I've been through wha Kamilah went through. I was the same age when it happened."

Something shifted in his eyes. But he said nothing.

"I lost my sister and my father to the sea, David. I know what that can do to a child, a family."

He stared at her, the shadows of flame and night dancing across the angles of his face. She knew she'd snagged some thing in him. But he was too angry to ask about what it wa she'd been through.

So she pressed further. "Kamilah's fantasy is to see th mermaid and the prince find a happy ending, David. Not th ending she's read over and over again in Andersen's tal where the mermaid sacrifices herself. She has a dream of see ing us together."

"That's preposterous. It'll never happen."

"I don't doubt it. But seeing the two us together will giv her a measure of faith that could end up pulling her throug the initial days after her capture. She needs stability, David."

He glared at her. "Damn you! You're the one who filled he head with this fantasy nonsense. I should've put a stop to i right away."

She held his eyes. "No. It wasn't me who put the fantasy in her mind. It was there already. I'm just the one she opene up to."

"You fueled it! You gave it form. You were a bloody curse brought in with that wretched storm. This is all your fault."

Her frustration piqued. Her fists clenched at her side and her nails bit into her palms. "This is *not* my fault. This is Tariq's fault. I refuse to shoulder the blame for his actions. Yes, at first I felt responsible. But not now. Yes, my actions have resulted in disastrous consequences. But I picked up that phone and called in because I couldn't lie to you, David. I picked it up because I cared, dammit."

Shock jolted through his body. His eyes widened. She could see the stark question in them.

"That's right. *I care.* For you. For Kamilah. For everything that is good and true and honest in this world. I lost my mind and I fell for you, David. And by God I'm sorry I did. Because look where it got us. But the reason we're here is precisely because I could never knowingly lie to you. And I swear on my life my amnesia was real. I swear I never meant to hurt you or Kamilah. When my memory returned, when I realized what was happening, I picked up that damn phone in your office to tell my handler I wouldn't, *couldn't* finish the job."

His features shifted. She was getting through to him. "Whether you like it or not, I'm going with you to Al Abèche. I'm going to do everything in my mortal power to make this right."

"Jayde—"

"I have nothing else to live for, David." Her voice wavered. "I've lost everything since washing up on your bloody island. Don't take this away from me, too."

Chapter 13

He clenched his jaw, biting in emotion. Hot orange sparks exploded into the black night and leaped above the flames of the bonfire. His heart hammered in his chest. He stared at her. What did she mean she had nothing left to live for? Was this all just another lie?

Not by the naked anguish in her eyes. But then, she was a trained agent, wasn't she? It was her job to wear fake emotions, to insinuate herself into peoples lives…into their very souls.

She took a step closer to him. His body braced. His fists clenched. He didn't trust himself this close to her. He didn't trust what was raging through his blood.

"You've *got* to believe me, David. The amnesia was real."

Could it be the truth? It sure as hell had looked real to him. Watson had said she could be faking. But he'd also said she may have dissociated from her identity to protect herself from some trauma, and that when her memories did come back she night go through great pain reliving them. Was she feeling that pain now? Was that what he could see shimmering in her eyes?

Guilt stabbed sharply. Deep down he ached to reach out, to touch her, to comfort. But he couldn't bring himself to crack out of the armor he'd barricaded himself behind. He could not bring himself to ask about her past, to ask about the sister and father she lost to the sea. He didn't want to know any more, to feel any more. He wanted to shut her out. He wanted to hate her.

So he turned away from her.

"David," she said softly. "Please don't hate me for this. The only mistake I made was to fall for you. I regret it deeply. It's the biggest mistake I've made in my entire adult life. But you have to understand, everything that has happened over the last hours relates directly back to that one fatal error. And if you look at it that way, you too must shoulder your share of the blame." She sucked in a shaky breath. "This is also your fault, David. You made it impossible for me not to...to love you."

His breath caught sharply in his throat. He clenched his teeth. His head pounded wildly. But he refused to look at her. *Love?* His heart twisted. He tried to breathe.

She was right. It *had* all been a terrible mistake. One that belonged to him as much as to her. The mistake had been not resisting the impossibly powerful force of attraction that simmered between them.

He turned, very slowly. And swallowed. Because it was still there. That force still simmered. It burned fiercer than ever. He only had to look into those emerald eyes to feel the heat of it smouldering deep down in his core. And right at this moment he couldn't hold on to the hatred he was so desperately trying to direct toward her. In its place was an overpowering urge to grab her and to squeeze her so tight she could barely breathe. He wanted to hold her so close she'd feel his pain

right through her skin. He wanted to share the feelings tha
boiled inside him, the anger and anguish of a betrayed brother
of a man who still was being rendered incapable of resisting
the force of the enigmatic woman in front of him, of a father
who'd lost his child.

He'd been through a meat grinder. But, hell, so had she.
And she was right. Kamilah would need her. No matter what
he thought about it, his child had formed a deep bond with
this woman.

"I'm coming to Al Abèche, David, whether you like it or
not," she insisted. "I'll be ready by first light."

He brushed her statement aside. "What happened…to your
family?" He wanted to know. Needed to know.

Her lip twitched. But her eyes held his.

"Tell me…Jayde." He used her name for the first time, and
it stuck in his throat on the way out. "What happened?"

She shivered slightly, in spite of the warm night air. "When
I was six…I was in a boating accident off the coast of Cornwall. I…I watched my sister…my twin…"

"Twin?"

"Yes. Identical twin. Her name was Amber. I…I watched
the sea swallow them. Amber and my father." Her eyes were
bright with emotion but her voice was flat. "My dad saved me
first. He went back for Amber but he…they never made it. My
mother wasn't with us that day, but it destroyed her anyway.
She killed herself two years later. That's…that's when I had
my first amnesia episode. When I was eight. After I found my
mother. I lost two whole years, just blanked out, forgot who
I was."

An odd ball of pain expanded in his chest. He knew just
what it was like to watch someone you loved being sucked
down by the waves. "Is that why you think you connected with
Kamilah like you did?"

"Even with my amnesia, a part of me deep down inside must have sensed the similarity of our pasts. I...I didn't want to see the two of you destroyed by this, David. I..." She looked away quickly, trying to hide the glimmering tear that escaped her eye. "I think that by trying to help you and Kamilah I must have subconsciously been trying to fix my own wretched past. I...I just wanted to put it all right."

She sniffed and angrily smudged the trail of tears shining on her cheeks, then gave a soft, derisive laugh. "I...I never cry, you know."

He ached to hold her.

She sniffed again, rubbed her nose and took in a deep, shuddering breath. Then she pulled her shoulders back, lifted her chin. "That's why I'm going to Al Abèche, David. I have to make it right."

He studied her in silence, the fire crackling. In spite of what he had done, he could only admire her strength, her determination, her desire to set things right. "It will not be easy," he said finally.

"I can handle it."

"The Sahara respects no man...or woman," he warned.

"I said I can handle it."

"We will fly into Tabara, the capital. But from there we will have to travel three days and nights by camel in order not to arouse suspicion. Any air or vehicle traffic into Al Abèche will alert Falal or rebel informants."

"I know."

"You ever ridden a camel?"

"I can ride camels. I can speak Arabic. I've worked in Algiers and in Egypt—"

"Right," he snapped. "How could I forget? You're a trained agent."

"Exactly," she retorted. "That's why you need me."

She spun on the heels of her army boots and stomped over the sand and up to the path that led back to his castle. "I'll be ready at dawn," she called out of the dark.

David blew out the pent-up air in his chest and turned to stare back out over the ocean. He felt as if he'd been shoved right up to the very edge of his existence. And beyond was wilderness. Uncharted territory. Tomorrow he would be over the ocean, in that wilderness, in the blistering heat of the desert under a wild, open sky. Alone with Jayde. With no place to hide from each other. He knew they would both be stripped naked by the blistering winds and harsh environment they would have to traverse to reach his child.

Summer in the Sahara held no mercy.

Jayde packed her backpack with grim determination. It was nearly three in the morning, but sleep eluded her. She needed to keep moving. She carefully checked through the supplies Lancaster had shipped to her. Among them she had a military issue compass, knife, binoculars, night-vision gear, pencil flares, sat-phone and cash. She'd also asked for some more serious hardware, and Lancaster had obliged by sending her some small but highly effective weaponry that included thin bricks of malleable plastic explosives along with strips of chemical reactant. He'd also thrown in chemical darts that would render a victim paralytic for several hours, and a small grenade launcher that could be fitted to her rifle. The launcher could be used to deliver an array of both lethal and less-than-lethal munitions including teargas rounds, smoke, signal flares and revolutionary electromagnetic pulse grenades.

Jayde studied the e-grenades. They'd only just come through highly secretive British military trials. They were hand-held versions of the bigger electromagnetic bombs the army now had in its arsenal.

Jayde knew the big electromagnetic pulse bombs could overwhelm the electrical circuitry of an entire city with an intense electromagnetic blast. Instead of simply cutting off power, an e-bomb literally overloaded and fried everything that used electricity. A big enough e-bomb could thrust an entire city back two hundred years or cripple a military unit. These mini versions in her hand would delivery enough power to knock out the communications and security capability of the Falal fortress. Not that she'd need them. That was going to be Sauvage's job. But she was now prepared for any eventuality. And that's the way she liked things.

"Thank you, Lancaster," Jayde whispered as she packed them carefully with the rest of her gear. She checked her watch. In a few hours they'd be on their way.

She prayed Tariq hadn't harmed Kamilah yet. She wasn't going to even entertain the negative. They were going to get her out. Safe. And to prove it, she was going to pack a bag for Kamilah. She would need some fresh clothes once they'd extracted her. And maybe something familiar and comforting from home.

Jayde made her way down the corridors to Kamilah's room. The palace was ablaze with lights even at this hour. David had lit up his castle like a beacon. He was letting nothing rest.

Jayde opened the door to Kamilah's room, and the instant she saw the unruffled covers on the little girl's bed, agony clawed at her heart. Where was Kamilah sleeping tonight? How had she reacted to the monstrous change in her uncle? Was there anyone with her to comfort her when she cried?

Jayde set the small bag she'd brought from her own room onto the bed and began going through the closets and drawers sorting out some clothes for Kamilah. She folded them neatly and packed them into the bag with military precision.

Some training died hard, she thought ruefully. Well, she might need that training to help get this child back.

Then she caught sight of the small teddy bear lying on Kamilah's pillow. Jayde hesitated, picked it up and buried her nose in the soft fur. It smelled so innocent. Like sunshine. Like a kitten or puppy…like Kamilah's hair. Emotion stabbed behind her eyes and ballooned in her throat. She swallowed it down. She tucked the teddy into the bag and began to zip it up, but something peeking out from under the white ruffles of the pillow sham caught her eye. Jayde reached for it. She pulled out a leather-bound book. *The Little Mermaid.*

She fingered the embossed gold lettering. This time she couldn't swallow the emotion away. It spilled hot and furious down her cheeks, and her chest jerked with a powerful sob. "Hold strong, baby," she whispered clutching the book to her heart. "We're coming…we're coming to get you. We're not going to let you down."

Jayde Ashton swiped away her tears. This crying business was the pits. She had a sneaking suspicion that this new part of herself wasn't going to squeeze back into any bottle now that it was out. She turned to search for a scarf or piece of fabric in which to wrap the book…and froze.

He stood in the doorway. Watching her. A dark and silent specter, a strange and unreadable look in his dark features.

"David?"

He stared at the book in her hands, then he looked up into her eyes. He held her gaze, and a current of connection surged between them. In that instant they were bound. She knew it. He knew it. They were in this together. They were joined by a fierce drive to save this child. And the very thing that united them was what also tore them apart.

Jayde swallowed against the sheer oscillating power of it. "I…I was just gathering a few things for Kamilah."

His eyes shifted to the small bag on the bed. Jayde saw his throat work, the muscle pulse rapidly at the base of his jaw. He nodded. Then he spun on his heels, and she heard the clack of his boots on stone as he marched down the corridor.

She let out a shaky breath. Through the window, dawn was already a peach hint on the distant horizon.

They had to get going.

Heat lay thick like treacle over the dusty desert capital of Tabara, and the air shimmered like a mirage above the ancient buildings. The sand was everywhere. Constantly moving, propelled by the kinetics of wind and gravity. The Sahara literally drifted along the streets, blowing into lobbies of crumbling hotels, frosting traffic lights and piling in drifts in alley corners and ancient doorways. It was so fine in texture it made table salt look coarse by comparison.

After being here only a few hours Jayde had simply given up trying to resist it. It was in her clothes, her hair, her eyelashes, under her fingernails, in her mouth. And the heat slowed her every movement, making her feel sluggish.

David had left her in a small earth-brick hut on the crumbling outskirts of the city where thin goats roamed and children played in ragged clothes. He'd gone to the bustling market in the city center to buy camels and grain.

Her job was to pack the food supplies they'd bought as soon as they'd arrived and to have the bags ready to load onto the camels.

Jayde secured the rice, tins of sardines and dates in the final bag and then she lugged everything outside to wait for David. He wanted to have their camels watered by the evening and he wanted to be gone by nightfall when the oppressive air cooled a little. They would travel through the night. The next day would be tougher because they would continue their trek through the blistering midday heat of the Saharan summer, stopping only briefly to feed and water the camels before pressing on again.

Their goal was to stay low-key and under the radar so as not to alert rebel spies. Jayde was dressed in the manner of an Azarian camel herder, with a loose-fitting muslin shirt that hung to her calves and covered her arms. Under it she wore light muslin pants. On her feet she wore battered old flip-flops and a head cloth hid her hair.

She shaded her eyes and squinted into the haze. The sun was already beginning to dip down toward the distant desert horizon but there was still no sign of David. Jayde felt her jaw beginning to tense. From this last ring of small earth houses that fringed the northern outskirts of Tabara, the Sahara stretched like an undulating ocean in tones of yellow, ochre, cream and amber as far as her eye could see. She felt as if she was standing on the very edge of civilization.

As they trekked into that sea of sand, moving north to Al Abèche, toward Libya, she and David would enter the most arid and hostile region of the Sahara, where moisture was virtually nonexistent and dunes reached four hundred feet and more in height. Al Abèche was a town that hung onto a thread of life in that desiccated wasteland, and they would travel an old Bedouin route to get there.

It was tough for Jayde to get her head around the fact that it would take three days to reach their destination while the urgency of the situation was so acute. But as Sauvage had said, Tariq's demands had afforded them the luxury of time to get it right. *"We have only one shot and we must make it a clean one,"* he'd said. And traveling into Al Abèche any other way would most certainly alert any informants or rebels in the area. They had to try and blend in as best they could. It was that or stay on Shendi and wait. And neither she nor David were the waiting sort.

And while she and David traversed the desert, Sauvage would gather his team in Egypt and Gio would keep the lines of negotiation open with Tariq.

Jayde heard a sound to her right. She swung around. It was David. She sucked in a breath of relief. He was striding toward her, camel stick in hand, three camels in tow. Two were a creamy white, the other one red. He'd already saddled them. Two goatskin water bags, or *guerbas,* were strapped to one. The others were loaded with grain. From one dangled a blackened cooking pot and an old kettle.

"What took you so long?" she called out to him.

"Camel shortage at the market," he called back. "They had mostly calves or untrained bulls that turn into frothing demonic man killers if the mating urge hits." He jerked his head toward the three beasts in tow. "Found these three geldings at the butcher's yard. I reckon they have some life in them yet."

David grinned as he neared, his teeth a slash of stark white against his skin, which was already darkening from the fierce desert sun. It sent a crazy spurt of desire through her. She hadn't seen him smile since they'd made love on his yacht.

He was dressed in similar garb to hers, but he had his *jambiya* thrust through a tie at his waist. But even in peasant dress he was regal. He looked like the sheik, the true leader that he was. And like this crumbling and once-majestic desert city of Tabara, he had one foot in an ancient world, another in a new one. If anyone was to build a bridge between the two ways of life, this was the man. Seeing him like this, she could suddenly understand him in a profound way. She could almost feel the spirit that drove him. And it only deepened what she felt for him already.

She brushed the sensation aside. She couldn't afford to feel anything. Because once they rescued Kamilah, he and his daughter would walk away from her. It would be over. She knew that. He hated her for her betrayal. He blamed her for this tragedy. And the only reason he'd brought her with him now was for the sake of his child.

But she couldn't take her eyes from him. She was entranced by his enigmatic presence, the way he moved in this environment with the elegance and ease of a man born to the sands of the Sahara. Right now there wasn't a trace of Anglo-Saxon about him, apart from the unsettling blue of his eyes against his dark skin. The color was made even more striking as it picked up the indigo blue of the cotton head cloth he wore.

"What are you staring at?"

"You."

He grunted and handed her the head rope of the red camel. "You sure you can handle these creatures?"

"I am." She took the rope from his hand.

David watched, ready to leap to Jayde's aid.

She allowed the beast to sniff her, then she tugged on the head rope and expertly couched the animal. He raised a brow in surprise. This woman was something else. She acted like a desert native.

His admiration flattened almost immediately. That's exactly what she was trained to do. To insinuate herself into situations and blend in like a native. She'd been trained to deceive, and because of this very skill he was admiring now, she'd been chosen by a government agency to betray him.

He felt his jaw clench. He watched Jayde proceed to lug her big bag over to the couched animal. She hefted it up and began to meticulously secure it to the saddle horn. It looked heavy, cumbersome. "What's in there?" David asked, watching carefully as she tied the knots, making sure he wouldn't have to recheck them once she was done.

"Nothing much."

"Put it on the other camel, the one for the supplies."

"No." she simply. "I need to keep this one with me."

"Why?"

She shot him an odd look. "It's my personal bag."

He frowned, watching as she secured a second bag to the camel. A much smaller one. His chest constricted. It was the little bag with Kamilah's things. His hand shot out in reflex. "I'll take that one."

Her eyes flashed to his. She hesitated. "Sure." She handed it to him. Their fingers brushed as he took the bag from her. The electricity of the touch stilled them both. Their eyes locked. And neither needed words to share what was going on their minds. This little bag was a symbol of why they were both here in the desert. And the magnitude of what still lay ahead hung heavy between them.

They worked in silence to load the rest of the bags. Then David watched again to make certain Jayde knew how to mount these notorious desert beasts.

She slipped into the saddle with ease, pressing her heels into the camel's neck. She tugged on the rope, made a clicking sound with her tongue, and the beast rose like a wobbly leviathan.

And in spite of himself, a grudging admiration arose in David. The woman knew what she was doing all right. He wasn't going to have to worry about her abilities. He could now focus solely on the task ahead.

With the three camels loaded and strung together, they left the outskirts of Tabara and made their way down the cascading dunes to a small wadi, a riverbed where dark water pooled and a few date palms straggled in sand as white as snow. There they would water their camels and set out as soon as the sun dipped over the horizon.

A handful of children ran behind them on skinny brown legs as they made their way down to the wadi. Their grubby little faces ranged in shades from dark chocolate to pale coffee. The colors of Africa. And in their eyes, David saw Kamilah's. And in their laughter, he heard hers.

His stomach clenched violently. His hand fisted around the head rope. He lifted his chin to the distant horizon. And in his heart he said a silent prayer. He prayed the gods of the desert would spare his child from the crazed wrath of his half brother.

By the time the sky turned to purple velvet and only a faint violet streak lingered where the sun had slipped behind distant dunes, they had their camels watered and supplies once again secured.

They set out at a rhythmic pace. David let Jayde take the lead. He followed up the rear, behind the camel that carried supplies and grain. Keeping distance between the two of them had been automatic since the moment their hands had brushed over Kamilah's belongings.

The air was still viscous with heat, but the wind was now smooth and soft against his face. They settled into the undulating and mesmerizing rhythm of their camels, traveling in absolute mind-numbing silence for hour after hour after hour.

The sky above them was vast. Stars moved across the heavens in a transcendent display as the hours ticked down toward dawn. Every now and then the movement of a falling star caught David's eye and he began to feel that familiar sensation descend on him as he traveled into the sandy void.

It was a feeling he didn't really have words for. It was spiritual, one of the reasons the Sahara had kept pulling him back throughout his life. Out here David was acutely aware of the fragility of his humanity. He got a sense of perspective he could only imagine was akin to the feeling space travelers got when they looked back at the brilliant blue marble of a planet they called home.

Quite simply the desert helped him put life in perspective. It was where time warped and everything seemed possible.

Even getting his daughter back.

As he rode he watched the hypnotic and sensual sway of the woman on the camel ahead of him and he found himself wondering if it was the same for her. What was she thinking as they headed into this void of sand? In so many ways she was a woman after his own heart. She challenged him in more ways than he could imagine. And she did things to his body he hadn't dreamed possible. As he let his mind go, he found himself wishing it had been different. That there had been a possibility of a future for them. That she could have been his *Sahar*, a gift to him and Kamilah from the sea.

He shook his head.

He was beginning to feel the effects of fatigue. They'd been going all night without a stop. He looked to his right and saw that a copper tinge was already beginning to bleed into the sky, heralding the arrival of the sun.

He settled back into the hypnotic sway of the camel. And almost instantly his mind took off again. He found himself wondering if perhaps there could still be a future for them.

No.

He jerked his mind back. He was being a fool. She was a government agent doing a job. And once this mission was over she'd simply move on to the next. She would slip as effortlessly into some other world as she had into his. And perhaps as easily into another man's heart. There was no room for him and Kamilah in a future like that.

Then her words echoed like a ghostly taunt in his head. *You made it impossible for me not to…to love you.*

His throat constricted. Yeah, so maybe she'd fallen for him. But it had been the biggest mistake of her life. She'd said so herself.

He swallowed the bitterness in his mouth. That was then. That was Sahar. This was now. This woman was Jayde.

But something still ate at him, something he just couldn' let go. The need to know began to, once again, burn in his gu as the copper on the horizon fired into a livid orange and the Sahara sands began to glow.

He clucked his tongue, urged his camel to move faste until he'd caught up and was riding alongside her.

"Jayde?"

She swung her head around and her eyes caught his David's heart stalled. She'd never looked more beautiful to him as she did right now in her peasant gear with a piece of cloth tied like a turban over her head. In the golden dawn ligh her eyes were a liquid and lambent green made only more beautiful by the deepening bronze tan of her skin. In spite of her obvious fatigue, she looked proud. Regal. A princess of the desert.

"What is it?" she asked.

He'd lost his train of thought the second he'd looked into her eyes. "I…ah…back on Shendi, you…you told me you amnesia was real."

"It's the truth, David."

"When, Jayde, when *exactly* did your memory return?"

She halted her camel, shifted around in the saddle to face him. "Why?"

The sun exploded over the horizon, and the sands around them caught fire. He squinted as his eyes adjusted to the flare "I need to know. Did you remember before…before we were together, on the yacht?" *Before we made love.*

The look that shifted into her eyes made his heart sink "David, you told me once you abhorred a liar. I'm not going to lie. Everything I tell you from now is the whole truth." She studied his face.

But he said nothing, just waited.

"I began to remember first in little bits and pieces. I didn't now what was happening and I thought I might be imagining things. It scared me. Then…then when you showed me nto your office and I saw the map of Azar with all those little pins, I got a big chunk of the picture. And then, at dinner…when I saw Tariq's face, that's when it all really started slamming home. It all just came down on me and I was totally confused. I needed to sort it out…in my mind."

He glared at her. So she *had* known. He clenched his jaw. She had known before he went to her on the pier. He kicked his camel forward.

"David—"

He ignored her. She'd known who she was when she'd made love to him. And that burned like all hell.

"David!" she demanded. "David, stop! Listen to me!"

He stopped, turned slowly back to face her.

"What I felt for you was true, dammit. *That* was not a lie. What we shared was *not* a lie!" Her eyes flamed like the growing globe of heat rising fast in the sky. "You put life back into me, David." Her voice caught. "Don't you see? I had *nothing* before I met you. Dead to emotion from the day my mother killed herself. You made me live again! And I didn't ask you to do it. I didn't ask you to make me feel again." Ferocious emotion brought angry spots of color to her cheeks. He could feel heat beginning to rise from the sand.

"And now—" her voice quavered "—and now that I've felt what it's like to…to love…I've lost it all. Everything. Every damn thing that means anything to me. I've lost you. Kamiah. My job." Her voice broke. Tears shone in her eyes. "Don't for one minute think I'm enjoying any part of this. I didn't ask for this. I didn't ask you to sneak in under my guard."

His chest cramped. "Jayde—"

She held up a palm. "Forget it. Just forget it. Don't say a thing. We've got a job to do and that's the only reason I'm here. You know it. I know it. So let's get on with it."

"Jayde, I…I'm sorry." And he truly was. For her. For himself. For his child. For what had happened to his brother. For the unfulfilled promise to his dead father. For his mother who could never love the desert. "I'm sorry," he said again.

Her mouth opened.

"Yes. I'm sorry. For everything. I…I wish it could have been different."

She stared at him. Then something shuttered in her eyes. She pressed her mouth into a tight line and kicked her camel forward in a spurt of dust.

He let his camel drop back. He felt shaken. Shut out. Unsure. And in love.

Yes. He couldn't hide from it. He was in love with this incredible woman. And there was a desert of distance between them.

Chapter 14

The sun shrank to a scorching white-hot ball as it climbed into its zenith. It bleached color from the world and set the land blazing with blinding light. The dunes swelled in size like monstrous waves, torrid and desolate as far the eye could see. And beyond the heaving sands, the horizons simply vaporized into a blur of white heat.

Jayde felt her breathing become labored, and she could see her camel was suffering. They had dismounted and were walking to give the beasts a break. Her feet burned, and sand rubbed blisters into bleeding patches of raw skin. The *guerbas* were almost empty and Jayde knew no man or woman could last longer than one day in this heat without hydration.

"How far to the next water?" She called out to David, her voice hoarse, her lips thick, cracked.

"Should be a wadi over the next ridge," he called back. "We can water there if it hasn't dried up already."

Great, she thought as they pressed laboriously on up on
dune and down the next, the distant ridge never appearing t
get any closer. Her calf muscles felt as if they were tearin
apart. Her back ached and her tongue felt swollen to twice it
size. The sides of her throat literally stuck together. She wa
seeing bright pinprick spots and swarms of black dots in he
peripheral vision. She was beginning to feel dizzy and slightl
crazy as desert madness and the sheer size of the place trie
to grip her mind.

She stumbled in the shifting sand, fell to her hands. It wa
blistering hot against her palms. David moved instantly to he
side. "Here." He reached for the *guerba,* held it out to he
"Take some."

She shook her head. "What if the wadi is *not* over the nex
ridge?"

"It will be. Here, drink."

She let a small sip of water moisten her lips, but she knew
how dangerous it would be to finish every last drop. Nothing wa
a given in this desiccated environment. There may *not* be wate
over the next ridge. She knew David was only saying that to eas
her mind. "Thanks." She handed the goatskin back to him. "
think I'm going crazy. I'm getting mad visions in my head."

"The jinns," he said. He helped her to her feet. "Wait her
with the camels. I'll head to the top of that dune and see if
can see the wadi."

She watched him move up the monstrous mountain of san
until his image wavered in the glistening heat and she though
he might be a ghost, a trick of her mind. She blinked agains
the glare trying to track his movement to the top. What if he
got lost? She'd be dead on her own. She didn't have a clue
where they were. Panic struck her heart. It boiled through he
blood. She began to scramble wildly up the dune after him
leaving the camels.

"David!" She yelled as she stumbled up the mountain of and, slipping back down as fast as she moved forward. David!" Everything turned to fire around her. The whole orld was burning. *She was going to die!*

"David!" she screamed. She fell to the sand, and a world f fiery flames spiraled around her.

"Hey, hey, it's okay." She felt his arms supporting her, lift-ig her up. Her focus began to return.

"It's all right, Jayde, take it easy."

She looked up into his eyes. His skin was even darker and is eyes more blue. Right now he looked like a god. Her sav-or. She gripped his shirt with her fists. "Don't leave me, David."

Something shifted in his eyes. He smoothed her cheek. "It's kay, Jayde, it's just the jinns talking."

"Don't leave me. Ever."

"Don't worry, I won't. We're in this together, all the way. he wadi is just over the ridge. Come. Before we lose the cam-ls and our gear." He helped her slowly down the dune. And he realized just how vulnerable she was without him. And vhat a terrible fate could have befallen them if the camels had vondered off because of her mad carelessness.

The water in the dry riverbed was almost nonexistent. It vas dark and smelled bitter. But it was water. And right now hat meant life. David used it to make *zrig,* a blend of water, owdered milk and sugar. They sat under a small rock over-ang alongside the wadi and drank copious quantities of it.

Jayde could feel her body and her mind slowly begin to re-urn to normal as the moisture and sugar seeped through her ystem. She took the last sip of her share and returned the owl to David. She watched as he cupped the enamel basin n his deeply tanned hands and lifted it to his lips. There was

something so basic and so beautiful and powerful about th
man, she thought. Something so honest.

Maybe it *was* the jinns. Maybe it was the effect of th
desert. Because she felt as though there was nothing to hid
behind out here, nothing to veil emotions. And she'd su
prised the hell out of herself by begging like a fool for him t
never leave her. It was as if something deep and primal ha
ripped loose and erupted out of her very soul.

Now she felt embarrassed. "I'm sorry, David. I think I lo
it back there," she said. "And I could have lost the camels.
was totally irresponsible."

His eyes caught hers, held. Then he grinned suddenly, hi
teeth impossibly white, fine wrinkles fanning out from hi
cool blue eyes. "Like I said, the jinns got you."

She nodded. "I guess they did. And they don't get you?"

"All the time." He sipped the dregs of the *zrig*. "We'll res
here a few minutes," he said. "Why don't you lie down, tr
and close your eyes."

The notion was overwhelmingly appealing. She desper
ately needed rest but she hadn't wanted to hold up thei
progress by telling him so. She tried to inch farther into th
thin line of shadow under the rock. She lay back on a faded
blanket and covered her head with the fabric of her head
cloth. Trying to hide from the heat and blinding glare of th
sun proved futile. She nevertheless drifted into a dazed an
delirious state somewhere between dream and sleep.

And in her dream she was drowning in the sea. The wave
sucking at her. But she could see the shore, the beach, his pal
ace up high on the ridge. She could see Sheik David bin Oma
bin Zafir Rashid, an untamed warrior galloping over ancien
dunes on his white stallion, the platinum-hot glare of sun a
his back throwing his profile into stark and menacing shadow
He had his arm raised high above his head, brandishing hi

mbiya, as a blood-curdling battle cry emanated from his throat. He charged over the dunes, over the sand toward the sea, toward her.

Fear clutched her heart. She began to go under, salt tearing at her throat, burning her nasal passages. But the thundering hooves bore down. David reined his stallion and rode over the beach sand and into the white froth of the waves. He swung low over the side of his horse and scooped her naked into his arms.

She clutched onto his shirt, stared up into cool indigo eyes under his turban. He grinned at her, a piratical slash of white against the deep brown of his face.

Then she was riding behind him on his stallion. Naked. Wild. Free. Laughing. She'd survived. She hadn't died.

And she felt the delicious ache of desire pump blood through her body. And for the first time she could remember, she realized she was truly alive.

Her eyes flashed open. Her heart was racing. Through the cloth covering her face she could see that the sun had moved across the sky. Panic kicked at her. He'd let her sleep too long. They would lose too much time. She jerked up. Her brain was thick. David was no longer beside her.

Her panic mounted as she squinted into the sun trying to find focus, to scan the surroundings.

Then she saw him. Relief swooped through her. He hadn't left. He'd moved into the meager shade of a rock. His back was to her and his head was bent low over something in his lap.

She got up and went over to him, the muscles of her legs aching with each step.

He looked up as she approached. And in his eyes was something unreadable. Then she saw what he held in his hands. A leather-bound book. *The Little Mermaid.*

She sat quietly beside him.

He closed the book and ran his strong brown hands over th cover. His eyes were liquid ink. "I'd never read it, you know

She nodded. She didn't know what to say.

"All this time and I never read her favorite story. Ho could I have let that happen?"

"David," she softly, "don't be so hard on yourself."

His eyes lifted to hers. "Thank you, Jayde." His voice wa low and full of gravel. "Thank you for being there for Kami lah…in…in a way I never was. I just didn't see it. I didn know how. *This* is what I should I have been doing all alon Reading to her. Fairy tales. Indulging her in her childish fan tasies. I should have been playing with her, allowing her t be a child. I should have let her know it was okay to hav fun…that it wasn't a slight to her mother's memory."

She placed her hand on his arm. "You needed to let *your self* know it was okay to live again, David. And that come only with time. Don't blame yourself."

He sucked in a deep breath, closed his eyes and held hi face up to the sky as if to stop the kinetics of gravity drawin the tears down from his eyes. "And time we've had. It's nov time to move forward. We'll get her, Jayde." He whispere up to the heavens as if convincing himself as well as the uni verse. "We'll get her. And we'll let her be a kid. I won't le her down again. *Ever.*"

Jayde's stomach tightened into a ball. He was saying "we. But she knew she would not be a part of the equation. No once they'd freed Kamilah. There wouldn't be a place for he He'd made that clear enough. "You have never let her down David."

"I did. By not saving her mother. She blames me. Sh holds me responsible for her mother's death."

"No, she does not blame you, David," she said softly. "She has never blamed you."

His eyes flashed to hers. "How would you know?"

"Because she told me. She told me what happened that day, what she saw through her own eyes. And she told me how hard you tried to save her mother and she told me how very proud she is of you."

His mouth pulled sideways as he tried to contain his emotion. "She *told* you that?" His voice was thick.

"Yes, David," she said softly. "Yes, she did."

He opened his mouth and let out a whoosh of air. Then he turned to look at her. "Thank you," he whispered, his eyes tunneling deep into hers. "Thank you, Jayde."

Then he clenched his jaw. His eyes turned cold and determined. He jerked to his feet. "Come," he said, holding his hand out to her. "Let's go and give my baby that happy ending. The one you promised her."

Jayde reached out, grasped his hand. And she felt a new connection between them. A solidness that hadn't been there before.

He strode over to the camels he'd hobbled near the fetid water, showing no sign of the fatigue that gripped her. "If we keep moving through the night," he called out as he untied the camels, "and throughout tomorrow, we could be in Al Abèche before next nightfall."

They stopped once more in the late evening and then pressed on into a night that was as stinking hot as the day that had preceded it. The moon was an almost nonexistent sliver, and the only light that guided them came from stars splattered over the huge black dome of sky.

The farther north they went, the drier the desert, the more hostile the terrain, the blacker the night. In places, sand dunes gave way to sharp rock ridges, and flint in the stone glinted at them like sharp teeth in the dying light of the waning moon.

Jayde knew that once they reached Al Abèche they would be only twenty miles from the Libyan border. The Falal fortress was only another ten miles into Libya. There they would contact Gio Moriati and they would wait for Sauvage and his team to bring Kamilah to them. They would then fly out by helicopter. Dr. Watson would be waiting to treat Kamilah or Shendi if all went according to plan.

She ran over the timeline again and again in her head, trying to stay awake on her camel as dawn once again seeped up from the horizon.

As the sun burst into the sky and rippled the sand with orange color, a wave of heat descended on them that was so oppressive Jayde thought it might just end up killing them by midday.

Even the wind had stopped, making the air thick and gelatinous. It sapped her energy and it slowed the camels. Jayde began to feel tense, edgy, delirious as they waded through the heat and sand. She tried to shake it off. But in each distant ridge of rock she saw monsters lurk. She couldn't tell north from south anymore. She felt alarmed at the hostile vastness of landscape. She tried to tell herself it was the jinns playing tricks with her mind again.

But this time she could see David was edgy, too. He kept peering at the horizon to the right of their little caravan, as if expecting something.

Then she saw what he was looking for, what he must have been sensing all along. A clot of angry red cumulous clouds began to boil up high over the distant horizon. She caught her breath as it changed before her eyes into a terrifying monstrous black claw of sand and wind. She watched in horror as t roared toward them, covering miles in seconds. She glanced round in panic. There was nowhere to hide.

David moved fast.

He yanked her down from her camel, thrust the animal's ead rope into her hand. He yelled above the screaming sound .s the wall of sand advanced. "Hang on to this no matter vhat! Pull that cloth over your face! Lean into wind!"

She couldn't move. She was held prisoner, awed by the sheer cope the advancing, twisting, spiraling whorl of blackness.

David worked quickly to secure the camels. "There should e a deep wadi up ahead," he yelled. "If we can find it in the torm, we'll have shelter."

The sound slammed into her head the same instant light vas blotted from the sky. It was a sound so awful it seemed o emanate from the very bowels of the earth itself, scream-ng up from the core into the sky, sparking a primal terror deep vithin her.

Then the sand hit, instantly choking her nose, her throat, ier lungs. She reeled back, then forced herself forward into he teeth of it.

It cut into her skin like a billion needles. She couldn't see thing. She staggered blindly forward, clutching onto the iead rope knowing her life depended on it.

David steered them into the raging blackness. As they nched forward, the wind and sand filled her head with whis->ering voices, senseless moaning, screaming, in a thousand ınidentifiable tongues.

She had no idea how long they battled against the storm. She noved like a dulled automaton, foot before foot. She no longer 'elt the pain. Then she felt his hands on her, pulling her, guid-ng her, forcing her down into a crevice of rock. She felt his solid >ody tuck in next to her. He pulled a blanket over their heads, ield her into him, shielding her from the worst of the storm.

They huddled like that, breathing in each other's hot ai
as the sound and sand tore at their senses for what seeme
like hours.

Then as suddenly as it had come upon them, it was gone. A
eerie silence filled the desert. David threw back the blanket
shaking out layers of fine sand. Jayde coughed and spluttere
as she tried to wipe the grit of sand from her eyes and mouth.

She looked up at David. He stared at her. They'd made it
They were alive. Behind him Jayde could count all three cam
els present. And beyond the camels, she could see water, life
giving water gleaming in a depression in the dry riverbed.

Her body shuddered with a crazy sob. She felt as if she'
been stripped of everything in that sand, like she'd stared int
the black maw of death. But they'd survived. And she wa
staring at a pool of water in a depression of snow-white san
fringed by a handful of straggling date palms.

She began to cry. And laugh. Crazily. Hysterically.

David grabbed her by the shoulders, pulled her into him
held tight. And she could feel the force of fierce life flowin
through his hands, his arms, his entire body. The same forc
seared wildly through her.

She laughed and sobbed into his neck until tears ran i
muddied rivers down her cheeks, until every last bit of ten
sion had been drained from her body.

She pulled back, stared up at him, and began to laugh al
over again. "Oh, my God, don't tell me I look anything lik
you do."

He grinned, and his eyes twinkled fierce blue through th
sand that caked his face.

He studied her. And he began to laugh, too, a sound tha
came from deep in his belly and burbled up through his chest
He laughed so hard it brought moisture to his eyes and it ra
in streaky trickles down the sides of his face.

He took her hand and they ran down to the water like abandoned spirits under the dome of empty blue sky. They furiously shed their clothes, tossed them onto the white sand of the riverbed and plunged into water that embraced their hot and burned and raw bodies like cool silk.

Jayde sank under the water and rinsed the sand from her hair. She surfaced. "This is heaven. This has *got* to be heaven. I have died and gone to heaven."

A strange look filled David's eyes.

She went silent at the darkness she saw in them.

Then he grabbed her, yanked her into him and kissed her brutally on the mouth. She kissed him back, hard. Tongues slipping, fighting, mating, teeth clashing. Breathless, Jayde pulled back. And in his eyes she saw the pure rawness of primal male hunger. It was as if the winds of sand had unleashed something savage in both of them. It scared her. "We...we should move on," she whispered.

"Yes." The muscle in his jaw pulsed hard. "We must water the camels," he said, his voice thick.

"Yes."

They stared at each other in silence.

He broke it. "Come," he said, his voice rough. "If we don't feed the poor beasts they'll never get us to Al Abèche."

The chores of living were paramount out in a place like this. Jayde could see that now. Wrapped in a *kikoi,* her hair drying in the sun, she worked alongside David to water the beasts that had brought them this far. Then she sat on a blanket spread under the shade of the straggling palms and watched as he spread a tarp on the sand. His *kikoi* was wound around his waist, and his chest was bare and strong and dark with hair that ran in a thick black whorl to his waist. She couldn't take her eyes from the way his muscles moved under his slick skin as he poured piles of grain on top of the tarp.

Then he stood back as the camels began to splutter and his
and bite at each other, serpentine necks fighting for the food
so that it scattered and spilled off the tarp and onto the sand

David chuckled. "That'll teach 'em not to share." He came
and sat beside her, his body touching hers. The electricity was
inescapable, and what happened next was as unavoidable as
the passage of the sun over these heavens.

He reached over and tugged her kikoi loose from her chest
so that it spilled off her. She sat as naked as the day she was
born. His eyes ran over her, sending a spurt of liquid heat
through her body. He reached up and grazed his rough palm
over her breast. Her nipples hardened instantly. "You have the
most beautiful breasts," he whispered, looking into her eyes

The warm, dulcet tones of his voice seeped into her blood
and pooled in the base of her belly.

He ran his roughened hand down the length of her leg and
slowly, very slowly, up along the inside of her thigh. Her
breath caught in her throat and she instinctively relaxed her
thighs, letting her legs fall open to him. Heat spilled to her
groin as his hand moved up to the apex of her thighs, his
roughened fingers searching her wet folds. He leaned over her
his lips finding hers as he slid a finger up into her heat. She
groaned, opened wider, moved against his finger. He plunged
it deeper into her, stroking her as he deepened the thrust of
his tongue in her mouth. The movement of his hand brought
her to an almost unbearable pitch of pleasure.

He straddled his leg over hers, used his knee to force her
thighs even farther apart, and as he did, his *kikoi* fell loose.
He was solid with need. She moaned, arched toward him.

David couldn't hold off a second longer. He leaned her
back onto the blanket, mounted her and thrust himself deep
into her slick heat. She moaned, bucked under him, and it
drove him nearly wild. Naked under the skies with camels

crunching grain quietly over to the side, they joined their bodies in a fierce obsession that knew no shame. They tangled their limbs in feral abandon. And for David there was no past and no future. Just the present. And the woman under him was not Jayde. Not Sahar. Nor a mysterious mermaid. He didn't know her by a tag. But he knew her nevertheless. In a most intimate way. He'd come to know her when she didn't have a sense of self. And he'd discovered the pure, giving soul that existed at her very core.

He'd come to know this woman in a way he'd never dreamed he could know any woman. And at this moment, he was not David Rashid, British aristocrat. He was not Sheik David bin Omar bin Zafir Rashid, descended from a line of fierce and noble nomad warriors. He simply existed. An Adam in the desert united with his Eve under the sky, only a raw and primal honesty between them.

He cried out in wild release as she shuddered under him.

And in this instant he knew in his heart that this was the only woman for him. Spent, he sank back and lay on the blanket beside her. In silence they stared at the sky through the dried fronds of the palm as the heavens turned livid orange and violet. He laced his fingers through hers, squeezed her hand. She squeezed back in response. He wanted to keep her by his side forever. But he couldn't allow himself to think of forever until he'd saved his child. He could offer nothing to the world or to any person in it until he rescued his daughter.

Jayde sat up, traced her fingers along the side of his jaw and over his lips. She smiled at him, a smile that reached right into her eyes and made them dance with pale-green life.

She opened her mouth to say something but a sound jerked them both back to reality.

It was the sat-phone. Ringing in the saddle bag. They exchanged a stunned glance. It could only mean one thing.

David grabbed his *kikoi,* wound it around him as he strode over to their pile of supplies and pulled out the phone.

"Rashid."

"It's Moriati, David, we've got bad news."

The muscles across his chest snapped tight like a steel band. "What news?" he barked. He was vaguely aware at how Jayde jumped at his tone, grabbed her *kikoi,* came over to his side.

"Sauvage and his team have been captured in Egypt."

His brain spun. "How?"

"Egyptian authorities were tipped off. It was Farouk, David. He's been working on the inside for Tariq. I've dealt with him."

"He confessed?"

"Yeah. He got word to Tariq and Falal about our plans to attack the fortress from the north using Egypt as a launch. The Falal then fed a line to the Egyptian authorities telling them Sauvage and his team were planning trouble in Egypt. It's tied them up in bureaucratic tape, David. They've got them behind bars. It will take weeks for Sauvage and his men to get out of this."

"We'll get another team together."

Moriati was quiet on the other end of the line.

"Moriati, what is it? What are you not telling me?" he barked.

"Tariq has lost patience. He demands to have all Force du Sable troops out of Azar by midnight tomorrow or he will harm Kamilah."

"Talk him out of it."

"David…there is no negotiating with this man."

"Buy time, dammit!"

"Can't. He's cut off all communication. This is his end-game, David. We have no choice but to give him what he wants. And—" Moriati paused "—I have to be brutally honest with you, even if we do deliver, I'm not sure he'll uphold his end of the bargain and give us Kamilah."

David's throat constricted, shutting off his air passages. His heart jackhammered in his chest. Adrenaline balled every muscle in his body. "Give him what he wants! Give the order, Moriati. Pull the troops out of Azar. And in the meantime, I'm going in myself. I'm going to get my daughter."

"They'll kill you."

"So be it. If my daughter dies, I die, too." He clicked the phone off. His limbs shook.

"What was that, David?" Jayde asked. But she could already guess.

"Sauvage and his team have been captured in Egypt. Faouk tipped Tariq off, and the Falal in turn tipped the Egyptians off. Now Tariq has brought his deadline forward to tomorrow midnight. I've given the order to move the troops out but I'm going in get my daughter."

Jayde studied his face, his eyes. He was serious. Deadly so. "They will kill you, David."

"They will kill Kamilah if I don't."

She knew he was right. She'd believed it all along. Only an extraction would save the little girl. Not negotiation.

"I'm going with you."

"No. No way in hell."

"Yes way. I'm in this all the way, David." Her eyes flashed to her bag. "I can help. You need me. I've been trained in covert operations. You haven't."

"I can't let you do this, Jayde. I can't ask you to endanger your life this way."

"No, you can't. But *I* can. And I'm not letting you do this alone."

"You said it yourself they will kill."

She reached up, grabbed his shoulders, her eyes lanced his. "Then we will fight, David. Then we will fight back."

Moisture filled his eyes as he stared down into hers. "Do

you realize what you are doing, Jayde? Do you realize what you are saying?"

"I do."

Emotion spilled out from his eyes. He grabbed her face in his hands, kissed her hard on her mouth, held her tight in his arms. "I can't…I can't let you do this."

She pulled away. Her eyes bored into his. "I've never been more determined about anything in my life. Give me that phone," she demanded. "What's Moriati's number?"

He handed it to her and watched her punch in the number.

"Gio," she said with crisp efficiency as she crouched down into the sand and picked up a small sharp piece of rock. "I need the satellite specs of the Falal compound. I need to know the layout of the fort. I want to know where you figure they're holding her, how many guards." She began to draw in the sand with her rock as she listened. David watched as the shape of the fort emerged in the sand. She marked Xs for guards and soldiers. This was her job. This is what she did for a living. This was what he had hated her for. And now he saw what good she could do with it. And respect for her swelled inside him.

She clicked off the phone, slanted her eyes up to him.

"See," she said pointing her finger at her map in the sand. "This is where Gio reckons they're holding Kamilah. Satellite heat-imaging shows a small and fairly stationary figure here in this room on the ground level. This—" she pointed her finger at an X in the sand "—is probably a guard. There's only one outside the door. And there are surprisingly few people in the fortress. Moriati reckons they might feel safe with Sauvage's rescue attempt thwarted and they might be mobilizing for the anticipated coup attempt once the Force du Sable troops are out by midnight tomorrow."

"We stand a chance, then," he said, hope blossoming in his heart.

"Maybe," she grinned up at him. "But only if you follow my orders."

He pulled a face. "I've never taken orders from a woman."

She stood up, bussed him on the mouth. "First time's the hardest, Rashid. Get used to it. Because I plan on being around for a while."

Incredulous, he watched her march over to the camels and cart loading their gear. She'd sown the seed of a promise in his heart. *I plan on being around for a while.* He let her words sink in, feed the promise.

She spun around "Hey, you gonna help or not? If we move now we can be in Al Abèche by nightfall. We can dump our stuff, regroup and be at the fort sometime after midnight. That will give us a few hours of new-moon darkness before dawn," she yelled as she hefted a bag onto her red camel.

In spite of the gravity of the situation he felt a delinquent smile tug at his mouth. "Yeah," he whispered. He was going to make damn sure she stayed around. He wasn't going to let his woman go. Not now. Not after she'd been through all this with him. Not after what they'd shared in the desert.

And suddenly saving his daughter became something even bigger in his mind. It became a need to kill the cancers of the past to ensure a future. It became a driving need to make all three of them whole…him, Kamilah and Jayde. A family.

Because all of sudden he could see with incredible clarity that the very thing that had been driving them apart is what ultimately bound them together—love.

With new fire searing through his blood, he set about loading the camels. And he began to plot. He knew people in Al Abèche. Loyal villagers. Men who would stand by them to fight the Falal. But they had to hurry.

The clock was ticking.

Chapter 15

A moonless night brought them invisibility. With fresh camels, eleven additional men from the village of Al Abèche, and a small cache of black-market weapons, including the stash Jayde had brought, they'd crossed into the Libyan desert undetected just after midnight.

They were all dressed in black. Jayde and David had extra clothes in their saddle bags for their return journey. Jayde had borrowed a chador from a Muslim woman in Al Abèche. The plan was to hide Kamilah under it and for her and David to pose as a simple Bedouin man and wife if they encountered any rebels as they fled. She and David would go one way. The villagers, who were to create a distraction to the north of the fort, would flee in another direction. They would all meet up in Al Abèche…*if* all went according to plan.

It was almost three in the morning. They didn't have much time until first light. Jayde and David lay flat on their stomachs against the warm sand of a dune that provided them cover. The village volunteers, all experienced guerrilla fighters who'd fought Azarian rebels for Sauvage and his team, had stolen around the west end of the fort and made their way into the rocks of the northern ridge armed with grenades, explosives, AK-47s, *jambiyas* and scimitars.

David scanned the fort with night-vision binoculars while Jayde rolled onto her side, carefully attached the grenade launcher to her rifle and inserted a small e-bomb canister, making sure she had another ready to go as soon as she'd fired this one. She checked her watch. "Two minutes," she whispered.

The seconds ticked by interminably as they waited for their men to detonate explosives along the cliff face to the north. That was where Sauvage's men were supposed to have been, according to the plan Farouk had given to Tariq.

Tariq would think David had found a replacement team, and the attention of the few Falal members left at the fort, the ones who had not yet mobilized for the Azar coup, would be diverted northward while Jayde and David crept in from the south.

The plan was for Jayde to fire her e-grenades over the compound as soon as the distraction to the north commenced. The e-grenades would knock out all electrical communications and surveillance equipment in the fort. She and David would then creep in using night-vision gear and neutralize the two guards at the southern entrance.

They would move quickly into the fort and find the room where they assumed Kamilah was being held. They would have to deal with one guard there, according to Moriati's satellite specs.

The first explosion went off on cue, cracking the silence of the desert night. Then the next, and the next. They heard yelling, gunshots, general confusion as the few Falal fighters still in the fort scrambled to cover the northern side of the compound and began firing into the dark.

"Now!" she whispered, firing the launcher. Equipment began to explode and cook under the massive electrical surge. Even from their vantage point a hundred yards away in the dunes, the acrid smell burned their nostrils. Jayde reloaded, fired again. The fort was plunged into blackness.

They raced like silent black ghosts over the sand, using night-vision gear. Through it they could make out the green-gray shapes of the two guards at the entrance. The two men were focused on the ruckus north of the fort.

They caught them unawares from behind, jabbing them in their necks with Jayde's chemical darts. The guards slumped with soft thuds to the ground.

Guns fired to the north. Another explosion rocked the ground. The Falal fighters were fully engaged by their men. David and Jayde ran down the right-hand corridor. They came to a sharp corner in the passage of the old stone fort. David pressed his back against the stone wall, peered carefully around the corner. Ahead, left unguarded, was a thick wooden door with metal hinges. His heart clenched. This was where satellite imaging showed a small and fairly stationary figure they presumed was Kamilah.

He motioned to Jayde that all was clear. They ran to the door, still using night-vision gear in the blackened fort. The door was locked. David fought with the bolt. Jayde touched his shoulder, gestured he move aside.

He watched as she deftly wound two different shades of malleable substance together. "One thread's explosive," she whispered. "The other contains a chemical that will detonate it in seconds. Be ready to get back." She moulded the plastique against the door lock. They both ducked back around the corner in the passageway.

A muffled thud sent shockwaves down the passage. They raced toward the door. David shoved it open. And in the corner, on a pile of old blankets, her eyes big and black in the darkness, was the gray-green silhouette of his baby girl. His heart clean stopped, then kicked sharp up against his ribs. She couldn't see them. She was clearly terrified. "Kamilah!" he whispered. "It's me."

Jayde stood guard at the door.

He rushed toward his child in the dark corner.

"Daddy?" said a tiny voice. Emotion exploded violently in him. She was alive. Speaking. His hands began to shake. "Oh, God, Kamilah, are you all right? Did they hurt you?"

"I'm scared, Daddy. I can't see you. It's dark."

He scooped her up, hugged her tight to his chest. "I've got you, baby, we're going to get you home."

"I knew you'd come, Daddy. I knew."

"Of course, baby. Of course—" He halted as he heard a muffled cry behind him and the sickening sound of a body slumping to the ground. He swung around, Kamilah still clutched tight in his arms.

David's heart stalled. Jayde was curled in a limp pile on the floor, a black stain spreading under her. *Blood.* Tariq stood over her, a bayonet in one hand. *He'd stabbed her!*

Then light from a flashlight cut the darkness. David winced against the pain that screamed through his eyes and into his brain. He whipped off his night-vision gear and, blinking into the glare of the light, slowly set Kamilah down. "Get behind me," he whispered to his child. "Get in the corner, cover yourself with the blankets." His fingers curled around the hilt of his *jambiya* as he spoke. Rage was boiling through him. A sick fear curled through it. *What had Tariq done to Jayde?*

With one hand, Tariq aimed his bayoneted rifle at David's heart. With the other, he pointed the flashlight at David's eyes.

David blinked again, a little more accustomed to the glare of the light. He stared at the blade mounted on the end of Tariq's gun, the blade stained with Jayde's blood. "Tariq," he said hoarsely, "let Kamilah go. Let Kamilah and Jayde go."

Tariq nudged Jayde's limp form with his boot. "She's not going anywhere. Neither are you." He stepped close to David.

Every muscle in David's body strapped iron tight. He slipped his *jambiya* slowly from its sheath as he spoke. "Let us talk, Tariq. Let us work this out. For our father's sake."

Tariq snarled. "My *father?* The man who took an English bride and made a bastard sheik?" He moved even closer.

David's teeth clenched. He angled the curved blade of his *jambiya* slowly up in front of him, poised should his brother take one more step in his direction. "Let my daughter go, Tariq." He waved his *jambiya* menacingly in front of him, feeling the familiarity of the hilt against his palm. "I'm warning you."

Out of the corner of his eye David could see Jayde move ever so slightly. *She was alive.* His heart kicked his ribs. Then he saw her hand move slowly up to her head. She lifted the night-vision scope still attached to her eye. *She was more than alive. She was preparing to make a move.* She caught David's eye, signaled to him to draw Tariq away from Kamilah.

New fire seared through David's blood. He edged slowly to the corner of the stone cell, away from his child, away from Jayde.

Tariq followed David's movement with his flashlight, his finger curling around the trigger of his weapon.

Jayde's hand inched across the crumbling stone floor, groping for a loose chunk of stone. David saw her fingers close around one. She hefted herself up on one elbow and flung the rock at Tariq's head.

Her aim was dead-on. The rock cracked against his skull.

A grunt escaped Tariq. He spun around, aimed at Jayde, and David hit him abruptly from behind. Tariq's shot went wild as he stumbled forward under the impact, the rifle and the flashlight skittering across the floor.

He spun instantly back to face David, his hands empty. Thick black blood was oozing down the side of his face from the gash in his head. He drew out the dagger at his waist, swinging it threateningly.

The light in the cell was dim, the flashlight lying on the stone floor pointing a halo at the far wall.

Out of the corner of his eye, David saw Jayde crawling over to the pile of blankets, to Kamilah. He had to hold Tariq's attention, give them a chance to escape.

Tariq's eyes were wild with anger. He inched closer to David, crouched, his knife swaying.

David raised the point of his dagger. "Don't move, Tariq. Don't force me to do this. Just let us go. We can put all this behind us."

"Never," Tariq snarled, inching even closer. "Even if you get past me, you'll never make it over the border. I have already alerted Libyan troops. There is a column moving in from the east as we speak."

David's heart clenched.

Tariq came closer. Then in the blink of an eye, he lunged at David.

David jerked back, just missing the thrust of the blade. His heart pounded like a drum. He could see Jayde gathering Kamilah into her arms and hunkering down over her as she shuffled out of the cell.

Tariq lunged again, taking advantage of David's distraction. David moved quickly, once again narrowly missing the swing of the blade.

Then Tariq came at him again. David jumped. But not fast

enough. This time Tariq's blade sliced his forearm. David fel
the searing burn, the warmth of his own blood. But he coul
not bring himself to lunge forward, to plunge his *jambiya,* hi
father's *jambiya,* into his brother's body.

Tariq now had him backed up into the corner. He came a
David with a final thrust. David swung to the side. Tariq stum
bled forward with his own momentum. Before he regained hi
balance he lurched sideways after David. David tripped back
ward over the loose stone floor, and Tariq came down har
on top of him, right on top his David's dagger, impaling him
self on the blade. A soft grunt escaped his body as the blade
sank deep into his chest.

David's heart stopped. Tariq's eyes were huge with silen
shock. David could feel the wet, hot blood of his brother
seeping thick over his hands. He rolled quickly over to hi
side, pushing his brother onto his back. The *jambiya* was bur
ied in his chest to the hilt. His brother gaped up at him. Bloo
started to dribble from the corner of his mouth.

David got to his knees. "Tariq!"

His brother groaned.

"By God, Tariq, what have you done?"

A sound bubbled up from Tariq's throat with the blood and
spittle. He choked as he tried to speak. "I…I die for my peo
ple. I…go in peace. You…you will not escape…" He
coughed, choked. And his head lolled to the side, his eye
wide and suddenly empty.

David stared at his father's *jambiya.* The symbol of his un
fulfilled promise. And tears spilled hot and furious down hi
cheeks. His whole body began to shake. "Why, Tariq? Why?'
The pain in his own heart grew unbearable. He bent his head
low over his brother, kissed his face and said a silent praye
for the salvation of his brother's soul. And for his own soul
He closed his brother's eyes.

Then he remembered the Libyan army. He could not afford to waste time. David left the *jambiya* stuck in his brother's heart. He would not be able to bear ever touching it again. He covered Tariq with a blanket from the corner in which he'd found Kamilah. And then he fled down the passageway after his woman and his child.

He found them in the dunes with the camels. Jayde had already donned her chador and was mounted on her beast with the folds of her garment wrapped around his daughter.

"How is Kamilah?"

"She's doing okay...considering."

"And you, Jayde...your wound?"

"Surface. He struck in the dark, missed his mark, missed the vitals. I was lucky. I'll be fine." She stared at his arm. "You're bleeding, David."

"It's nothing." David couched his camel, mounted. "The Libyan army is on our tail," he said quietly. "We must flee. We'll take the southeast route and circle back into Al Abèche. They'll be looking for us to the southwest, the direct route. Have our men gone?"

Jayde nodded. She clucked her tongue and kicked her camel into action. The southeast route would take them into the worst desert, and they had little water. But no choice.

They raced through what was left of the night. They slowed as dawn leaked blood-orange into the sky. "We must be over the border now," David said. "Are you all right, Kamilah?"

His daughter was burrowed into Jayde's chador. From under the folds she nodded her head, eyes still wide. She was in shock. They needed to get her treatment as soon as possible.

"Do you think they'll cross the border?" Jayde asked.

"I don't doubt it. We must keep moving." He dug into the saddlebag and pulled out the sat-phone. Moriati picked up on the second ring. "We've got Kamilah. We're in Azar, heading into Al Abèche from the east."

Gio was silent. Then he spoke. "I don't know how you pulled it off. Congratulations."

"Halt the withdrawal of Force du Sable troops, Moriati. Ready them for a coup attempt."

"Done."

"And we need a chopper in Al Abèche ASAP. And have Watson on standby in Shendi. We have to move. The Libyan army is on our tail."

"Jesus, have they come over the border?"

"We're not sure but not risking it, either. We hope to make Al Abèche before nightfall."

The sun was high in the sky. Jayde's mouth was bone dry. She could see David was suffering, too. They'd given Kamilah what was left of their water. Their camels were under strain. They rode in limp and undulating silence as the desert sand blazed relentlessly and the sun beat down on their heads. They had only a few miles left to go by David's calculation. They'd made record time. And were paying for it.

Then something caught David's attention. He halted his camel, squinted at the northern horizon. A faint plume of orange dust rose in the air and feathered into the blue sky.

Jayde's heart clenched. "What is it?"

"Trucks! Move!" He whacked Jayde's exhausted camel on the rump, kicked his own into a gallop. They began to race across the dunes.

But the dust plume across the ridge grew at an alarming rate and began to close in on them, circling around to the west, cutting off their access to Al Abèche.

And for the first time, Jayde felt defeated. She was exhausted. She'd lost blood. She was in pain. Her thirst was exruciating. Then she looked down at the little child that clung o the saddle in front of her. She couldn't let her down. She ad to make good on her promise. A happy ending. She gritted her teeth, tightened her grip on Kamilah and focused on speed.

But their pursuers were closing in. They could see the black line of vehicles clearly now like huge ants crawling across the sand ridge. Jeeps and a truck.

They could never outrun them. They were being cut off from their only hope of survival. If they were forced back into the desert, they would be dead by tomorrow.

The caravan of vehicles crossed around the ridge and started coming at them from the south.

They were done for.

David halted his camel. Jayde halted hers. They were both breathless. David stared at Jayde. And she knew what he was thinking. They had both known it could come to this.

But as she opened her mouth to speak she heard a chopping sound in the shimmering white-hot sky, growing louder and louder. Helicopters. She squinted into the sky.

Two black choppers materialized like prehistoric beasts over the shimmering heat of the desert. Goose bumps ran over Jayde's skin. The three of them stared in stunned silence as the copters bore down over their heads…and straight onto the convoy ahead of them.

Flashes of light and sound streaked from the machines, and instantly the jeep convoy erupted in explosion. Flames and waves of sound roared over the dunes. Black smoke spiraled into the sky. Fire crackled from the burning out hulls of vehicles in the distance.

Jayde stared at David, dumbfounded. "What was that?"

David smiled wryly. "Force du Sable. Sauvage's men. The best damn private army in the world." He blew out a huge breath and grinned. His eyes were alive with light. "Ladies, think we made it."

"I think we did," she whispered.

"Yaaah!" he cried, whacking her camel on the rump. And they galloped over the last stretch of sand into Al Abèche.

A week later Dr. Watson gave Kamilah a clean bill o health. According to him, she'd fared exceptionally well. He credited this to the fact Jayde and David had arrived as a team to rescue her, restoring her faith in the world.

David stroked his daughter's silken hair. Her eyes smiled up at him. Warmth spurted through his chest. "You sure you don't want another bedtime story."

"Daddy," she said. "You've read nearly *all* my stories. I have to get new ones now."

He kissed her on the forehead. "I'm making up for lost time, sweetness." He tickled her in the ribs. "Just one more? Huh? Huh?"

She squealed and giggled as he tickled her.

"*The Little Mermaid,* maybe? How 'bout I read you that one."

She stilled, her eyes suddenly dark and serious. "Nope. I don't need that one anymore."

He sat up in surprise. "You don't?"

"Uh-uh. I don't like the ending of it anymore." She grinned. "I can make my own happy endings now."

Emotion pricked hot behind his eyes. "Yes, sweetness, that you can." He kissed her and closed the shutters. "Good night, baby."

"'Night, Daddy." And again his heart squeezed at the sound of his child's happy little voice. He made his way out of her room.

"Daddy?" she said as he was about to close the door.

"What is it, sweetheart?"

"Will she stay?"

He was silent for a while. "I sure hope so. I'll let you know 1 the morning."

David made his way out onto the terrace. The moon was ising and the swells were slow and languid out over the cean. Jayde stood at the end of the terrace, the hem of her white dress ruffling in the breeze around her calves, the tenrils of her hair blowing with the warm wind. He slipped his rm around her waist, and together they stared out over a horizon as clear and vast as the future that lay before them.

"Jayde," he said. And inside he quaked. Because he was errified of what she might say when he asked her.

"What is it, David?" Her eyes were so big and so green. He wanted to wake up to those eyes every morning for the rest f his life. He wanted to drown in them forever. "Jayde, if I asked you to stay, would you?"

Her eyes searched his in silence.

His heart balled into a knot. He wanted this above anything lse in the world. He wanted her at his side forever. He wanted hem to be a family.

She sucked in her breath.

He braced, waiting for her words.

"David," she said, "out in the desert, I said some things. And you said it was the jinns talking…"

His stomach bottomed out.

She lifted her face to his. "It wasn't. It was *me*. It was me alking from my heart, me stripped of every damn defence I'd ver built up around myself. In those dunes I pleaded with you o never leave me. I also told you I intended to stick around." She smiled. Her eyes shimmered. "I meant it, David. All of t…if you'll have me, that is."

Tears filled his eyes. He grasped her face with both hands nd kissed her hard. Then he stopped, backed off. "What bout MI-6?"

A wicked twinkle lit her eyes. Her hair billowed softly ou
behind her in the jasmine-scented breeze. "I have a new job.

"What?"

"I work for Sauvage now,"

"I don't understand."

"He wants me for the North African intelligence and re
search team he's putting together. It's part of a new servic
he will be offering his clients. The mercenary business i
shifting more and more into this field. He says I can do th
bulk of my work out here, as long as I make myself availabl
for client briefings and meetings in London and at the Forc
du Sable base on Sao Diogo."

His face was priceless. She'd rendered him speechless
She loved him right now more than anything in this world
This powerful man who'd become her one weakness was th
very person who had made her whole again. He'd put the feel
ing back into her soul. He'd given her life. Real life. In all it
messy guts and glory.

"How long have you and Sauvage been in cahoots?"

She chuckled. "A lady has to have some secrets, no?"

He took her face in his hands. "Damn, I love you, woman
You truly *were* a gift from the sea," he said. "Marry me, Jayde
Be my happy-ever-after."

Her heart clenched. "You mean Kamilah gets her fairy-tale
ending?"

"We all do. She gets her voice back...I get the mermaid.'

"And I get the prince." Tears pooled in her eyes. She kissed
him. "Yes, David. Yes, I will marry you."

And for the first time in Jayde Ashton's life, she believed
fairy tales really could come true.

* * * * *

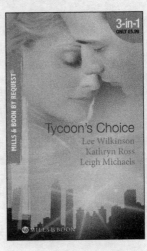

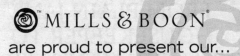

are proud to present our...

Book of the Month

Their Newborn Gift
by Nikki Logan
from Mills & Boon®
Romance

When Lea became accidentally pregnant she
decided that she would go it alone. Rodeo star
Reilly wasn't the sort of man who'd want to
be tied down. But five years later she needs
to tell him her secret...

Mills & Boon® Romance
Available 4th June

*Something to say about our
Book of the Month?
Tell us what you think!*
millsandboon.co.uk/community

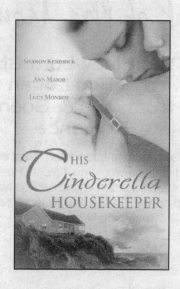

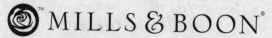